This book belongs
to:
Kathryn A. Denny
— 2002 —

PASADENA

PASADENA

a novel

DAVID EBERSHOFF

RANDOM HOUSE

NEW YORK

Copyright © 2002 by David Ebershoff
Map copyright © 2002 by David Cain

All rights reserved under International and Pan-American Copyright Conventions.
Published in the United States by Random House, Inc., New York,
and simultaneously in Canada by Random House of Canada Limited, Toronto.

RANDOM HOUSE and colophon are registered trademarks of Random House, Inc.

Library of Congress Cataloging-in-Publication Data
Ebershoff, David.
Pasadena : a novel / David Ebershoff.
p.   cm.
ISBN 0-375-50456-7
1. Pasadena (Calif.)—Fiction.   I. Title.
PS3555.B4824 P37 2002
813'.54—dc21   2002020684

Random House website address: www.atrandom.com

Printed in the United States of America on acid-free paper

24689753

First Edition

Book design by Casey Hampton

IN MEMORY OF MY GRANDPARENTS

Rebecca Jane Erikson Rutherford   1912–1992
Robert Bruce Rutherford   1914–1996

John Henry Ebershoff   1908–1999
Maxine Malsbary Ebershoff   1909–1999

RUNOFF

prologue

O God of heaven! the dream of horror,
The frightful dream is over now;
The sickened heart, the blasting sorrow,
The ghastly night, the ghastlier morrow

EMILY BRONTË

THE DAM BROKE and Linda looked up and saw the bluff collapse, a waterfall of mud.

She held her breath as the sludge burst from the swamp, as it funneled down the sandstone cliff, down the scaffold of steps, swallowing her. The mudflow slapped her face and plugged her ears, sealed her eyes, stopped her mouth, shoved cold between her thighs. She was a girl of seventeen, now dragged under by the grimy hand of a broken single-arch dam. The dirty water was in her throat, the air stolen from her lungs. A torrent of silt plucked her down to the cove, where her outrigger canoe rested against a rock padded with rubbery laver. Linda tumbled as if wrestled by a wave—no air or light, up turned down, the mud's tide carrying her. It was rocky like the oozy water-bound macadam poured to pave the roads to and from Baden-Baden-by-the-Sea, the gravel and the dust-water devouring the old wagon trails and the weedy surrey routes and the former cow paths. The earthflow rolled Linda, stones attacked her, shredding her workdress, bruising her pale flesh. Linda Stamp, a fishergirl with eight lobster pots at the bottom of the Pacific, was transported in a coffin of mud.

The January rains had swollen Siegmund's Swamp, home of the winter runoff and the red-eyed vinegar fly. The downpour had prodded the dam, while Linda toiled below, nailing the planks into the staircase. She was not alone: Bruder was a few steps above and her mother, Valencia, was next to her, handing her wagon-box nails and brushing the hair from her eyes. There'd been five days of rain, sometimes an inch an hour, flocks of clouds soaring off the Pacific, wings of thunder, a vulture-black sky. The rain had flooded the earthworm holes and the vole dens and uprooted a crooked digger pine.

But this morning the rain had stopped; a slit of pink sunlight pierced the sky. "Maybe we should wait another day," Valencia had warned, but Linda wouldn't listen. They returned to erecting the staircase, one hundred steps up the bluff's seventy feet, from cold-sand beach to the little onion farm: Valencia, her black hair streaked with silver, her tongue clucking *¡Jovencita!;* Bruder, nineteen or twenty ("Orphan boy!" Linda would tease); and Linda. The three hammered step after step, cross-beams and hand-hewn two-by-fours, into the tarred-wood foundation. They worked steadily in the dry morning, anxious to complete the stairs, watching the sky swell and sag. "The worst is over," Linda predicted. "The rain won't return." Her mother's screwed-up eye disagreed. Bruder said nothing, the nails stored between his teeth, a T-head bolt behind each ear. Linda sang while they worked—*O, she was born in the Ocean, and died in the Sea!*—as Valencia and Bruder hauled the lumber with the log chain and hammered with the mallet. They worked as the ocean chewed the beach, foam spraying the steps, bull kelp spit from the mouth of the waves, hermit crabs skittering like crumbs across the table of sand. Up on the farm, Dieter shod the hinnies in the barn and sorted the white onions from sack to crate and napped on a hundred-pound bag of scratch feed.

Then the sky reopened and the rain fell again, pecking anew the farm and the sea, and the dam broke and Linda looked up and saw the downpour of mud: mudflow ferrying uprooted ice plant and mica-flecked stones and pale-yellow kangaroo rats and kitchen garbage and everything ever buried in the arroyo. Stewy mud, both liquid and solid at once, penetrated the dam and devoured her in less time than it took to say her name: *Linda Stamp!*

She said it and she was gone, the landslide pushing her down, yanking her under, pulling her in. Everything turned black, and the mass of moving earth trapped Linda. Valencia, reaching for Linda's hand, was ripped away; and Bruder, too; each gone, each interred.

When the river of mire halted at the beach, Linda was lying in earth as dense as the fresh pavement on El Camino Real. She struggled to raise herself, but the muddy tomb held her. All at once, her past and her future had become sealed together in a dreamless, bottomless cave, everything as cold and quiet as the bottom of the ocean. Linda couldn't see and she couldn't move and she felt only fear. The mud settled like water stilling in a trough, and Linda heard the silence, as if there was nothing left, no one there. In the landslide Valencia and Bruder and Linda breathed mud and darkness, each aware of entering the grave alive.

Yet one, only one, gasped and fought and shuddered and died.

SPECULATION

part one

Will the day be bright or cloudy?
Sweetly has its dawn begun;
But the heaven may shake with thunder
Ere the setting of the sun.

EMILY BRONTË

1

ON A DECEMBER MORNING in 1944, Mr. Andrew Jackson Blackwood—a young-faced, self-made man who had been in California
twelve or fourteen years, depending on whom you asked—was making
his way down El Camino Real. He was driving his yellow Imperial Victoria on his way to a real-estate convention in San Diego. At present he
was somewhere between Dana Point and Oceanside, but many miles
back his Automobile Club map had flown out the window, the wings of
its paper-folds extending and flapping away. The fluttery movement—
and the car's sudden swerve as he lunged for the accordioned map—
made him think of a large, ancient bird lifting itself into extinction.
This was a more morose thought than Blackwood was used to, and it
didn't stay with him, flitting away like the map itself. But Blackwood
had a sense of direction, he liked to tell himself, and he continued on
his way.

Yet by now he could no longer be certain that he was still traveling
down El Camino Real; had he made a wrong turn somewhere back?
The road cut through dormant pea fields and lettuce farms and a patch
of shallots, passing an avocado orchard and a lemon grove protected by
eucalyptus windbreak. It climbed a scrub-oak terrain burned gold in
autumn where at hillcrest a rattler stretched belly-up in the sun. Thin,
shabby utility poles stood across the fields like a line outside a poor-
house, and upon the drooping wires sat a family of garbage-fed gulls.
Every now and then the road turned sharply and the hammered pewter
of the Pacific would appear in the distance and Blackwood would inhale, tasting the salt on the breeze. He was listening to the kid an-

nouncer on the KCRO radio news, and lately word from Europe was better than expected, the Americans marching swiftly up the wine-cold valleys of the Moselle. Blackwood thought of the boys weighted down by carbine and canteen, and it occurred to him just then, as he descended a hill and the ocean lay before him, that the war would end sooner than most dared to hope. The soldiers would return en masse and many would request passage to Long Beach or Coronado and each would need a bungalow and a patch of ryegrass for himself and his honey-haired girl. The world after the war would be different. There would be an unprecedented demand. Someone would supply it. The idea came to Andrew Jackson Blackwood, complete and formed.

And this was what distinguished Blackwood from the rest, he liked to tell himself—whether when meditating upon the passage of another day while falling asleep in his mint-green pajamas, or at the closing of yet another deal around the bank's white-oak table. Blackwood looked only forward, never back: the cuffs of history never locked about his wrists and throat.

In an open stretch of flatland close to the shore, he spotted a farm stand tended by a girl with dark, nostalgic eyes. A tulip tree shaded the stand, and Blackwood slowed the Imperial Victoria as he passed it. The girl looked sad, perhaps because of her skimpy display of onion and the day's catch in a box of ice: three cigar-shaped flyingfish on their sides, their woven silver wings catching the sun. Behind the stand was a small farm, its turned onion field edging an arroyo dense with lemonade berry. The farm extended to the ocean, a perfectly underutilized tract of land, and Blackwood—whose first speculation in California real estate all those years ago had hauled him north across the border from poor to rich—swerved and turned down the dirt road.

He was a thin but strong man whose Broadway Brothers suits fit him well. In 1931 he had arrived in Pasadena unnoticed, an import from Maine who, with a small wad of money of questionable origin and a full, boyish smile, bought an abandoned whitewashed mansion on Orange Grove Avenue that had once belonged to a family whose money had been made and lost in ice. Blackwood converted it into a rooming house open to anyone who could push the nightly fee through the slot in the cashier's cage. Because he was sympathetic to the outsider, from the beginning Blackwood accepted the money of any and all men—Negro, Mexican, Chinese, even a girl or two in dire straits—at a time when most other landlords turned away those with a hue in their flesh or a pickled breath. This and a general distrust of the police kept Blackwood's rooming house full and brought him rapid success in the world of the down-and-outs. Eventually, other properties followed, dilapidated and distressed, picked up for pennies on the dollar. Early on, Blackwood became friendly with a professor of economics at Cal Tech, a man they called Stinky Sweeney, and together Blackwood and Sweeney pondered the many ways to expand their pies while most others watched theirs shrivel in the pan. And oh how Blackwood's pie had grown since he'd come to California! Spanish-tiled mansions divided into by-the-week apartments; long-closed dress and millinery shops on Colorado Street reconfigured as pawn emporiums and pool halls and even a lounge where girls danced in their rationed silk underwear; and the plots of sandy land bought for almost nothing from desperate, tax-hounded people who sometimes paid Blackwood to take the property off their hands! He padded his real-estate holdings with a position in steel stocks, in oil shares, and in a piece of a rubber-belt company that held a patent. But Blackwood knew that there was no asset in California like the parched terra firma that could crumble in the hand.

The dirt road ended at three small cottages on a headland bluff. They overlooked the ocean, their foundations close to the eroding lip, where ropes of ice plant grew in rappel and belay. The cottages were on the verge of decrepitude, shredded tar paper and horizontal plank warped white with salt, and the arroyo-stone chimneys leaned precariously against the scabbed corrugated roofs. The wind was throwing dirt and sand in the bantam-pecked yard, and from the barn Blackwood heard a horse sneezing and the groan of an udder-sore cow. Blackwood, so skilled at this sort of evaluation, noted that there wasn't a telephone pole in sight. What was it he had first taught himself when he arrived in California all those years ago? *The true developer sees value where others turn away.*

Blackwood got out of his car and called hello in a friendly way. What Blackwood didn't know about himself was that pink-cheeked friendliness came naturally to him, and that others sensed it and trusted it, perhaps even when they should not. He was handsome in a safe, pale-featured way—handsome enough for success to have come to him just a little more easily than to most; but he was unaware of this slight advantage. In fact, Blackwood was certain that he had started off with no advantages at all. He was equally unaware of his natural powdery scent, much like a baby's, not unpleasant but unusual for a man of forty-four.

Oddly, however, on this December morning his typically cheerful "Hello! Anyone home?" emerged shrilly, as if he was nervous—like the call of a red-tail hawk. But Blackwood wasn't the type of man who knew about birds and their calls. Since moving to California he had failed to grow curious about habitats and ranges and migration paths interrupted by the reach of man. Like most Pasadenans—and certainly he thought of himself as one, although others, many others, did not—he delighted when a bald eagle alit in the Arroyo Seco. Why, the *Star-News* had run a picture of such an event this very morning!—but this was the extent of Blackwood's ornithological interest. Had it been greater, he might have noted earlier the sign along the dirt road that read:

CONDOR'S NEST
STAY OUT

"I'm afraid you've made a wrong turn," someone said.

The voice came from behind one of the cottages, and Blackwood turned and removed his hat and said in that cheerful way of his, "Who's there? How do you do? My name is Blackwood. Andrew Jackson Blackwood. Sorry to barge in." A man appeared on the porch, and Blackwood offered his free hand.

"This is private property."

"Yes, I'm aware of that. And I'm sorry to intrude, but in fact that's why I turned down your drive. I thought we could have a chat."

"You'll have to leave." The man was taller than Blackwood, broad in shoulder but weary in whiskered cheek. His hair was as black as crude oil, his eyes too, and this made Blackwood think of his thousand shares that had doubled in value three years in a row. Only then did Blackwood realize that his hand was still extended. He wondered why the stranger hadn't offered his own, but the paw of the man's right hand, Blackwood now noted, was wrapped around the deer-foot handle of a hunting knife, and this caused Blackwood's heart to sit up in his chest. A waxy sweat broke out on his face as he noticed that the man's shirt was sprayed with blood. On closer inspection, Blackwood could see that blood splattered the man's pants as well. In the man's hair, tiny rubies of blood sparkled, and there was a drop of blood on his lip, bright and round and trembling. Blackwood didn't want to believe it, but the evidence suggested he had stumbled across a murder. Blackwood was silent, and his hand reached behind him for the Imperial Victoria's door. He would try to leave.

"Who sent you here?"

"I . . . I . . ."

"Why did you come?"

"I . . . I . . ." But Blackwood couldn't.

Suddenly there was a noise, like a log smacking the side of the cottage, and Blackwood's knees, tender since his days kneeling in the flinty Maine soil, buckled, and he found himself huddled against the car, its door warm against his cheek. He heard the smacking noise again, and Blackwood, teary, looked to the man and was prepared to beg, to offer anything to be sent on his way without harm. The tears were hot on Blackwood's lip.

The smacking repeated, and Blackwood peered through his fingers and finally noticed the large barracuda hanging on hook and chain from the cottage eave. Its yellowish, bat-shape tail fin whipped the side of the house, and its long, bulleted head surged up the chain and then fell back, its mirror pelvic fins quivering. Its silver belly had been sliced from anal fin to gill, and blood dripped from the fish into a puddle, attracting tiny blue Euphilotes butterflies.

How could Blackwood have been so silly? The man was no more a murderer than Blackwood himself; Blackwood had panicked, something he had long ago taught himself to avoid. Fear keeps a man from accomplishing things, he knew; fear chains a man to his past. He was both disappointed in himself and aware of the man staring at him down in the dirt. Blackwood pulled himself up, attempting to wipe the distress from his brow. "Did you catch her?"

The man nodded and stared in a way that made Blackwood feel as if his skin were being penetrated. The man's flesh was warmly brown. Blackwood noted more than a drop of Mexican in him, and wondered where the man was from.

"Do you eat barracuda around here?"

"Not much anymore. The schools are thinning out." The man turned his knife in his palm as if he were a child showing it off and then, with a wrist-snap, flung it into the barracuda's head, sinking the blade between the fish's feline eyes. Her jaw popped open and a ribbon of blood rushed between her fangs and she stretched herself to her full three and a half feet and died on the hook.

The sight of it pressed the breath from Blackwood's chest. Then he managed, "May I ask how long you've lived here, Mr. . . . ?"

"Why do you want to know?"

Blackwood refilled his lungs. "Well, you see, I'm a real-estate developer." He said this as if he were announcing that he was a teacher or a fireman or a member of the clergy; that was how vital Blackwood thought of himself to the community, to the great goal of California's progress. "I was wondering if you'd ever be interested in selling your land, Mr. . . . ?"

The man walked to the fish and pulled the knife from its head. He wiped the blade clean on his pants and said he'd never thought about selling anything at Condor's Nest.

"I would imagine," Blackwood tried again, "you might be able to sell this piece of property and buy yourself a nice house in town somewhere. Someplace where the roads are paved, perhaps?"

"I don't want to go anywhere. I've traveled and now I'm home."

"Do you mind if I ask how much land you have?"

"Ten and a half acres."

"Ten and a half, is it?" Blackwood scanned the property; he wondered if the arroyo behind the barn would make subdivision difficult. Probably not, what with the way they're putting up houses in the canyons. All you need is a pair of stilts and a concrete mixer. Easy enough these days. Or maybe Blackwood could dam up the arroyo and create a little green pond; people would like that, people would pay more for that. It'd be easy enough: throw a wall of soil across the arroyo's mouth and catch the winter runoff. He'd have to be careful about flash-flooding, but Blackwood knew what he was doing. On closer inspection, it appeared that perhaps once someone had tried this: the foundation of a collapsed dam remained in place. He thought to ask, "You ever think about closing it up? Make yourself a nice little casting pond?"

Then for the first time the man's hard face softened. "How much is it worth, Mr. Blackwood?"

"The arroyo?"

"The whole farm."

Blackwood hesitated, thinking that this might be some sort of test.

"I'm sure you'll understand when I say I don't go around tossing out
numbers if the other party's not interested." He added, "I'm sorry, sir. I
didn't catch your name."

"Bruder."

"Bruder? A pleasure, Mr. Bruder." Blackwood moved to tip his hat,
but then he realized that it was gone and he ran his hand through his
hair, which was so fine it parted randomly when the wind blew upon it.
The hat sat overturned in the dirt, a sagebrush lizard inching toward it,
and Blackwood felt the sun burning his ears and his neck. His skin was
more sensitive than most people's. Whenever he appeared in a terry
bundle at poolside or on the beach, he would say he had a northerner's
complexion, careful not to be any more specific than that; he knew that
some people thought he was from Canada, and that was fine with Andrew Jackson Blackwood.

He went to retrieve his hat when Bruder said, "Would you like to
come inside, Mr. Blackwood?"

In the middle cottage were two rooms, a kitchen with a coil-handled
stove and an alcove hidden by a rose-petal sheet strung along a wire.
There was a terrible bareness to the place. Dark kerosene smoke painted
the walls, and Blackwood took this as a sign that he was dealing with an
unsophisticated man. He supposed that Bruder was one of those farmers who could no longer make a go of it; and something in Blackwood
wondered why Bruder would even try. Bruder opened a cupboard that
held nothing but a tin of sugar, three white onions, a jar of apple butter,
and a hard round loaf of bread. Blackwood sensed things turning his
way, and that was what he had learned over the years: to keep a wet finger in the wind.

"Coffee, Mr. Blackwood?" Bruder lit the stove.

A few minutes later, Blackwood took the cup of coffee and Bruder
poured himself a jelly jar of jug wine. "There's a long history at Condor's Nest," Bruder said. "I can't think of anything that would convince
me to sell it off."

"There's always a history, Mr. Bruder."

"A lot has happened here."

"I'm sure that's true."

"I've never wanted to sell this land."

"Sometimes it's hard to think about." All those years ago, it had been
so easy for Blackwood to don a developer's hide. The trick was to look

them in the eye once, and never again. A few months ago, he'd read an article in the *Star-News* about a tennis champion who was asked about the key to winning Wimbledon, and the man—there was a photograph of him in his white sweater-vest—had replied, "Just keep moving forward." Blackwood couldn't agree more. He looked forward to reporting to Stinky about the ten and a half acres and the strange man, who had a blue-black scar at his temple that eerily darkened and lightened like the shifting winter ocean. "It was like stepping back in time," Blackwood would say on the telephone. "Like meeting a forty-niner in person."

"Do you live alone, Mr. Bruder?"

Bruder sat up, and Blackwood could see that once he'd been handsome. Could've been in pictures, thought Blackwood, with those heavy lids and that nose, long but not fleshy, like John Gilbert's; it was Blackwood's one vice: Saturday night at Grauman's Egyptian, staring up into Gable's huge, mattress-size eyes. That, and reading the *American Weekly* insert and the *Star-News* society page for the latest breeze. Blackwood took perhaps a little too much pleasure in the misfortune of others, but he had no reason—at least not yet—to believe that he would come to regret this glee.

"I have a family," said Bruder, standing and taking Blackwood's cup. "Now you'll have to leave."

Bruder walked Blackwood outside, and a pride rose in Blackwood's swift and lean heart as he saw the yellow car sitting in the sun, the ocean reflecting in the gleam of its hood. He expected Bruder to say that she was a hell of an automobile: every now and then that's what strangers said on Colorado Street—not that the Imperial Victoria was the fanciest car running around Pasadena, heavens no, Blackwood wasn't one to waste his dough. But the car was the first substantial item Blackwood had ever bought for himself, and he loved her as another man might love his dog, or his wife. Its wheels were white, and its yellow skin was as bright as a Model's banana, and every now and then he would click his heels when he realized she was his. It's because Blackwood had never thought he would one day own an Imperial Victoria. Certainly he'd never thought he'd be sizing up ten and a half acres of subdividable farmland. You never know where a dirt road will take you in life; that's what he had told himself back in muddy Maine, and now look at Andrew J. Blackwood.

"Why don't you think about it, Mr. Bruder?"

"I'll never sell my land. Not at Condor's Nest."

"Never's a long time, Mr. Bruder. I can stop by another day and we can continue our chat."

"That won't be necessary."

"But I could if you wanted."

"No thank you, Mr. Blackwood."

"Is that your daughter tending the farm stand, Mr. Bruder?"

"Drive carefully, Mr. Blackwood. A lot of rocks round here. One might fly up and dent your hood."

Andrew Jackson Blackwood climbed into his car and turned it around and drove down the long dirt lane. In his mirror, Bruder and Condor's Nest fell away, the dust and the dead mayweed blossoms rising, and the endless ocean. When he reached the road he waved to the girl, who was busy shifting the box of flyingfish into the tulip tree's moving shadow. "What's your name?" he called.

"Sieglinde!"

"*What* is it?"

"I'd get out of here if I were you!"

Blackwood waved again and then drove on to the convention in San Diego, certain that Mr. Bruder would be glad to see him when he returned on his way home in a few days.

2

THE TRIP TO SAN DIEGO turned out to be a waste of time. Blackwood met with men from City Hall whose minds were clogged with
regulation, and chatted with halfhearted developers who feared "the
uncertain times." A lady developer declared that she was sitting things
out for the time being. It had been a sorry bunch indeed. But one young
man from Ocean Park, who turned out to be nothing more than an ambitious bookkeeper with a keen eye, tipped off Blackwood about the
values along the farmland coast north of San Diego. This conversation
had proved so interesting that Blackwood bought the man a second
bourbon, and then a third, while Blackwood nursed a golden beer, and
eventually the young man spilled to Blackwood everything he knew
about North County. He said that the place to look was around a tiny
village called Baden-Baden-by-the-Sea. "Never heard of it," said Blackwood. "That's the point," said the young man. "No one has. Long ago
it was known for its mineral spring. People would come from all over
to drink its water and to bathe. But the spring dried up in the Great
Drought way back when, and the hotels closed and most of the farms
collapsed. The village was almost forgotten."

The conversation proved invaluable, but it kept Blackwood from
hitting the road until nightfall. He hoped Bruder wouldn't mind his
late arrival, but why should he? Thanks to the honest-faced young
bookkeeper, Blackwood had calculated a modest but fair offer for Condor's Nest. It did not occur to him that Bruder would turn him down;
after all, what did Bruder have to hold out for? Not nostalgia, for Blackwood was certain Bruder was a man with little worth remembering.

It was raining when the Imperial Victoria reached the farm. A dense fog hid the ocean, and the mud sucked on Blackwood's shoes as he stepped out of the car. He heard the waves thrashing angrily, the high tide throwing rocks and kelp and limpets. Miserable spot in a winter storm, thought Blackwood, and he knocked on the cottage door. There was a light in the window, but no answer came. Blackwood peered inside and saw a small bulb—one he hadn't noticed before—burning dimly above the kitchen table, and a gentle disappointment touched him: Condor's Nest wasn't trapped as far back in history as he had first believed. Even so, he rapped the glass, and nothing in the cottage stirred except the fire dying in the stove. He wondered where Bruder would go on such a night, and whether the girl was with him. The salty rain slanted down, falling sharply on Blackwood's neck and face, and he pulled his hat over his ears. He feared that perhaps he'd left the Imperial Victoria's window cracked, but such carelessness wasn't like Blackwood, and he assured himself he was anxious only because of the night and the rain, which just now hardened to hail.

Blackwood was certain that Bruder would return sometime soon, and so he thought about perhaps waiting at the kitchen table. He had a feeling about Condor's Nest, something he could describe only as a sense of possession, as if the process of transferring the property from Bruder to himself had already begun. He turned the doorknob, but found it locked.

"Looking for someone?" came a voice.

"Mr. Bruder," Blackwood began, but when he turned around he discovered it was someone else.

There stood a young man, locks of dark hair pasted to his throat. His cheeks were red, as if he'd been running. He was coatless, and the rain ran off his shoulders and down his overalls, which were oddly patched in the hem and seam and had a red satin heart sewn on the bib. He wasn't wearing any shoes, and his feet were so huge and white they were like lanterns on a path. "He didn't invite you back," the young man said.

"Are you Mr. Bruder's son?"

The young man shook his head and told Blackwood to follow him. They walked round the cottage to the back, where the wind off the ocean snapped the clothesline and bent the digger pines. The young man said something, and Blackwood had to shout "Sorry?" but the young man shook his head again. Blackwood moved to the edge of the cliff, peering over. The waves heaved and exploded against the bluff, which was sixty or seventy feet high, Blackwood guessed. He saw the ghost of a wooden staircase leading to the beach. An image of a falling man quickly entered and left Blackwood's mind, and he chided himself for staring into this pool of fear. "Wouldn't want to be at sea tonight," Blackwood called, but the young man ignored him.

He led Blackwood to the second cottage, into a room dark except for the glow in the fireplace. When the door closed behind them, the howling in Blackwood's ears died. The room was more pleasant than the first cottage; there was a mantel carved with blue whales, a shelf displaying books and abalone shells, and two bentwood rockers atop an oval braided rug. Someone had hung a baleen above the door like a strip of bunting. It was a handsome-enough place, but certainly not worth saving from the clearing crew. Blackwood imagined the bungalow with the detached garage that would replace it; this alone would return the price of all of Condor's Nest. But Blackwood was getting ahead of himself. And so he offered his hand in introduction.

"I know who you are," said the young man.

"Do you?"

"Bruder told me."

"That was kind of him. But I don't know who you are."

"Me? I'm Palomar Stamp." He said this gently, as if the name required care in delivery.

"Palomar Stamp?"

"They call me Pal." He sank into one of the rockers, and as he dried by the fire, steam rose from his thighs. He said, "Did you meet Sieglinde?"

Pal pointed behind Blackwood. On a bench by the window, the girl from the stand was busy sharpening knives. As she scraped a blade over a disk of sandstone, her curls fell into her face. Blackwood couldn't be sure, but he thought he recognized the deer-footed hunting knife. Half a dozen knives waited for her whetting stone, sharkskin handles and double-blades and a crescent-shaped handsaw, rusty at the tip.

"Did you manage to sell all your flyingfish the other day?"

"He won't want to see you," she said. She was a strong-limbed, dreamy-faced girl of nineteen or twenty, and her voice was surprisingly low, like that of an adolescent boy.

"Are you two brother and sister?"

Pal shook his head.

"But Mr. Bruder is the father of one of you, yes?"

The girl's chin moved from side to side. "You'll have to find out for yourself, Mr. Blackwood." She returned to her knife-carving, the delicate, circling *shhhhhhhh* of the grinding competing with the roar of the storm. Pal unhooked the bib of his overalls and let the flap hang down, the satin heart upside down and hidden in his lap. He folded his hands behind his head and closed his eyes. The rain had soaked his thin cotton work shirt tight to his chest, and even in the dim room Blackwood could see Pal's small pricked nipples and the two mats of hair beneath his arms.

Blackwood remained standing in his coat, and an uncertainty approached him: perhaps he should leave? The drive to Pasadena would take several hours, and he had an early-morning appointment out at the old orange ranch. He had failed to replace the Automobile Club map, but this didn't particularly concern him. He did, however, want to speak to Bruder—get the offer on the table, at the least. The young bookkeeper, whose face had flared candy-pink as he plunged into his fifth and sixth bourbons, had described North County as the last bargain around, and said that if he himself had the cash he'd buy up a farm or two. "Untouched" was the word the bookkeeper had used, and it stuck with Blackwood; there was so little left in the Southland one could describe that way, so little left in the world. The advertisement in the *Star-News* had called the ranch in Pasadena and its abandoned groves *untouched* as well. It was a word that could cause a developer's heart to swell, the freedom it implied. Nothing better than starting from scratch, transforming the pale scrubland into neighborhood. Since arriving in California, Blackwood had played a part in a number of developments that had begun with the untouched—dividing up the remains of the Rancho San Pasqual, and the old homesteads above Santa Anita and at the head of Eaton Canyon, and the buckwheat hill around the burned-down Hotel Raymond. He knew that some people thought he was crazy, running a road into a canyon where only the coyotes lived. What precisely did he enjoy in real-estate development? He couldn't articulate it exactly, and liked to believe it was something more than the money; perhaps it was the flattering custom of naming a street after the developer. He could already imagine the street sign at Condor's Nest: Blackwood Lane, a road dead-ending at the ocean and leading fifteen or twenty G.I.s and their families (maybe more, depending on how that arroyo checked out) to their bungalows. Blackwood wasn't just any old developer, oh no; he set strict guidelines for design, in Pasadena often emphasizing the Spanish: red tile roofs and tinkle-fountain patios and climbing bougainvillea. He had learned that, for whatever reason, people liked a delicate whiff of the past. Blackwood also felt that he respected the land more than most developers, and this despite the fact that he wasn't born on California soil—but then, really, who was? Thinking of Condor's Nest, he wondered if it might be best if Blackwood Lane were set up to resemble a village road on the moors of England, thatched cottages with Tudor beams—not that he'd been to England himself, but in his youth Blackwood had been a reader. A reader and a collector of postcards.

"Did you want something, Mr. Blackwood?"

"I was hoping to speak to Mr. Bruder."

"I realize that," said Sieglinde. "Did you want something from the kitchen? Some tea?"

Her feet were also bare, but this didn't stop her from heading out into the storm. The violent night intruded through the open door as she left him alone with Pal.

"Is he around?"

"He'll be back. He's down on the beach."

"On the beach? What's he doing there?"

"Fishing. Checking her lobster pots."

Blackwood wondered if this could be true and thought that Pal might be teasing him; or maybe Pal didn't have it all in the mind. There was something about him, after all; his head large on his shoulders, the skull massive in the brow. Certain words—like "Condor," for instance—seemed to catch on his tongue, not like a stammer but almost as if he didn't comprehend them. "Sieglinde," as well. *Sieg-l-l-l-linde.*

"Does he usually fish on a night like this?"

"Most of the time."

"Is that wise?"

"You'll have to ask him." Pal's finger touched the spine of a book on the shelf, a German edition of Gibbon. It made Blackwood wonder who at Condor's Nest was reading Gibbon, and the other books of history, Carlyle and Tacitus and two volumes of Plutarch.

Sieglinde returned with a kettle, and she leaned over Blackwood to fill his cup, the rain dripping from her face onto the top of his head. Then she returned to the bench and her knives and said, "He's come back."

"How is he?"

"Cold."

"Do you mean Mr. Bruder?" asked Blackwood.

"I told him you were here."

"What did he say?"

By the time Bruder entered the cottage, Blackwood had begun to dry out and sleep had nearly overtaken him, but the storm rushing through the door triggered Blackwood's heart.

"There's a leopard out there waiting for you," said Bruder. Obediently, Pal stood and buttoned his overalls. "A girl-shark. She won't take much time. Watch out, she might be full." Pal took two knives from Sieglinde and a club hanging on a leather string by the bookshelf.

"Go with him," Bruder said to the girl, shaking off the water, and for the first time Blackwood saw the canine in him, in the strange yellow rimming his eyes. Blackwood figured he'd be able to get a good deal out of a man so crude. Pal and Sieglinde left silently, the wind greeting them at the stoop.

"The children don't like it when she's loaded."

"Excuse me?"

"When the shark's pregnant. A baby shark can flip out of the gut, as alive as you and me."

The cottage, a dainty room with a second room behind the fireplace barely big enough for a bed, was nearly too small to hold Bruder, it seemed.

"What do you want, Mr. Blackwood?"

"Nothing more than a friendly visit."

"Shouldn't you be home on a night like this?"

"I was on my way home but thought I'd stop by. See if you'd given it any thought."

"I gave it thought the last time you were here. This is my land." And then: "My home."

"Yes, but these are interesting times. Things are shifting these days, places changing. The second half of the twentieth century is approaching, and they say it won't look anything like the first."

"Is that what they say?"

"I believe so. The word is the war will end."

"Of course it'll end. They always do."

"But soon, Mr. Bruder. In the next year, year and a half. All I'm say-ing is you might want to think about being ready."

"Ready?"

"For life after the war."

"I've been ready for life after the war since the last one." There was a foreignness to him that Blackwood couldn't place: his formal syntax contrasting with his plodding movements; his large body so quiet and contained. More than anything, Bruder seemed to be a frontiersman, and looking at him Blackwood felt as if he were staring at the history of California itself.

"I see you noticing the books, Mr. Blackwood. Do you like Gib-bon?"

"I'm not much of a history man myself. I go more for numbers and that sort of thing. You know, adding things up."

"I can tell you're not from California."

"What would make you say that?"

"You strike me as a man from back east," said Bruder.

"I've been living in Pasadena for more than a dozen years. Some would say that makes me more Californian than most."

Bruder pulled off his wet sweater, the collar catching his hair and re-vealing again that picture-star profile and the night-dark scar. Some-times Blackwood's boyish face left him feeling a bit insubstantial, and he would stand at the mirror and imagine himself transformed, with the bursting, manly features Bruder possessed in full supply: bushy hair thick enough to snare a hand, a granite-hard profile, a sturdy chin. Bru-der probably didn't even know what he had, and a flea of insecurity bit Blackwood's sensitive flesh.

"You're from Pasadena?" said Bruder. He was busy unlacing and opening his boots to dry them at the fire. "That's a long way from here."

"Not so far. The Imperial Victoria gets me there in a few hours."

"I remember when it would take a day."

"You've been?"

"You could say that. It was long ago."

"You might not recognize it. It's become quite a city. And we've got a concrete parkway that runs along the bottom of the arroyo all the way to Los Angeles. Three lanes in each direction. They're thinking of extending it out to Santa Monica Beach."

"I've heard."

A flame rose in the fire, eucalyptus sap cracking, and the two men sat silently until Blackwood cleared his throat. "I'm prepared to make an offer."

"I'm not prepared to sell."

"Why not?"

"I'll never leave Condor's Nest."

"Don't you think one day you'll grow tired of winter fishing and tugging up a couple of acres of onions?"

"I plan to die here, Mr. Blackwood."

"You want to be buried *here*?"

"I didn't say that."

The conversation had turned ghastlier than Blackwood liked, and he tried again. "Think about your daughter."

"My daughter?"

"Yes, Sieglinde."

Bruder sat frozen, his lips pressed together so hard they were turning white. Then his hand reached out and delicately stroked a twig of pink coral that sat upon the bookshelf.

"I'm sorry. That was her name, wasn't it?"

"No one has told you that Sieglinde is my daughter."

"Of course, I'm sorry. My mistake, Mr. Bruder. But tell me, what kind of name is Sieglinde, anyway? Rather unusual for a girl these days. Is it a family name, by chance?"

"I'm afraid it's time for you to leave, Mr. Blackwood. Condor's Nest is not for sale."

"I hope I didn't say anything to upset you."

"You've said nothing that I'll remember in the morning."

"Can I give you my card? In case you change your mind?"

"My mind is firm."

"But just in case," and Blackwood left it next to the pendant of coral, which was intricately carved and strung along a leather thong. He held the coral to his eye and saw that there were words inscribed on it, but he couldn't read them in the dim light. "Beautiful piece," he said, holding it in the space between his face and Bruder's.

Bruder took it and folded it into his palm. "Yes, she is." An eerie calm veiled him, as if for a moment he were traveling somewhere else. Blackwood tried to shake his hand good-bye, but Bruder was motion-less, propped against the wall, his eyes glassy. He was staring at nothing in particular; Blackwood stood beside him and could hear their breath rise and fall in unison. Blackwood didn't want to leave just yet, not until Bruder shook himself from his daze, and standing next to the bookshelf Blackwood pulled out the volume of Gibbon. Stinky had recom-mended it once, but where would Blackwood find the time? Black-wood and Bruder were close, their shoulders nearly touching. The rank odor of salt and fish scale seeped from Bruder. Lightning flashed over the ocean, and the bulb on the wire went out. The cottage fell dark, and then, eventually, the weak yellow light returned. Blackwood opened the book and found on the endpaper a name written over and over: *Sieglinde! Sieglinde! Sieglinde!* There was also written, "This here book belongs to my brother Siegmund and to no one else and to those who crack its pages and smudge its ink I curse you, all of you, to your death! And beyond!" It was dated 1914. Because he was a man of numbers, Blackwood knew the dates didn't add up. "Was this written by your girl?"

"Who?"

"Sieglinde?"

But Bruder said nothing, and Blackwood returned the book to the shelf. "Good night, Mr. Bruder."

Bruder failed to respond.

"I'm sure we'll see each other sometime soon," Blackwood added, but after he'd buttoned himself into his coat and pulled down his hat, a tic rose in Bruder's jaw and he said, his finger caressing the coral, "I doubt that, Mr. Blackwood. I should think we'll never meet again."

3

MRS. CHERRY NAY WASN'T from Pasadena, nor did she pretend to
be, but by 1944 she knew as much about the city as anyone born at the
Arroyo Seco's lip. Her name as a girl hadn't been Cherry, and certainly
it hadn't been Nay, and when she arrived in Pasadena on New Year's
Day 1920, she quickly shed a few pounds from her past. Cherry walked
with small strong legs and a sturdy gait, her pistol-gray curls shooting
from her head. Since the outbreak of war, the simple, colorless clothing
she had worn all her life had become fashionable among the women of
Pasadena; over the years, Cherry had begun to blend in in other aspects
too. She was forty-one, and only once in her life had she lied about her
age: when she was seventeen, she told the editor at the *Star-News* that
she was eighteen and a half; during this interview she also embroidered
her experience reporting society gossip, inventing a story of lurking in
a hibiscus to catch a railroad heiress in illicit arms. On the spot, the editor had hired Cherry, and she'd worked for him for more than ten
years, stringing for the *American Weekly* insert too, eventually becoming
a well-known and sometimes feared columnist. But long ago, Cherry
Nay had given up that sort of life. Now she and her husband, George,
ran Nay & Nay, real-estate brokers and development. She left the development to George and handled the residential sales, and over the
years Cherry had learned that a real-estate broker could uncover as
much as a reporter, often more. Because she no longer considered herself a snoop, she tried not to peer into the yawning drawers in her
clients' bedside tables, but there they were, open like infant coffins,
offering her a full view into their lives, the Bible next to the sleeping
pills. Ever since her childhood, Cherry had taken pride in her ability to

piece together a person's life with only a few scraps of information, a Holmesian skill she put to use throughout her day. Back in 1930, she had first met George at a City Hall hearing over the proposed motor parkway, six lanes of concrete he and the others wanted to pour along the bottom of the arroyo. George had an attractive, muscular build and pretty, almost girlish blue eyes, and he carried a volume of Marcus Aurelius shoved up under his arm. He looked like the type of man who was prone to yelling, but in fact he spoke softly, choosing his words with care. He was determined to build the parkway, and he told the hearing in nearly a whisper that he wouldn't give up until the concrete had dried. At the time, Cherry had known nothing else about him, but just this was enough for her to be able to imagine his entire life; and it was enough for her to know she wanted to give up reporting—"It's a dirty business," she predicted George would say one day—to become Mrs. Cherry Nay.

But on this December morning in 1944, all that felt like another life, one she had reported on, filed, and tossed away. She had a near perfect memory, recalling everything of the years when she had signed her columns "Chatty Cherry," but there was an uncomfortable, telescoped distance between that woman and Mrs. Cherry Nay, who had to get across town for a nine o'clock showing at the Rancho Pasadena. The seller was a man by the name of Bruder; she had known him since she was a girl, and she liked to think that if she had done any good as a journalist, it had been with him. He was selling the old orange ranch, 160 acres, a place where quite a few things had happened in the last generation, and as Cherry drove west on the Colorado Street Bridge— "Suicide Bridge," they'd been calling it since it opened years ago—she promised herself not to get bogged down in its past. That was the trouble of a perfect memory: at any time it could flood Cherry, the dam loosened by the scent of orange blossoms on the breeze or the way the morning light cut into the hillside, and especially when she drove down the coast to Baden-Baden-by-the-Sea. Cherry hadn't spent much time at the rancho herself, but her old friend Linda Stamp had seen her life change there, end there too, and in some ways, Cherry had to admit, her life as well had turned the corner because of the Rancho Pasadena. Cherry preferred to keep herself removed from the narratives of others, but in this case she hadn't entirely succeeded, becoming a bit player in a larger story, a fact she was reluctant to admit, especially to herself.

Her appointment was with a man named Blackwood, whom she knew of but had never met. George, who had gone to Washington to draw up contingency plans for the real estate of German cities, had warned that Blackwood was a small-timer; "a bit of a looky-loo," George had written in one of his nightly letters. Yet few others had called about the rancho—it had become something of an anachronism by 1944—and Bruder had reminded Cherry that he was anxious to strike a deal: "Do what you can to relieve me of it," he had said. The pain in his voice would be apparent even to those less observant than Cherry Nay.

On the telephone, Mr. Blackwood had spoken in a somewhat child-like voice, one that Cherry had found sincere, and she pasted this observation to her developing profile of Andrew J. Blackwood.

She was driving quickly through the Linda Vista hills, where the live-oaks canopied the streets and the scent of run-over skunk hung noxiously in the dewy morning; she was in a hurry to reach the house and open things up prior to Mr. Blackwood's arrival. And at precisely the same time that Mrs. Cherry Nay was turning her key in the door of the Rancho Pasadena mansion, the Imperial Victoria was crossing Suicide Bridge, the morning sun burning in Andrew Jackson Blackwood's rearview mirror.

On the seat beside him was the advertisement from the *Star-News:*

EVERYTHING FOR SALE

BEAUX-ARTS MANSION

100 ACRES OF ORCHARDS

60 ACRES OF GROUNDS

YOUR OWN ARROYO!

THE RANCHO PASADENA

LAST CHANCE TO OWN A PIECE OF CALIFORNIA HISTORY!

He had had to phone twice, eventually securing an appointment with George Nay's wife. Mrs. Cherry Nay had given him directions in a friendly but distracted voice, as if she had just realized she had lost something, a diamond ring down the drain or something of the sort. Blackwood interpreted this as an encouraging sign that he was dealing with a birdbrain. But her directions had proved topographically precise, including that the asphalt would end at a black walnut, and that the street would become a white dirt road, and that at the road's end there'd be a gate covered in wild cucumber. "A dirt road? In Pasadena?" This had brought a ripple of hope to Blackwood, who wondered if much of the rancho remained undeveloped, a crude piece of arid scrubland. Over the telephone he had inquired about the price, but Mrs. Nay had said, "Now, Mr. Blackwood! You know as well as I that I'd never give that out over the phone."

Over the years, Blackwood had heard surprisingly few stories about the ranch and its family, the Poores. As far as Blackwood knew they all were dead now, Captain Willis Poore the last to go, a heart attack last year while doing calisthenics on his terrace, or so Blackwood had read in the obits. The captain's wife, a woman by the name of Lindy, who, according to the *Star-News,* wasn't from Pasadena, had been dead for a number of years; his sister, Lolly, too, a girl who had once kept the largest rose garden in Southern California. The obit had gone on to say that the rancho "had seen its best days pass," and Blackwood had made a note to keep his eye on the auction block. The rancho sprawled at the western edge of Pasadena, tucked between Linda Vista and Eagle Rock in a small valley that most people didn't know how to find, including Blackwood. He thought, vaguely, that he had heard Stinky say that the family had something to do with the founding of Pasadena; but Stinky also added that the Poores weren't a Cal Tech family, that was certain. "Goodness, now take a look at this," Stinky had said on the telephone. "I'm looking at a 1925 Valley Hunt Club roster, and sure enough, here they are. Captain Willis and Miss Lolly Poore, Junior Members."

The dirt road was in bad shape, toothed coyote brush and thickets of poisonous buckeye creeping into the car's path. Blackwood drove carefully, worried about his paint job, making his way up the chaparral hill. The rains had left everything blindingly green, the deerweed in bloom with tiny butter-colored flowers and the sagebrush tipped with yellow blossoms. Vines of Pacific pea climbed the live-oaks, their ovate leaflets shimmering in the December wind. A row of bluish leaves sprouted from the road's center hump, an early sign of a poppy trail. The car continued its climb, and the pitch of the road steepened. Soon the ceanothus and the lilac and the twisted-trunk madrone were nearly choking off the car's path. The morning's blue shadow pressed the side of the hill, a chill touching Blackwood's neck, and he thought about turning around. But at last the car approached the tall black gate. As Mrs. Nay had said, vines of wild cucumber twisted through the wrought iron; Blackwood got out and shoved the gate, and to his surprise it opened easily, as if a hand were pulling it from the other side. It was warm from the sun, and he dragged it across the road; dust rose in a line that seemed to mark the rancho's boundary, a border to another world.

Back in his car, Blackwood continued up the hill, switchbacking through thickets of holly berry and pink-veined laurel sumac and minty eucalyptus. He was listening to the Saturday "True Stories" program on KHJ, and just as the actress on the radio whispered in a panic "I think there's someone in the house!" reception was lost. Blackwood stretched to fiddle with the dial, and to his great disappointment the white plastic knob snapped off in his hand. The road turned sharply, but Blackwood, whose eye was on his dash, failed to turn with it, and the Imperial Victoria's front wheels ran off the road and the car teetered over the edge. With no time to spare, Blackwood's frightened foot found the brake; he was on the verge of a terrible plunge into the arroyo below.

Yet when put into reverse, the car performed for Blackwood. With sweaty palms he steered back onto the road. He mopped the moisture from his face and, reminding himself that caution was the developer's guide, continued up the hill. Beyond the bend, the one he had almost missed, the road crested and the wildbrush fell away and before him was a wide, untended lawn surrounded by tight-budded camellias and yews and fan palms swaying high above. The grass needed reseeding, but immediately Blackwood began to tally the acreage. The great lawn alone must have added up to nine or ten.

The road skirted the lawn, and soon the dirt gave way to pavement, a strip of white concrete cracked and sprouting branchlets of ricegrass. Blackwood reached for his hat with the maroon band and the tiny golden feather, propping it on his head, and it was then that he saw the house. The Poore House, as Mrs. Nay had referred to it on the telephone, dwarfed the mansions on Orange Grove—"Millionaires' Row," they used to call it long before Blackwood moved to town. The house seemed to Blackwood even bigger than the Hotel Vista, but that wasn't possible; in its heyday the Vista could sleep five hundred. Blackwood thought about how Pasadena's richest citizens, tucked behind hedgerow and hairy-leafed arroyo willow and pillared gate, called their Mediterranean villas *casitas,* their slate-roofed palaces *cottages,* their

Greene & Greene redwood mansions *bungalows.* "It's how they are," Stinky had remarked, in his analytically detached way. "There's no economic rationale for denying one's wealth, the way some people do around here. But it wasn't always like this. A generation ago it was just the opposite, everyone flaunting about. Things change, don't they, Blackwood?"

Blackwood would have to present himself to Mrs. Nay as unimpressed, not letting on that he'd never seen an estate like the Pasadena; as if he were used to surveying private kingdoms. She had described the mansion as Beaux-Arts, but it was more than that: it was a twisted California mélange of Italian villa and Andalusian farmhouse and French château, three stories, plus attic, whitewashed with a red pantile roof supported by a cornice decorated with escutcheons bearing navel oranges and bobcat heads. A wide terrace ran along one side of the house, its chipped balustrade topped with marble urns potted with dying yucca—Blackwood guessed this was where Captain Poore had fallen dead. Creeping ficus jacketed the eastern half of the house, tangled with a dying passion-fruit vine.

Blackwood drove through the portico's narrow columns and parked the car. He saw no one and heard only the chime of the yew leaves and the calling jays. In the distance, the Sierra Madres were limey yellow in the early sun, their peaks protected by snow, and it occurred to Blackwood that he had found a private world separated from the rest of Pasadena. It was not altogether impossible that they'd be asking too much for the Rancho Pasadena; right away he'd have to get the price out of Mrs. Nay.

"What are you talking about?" said Cherry Nay. "You haven't even seen the place. Let's not talk about prices until I've shown you around." She was the forty-and-over ladies' tennis champion at the Valley Hunt Club, and ten years of rushing the net—how Cherry Nay loved to volley and smash an overhead!—had worked her skin into a supple brown leather. In person there was nothing birdbrained about Cherry, and she sensed that her very presence had surprised Blackwood, as if the most apparent facts about her didn't add up easily: her girl-size body and her sun-worn face and her old lady's hair and her pleasure, and enviable skill, in assembling information and relaying it with authority. She had a habit of closing her sentences with the firm statement *And that's just the way it is,* and she said this now as she told Blackwood that since he had bothered to come out to the ranch, he might as well stick around for the tour. "Now let's see this big old house!" She said this with the giddiness that had greeted Blackwood on the phone, and he was disappointed in himself for misjudging her; he wasn't dealing with a rube at all.

They moved down the gallery that ran the length of the mansion. The house was empty except for a row of gilt-legged chairs draped in muslin and, at the base of the main staircase, a six-foot marble statue of Cupid blindfolding a half-robed woman whose bare stone breasts caused Blackwood to avert his eyes, a modesty Cherry noted as she explained, "The owner is selling everything as is."

The house had been built in 1896, she said, for a land speculator and orangeman by the name of Willis Fishe Poore I. "Carved out of the old Rancho San Pasqual. It replaced an earlier but also grand mansion," she said over her shoulder, moving quickly, assuming that Blackwood could take everything in at her rapid pace. What Cherry was careful to keep to herself was that Bruder had called from the village booth early this morning and asked if she knew anything about a man named Andrew Jackson Blackwood; he'd been poking around Condor's Nest, Bruder had said, and Cherry, careful not to lie, had said that she'd never met Mr. Blackwood. "Is he a serious fellow?" Bruder had inquired. "There's something about him that makes me think he might be the one." Cherry had said she would try to find out. She hadn't revealed that Blackwood would be inspecting the Pasadena in a few hours, and Cherry somehow understood that it would be best for her to mediate. She knew she had something to gain by keeping each man away from the other for as long as possible, allowing information to transmit through her.

"Willis Fishe Poore?" said Blackwood.

"The first."

"The first?"

"Mr. Poore, as I'm sure you know, was one of Pasadena's founders. He kicked off the Indiana Colony back in 1874. Not that George and I care about those things—whose homestead was here first and all that rigmarole of the past. But as I'm sure you know, there are those around town who take great pride in their antecedents." When the house first rose on the hill the ranch totaled 2,500 acres, but that was long ago, said

Mrs. Nay. Now the Pasadena was a not-unimpressive 160: 60 acres for
the estate and its gardens—"what's left of them"—and 100 acres set
aside for the orchards, half dead and the other half gone wild, producing oranges as black and filmy as coal. "The spreading decline hit during the Great Drought back in 1930, doing the grove in once and for all.
It's too bad, really. It was mostly navel, that was the crop. But there was
grapefruit, tangerine, cherimoya, mandarin, apricot, blood orange,
peach, walnut, sapota, and Kadota fig. It was quite a place, Mr. Blackwood." Once there'd been a staff of six gardeners, Japanese men in
green rubber boots who swept the lawn with bamboo rakes. In the
house there'd been secretaries and chambermaids in lace pinafores and
a seamstress and, later, a chauffeur who parked the cars in the converted
stable. It took Willis Fishe Poore four years to build the house, and
thirty mules to level the hilltop and dig the trout pond and clear the two
acres for the thousand rosebushes. The house resembled the Château
Beauregard, said Mrs. Nay. "Elmer Hunt—you've probably heard of
his nephew Myron—transformed it into a . . . I suppose the best description is a California *castillo*." There was a bowling alley in the basement and a billiard room where Mr. Poore used to gamble with his
ranch hands and a loggia off the portico where delicate Arcadia orange
trees, planted in porcelain saki barrels, blossomed so sweetly that Lolly
Poore, Mr. Poore's daughter, once collapsed from the onslaught of their
perfume. There were twelve bedrooms, each with a view of the orange
grove, and eight baths—"The first full-service in Pasadena, George always reminds me to point out"—plus a back wing big enough for a staff
of twenty-four.

"But those days are over," said Mrs. Nay. "Nobody lives like that
anymore." She doubted Blackwood intended to live like that. He could
turn out to be the type of man who would raze everything, denuding
the hill even before he had a plan of what to do with it. It was a shame,
really, and although Cherry wasn't a sentimental woman she held out a
tiny hope that someone would come along and roll a carpet down the
hall and replant the groves. Nothing wrong with keeping a little bit of
history alive, Cherry liked to say.

On the landing between the first and second floors, they looked out
the window toward the North Vista and its dolphin fountain, now dry
and cracked, and a camellia garden reclaimed by a bramble of red-
berried toyon. From this view, Cherry realized, the ranch appeared

rather forlorn, as if it were straining to expose its true sadness to its visitor.

"How long has the house been empty, Mrs. Nay?"

"A year or so. But it was on the decline for quite some time."

"Like so many properties around town, Mrs. Nay. They say Pasadena isn't what it used to be."

"I suppose you're right, Mr. Blackwood. When was the last time anyone built himself a mansion? Years ago, probably 1929 or 1930 at the latest. I can remember when they went up two a week."

Blackwood sensed an opening, although he didn't understand where it might lead him. He said, "You mustn't forget the war, Mrs. Nay."

"Of course, Mr. Blackwood. I don't want you to think I'm not doing my part. We save our cooking fat in a tin can like everyone else, and the cook and I have learned more cottage-cheese recipes than I ever thought possible. I'm not complaining. Surely the war will end one day, but I have a strong feeling Pasadena will never be the same."

"Nothing will be the same, Mrs. Nay."

"That's true, Mr. Blackwood." And then, "And that's just the way it is." She paused before saying, "But that's not why we're here. There's plenty more to see, Mr. Blackwood! Note the Diana statue. That comes with the house as well."

She was having a hard time piecing Blackwood together; he was both rough and sophisticated, confident and self-conscious, adolescent and middle-aged. She knew he wasn't from Pasadena, and she knew that his application for membership at the Valley Hunt Club had been rejected. The same was true for the Athenaeum over at Cal Tech, even his friend Stinky Sweeney hadn't come out full-hearted on Blackwood's behalf; and the Playhouse had voted not to elect him to its board. But Cherry's sympathy for outsiders far surpassed her husband's and that of most of the people she knew, and she wanted to take Blackwood's hand and advise him to stop trying: some people will pass through the gates, and some never will.

On the terrace, she pointed out the orange grove and the ranch house and the outbuildings. "It comes with all sorts of picking and packing equipment. If you're interested, if you're serious, Mr. Blackwood, I will supply you with an inventory."

He felt obliged to say, "I am serious, Mrs. Nay."

Her finger traced the property line: "From that hill with the fire scar in its side to that one shaped like a camel's hump, including that little arroyo over there."

"What's that noise?" asked Blackwood.

"What noise?"

"That whirring noise?"

The two stood on the terrace, its red Welsh tiles casting a glow about their feet.

"That's the parkway, Mr. Blackwood."

"Is it *that* nearby?"

"Yes, it's just beyond that first hill over there. Captain Poore, who was Mr. Poore's son, sold some of his land to the men who dreamed of paving the Arroyo Seco with a six-lane road." She failed to mention that one of those men was her husband.

"I suppose you can hear it night and day?"

"I'm afraid so. They say a thousand cars use it every hour." She and Blackwood exchanged a look that they both understood to mean that the parkway's proximity would knock something off the price; she held private the thought that the parkway had made her and George very rich. "Except for the automobiles, we really could be stepping back in time, couldn't we, Mr. Blackwood."

He thought her a handsome woman, small and mulish, like the few lady professors scuttling around Cal Tech. He thought to ask, "How about you, Mrs. Nay? Were you born in Pasadena as well?"

She said that she was from Baden-Baden-by-the-Sea, and that George was from Bakersfield. "We're both upstarts in Pasadena, but we've done all right for ourselves. We've been over on Hillcrest for the past ten years and we've seen the changes, Mr. Blackwood. And we know the next ten will bring even more." She was of two minds about what she did in real estate—ushering in progress and stamping out the past—and sometimes it was as simple and innocent as shepherding a bungalow with a swing on its porch from one generation to the next, but other times, especially with George's deals, it meant deciding that the past should come down altogether: choosing one hundred tiny new houses over a citrus grove.

Blackwood noted that in the past several years the changes had been especially rapid: the Hotel Vista converted into an army hospital, the candied-fruit shops on Colorado Street boarded up, and a dozen Orange Grove mansions abandoned in the night and turned into rooming houses, or pulled down by rat and ivy. A nearly imperceptible brown veil hung over the rancho's valley, blurring the landscape like one of the *plein-air* paintings that hung in the ballroom of the Valley Hunt Club— or so Blackwood had heard.

"And what's that over there, Mrs. Nay?"

"What?"

"That white structure at the far edge of the grove? Is it a folly?"

"Not at all. That's the mausoleum. They're all buried there, the whole family."

"Who?"

"The Poores. Most recently Captain Poore. He followed his wife and sister by more than ten years." And then the memory washed over Cherry and she said, although she didn't intend to, "She was an unusual woman."

"Who?"

"His wife."

Continuing her tour, Mrs. Nay explained that the library's mahogany paneling had come from a manor outside Windsor, pried from the walls of a cash-poor earl and crated to California by the Duveen Brothers. The roller shades were drawn and the seams in the herringbone parquet collected dust, and the room was gray and vacant, except for the six thousand books on the shelves. "The present owner chose not to take them. He says he doesn't like to read another man's books. He's not from Pasadena, Mr. Blackwood. Or, I suppose he is, but not like anyone else."

"How do you mean?"

"He was an orphan. Raised at the Children's Training Society, out by the old City Farm. It closed a while back now. You probably don't know it. There's no reason you would."

"I'm afraid not." Blackwood pulled a volume of Gibbon from the shelf and found a bookplate that read, *This book belongs to the library of Lindy Poore, 1930.* The pages were heavily underlined and annotated. On the inside of a schoolroom edition of *The Three Musketeers* he found a signature, written over and over, *Sieglinde Stumpf.*

"Sieglinde Stumpf?"

"What's that, Mr. Blackwood?"

"Who's Sieglinde Stumpf?" He pointed to the signature.

"She was the mistress here."

"Here?"

Mrs. Nay nodded, and her hand fell to his wrist. Sometimes Cherry would say to George that she hadn't thought about Linda Stamp and Bruder in years: "It feels like someone else had known them, not me . . ." But in truth, a day didn't pass when she didn't turn over the details, the stones of the story tumbling and polishing in her mind. "Tell me, Mr. Blackwood. Is it the house or the land that interests you?"

"Both, Mrs. Nay."

"Do you have any intention of preserving things as they are?"

"No plans yet, Mrs. Nay. But anything is possible. I'm most interested in what's best for the property. And for Pasadena."

"I was hoping you'd say that," she confessed. "We shouldn't rip up every last thing, should we? On most days, I find the past a useful thing to keep in mind. I had a gentleman in here who had an idea to turn the mansion into a halfway house. Another fellow wanted to build an apartment complex where the roses are. You can't imagine what he had planned for the orange grove. Still, the present owner has little reason to seek preservation. If it were up to him, he'd tear down the whole thing. He says the only thing the mansion could be used for is a home for old ladies."

"A home for old ladies?"

"That's what he says, and I know he's probably right. But I'm sure you can see this is a one-of-a-kind. In the end I am a realistic woman, Mr. Blackwood, and my only hope is that the future owner thinks carefully before he raises his ax."

"There aren't many people who can take on a mansion and one hundred and sixty acres just for themselves these days, are there, Mrs. Nay? Few people set themselves up as barons anymore."

"That's what the present owner says." In the dim library, her eye gleamed and she made a little swing with her arm, as if she were on the tennis court.

"Did you mention who the present owner is? Is he Captain Poore's heir?"

"I didn't mention the name, Mr. Blackwood. He has asked me not to say."

"I understand."

"But he is an unusual man." She said this to test Blackwood, to fillip the crystal of his interest to hear how it rang.

"Is that so?"

"I've known him for years and years." She added, "He once worked the orange ranch here."

"And now he owns it all?"

"It's a long story, Mr. Blackwood. Mr. Bruder's history is complex." She knew that the revelation of Bruder's name would startle Blackwood. Cherry wanted to grade his resourcefulness, to see if he was the type of man who could stitch together a story with the little scraps she had meted out.

"Mr. Bruder?" said Blackwood, pressing his lips together so as not to give anything away. He peeled back the window shade: the small valley lay before him, the hills fighting off the fiery reach of the new houses, the roof tiles as orange as flame and the fresh roads the color of smoke. What was the likelihood that it was the same man? On the other hand, what was the likelihood that there were two? "Do you have any idea why Mr. Bruder is selling?" asked Blackwood.

"As I said, it's a long story."

"I have time."

"I really shouldn't say. After all, I'm representing the seller."

"It would help me in my decision. And my decision might be for the good of things in Pasadena." Cherry didn't say anything, and Blackwood tried again. "Who is this girl named Sieglinde?"

"Which Sieglinde? There are two." Cherry checked her watch. She didn't know why she felt the need to tell the story, but it pressed at her from beneath her skin, an angry fist punching out. Like Blackwood, she sensed that an era was coming to an end, and perhaps she wanted to set things straight before the world moved on. And unlike Bruder, Cherry had never made a promise to keep a secret; and oh! how from the day she first heard Bruder's name she had known he would change their lives. Now they were allies of a sort, she and Bruder, hooked together to a past that was receding quickly. She had recounted the story to George early in their marriage, and he had said, his lips gentle upon her forehead, "Cherry, I'm glad you've given up newspapering. It makes you ponder such horrible truths."

"Should we pull a couple of chairs onto the terrace?" she said to Blackwood. "Beneath the coral tree?"

"After you, Mrs. Nay."

The transition from the library to the white sun erupted a flash in

Blackwood's eyes. For a second he couldn't see, and then his pupils readjusted and Mrs. Nay was waving her hand, "Over here, over here."

On the breeze was a lingering scent of citrus. The past blossomed on its sturdy stalk. The memory carried Cherry upon its sweeping flood and she said, but not to Blackwood, "Where to begin, where to begin?" She hesitated, and then, with her eyes sealed, said, "Where did the trouble first begin?"

SPRING

part two

A mute remembrancer of crime,
Long lost, concealed, forgot for years,
It comes at last to cancel time,
And waken unavailing tears.

EMILY BRONTË

1

DOWN THE COAST, along the old El Camino Real, in a flatland between the ocean and a rancid salt lagoon, not quite midway between the
bougainvillea-buttressed missions of San Juan Capistrano and San Luis
Rey, was the village of Baden-Baden-by-the-Sea. At the turn of the century it was a handful of acre farms and fishing shacks—"blackies," they
were called—and a straight strip of gray-sand beach. At one end of
town, on the bank of Agua Apestosa, the long-dead virgin Donna Marròn had built a schoolhouse, where generations of student eyes had
reddened in the swamp-ripe afternoon breeze. At the other end, on Los
Kiotes Street, was Margarita Sprengkraft's P.O. and general store, where
the twine of gossip wrapped up every purchase. A hundred yards from
Margarita's porch stretched the village pier, which groaned under the
pressure of high tide and the weight of fishermen leaning perpetually
against its rail. Up on the bluff above the village was the Fleisher gutting house, a lean-to warehouse that swayed in the wind and dumped
buckets of fish blood into the sea and employed fishergirls from the
farms, young women whose fingers stank and whose clothes at day's
end sparkled with the sequins of scales. Each March, after the last winter storm, the farmers came to town to rebuild the pier, but the gutting
house never fell to the January storms; the fishergirls were always busy,
day after day, year after year, knifing open the pale pink shells of quivering rock scallops, or slitting open mackerels and turning their delicate
flesh inside out.

And in the village center sat a large round boulder of red chert. At
sunset, the fiery rays playing on its dimpled surface made it look like a
ten-ton navel orange. It was surrounded by a bunting-draped viewing

platform that resembled something out of a small midway or carnival.
The villagers called this rock Apfelsine, and perpetually trickling down
its stone-rind face was the mineral water that gave the town its name.
Since the 1870s the Apfelsine mineral spring had drawn settlers to this
part of the coastland, and it had drawn real-estate speculators too, men
who erected hotels for the tourists who journeyed here to buy tin cups
of Apfelsine water for twenty-five cents apiece. The waters were of
such a rich mineral complexity that the village promoters guaranteed
that their imbibement would deliver not only rejuvenation but transformation: "Drink a cup of pure Apfelsine water and be the man you
were meant to be! Become the girl you've always dreamed of!" The
tourists arrived with hopes of changing their lives and their fates, and
they drank at the spring and departed certain of their altered, and im-
proved, destinies: ugly girls went away hopeful of husbands, slow boys
left hopeful of fortunes, hard-luck men and women wet their lips with
spring water and returned home believing they would rise beyond their
lot. Every few years, when the real-estate speculators became swamped
by debt, the hotel at the spring's side would burn in a mysterious midnight fire, guests in white sleeping dresses running from the smoke.
But within a month a grander hotel would always replace it, its veranda
wider, its mineral baths deeper, its views of San Clemente Island forty-
nine miles offshore expanded.

And the villagers of Baden-Baden-by-the-Sea would laugh at the
visitors and the speculators and sell them sips of water and souvenir tin
cups and lobster dinners. But they would never turn to the Apfelsine
for their own thirst. For everyone on this particular stretch of coastland
knew better than to challenge his fate.

Almost everyone, that is.

Inland, tucked among the gold-grass hills, was an abandoned silkworm farm called the Cocoonery, which Herr Beck had refashioned
as a flower house and depot. Where millions of silkworms had once
devoured themselves cannibalistically, now Ensenada girls pruned bird-
of-paradise and long-stemmed lilies, packing the stalks in wet newspaper for train delivery. All around the village, nitrogen laced the soil,
and when the year saw thirty inches of rain the farmers made skimpy
but reliable livings rotating their crops among sweet onion and alfalfa,
red-leaf lettuce and white corn, leeks and chives and a little cotton. During the wet years, a few farmers dabbled in gladiolus and the hundred-

petal ranunculus. Once, a German farmer named Dieter Stumpf tested fate by planting thirty rosebushes on his ocean farm. But the salt in the wind pickled the buds and everyone told him to leave the rose briars to Pasadena, where they had better luck with their blooms.

But when drought blanched the year, the mineral spring ran dry and the tourists stopped coming and the speculators turned brittle, and no one could make a living at all.

A regular morning fog shrouded the bluffs and the fields of Baden-Baden-by-the-Sea, the heavy dew bending the brittle bush and the monkey flowers. On some winter days the fog never lifted, and the villagers—Spaniards and Mexicans and Germans twisted together into a wild Californian vine—padded through their work in damp ponchos while the greedy lips of the few remaining longhorn cattle worked the succulence from the cholla and the live-forevers pushing up from the crags. Yet for much of the year the fog would ascend early to reveal the hills and the scrub, the farms and the sea—an unknown paradise emerald in January and February and March, gold and gilded the rest of the year—through which the Santa Fe passed but didn't stop. The village had once been a marine outpost on the Rancho Marròn, a parcel of cattle land that stretched a half-day's ride between the Pacific and the first wandlike creosote bushes of the desert. But that was long ago, when the rancho's allegiance ran to the Spanish king—for whom the highway, still running north and south, was named. But the world of missions and padres, Mexican governors and suede-legged rancheros, fields littered with the sun-bleached debris of steer—horned skulls and carrion and carcasses skinned for hide and tallow—had disappeared by the time Dieter Stumpf beat the odds of side-wheel oceanic voyage and arrived in California in 1866.

The Stumpfs—faithful family of Schwarzwald—owned, through land grant, the sea cliff known as Condor's Nest, two score acres two miles outside Baden-Baden-by-the-Sea. The sandstone-and-blueschist bluff rose seventy feet above the Pacific, crowned by a trapezoid of field and an arroyo where a lonely puma prowled. The property had come as compensation for the tin cups Dieter and his brothers had produced for the Union Army in the Stumpfs' tiny hammer-tapping shop. The shop sat deep in the misty Black Forest on the outskirts of Baden-Baden, where waters heavy with minerals had long before earned a reputation for therapy, both hygienic and Providential. For more than two years,

young Dieter had worked late at night tapping his small-headed mallet
against the circular sheets of tin, *tap-tap-tap*ping cup after cup into
shape, curling over the lip with pliers. He produced his cups for the
Yankees and the Confederates and didn't care who won; all he cared
about was staying busy and receiving an eventual, if currently unspecified, reward. Dieter was smaller than most boys, with a head almost
pointy at the crown, and his face and hands were pruned like an old
man's. Nothing made him happier than working alone, tapping and
bending tin, out of teasing's range. When the Civil War—which from
Schwarzwald seemed more like an opera raging on a prince's distant
stage than anything with actual bloodspill—came to a halt, the federal
government of the United States offered Dieter and his brothers a piece
of land to pay for the tens of thousands of tin cups. But Dieter's older
brothers weren't interested in land on the other side of the world. In
exchange for his share in the Stumpf tinnery, they gave Dieter all rights
to the land grant, and happily sent their odd little brother on his way.
Yet to Dieter the reward was so great that his immediate hope was for
another war. Some might say that Dieter had been duplicitous in supplying both sides, but Dieter himself realized more than others that he
had been wise. For he believed that a boy could pave his own path, and
that was what he had done, with a mallet and thousands of dull, circular sheets of tin.

The official papers were slow to reach the thatched shop deep in the
fir wood, but when they did, and after the pale-faced sister at the moss-
walled nunnery downstream translated them, Dieter learned that his
offer for compensation was for one of three pieces of genuine American land: a wooded parcel described as prettily situated at the tip of Illi-
nois; a cottonwood plain at the foot of a mountain range he'd never
heard of, "the Stonies," as Sister Anke translated it; or a plot of California soil, up on a bluff, that stretched from an ocean-thrashed precipice
inland to a hill rolling with soil the color of caramel. This oceanside
land lay situated in a newly formed settlement called Baden-Baden-by-
the-Sea, named for its own mineral-heavy spring in which the old and
the infirm and the barren and the lovelorn and the Christ-scared
washed their feet and hands. One of young Dieter's repeating night-
mares was about meeting a girl—dark-eyed, hair wild round her face—
in the dawn but not knowing how to speak, how to shout "Wait! It's
you!" In the nightmare, language failed him, and so he chose the piece

of land, forty acres, where it seemed most likely people would shout and sing in his German tongue.

He arrived in California in September 1866 on a side-wheel steamer called the *Elephant Seal*. Upon taking deed to his land, Dieter, only fourteen but telling the world he was twenty, mistakenly believed he'd better get busy with his mallet or else he and his hinny, Caroline, would find themselves freezing beneath the cruel veil of the first snow-fall. That was how little he knew about where he had landed. The first cottage rose from the pounding of Dieter's mallet in twelve days. This was the same tool that had hammered a war's worth of tin cups, and somehow Dieter knew that this mallet would determine more than a few things in his life. At the eastern edge of his new land—which the Baden-Badeners had dismissed as too windblown to be worth anything—tilted a eucalyptus grove, their trunks pink and buckling like the skin on elbows. The grove had been planted by Donna Mar-ròn, who had possessed ill-conceived dreams of a rancho lumberyard. Those trees, gone wild over the years, provided Dieter with his first plank. The cottage's floors were green and weepy from the freshly cut wood, and the chimney leaned with stream stones. A coal stove, pot-bellied, coil-handled, disassembled and shipped to California in a crate on the *Elephant Seal,* sat portly on a large flat beach rock. In the alcove, beneath a shuttered window, Dieter first unrolled his horsehair blanket and slept, so tired that he dreamed of no one at all. This sensation would carry him through the years: nightly dreamless exhaustion from the hours in the field, clearing and tilling and planting and harvesting and separating and packing—all that work and only getting by. The hinny and the nitrogen-rich soil and the months of relentless sun brought Dieter no riches at all, only a steady hard life of rising with the bantams and retiring with the silvery moon peeking through the gaps in the tar paper. Each October, before anyone could guess whether the winter would be wet or dry, Dieter would twist himself with worry, wondering if this would be the year he'd be unable to feed his hinny and his hens and himself. His agrarian skills earned him enough of a reputation for the gimpy horsemen who hung around Margarita Sprengkraft's front porch to tip their hats and call him by the friendly nickname Cebollero, "Onion-seller," which he translated in his head as "Herr Zwiebel." The other villagers, some German but many more of Spanish and Mexican blood, trusted him enough to grant him the right to work the scale at the gutting house or borrow a double-barrel to shoot a bold coyote or kneel at their pews in the adobe cathedral where the waxy hands of Padre Vallejo caressed their chins as he offered the chalice. They asked Dieter to play his fiddle at the harvest dances and join the crew in burning the sumac creeping alongside El Camino Real, and not once did anyone claim he had succumbed to what was called "Californio fever," something Dieter eventually understood as old-fashioned laziness. The villagers of Baden-Baden-by-the-Sea accepted Dieter in every way but one: they refused to let him marry one of their own. And when he asked why, Margarita, at her counter, arranging bolts of calico, told him how Baden-Baden-by-the-Sea perceived him. "You're a funny little man. You're smaller than most ten-year-old boys. Your face is wrinkled and fat like a baby's. You make us think of a tiny creature stepping out of an enchanted forest. We've read about you in fairy tales. You own the worst piece of farmland around, right there at the ocean's edge. You weren't meant to marry." Did she say the word *Erdgeist*? Dieter wasn't sure, but afterward he would recount it as if she had: *Who would let his daughter marry a gnome? a stranger? he who is not one of us?*

Many years later, after Dieter married the girl from Mazatlán with the heart-shaped face, he built a second cottage. By then he was familiar with every pebble in the arroyo and every golden chinquapin and cinnamon tree cresting the hillocks and the intertidal marshes abutting Condor's Nest. Out by the eucalyptus stand, a great blue oak grew in yellow grass. Lore claimed that a Spanish settler had married an Arcadian princess beneath the oak's canopy, but Dieter was Teutonically suspicious of any myth that didn't involve Norns and Valkyrior. Regretting nothing, he axed the blue oak to a stump; and just as easily as the myth had billowed over the years, so it disappeared with the felled tree. But Dieter wasn't one to consider preservation, nor was anyone else those days in Baden-Baden-by-the-Sea. His handsaw, won in a poker game on the deck of the *Elephant Seal,* drove wide kerfs into the logs, splitting them into planks later smoothed with a file. The second cottage was no bigger than the first. There were three windows facing the Pacific, which for years Dieter had done his best to ignore. But the new cottage was more refined, with a bookshelf and plastered walls and a mantel carved with blue whales. Dieter strung his old horsehair blanket along a wire, securing privacy for the bedroom, and hung, in a ges-

ture he believed would be inviting to a female presence, a string of
washed-up baleen over the door. This cottage, lullabyed with the night
ocean, warm from the chimney, cocooned old Dieter and his young
bride in their conjugal bed, where they would retire stunned by fate and
fatigue. Dieter would smell of the chives and the leeks and the white
globes of onions, and Valencia would be perfumed by the owl limpets
and the hairy hermit crabs she'd learned to collect during an ebbing
tide. The shrouded bed, a mattress stuffed with mule hair, served as the
nativity pallet for Siegmund, in 1897, a runt of a baby, bright and dark
as a ruby grapefruit, eyes squinty and struggling, and then, six years
later, on New Year's Day, Sieglinde, a mass of black hair marking her
from the beginning.

Years later, Dieter would tell her about her infant gray eyes. "Gray
as gull," he'd say, in his accent that Sieglinde thought of as iron and
rust. "And we couldn't tell what color they would end up. One day they
looked like they'd fire up and turn permanently blue, and the next day
they seemed as if they'd turn as black and slick as a moray. Back and
forth, blue and black, black and blue, your eyes changing like a witch's,
as if there were a fire smoldering in you. Blue, like the belly of one of
your lobsters, black as that old tooth of mine that one of these days I'm
going to ask you to yank out." Eventually baby Sieglinde's eyes sim-
mered permanently black, and Dieter, who was well past fifty now and
somehow at last suited for his small, wrinkled *Erdgeist* body, attached
the plow to his burro Beatrice and cleared the land for the third cottage
of Condor's Nest.

He built it for the children with his mallet, a one-roomer with
diamond-paned windows and a tin-and-tar-paper roof and a porch
where chilies and laundry dried in the sun. Sieglinde's bed sat beneath
the window that faced the ocean; Siegmund's pitted-iron bedstead
pushed beneath the window that surveyed the fields. Before she was
six, Sieglinde had caught a puma pup in her claw-mouthed trap. She
spread the cat-skin cozily between their beds, ignoring Siegmund's
complaints that it was like sleeping with a feline ghost. Electricity had
yet to reach the farms surrounding the village. The lone kerosene lamp
was nailed to the wall above his bed, its circle of light failing to reach
Sieglinde's pillow. At night Siegmund would stay up reading, the lamp
reflecting off his spectacles, while Sieglinde would roll into her nightly
heaving slumber. She didn't understand where her brother's reading

appetite came from, but there it was—a longing that was foreign to her. Dieter made Siegmund read certain books: *A Guide to the Soils of the West; The Gentleman and His Ranch; The Benevolent and Proper Thinking of Today's Young Farmer.* But whenever he could, Siegmund would open a volume of history or literature. "You'll die with a book in your face," Sieglinde would declare, yawning, pushing her hair into her sleeping cap. Siegmund wouldn't respond, his body and his books huddled together. And Sieglinde—who even at age six had visions of the world beyond Condor's Nest and Baden-Baden-by-the-Sea—would pull the quilt to her chin and shut her eyes.

Her brother didn't see well, and she'd always say he had damaged his eyes reading in the weak light. Though his wire spectacles were expensive, he was careless with them—or so it seemed to Sieglinde—the arms snapping or the lenses popping out in the ocean or Siegmund simply forgetting where he'd left them, even if they were propped atop his head. "You'll go blind from reading," she'd say, unaware of her maternal tone. His lips would move as he read, and sometimes a whole word would emerge from his throat, as if he were testing out its meaning and how it might apply to the Stumpfs of Condor's Nest. Sieglinde could see that it was a struggle for him to comprehend the books—it would take him many months to finish one, sometimes even a year— and she wondered what made Siegmund try. "I want to learn for myself. I want to become an educated man," Siegmund would say shyly, as if such an utterance would expose his soul too rawly. And maybe it did: for already people said things like *Sieglinde's the bright one* or *I don't know why he even bothers* or *What on earth can he learn from a little History?* Sieglinde too possessed a vague notion that Siegmund was fighting his destiny, a battle that inevitably he would lose. Even at a young age, she had enough sense of the way things worked in the world to understand that he was meant to be an onion farmer, nothing more and nothing less, and that any attempt to climb out of the hole of his fate would prove futile—and, perhaps, even dangerous.

But Sieglinde also believed that certain people—like herself, like her father—could leave behind the world they came from. Certain people lived off the blood of free will.

She was an early riser, up with the coydogs, their blood flooded with spaniel and shepherd and retriever and rufous-eared coyote; up with the tide, up with the sun yawning above Siegmund's shallot field, where it reflected against the white bulbs peering through the soil. In many ways young Sieglinde was like her mother: dark-haired, strong in arm, long in throat, possessing a general loathing of idleness and imposition. The one difference—and this Sieglinde realized only gradually—was the color of their flesh: she had inherited her father's Teutonic paleness, while Siegmund's skin was a muted version of their mother's, like cinnamon atop a bun. When Sieglinde asked about it—*Why would we end up as if we're from different litters?*—no one could answer, nor did they try. Instead, Valencia would read Sieglinde the Bible—*There was a man in the land of Uz*—and she'd sit in her mother's lap both frightened and angry about the improbability of the stories: pillars of salt and a man in the belly of a whale. From the beach Sieglinde had seen the short-fin pilots and the migrating grays, and she knew that were one of them to swallow her she wouldn't survive; the yellowish baleen would end it for her, and maybe the only memorial would be the bunting of whalebone strung above the door. Did her mother believe that all this was true? Valencia revealed nothing, only hinted at what she believed by wrapping her arms around her daughter. Because Sieglinde always felt a tiny chip of pity for her mother, she decided to believe the tales. Did Sieglinde have a choice? She didn't think so: no, instead it was a matter of demonstrating to her mother the purity of her love. And so she believed what Valencia read, especially the story of Delilah and old Samson. That one was easy to understand, and Sieglinde thought of Siegmund. She realized, maybe for the first time, how simple it was for some people to transform themselves, to invent their lives.

There were other things, too, that separated Valencia and Sieglinde from Dieter and Siegmund. Their love of water, for instance. "Why do you suppose Siegmund hates to swim?" Sieglinde would ask. As a fishergirl she believed that wealth would come from the waves and the murky ocean floor, not from a fistful of seeds planted in a row. Early on she had learned to cast and catch, scale and gut, flay and ice, pound after pound of fish: sharp-snouted halibut, black-speckled sea bass, righteye starry flounder, lateral-keel bluefin, swell shark, mako, butterfly ray, priest, the loud black croaker, scaleless marbled cabezone, rubberlip seaperch, steep-profiled sargo, blunt-headed blacksmith, thrice-striped shiner, white-bellied opaleye, yellow-orange señorita, half-moon, turbot, skipjack, and the spiny clawless rock lobster pulled from the pots she built herself, their antennae tapping her wrist as if to remind Sieglinde that the world was hers to snare.

"Why do you suppose at supper Papa blesses only the earth?" Her mother would say that Dieter and Siegmund would never know certain things. "It has to do with where you come from." *De donde* . . . and Valencia would set to plaiting Sieglinde's hair and tell her the stories of her own youth.

Sieglinde loved her mother for many reasons, but especially because Valencia had survived misfortune—or had survived it thus far. After all, Valencia had arrived in Baden-Baden-by-the-Sea not by train or wagon but on an iron-hulled freighter, the *Santa Susana*. The ship had flown a Royal Hawaiian flag, and it smuggled Spencer pump shotguns with damascus-twist barrels between Los Angeles and Mazatlán; and Valencia, in 1896, first saw Condor's Nest from the ocean, from five hundred yards out, on a run up the coast. She was seventeen at the time, indentured to the ship's owner, a man named Moya, forced, along with a flat-chested girl four years younger than she, to comfort the captain and his crew through the roll of the night sea. It was dusk when Valencia first saw the sunset shimmering on the cottage's tin roof. Before she could talk herself out of it, she slipped over the *Susana*'s gull-caked rail. It never occurred to her that she wouldn't make shore; her arms, thin but muscled from years of shoving men away, brown from the sun, soft with a pale fur, turned again and again, propelling her toward the bluff. When she emerged from the tide—her blouse clinging, her skirt lost to the waves, kelp braided through her hair—she began to sob.

By now it was dark and the full moon had become Valencia's torch, and from the beach the sea cliff appeared too steep to scale. It loomed—seventy feet, she guessed—craggy friable rock and eroding sand and vines of ice plant and beach morning glory and evening primrose, their blossoms open demurely for the night. She walked up the beach, from one cove to the next, balancing herself with extended arms as she stepped through the pools of the splash zone, slipping on a loose stone, turning her ankle in a sinkhole. Each cove was more difficult to reach than the previous: rocks slick with the rising tide and red sea urchins, with skittering hermit crabs, with the greasy Pacific laver, with sea cucumbers like banana peels on her path. One cove had a secret cave in its wall, a dark room in the stone that looked like a nave, Valencia thought, frightened and moving on. Ramparts of rock isolated each cove, loose scree obstructing her. Eventually she became trapped by an impassable cliff that thrust itself up from the sea. Her attempt to scale it ended in a pair of bloody palms. Valencia turned around.

The tide was rising quickly, the waves exploding, so much louder than the Spencer shotguns the captain had shot off the starboard rail when showing his crew what he would do if a customs agent tried to board his ship. She worked her way back, past the cliff where she had seen the cottage, and beyond, hoping to find a beach where the bluffs turned to hills and a crevice or a chimney would announce itself as her exit. But she only stumbled into more coves—coves, she imagined, where on a fine summer afternoon a man and a woman might retreat, in fear of nothing, their pasts washed away and their futures undetermined. But on this early spring night, with the tide shoving forward, with her bloodied blouse, Valencia found herself once again a captive. She might as well have stayed on the *Santa Susana* and got herself shot on the bow, she was now thinking, perched on the sole dry rock she could find, her knees pulled to her chest, blinking back the tears. They tasted no different than the ocean, and to her the Pacific became an endless bowl of crying, filled by girls like herself, crow-haired girls who would do anything to escape their lives. How had she come to this? It was just like her, to leap into the ocean without any sort of plan. The moon was fat above the water, guiding the *Santa Susana* into port, Valencia imagined; guiding Valencia nowhere at all. She didn't know what she wanted—rescue or death—and she was too young, on that first night on the shore of Condor's Nest, to imagine anything else. The water pushed closer, splashing and shattering, crashing and battering, the reach of each wave an inch farther up the sand than the preceding one, so that before long rounds of water shot her in the face.

Then at once, as if from nowhere, a snowy plover pattered by her feet, happily singing *chu wee, chu wee.* Next followed its mate, nearly hopping over Valencia's foot: a soft white ball, legs orange and thin as candy-sticks. The two birds, gleaming in the night, scurried together as if in love. Where were they going? They hurried to the back of the cove, where a log of driftwood wobbled with each shove of the tide. Then the plovers disappeared. Aloft, Valencia assumed, although she couldn't see them above her, and something told her to check where they had gone. The sand was soft, swallowing her ankles. The water flushed around her shins. Ledges in the walls of the cove looked to Valencia like balconies, and she wondered if the plovers were up there, watching her like a pair of white-haired patrons in a horseshoe-shape theater.

Then she saw it. It was more of a chute than a path, erosion-carved, a long trough through the soft-stoned bluff. From its base, littered with the froth of tide, Valencia could tell that it would lead her out of the cove and up off the disappearing beach: a narrow gash in the bluff that would rise and widen and spill into a dry arroyo next to the cottage. The path would save her; she knew this the moment the pebbles pressed into her feet. And she would rise to the top of the bluff where Condor's Nest huddled, then a lone cottage aglow with the light of the coil-handled stove. She wouldn't meet her future husband that night. No, that night she would pass in the barn with Beatrice's serape and steaming dung warming her. Her meeting with Dieter would come the following morning, when her blouse had dried stiffly and a burlap sack, split open and tied with rope, revealed her long legs, and that meeting would prove fateful: nine months later Margarita Sprengkraft would be calling Valencia "Frau Stumpf," and Siegmund, with his poor eyesight, would be born.

And Sieglinde would always assume that because her mother had come from the ocean, she herself was in some way its child—a statement Siegmund found excessively dramatic. "Only a girl would say such a stupid thing," he'd sniff, the red tail of his sleeping cap snaking across his shoulder and his spectacles slipping down his nose.

"Only a boy would care about what a girl had to say," Sieglinde would reply.

She was thinking of this one afternoon in the late summer of 1914. Dieter had asked Sieglinde and her brother to sit down to the kitchen table. She knew something had happened because it wasn't suppertime and it wasn't anyone's birthday. She was eleven, already a busy lobster-girl, and she said, "Will it take long? I haven't much time." She'd been on her way to the beach when Dieter and Valencia called her inside. Sieglinde was planning to swim out to her pots before high tide.

"Sit down and be quiet for once," said Siegmund, pinching her arm. At the table, she could hardly sit still in her bathing dress, which revealed her shoulders—much to Dieter's, and Siegmund's, concern.

That very minute the tide was so low that she could have, had she been out on the beach instead of trapped in the dark cottage, snatched up purple sea urchins by the dozen, to say nothing of her potential lobster haul. She had struck a deal with her father—one that only years later would come to seem unfair—that for every dollar's worth of fish and lobster she sold at market, Sieglinde could keep a penny; she was no more greedy than most children, but a penny gleamed perhaps just a little more brightly in Sieglinde's eye.

The shuttered window in the alcove left the kitchen dim while the day outside the split-gate door pulsed brightly. Waiting at the long table where every night she ate her *papas locas,* their red skins bitter in lime juice, Sieglinde—possessed of a fearlessness she doubted she would ever outgrow—impatiently swung her legs from the bench.

"There's something I have to tell you," Dieter said at last. "Something quite serious."

"Now what?" said Sieglinde, dreading September, which meant the return to the schoolhouse at the edge of the stinky salt lagoon where Miss Winterbourne, pinned up in blouse and bun, patrolled the aisle with a flyswatter that would land on any young student's hand whenever a stray chirp flew from a mouth. *Swat, swat, swat,* Miss Winterbourne had snapped the flat of the swatter against Sieglinde's hand so many times that it no longer hurt; once during the previous school year Miss Winterbourne had struck Sieglinde all day and the girl had never flinched. Sieglinde had sat tall and extended a hand for another swat, like a princess waiting for a kiss. And oh! did she think she was smart, certainly smarter than sour Miss Winterbourne, smarter than anyone else in that mouse-guarded school, especially Charlotte Moss, who sucked on the end of her hair curls and asked for extra-credit homework in expository writing. Sieglinde thought this until the last day of school, until a minute before Miss Winterbourne rang her handbell for the final time that term and moved to Sieglinde with the flyswatter and smacked her across the cheek. Then Miss Winterbourne rang her bell, and Sieglinde, against her will, broke into tears. Siegmund had to carry her home, her legs wrapped around his waist.

Now, in August, with Miss Winterbourne waiting around the corner of month's end, Sieglinde couldn't guess what could be more serious than what lay ahead for her.

"A war has broken out," Dieter began.

"In Europe," Valencia added.

"And Germany's at the center of it."

"What does this mean?" asked Siegmund. A grim seriousness had overtaken him.

"It means that the world has changed before our very eyes. In one long day, everything has changed. We'll have to change too."

"What does this have to do with us?" Sieglinde asked.

"Germany has become the enemy," her father said.

She wasn't listening to him; she was thinking about her lobster haul: she could expect six in each pot at this time of year. Already she counted the coins those would bring at the gutting house, and the palmful of pennies she would keep. She'd been saving for a felt hat with a snowy eagle feather she'd seen at Margarita's; it would take her more than a year, but she had set the trap of her mind upon that hat. Once a month she would visit Margarita's to try it on, cocking her head in the mirror and announcing that one day she'd return for the *chapeau.*

"How can you be sure this business in Europe has anything to do with us?" she asked her father.

"Sieglinde, *jovencita,*" said Valencia. "It's the world we're talking about. The world's in trouble."

"I don't care."

"Would you shut up for once?" snapped Siegmund. "You wouldn't know anything serious if it hit you over the head." And despite how much she teased Siegmund, it stung her worse than anything, certainly worse than Miss Winterbourne's swatter, when he scolded her. At eleven she was in love with her brother, the way other girls were in love with their horses, or their fathers.

"We're going to have to change some things around here," said Dieter. "Starting with our names. People will begin to blame us."

It made no sense to Sieglinde that just because some Germans wanted to kill some Belgians on a mustard field she'd have to change her name. Her German name meant everything to her—because it was hers and no one else had it and it sounded pretty on the tongue, like a command. She nearly asked, "Just where is Germany, anyway?" But she knew this much: she knew it was much farther than her mother's Mexico.

"What are we going to change it to?" asked Siegmund.

"We can't call ourselves Stumpf anymore. We're going to change our name to Stamp."

"Stamp?" Sieglinde cried. "You mean like a postage stamp?"

Valencia took her hand and reassured her that most girls dreamed of growing up and taking another name. "It's only happening to you earlier than the rest."

But Sieglinde hadn't dreamed about this, and she said, "You mean like stamp out your brains? I'm going to jump on top of you and stamp, stamp, stamp you to death?"

"Please shut up." Gently, Siegmund's hand fell on hers.

"And, Siegmund. From now on we're going to call you Edmund."

"That sounds all right." He was seventeen, and recently a downy mustache had pushed forth upon his lip, and a creep of hair up his thigh, and a wet-soil scent, musky from his body's coves.

"Edmund?" Sieglinde cried. "Look at Edmund. Master Edmund! Ha ha ha on you!"

Then they turned to her, and she saw herself in all of them. The Stumpfs of Condor's Nest weren't Mexicans or Germans, she realized. They were Californians, a jumble of history that had become their own.

"And for you," Dieter began. "We'll call you Linda."

Her legs stopped swinging from the bench. "Linda? Do I look like a Linda to you?"

Her mother said she did.

"But that's silly. My name's Sieglinde. You can't change my name just like that." She hesitated. "Can you?" She sat motionless. Their eyes fell on her; she felt something move beneath her—was it the bench, or something else? Then she knew, in the late afternoon in the late summer—with the Euphilotes butterflies fluttering above the bluff, with her buoy bobbing in the ocean—that something in her life, something beyond her name, was changing today. The sunlight pressed through the crack in the split-gate door. Something waited for her outside in the yellow light. And before she knew what she was doing, Sieglinde Stumpf, now Linda Stamp—eleven years old and already with a history of improbably surviving scarlet fever, a spooked horse's hoof, and a baby stingray—ran from the table, bursting into the dooryard where the bantams preened and the hinny grazed, running down the arroyo to the beach, screaming, not aloud but in her head, "Linda Stamp! Linda Stamp! What kind of girl will be Linda Stamp?"

2

NOT LONG AFTER THE KAISER rolled across the hillocks of Belgium in the lavender-skyed summer of 1914, Dieter Stumpf, who now introduced himself as David Stamp, packed a roll of canvas trousers, a Catalina-wool sweater, his little cap with the earflaps, a rifle, and a pair of pliers. "I'm off to war." It seemed like an impossible outing for the old onion farmer: gray in the beard, freckled over, knuckle swollen like a mutton joint. As he set off, his rucksack was stooping him, the rifle oversize in his hands. "Are you sure you should go?" Linda asked. But her father saluted farewell, and Linda watched him move over the ridge, his roll strapped to his shoulders, whistling "Born in the Ocean, Died in the Sea." Charlotte Moss, whom by default Linda considered her best friend, came to witness the departure, scribbling notes about it in a little pad. "Where do you think he's headed?" asked Charlotte, the daughter of a seal hunter, her head spun with woolly hair. When he returned an hour later because he'd forgotten his lucky mallet, she asked him. "To the front with the boys. Don't worry, I'll be back." With the mallet swinging from his belt, Dieter departed again, this time for good.

Four letters arrived in four years, each at Christmas, each from a town along the front: Rheims, Soissons, Vimy, Ypres. Linda would watch Valencia read the letters over and over during the following winter months, pulling the pages from her work dress and tucking them back in until eventually, usually by Easter, the paper had flaked apart. Linda didn't understand it—how her mother had come to miss him so—and she was vaguely certain that such longing would never occur in her own life. Linda promised herself that she'd never miss anyone more than he missed her. She'd study her mother and wonder precisely when Valencia had become the woman she was now: bent at the wash-tub, lye-scrubbing the floor planks, prodding Linda to her chores. "Back to work," Valencia would say, steering Edmund to the fields and Linda into the ocean. Sold at market, Linda's winter catch of the kelp-colored tidepool johnny and the long-nosed baby shark would bring more money than Edmund's sweet onions. He always stored a hundred-pound sack beneath his bed, and in the dark morning, when Valencia called them to rise, they would look at each other in that stunned moment of waking, and each would find the eyes of the other red and slick with tears.

With their father gone, Linda proposed that they revert to their old names.

"Sieglinde Stumpf is dead. Why can't you get used to Linda Stamp?" Edmund would say this seriously, with a touch of pride in his cocked chin. Sometimes, Linda hardly believed they were of the same blood. She thought this more and more as time went on, late at night while the kerosene lamp burned. With the quilt taut at her chin, she'd try to sleep while Edmund read. In Dieter's absence he tried to teach himself to read German, borrowing the three books Dieter had brought over in the same crate as the coal stove: the three volumes of Gibbon, nearly three thousand pages, all in a language that felt to Linda as foreign as Chinese. What was he thinking, staying up late with a little dictionary and a pencil, wasting all that kerosene? "What could you possibly learn from the Romans?" she asked, only to receive a hurt frown in reply. Once she stole one of the books and wrote her name on the inside cover and a message to deter a potential thief. She hid it within her sheets, sleeping with it, its hard spine pressed against her thigh. In the morning, Edmund's eyes were redder than usual, as if he had whim-pered for the missing volume through the night, and when she pulled back her bedclothes he cautiously removed the book from her sheets, his head turned and his lips pursed, as if he were performing an un-bearable task.

But often at night Linda couldn't sleep, what with the lamp shed-ding its light past midnight and Siegmund perpetually turning pages in their quiet cottage. She tried to focus on the waves breaking against the bluff, counting their intervals, always surprised when one crashed stronger than the rest. She'd lie awake, her fingers threaded behind her head, and she'd listen to the ocean and to her brother clear his throat or produce a tiny, gentle *hmmmm,* and even after he at last extinguished the lamp her eyes would remain open and her ears would register the farm's every sound, her brother's every soft dream-groan. When the moon was full, she could make out his face across from her, the way he sucked his lip in his sleep or brought a curled fist to his eye. He'd grown sturdier in recent months, transforming in an almost secretive manner: his short arms thickened with muscle, and as if out of nowhere, a tiny tomahawk of an Adam's apple had appeared in his throat. In the dark, the hours passed more slowly, and Linda had time to think of another world, where the fields didn't reek of onions and they didn't have to go to school and Edmund and she could live together. She'd imagined a house on a hill somewhere, overlooking a valley, and this imprecise but gleaming notion of the future would keep Linda up through the night. No matter how tired she was, she'd rise before dawn and wrap herself in the rusted-button sweater knit by the Alsatian who lived next to Margarita's and pull on her rubber boots. Edmund would turn his back to her and step into his trousers, balancing clumsily on a single foot. She couldn't help looking, and she'd notice the fine hair on his legs, like the thin fur on the dogs' bellies. It occurred to Linda that her brother was leaping ahead without her, physically becoming someone else. She wanted to whisper across the narrow gap that separated their beds: "Edmund, what's happening to you?" She wanted to ask Valencia as well: What had happened to the girl Linda had heard about? The one who boldly fled the *Santa Susana?* Why had she changed when she took the name Stumpf? And changed even more when she called herself Mrs. Stamp? Linda didn't understand that one misstep could determine the outcome of a girl's life; despite the evidence, she didn't want to believe that a life, her life, was a scaffold of fragile constructions, flimsy and easily toppled. If Dieter had been around, she'd have asked him too: Do you remember anything about your youth in the Black Forest? Tell me about Schwarzwald! But she doubted that Dieter recalled anything more than how to hammer a sheet of tin and bend back the lip of a cup. And this was one of the first things Linda would profoundly misunderstand: she was wrong to think a man could cleanly shed his past when trying on a new identity. No, it was more like the silt at the bottom of a swamp, a new layer churning over the previous, sifting into a mucky stew, black and moist and eventually becoming deep enough to swallow a girl alive. And so each morning, after a night of sleepless sleep, Linda would pick her way down the arroyo's path to the beach and cast her rod. As the sun rose, her snelled hook and gut line would haul in redtail surfperch and three-finned tomcod, she'd struggle with a wandering baby barracuda and throw back an undersize green opaleye, and Linda would cast and reel until her sack was full and writhing with life.

3

BY THE TIME she was sixteen, Linda was known as the best lobster-catcher in Baden-Baden-by-the-Sea—acclaim she welcomed but would later regret. It wasn't because she had a dozen buoys; in fact, she had floated only one, yellow with a red stripe. It wasn't because she had strung dozens of pots along the pot warp; no, in fact she had lowered only eight to the ocean floor, hooking them to the line and laying the traps in the silty sand like a family of coffins. "Only eight!" one fisher-man declared. "My buoy has fifty!" Truth to tell, Linda was known as the best lobstergirl on this part of the coast because of a customized lob-ster pot that she never discussed, not because she thought of it as a se-cret but because there was no one to tell—except Edmund, and he said he wasn't interested. If he had been, she would have told him that her pots were longer than most and were made up of slender live-oak slats with gaps between them so wide that the pots looked incapable of trap-ping anything. Were you to stand one of her pots on its side on a dark night, you might not see anything but a box of air. Inside the pot, though, was a fatal lair. There were two rooms separated by a gut-line netting that Linda, lying awake in the middle of the night, knitted on her needle. The netting too was almost invisible, and more than once Edmund had tripped over a pile of it coiled between their beds. The lobster would pass through the entrance into the first room—the par-lor, Linda called it. Then it would slip into the second room, the kitchen, where the bait waited. The bait was another secret: Off Con-dor's Nest floated a dense kelp forest, and at its roots lived both the rock lobster and the sheep crab. Over the years, Linda had tried herring, sardines, pogies, mackerel, the head and backbone of a redfish, even a jelly. But more than anything else, Linda had learned, lobsters devoured crabs. So as part of her daily work, Linda would catch eight large sheep crabs and give the lobsters a hand by cracking their saucer-shaped shells. There wasn't a day, except in the blackest winter storm, when Linda didn't swim through the kelp forest to catch the crabs and lay them in the kitchens.

One day in the spring of 1918, she caught the biggest lobster anyone could recall: it weighed in at almost thirty pounds on the scale at the gutting house and measured nearly three feet in length. Mr. Fleisher called it Lottie, and sold it on Linda's behalf to someone in Pasadena who was throwing a banquet for the governor. Charlotte Moss came to see Linda to ask about the lobster. She told Charlotte everything, proudly revealing the secret of the sparsely slatted pots and the sheep crabs. Charlotte was compact and walked with an awkward gait, as if something had fallen on her hip and left it dented. In an attempt to bring her wiry curls under control she often employed a blue satin bow and palmfuls of Seroco Princess hair tonic, but nothing worked better than scissors and a baseball cap. Charlotte liked to wear trousers with a matching epaulette jacket, and if anyone ever said anything to her she'd answer, "This is just the way it's going to be." Linda liked this about Charlotte—not the somber uniform itself, but Charlotte's vision of herself, the sense of her already having transformed herself into the person she wanted to become.

It was Lottie the lobster that revealed Charlotte's ambition to be-come a newspapergirl; for Charlotte, who had sat in the yard biting her lip while Linda went on about the netting and the sheep crabs, left Condor's Nest and walked directly to the weekly Baden-Baden *Bee,* where she handed in her first thousand-word article. Not five days after Linda's greatest catch, the story ran on the front page, proclaiming Linda the best lobstergirl around. The article also informed the lonely-eyed fishermen who lived in the blackies of her secret pots and the sheep crab. Within a year, Linda, who had thought of the kelp forest off Condor's Nest as her very own, could count twenty-three buoys, each painted a different color, floating around hers. And it didn't even take twelve months for her to have trouble catching eight sheep crabs in an afternoon; and the crabs she managed to haul were smaller, almost im-perceptibly at first, but narrower across the shell nonetheless. And soon thereafter the lobsters too, although always waiting in the kitchens, had less heft in their tails, less reach in their antennae. Linda's lobsters now left little impression on Margarita's great fat face as she weighed them and gave Linda, in exchange, an increasingly meager stack of coins, all of which Linda had to hand over to Valencia, everything but the promised penny on the dollar.

It was because of this diminished stack of coins that in March of 1919, as Edmund's birthday approached, Linda found herself short of the necessary funds to buy her brother the gift she knew he wanted most: an atlas of California, two feet tall by two feet wide, with accordion maps and a red ribbon marker and gold lettering stamped on the morocco spine. For months she had eyed it behind Margarita's counter, and when she finally asked to see it Margarita's eyebrows rose. "I'm afraid that's twelve dollars." And then, "Linda, you and I both know your lobster haul isn't what it used to be." Linda proposed paying for it on layaway, but Margarita never sold to the Stamps on credit. "They're good enough people," she'd say at her counter to anyone who would listen. "But a little too close to the edge to extend a loan. It would take only a fire or a flood for everything to collapse around them." Instead, Linda decided, she would throw Edmund a picnic, although it wouldn't be much of a party: just herself and Edmund and Valencia and Charlotte Moss, who by now wrote a weekly column for the *Bee* called "The Whisper of the Sea."

Linda read in *Rob Wagner's California Almanack* that at sunset on Edmund's birthday the tide would be low and the beach wide. She spent the day at Valencia's stove, stirring the pot of chicken à la Providence, frying the oysters and the salsify fritters. On the beach, she secured an old blanket in the sand and pitched an awning over it with four fishing rods and the sheet from her bed. From above, the fluttering white sheet looked like the sail of a grounded schooner—a shipwreck on the beach.

She spent the afternoon hiking up and down the bluff, carrying the sandwiches and the jug of lemonade and collecting driftwood for a bonfire. How much easier things would be if there was a staircase leading to the beach, and not for the first time she thought of cutting the lumber and buying the two thousand wagon-box nails and erecting the one hundred steps herself; she had tried to interest Edmund in the project late one night but he had only turned away and told her to go to sleep.

She felt that some sort of ritual should commemorate Edmund's advancement into adulthood. She thought of a Maypole, but didn't know how she could get a big-enough pole down to the beach. She thought perhaps they should sacrifice something in the bonfire, something horrible like a leopard shark, but she had never caught a leopard shark in her life. Maybe she should prepare songbooks for singing around the fire, but what would they sing? "Born in the Ocean, Died in the Sea"? "The Farmer from France"? "True Love in the Afternoon"? None of those sounded right, but as she shoveled out the bonfire pit she sang to herself:

> O, she was born in the Ocean
> And died in the Sea
> A girl of emotion
> In love with me

With each thrust of the shovel, Linda feared more and more that the party would disappoint her brother. Edmund would hike down to the beach and they would look at one another and have nothing to say or do. He might say, "I'm too busy for all this." She imagined his voice: "Linda, please leave me alone." He would climb back up the sea cliff, and Charlotte might whisper, "That Linda. She lives in her own world, doesn't she?" Linda overheard Margarita say just that once down at the store, as Linda was off in a corner of the shop trying on the little felt hat with the bald-eagle feather. Over the years, the hat had become known as "Linda's sombrero," and Linda knew, even if no one believed her, that one day it would be hers. "I wonder sometimes why Linda just can't keep her feet on the ground," Edmund once said to Valencia. "Who on earth taught her to reach for the stars?" And Charlotte Moss once wrote in her breezy column: *Guess which Baden-Baden fishergirl dreams of one day leaving us behind?* What was wrong with them?, Linda asked herself, her shovel sinking into the sand and then flipping each spadeful over her shoulder. Sink and flip, sink and flip, and Linda's bonfire pit deepened, and only when she struck water did Linda turn and see that for the last several minutes each spadeful of sand had landed on her box of oyster sandwiches and chicken à la Providence.

The picnic was ruined. Linda looked to the sky and realized that it was nearly five o'clock and that Edmund and the others would arrive on the beach within the hour. There was no time to climb back to the cot-

tage for her bathing dress. She pulled her clothes over her head and
rolled her wool underpants into a ball, and there Linda stood, naked on
the beach, her chest goose-pimpling, her hips white and bright in the
fading afternoon. During the past few months, much to her regret,
she'd begun to develop a sense of modesty. It would shame her deeply
were Edmund to see her like this, fleshy and vulnerable. And so, with
her lobster satchel around her waist, she pushed forward into the cold
March ocean.

The tide slapped at her shins and her thighs and between her legs,
and Linda paddled on, through a bed of bull kelp, the long stalks parting around her. From twenty feet out she could see Condor's Nest up
on the cliff, the tin roofs throwing back the setting sun as if in protest.
Edmund, she knew, was in the fields, riding his burro as long as he
could before Valencia would make him change his shirt for the picnic.
Valencia was in the kitchen, embroidering the blouses she sold at Margarita's. Charlotte, Linda imagined, was walking toward Condor's
Nest, pulling a notebook from her pocket, ready to record a thought.
From this sea view, Linda's world appeared calm: the three cottages
alone on the bluff, ghostly smoke rising from a chimney. It was a world
Linda loved more than anything, but she knew it couldn't contain her;
she was sixteen, and she believed she was capable of taking care of herself. She longed for the day.

Her skin blue and cold beneath the water, Linda propelled herself
out to the buoy that marked her underperforming lobster pots and
tugged the lines. The pots would be stuffed, she could only hope, with
three-year-olds banging their tails. She inhaled and began swimming
straight to the bottom of the Pacific, her hand around the pot warp
guiding her down. At once everything around her was silent, the water
dense and icy and black and touching her everywhere. The pot warp
was slick with algae, and her hair fanned around her and she motored
onward. On the ocean floor there was just enough light to see a few
inches in front of her. The pots nestled against a rock covered with a
giant green anemone, its tentacles swaying. Surfgrass and sea lettuce
and lime-green dead-man's-fingers and a giant drooping sea palm
waved in her wake, as if welcoming her. The sand was fine and scat-
tered with broken-up buckshot barnacles, and the ocean floor swallowed her feet.

She inspected two pots and found them disappointingly empty.

Nothing in the next two as well. Worry rose in her as she turned to the almost invisible slats of the fifth and sixth pots. Both empty. In only a few years the bottom of the ocean had changed, and if she hadn't seen it herself she would never have believed it possible; hadn't Linda once gone around saying that the ocean was so big, no man could change it? In the seventh pot, three lobsters waited inside, and in the eighth one hovered mournfully. These lobsters were almost five pounds each, and one of them was so fat and long it was the biggest she had ever caught after Lottie. It barely fit through the mouth of her satchel, and just as she was tucking its tail into the bag and buttoning the flap, Linda sensed something move at her feet.

She nearly gasped.

It could have been a tidepool sculpin or some other bottom-scraper she'd never bother to haul. Near the pots she'd once seen a two-spotted octopus, but when it saw her it had billowed away, a rubbery tablecloth caught in the watery wind. And that was probably what this was, Linda reassured herself, an old two-spotter, with its pear-shaped head and its green-brown skin and its arms sucking mollusks from the rocks. They were the biggest cowards in the Pacific, dashing away at the sight of anything bigger than themselves, and Linda took hold of the pot warp and swam to the surface.

The light poured from above, green through the water, and now she could see the bottom of the buoy. In another few seconds she would push her head into the daylight, but just as she was about to crack the surface and fill her lungs with air and wipe her hair out of her eyes and turn toward shore—where she'd dress on the beach and then show Edmund the giant lobster—just then, still in the clasp of the ocean, still ten feet under March water, Linda saw the slender snout of a blue shark.

It was about five feet long, not quite full-size, its pectoral fins extending from its side like two crescent moons. Its belly was white, its back was dark blue, and its two black eyes were sunk deep in the side of its snout, which was now only a few feet from Linda. At first she couldn't believe it was a shark, because the blues usually didn't come this close to shore, and she thought that maybe it was a swordfish that had lost its sword, or a large barracuda—so long and skinny it was—but then it opened its mouth and revealed a row of rounded but deadly-looking teeth.

Linda stopped kicking and floated silently, hanging on to the pot warp. She couldn't tell if the shark was eyeing her or her lobsters. It was a dark-eyed silent creature, its intentions all mystery, and if Linda hadn't been so frightened she would have recognized the shark's sleek, dangerous beauty; she would have pondered the fast fury that ran electrically through its brain. She knew she should try to escape, but she didn't know how; she was transfixed. She and the shark floated in the ocean, as if suspended from something above, its fins paddling, her lungs aching for air. She thought about the party that was about to arrive on the beach looking for her. A part of her was already resigned to the fact that the shark would devour her, nudging up its snout and flinging open its mouth and snapping those teeth into her thigh, penetrating her flesh. She would release an underwater scream, one that only she and the shark would share, and her blood would seep as slowly as ink clouds, staining the sheets of the ocean. And later, when Edmund arrived on the beach and couldn't find her, he would shrug his shoulders and say, "Where'd she get to now?" She thought of the story her death would provide Charlotte's pen: a girl disappeared, stolen away as if by a large, cruel hand. Linda hoped that Charlotte would notice her clothes on the beach and piece together the facts, and Linda wrote the final sentence for Charlotte: "Did Linda Stamp drown, or was she eaten alive?"

The shark's eyes were the size of sand dollars, with a gelatinous sheen. They didn't seem to have eyelids—they were simply two dark, oily disks staring into the still world of the ocean and finding Linda. All of it—her desperate need for air, the winter current, the threat of the mouth curving prehistorically beneath the blue snout—made Linda think of her life at Condor's Nest, with its surrounding thicket of hottentot figs blooming with yellow flowers; of Dieter, still in Europe, even though the newspaper pinned to Margarita's bulletin board indicated that peace had arrived and that Wilson himself had gone to France to sweep things up; of Valencia, who had recently pulled Linda aside and told her a few shocking secrets of the world, most of which involved womanhood; of Edmund, her Siegmund, who had recently complained to Valencia that he no longer wanted to sleep in the same cottage as his sister. She thought of them all, but mostly of her brother, his face invading her mind: and she felt the urgency to make a final choice, a choice of devotion, to settle her heart upon one single thing before it was too late. Linda chose Edmund: If I can think of only one, I shall think of you. She wondered what the shark was thinking of, what it—*he?*—had chosen. And just as she was about to go limp and offer herself, the shark whipped its tail and turned around, its snout leading the long dark hunting way.

As she broke the surface, Linda was crying and gulping for air. She started for shore; in front of her waited the pitched bedsheet and the bonfire pit and, above, Condor's Nest. She thought she saw someone moving in the garden on the bluff, but she couldn't tell who it was. Someone in a white shirt—was it Edmund? Would he believe her when she told him of the blue shark? She could hardly believe it herself— those shallow black eyes the most evil thing she had ever seen! Her satchel was heavy with lobster and water as she paddled on. There'd be time to dry off and rehook the buttons of her dress and run up the bluff to the kitchen to fetch a deep pot. She would pull Edmund aside and describe the snout and the dorsal fin and how frightened she'd been, and she wanted him to know that he had been in her mind as those teeth gleamed in the dusky water. It was he she'd been thinking about, only Edmund, dear Edmund; everything else had fallen away. And she didn't care what he would say, didn't care if this would embarrass him or lead him to call her a stupid girl—because this was the truth, and Linda Stamp had faced a grinning blue shark, and so what if it was little more than a baby, its teeth made Linda's puma trap look like a nut-cracker. She had to tell him, she had to take Edmund's hand and tell him what really ran through her mind during the moments that mat-tered most: that she would always think of him first and last, that she was his, and *Oh please Edmund tell me that you are mine.* She reached the shallows, the waves crashing around her, and she stood, the water reaching her waist. She had made it to shore, and despite her fear she knew that she would return to the ocean floor; either the shark would come for her or it wouldn't. Linda's optimism set in, and just as she began to emerge from the water, naked except for her satchel and a stalk of kelp across her shoulders, Linda saw a man appear on the beach, fol-lowed by someone else, and Edmund trailing behind.

"Linda!" her father called. "Is it really you?" He was waving his arms over his pointy head, and he began running toward the water. He was skinnier than she remembered, and his beard was like a bib across his chest and over his green wool jacket.

Linda stopped, crouching and covering herself in the tide. She waved demurely. Something in her had assumed she'd never see her father again. And something in the expression on Edmund's face—a face that had turned hard and old as he became a young man—told Linda that he too hadn't expected to see Dieter again. He'd come to believe that the farm was his, and he'd begun to dig his toes into the windswept land.

"Come out of the water and give Papa a hug," Dieter called.

But between Dieter and Edmund was a stranger, a tall young man in a white shirt that billowed to reveal a patch of black hair on his chest. He held his chin down, and his shoulders hunched against the spray, and his mane of black hair blew about. He followed Dieter to the water's edge, and when he looked up, Linda, naked in the waves, the lobsters' antennae tickling her thigh, saw his face: eel-dark eyes, a mouth split apart as if he were about to say something, as if he recognized her, his brow buckled with a worry Linda knew just then she'd forever wonder about.

"There's someone I want you to meet," Dieter said.

Behind the stranger hurried Edmund, his cap pushed far back on his head as if he'd been scratching it while figuring something out. He squinted and his face was blank and his glasses slipped down his nose and off his face, and Linda saw that his resemblance to Dieter had magnified. She knew that Edmund was sensing something shift beneath him. The four years of their small world, Edmund and Linda's tiny circle of a world, had closed upon itself, a locked globe. Then Valencia appeared, and Charlotte Moss with her notepad.

"I want you to meet Bruder, Linda. He's made the journey back with me and he's here to stay. Come out and say hello."

But Linda couldn't come out of the water, not just yet. First she'd have to resign herself to the fact that the interim years of war now belonged to memory—but whose memory? Then she'd have to think about the bag of lobsters and realize that she didn't have enough for Bruder but would have to offer one to the stranger anyway, and she already knew that she would hand over the largest to the young man, saying something silly like "Doesn't all that hair get in your eyes?" And then, before she could emerge from the ocean, she'd have to beg her father and her brother and the boy who'd go on to sleep in the bed across from Edmund's to turn around and allow her to dress in privacy. Upon realizing that she was naked, Dieter and Edmund skittered nervously up the bluff to Condor's Nest, saying, "We'll be back, we'll be back!" But Bruder looked up alertly; his eyebrows lifted and he sealed his lips and he hesitated before he followed the others. The wind flapped the wings of his sleeves, and slowly he left Linda alone on the beach, a glance stolen over his shoulder. And when at last he was gone, Linda ran from the ocean and pulled her dress over her blue cold chest, and she dried as the weak sun set and the salt hardened upon her flesh and turned into bitter crystals in the night.

4

BRUDER WAS ABOUT NINETEEN, or maybe twenty—no one knew his birthday for sure. His mother had deposited him as an infant at the Children's Training Society in an orange crate lined with newsprint. Mrs. Trudi Banning, the long-faced Prussian widow who ran the orphanage, had given him his name. She'd been holding him up to the sun, turning him this way and that, finding the baby strangely large and of a warm, wooden color, when the mailman delivered a perfumed letter from her brother, Luther—a petal-skinned poet to whom Mrs. Banning's heart was devoted. She was thinking of her brother and holding the new baby, and his name came to the orphanage's mistress like a chill on the spine.

Over the years, gossip about the boy traveled on the breeze and Mrs. Banning told Bruder what she knew, and what she speculated to be true: "Your mother was a hotel whore. She was a chambermaid first at the Raymond, but then it burned down, and then at the Hotel Maryland, where she was caught *nakt* beneath the pergola. Who your father was, I'm sure even she couldn't say. She was from Mazatlán, your mother, smuggled up the coast, and that is all I know, my lad, but it should be enough to tell you who you are. And what kind of man you are destined to be." Until the war, Bruder had spent his entire life in Pasadena at the Training Society, and as soon as he was old enough to understand that Mrs. Banning didn't want him to know how to read anything more complex than the stenciling on the side of a grove box, he walked to the library and found a copy of *Kidnapped* and began reading about boys in worse straits than himself. He was always big for his age, and black-haired puberty came early, and by the time he was twelve years old and nearly six feet tall, he was easily spotted prowling the streets of Pasadena in a lonely lurch, to the library and back to the orphanage, books clutched in his paw. Rumors about him spread around town—*He's a mutant! He's the devil's son! He only* pretends *to know how to read!*—but there wasn't an invented story or whispered fallacy of which Bruder was unaware. He knew that people called him "El Brunito," and that they said that the accident with the ice-delivery boy wasn't an accident at all. He knew he frightened women on Colorado Street, young fragile-wristed ladies whose faces would blanch whiter than their tennis sweaters when his long shadow crossed theirs. He had been born in Pasadena, but there was a segment of society—the 100 Percenters, he knew they called themselves—that ruled the little city in the valley and considered him and everyone like him to be "from somewhere else." Then, in 1918, Bruder went to war with the Motor Mechanics Co. 17, First Regiment, and he returned with a penny-size burn scar in his brow. He journeyed back to California with Dieter Stamp, the two of them having struck a deal. On the way, Dieter told stories of his youth and his family and his farm at Condor's Nest, and Bruder, who early in life had learned that he could gain more by listening than by speaking, arrived in Baden-Baden-by-the-Sea in the spring of 1919 knowing everything about Dieter's daughter, Linda Stamp.

She shrieked like a spoiled child, he thought, when her father informed her that he had gone to war and never changed his name. "I left Condor's Nest and I thought: I am not David. It is not who I am. I tried calling myself David, but after a week I gave it up. I am Dieter." Linda hollered over the betrayal: "It isn't fair!" It was a cry Bruder would hear again and again during his first days at Condor's Nest.

At the supper table one day shortly after Bruder arrived, Linda told her story of the blue shark, exaggerating her courage in the glare of its teeth. "There we were, just me and the shark." Her account brought fear to her parents' faces, and to Bruder's, if not fear, certainly a quiet respect. Linda could see that he was asking himself, What sort of girl is she?—but in fact he was warning himself because he knew exactly what kind of girl she was.

The shark story left Edmund anxious. "I don't think you should be out fishing by yourself anymore. It's too dangerous for a girl."

Linda turned, barely aware that he was referring to her. "Too dangerous?"

"You could've been killed."

"But I can—"

"Edmund's right," Dieter broke in. "Maybe you should stay out of the ocean unless you're with Bruder." Over the years Dieter's beard had grown lacy, a grid of white wire cut and bent like latticework. The years of war had folded twice again the creases in his throat, where his skin bunched up, and he fingered this loose flesh as he ate a shrimp ball.

"With *him*?" said Linda. "Does he even know how to swim?"

"With *Bruder*?" said Edmund.

"Of course he knows how to swim."

"Does he know how to fish?"

Her father assured her that he did.

"Why would we send her out with *him*?" asked Edmund. But Dieter ignored his son.

"*Do* you know how to fish and swim?" Linda asked the young man.

"No, but you'll teach me." And he left the table and climbed down the bluff and stripped to his waist and rolled his trousers up to his knees. Linda followed and watched him from the beach. She doubted he would venture into the ocean without her. She assumed he would be a slow student, requiring months to learn, and something in her looked forward to the many days of him paddling tentatively at her side and heeding her instruction; days when Bruder's face would float awkwardly in the water; days when he'd be nervous and careful to stay close to her.

But Bruder didn't wait for Linda. He pushed himself into the waves. At once the tide pulled him under, and his fist rose in a way that she interpreted as a call of desperation. She couldn't believe it: the boy had been at Condor's Nest not two days and already he had drowned. She ran to the tide, tugging her dress over her head as she went, and in her underwear she swam out to where the waters had closed around him. There she paddled and panted, her underclothes heavy and pulling her down, and then something warm and firm took her by the ankle and climbed the ladder of her body and Bruder's slick, otterlike head punched through the water. He was gasping, the sunlight flashing in his face. "You'll give me my first lesson now?" He added, "Linda. It's a pretty name."

The next morning, he pulled her from bed and told her to watch from the bluff. "Don't rescue me this time," he said. On the beach, he stripped to nothing and swam jerkily but steadily to the horizon and beyond, hundreds of yards past the colony of lobster buoys, his pale behind humping through the water like a dolphin head. He returned to shore as if powered by steam and shook the water from his wine-blue body and stepped back into his clothes. "Now I've learned," he said when he returned to the bluff, where he found not only Linda but Edmund, who threw a swimsuit at him and said, "We wear clothes around here." Bruder went to the cottage and reemerged in a worsted-wool tank suit that was so tight across his chest and around his groin that it was more obscene than if he had been standing before Linda with nothing on at all.

But even if Bruder could now swim, he still didn't know how to fish. A few days later, Linda led him to the beach, hauling a pair of bamboo casting rods and a tackle box. The ocean was calm, and she baited a hook with a greenish-blue jacksmelt, hung a weight to her line, and waded into the surf. Bruder watched her from the shore. She maneuvered the tide and the rod with skill and experience, and Bruder realized that everything Dieter had promised about his daughter was proving to be true. And more.

"Just watch," she cried, casting again. He possessed an unusual reserve of patience, she sensed, but this for some reason made her even more impatient. Soon, however, something yanked her rod, and its tip bent like the handle of a cane. Linda pulled, and the rod curved so sharply it looked as if it would snap. She planted her feet into the sand, bent her knees, and steeled herself against the waves crashing at her thighs. Linda reeled and snapped her rod back and forth, fighting the fish, and after five minutes she cranked her reel one last time and pulled up a brown-back barracuda. The fish, almost three feet long, thrashed in the surf, and Linda held it aloft and walked it over to Bruder, who backed away as she approached. On the shore, the barracuda flopped around and sank its fangs into the sand, and Linda didn't think she'd ever seen a boy as frightened as Bruder was now. "You've got to kill the 'cudas straight off," she said, pulling a club from her pile of gear and whacking the fish on its long pointed head; the fish flipped itself over and died. "Now it's your turn."

He hesitated, sitting on the rock next to Linda's outrigger while she rebaited the hook. On the journey home from Europe, Dieter had told Bruder about his children, describing Edmund as impractical and soft-breasted and Linda as a girl with the soul of a diamond ray. Having never seen a stingray, Bruder didn't know what Dieter could mean, and he imagined a dark-haired girl who was both graceful and wing-fast and who lurked prettily until provoked. He was thinking of this when she startled him by sliding the rod into his hands. She worked her fingers around his wrists and demonstrated how to cup the pole's handle and spin the reel. She asked him if he understood and prodded him into the water. "Go on, give it a try. What's the worst that can happen?"

Bruder waded into four feet of water and stood for several minutes while the waves passed through him, his body rising up and falling with the tide. He had harvested alfalfa and picked a walnut tree clean and fixed a hundred truck engines, but this task with the delicately thin rod felt strange to him, and he worried that Linda hadn't told him all he needed to know. "Plant your feet," she called. He ground his feet into the sand, swung the rod back over his shoulder, and then cast, flipping his arms and wrists. Together, Linda and Bruder watched the fishing rod fly out of Bruder's hands and up over the little waves, hurtling like a javelin fifty yards to sea. Bruder returned to shore, stripped down to his skimpy tank suit, and dove back into the water. He swam to the fishing rod and returned with it held aloft and crawled up out of the waves and slipped it into the hole of Linda's cupped hands. "Show me again."

Linda told him to watch more closely this time. Then she stepped into the waves, planted her feet, called "Here goes!" and cast her line. But as the hook flew back over her shoulder, the gut line an invisible arc, it caught on something and she heard a tiny moan and turned to find it snared within Bruder's cheek. Who was more surprised by this, neither could say. Their eyes were wide and upon each other.

But over time, where both Linda and Bruder expected a scar to buckle and shine, instead a scab formed and fell away, and even the most careful eye couldn't see that a snelled hook had once snared Bruder. Within a month there was no evidence of it except his word and hers, a story that would either tumble around the flatlands and collect into myth, or break up and crumble away.

It didn't take long for Bruder to grow used to—and even to look forward to—listening to Linda, to her questions about where he came from and how he had met her father, to her tireless inquiry into what he thought of her. Bruder would listen to Edmund too, as he warned him to stay away from his sister: "She's not like other girls." He listened to Dieter tell him not to mind Edmund—"He's a funny boy"—and slowly Bruder realized that the only one who listened as closely as he did was Valencia, whose face would turn and lean in and betray nothing when the others spoke.

Bruder had never been like the other orphans at the Training Society, boys who would long for a family and would wet down their hair whenever the Sunday picnickers spread their blankets in the orphanage's walnut grove. These boys were desperate for a mother and lonely for a father, and in their eyes Bruder had seen a pathetic fear he promised himself, even as a child, never to succumb to. When the other boys whimpered themselves to sleep in the dormitory, Bruder would stay up reading by the lamp. He had always taken solace in the books he stole from Mrs. Banning's shelf, even greater solace in the comfort of his own quiet mind, and for many years he carried in his pocket a piece of advice he'd written out on one of Mrs. Banning's alms cards: *Dumb's a sly dog.* The same was true for a horse, Bruder often thought, and even though he was a motor mechanic he had befriended more horses than people in his short long years of life, and what was it the poet had said in the book Mrs. Banning had snatched from his sleepy teenage lap?: "My horses understand me tolerably well; I converse with them at least four hours every day."

And this was what Bruder was thinking of when Linda came to him with the news that Dieter's horse had caught his hoof in a railroad tie and snapped his hock. Dieter would have to shoot Kermit on the track before the 1:52 hurried north to Los Angeles. Linda and Bruder ran across the onion field to witness the execution, but they found Kermit's long nose resting against the rail, a bullet from Dieter's Colt Peacemaker sunk into his white-patched haw. Next to him, Edmund was weeping.

"Papa, you killed him?"

"He was almost as old as me."

"Where will you get another?"

"Another horse? It's time I buy a car. Ask the mechanic from Pasadena. Nobody's riding in the cities anymore." Dieter went on to say that he'd seen a water-cooled International MW with a blue leather seat and a rear bed that could cart more than old Kermit on his best day, "May he rest in peace."

"But, Papa?" sniffled Edmund. "Where will you get the money?"

Dieter told his children not to worry about such things. "Let's get the old guy off the rail." As the sun shone on the tracks, Dieter and Edmund began to argue about what to do with Kermit. Dieter thought they should leave him to the coyotes—"He'll be gone by morning." But Edmund reminded his father about the new regulations against dumping equine carcasses—so many people were doing it in their rush toward the automobile. There'd be a fine that none of them could afford, Edmund warned. "We should burn him down."

But Bruder pulled from his boot an Ames bowie knife with a shark-skin grip and told the others he'd take care of Kermit. He had quartered horses at the City Farm, and the job was easier but bloodier than it looked. Bruder noticed the way the knife caused a stir in Linda, a flame in her ever-flickering eyes; he slapped his palm with the blade, and the little *smack!* of steel on flesh drew Linda closer to him. She watched the blade slice the horse's belly from stifle to brisket, and a red jelly mass lurched out. Blood splattered Bruder's shirt, and a spigot shot Linda's legs; she was shocked by its salty warmth. "Get me a wheelbarrow," Bruder instructed Edmund. Bruder sank his hands into Kermit's gut, scooping out the yards of wormy intestines and the wine-red liver. Then he sliced the belly horizontally and plucked out Kermit's still-quivering ten-pound heart. "Edmund! Fetch the butcher saw."

As he proceeded with his work, Bruder tossed the salvageable pieces into the wheelbarrow, where white rattlesnake moths landed on the muscular hamstring and gaskin and loin. It was the knee joint, connecting forearm and cannon, that most impressed Linda: the blade of the bowie *hack-hack-hack*ing through it. "Strong bastard," Bruder said as he tried to rip the knee free of ligament. He looked up from his work and saw her, her toe tracing an arc in the dirt. "Get down and help me," he ordered, and she sank to her knees as if forced by a large invisible hand and found herself so close to Bruder that his hair blew against her brow. Linda worked her hands around a shank. She didn't expect Kermit to still feel like a horse; she thought that handling this piece of him would feel no different than handling a quarter of meat. But Kermit's coat bristled coarsely, its grain changing hue from brown to cider-orange as she ran her hand over it. She felt the exactness of the tissue beneath the coat, the pads of shifting muscle she had watched for years as Edmund rode around the farm and along El Camino Real.

Now, crouching, the railroad ties pressing uncomfortably into her knees, Linda helped Bruder yank free Kermit's kneebone. Dieter, impressed, and Edmund, aghast, stood in the shade of a red elderberry. When the bone snapped loose, Linda and Bruder fell down the little hill the railroad track sat upon, laughing as they tumbled, the horse leg between them, finally landing in a thicket of bladderpod. The shrub was heavy with fruit, its green pods resembling two-inch peas, and Linda felt the fruit crack beneath her. She sat up and looked down her chest and down Bruder's too and saw that they were both smeared with blood. The blood had soaked deeply into her dress, reminding her of what Valencia called *la carga*—an event Linda had done her best to always hide from Edmund. But now she and Bruder looked at each other with open, blank eyes, and he took the leg and hurled it into the air and they watched it rise and arc and fall, like a strange long-extinct bird. When it hit the ground, dust rose and the day was clear and the sun was white and the buzz flies arrived and Bruder's eyebrows danced and he stared longingly at Linda. He was thinking that she was beautiful when she was silent, and the blood somehow made her seem even more alive, the blood dripping from her hands, and Linda realized that Bruder was the first person she had ever really known from someplace beyond Condor's Nest and Baden-Baden-by-the-Sea. She had dreamt of the world far from the village, up the coast or down, and she had expected one day to rush off and see it, but now a glimpse of the world had come to her. Bruder had taken pleasure in dismembering the horse, but this didn't frighten Linda, and only when a cloud passed before the sun and the glint faded from the railroad track did she notice Edmund standing by himself, his finger nervously at his collar. His face had gone pale and he was mumbling, "They've gone crazy. He's turning her crazy."

Dieter swatted him with his cap. "Leave them alone. They're learning to live, that's all." Edmund's cheek trembled as he watched Bruder head off to the barn. When he was gone, Dieter added, "He gets more done than you."

As he said this, Charlotte Moss appeared along the railroad track. Her curls were pushing from beneath her beret, and she tapped her

5

ONE DAY AT THE END of April, Linda took Bruder into the village to visit the mineral spring. She explained that scientific analysis had long ago determined that the Apfelsine waters were chemically identical to the thermal springs of Hoellgassquelle in Baden-Baden, not far from Schwarzwald. But on the journey home from France, Dieter had already told Bruder about the Black Forest, where the wood was dense with fir and holly underbrush and blackwood and the mouse owls that called sinisterly at dusk. "The tourists would travel from Berlin and Paris and London to rinse away their sooty maladies. I'd sell them little tin cups with the date of their visit imprinted into the handle." Whenever he told this story, Dieter would hold up his mallet, as if in proof. Since the 1880s, California's tourists had journeyed—first on horseback, then briefly by stage, then by rail, and now by car—to Baden-Baden-by-the-Sea in the same pursuit. There'd been a hotel built on the bluff just beyond the spring, with gingerbread trim, balconies with views of the ocean, room rates of $1.50 a day, and a motto of "To read, ponder, drink—and Live." Dieter had worked there before Valencia arrived. He had ported dusty imitation-alligator trunks and delivered ices made with Leucadia lemons to ladies sunning themselves in wicker chaises. "But I lost my job because I'd always arrive at the hotel smelling like onions," Dieter told Linda many times, the story embellishing itself seemingly at its own accord, so that the final version, the one Dieter had recounted at the supper table just the night before, included a blind widow who wore the world's largest emerald, a white-blond bachelor with a Siamese butler, and a wirehaired terrier, property of one Mrs. P. G. Furnass of Pasadena, the dog drinking the lemonade and falling over dead at Mrs. Furnass's feet, which were crammed into buttonless half-Congress shoes a size and a half too small.

On the Apfelsine platform, Linda said, "Tell me about the war."

"There's too much to tell," said Bruder.

"Just one story."

He thought about this and then offered a simple tale. "There was a kid in my company, a terrible mechanic, lost every wrench issued to him. Each morning he woke up certain his number would come up that day. At night, he quoted the poets as the howitzers lit up the sky. It was his way of praying, and most of the other boys huddled around him in the dark, listening to the cantos and the couplets. After he was killed, the captain gave me his books, and there's one thing I read that makes me think of you."

Linda leaned closer as Bruder began to recite, almost as if it were a song:

> *Her silence, her transfigured face ablaze*
> *made me fall still although my eager mind*
> *was teeming with new questions I wished to raise*

Linda thought it sounded nice, but she didn't understand what Bruder might mean by it, and years would pass before she learned—at the bookstore in Pasadena, where the scent of pine shipping crates drifted up from the stockroom, in the Spanish Library Room—where these words came from. She had never known anyone to memorize poetry, and it left her even more curious. He was both worldly and crude, citing the poets and the saints and staring her down and grunting when she served him *bolitas de masa* and black coffee. When he spoke of the Training Society, she imagined Bruder as a boy in a place similar to Mission San Luis Rey, with its stucco façade breaking apart in great brittle flakes and the two-tiered bell tower shadowing the courtyard; she imagined the light through the rose window above the mission's double door, the slanted rays falling on Bruder's young face as he studied silently with nuns in squirrel-gray habits. Once, while Dieter was at war, Linda and Edmund had run in the fallow field abutting the mission, where, years before, grapes had ripened and sheep nibbled the smoke trees; and in the side cemetery, shaded by a small stand of conifers, Linda had collected golden poppies for her hair. Had Bruder grown up in such a place?

"It was nothing like that at all."

He lit a cigarette, and the bluish smoke curled around his face as he described the Mexicans and half-Mexicans and slow-wits and misdemeanants and the handful of Negroes and the pair of Chinese brothers he had slept with in an attic dormitory. "We lived in a big house called Casa Angélica, forty boys and four ladies, one who was too fat to walk. It sat at the edge of the City Farm, and after the morning classes, where Mrs. Banning taught us not how to read and write but how to properly grade citrus and grow rootstock, she'd scoot us into the fields to take up picking sacks with the ranch hands. It was a big farm, five hundred and seventeen acres, fertilized by Pasadena sewage, and until nightfall we'd climb the walnut trees and clear the orange groves and harvest the seed potatoes and the alfalfa. The effluent of municipal waste ran around the farm in an open brown ditch, and not a single one of us at the Training Society realized until after we left the orphanage that we had come to smell forever like shit."

"Are you telling me the truth?" said Linda.

"Why wouldn't I?"

She proposed that they buy a cup of water and led him to the vending stand. The spring water had etched a pair of oblong impressions into the boulder's surface, and the villagers had seized upon the indentations' vague but reasonable likeness to a pair of vigorous lungs. HEALTHY WATER HEALTHY SUN HEALTHY LUNGS, proclaimed the banner perpetually draped across the veranda of the Twin Inn, the most recent hotel. A sign next to Margarita's door read: CONSUMPTIVES WELCOME ON MONDAYS. Six-inch pipes hurried the water to a public bath, where Bavarian widows boiled it in bell-shape vats, a towel draped over their lumpy shoulders. *Nein nein nein,* they'd say, a soft arm extended in barricade when a modest tourist tried to enter the bath covered in bathing gown and cap. A three-quarter redwood wall separated the men's bath from the ladies', and across it, back and forth, traveled squeals and deep-settled moans of relaxation and regeneration and release.

A platform with a rail surrounded the Apfelsine, and over the years the villagers had built it out toward the sea cliff and the lagoon. There was an arcade for throwing rings around orange-soda bottles and a shuffleboard gallery where first prize was a baby octopus origamied into a jar of formaldehyde. In the middle of this, the weeping rock stood protected by a small orange tent with a California grizzly flag flying from its peak, and a stand decorated with bunting sold cups of water for twenty-five cents.

Behind the counter was Charlotte Moss, who would say she liked to work at the mineral spring not for the money but for the news. By now everyone in town knew that Charlotte wanted to become a full-time reporter at the *Bee.* Already her column was more popular than the tidal report and the real-estate exchange. She never printed a name—this would become her trademark—and with each new edition her stories set off a sporting speculation over their subjects' identities. If it's news, it'll swirl around the Apfelsine, Charlotte liked to say, and although this may have been true, she failed to add that she needed money for the berets and the smocks she had taken up as her reporter's uniform and—a secret held even more tightly behind Charlotte's breast—for food. Her father would go to sea for months with the promise of future fortune, but when he returned his pocket was never lined with wages; no, his pocket was always drained, in debt to the liquor chest, the poker table, and a whorehouse in every north-water port. Early on, Charlotte had gone hungry in life, and as a teenage girl she promised herself that she would never starve again.

"Two cups, please." Bruder fished through his pocket, produced a dollar, and slid it across the counter.

Charlotte handed the first cup to Bruder with something of a leer. "I see you brought your new friend."

"His name is Bruder."

"I already know his name." Charlotte ceased pumping the water to take him in, and Linda nearly expected her to pluck her notebook from her pocket and write a few things down.

"Welcome to Baden-Baden-by-the-Sea," said Charlotte. "Home of the Navel-Shaped Rock, the Restorative Mineral Spring, the Lagoon of the Hideous Stench, and the Prettiest Fishergirls in the World."

"I gave you a dollar," said Bruder. "You owe me fifty cents."

"Here's to your health," said Charlotte. "And here's your change."

"What makes this water so special?" he said.

"Depends who you ask."

"I'm asking you."

"If you ask me," said Charlotte, "it holds nothing more than you'd expect. But if you ask Margarita or Mayor Kramer or the owner of the Twin Inn, they might tell you it'll purify your lungs and cleanse your blood. The Apfelsine's been known to attract even one or two syphilics, desperate as they are."

Bruder was standing close to Linda, and the breeze off the ocean was salty and passed through his hair: and she could see how small and pink his ears were, like two tight roses. The wind was whipping Bruder's trousers, the baggy thighs brushing her yellow skirt, and it felt as if just at that very moment both Bruder and Charlotte noticed that Linda was wearing a Sunday dress on a Saturday afternoon.

"Here's to the Well of Life," said Bruder, and he recited.

> For unto Life the dead it could restore,
> And guilt of sinfull crimes cleane wash away,
> Those that with sicknesse were infected sore,
> It could recure, and aged long decay
> Renew, as one were borne that very day.

Upon hearing this, a nervous panic overtook Charlotte—she could hardly believe that someone knew something she did not—and she plucked the pencil from behind her ear. "What's that? Where'd you hear that? Can you repeat that?"

But Bruder steered Linda away from Charlotte to the other side of the deck. They sat on a bench, and their knees were close but not touching. "Be careful around her," he said. Linda protested that Charlotte was her best friend, and she couldn't know it at the time, but these were the first days in Linda's life when the hand of fate was beginning to swat her around.

It was a bright afternoon, and the lagoon's cattails bent in the wind. Other than Charlotte, there was no one else on the platform, and Linda and Bruder leaned over the bench and looked out at Agua Apestosa and the schoolhouse on its far shore. Sharp grass stood tall in the black water. In the distance, the hills were yellowing from the early heat; in another month, all would be dry and brown. A pair of yellowthroats flew over the water, and Linda pointed out to Bruder two California least terns, small white birds with orange legs and black-tipped yellow bills.

The wind played with Bruder's collar, revealing fine wisps of chest hair. His lips were full and faint in color, like an early grape. When his fingers fell to her bare arm, the sensation caused her breath to catch in her throat: as if he'd found a patch of her skin never before exposed to another's hand. But as soon as it happened, his hand jerked away and he muttered, "Sorry." It was the first apology out of him, although there were other times when he should have excused himself: the time he spit out the canned tongue and barked, "Don't feed me this!"; and the evening when he walked in on her preparing her bath: their faces frozen in the instant of orange sunset and gull-squawk outside the window, and had it been a moment later he would have found her naked, a washcloth cupping her breast. So many things Linda didn't understand about Bruder. The simple question of his age resulted in further misunderstanding: "I'm about as old as Edmund, more or less." But if that were true, then why did the mat of hair grow on his chest and not her brother's? And what about the beard that required a blade sharp enough to slaughter fowl? And the odor, unmistakably male, both fruity and rancid at the end of the day? Linda would lie in bed wondering if it kept Edmund from sleeping, that smell and Bruder's large body cocooned by slumber so close to his own. More than once she had tiptoed across the yard, shushing the goats, to stand on a crate and peer through the window. There she found Bruder, big in her former bed, his heavy face sunk into the hen-feather pillow. And no matter how late it was, she'd find Edmund sitting up in bed, glasses slipping down his nose, the light cast across the volume of Gibbon in his lap. Once she heard Bruder say, "Are you still reading *him*?" And then, yawning, shifting beneath the blankets, "I finished Gibbon in a week." Three nights in a row she had stared in at Edmund and Bruder, and her chest had filled with longing, a desire that emerged with the ponderous night surf and the contemplative moon and the sleep-groan of the burro. Finally, on the third night, Edmund looked up from the book and met her eye in the window. He seemed to want to say, "I wish you'd come back, Linda."

Other things, too, caused Linda to sit on the bluff with her chin in her fist and wonder about Bruder: the burn-scar in his temple, and where it had come from. "The war, Linda," he'd say. "The war." Along with the bowie knife, he owned a bayonet that he sometimes wore in his belt; not a month after their first fishing lesson, Linda witnessed him use it to flay and gut a sea bass the size of a hound. "That from the war too?" If in reply he might have had some story from the front, she couldn't pry it from him. But once, when Edmund was in the fields, Bruder waved her into the cottage and told her he had something he wanted her to see. He reached into his rucksack and brought out a folding fan with a blue silk tassel, a Bible swollen with warp, and a delicate stick of coral dangling on a leather thong. Carefully he placed each on the bed, and he cuffed Linda's hand as she reached for the necklace. "They came from my mother," he said, and Linda screwed up her eyes and said she thought he didn't have a mother. He said he didn't, but these were next to him in the orange crate when he was delivered to the Training Society's door. Again, Linda reached for the coral. It was as orange-pink as a rose's heart, and this time he let her inspect it, on condition that she never tell anyone what she'd seen. "Something's written on it," she said, bringing the coral to her eye. "Pavis?"

And Bruder dreamily reclaimed the pendant and folded it away in his palm. "I only know her name."

He was the heir of a mother's name and a few belongings and nothing else. He knew that some took pity on him, especially when he was a boy, but Bruder had always felt blessed to possess no past, no antecedents tugging him down, steering him this way and that. He had been a boy, and now he was a man whose life was his own. Bruder liked to think he was fearless and this was almost true; his only fear was of losing himself to someone else.

Far off in the distance, beyond the village edge, Mt. Palomar was dark in the afternoon shadow, its ridge a lonely peak above the hills. Linda told Bruder the story of the picnic she and Edmund had once made on the mountainside, on a path originally carved out by the Indians who used to call the mountain Paauw. They had hiked through a cluster of waist-high brake ferns and stalks of lupine, and a cloud of gnattish no-see-ums had flown out of the belly of a felled mulberry and attacked Linda and Edmund, whining in their ears. Linda convinced Edmund to continue up the mountain, but soon they smelled a brushfire, and when they looked above them they saw flames leaping across the hairpin road. The fire was burning another thousand feet up the mountain, never putting Linda and Edmund in danger, but now she told the story to Bruder as if they had felt the heat upon their faces. She recounted the marigold-orange flames gnawing at the dry azalea and chestnut trees, and the abandoned vineyard succumbing in a hot swift *whoosh,* and the tree squirrels leaping from the burning oak branches, and the horrible cackle of the fire's appetite . . . and Bruder took her wrist and said, "That's not the way it happened. Edmund already told me you were safe on the valley floor."

She was a funny girl, he thought, and a liar too, and a warning signal drifted from her, like early white smoke. But even so, Bruder couldn't let go of her hand. The journey home from the front had taken months, and Bruder had carried Dieter's rucksack, bulky with sheets of tin, and every now and then Dieter would speak of his daughter as if she were a princess whose life had already become myth: "She was born on New Year's Day," Dieter would say, "with eyes that were both black and blue." Once, when they were within days of Condor's Nest, Dieter had said, "Consider yourself forewarned, my young friend. Her heart is her own." And Bruder had replied, "So is mine." On the long journey home, Dieter had also told Bruder about Edmund, and once Dieter admitted that Edmund was not the boy he had hoped for. Bruder had made the mistake of repeating this to Edmund one night as they lay in their beds side by side, and Edmund had replied, "One day you'll regret ever coming to Condor's Nest."

Now on the bench, Bruder said, "You realize, Linda, that Edmund and I are enemies."

"What are you talking about?"

"We're rivals."

"Rivals for what?"

"Linda. Don't you see?"

Over at the water stand, business was slow. Charlotte leaned on the counter, her ear pricked up. "You two need more water over there?"

"Where'd Papa find you, anyway?"

"Why don't you ask him?"

"I already did."

"What did he say?"

"He said you'd tell me one day."

In profile, there was a delicacy to Bruder. Nose sharp along the ridge, eyelashes curled, the throb of a tiny vein in his temple beneath the scar. He brought a foot up on the bench and rested his chin on his knee, and the heft of him touched something within Linda. His pants stretched tightly around his thigh. She could see the outline of the knife in his pocket, and he sat erect on the bench as the mineral spring trickled down the face of the Apfelsine. Charlotte coiled her hair around her finger and sucked on her pencil tip and thought about her next column. And Linda thought to ask Bruder, "Will you be staying with us for good?"

He said it would depend, and the next morning he set to the task of building himself a cottage at the rim of Condor's Nest, rising at dawn to clear a plot dense with Our Lord's Candle scrub.

In the afternoon, Linda followed Bruder to his building site, chasing a fence lizard, her quick hand nabbing its tail, and she climbed a pepper tree and hooked her knees over a branch and hung upside down, the lizard dangling from her fingers as she watched Bruder level the soil. She recognized something in him although she couldn't name it, and she knew, bright with impatient blood, that the years would have to pass before she would come to understand. "Why would you want to live all the way out here? You can't even see the ocean." She released the lizard, and it disappeared down an ant hole. She pulled herself up, taking delight in the muscles in her upper arms—triceps, Edmund had taught her, pointing to an anatomical diagram of a man that had embarrassed him more than her. Once on her feet again she shook out her skirt, a dull thing of iron-stripe sewn from a bolt Edmund had traded a hundred pounds of onions for.

Bruder began to sort the delivery of lumber from the Weltmeer yard. Linda couldn't guess what exactly he'd build himself with so little plank. Was he building a single room with a tin roof? Way out here on a northern slope, where the afternoons fell with bitter shadow? His face was intent with his task. Linda couldn't be sure, but she thought she recognized hurt in the fold of his brow. But she was wrong. No, he simply wanted to live alone, it was all he had wanted since the long days of his youth when he shared a dormer room with forty sniffling, smelly boys, their flesh crusted with sweat, their mouths and asses gasping through the night. There were a few years when he was a teenager, after the delivery boy was killed by the block of ice, when Bruder refused to speak, and Mrs. Banning, fearing that Bruder was dangerous, made him sleep in the henhouse, on a bed made from packing crates, and he'd never been happier, alone with the feathers swirling in his breath.

The henhouse smelled, and the birds clucked and cooed through the night, but Bruder didn't care—at least he was alone, where no one could peck at him, scratching at his heart.

Linda could sense only some of this, and she offered to help him build the shed. He slit his eyes as he ran the measuring cord along the planks of Douglas fir, and his shoulders lifted like wings as he laid the bricks in the foundation; and the shack rose with a tilt, as if grudge and grievance were in its design. On that day in the late spring of 1919, Linda knew that she was capable both of building a tiny cottage, and of love; she had the great desire to risk everything for pleasure and a sated heart. Although she couldn't articulate her longing, the feeling, the entombing sensation, held her firmly, and again she presented herself to Bruder as his builder's assistant. This time he didn't turn her down, and the lean-to went up with the aid of her mallet—Dieter's mallet—and for four weeks she lived with hard fir splinters sunk preciously into the pink meat of her palm.

Edmund dubbed it "the Vulture House." He said that the name came to him one day when he saw a condor flying over the onion field out to where Bruder and Linda were busy with mallet and nail. "Those huge wings, almost ten feet across, it's the most beautiful sight in the sky, and there it was swooping over the field, hunting for some sort of kill, its big head bald and ugly. They've been coming less and less, and everyone's wondering what's happening to the condor. Margarita says God's taking them away, and Papa says 'Good riddance,' and when I asked Mama she told me that one day we'd understand. And then one appeared out there as you and Bruder were finishing up his crummy little shed. It came out of nowhere. Do you remember, Linda, how they'd swarm when we were little? When it was just you and me and we'd spend the day looking into the sky? Remember how we'd shoo them out of the arroyo? Their nasty beaks stuffed with the gut of a mule deer? I don't know if you noticed, sister, but we haven't seen one since Papa came home. And then all of a sudden one appeared low in the sky above you and Bruder."

As he told Linda this, she noticed for the first time a severity creeping into Edmund: a crease at the corner of his eye; a curl in his knuckles, as if he were on the verge of forming a fist. "For a while I thought

Bruder had driven the condors away, but that wouldn't make any sense, would it? Could he do that, Linda? You two were out there hammering away, nails in your mouths, sun beating your necks, too busy to lift your eyes to see the most beautiful sight in the world flying overhead. Remember how they used to run in gangs off the bluff, throwing themselves down toward the ocean? Don't you remember, Linda? They'd run fat and slow over the cliff and fall and then at the last possible second their wings would catch the thermals and up they'd go, up and up over the bluff and off into the foothills to find a dead tule elk or a pronghorn. Don't you ever ask yourself where the birds have gone? Don't you see things changing, Linda?"

Linda hadn't noticed this, and the condors were so big and ugly she couldn't imagine why they'd want them around anyway. "And there that one was, returning to the farm," said Edmund, "and I don't know why but I thought it was some sort of miracle, and that just maybe Bruder was responsible for both sending them away and then bringing one back. Can you believe it? Bruder, with those eyes like a pair of sinkholes, bringing us any sort of good! But the bird in the sky told me otherwise, and I hitched the hinny and followed the bird across the field. A Santa Ana was keeping him from flying away, suspending him. He was held aloft as he tried to make his way inland, as if God Himself had run wires through the bird's wings and was dangling him there for me to see. He flew in front of the sun, and looking at him was nearly blinding, and I thought to myself, This is it, this is it."

"This was what?" asked Linda. They were on the bench outside the kitchen, and without either of them realizing it, Edmund had taken her hand.

"I didn't know, but I knew it was something. You know, Linda, those times when you don't know what's going on but you know there's something. That the world is shifting and at first you don't notice it but then God sends you a signal telling you to pay attention. That's what I thought, and I'll never forget the feeling when I headed into the arroyo and walked up the riverbed. It glittered with mica and rock and the day nearly blinded me and there the bird sat, wings hunched up like a pair of great shoulders. I got closer and closer to him, closer than I ever thought it would be possible to get to a bird. I was convinced the condors were all but gone from the farm, but this bird, that just maybe was the biggest God had ever created, was on our land, in our arroyo, there for me to see. So ugly he was beautiful, that pink bald head wrinkled and tender like a newborn, and as I stepped closer the bird didn't move and I was nearly convinced that I'd get close enough to lay my palm across his round head. And just then, in the glare of the white sun, I stepped on one of those broken-up planks you and Bruder were dumping in the arroyo, and a nail pushed through the sole of my shoe and I let out a scream. My foot was bleeding, the nail driven up into my heel, and Mr. California Condor turned his horrible head and revealed himself to be not a condor at all but a stupid old turkey vulture hunting for kitchen garbage. He stared at me and cackled, laughing the way you sometimes laugh, Linda, and the vulture swooped, his wingtip slapping my face, and flew away."

6

BY THE LATE SUMMER, Bruder was working next to Edmund in
the fields, and as the stink of onion seeped deeper into his fingertips,
Dieter realized what Bruder had known all along: Bruder was a better
farmer than Edmund. Bruder promised Dieter profits he had only
dreamed of, "If you let me run the farm for a year. All I need is a year.
Just keep Edmund out of the way." Dieter struck the deal without regret, and went to his son to break the news, but Valencia called him to
the kitchen and fed him a *chollo* and a cup of warm milk and soon Dieter
forgot about his task. The next day, Bruder stopped Edmund from entering the field by placing his boot upon the irrigation standpipe. "I'll be
running the water from now on," he said. With his heart rattling, Edmund ran to his father, who said, "It's just for the year." "What am I
supposed to do?" "Now you have time to build the reservoir you've
been talking about." It happened on a day when the winds blew hot
down the slope of Mt. Palomar, shifting the sands of Condor's Nest,
and the grit caught Edmund's eye as he watched Bruder shove his old
wheelbarrow into the field.

Linda found Edmund in the shallow crook of the arroyo where the
vulture had landed. Linda asked her brother how she could help. She
wished she could say that Dieter had made a mistake, but she knew that
Bruder would bring the farm greater prosperity than Edmund, who
had spent more time studying manuals and encyclopedias and drafting
plans in his log than tilling and sowing and negotiating at market. "Do
you think he'll fail?" asked Edmund, and Linda said no. "He'll do all
right, but so will you," and she touched her brother's arm, and he let
her, and then he sent her to the beach for a load of rocks. "Bring back

anything bigger than a cat," he said, and together, over the next several weeks, they constructed a small single-arch dam. They bought chipped bricks from Heisler's masonry and broken terra-cotta pots from the Cocoonery, and slowly the dam rose in a compact but stern mass. It was nothing more or less than a slightly curved wall of boulder, masonry, pine log, concrete dollop, packed earth, and, at its very heart, bales of hay. When they hauled the last stone into place, the dam stood nine feet high and six feet thick, and Linda could stand on one side and Edmund on the other and they could tap the rocks with their hammers and neither would hear the other. "You're sure it'll work?" she asked, and Edmund replied, "We'll have to wait and see."

Not long after, Edmund took a job as a clerk at the Twin Inn. The hotel was known both for its ocean views and for its pan-fried turkey, the birds freshly slaughtered by Señora Sara de Jesús Robledo in a shed out back. In the kitchen, the lard melted in a skillet as wide as an auto wheel, and Señora Sara—aproned but never without her carbuncle rings—fried the turkey whole with the feet, the giblets, the crimson flabby flesh from beneath the beak, and the beak itself, pulverized in a corn-grinder and sprinkled across the batch with pinches of *buenaventura.* Turkey *escandoloso,* it was called, and combined with mineral water and ocean breeze it brought a swift health to the lungs and soul—or so the tourist pamphlets and the advertisements in the Wisconsin and Indiana newspapers declared. And because of this, more guests visited Baden-Baden-by-the-Sea in the summer of 1919 than ever before.

But Dieter, recalling his own rejection at a hotel, didn't want Edmund to take the job. There were still plenty of tasks at Condor's Nest: clearing a fire path from the arroyo, fixing the backshed's roof, planting a row of grapevines on the hill, building a staircase up from the beach. "You won't be idle. Bruder will find plenty of work for you."

But Edmund was determined. "Why do you want to leave us?" Linda asked as he was preparing for his first day at the hotel. He was sitting on the bench in the kitchen yard, proud of his uniform of black gabardine trousers and a matching satin puff tie. A shoe was clamped between his knees, and he was buffing the toe cap.

She asked if she could visit him at the hotel, but he said he'd be busy keeping track of the guest rooms and making sure that everyone had what they wanted. He bent to lace his shoes; they were Dongola oxfords with a military heel, bought at Margarita's for $1.45. Edmund had admitted his anxiety over such a steep purchase, but Linda had swatted her hands through the air and said, "Why worry about it?" She wondered where he got it from: his timidity, his caution. He was unlike the rest of them, she knew, unlike Dieter and Valencia and certainly unlike herself. It was as if he had come from a different world, and again Linda was struck by the notion, vague as it was, that another world heaved and cleaved beyond the reaches—the San Luis Rey River, Mt. Palomar, the black lagoons—of Condor's Nest and Baden-Baden-by-the-Sea.

"Do you have your lunch pail?"

"I get a free turkey dinner with every shift."

"Can I pack you some *conchas*?"

"Muffins come with every meal."

"Is there anything I can do for you?"

He said there wasn't, and just as he was about to depart, Bruder appeared in the yard. His feet were bare, his pants rolled to his shins. He was carrying Edmund's book, *The Gentleman and His Ranch*, and Linda watched the twitch in Edmund's face, the blink, the sniffling nose. "Off to the hotel?" Bruder asked. Edmund continued packing his satchel and then set out down the dirt lane, careful to keep the dust from his cuffs, and when he turned to wave good-bye to his sister he found that she was already gone, on her way to the beach with Bruder, nothing in the kitchen yard but the short shadows and the white glare.

It was a cloudless day and on the sand, Bruder stripped down to his tank suit. Linda was wearing her cotton swimming dress, and as she jumped the waves, the water pulled on the frilled trim, and she envied Bruder, free as a seal in his skin. She watched his shoulders turn as he paddled through the ocean. From his mouth he spouted water five feet into the air. He liked to chase her, circling with a shark's precision, and a dark intensity would hood his eyes and she'd become nervous, a hundred yards out, as he swam, the fin of his arm crooked through the water, around her, and he'd refuse to stop or to speak when she'd say, "Bruder, please let's float here for a minute. Look up there. You can see the cottages and our dam. Isn't it a beautiful little dam?" But Bruder wouldn't stop, and once or twice he would dive, abandoning Linda on the surface, swimming so deep that even his air bubbles disappeared, and then a sudden tight grip would yank her cold foot. Once or twice she felt something soft against her skin, as gentle as a pair of nibbling lips.

They swam for more than an hour and then returned to shore for the outrigger. She had taught him to canoe the waves, the bamboo float facing the wind, and they would paddle until her arms ached and Bruder would yell for her not to stop. There was a ferocity to him as he sank his oar into the water and propelled the canoe through the surf, and it triggered a lurch within her chest. He knew what he was doing to her at moments like this, and it was his intention to make her realize that there was no one else in the world. Before he could admit to himself that he loved her, he wanted to be certain that she loved him. Before he could claim what was already his, he wanted to be sure that she longed to be possessed.

When they finished canoeing, they ran up the beach, to the gully path that led to the farm. Her bathing dress was heavy on her breasts and thighs, and the sun was warm through the cotton, steam rising. As she climbed the path she pulled on the ice plant, its snapped leaves secreting a sticky clear fluid that reminded her of something—something that even the thought of, in Bruder's presence, caused her to blush. She turned around and he was a step behind her, his arms stretched toward her; was he trying to capture her? With the arroyo dammed up, they now had to climb a steep path up the bluff's face, and again Linda was saying that they should build a staircase and that she would do it herself, if only someone would volunteer to be her builder's assistant. She was shouting like a golden eagle *kee-kee-kee,* and as they reached the top, Linda wanted to collapse with Bruder at her side, and just then Valencia called out for Linda, asking her to come help with the wash.

She told her mother she was busy.

"No, no, come now. And leave Bruder alone. He has work in the field."

Linda bent to catch her breath, and Bruder's hand fell to the small of her back. The sun burned the water from her skin, and Linda felt the quick rush of blood as she lifted her face.

"Linda!" Valencia called again: *Lean-da! Lean-da!* Her mother appeared with the wooden laundry paddle. Valencia's skirt ran to her ankles in the old-fashioned way, and she made a face that said she was too busy for games. Linda cooled with the disappointment of daily life. Her mother's interests were narrow, Linda had observed, her energy reserved for the cooking and the wash, the kitchen garden and the henhouse, the Friday-evening suppers in the schoolhouse where a dozen hands slapped out the *masa* and the wood smoke mixed with the semi-sweet smell of *tortillas* cooking on the comal. Valencia wasn't interested in the world beyond Baden-Baden-by-the-Sea, and as far as Linda could tell she knew nothing of it. Of her mother's early years in Mexico, Linda knew little. Once, for her birthday, Linda had asked her mother for a trip to San Diego, to ride the trolley and peer into the carpeted lobby of the Ulysses S. Grant Hotel. But Valencia never expressed any desire to step onto city pavement. "Everything I need is right here," she was fond of saying. That, and "Ay, Linda. You too will come to see."

Now Valencia was hauling the wash into the yard. There hadn't been rain since April, and there wouldn't be rain until November, and the garden had withered into a sandy bed of lavender-petaled horned sea rocket and a thicket of white geranium that lived off dishwater and a patch of scraggly myrtle white with sea salt. Years ago, Dieter had cut a picnic table and bench out of the hull of a schooner called *El Toro* that ran aground in La Jolla cove. The sailor graffiti remained in the plank, and Linda couldn't count the number of suppers she'd sat through running her finger over their carvings: a crosshatch count of days at sea; a crosshatch count of days since a woman was touched; the sketch of a huge-eyed girl lifting her petticoat. Storm and sun had faded the graffiti, but they remained firm enough in the wood for Linda to imagine the sailors in their canvas hats pulling in a topsail and sleeping four to a bunk. Linda wondered if she was the only one who saw the traces of the jack-tars' passions, but recently Bruder had said that he saw them too.

Valencia set down the laundry and fetched from the stove the pot of boiling water, pouring it into the half-barrel and instructing Linda to clamp the roller-washer to the rim. It was late morning, and Linda looked to the sun and to the mound of laundry and knew she'd still be washing in the afternoon, and that the day would pass at the washer's hand-crank. It was a mindless task, and after a few minutes—sorting out the clothes, submerging a checked shirt in the boiling water and wringing it through the roller—she began to wonder if she would stand at the picnic table and wash other people's undershirts for the rest of her life. "Mama, may I ask you a question?"

"Where do you think Papa met Bruder?"

"Along the front. You heard him say that." She was preoccupied with unraveling the arms of a pongee shirt.

"Why do you think Papa brought him home?"

"Because Bruder doesn't have anywhere else to go."

"But if he's old enough to fight in the war and carry a rifle, isn't he old enough to go wherever he wants?"

"I don't know, Linda."

"Do you think he saved Papa's life? Rescued him from the Germans, maybe?"

"So many questions, Linda."

"Do you think Papa owes him something?"

Linda felt let down by her mother—let down that Valencia didn't share her curiosity. Other things, too, failed to interest Valencia. Like what the men did in the evenings at the Twin Inn tavern, a room drenched in an unearthly yellow glow from the electricity in the crystal-dagger sconces. Why didn't Valencia wonder what went on in there? Or wonder what lay down the coast in the village above the cove, La Jolla, or even farther, on Union Street in San Diego, where Linda had heard—but certainly hadn't seen—that a horseless omnibus rattled up and down the street ready to take anyone anywhere for a nickel?

Valencia passed Linda one of Edmund's shirts with the detachable collar. It smelled of him, of chipped redwood and onion; she could nearly feel his flesh beneath the worn cloth. "I know what you think," said Valencia. "But you're wrong, Linda."

"Wrong?"

"I was like you too."

Linda didn't understand.

"It was a different world when I arrived. Everywhere you looked, there was nothing but chaparral and oak scrub. The arroyo seemed bigger then, a gash flowing to the ocean. Agua Apestosa was wider, blacker too, before they built the bridge. Ay, Linda, if you think it stinks now, you should have turned your nose to it then. When the Santa Anas blew, we'd have to tie rags over our mouths."

Linda scrubbed the shirt with the wire brush. She wondered what her mother was trying to tell her, and what any of this had to do with Papa and Bruder, and with her. But Valencia continued, describing the dirt road that once connected the village to the rest of the world; it was an overnight trip to Los Angeles, she reported. How did she know this? Because that first morning, after Valencia swam ashore and woke in Dieter's barn, she tried to escape again. She'd never forget it, she told

Linda. Waking with the bantams, the fold of her elbow lined with sea salt, her sleepy cheek impressed by the straw. At once she knew that everything had gone wrong for her. Valencia had hoped to jump from the *Santa Susana* off the coast of Rancho San Pedro. When Linda asked where that was, Valencia explained that it was a place that officially traded in tallow and hide, and unofficially, according to rumor passed from the fern-planted windowsills of Mazatlán, traded in opium and girls with hair as black as Valencia's. That was the way Valencia's best friend, Pavis, a strong girl with an upturned nose and a braid coiled atop her head, had put it as Valencia was preparing to sign up for service on the *Santa Susana.* Such a prospect had frightened Valencia, but she also knew that just beyond San Pedro Harbor and the muddy salt flats of Wilmington lay a road, white-dirt and two-lane, that cut through the yarrow and the live-oaks and the dried-out river washes, across a flat stretch of land once grazed by fifty thousand head of cattle, through the citrus orchards, toward a pueblo, already a village, already a town, with whispery promise of metropolis, they called Pasadena. Even girls in the back streets of Mazatlán, girls who ran shoeless and taught themselves to read by sitting in the laps of old men in the bar of Hotel San Poncho, a glimpse of breast cracking like a smile, and studying day-old issues of *El Diario;* even these girls, even in 1895, had heard of Pasadena, of the resort town blossoming in the orange groves, where five-hundred-room hotels sprouted beside the arroyos, and chambermaids and seam-stresses and silver-polishers and ballroom-floor waxers were in greater demand than water.

"Why did you want to go there?" Linda pushed another load around the barrel. She herself had never seen Pasadena, had never thought much of it, had assumed it was a valley of rich girls, their shadows ex-tending across croquet lawns.

"We had heard that peacocks lived in the trees and that every man had his own orange grove." That, and there wasn't a hotel in Pasadena that didn't need a thin girl with quick hands who could bow to guests on the loggia and tuck satin-trimmed sheets beneath a bed's corner. Va-lencia had also heard that Spanish was still useful in Alta California, es-pecially in the kitchens and butler's pantries and back staircases of Pasadena. Valencia had also heard it described as a land of freedom and prospect. "Because it's all new up there," Pavis explained as Valencia boarded the *Santa Susana.* "A girl like you can go there and in no time marry a railroad baron or an electricity tycoon or a gentleman with five hundred acres of orange grove!"

"But how will I meet such a man?" asked Valencia.

"You'll find a way!" said Pavis. "Be sure to wear a pretty dress when you arrive! Be sure to brush the nest out of your hair!"

With this counsel Valencia had boarded the *Santa Susana*. After the ship laid anchor in San Pedro Harbor she would slip ashore and never be seen again—at least that's what she told herself on the voyage out, belowdecks, in an old side chair upholstered in bald velvet, where she slept sitting up. Soon, however, she learned that the captain, Señor Carillo—wide-pored and broader in the middle than at the shoulders—never intended to allow Valencia to leave the ship again. In the first month, Valencia sailed to San Pedro and back to Mazatlán, all the while studying the endless turning, denting, jagging line of the coast. When she returned to the waters off Mazatlán, the captain wouldn't allow her to visit shore; from the ship's rail she could see the distant Sierra Madre and the city's red pantiles and she'd wonder, Where is Pavis? Beneath a fern hanging from a window? On a lap at the San Poncho? On one of the other freighters floating lazily in the harbor?

"It was on that second voyage," Valencia told Linda, "that I swam ashore to Condor's Nest. I thought I was swimming to Los Angeles. Turns out I was wrong."

Wrong indeed, thought Linda. Her mother handed her a bundle of laundry wrapped up in a shirt, the sleeves tied like a bow. When Linda opened it she discovered a pile of undershirts made from a ribbed cotton that wasn't sold at Margarita's. Edmund's undershirts were long-sleeved and of a thin wool that pilled; more than once, Linda had held up one of them and peered at the sun through the tiny holes in the wool, his faint odor fresh and warm on her face. But these undershirts were Bruder's, stiff with sweat. They were larger than Edmund's, hanging to Linda's knees, almost as big as the sail she used to pitch on her dory. "He's tall, isn't he?" she said.

Valencia murmured, busy with Dieter's long johns, unbuttoning the flaps.

"He's got a funny smell, doesn't he?"

"Who's that?"

Linda, under her breath: "Oh, never mind."

She wondered about it, about what type of body would heat up and boil over in the pit of the arm like this, releasing an odor so powerful that it would have to pass twice through the roller. She pulled the shirt over her head.

"What're you doing?"

Linda didn't answer.

"Take it off. There's work to do."

"Look, Mama! It's as big as a dress!" She held out her arms and twirled around, the ocean and the bluff and the fields becoming a blur, blue and sand and brown and green. She shut her eyes, and the roar of the ocean increased and the scent of the undershirt flooded her nostrils. It brushed her shins, the buttons tickled at her throat, and Linda continued to spin. Valencia said, pausing from her task, "Ay, Linda. Don't you remind me of me." She snapped her tongue nostalgically.

And that was what Linda was thinking, too. She wondered how her mother, who had proceeded with her young life so bravely, who had been beautiful too . . . how such a girl—a girl who could leap into the sea!—had settled into life at Condor's Nest, hoeing the garden and feeding the mules and grinding the wash through the roller. How had her mother become her mother? Yes, that was the question Linda asked herself. How does anyone become who she is? Yes, the stories of Valencia's youth reminded Linda of herself, but then something had happened. Valencia had become someone else—had it occurred overnight?—and all of this, while she twirled in Bruder's undershirt, made Linda ask herself: What will happen to me?

"Give me that shirt." Valencia pulled the shirt over Linda's head, and Bruder's scent drifted away.

Linda wondered what had changed since Valencia first swam ashore. El Camino Real had widened since then, the shoeless burros and the horses making way for the macadam and the automobiles. Not long after Linda's birth, Dieter sold his easternmost land to a man expanding the width of the road to two lanes. The transaction reduced Condor's Nest to twenty acres, including the arroyo. "Those automobiles are changing the world around us," Linda could recall Dieter saying excitedly when she was very young. But by the time she was seven or eight, he began to say sourly, "Those automobiles are ruining everything around here. Next thing they'll do is pave up the lagoon." And that turned out to be almost true, as a bridge was run across Agua Apestosa so that the cars could save two miles rather than have to skirt its edge.

Linda learned that she liked the notion of progress more than her father did, and it puzzled her, her father's grumpy acceptance of the future— the way his forehead would wrinkle and his nose would seemingly extend into a hook and his spiderweb beard would flap in a sunset breeze. He was becoming an old man, Linda could see.

Of course, Dieter resented the roads and the automobiles because, as he put it, everyone got rich on them but him. "That man made me hand over my land," he'd say as he stood in his fields and watched the traffic hurry by.

"Why'd they make Papa sell his land?" Linda asked her mother as they continued with the wash.

"Nobody made your Papa do anything. He sold it to the first man to come along. If he'd waited another month, he would have gotten twice as much. Another year, four times."

The clothesline was a triangle of rope staked to three cottonwood poles, protected from the wind by a screen of fan-palm fronds. The mayweed was in bloom, clusters of it around the poles, and Linda, soon bored, stopped pinning the clothes. She plucked the flowers, which looked like daisies but were, according to Edmund, poisonous—which had seemed unlikely to Linda, but since Edmund insisted it was true, she believed him. She linked the mayweed into a wreath and crowned herself, the flowers' tiny weight as imperceptible as a tick on the scalp.

She returned to Bruder's undershirts. They were heavy with water and now smelled of lye and the barrel's hooped oak. The stains were gone, his smell was gone. She held a shirt up against the sun. All she could smell was the ocean and the light burning the shirt dry. She took two pins from her lard tin and clamped each shoulder to the line.

"You don't have to do that."

"Who else is going to do it?"

"I'll do it myself," said Bruder.

"That'll be the day."

"I didn't ask you to do this."

He was leaning against one of the poles, his dungarees wet up to the knees, and staring at her in that way of his, with his chin hard with whisker, the corner of his mouth up as if he were about to make a rude sucking noise. What did he want? He sometimes wished Linda would cough up the question. If she were to ask, he would tell her. What no one knew about Bruder was that he was a cautious man, careful not to step into unfamiliar danger. He had learned as a boy in Pasadena to know his enemy; it had saved his life at the Children's Training Society, and in the beechwood forest in France—his enemy had never been who he seemed.

"Why are you wearing daisies on your head?"

Linda touched her hair and felt the wreath. She must've looked silly, like a girl who thought she was a princess. "Oh, this . . . ? Why, these aren't daisies. You don't know very much, do you? This is mayweed. And you better be careful, because it's poisonous. You better be careful if you can't tell the difference."

"No, it isn't."

"No, it isn't *what?*"

"Mayweed isn't poisonous." And then, "No more poisonous than you or me."

She was about to curl her fist and say, Oh yes it is! But she stopped herself. Yes, Bruder would ask her where she had learned something like that, and she would have to tell him it was Edmund; and Bruder would laugh, his mouth open so wide that she could see into the black cave of his throat.

From behind his back he produced an orange, and he began tossing it in the air and catching it. "Come with me." Bruder moved to her. He threw her the orange. Imprinted on its rind was a faint blue stamp:

PASA

"What's that supposed to mean?"

"I want to show you something."

"What?"

"Just come." His shadow fell across the laundry basket. Linda felt a rise in her pulse as he stole the orange from her palm.

"I've got laundry. What about Mama?"

"We'll be back."

"Where are we going?" His hand took hers, and it seemed as if her hand belonged to someone else: a free little hand caught in Bruder's hot paw.

He ran to the edge of the bluff and Linda followed, the basket of laundry turning over behind her. She wondered if anyone could see them, if Valencia, whose eyes were puffy and bruised with fatigue, was standing in the kitchen and looking out to the ocean, witnessing them sprint away.

He had seen something on the beach that frightened him and he wanted to show Linda, to see if it frightened her as well. They would share their apprehension, and Bruder predicted that Linda would reach for him and then he would hold her and his arms would fall around her and he would have her and they would rock as the tide ran over their feet.

They ran quickly down the path, Bruder's feet kicking dirt and rock, his hands, extended for balance, grabbing vines of ice plant, the fleshy triangular leaves snapping. Linda followed, losing her balance and grabbing for the purple flowers. She didn't stop, she slipped and ran farther, one pace behind Bruder. When he turned and called "Are you all right?" she hollered, "I know this path better than you." The truth was, she'd never run down it so fast, and there was a part of her, a dark pulsing part, that feared she would lose her balance and tumble forward into Bruder and pull them both off the face of the cliff to the rocky beach below. This didn't scare her, only sent her heart racing faster, so that she became overwhelmed by her own heat, her forehead releasing a sheet of sweat across her face. Her blood was flowing so fast through her body that it felt as if something in her was changing just then, as if what she felt for Bruder was somehow replacing an earlier emotion. Bruder's arms stretched parallel to the earth, as steady as the line of the horizon, and he transfixed Linda: the smooth bump of bone that grew at the base of his neck, the tendril of hair creeping down toward his spine, the chapped elbows, pink and white like valentines, the rear pocket in his dungarees stuffed with an old kerchief that Linda had seen him use to pull back his hair in a warrior manner. She was wet with her own perspiration and dizzy, and then she lost balance, the soil crumbling beneath her. Linda fell forward against Bruder, and he fell as well, downward, their bodies pressed, but they were only a few feet from the beach and they landed, chest to chest, in the sand.

Her eyes were closed, and her heart slowed. Bruder's pulse reverberated through her breast. She felt something she had never felt before, and she told herself she'd never forget it, whatever it was. Bruder felt something too, but he knew precisely what it was; he jumped to his feet and pulled her up. "Come on now. She won't be there forever." And then, in a quiet voice she nearly didn't hear, "My Linda."

"Who?" Linda called, trailing Bruder. He had scraped his elbow in the fall, and it was red with dots of blood. He dabbed at it with the kerchief and then held it up for Linda to see the stain.

She chased after Bruder and grabbed the kerchief. It was stiff with sweat and now spotted with blood and heavy with the smell she'd been wringing out in the washer barrel. Linda hurled the kerchief toward the ocean. The wind caught it, the white cotton fluttering, and Bruder and Linda stood, shoulders touching, and watched the kerchief dip and rise, like a lazy gull, like a pelican loitering before its plunge, until the wind, as it sometimes does over the lip of the Pacific, died, fell flat immediately, and the kerchief, white with red stars of Bruder's blood, collapsed on itself and sank into the sea.

"Where are we going?" she asked.

"You'll see." He was hurrying along the sash of the tide, the lacy foam collecting on his ankle. "Down in Cathedral Cove," said Bruder. "There's something you should see." He said they should hurry and he offered his hand, but Linda didn't take it, instead running ahead and leaping over the driftwood logs and the clumps of kelp. One other thing Dieter had told Bruder about his daughter: "She doesn't know herself. She doesn't know what people think of her and she doesn't care. She's free that way. But then, so are you!" But Bruder knew himself, and running along the beach one step behind Linda, he thought of the girls who had sent him notes bound in Belgian lace handkerchiefs: *I love you!* Not too many girls, but one or two from the whitewashed mansions along Orange Grove Avenue, one girl slipping away from a governess and rushing high-waisted into the crowd on Colorado Street and taking Bruder's hand and forcing his fingers around an orange-oiled square of lace. *I love you, Bruder, and you must love me!* The girl vanished into Dodsworth's dress shop, and Bruder was left with a hand reeking of an heiress, the citrus perfume sickly sweet, and he rinsed his palms in the lily-pad fountain in Central Park. He threw away the note and burned the handkerchief in one of the grove-heaters at the City Farm. He never knew the girl's name, but he knew enough about the rich girls of Pasadena to be sure that she, whoever she was, assumed that everyone in the valley knew her name. He knew that somewhere a girl was resting her chin on an iron balcony rail that even at night radiated the heat of the day's sun, waiting for him, and he laughed, for he knew that he would never go to her. He would sleep with the dogs before bedding a woman like that; even as a boy bursting out of his teens, Bruder knew himself enough to know that a girl with pearls choking her windpipe would never mean anything to him. He had assumed that no one would, but now here he was, running down the beach, at Linda's heels.

Cathedral Cove was almost a mile south of Condor's Nest, around the far bend, past Jelly Beach, where the helmet-shape by-the-wind sailors hovered like incandescent ghosts in the summer waves. For as long as Linda could remember, Dieter had warned her not to swim there, Edmund repeating the words of caution: *You could lose your leg to a sting.* Linda, whose natural inclination was to run past any NO TRES-PASSING sign, had heeded their advice because one of the few things that frightened her was a jellyfish. Shapeless and colorless—blobs of nothing that you can't put your hands around! She used to ask Edmund, "If a jelly is nothing, how can it hurt me?"

The previous night's moon had been full, and the tide on Jelly Beach was so low that it revealed a table of tidal pools Linda hadn't seen in nearly a year, a plane of shallow puddles undulating with red-mouthed anemone and paved with abalone. Linda noticed a small or-ange globe bobbing in a wave far out in the water, and then a second, and a third, came into focus. In the glare she saw more oranges floating atop the tidal pools and out in the waves, at first dozens but then hun-dreds and then thousands of oranges floating on the horizon, the sea decorated with perfect round knobs of citrus, as bright as the golden-orange garibaldi. Suddenly they were all over, as if dumped from the crate of the sky, and Bruder picked one up from the sand. He threw it high into the air, and together they watched its long arc and its faraway plunge into the surf, its disappearance, then its reappearance, as it popped through the water, perpetually afloat.

Linda asked where the oranges had come from, and Bruder said, "A wreck."

The sea was littered with oranges, and the pelicans had found them and were diving in noisy swoops, mistaking the oranges for rare fish, the fruit bulging obscenely in their black pouches. How could there have been a shipwreck on such a fine day? Maybe a freight car had over-turned on the bridge spanning Agua Apestosa, its load of citrus spilling into the marsh and then drifting out to sea.

Far out in the tidal pools, a figure in a broad hat stood bent over the shallow water, collecting something, kicking the oranges, turning over shells and crabs. Linda couldn't be sure, but she thought it was a young boy. She didn't recognize him, but things were changing so quickly in the village that lately she could walk down the beach and pass people she'd never seen before, people who had motored over from Escondido and Julian and stumbled down the paths to swim and fish and chase one another in the surf. The world that she had once assumed belonged only to her was quickly opening itself to a surging crowd of strangers, with their car exhaust and their trammeling beach sandals and their habit of leaving wax paper and pipe ash in the sand. "The ocean will sweep up after us," they would say.

"Is he waving at us?" Bruder asked about the boy in the tidal pools.

Linda couldn't be sure; he was more than fifty yards away, shaded by a white straw hat. His hand moved quickly, and Linda wondered if the boy was saying hello or if he had discovered something, maybe an oyster with a pearl the size of a baby's fist; or maybe the boy needed help, maybe his foot was trapped in a moray's cave. The figure waved again, this time with his entire arm, but Linda thought she saw the flash of a smile. She thought she heard something, but with the wind skimming the water and the flushing waves and the gulls crying as if they had lost something, she couldn't be sure.

"Did you hear anything?"

Bruder shook his head. He had heard nothing, and he wanted to get to Cathedral Cove. "We have to hurry. She might be gone."

"Who?"

Bruder tugged Linda, his hand around her wrist; a hand as big as her face, Linda knew, because once he had held it over her nose and his pinkie had touched one ear and his thumb the other; through the mask of Bruder's hand she had seen Edmund avert his eyes.

The oranges distressed Bruder, for he knew where they had come from and he knew what kind of mismanagement would lead to such a spill. In the beechwood forest of France, he had promised to keep a secret, and he couldn't tell Linda that the spilled oranges had anything to do with him, *with us, Linda.* Sometimes when Bruder was restless, he would remind himself that only patience would ferry him into the future, and this would slow his overworked heart.

Cathedral Cove was a small inlet, its waters churning with riptide, potato-size rocks covering the beach. At the back of the cove, a row of boulders covered in velvety moss attracted green-eyed flies. The cliffs rose sharply to a bluff above, where an abandoned Lutheran church lurched in the wind, its planks stripped and rotted and occasionally pried free for a bonfire set by ranchless rancheros. A small passage opened in the cove's back wall, an arched hole that forced even young children to crouch to get through it. Inside was a small cave lit by a rose-shape hole above the passage, a cave smaller than Miss Winterbourne's schoolroom, but with a vaulted ceiling and, at one end, a flattened rock like an altar. When she was seven or eight, Linda had wandered from Condor's Nest down the beach, reaching the cove for the first time in low tide. She'd always remember her own little-girl's gasp as she peered into the cave, seeing the sunbeams slanting through the hole above the passageway, landing on the altar rock. It was like a miniature church, a dollhouse cathedral, like the pictures in Dieter's book on the Catholic churches of Germany; the book was illustrated, tissue paper shrouding each print of the cathedrals—in Köln, in Dresden, in Leipzig, in a place called München. Someone had tinted the prints with colored pencils. In the book, each cathedral's nave lay lit in a slanted column of sunlight, just as the sun fell into the little cave on the beach. Its discovery—*A chapel on the beach! A cathedral in a cove!*—had excited her so much that she ran all the way back to Condor's Nest to tell Edmund. *I'm going to call it Cathedral Cove*, she'd decided. She ran so fast that she could nearly see her heart leaping against her dress, and when she finally reached Edmund, who was lying on his bed reading an agricultural dictionary, she found it difficult to put the words together to explain what she had come across. "Down the shore . . ." she tried. "I found something, I discovered something. Come and see!" "Did you make it to Cathedral Cove?" Linda's heart fell quiet as Edmund explained that she wasn't the first to discover the little cave; in fact, she may very well have been the last.

When they reached the cove, Bruder and Linda stopped at its edge. The oranges sat brightly atop the black rocks like planets in the sky, and Bruder's hand fell to her shoulder tentatively; he had warned himself against touching her, but his hand moved to her neck nonetheless. He had wanted to feel her flesh since the first time Dieter had said of his daughter, "Her eyes are as black as yours."

"Maybe we shouldn't," said Bruder.

"Shouldn't what?"

"I brought you here to show her to you."

Was there a grounded ship just beyond the cove? A beached dolphin, bloated and heaving in the sun, a fin flopping desperately? Those seemed possible, or maybe a sea lioness mourning a lost pup, wailing in the tide, her eyes weepy and her whiskers limp. And then it occurred to Linda that just maybe Bruder had brought her here to be alone with her. Maybe his hand would lead her through the mouth of the cave and into the damp hole in the bluff. What would she do were he to lay her upon the stone altar? Her longing for him had been deep, a remote ache rising within her at night.

Then she saw something on the beach. "What is that?"

Fifty feet away, in the passage that led to the cave, something white and blubbery lay sprawled, a few oranges glowing around it. At first, Linda thought it was a baby sperm whale caught in the riptide and thrown ashore. But there was something about the shape—long but tapered at the end, with something resembling a head—that told Linda it wasn't a sperm whale. A dolphin perhaps, or a bluefin tuna, its belly silvery white in the afternoon. And maybe that would explain the smell, which just then reached Linda's nostrils—a black odor of decay and rot and overripening beneath a fat sun. Her hand took Bruder's.

"Do you want to see her?" he said.

He moved and Linda followed, her hand over her nose and mouth as the odor erupted, the way a light you're inching toward widens and floods the eyes with its whiteness. Except that this smell was black, it was dead, but not like a dead fish—already, Linda could tell that it, she, wasn't a bluefin tuna or a dolphin astray from its swimming grounds off San Clemente Island. No, she was something else. Someone else.

Bruder picked up a stick smooth and glossy from the tide. "I found her like this," he said.

And as they approached, Linda began to wonder who the girl might be: a girl like her mother, flinging herself from the stern of a ship; a girl praying in the abandoned Lutheran church above who slipped at the bluff; a girl pulled under by the greasy hand of the riptide; a girl not unlike herself, traipsing and hunting the ocean and the beach, who somehow found her death.

She was a tall girl, naked, with her arms at her sides and her knees at an awkward angle and her ankles crossed. Her mass of mossy blond hair fell over her shiny cheek. Her back was a silvery-blue hump, and

Linda, now only a few feet away, could see that hours in the water had bloated the girl, filling her flesh with a layer of saltwater that made her look something like an oversize doll: arms padded and soft, feet white and jellyish. Her hair reminded Linda of the horsehair sewn into the porcelain heads of the dolls kept on the upper shelf at Margarita's, behind the register. How frightening were their painted blue eyes, following Linda round the store whenever she went to try on the eagle-feather hat.

Bruder poked at the girl with his stick, nudging her shoulder, releasing a cloud of flies.

"She's dead," Linda heard herself say. "What happened to her?"

"She must have been in the wreck."

"Who do you think she is?"

"Probably a captain's girl." He nudged the girl's head with the stick; it flopped heavily, waterlogged; her spine was limp, apparently snapped—and the thought of it filled Linda's head with the bright crackle of an imagined *snap!* She could hear it, the girl's neck cracking in a thrust, in an unexpected jolt, the girl once alive and pretty and fearless and proceeding happily with her young life, expecting nothing, expecting everything, and then a sudden whip that snapped her throat; it was as if Linda had been there when the girl's life had come and gone, and now she watched the neck turn limply with the shove of Bruder's stick, and suddenly Linda realized that that horrible sound, that sound she had actually never heard, would linger with her for as long as she lived, and that this day, with the tide creeping forward and the gray gulls hanging motionless in the wind and the sun shifting perpetually and Bruder's hand falling to her hip and his voice, deeper than any boy's she had ever known, saying, "Are you all right?"—that all of this, the foul black odor and the shimmering hump, and the puffy ankles crossed and the golden flash of pubic hair as Bruder continued to prod the girl's body, trying to flip her over but, when they saw the swollen stomach, the expectant stomach, eventually giving up: "Oh God, she's pregnant!" Yes, she realized that all this would someday come to mean something to her, and to Bruder, too, and then the boy with the stick, the boy who had come home from the war with her father and slipped into her former bed and snatched away Dieter's filial affections for Edmund, and maybe *her* feelings for her brother too, the boy with the hair as black as her own and the body—once, through the window of the cottage, Linda had seen him undress—like a roan's, strings of muscle in the thigh, across the breast, in the black pit of his groin, then this young man named Bruder pulled Linda to his chest. His heart knocked against her breast, and she felt it echo within her and sobbed softly into his shoulder, and he stroked her head; and Linda wanted him to hold her forever, but the stench was too much for them to remain at Cathedral Cove, and she said, "We'll come back on a nicer day," and Bruder released Linda, and he hoped that that would be true but he couldn't be as sure as she, and they moved up the beach in silence, and each imagined the future differently.

On Jelly Beach, the tide had begun to move in and the waves were throwing hundreds of oranges onto the sand. Linda and Bruder saw the boy from before sitting on a rock taking inventory of what he had collected from the tide pools. His back was to them, and the disk of his straw hat hid him completely as he bent over his task. Bruder said, "Let's not tell him about the girl. It'll frighten him." Bruder called to the boy, and Linda called out as well, and as they approached him he turned around and they were surprised to see that he wasn't a boy at all. No, in fact the boy in the hat was Charlotte Moss.

On the rock she was examining a freshly broken piece of teakwood and a silver fork and a coil of rope and two or three oranges. "There's been a wreck," she said. She was busy writing in her notebook, a pencil behind each ear.

"Do you know the ship?"

"A freighter out of San Pedro. Carrying half a million oranges to Maine." She seemed pleased with her acquisition of facts and pointed out the flotsam as if to prove her story. Then she said, "Everyone lost, it seems."

"How do you know?"

"It came on the wire. The *Bee* sent me down here to see what's washing in. Where'd you two get off to?" Charlotte asked.

"A long walk," said Linda.

"Boy, I'd say. You passed by here more than an hour ago." Charlotte's chin, soft and soon to require plucking, twitched, and an idea struck her and she wrote it down.

"We went to Cathedral Cove," said Bruder.

"Anything down there?"

"A few more oranges," he said. "And a girl."

Charlotte opened her mouth skeptically and said, "Then I must get to work. It might be my biggest story yet." And she returned to the debris, holding it to the light. She screwed up one eye as she thought of the best phrase to describe the washed-up sterling filigreed hairbrush that must have belonged to the captain's wife or the ship's owner or a rich patroness seeking clandestine passage to another world. Only then did Charlotte say, "You mean an actual girl?"

Linda and Bruder said good-bye to Charlotte Moss, who moved in the direction of Cathedral Cove. She called, "Look for me in the paper tomorrow!" Their throats burning with salt, Linda and Bruder returned to Condor's Nest. At the foot of the bluff, Bruder reached to kiss Linda, but she instinctively looked up the cliff and saw Edmund peering over. A cloud of uncertainty shadowed her face as Linda left Bruder and climbed the bluff. She ran to tell her brother about the wreck and the thousands of oranges and the silver-fleshed girl.

7

OVER THE YEARS, Bruder had learned that nearly everyone wanted to tell a story—forging the past and inventing the details along the way. The boys at the Training Society wove their family histories around the few scraps they knew: "My mother had green eyes and a beautiful mouth, and she fought off a hundred and one men before she accepted my father's plea for her hand." The soldiers in his company had told stories of the girls waiting for them at home: "She works as a telephone operator, and she's so beautiful that men ring her up just to hear her voice—but she loves me, only me." And on the long journey home from France, Dieter had described Valencia and Linda as "my little mer-maids."

And this was how Charlotte described the drowned girl in the *Bee.* "Her hair grew in long kelp-like strands, and she lay curled on the beach. She was a child-maid, whose life ended before she knew what had happened to her. She went down with the ship, and no one will ever know her name, nor her baby's."

"Charlotte made up most of her column," said Bruder.

"In the end, what difference does it really make?" said Linda.

Her response touched him with regret, and one night he was study-ing her as she opened the case that held Dieter's violin and wondered if she was like the rest: inventing the past to invent the future—ready, eager to tell a lie.

But Linda studied him as well, confused about why he never told his own stories. Since that day on the beach, Bruder had ignored her, working late in the fields and eating alone in the Vulture House. "Are you afraid of Edmund?" she teased. "No," he said. And this he with-held: *I'm afraid of you.*

She handed the violin, burnished red with ebony pegs, to Dieter. These were the nights she used to love, when Dieter clamped the vio-lin between his chin and chest and the *Lieder* wept from his bow and Valencia told stories of Mexico, and Dieter told stories of Germany; of California when the scrubland stretched endlessly, untouched, untram-pled.

When Dieter began to play one of Linda's favorite songs, "Früh-ling," she pulled Bruder up to dance with her. He refused, but Dieter prodded, saying, "Go on. She doesn't belong to anyone else."

Bruder held Linda, her breast against his. He kept an eye on Ed-mund, who was reading on the window bench, doing his best to ignore them, his pout reflected in the glass. Years ago, Bruder had peered through the Valley Hunt Club's kitchen-door window into the white-tie balls, and he had seen men's fingers intertwined with women's, hands guiding hips, but he didn't know how to dance and Linda sensed this, guiding him around the cottage. He was clumsy and self-conscious and wanted to please her, and she wanted him to trust her. "Follow me," she whispered. And he did. Outside the window, the moon was full over the ocean and the waves crashed gently in the low silver tide.

Dieter continued playing the *Zeltmusik* and described how back in Schwarzwald at the end of harvest he and his brothers would use their mallets to pitch a canvas tent in the barley field. For three days they'd play their violins while a pair of singers, usually lovers, would perform *Lieder* and *Spiele,* and the village would dance through dusk and dawn, but the singers wouldn't stop until Dieter was the last one standing in the tent. It was a contest—who could fiddle the longest—and Dieter al-ways won. They used to call his mother *Der Waldvogel,* and his nick-name had been "the Chickadee." His brothers would ask him to play his violin in the tin shop to help the hours pass, and when the orders had flooded in from the American armies and the hammering in the tin shop lasted through the night, sometimes it was Dieter's music that would keep the mallets tapping.

Bruder returned Linda to her chair, and he took Valencia's hand and asked her to dance.

"Mama never dances," said Edmund.

Bruder could see that the subject had touched Valencia, like a finger stroking the cheek, and it made him wonder about his own mother; he tried to hold back the longing, to fight down the curiosity. More than once he had told himself that it was a waste of time to wonder about the void of the past. But in spite of himself, Bruder couldn't always resist.

"It was years ago," said Valencia.

"What was?" asked Linda.

"The world I swam into, on that night long ago."

"Why did you leave Mexico?" asked Bruder.

"It's a long story."

"Tell us," he said.

"It's late. Bed is calling."

"Then start now," said Bruder.

"And then you'll tell us how you first met Papa," Linda said to Bruder. "First Mama, and then you."

He said nothing, he did not make a deal, but Linda misread his grimace as agreement, and perhaps Valencia did as well, or just maybe, weary from the endless months of sun, she thought that there was no longer any reason not to tell her daughter. Did Dieter know? Yes, although he had forgotten the details over the years. And what about Edmund? He had heard from his father that his mother was an orphan; that was as much as he cared to learn. This scrap of history Linda had already collected. When Dieter picked up his violin again, Valencia said, "It reminds me of the music in the hall in Mazatlán, just off the Plaza de la Luz, where on the first Saturday of each month, a three-member band opened their velvet-lined cases and played to a crowd of sailors and miners, *banditos* and mercenaries, at a *fiesta* that the regulars called Café Fatal." There, years ago—*estaba una otra centuria, un otro mundo*—young Valencia, not much older than Linda was now, first learned to dance.

She had been tall for her age, with the legs of a crane; she wore her hair pulled from her face, and her skin was softened by a weekly smear of butter. She first attended Café Fatal with Pavis, who was two years older, already full in the blouse, the suede pouch she wore around her waist already filling with silver. Pavis wore a turquoise ring, a child's ring that no longer fit, but she would grease her finger in a jar of lard to slide the ring past her knuckle. Valencia would watch this ritual, the finger sinking into the mass of pearly grease, as she ran the butter knife over her arms and legs, over her throat and the thickening pad of her heel. Both girls were orphans, Pavis having never known her parents, Valencia having watched hers, when she was seven, drown in the flash flood that swept away the village of Villa Vasquez. Thirty-seven villagers disappeared, along with the village itself, which had been known for its hammered silverwork and necklaces set with coral. Valencia's mother, in the few minutes before the flood, just as the village realized that it was about to drown, had taken Valencia to one of the adobe bell towers of the Cathedral of Magnificent Salvation and then returned to the *casita* to fetch Valencia's crippled younger brother, Federico. It was from that height that Valencia witnessed the brown water pounce toward the village like an enormous beast, two boulders as its eyes, and swallow the houses and the silver factory and the chimneyed smelter and the stables and the market where Valencia's mother bought corn oil and dried beef and jars of pickled sea bass imported from Mazatlán; Valencia watched the churning water inhale the wagons and the cottonwood trees and the shrubs of wild mustard and the thirty-seven villagers, each running frantically, squealing like a nest of mice scurrying at the meow of a cat, the entire village reduced, from the viewpoint of the bell tower, to fleeing squeaking rodents. But not Valencia's mother and her father and young Federico: the three of them did not turn into mice at the moment of their death; no, instead they looked toward the wall of water and simply leaned against a ponderosa pine and crossed themselves and let the water crash over them. As she watched the flood swallow them, Valencia was terrified for her family, and for herself: for the cathedral, with its twin bell towers, was in the flood's path as well, and only seconds after it consumed the ponderosa pine, the water rushed toward the cathedral's iron-studded door, where Padre Cid shielded himself with a Bible. The church disappeared, and the water rose to the bell tower's rail; and surely it would rise beyond the rail, Valencia assumed just then, waiting, crossing herself, and praying. But the water peaked, and Valencia, who never once shut her eyes, watched the flood's froth, a stew of debris—porch chairs and latticed shutters and wagon wheels and iron ice tongs, and over there was a horse tossed about like a twig, and just up there was old Señora Viquario, fat as a cow, chained to her bull, Carlos, the two of them dead and bobbing like buoys—Valencia watched the flood's churn slow and settle and retreat, so that by the following dawn, all glittered in the sun and all was gone, nothing left but the twin bell towers and the lone, stripped trunk of the ponderosa pine.

That was why Valencia grew up in the orphanage, La Casa de la Naranja, where she and Pavis first became friends. The orphanage was run by five nuns whose habits swept the floorboards. Each morning the nuns sent the girls to the dairy to milk the sheep and churn the butter and skim the goat cream. The orphanage, although lonely, never became a house of misery. No one beat Valencia or rubbed her nose in her own excrement or forced her onto the straw mattress of the dairy hand, Señor Ferrero, who eyed the girls while fingering his shoebrush whiskers. No, not once did he move his hand from his face to one of the girls. At the same time, never once did the nuns hug Valencia with their stiff woolen sleeves or help her comb the snarl out of her hair. No, only Pavis helped her, using a silver comb spared by the flood: deposited at the foot of the bell tower along with a stick of pink coral with a silver-filigree cap and Padre Cid's Bible, its pages damp and fleshy like a mushroom. Pavis would comb out Valencia's plait, telling her that soon it would be time for them to leave the orphanage and take up positions as chambergirls at the Hotel San Poncho. There they would serve the guests, mostly sailors and miners and men trading silver for guns, gold for bullets, rocks of turquoise for candy-red sticks of dynamite. The chambergirls would offer coffee with milk, shark stewed in lime, and corn baked in its own husk. The men would say, "Here's a piece of silver if you come and sit on my lap," and Señor Costa, the hotel owner, would nod from behind the front desk, where he counted his money and locked up in a safe his guests' pocket watches and wedding bands. And this sort of work, led to the first and then frequent visits to Café Fatal, on the first Saturday of each month, where Pavis and Valencia would sit at a table in the corner drinking rum sent over by an admirer with gold teeth. He would ask one of them to dance, or both of them; and a moist hand would cuff Valencia's wrist and pull her to the center of the hall and place itself at the small of her back, its sweat seeping through her blouse. The men smelled, she learned that first Saturday night: like the rind of a ham or the tail of a fish or the bed of a bull or the heap of apple cores beneath the hotel's kitchen window. She nearly expected a swarm of flies to emerge from the collar of each man who paid her to dance, or to find flies caught in the sticky trap of his nostrils. Handprints on her blouse to wash away in the morning, grease on her wrists, salty slobber behind her ear. Valencia pressed against a man softer in the breast than she, clammy breath fogging up her face, the jab of a revolver in a pocket. Pavis would dump out her suede pouch onto the bed they shared and count her coins and tell Valencia what she would buy with the week's take: a hand mirror, a hat with a wide brim decorated with yellow feathers, a bigger purse. "Wasn't it fun last night? All those men? All these coins?" Except Valencia never thought of it that way.

She was just a girl when she first visited Café Fatal, arriving with a fan looped around her wrist. Not ten minutes after her arrival she was dancing with a man with a bump on his bald, thumping-veined crown. She tried not to look at the soft gray egg-size lump, keeping her eyes on the three-member band, wrongly believing they would come to her aid. The money she and Pavis earned at Café Fatal paid for the room in the hotel basement where they slept and stored their few possessions in a blanket chest. In that dark, cool room, Valencia had learned to dance with the son of the hotel owner, a boy named Paco, fifteen years old, shell-white hands and small, hairless arms, a perpetual tremble in his lip. Pavis called him Paquito: "What a pretty little boy!" And Paco didn't mind, he preferred hiding in the basement with the chambermaids who worked for his father to sitting behind the reception desk and requesting, in a quavering voice, the hotel's guests to deposit their guns and knives in the bronze-cast safe. Paco would bring the two girls plates of sugar dough and cups of milk warmed on the stove; he stole satin ribbons to braid through their hair; and one day he arrived at the foot of the basement stairs with his hands behind his back. "For you," he said, offering a silk fan with a blue tassel. Valencia snapped open the fan, its panel painted with the scene of a smoking volcano. And then, blushing, he said, "You're like a sister to me."

Valencia wondered why he was saying such a thing, why he had given her the fan, looping it around her wrist. She had been living in the basement for only four weeks. A sister after four weeks? But there was something brotherly in Paco, in the way he would stand close to her but never touch her, in the way he eyed her lovingly but never with longing, with overwarmed breath. There was a song that he'd taught her: *You are the spring for which I longed in the frosty wintertime.* And he would sing to her, and on the day he offered her the fan, he also offered to teach her to dance, his hand fluttering to her shoulder. His lip started to quake, and Paco began to sing in his head voice: *O, let me come close to see the noble light in your eye.* He guided Valencia around the room until they bumped into the blanket chest and fell onto the bed. She felt the fast thud of his heart as they landed, but soon it slowed, her own following, and to Valencia's surprise and relief, they fell asleep in embrace.

And so Paco became Valencia's secret friend during those first months at the San Poncho, sneaking into her room to dance when Pavis was busy sitting on the lap of one of the men at the hotel bar. He would say, "You shouldn't have to spend time with those men." He would say, "You shouldn't have to visit Café Fatal."

"Easy for you to say," Valencia would reply. "Not only do you own the Hotel San Poncho, you also own the candle factory and the livery and I understand you own a rancho somewhere between Mazatlán and Villa Vasquez that stretches for the length of Spain."

"Nothing stretches for the length of Spain but the length of Spain itself." And he would brush the hair out of her eyes and take her hands and move close to her, but never kiss her. *Mi hermana.*

And so it was on that night at Café Fatal, when the man with the tumorous bump atop his head led Valencia around the hall, that she vowed never to dance again. The man paid her for the dance, and Valencia returned to the table where she had left Pavis and the silk fan. The man had left her with two silver coins and a grimy feeling that made her think that his oniony stink would never wash from her blouse. "He wasn't all that bad," said Pavis, her lips clamping around a paper straw. The gold rum rose through the tube and filled her cheeks. "They can be worse."

And Valencia knew that Pavis was right; why, hadn't Valencia witnessed a menagerie of men pawing at the mole on Pavis's throat: a man with a radish nose; a man with the hair of his armpit creeping from his sleeve; a man with stains on his trousers; a boy no older than Pavis with a cigarillo stub lodged in the corner of his mouth. So many, so many more to come, Valencia knew, and she was at the age when she both wondered about her future and doubted it: for she knew in the pit of her heart that her life would have to change, that she would one day flee the San Poncho. Yet, even so, it felt that life had condemned her to this: to the windowless basement, to the steaming stove where she boiled the sheets, to the endless chatter of Pavis, who rattled off her dreams of a villa overlooking the sea and a team of chambermaids to sweep her tile

floors and to carry her on a crêpe de chine chaise to the outhouse carved
into the volcanic rock. "It'll happen," Pavis would say. But Valencia
doubted it. No, she couldn't imagine anything beyond the present,
even though she knew there was a future; there had to be. But she worried that she would pay the rest of her life for surviving the flood; that
her life would be the payment, her debt to the silent, already-dead faces
of her father and mother and little lame Federico as they watched the
flood descend on them with the vastness of something Valencia could
attribute only to her God—whom she abandoned from the next dawn
until the day Sieglinde was born.

"Go on," Pavis said. "Have a sip of rum."

Valencia pressed her lips around the straw. It wasn't her first time
tasting rum, but the heat surprised her nonetheless, the burning in her
throat. She returned the glass to Pavis, and it was just at this moment,
as the rum burnished the color in Valencia's cheek, that a man neither
girl had ever seen before entered Café Fatal.

He was tall, but not tall like the man with the overbite who had paid
Pavis to dance with him behind the café. No, this stranger was tall in a
head-turning way, with black hair feathered around his face and a trim
black beard. Valencia and Pavis both noted that his clothes were finer
than those of the other patrons of Café Fatal: a waistcoat with a standing collar and high Hessian boots, the soft black leather folded just
under his knee.

"Who's that?"

"I don't know," said Valencia.

"What do you suppose he wants?"

The man walked about the room, Panama hat in hand, nodding at
the girls who huddled at tables or along the wall, their collars yawning
open around their throats. He shook hands with a few men, stopping to
laugh with a pallid clerk who was sweating as if he owed money: Valencia had danced with him last week, her hand sinking into the damp
folds of his back. Then the stranger approached Pavis and Valencia.

The girls turned their faces in his direction. If you were to look
at them like this—two young faces, one, Valencia's, shaped like a
valentine—you would notice the small differences that would change
the course of their lives: Valencia's forehead was higher, and smooth;
her eyes were imperceptibly wider than Pavis's, her nose possessed of

one less scrap of flesh. The careful observer, the evolutionary eye, would register the subtle differences in beauty. The stranger asked Valencia to dance.

He asked her name, her age, where she was from.

"Yes, Villa Vasquez," he said. "Swept away in a flood."

Out of the corner of her eye, Valencia could see Pavis's shoulders pinched over her rum.

"Have you returned since the flood?"

She shook her head.

"Yes, well. New families have moved in. There is corn in the field, the silver mine has reopened, the smeltery belches filth once again into the sky."

"I had no idea."

"How would you know, here in Mazatlán?" And then he asked, "Do you want to return?"

"To Villa Vasquez? No, there's nothing there for me."

"The bells in the tower are ringing again."

"They never stopped."

He pressed her closer, and she could see the needles of whiskers in his throat and the dense curl of his beard. He smelled of salt. His eyes were small in his face, the pupils nearly filling his sockets, and they narrowed on her.

"Where do you live?"

She told him.

"Do you want to leave?"

"For where?"

"Do you dream of leaving Mazatlán? Of your life changing forever?"

"Sometimes."

"I didn't come to dance," the man said.

"If you think you're not going to pay for this—" Valencia said, pulling away.

"No, no, hush. Of course I'll pay you for this dance. I'll pay you more than you've ever earned."

She stood erect, fear filling her.

"I run a shipping company," the man said. "My ships always need a girl or two to feed the sailors and to scrub the cabins."

Something in Valencia sank; at first, the man had seemed to promise so much more.

"If you ever want another job," he said, "you can find me at the harbor. My name is Fernando Moya."

"Señor Moya."

"Ask anyone at the harbor. They'll know how to find me."

"All right then," she said. The music had stopped, and Moya paid her. He tipped his hat and said good-bye.

"What did he want?" asked Pavis.

"He's hiring girls for his ships."

"Is that all?" And then: "By the way, Paco came by."

"Paco? Just now?"

"Yes, Paquito. He was looking for you. But then he saw you dancing with the stranger and he ran away."

And so that was the mix-up that would change Valencia's life: later that night, after Pavis left Café Fatal with a butcher who had blood beneath his fingernails, Valencia returned to the Hotel San Poncho, and upon descending into the basement, she found her room destroyed—the mattress hurled to the floor, her clothes ripped apart as if by an animal, her Bible open, a page torn from it, and the blanket chest gone. Valencia stood in the room, a candle close to her face, and then heard the creak on the stairs. She knew that Paco had ransacked her room, and she knew that it was he coming back for her. She wasn't angry, and she imagined the remorse in his face as he reached the bottom of the steps, she imagined his hands clutched over his heart, and as she looked up to greet Paco's eyes, she saw that it wasn't Paco at all but Paco's father, his face slick with kitchen grease, feet bare and thick with callus, his few strands of white hair adrift on his head. "What did you do to him?" Señor Costa demanded.

"Nothing."

"Why'd he do this?"

"I have no idea."

Paco's father didn't believe her—*You're lying!*—and his voice rose as ropes of spittle swung from his lips. Valencia dropped her candle and the basement fell black, and nothing moved in the room except her feet pushing her back until she was against the stone-cold wall, in the corner, and Señor Costa, the man who fed her and paid her and ogled her and told her she was worth no more than a load of soiled sheets, descended upon her, as Valencia somehow had always known he would. Her eyes—which had been open and alert since the day of the flood—closed, and the world around her, her small world, closed, and there was the jolt of a fist to her cheek, but it didn't matter; there was the child's cry of a grown man: *He said he'd never come back, you drove my Paquito away!;* there was the grunt of a man forcing himself into ecstasy, and her own muffled sob. And the world was closing, and soon she would flee the Hotel San Poncho and Mazatlán, and in the blackest instant of this one night, Valencia told herself to remember the name Moya. And even before it was over she imagined herself asking the fishmongers at the harbor if they knew a Señor Moya, and she imagined an office on the second floor across the street from the pier where Señor Moya sat in a room with maps on the walls, and he, less handsome in daylight, would light a cigarette and tell her that he wanted her to join the crew of a ship called the *Santa Susana.* "It's sailing for Los Angeles tomorrow," he would say. "Join the crew. You'll be gone for three weeks. When you return, we'll see if you want to stay aboard or not." And because Señor Moya had turned out to be nothing more than a businessman, a man who counted pesos in his sleep, a man whose wealth was measured in the heads of horses and sailors under his employ, a man who saw a pretty girl and didn't think about keeping her for himself, no, figured out a way to turn her beauty into a small but desirable mound of gold, he shook Valencia's hand and said that the ship was sailing at dawn, and that she could take nothing more than a change of clothes. "You'll be provided for on the ship," he said. Valencia, who had no other choice, both believed him and did not, and thought of the anchor dropping into the harbor off Los Angeles; she thought of the slap of the dory's oar as it hit the sea, carrying her from ship to shore; she thought of the pavement of a city she knew nothing about, and the town called Pasadena where Pavis assured her the hotels always needed a chambermaid. It would be a place where no one knew her, where she could look into a stranger's face and introduce herself as someone else, in possession of the dreams and history and future of someone other than herself. Where no one would ever know that Paco's father had ever touched her. She passed the fan and the Bible and the coral pendant to Pavis—"I'll send for them when I can"—and in the morning, Valencia felt the *Santa Susana* sway beneath her as it set sail up the blue coast to Alta California.

Much later, after Valencia had finished telling her story, Linda lay atop her blankets in her white nightdress, and after a long time she got up and crossed the onion field to the Vulture House. There was no light in the window, and as she pressed her face to the diamond pane in the door, Bruder greeted her.

He opened the door and led her inside. He had been expecting her, and he told her so. His suspenders were tight across his shoulders, and he had scoured the onion from his fingertips, and he didn't own a mirror but tonight he had wished for one. The Vulture House was empty but for his bed and a small table and a shelf for his books, and Bruder gestured for Linda to sit on the bed and he sat next to her, the mattress denting beneath them. The moon pulsed through the window and lit Linda's face and made her nightdress glow.

She wasn't aware of Bruder's anticipation; his back was to the window and his face was darkened by the night, and she had come because she had learned something and she wondered why no one else had learned it too.

Bruder pulled the rucksack from beneath the bed and moved to spread out its contents as he had done before. "They're hers," Linda said. His shadow fell across the Bible and the fan, and he startled her when his fingers peeled open her fist and placed the coral pendant in her palm.

"No," he said. "They're mine."

"But they were hers."

"They were my mother's. And now they are mine."

The coral was slender and fragile and cold upon her skin. His firm sense of possession startled her, and she saw that he would do anything to protect what he believed was his. "Does she know?" she said.

"Linda. Don't say anything."

She didn't understand.

"Must everything be said?" Bruder took the pendant and slipped it between her lips like a slim cork in a bottle's mouth. He wanted her to stop talking and he wanted to kiss her and he knew that she wanted him to, and as the mattress sagged deeper and their thighs pressed together,

her thighs bare but for the sheer nightdress, Bruder leaned into her and Linda let the coral drop from her mouth and pushed her face to his—for Linda was sixteen and determined to live a life other than her own—and just at this moment there was a rattle at the door and a pool of moon-shadow spilled across the threshold and Edmund snapped his tongue and said, "Linda! When will you learn to leave him alone?"

8

IN THE FALL OF 1919, with the memory of war receding and the hospital ships in San Diego Harbor rising as the casualties healed, Linda returned to Miss Winterbourne's schoolhouse. On that first Monday, she set out for school with Bruder one pace behind. Edmund walked with them, on his way to the hotel's front desk, where throughout the summer his elbow had worn away the varnish from the oak.

A car sped by, driven by a man in leather gloves with a standard poodle sitting primly in the passenger seat. The man honked cheerily as his wheels spat gravel at their feet. Only six or seven years before, the road had been barely wide enough to let a buckboard and a Tin Lizzie, snout to grille, pass at the same time; now the push of the pneumatics had cleared the scrub in a wide-open swath. One day, someone would give the road a name, and the collective memory of it as nothing more than a dusty horse path would drift away.

Bruder had surprised her again, when she'd asked him if he wanted to go to school with her. She had asked for no other reason than to see his face twitch as her voice landed upon his ear. He had said, "All right. I'll go with you." There had been an awkwardness between them since the night in the Vulture House, as if neither knew whether the other recalled what had nearly taken place. But though Linda remembered everything, she was just young enough and too trapped in the circumstances of her life to know how to re-create the night, the moon, the treasury of the items spread between them on the mattress. Edmund's eye had remained watchful upon her, and he had searched for further clues of indiscretion. He had whispered to Linda, "Don't make the mistake so many girls do." What Linda didn't know was that Valencia had said to Bruder when they were alone next to the onion cart, "First she must discover what she wants. Give her enough time for this." What Linda didn't know was that Dieter worried as much for Bruder as he did for her.

Over the days and the weeks the tension had risen within Linda, leaving her with a tender longing beneath her flesh. She wondered if Bruder felt the same, but in fact he did not. Bruder had begun to love Linda, yet at the same time he remained self-contained. He existed contentedly with the firm knowledge that he wasn't in debt to anyone, that in fact others owed him. Bruder stroked his power, as if it were a coin in his pocket. He didn't think about it throughout the day, but he knew it was there, jingling as he walked. Others would come to him; eventually, Linda would come to him again. Bruder didn't doubt his future; he was a patient man because he had seen so many others destroy themselves with impatience. On the way home from France, Dieter had said, "When we get back to California, I'll take care of you." There had been a deal, a tit had been laid out for a tat—like that other deal Bruder had struck in the beechwood forest—and Dieter and Bruder both knew what hung between them. "You may stay at my farm," Dieter had said. "You may do what you want." Did this extend to his daughter? Only Bruder and Dieter knew.

But Linda would perceive none of this; how could she? She saw only the clear September morning and the rolling ocean and her brother in his hotel uniform and Bruder in the pair of railroad-stripe overalls she had given him, with a red satin heart sewn to the breast. The sun gleamed upon the satin, and it flashed in Linda's eyes, and she believed it was proof of how things would turn out for her.

Just last week, Linda had gone to Margarita's to buy for the first day of school a new red dress and the eagle-feather hat. But while trying on the little hat, Linda had seen the curious pair of overalls, folded on a table next to a stock of fisherman sweaters and pants waterproofed with wax. "Those came by mistake," explained Margarita. "I ordered three pairs of ladies' candle-toe boots, and this silly pair of overalls was at the bottom of the box. Nobody will buy them."

Linda held them to her chest. There was something about the overalls—the blue and white of the stripe, the pocket in the front bib too slim to hold anything but a comb, the satin heart the size of a large button sewn curiously between the two front clasps—that made her think

of Edmund. She didn't have to close her eyes to picture him: the overalls hanging from his shoulders; the long stripe running down his leg;
his cowlick, wet from a bath, erect. "Do you think Edmund would like
these?"

"Can't imagine why."

Linda emptied the sack of pennies onto the counter, and Margarita's
fast, fat fingers counted them in fives. "You've just enough for the overalls and the dress, but you're short for the hat." "Will you spot me?"
asked Linda. "Never," said Margarita, folding the overalls into a box.

When she got home, Linda found Edmund in the barn, watering the
hinny. He was in a pair of drooping brown pants held up by a strip of
old notch leather. It struck Linda that he was somewhere between his
life as a boy and his life as a man, but in a different way than Bruder.
Linda imagined Edmund in several years, grown with a farm of his own
and a small, bony child with a peeling nose and a wife of some sort—
but who she was Linda couldn't guess; she couldn't even picture a face,
a cheek, or the color of her hair.

She told Edmund she had something for him, and he said, "What is
it? I'm busy."

"I bought you something. I saw it and thought of you."

Edmund lifted his eyes, and when she offered him the box his face
moved, as if an itch of gratitude were running up the ridge of his nose.
Linda suspected that he wanted to tell her that he wished more than
anything that they could return to the days during the war, when it was
just the two of them; but she knew he wouldn't be able to say it.

Edmund moved to accept the box, holding up his greasy hands.
"Maybe I should wash up first?"

"I'll open it for you." Together they sat on a sack of feed, their knees
touching.

"Did you buy a present for Bruder?"

"Only you."

The color rose in his cheek. He was whispering. Beyond the barn
door the sunlight was white and opaque. The hinny brayed, shaking
her neck, and a cock scratched at the thrown straw and then paddled its
way to the rafters. Except for the noise of the farm, the world fell silent,
and it was only the two of them.

The box lid fell to the ground, the tissue paper opened, and Linda
pulled out the overalls. "Aren't they beautiful?"

"Those are for me? I can't wear those. It's what a clown might wear, or a circus bear."

"I think they're dashing."

"I don't want to look dashing." He shook his head and said that she would never understand him, and she said that she was ready to give up trying. The cock cooed from above, and the mongrel Madame, heavy in pregnancy, appeared in the barn door. She began to bark. "Linda, you want me to become someone I'm not. I can't change for you."

"Of course you can. Everybody can. Isn't that what growing up is all about?"

He shook his head again and he was trembling, as if someone were pressing a bar against his chest. His eyes darted, and Linda could see that he felt trapped.

"I was trying to help you."

"Try it with someone else." Edmund held out his hands, palms open, and he looked incapable of ever speaking to her again. But then, almost inaudibly: "Please leave." He spoke with such fragility that Linda rippled with shock when Edmund next threw the overalls at her. A metal button, imprinted with the horned-ram logo of a manufacturer in Lowell, Mass., hit her beneath the eye. A red fury erupted within her chest: she was certain she was bleeding, but when she touched her face she found nothing; a small bruise would bloom, and it would fade away.

Later, Linda fetched the sewing kit and the scrap basket from Valencia and went to her cottage and threaded a needle. She hated sewing, and hoped for the day when she'd never have to darn again; but like every other girl, she could stitch a hem in her sleep. As she dumped the basket of scraps onto her bed, Linda peered into her future—as she did more and more every day—and vowed not to be like every other girl. The pant legs would need another eight or ten inches; the seams would have to be let out. Linda fished for some spare cloth that would match the overalls, but she found nothing. When their clothes became worn and stained or shredded by barbed wire or fishing hook, Valencia and Linda would force the shearing scissors up the seams and store the loose pieces of fabric in the basket. There was a swath of flannel printed with edelweiss that had once been Valencia's Sunday dress. There was a square foot of bald wool from Dieter's wartime long johns, and a yard of yellow muslin that had once fallen to Edmund's ankles as his nightshirt. Cuts of teamster's cotton blue twill, of heavy orange chambray, plaid cotton cassimere, black moleskin, falcon twill with an apple-red stripe: all from clothes that hung on the line of her family's memory. Shirts resewn into blouses; sweaters reknitted into caps; skirts hitched to become half-leg pants or a middy or, finally, a handkerchief, embroidered by Linda and Valencia. Among the scraps, Linda found half of the white flannel sheet that had come from her bed, shredded in two after she had menstruated in her sleep one night. She had wanted to burn the sheet—the blots of blood bright and vulnerable and shaped like a pair of eyes—but Valencia had said, "No, no. The clean half is still good." And Valencia had been right, for now the flannel would work in tailoring the overalls for Bruder—adding long cuffs, extending the seams in a way that would let his thighs and chest breathe. If only the satin heart on the breast could grow as well—how small it would be on Bruder, like a tiny stain.

When they reached the schoolhouse, Linda called "So long" as Edmund continued on his way. She watched him head down the road and waited for him to turn around and wave, but his back remained to her. Then a truck's cloudy exhaust engulfed him, and when it dispersed he was gone.

Miss Winterbourne was on the schoolhouse steps, welcoming her students. Over the summer, she had bobbed her hair in a style that Linda had seen in the merchandise catalogs; she looked like an old woman trying to pass herself off as young. Her collarless blouse revealed her throat, which flushed when Linda introduced her to Bruder. "What level were you last term?" Miss Winterbourne inquired. He didn't respond, and this caused the blush to boil up over her chin and into her cheek. "He was at war," said Linda. "With my Pops."

"Then welcome to the Calvera schoolhouse," said Miss Winterbourne.

"I'm not here to go to school," said Bruder.

"You aren't?" said Linda.

"I said I'd walk you to class, and I'll pick you up, but you didn't think I'd be—?"

"You mean, you're leaving me?"

"Linda," he said. "I'm a grown man." He laughed, and was reminded that she was still living in the narrow antechamber between a girl's life and that of a woman, and sometimes he forgot this about her because he himself had departed the room of his boyhood both early and fast. By the time he was six he'd grown used to eating in the yard with the dogs; by the time he was eight he'd learned to ignore Mrs. Banning's screaming voice, "You'll have to earn your way!" A mat of hair had grown upon his chest at twelve, and a hard beard on his chin at fourteen, and the last time Bruder had thought of himself as a child was years ago, just before people began to spread the cruel rumor that he had killed the kid from the Pasadena Ice Company. Bruder didn't know his birthday, and Mrs. Banning used to corral all the boys at the Training Society whose birthdates were lost for a joint celebration on January 1, each unlucky child receiving a pair of socks with a grapefruit in the ankle of one, and an orange in the toe of its mate.

But Linda wasn't like him, and if he didn't envy her lingering childishness, he nevertheless admired it. Even so, he wasn't returning to school. "I'll pick you up at the end of the day," he said, and then he too was gone, a figure receding slimly upon the horizon, and Linda was left alone with Miss Winterbourne. She felt her teacher's fingers upon her neck, guiding her inside, and just as Linda was resigning herself to despondency, Charlotte appeared, chirping, "Ready for another year?"

The first day of school was long: Linda and Charlotte and the other girls were assigned to read *The Three Musketeers* while the boys studied algebra. Linda had trouble getting beyond the first sentence: "Meung, a pretty market town on the Loire and the birthplace of Jean de Meung . . ." So many things that seemed to have nothing to do with her. She wondered if Bruder had visited Meung during the war, if he could explain over supper just how wide the Loire ran, what was sold in the market, just who Jean de Meung was, and why she should care. Had he met her father nearby? The other girls—Margie Gutter, Hedda Strauss, Inga Serna, and Charlotte—each sat with her book on her desk, fingertip moistened and ready. Linda thought about sending Charlotte a note, but the flyswatter—hanging from a rusty nail next to the photograph of Donna Marròn—caused her to hesitate. She continued reading but could think only of Bruder, and she found herself writing something down:

Did you see his overalls with the little heart?
Those were from me!

Linda sent the note to Charlotte, who read it while nibbling her lip. She wrote a note and returned it to Linda. It arrived safely, unnoticed by Miss Winterbourne's patrolling eye, but when she read it, Linda let out a little gasp.

Linda Stamp is in love!

She didn't know what was more shocking, the note itself or Miss Winterbourne's claw landing on her desk and plucking the note and raising it to her face. Miss Winterbourne's eyes narrowed, and she said, "Class, I have some news." The students perked up, hair bows and cowlicks rising and ears warm and red from stale schoolroom air pricked up too.

"You'll be interested to know that our very own Linda Stamp is in love. Unless one of you claims this note, I'll assume Linda wrote it herself, and she will spend the afternoon clearing the brush around the outhouse." The students sat upon their hands and Charlotte pushed her nose into her book and Linda was alone, and although she had expected life to treat her differently, she hadn't expected life to mishandle her so unjustly. Nor had she expected the betrayal from Charlotte, who at that very moment closed her book and claimed the note's authorship.

At the end of the day, Miss Winterbourne sent Linda and Charlotte with a pair of scythes into the thicket at the top of the hill, and she sent Bruder, who had arrived to fetch Linda, home.

"He didn't even argue with her," Charlotte pointed out. "He left without you."

"No one can argue with her."

"But didn't you say he does whatever he wants?"

For two hours they cleared the brush, the spiky branches scratching their forearms, and when at last Miss Winterbourne released them, they walked down to Charlotte's house. A certain bond, too tentative to discuss, had looped the two girls together this afternoon, and each sensed it, although differently: Linda believed that Charlotte was her friend, and Charlotte believed that she would keep Linda honest. As they walked down the hill, their swinging arms brushed, and the blood from their scratches, just two tiny drops, mixed.

Charlotte lived with her father in a blackie on a strip of beach where the widowers and the loners and the gimps huddled in a village of outcasts who scraped the sea for their living. People said that these men were too grimy, too greasy with fish oil, too accustomed to scratching in impolite corners of the body, to marry. "Who would have them?" asked Margarita. "You'd be doomed to filth." The blackies were lined with tar paper, their walls smudged with kerosene oil and pipe smoke, fingerprints and fish scales and, in the loneliest cottages, missiles of mucus launched from the nostril's silo. Any metal that wasn't brass, even a belt buckle or a trouser button, would pit up with salt and flake away with black corrosion. The shacks stood so close to the surf that they didn't have front windows, only a door on a perpetually crumbling hinge, and when the wind blew and the men were too drunk to remember to properly latch things up, the storm gusts would strip the doors from their frames like a bandage torn from a wound.

As they reached Charlotte's blackie, the sun was setting and the ocean lay calm and golden and broken by nothing but the splash of a flyingfish. Charlotte offered Linda a cup of milk and lit a lamp and then a cigarette. Linda had never seen a girl smoke: the purply-gray smoke oozed in Charlotte's mouth. Charlotte gave Linda a cigarette, and it dangled between her lips as she tried to figure out what to do with it.

"Did you hear they're making plans to run electricity down here and out into the fields?" said Charlotte. "Finally someone's remembering the blackies. Pup's up off Point Conception chasing otters, but they say there might be lights in here by the time he's home. I'm writing a story about it, from the rise of the first pole until the bulbs illuminate." Lately when she set out to cover a story, she'd wear a broadcloth skirt and, hanging from her waist, a nickel watch with a shamrock etched into its case. She had started to say things like *Time's a reporter's enemy* and *And that's just the way it is* and other sayings that Linda was sure Charlotte had learned from reading in the library the month-old newspapers from back east. "I'm going to tell the truth, and that's just the way it is." And soon Linda learned that the way it was in Charlotte's stories, no matter how far from the truth, was accepted without skepticism: Margarita's counter buzzed with items from the *Bee* whether they were correct or not; it was as if it almost didn't matter. "It might as well be true," she'd heard Charlotte say.

"Do you ever worry about getting things wrong?"

"I haven't yet."

They were as close as either would get in her life to having a best friend, although certainly at this point neither pondered such a fate. But they mutually understood that each was in need of an ally before taking on the larger world. A few years ago, Linda had tried to teach Charlotte to fish, but out in the dory, Charlotte had tripped on the anchor line and plunged overboard. "I guess I was meant for terra firma," Charlotte had said. "Hard land for hard facts," she had said, laughing at her own humor, as she always did.

Now Charlotte said, "Did I mention that I've got my nose into something else right now? I'd tell you if I was sure you could keep a secret." Linda assured her that she could, and Charlotte summed her up with her steel-colored eye. "Did you know that something funny's going on out at the Cocoonery?" Linda asked what, and soon Charlotte, like a split melon, was spilling what she held—for even more exciting to Charlotte than discovering a good story was passing it on.

The Cocoonery—every town has one or two such buildings—had risen opulently years before for a purpose long since gone obsolete. Sometime around the turn of the century it first opened as a silkworm farm. A Minnesota real-estate developer by the name of Mina Van Antwerp, birch-faced and set with a Nordic jaw, had settled one hundred acres in the hills east of Baden-Baden-by-the-Sea, establishing what she called the Minneapolis Beach Colony. She arrived in California with a plan to turn the soil into gold or, in this particular case, raw fluttering spinneret silk. Miss Van Antwerp placed ads in the newspapers of dug-in snowy northern towns, Duluth and Boulder Junction and Fargo and even Winnipeg, offering five-acre get-rich-quick plots to anyone interested in growing mulberry trees. With a team of ranch hands she built the Cocoonery: thirty feet high, crossbeams of ponderosa tied with strips of leather soaked in oily water, tin roof, sliding barn doors on all sides to let in the sun and, eventually, a railroad car. Inside, the trays of silkworm larvae were stacked to the ceiling, each drawer incubating hundreds of thousands of silkworms. But Miss Van Antwerp was a better saleswoman than sericulturist, and—to her great shock—the silkworms hatched while the mulberry trees were still saplings. With nothing to eat, the hundred million worms devoured themselves, and the most Darwinian cannibals, engorged for a single night, proceeded to starve to death. The collapse of the Minneapolis Beach Colony followed immediately, homes abandoned months after they were built, deeds to worthless land crinkled up and tossed from fleeing buckboards. For years the Cocoonery stood empty on the hill-crest, where the winds blew from every direction and the grasses dried to every shade of gold. Then, just before the war, Herr Beck, whose in-heritance had come in the form of gladiolus bulbs, bought the building and reestablished the Cocoonery, this time as a co-operative where the growers brought their plants and cut flowers. Under Beck's organiza-tion, the produce was sold to distributors from Los Angeles and River-side who backed their railroad cars into the building and pulled out with their perfumed freight: poinsettias in autumn, secreting narcissus in winter, ranunculus in spring, honking gladiolus in June, bird-of-paradise flapping across the yellow span of summer; and asters and blue-belled delphiniums and cabbage-size peonies and roses as big and white as eggs on two-foot stems. Those trains, chugging along a special track that ran to the Cocoonery's gate and up its little hill, hacked coal-cough across the surrounding farms, including Condor's Nest; the en-gineers tossed their Hapsburg root-beer bottles into the gully along the tracks and, embarrassingly, the limp, deflated balloons of their syphilis-avoiding condoms. And now a fleet of pickup trucks pop-gunned their way across the fields out to the Cocoonery: *crack! crack! crack!,* their wheels digging rutted shortcuts into the scrubland around the hill. The trucks drooled tarry oil into the roads, leaving Linda with another farm chore, to scrape the black gunk from the hinny's hooves. And the girls who worked at the Cocoonery, cutting stems with dull knives and pot-ting three hundred poinsettias a day with bloodied fingertips: some-times they'd come into the village and smoke on Margarita's porch and whistle at the traffic. Even Linda knew that the Cocoonery had rapidly changed the eastern hill country. Last year, one of the girls had been stabbed in the throat with a pruning knife; and every few months a girl fled, her swelling stomach hidden under the folds of her apron. No, flower distribution wasn't all that went on out there, Charlotte ex-plained. "It's turning wild."

Linda asked Charlotte what, exactly, she meant.

"Why don't you come with me on Saturday night, and together we'll have a look-see."

It was a few miles past the village, beyond the lettuce fields and the dairy farms and up in the folds of the foothills. On this Saturday night in October, stars and the dimpled moon lit the way along the railroad track, and it was colder inland than by the shore. She and Charlotte didn't speak, the gravel loud beneath them. Charlotte had told Linda to wear shoes she could run in. "Run?" "Just in case." Charlotte said that they shouldn't take the main road out to the Cocoonery—"Then they'll see us, and we most definitely aren't supposed to be there"—and Linda's heart quickened over what they might find.

She had lied to Bruder: she'd told him she was spending the night with Charlotte, and she hadn't been prepared for him to ask, "Doing what?" "Doing what?" she repeated, wondering if her promise not to tell anyone included him. "We'll be mending socks. Her Pup's coming home soon." As it slipped from her mouth, the lie stung her with regret, and she knew he didn't believe her. "I'll tell you later," she tried, but the lie was told, and what was it Valencia used to say when Linda was little? "You can't unsay a lie." Was that it? Was that what Valencia had said?

"Do you hear the music?" said Charlotte.

It greeted them, running down the canyon, a fast river of rhythm. Linda and Charlotte continued along the tracks in a ravine between two hills, and then the tracks turned and the hills fell away and they saw the Cocoonery. It sat atop a lone hillock surrounded by live-oaks, its glass walls lit and glowing, and *Zeltmusik* throbbed from the open doors. The tin roof reflected the torches staked around the building and on the hillside, the flames bent and broken in the wind and snake-black oil smoke slithering through a hole in the sky. Linda and Charlotte crept closer and found a sycamore's Y-branch to sit upon to inspect the scene. Through the glass walls they saw a *banda* on a stage, the musicians in white silk shirts with ruffled sleeves: one man at a 750-pound parlor piano, a boy surrounded by bongos, a man in spectacles with a Sevilla mandolin on his lap, a fourth plucking a nickel-shell banjo. People were dancing in a line, men she didn't recognize and girls more or less

Linda's age, their faces shiny with heat and their blouses split open to
reveal their breasts. For the most part the men looked like the fishermen and hands and migrants who traveled with the seasons; their shirtsleeves were rolled past their elbows, their denim jeans crusted with
field soil, and their eyes bright with greediness and a vulnerable uncertainty and awkwardness about how to dance. Linda guessed they'd
come from Oceanside and Escondido and maybe even from the apple
orchards in Julian, and perhaps some of them were the bachelors who
lived in the earth-hovels on the slope of Mt. Palomar, men who formed
a disorganized but heavily armed regiment that made its living charging
tolls to the Sunday drivers who ascended the mountain's peak.

On the hill around the Cocoonery were dozens of motorcars, reflecting the torch flames in their spoked wheels and running boards and
in the brass-trimmed bulbous horns screwed to their dashes. More cars
than wagons, and Linda knew that the cars belonged to men who
weren't hands—men perhaps all the way from San Diego, shop owners
and insurance salesmen and maybe even one or two of the real-estate
developers who'd been turning up at Margarita's counter in recent
months, asking around about the ocean farms. At the foot of the hill,
horses were hitched to the rail fence; the torches caused them to stamp
nervously, and their rubbery nostrils flared, and the horses looked out
of place. The music floated down the hill *car-rum-dum-dum! car-rum-
dum-dum!,* the melody mixing with the men laughing and the loud girls
telling jokes with punch lines Linda couldn't hear and a happy, stumbling brawl over a bottle. There were four or five fishermen Linda
knew from the pier, Barney and Beet Pete and H.D., who was really just
a boy, too young to shave, as hairless as a honeydew, which was where
he got his name. The fishermen were sitting outside the Cocoonery on
overturned crates labeled LIVE PLANTS, rolling cigarettes and passing
around a small jug; fish-faced men with popping, gelatinous eyes and
mouths shaped like O's as they tilted the jug toward their pouts. Other
men sat outside on logs and crates, in circles lit by a fire in a ditch, and
dogs were snapping at the sparks and chasing one another, and a pair of
mongrels were stuck together in intercourse and a couple of men had
to pull them apart. Men were humming and pouring wine from bottles
and whiskey from burlap-wrapped flasks, and the torches revealed the
wink of drink in their eyes.

"Look over there," whispered Charlotte. "It's Mr. Klift." She wrote his name in her notepad, the first in a list entitled "Who I Saw." Marcel Klift was a lawyer with offices in both Baden-Baden-by-the-Sea and Del Mar, and he was dancing with a woman with a red fox tippet around her plump shoulders and a net-veil hat. Next to them was Dr. Copper in the black suit he wore when visiting the dying, but tonight with a cactus rose in his lapel. On his arm was not his doctor's bag but a girl in a carelessly sewn dress. She was twirling around him, trying to get him to dance, saying, "Come on, Hal, move your feet!"

"What are they doing here?" whispered Linda.

"They're drinking."

"Who are all these girls?"

"They're the girls who work for Herr Beck."

"Why are they here at night?"

"To get paid. To earn a living."

Linda and Charlotte scuttled over to a greasewood shrub near a window, the needles pressing into them. Charlotte warned Linda to be quiet as they parted the shreddy branches: "No matter what happens, be still!"

And from here Linda could see everything: the *banda* with their shirts sweat-pasted to their chests; men's hands on the girls' narrow hips; a huddle of girls in a corner, each with a rope of baby-clam shells around her throat; six boys in the opposite corner, their bangs slicked down and on their feet shiny new trench boots made for the war but never shipped over. "You see Margarita's nephews over there?" Charlotte noted it in her pad. They were sucking whiskey from root-beer bottles and they swayed awkwardly, their arms around one another, propping themselves up.

The *banda* was playing a German maritime *Lieder—Der Sturm ist da, die wilden Meere hupfen*—that Linda knew from Dieter's violin. Many years ago, Dieter used to come to her and Edmund at bedtime. He'd stand between them and play his fiddle, singing more and more softly until at last his voice trailed off . . . *Guten Nacht*. Linda would pretend she didn't understand the lyrics, and after Dieter left she'd beg Edmund to translate the songs, and though now it seemed like another lifetime she could still recall how he would sit up proudly and recite the words like poetry and teach her how to sing. "No," he'd say gently. "It goes like this . . ." And finally he too would say, *Guten Nacht, Sieglinde, Guten Nacht.*

Next, a woman joined the *banda* on the stage, her green velvet dress dragging across the mandolin player's shoes. The sight of her caused all the men to stop, their hands falling from their dancing partners, and the hall fell silent except for gulps and pants and a whispered "There she is!" The woman moved to the center of the stage and raised her arms, presenting herself to the crowd: black hair oiled up in a swirl, glass earrings catching the light, a generous display of breast, a ring set with jade, a mouth like a small tomato. The mandolin player introduced Fraulein Carlotta to the crowd, and the men cheered and the girls applauded skeptically and Carlotta shifted her velvet-draped hips from one side to the other and began singing:

> *Das Leben froh geniessen*
> *Ist der Vernunft Gebot.*
> *Man lebt doch nur so kurze Zeit*
> *Und ist so lange todt.*

Through the window, Linda heard one of the men say to his pal, "She's famous round San Diego, but one day every man in California will know her." And his pal said, "You can know her tonight if you got the green."

Carlotta clenched a fist as she brought her song to climax:

> *"Enjoy your life, my brother,"*
> *Is gray old Reason's song.*
> *One has so little time to live*
> *And one is dead so long.*

The green velvet shifted like a dirty stream passing over a rock. She was older than the other girls, powdered and plucked, waxy eyebrows drawn in place, and unlike any other woman Linda had ever seen, Fraulein Carlotta seemed entirely aware of the power she held over men. She possessed the voice of a sad but experienced woman, and her breasts rose and fell as she sang, and her hand with the ring—the jade cut into a rose—swabbed the base of her throat as the audience applauded and hollered and someone yelled, "Carlotta, will you marry me?"

Carlotta leaned from the lip of the stage and said, "How much money do you have?"

The men hooted even more, especially the men who had no money in the world and never would, and feet began to stomp and the Cocoonery ripened with a warm compost smell. *"Danke, danke,"* she said. *"Muchas gracias,* boys and girls." The crowd clapped and whistled, and the boys sitting on the windowsills swung their feet and kicked the walls, and even the shy girls who were making promises to themselves to run away from Baden-Baden-by-the-Sea before the dawn applauded vigorously. And the more noise everyone made, the larger Carlotta appeared on the stage, and she seemingly towered over the members of the *banda,* and the spotlights transformed her stinky sweat to glitter. "How 'bout a little *mayate?*" she called. The crowd cheered, and the men took the girls' wrists, and together the dancers formed a line. To whistles and howls, Carlotta left the stage, and the *banda* took up a *rumba* accented with tambourine. The music shook the glass walls and the dancers flapped their arms like wings, imitating a swarm of June bugs aflight in the night and drawn to the great electric bulbs hanging from the Cocoonery's ceiling.

A carved figure of Miss Van Antwerp hung over the door like the wooden bust on the prow of a ship, and her stingy smile looked as if she were enjoying what her silkworm hall had become. The *mayate* was one of the favorite dances of the day, and Linda watched more men and girls pour into the Cocoonery beneath the oakwood face of the failed real-estate developer: railroad men too sooty to clean up properly; travelers with half-smoked cigars tucked beneath the bands of their hats; men in suit trousers and suspenders, with greedy spittle on their lips— these men looked like the developers who Charlotte had said planned to string electricity lines out into the open scrubland "on spec." "They're speculators," Charlotte had said in a way that had made Linda envious that her friend knew so much. And now fans suspended from the ceiling pushed warm air around the dancers' heads, and the great greenhouse ripened the spirits of all its revelers—or of the men, at least, for Linda saw the bloom in the girls' faces fold tightly against the oncoming, pawing night.

"Here's my story," said Charlotte, busy taking notes. "It's got all the goods: bootleg, debauchery, and girls bought for a price."

Linda watched a fat man in a hat too small for his head pull a gold-eyed girl from the dance floor and out into the torch-lit night. She was pounding his doughy chest, but he was smiling and no one seemed to notice that the girl didn't want to go. A narrow-nosed girl struggled for breath in hairy arms. Another girl sniffled into a handkerchief embroidered with a violet as she slotted several coins up her sleeve. In a corner, a group of boys groped themselves as they surrounded a girl with an overbite and a frail tin crucifix about her throat.

"I want to go," said Linda.

"I'm just beginning."

Linda was climbing out of the greasewood when Charlotte took her by the shoulder and said, "Linda! Look in there." Linda followed Charlotte's pointing finger through the crowd, and she was just about to say "I've seen enough" when she saw the small thick frame of Edmund.

His hair was slicked behind his ears, and his collar was starched and erect, but more shocking than the very sight of him was who he was dancing with: he was in the arms of Carlotta, who had changed into a tuxedo and now wore a white rose behind her ear. Her hair was pasted to her skull with pomade that made it look like the skin of a black plum, and Edmund hung from her chest like a small boy clinging to his mother and his fingers gripped her lapel and her arms held his face to the cushion of her breast. Carlotta plucked Edmund's eyeglasses from his face and tucked them deep within her blouse. They moved in a circle, and Edmund's eyes were dreamy with blindness as his face rose and fell with her breath. The violinist was playing a waltz, and after a few bars Linda realized it was "The Leipzig Fancy," one of Dieter's favorite songs, and Edmund's mouth was moving, as if he was singing to Carlotta.

Even more people were dancing now, the floor crowded and shoulders bumping, and the pulse of the music rose as shoes and boots shuffled and dress hems rippled against stockings that would shred before morning light. Ropes of wood-clack beads rattled, and all at once many of the girls handed themselves over to the night's duty, and in pairs men and girls left the Cocoonery for the privacy of bushes or a backseat or a back-numbing felled oak or, for those who didn't care, a firm bed of dirt. The lapel of Carlotta's tuxedo was shiny and her large hand ran down Edmund's back, and they danced and turned and then shifted toward the window by the greasewood shrub; and when the music lunged, Carlotta turned her hips and the white rose behind her ear came within a few feet of Linda, its heart stained red.

And there Edmund was on the other side of the glass, the grain of his beard greasy, his shoulders spread in his church suit. His hand cupped one of Carlotta's breasts through the tuxedo jacket, fondling it clumsily, and she smiled not out of pleasure but out of the satisfaction of a job completed, and Edmund's face had gone blank and Linda knew there was nothing in the world that could pull him out of his reverie. In the Cocoonery's warm damp air he had been transformed, and her brother was a man she no longer recognized.

"Just like the rest of them," said Charlotte.

The dancers shifted, Edmund and Carlotta waltzed away, and Linda strained to find them through the crowd. But the Cocoonery was filled with the Ensenada girls and the men willing to pay, the strangers up from Ocean Beach and Leucadia and in from Riverside, and the country folk from the desert side of Mt. Palomar. Strangers here, their snapping diesel engines chasing the rabbits permanently from the fields, they insisted on pavement through the village and on the road leading to the pier, and hurled all sorts of things from their windows to the side of the road: only this morning, Linda had picked up a pie tin and a green seltzer bottle and a pickle dish painted with sprays of arbutus and an empty box of Dr. Rose's Arsenous Tabules *"For the Treatment of Bad Complexion and Skin Diseases of Every Nature."* All sorts of people coming to Baden-Baden-by-the-Sea or merely passing through, and one day the road had brought Carlotta to Edmund. Why hadn't he told Linda about the Cocoonery? Disappointment overtook her as she clung to the greasewood branch. The music continued and Edmund and Carlotta were a pair in the sea of pairs and partners and lovers and buyers and sellers—"Quite a flower market," said Charlotte—and Linda, who had assumed that she would keep secrets from the world, not the other way around, felt a catch in her chest and began to cry. She pushed herself out of the bush and began to run down the hill, past the heavy farmer's boots and the cheap dresses cut from discount cloth. Linda ran with her arms extended, a sob lodged in her throat, and her outstretched hand hit someone who said, "Watch it, Miss," and a girl snapped, "Don't push *me*!" The heat within overtook Linda, a fever on the spine, the sweat collecting in the pit of her arms and between her legs, and she felt hot and sticky and trapped. The long painted finger of a woman she didn't know caught in her hair, releasing its mass from her bow, and it felt heavy and moist on her nape and around her face, and Linda would run all the way home and return to her cottage and pray to Valencia's

God to let her forget the night, to let her believe that all she had seen was a dream and not a glance into the future. She dashed through tequila picnics and over benches and past groups singing around pit fires, and she was crying now, aloud, "Stop! Stop!" and her arms were out as she ran down the hill, kicking paper boxes and abandoned newspapers and aluminum spoons so cheap that it was easier to toss them over one's shoulder than to carry them home. She knew that people were staring at her, but they didn't know her. Or maybe what they knew was that men and girls lived like this; maybe everyone knew it but Linda Stamp. She was prepared to sprint all the way back to Condor's Nest, where the greatest noise was the call of the ocean and the only litter in the path was the chucked mussel shell; where she would find Bruder in his little house, waiting for her on his bed, his arms at last ready to take her in. The pitch of the hill steepened, and all at once, gravity's pull overtook her and she was skipping out of control toward the bottom of the Cocoonery hill, and just as she was about to lose her balance and tumble forward, her hand hit a man who appeared from nowhere and her finger caught on the leather thong around his throat and the necklace snapped and the coral pendant broke free, and just before she fell to her face, Bruder caught her and held her and stroked her head and each said to the other, "What are you doing here?"

9

WHAT DID EDMUND HAVE to offer Fraulein Carlotta that other men did not? Not a more handsome face or more experience with women, and certainly not dancing skills or eyes strong enough to peer into the future. No, she made the mistake that many women have made over time: she thought he was rich. If not filthy rich, at least in possession of tracts and tracts of land, acres that could be sliced off and sold. Why would she think this? Because Edmund, transfixed in the way every man is at least once in his life, had told her whatever it was he thought she wanted to hear: "Why, it's just an old rancho out by the ocean," he said of Condor's Nest. "How big?" asked Carlotta. "How big? How big? I'm not really sure. Big enough. It'll suit you just fine," he said leadingly, and indeed his statement meant one thing to him and something entirely vaster to Carlotta. But as it turned out, his singular asset was precisely what Carlotta was in need of then: land or, in other words, a home. "I've been thinking about settling down, and I've always wanted an ocean view!" she cooed, fingers drumming the tightening skin of her belly. She held Edmund to her breast at the Cocoonery and didn't let go for a week—a week spent in a flimsy tent pitched behind a series of illicit singing halls, on a canvas cot that creaked and sagged beneath their rocking weight. She released him just long enough for him to return, dizzy with her orange-oil perfume, to the farm to lay claim to its deed.

"Papa," he pleaded with Dieter, "if you give me the farm now, she'll become my wife!"

But the one thing Dieter would never forgive was betrayal, and he sent Edmund back down the dirt lane: "Back to your harlot, my son.

Fraulein Carlotta at Condor's Nest, indeed." It was a scene lit by the autumn moon, and Linda witnessed it from the window above her bed, and across the fields Bruder held a lamp close to his copy of Homer and ignored the yelling, but then it became too loud and he opened his door and saw Edmund's silhouette slip by. It looked to Bruder like a ghost flying above the onion tops, but Bruder didn't believe in ghosts—no, Bruder believed only in the horror of fate and reality.

"No son of mine succumbs to the wayward heart," Dieter said with a shiver, and in private he made a proposal to Bruder, an adjustment to their earlier deal. "You've been like a son," said Dieter. "You've never betrayed me. One day, maybe soon, Condor's Nest will be yours." Dieter said he wanted to make sure that the farm never passed to Fraulein Carlotta or her offspring. "So I'm leaving it to you." He paused. "Ah, Bruder. Didn't I say in the forests of France that I would repay you?"

"We made another deal."

"Yes, but this is a better one. The farm will be yours when I die."

"Why not give it to Linda?"

"To my daughter?"

"If it's Linda's, then it will become her husband's. Do you see how we can accomplish two things at once?"

"But what if I don't approve of her husband?"

And Bruder understood. Dieter was trying to back out of the deal they had made in France, the deal that had first brought Bruder to Condor's Nest and to Linda. If he didn't take Dieter up on his new offer, perhaps in the end he'd wind up with nothing; and if things worked out as he hoped, Bruder would have both Linda and the farm. Bruder pondered the inevitable: for as he saw it, fate would always have its way— its hand large and strong-fingered and turning each of them here and there upon its great checkered playing board. He felt that if Condor's Nest was to become his, it was meant to be. And what about Linda? Bruder had begun to feel that she too was meant to be his. That he no longer needed a father's promise to gain a daughter's affection. Of course, deep down Bruder was a paranoid man; hadn't Captain Poore pointed this out behind the lines, forest-dappled sunlight across his face? But Bruder did not think of himself as paranoid; what man does? Yet he would saunter on instinct, strike out of self-preservation. And what Dieter was offering—"She's a humble farm, but she will be yours; I have the papers right here"—was the type of preservation Bruder understood best. What was it the newspaper once said?: "Back east a man is defined by his education and his clubs. Here in California it is by his parcel of land." An unanswered letter to the editor had asked: *And where, my good sirs, is a man defined by his heart?*

Dieter spoke to Bruder in the night. The moon was a bright, feminine frown behind a cloudy veil, and neither Dieter nor Bruder could see clearly the other's face; but each was certain that the other was recalling their private scene in the forest—the night one man discovered the other in treasonous pursuit. "Let's forget about this," they had agreed under the shells of battle, in the summer of 1918.

Except nothing is forgotten, not in war, not at home; not when a man is owed.

"You're my son now," Dieter said after the papers were signed. "Do you know what this means?"

Bruder said he did, but he did not.

"It means you'll grow old on the farm and watch over me and the land, and you'll be picking onions until your back breaks, but at least you'll have a place to call home, a stretch of land no one can take from you for anything."

Bruder thanked Dieter, although he knew that this deal would mean more than that.

"And another thing," said Dieter. "Part of this deal has to do with Linda."

"Yes, I know."

"You're my son now. She's my daughter. As a matter of speaking, you're brother and sister. Siblings."

"Siblings?"

"Everything you see will be yours, but you'll have to forget all about Linda. Trust me, it's for the best." He paused, and then said something that revealed how Dieter truly felt: "She's too much. And you're not enough."

"Even with the farm?"

"One or the other," said Dieter, whose assets were few and who could not afford to give them away unless a debt was due. He set his weakening hand upon Bruder's shoulder and tried to rock him playfully, but Bruder didn't budge.

It wasn't a gift, Bruder saw, but a proposal, and Bruder instinctively pushed its ring past his knuckle and wed himself to its terms. Like any good speculator, in the end he was a cautious man. He was risk-averse, certain that destiny was set against him. And in the end, like every proprietor, he would crave more.

Bruder accepted Dieter's offer. He would live with it, as best he could. And then one day she would come to him, and he would have both.

But Linda, almost seventeen, knew nothing of deals and terms and compromise; nothing of promises made in secret, especially those concerning her. The conflicted heart Bruder presented her she simply didn't understand: the man who had held her outside the Cocoonery, his hand raking her hair, a week later declined to join her in the outrigger canoe. He ignored her plea to go fishing; he took no interest in the reslatting and the netting of her lobster pots. He said "No" when asked if he would stop by her cottage in the evening. At this point in her young life, Linda was capable of love, capable of giving and receiving pleasure, certain in her ability to grip the bloody handles of a throbbing heart. But she was incapable of accepting rejection. And the autumn turned to winter and the first rains fell, and Linda's complaints to Valencia went unexplained, and how does a girl whose own heart has flip-flopped like a fish dying on a dock withstand another heart's turning against her? Within a few weeks she had lost both Edmund and Bruder, and lying awake at night, listening to the ocean crashing violently, she came to regret that neither had ever been hers. And she asked herself, over and over: What have I done?

"In time," Valencia would say, and it was all Linda had to go on: her mother's knowing words, a soothing voice paved by the long years of life.

And when Linda told Charlotte that Bruder had gone cold, Charlotte said, "I'm afraid that's just the way it is." It was brittle solace. "There's no resetting a man's heart. What's done is done is done forever." But Linda thought that Charlotte didn't know—why, Charlotte knew nothing but the daily breeze!—and Linda propped her chin upon her knees and picked at the scabs with her teeth and told herself that if anyone could defy destiny, it was she.

10

IN JANUARY 1920, Linda turned seventeen and a winter storm arrived gray-fisted and angry-faced, running off the Pacific. Dieter celebrated her birthday with his violin's *Zeltmusik,* and Valencia told Linda that when she was a girl in Mazatlán she had hoped to become a shrimp fisherman. One day she and Pavis had entered the children's *torneo de pesca* with nothing but a stolen rowboat and their eyelet skirts sewn as trawls, and they rowed back and forth off the peninsula where the lighthouse loomed, with the Sierra Madre behind it, and they hauled more pounds of shrimp than anyone else, boy or girl, but the fishermen refused to give two girls first prize, a tiny sterling shrimp with coral eyes. This was when Pavis first decided she had to lead her friend out of the city, and years later, at the little birthday celebration for Linda, Valencia said, "And now, Linda, here you are." But this time Linda found no comfort in her mother's tale, and she turned to the cold window, its glass streaked with salty rain.

The rains fell for five days, melting footpaths across the onion fields and eroding the route to the beach. The ocean's rage was so fierce that one morning it hurled a barking grouper against the door of Linda's cottage, its gills gasping with plea. Over the years, Linda had come to expect the January thunderheads: the flooding rains evicting the earthworms from their holes, their slimy trails iridescent on the threshold; the hailstones snapping the clothesline; the tide boiling and exploding against the bluff, tufts of sea-foam tossed against her sill. Linda believed she could manage in a January rain: she had launched her outrigger into a nine-foot surf on New Year's Day; she had held back a shiver in the schoolhouse, her stockings draped across the stove's belly; more than once she had caught what Edmund used to call *the end of her,* her lungs as sodden as the soil.

But this year was different, she believed. "Have you ever seen rain fall for this many days?" she asked Dieter, who wrung the water out of his beard and told her that once he'd lived through a storm in Schwarzwald that raged for exactly twenty-one days in a flimsy house with rafters greasy from the pork smoke rising from the stove. When she asked Valencia, her mother only said, *"El diluvio."* Had Bruder ever experienced rain like this? "I fought in France in an open trench," he said through the screen door. "Now go on. I'm busy." "You're always too busy for me," she complained. "Not always," he said. "Only lately." And then: "Linda, one day you'll understand." Through the wet screen he seemed to want her to linger on his stoop; and it was true: Bruder wanted to invite her in, although not quite as much as he wanted his future secured to the anchor of a plot of land. Was he too young a man to have such a cold heart? No, once the compromises begin, they never end. Even so, the heavy weeks of avoiding Linda had begun to pile upon his shoulders, and several times a day he wondered if he had entered into an arrangement he could not uphold. "I'll speak to you later, Linda," he said. And when she was gone: "Be patient, Linda."

Linda would have taken her question about the rains to Edmund, student of almanacs, but after his argument with Dieter, Edmund set out to follow Fraulein Carlotta through foothill towns up and down California, waiting for her each night in the flimsy six-sided tent as she sang and revealed just enough flesh—breasts and belly swelling heavier by the day—to inspire showers of coins. She'd dance with the men who would pay to stroke her hips, and when she returned to the tent the money went into a headless kachina doll. "When are we moving back to that little farm of yours?" she kept asking, for Carlotta was in a hurry, and he would say, "As soon as they finish building our new house. It'll be two stories, with a fireplace in every room," he promised, nearly believing the fantasy himself. He married Carlotta before the cold hearth of Salinas's justice of the peace—a marriage reported home on a postcard.

No, Edmund wasn't around for the January rains. He had left before he could see his dam in the arroyo successfully catch the runoff. As the rains continued and the water rose, Linda, sitting on her brother's empty bed and stroking the mattress lumps, decided to name the yawning black pond "Siegmund's Swamp."

She might have asked Charlotte what she knew about rainfall records and the history of storms. But not a month after Edmund's departure, Charlotte was gone too. Her father, a tall eel of a man, returned from his seal runs up north. After her story about the Cocoonery appeared in the *Bee,* nearly every fisherman within thirty miles wanted to tie Charlotte up and drop her to the bottom of the ocean, and Hammond Moss didn't want to have a daughter loathed by men of the sea. "What good will it do you?" he said. And then: "Enough of this newspapering for you." He was a man who spoke slowly, as if he had a limited pool of words to choose from, and he was more interested in getting along with the other sealers than in his daughter's hopes and pursuits. His wife had died in childbirth, and that was the last time he had shed a tear. He liked that his daughter was a tough-hearted storyteller, but he didn't like her planning a life that might somehow surpass his. Hammond Moss was an average shot, his rifle not always steady in his hand, and there were many men who harpooned more elephant seals, but nobody in the poop could tell a better yarn than he. He kept many a crew awake through calm, ice-starry nights, and what made Hammond Moss such a good storyteller—although he never knew this about himself—was that he didn't worry whether or not he was telling the truth. "It all might as well be true," he would say, and the men would shake their damp beards and agree. He had expected his daughter to marry another sealer so that he could retire to his blackie, Charlotte tending him while her husband was at sea. But upon returning from his latest run, Hammond could see clearly that Charlotte possessed—was possessed by!—ambitions that precluded him. Ritualistically, he dropped Charlotte's notepads and pencils into the ocean and returned to his chair with the springs poking lumpily and said, "Now what's for dinner?" And within a week, Charlotte was gone and it would be a long time before anyone heard from her again.

And so during that wet January, Linda found herself moping at Margarita's counter. "Linda, forget about the rain. Why don't you go over to the beauty cabinet and fix yourself up?" She scooted Linda to the far side of the shop, all the while *tsk*ing that Edmund would return, *Wait and see.* "Give this one a try." Margarita passed Linda a sample tin of La

Doré's Rubyline rouge, an eighteen-cent bottle of milk of cucumber for the throat, and a jar of orange-flower skin food for the buckling brow. "Nothing like a little beauty to help the days go by." And Margarita, who every night applied a Parisian depilatory to her upper lip, sent Linda home with a contraption called the Princess Bust Developer Kit. It came with a jar of bust food, a white cream prepared, according to the label, from vegetable oils and charcoal by an eminent French chemist at the Seroco Chemical Laboratory in Chicago, Ill. "Before you go to bed, work the cream into your . . ." And Margarita had kneaded the loaves of her own breasts in demonstration. Later that night, in the quiet of her cottage, Linda followed these instructions. With the rain steady on the roof, Linda carefully unbuttoned her blouse and worked the lardy cream into the underside of her breasts, into the inner flesh where they met, into the coin of her penny-hard nipples. The label promised "a plump full rounded bosom," but Linda wondered if she wouldn't be able to grow that on her own. She couldn't precisely say why she was doing this. She doubted the bust food's claims even as she scooped more cream from the jar, following Margarita's instructions to do so until her breasts were as slippery as a skinned hen.

The next step involved an instrument called the Developer, a plungerlike contraption made from nickel and aluminum, with a rubber cup at the end. "You'll know what to do with it," Margarita had said. The nickel rim was cold on Linda's flesh, and she thought of the etching of the Norse goddesses hanging above Dieter's bed: the breastplates, like helmets, worn by women with long double braids. Linda gently pushed the Developer's handle and it squeezed her right breast. A heat rose in her chest; and then a remote ache surfaced between her legs. She pushed again and a sucking noise emerged as the Developer clamped her flesh, brushing her nipple and sparking something deep in her lonely chest. She had never felt this before: the longing intensifying as she pushed and pulled more and more. It was somehow connected to a tingle between her thighs—an unfamiliar yet distinguishable desire linking every point in her body. She shifted the developer to her left breast. The sense of swelling expanded. Perspiration collected around her mouth, on her nape, on her inner leg. She tasted her own heat on her lip, wondering if it was saltier than ever before, but could that be possible? Margarita had told Linda to repeat the pushing action on each breast twenty-five times, but no more. As she applied the final sucking pressure, regret and dissatisfaction flooded Linda, and her life—which just months before had seemed full of promise—loomed dully. She fell back onto her bed and the Developer dropped to the floor and her breasts were greasy and slick and the air in the cottage was warm with effluvia. The rain was violent at the window and the ocean thrashed and Linda couldn't fall asleep, and she expected to spend the rest of her life awake and waiting, a girl with nothing to look forward to.

When Linda returned the kit to the store, Margarita offered a discount on its purchase. "Typically it's a dollar and a half, but I'll give it to you for ninety-five cents." Linda declined. A vague fear had descended upon her, a worry she likened to the dread of not being able to feed herself. She had looked up the word "passion" in Edmund's abandoned dictionary and skipped ahead to the final definition: *lust.*

"I know you think you don't need it," Margarita said, unpacking a shipment of barber's egg shampoo. "But you will. It'll happen even to you."

Linda left and stood on the store's porch; the rain ran in sheets from its eave. Los Kiotes Street, paved two summers before, looked slippery and dangerous, and she watched an automobile skid cheerfully into a hitching post. What she knew was this: She wasn't like Valencia or Margarita, or anyone else. Her needs were different, and they'd remain so. But what waited ahead for Linda she couldn't say. Would she one day work at the Cocoonery, separating the stalks of bird-of-paradise and packing the bundles of gladiolus and transplanting the Christmas poinsettias? It's what girls from the ocean farms did. Or they would marry a hand and move into a shadowy hacienda in the foothills, giving birth in a back room. The unlucky ones had a sick father to tend to, each morning dampening a rag in a basin and dragging it across his underside. A few girls tended shops in Oceanside, selling sun hats to tourists or bolts of lace to daughters of men whose pockets had become lined in the latest rush for real estate. One girl she knew put on a pair of dungarees and took a job at the first filling station in town, Walthau's, pumping gasoline and wiping the inland dust from the grilles. A couple of girls headed south to San Diego, donning the gray uniforms of the trolley transport, tearing tickets in two as the cars jangled along Union Street. Each waited for marriage impatiently, or so Linda had heard them say. Only Charlotte had escaped, but to where?

It caused a shudder to rise in Linda as she pulled down her hat and stepped into the rain. Then she saw the flyer nailed to Margarita's bulletin board:

Join our Crew as ELECTRICITY and TELEPHONY make their way to ALL of Baden-Baden-by-the-Sea. Come help our Village GROW and PROGRESS!

On the porch, a stranger was handing out employment forms, shouting, "Join our crew! Join up today!"

"What exactly are you doing, anyway?" asked Linda.

"We're stringing electricity out into the scrubland around town. I've got miles and miles of wire ready to go up."

"Why would you want to do that? Those are nothing but sand fields and dried-up river plains. Nobody lives out there but a family of coyotes."

"We're making the way for progress, young lady." The real-estate developer's name was Paiver; his padded throat supported his greasy round face, his cheeks bright with burst capillaries. He used his overworked, nail-bitten fingers to cup his mouth and shout, "Come help your village grow!" Paiver was busy handing out flyers to the men entering and leaving Margarita's, and he assured anyone who would listen that he paid the best wages in the village. He handed a flyer to Hammond Moss, who didn't know how to read but said he'd sign up anyway. "About time the countryside gets some lights," he said.

"Now, young lady, if you'll excuse me," Paiver said, "I've got to put a crew together to raise a thousand electricity poles."

He went into the store, and Linda stood on the porch and watched the silver rain run from the roof. Margarita's father, curled on an avocado crate, was drying a cat with his bandanna, and he reminded Linda to sign up inside for the electricity-pole crew. "It's our civic duty." He was a Sprengkraft, bulbous-nosed, white-haired, Rhône-blue eyes, a mind as foggy as a winter beach, and he cooed over the cat, *"Spaten, Spaten."*

By morning the rain had stopped, but the sky remained a swollen hide, and the muscular gray nimbostratus was hanging so low that Linda thought perhaps she could touch it were she to climb the first electricity pole. And Linda decided she'd join Paiver's crew.

"You can't join his crew," said Dieter.

"Why not?"

"He's not looking for little girls."

She was learning not to get angry, to ignore her father instead, and she said, "I know for a fact that Mr. Paiver needs as many people as he can get."

"You're too busy here," he said.

"I am?"

"You and your mother and Bruder have got to finish the staircase." The three had begun erecting the one hundred steps before Christmas, and now the scaffold of stairs clung to the cliff face half-finished and skeletal. Valencia had worried that the rains would weaken the foundation, but Linda had insisted that each morning they rise and continue pounding through the winter patter. But now Linda was bored with the project and wanted to sign up for the pole crew, and a clenched fist pushed its way up her throat.

Again, Dieter told his daughter she couldn't work alongside the men, and the two fought, each turning red and hot-throated, and Linda and her father simultaneously regretted that each did not understand the other, that neither tried to listen, and the shouting rose over the steady surf until at last Bruder said, "Let her go if she wants."

The cottage fell silent and Linda and Dieter looked at him as if neither understood what he had said.

"Why shouldn't she join the crew?"

It was settled, and Linda slipped Dieter's slim-handled mallet into her pocket and laced up her boots. And even more astonishing than Bruder's taking Linda's side was his subsequent announcement that he would work alongside her on Paiver's crew: "We'll dig some holes and lay some poles." And the two left for Margarita's porch one gray-skyed morning.

Bruder was a deliberate man, and he had understood the implications when he and Dieter had struck their terms, but every night since then he had sat erect upon his bed and picked at the plaster in the wall and ignored the book in his lap and looked through his window across the fields to Linda's cottage. He had become miserable in a way that he hadn't thought possible, and equal to his disappointment in himself was his suffering. It was difficult to live near her and not reach to stroke the soft fur upon her arm. There had been an hour not long before when he had assured himself that patience would bring him life's riches, including Linda, and he had violated his own philosophy. At night he would descend the bluff and walk the beach, the surf rushing past his thighs, and the moonlight would guide him and he would test his voice against the ocean's roar and his hollering would be lost to the waves and his face would become damp with salt and mist. He would call her name as loudly as he could, and he would realize that his yells were nothing against the Pacific—Linda's ocean, as he thought of it—and his throat would hoarsen and Bruder would return to the Vulture House worried about his future. He realized, during these weeks, that he was as obsessed about future and fortune as the next man, maybe more so, and this disheartened Bruder, for it meant that his scorn for most men in the world would fit snugly around him too. He had never had Linda, yet he had managed to give her up; a few acres of onion fields separated them, and the knowledge that those acres were on their way to becoming his own brought no comfort at all. An image entered Bruder's mind: of himself as an old man alone with his land; and although he had planned for that moment since he was a boy at the Training Society, hiding with a book in the walnut grove, sleeping like a bear in the trees, now the image, obtainable and true, delivered cold fear. Bruder, who had always wanted to be alone, now wasn't prepared to live out his fate. And on the road into the village, he took Linda's hand.

"What's this?" she said. "You don't talk to me for weeks and weeks, and now you want to lay your hand on me? Not so fast!"

"Linda, things aren't so simple."

"They never are."

As the crew assembled on the porch, Paiver said that he wasn't hiring girls, but Bruder defended Linda's skills and Paiver folded his fat arms across his fat chest and Bruder stood close to the man and said, "I don't think you understand." Most of the other men who had signed up for the crew were hands and fishermen who all knew Linda, and they said, with morning-whiskey breath, "She's all right. You can't ask her to leave. She's just one of us." Linda let the others defend her, and eventually Paiver was persuaded to hire her.

But laying poles turned out to be even duller work than building a staircase. They stood around for an hour waiting for Paiver's orders and at last he said, "All right, men. You're off to bring some civilization to the dreaded frontier." He cupped his fingers around his mouth and warned the crew that a drooping electricity pole was a disaster waiting to happen, either today or down the line. At first he was unaware of his pun, then he chuckled over it and felt smart: a man who deserved to be developing the land. "We were all put here for a reason," he liked to say, and Paiver—who would run out of cash before the lines were strung, abandoning the scrubland with one thousand utility poles sticking out of the ground—sent the crew on its way.

They boarded a buckwagon and rode to the edge of town, where the roads ended and the fields and irrigation ditches stopped at the scrubland's sagebrush gate and the chaparral stretched into the foothills, as it always had. The wagon halted at the corner of Miss Winterbourne's property, her little lettuce field waiting for spring, and in the front window of her bungalow a roller shade descended and a long finger curled back a corner for a peek. A second wagon, rickety on narrow wheels, waited in the gully between the road and the field, its bed stacked with dozens of poles of stripped Sierra Nevada pine cleared from the western slopes not far from Yosemite and sent south on rail. The wood was a pale blond, the knots smooth and dark, and the poles were shorter than Linda had expected. She worried that the wires might droop dangerously low, tripping a mule deer or, even worse, catching a condor's white underwing. When Paiver arrived in his car, she pointed this out to him. "Another word from you and I'll send you home," he growled, and Linda stepped back and bumped into Bruder, his chest hard against her shoulders.

It was a Saturday morning, and the men would be working Saturdays for a month, burying the poles in what Paiver called stand-up graves. "Six feet under. The trick to a sturdy pole is six feet under."

Above them, the sky was balling up with westerly clouds and storm. In the distance, the ocean was fighting itself, the waves slapping the face of its surface. The water punched itself black, and wind lanced the boiling surf, releasing the whitecaps' ooze. Three pelicans hung low, suspended in their wait for ink squid. The brief and violent California winter excited Linda, the four or six weeks in January and February when everything donned a coat of gray and damp. There was something dramatic about the rainy season that Linda looked forward to. It made her think of her mother's youth—why, sometimes Linda doubted she could believe Valencia's nearly biblical tales of flood and fire if she didn't live at Condor's Nest, where the winter drowned the soil and had swollen Siegmund's Swamp to its toyon rim; where the brittle autumn torch-lit the canyons, casting an orange glow brighter than an electricity pole could ever transmit.

At last Paiver began to divide the crew into pairs, assigning each team a spot every thirty feet along an old cow path. When he got to Linda, Paiver said to Bruder, "She's yours, my friend," and Bruder and Linda walked for about half a mile with pickax and shovel. There was nothing out here but the sandy land and the wiry wild sage and the rosemary shy in winter and the flooded gopher holes and the trails of shrew shit. On a sunny day there'd be a rattler or two sunning on the flat rocks, and lizards fast and colorless, and the spearmint smell of California burning itself to death. But today smelled of nothing but the future of rain. Far off, the ocean churned coldly, and barely visible was a thread of smoke stitching its way out of Miss Winterbourne's chimney.

"Why on earth is he running poles this far out of town?" said Linda. "There's nothing here."

"One day there will be," said Bruder.

"You can't farm this soil."

"They won't be farmers. They'll just be people needing a place to live."

Lately there'd been more talk of it, at Margarita's counter and in the *Bee* and even between Dieter and Valencia: the clearing of land, the rise of the bungalow, the people arriving in six-seater automobiles. Things had slowed down during the war but nothing would stop them now, the *Bee*'s land-listing column liked to say. A stuttering doughboy and his French bride had built themselves a beam-and-stucco house up the road from Condor's Nest on land Linda had assumed uninhabitable; the well they had dug was questionable at best, and the acre of property didn't come with an easement to the ocean. The vet couldn't farm or fish, and so he introduced himself to the village as a housebuilder. By the road he erected a billboard that said: NEW HOMES IN 20 DAYS. But it was hard for Linda to imagine people living this far out of town, this far from the ocean, on land without a tree. So the story went: even Donna Marròn's cattle had turned around at what was now the far edge of Miss Winterbourne's lettuce field. The land was so dull and red-soiled that even at Margarita's counter it was dismissed as worth less than the patch of soil at Condor's Nest.

Bruder began to open a hole with the pickax, but on his first swing the point sank dully into the mud. He took the shovel and dug up a spadeful of sludge and tossed it over his shoulder. He had repeated this no more than five times when Linda asked, "And what am I supposed to do?"

"Watch me."

"It's going to take all day. I thought maybe there'd be some sort of hole-digging machine. Like an apple-corer."

"Linda, can't we just work side by side?"

She didn't know what he meant by this and doubted its tenderness, but then she stopped herself; and for a long while he worked and she watched him silently. The sky continued to darken, and Bruder rolled his sleeves past his elbows, and as he swung the shovel, the hairs on his arms danced and his throat filled with blood and his shirt dampened and Linda could see all his flesh. She lay down and propped her cheek with her hand, and Bruder swung and looked to her, swung and looked again, and the rhythm overtook them and the day slipped on, and Bruder forgot what he had promised Dieter, and Linda forgot that Bruder had ever withheld his love. Bruder forgot that Dieter had warned that she was a dangerous girl, and Linda forgot that Bruder was an unknowable man. They were young, and each hoped to become another person in another life, and the shovel dug a hole in the soil never before touched by man.

"Do you want to dig?"

She took the shovel from Bruder and jumped into the hole. It was about three feet across, and the pile of mud and earth was rising, topped with stones scarred silver from the shovel. Then her shovel hit something with a *ping!* Linda shifted the dirt away and discovered an old bronze arrowhead, hammered and dull at the point. "Probably from the Luiseños," she said, and Bruder turned the arrowhead in his palm. She had learned this bit of archeology from Miss Winterbourne, who had explained that the Luiseños were a matriarchal society. Something vague had stirred within Linda upon hearing this historical scrap, although if she'd been asked to report precisely what a matriarchal society might be she wouldn't have been able to say.

She continued deepening the hole while Bruder sat on the pole. He whittled a stick with his deer-foot knife and then he practiced his aim, hurling the knife over and over into the pole's long flank, stepping back a few more paces each time. From twenty feet away he threw the knife and it missed the pole and whizzed by Linda's hand into the side of the hole.

"Are you bored?" she said. "I wish there was a way both of us could dig together."

"There isn't."

"What should we do?"

"We'll have to keep switching off," he said, and just then Paiver arrived in the buckboard and said, "These teams of two aren't working. I need to break up the pairs. Bruder, you come with me."

"I'm staying with Linda."

"You're on my crew and you're coming with me."

But Bruder refused and he leapt into the hole with Linda, and Paiver hopped heavily down from the wagon and the wind from his lungs fluttered his nostrils. Paiver fired Bruder and told him to get off his land. For emphasis, he coiled his hands into fists and turned up his mouth.

"You can't fire him," said Linda, inserting herself between Bruder and Paiver.

"I can't?"

But Bruder whispered into her ear to forget about it, *We weren't meant to work on this crew,* and she didn't understand him when he accepted fate so easily. Didn't he know how to fight? Didn't he know that one's destiny lay within one's own palm? His breath was warm and touched her ear and he said, "So long." He climbed out of the hole and walked off, and Linda remained four feet into the earth, her chest and head sticking out of the hole. Bruder turned once and said, "Are you coming, Linda?"

She began to move, but Paiver said, "Why don't you stay? I need a good worker like you." Linda said she wanted to go with Bruder, but Paiver said, "Linda, why? You'll see him later. Listen, Margarita told me she had a little hat with an eagle feather you've been eyeing after. I'll tell you what, put in a full day's work and I'll see what I can do about that cap. It'll look pretty on you." By now Bruder was too far away to hear their conversation, and Paiver went on, "Imagine wearing that hat when you go to see him tonight." She watched Bruder as he crossed the scrubland, the milky-sapped chicory parting around his ankles. For a long time he remained a white sail on the sea of the open land, and

Linda rested her chin on the handle of the shovel. "Okay, Linda? You'll stick around?" And she agreed and felt a heaviness in her chest, as if the mud had settled about her lungs, earth-packing her heart.

"Now dig that hole six feet deep!" cried Paiver and he left, the buckboard making its way up the line. Linda hummed to keep herself company, and she remembered the jazzy "Horse-Trot" and "The Heavenly Rest" and "The Figure-Eight" played by Fraulein Carlotta's *banda.* Linda sang as her silver shovel arced against the sky, and the clouds blushed black, and the winter day pressed upon her. She was determined to finish the hole before the rains returned, and she continued digging until her thumbs popped with blisters and tears of blood ran down her wrists. But she kept fighting with the soil and opening the dark hole, and by three o'clock the early drops of rain fell.

She didn't stop digging, but soon she was standing in a puddle and the walls of her ditch softened to mud, loosening with rocky ooze, and then a curtain of rain descended upon the field, so dense that the ocean disappeared behind it. At once, the weed-roots interlocking beneath the coastal range drank in the water, and almost magically wildflower buds swelled. The mud swallowed her boots and the hole began to erode, earthworms inched their way to higher ground, and Linda easily jumped from the hole just before it collapsed upon itself into a mound of black muck. She shivered on the sprawled telegraph pole and waited for the crew wagon to come fetch her. The rain fell in cold blankets, the clouds sagging so low that Linda thought if she had successfully erected her pole it would have reached into the mist. Lightning snapped flirtatiously over the Pacific, followed by the fraternal call of thunder, the girlish capering of electricity, and the mournful howl of thunder, again and again, one chasing the other, a cycle of tease and torment, and Linda held herself, not worried but alone. The wagon would come, her boots would dry at the coil-handled stove, a hand would extend to brush her wet hair from her face, from her throat and breasts. She felt an ache, remote and unfamiliar, and Linda sat with it as she thought of Bruder lying on his dry bed in the Vulture House, hands behind his head, shirt tight to his chest; she thought of rain catching in Edmund's fine hair, wherever he was. Was Carlotta pulling his cap around his ears just now? Linda waited for the buckboard, but eventually Paiver's car pulled up, its headlamp burning. He opened the door and said, "Get in," and she slid onto the split-leather seat beside him, happy to be out of the rain. She found herself in a small cabin warm with his breath, and they were alone and the rain fell so heavily that everything outside was a gray blur. Paiver cut the motor and the headlamp went out, and he leaned into Linda and said, "Now let's see how badly you want that little hat," and his greasy mouth was upon her and he was pawing at her wet clothes and he was saying, "Was it an eagle feather you wanted so bad?" and he was heavy, his chest barrel-dense, and his hands were both small and fat and the wiry hairs shocked her and his tuna-fish breath caused her to gag and Linda was sobbing but she wasn't going to let this happen, she believed she knew how to fight any danger hurled her way, and she shoved Paiver back. He pushed her against the seat and she kicked this time, and at first her knee landed in a flank of fat and he merely gasped but it didn't stop him, and she kicked harder, again and again, and now Paiver was cupping his palms over his stomach and his crotch and he was yelling at her as she opened the door and spilled into the mud and his words *You little whore!* cracked like thunder and Linda ran across the fields, home to Condor's Nest.

In her cottage, she stripped out of her clothes and dried in a towel and told herself that she would never tell anyone what had happened. She trembled in front of the mirror, her flesh milk-blue and goose-pimpled, and she saw the recklessness in her mass of damp hair. Linda cautioned herself: it had been her fault, she believed, and evening came and the farm was dark and a tiny light burned in her window, and until dawn Bruder watched it, wondering if she would come to him. If she didn't, he decided, tomorrow night he would go to her.

But the next morning the rain held its breath long enough for them to resume work on the staircase. Linda convinced her mother that the worst rains were over—"It could never be as bad as yesterday"—and she and Valencia climbed up the unfinished stairs, mallet and T-head bolts in hand. Valencia knelt and fingered the dirt and said, "It's too soft today," but Linda ignored her and said, "Then I'll build it without you." But Valencia surprised Linda when she said, "No, I'll come too." Linda couldn't think of the last time her mother had done anything to surprise her; and Linda would be thinking of this as Bruder surprised her too, appearing with his toolbox and kneeling at her side. The three spent the morning malleting wagon-box nails into the wooden frame. While they worked, Linda sang and talked about the hole she had dug, skipping over the horrible sight of Paiver in his car. She thought to her-

THE BURIED

part three

The waste of youth, the waste of years,
Departed in that dongeon's thrall;
The gnawing grief, the hopeless tears,
Forget them—O forget them all.

EMILY BRONTË

1

MRS. CHERRY NAY APOLOGIZED, but her tennis match over at the Valley Hunt Club was starting soon. She stood and moved to close up the mansion. "Do you play, Mr. Blackwood?"

"I'm sorry?"

"Tennis?"

"Not enough." But the truth was that Andrew Jackson Blackwood had never gripped a racket, had only thought over the years that he should take up the game for the sake of fitting in. Stinky Sweeney had rolled a north-south court behind his house over on Oak Knoll; others too. He didn't admit it to himself, but Blackwood sometimes stared at the phone waiting for the right invitation to come across the line. He'd bought a pair of white tennis trousers, just in case.

"Perhaps one day I'll see you across the net in a mixed doubles."

"It would be my pleasure, Mrs. Nay."

She chuckled in that knowing way of hers; again, she felt sorry for Blackwood—a successful man who was doomed to fail in matters of society. Maybe that was why she had felt the urge to tell the story of Linda and Bruder: to give Blackwood a bit of an edge in his negotiations—more than ever, she was possessed with a sense of justice. Or maybe it would teach Mr. Blackwood that Providence was a nasty thing to try to manipulate: follow your given path, and all the rest. Not that Cherry wholly believed in this sort of resignation, but sometimes she couldn't ignore the evidence that each of them had been put there for a specific and appallingly limited purpose. "But enough of such thinking," she said, and moved to return the chair to the library.

"Did you say something, Mrs. Nay?"

"Nothing, Mr. Blackwood."

"Then let me help you with the chair."

After the long morning on the terrace, the dim library welcomed them with its coolness. The tapestry on the wall, stitched in gray-blue silk, depicted a medieval prince beneath an orange tree. "That comes with the house as well?" Blackwood inquired for no particular reason.

"Mr. Bruder instructed me to sell everything 'as is.' " Mrs. Nay shuddered. "It's a term I don't care much for. The truth of the matter is, nothing is as it is. Or what I mean is: nothing is as it seems." She turned the bolt in the terrace door.

"Yes, it does imply that something is *wrong,* doesn't it? 'As is' indeed," he sniffed.

"I'm sorry we didn't see much of the land."

"Another time, perhaps."

"If you're still interested." A blank look of concern had quieted her. "If I haven't said too much."

"Of course not, Mrs. Nay. I don't want you to think about it again. I should know the history, shouldn't I?" He said this without fully understanding what he had learned from Mrs. Nay; the girl named Linda Stamp—what did she have to do with the Rancho Pasadena? He had yet to piece it together, and Cherry Nay saw this in his buckled brow. It was clear he had no idea who she was. On the telephone, Bruder had said, "There's something about Blackwood that I like. Something that I trust. See what he wants, Cherry."

Mrs. Nay led him back to the gallery. Blackwood laid his hand across the Cupid's cold marble foot and again turned his eyes from the stone breasts of the blindfolded maiden: so bare and round and white. "But tell me, Mrs. Nay. If you don't mind. How do you know so much about all this?"

"About?"

"About Mr. Bruder and that girl? About Condor's Nest?"

Cherry felt disappointed, as she imagined a mother might after failing to teach her son a cautionary tale; of course, Cherry wasn't a mother—she and George had agreed that parenthood wasn't for them: "Let's stick to real estate," George had said realistically. "To destinies where we can manifest our control." They'd made a joke of it: *Manifest Destiny*—one of those private conjugal jokes that reside deep in the hearts of only two.

Cherry said, "I knew Linda."

"You knew her?"

"Yes, of course. All my life. Don't you see?" But Blackwood did not. "She became well-known in Pasadena. Many people still remember meeting her for the first time at the New Year's ball. All wrapped up in a grizzly bear at the Valley Hunt Club."

"A grizzly bear? At the Valley Hunt Club?" One thing Blackwood never told anyone was that he had once applied for membership; the rejection had come swiftly, in a letter printed on paper the color of urine; they had gotten his name wrong, "Dear Mr. Blackman . . ."

Now he thought to ask, "When was this?"

"New Year's Eve, 1924. I remember it precisely. And so would she. But of course I wasn't Mrs. George Nay then. I was an outsider too, looking in at Pasadena, reporting on its comings and goings. At times it was something of a dirty business, scooping around for news. But that's just the way it is, I suppose. When I look back, what I remember most was how good those days were to this town and nobody even knew it, did they, Mr. Blackwood? At the time, everyone thought it would go on forever."

Blackwood didn't quite understand what she was referring to but responded, "No one could have predicted what would come next."

Mrs. Nay concurred, fetching her key ring from a chair.

"Did she tell you all this?"

"Yes and no. You learn things over the years. Linda might say something, and now and then it would get passed around town."

She was standing close to him, and beneath her loose leathery skin Blackwood could see the bones and frame of a girlishly small woman. "Captain Poore wasn't always careful about who worked for him."

"What do you mean?"

"People under the employ have been known to speak. It's just the way of the world."

"I'm not sure I understand."

"Stay right here," said Mrs. Nay, and then, slim in her dull gray dress, she ran down the gallery and up the stairs, leaving Blackwood to contemplate the long hall and the naked statue and the cool cavernous air. It didn't take much for him to imagine returning home nightly to this: for all this to be his. But Blackwood knew that manor life was not in his future; he lived modestly and through the rest of his days he always would. Most everything he amassed he poured into amassing more. It had become habit. Blackwood bristled if someone accused him of greediness: "My good sir," he'd say. "You have no idea from whence I come." Once or twice, Stinky Sweeney had advised him to "slow down," to "sit back and relax," to "enjoy your good fortune, Blackwood, my friend." It was common counsel from someone who'd been born with an agreeable life laid out before him. But that wasn't Blackwood's case. As a young groundsman in Maine, Blackwood had imagined himself as someone else, and he had become that man, obliterating his history along the way. Hadn't he wrestled down his own destiny with brutally expert hands? He was thinking that his personal reinvention had been both simpler and more difficult than he might once have predicted when Mrs. Nay called, "Oh, Mr. Blackwood!"

"Mrs. Nay? Is that you?" Her voice was ghostly and distant, reaching his ear from nowhere he could identify.

"What are you doing, Mr. Blackwood?"

"Waiting for you. Where are you?"

Her mischievous laugh filled the hall, much in the way a voice on "True Stories" could fill the Imperial Victoria's cab.

"Mrs. Nay? I can hear you, but I can't see you."

"Mr. Blackwood, this is what I mean. The heating ducts and the dumbwaiters in a house like this carry voices in an uncanny way. It's almost as if the house were wired with radio."

He wondered if she enjoyed the violent suspense of "True Stories" but instead said, "Every secret passed along, is that what you're saying, Mrs. Nay?"

"Yes, exactly," and again the naughty laugh, and he imagined Cherry Nay as a schoolgirl in a hair bow, passing a note to her best friend. "A maid hears something, and she tells a maid in another house. That is how things pass from back room to front. And sometimes from private conversation to newspaper story. There was a girl here named Rosa. She once peddled in gossip. But not maliciously, I should add."

"Rosa, did you say?"

"But that's another story. For another day, Mr. Blackwood."

In the gray light, Blackwood was left to think about all this. He had never employed anyone at his house other than a carpenter, a burly man who had lingered one night in a confusing way. Again Blackwood was reminded that he was living at the edge of a world distant from the one he had come from. He had no training other than how to lay a slate-stone path, and because he had traveled so far from his dirt-floored days, he sometimes had difficulty recalling the precise moment that had prompted him to pack up and pursue a new life. He'd grown adept at stating, "The cold drove me west." Or, "A friend telegraphed with a tip." When asked about his own history, Blackwood proved adroit in the vague. There was the fogbound reference to the defunct women's college in Brooklin, Maine. Occasionally he would allude to his flinty New England blood. But he was certain that no one in Pasadena knew that he had fled Penobscot Bay in a railcar, scandal trailing him across New England, only dissipating like coal exhaust polluting the sky by the time he transferred in Albany. No, no one knew of such things, for Blackwood had a talent for shifting the snowbanks over the bones of the past; he didn't think of it this way, but such was the truth. At the tiny women's college, there'd been a girl from Isle au Haut, sixteen and hair as red as a boiled lobster. Her name was Edith, and she was so thin that Blackwood could see her heart thump in her ribcage, and this raw display of mortality, like a pink trout dying at the bottom of a dory, had stirred Blackwood deep within. She had come to him that final night. She had pressed her face against the glass panes in his door: "Mr. Blackmann, let me in. Mr. Blackmann? It's me, Edith. I must talk to you! Please—" She was the only person in the world who called him Mr. Blackmann; the rest would snap *Andy* or *Blackmann* or *Boy!* Even after two months of intimacy she continued to give his name that respectful handling, and every time she said it, *Mister,* his chest would puff up a bit. She held hopes of becoming a singer—a coloratura soprano, she would say, lying in his arms; Donizetti was her favorite, the endless trills, "like cresting the Atlantic waves in a storm." Her lungs would fill with air and she would sing for him, and her throat would flutter with the high C's, and he would shut his eyes and think of a woodbird, flitting freely here and there. But that night when she came to his cedar-shingle cottage at the campus gate, where dirty-fingered groundsmen, one after the other, had lived for a hundred years, she wasn't singing, she was sobbing as she tapped the window in his door. "Please let me in. There's something I have to tell you." He admitted her and was immediately alarmed by the red flushing in her throat and by her red-rimmed eyes. She fell into his arms, and he stroked her tentatively; for even before she spoke, he sensed that she needed something from him, something he might not be able to provide. "At first I thought it might be nothing," she said, kissing him. Her body, the body that once he thought he might love, was frail, and he feared that if it were to fall into the wrong hands it could snap in two. "Then I prayed for it to go away," she was saying, her tears spilling over onto his cheek, and he wondered if she expected him to cry too? "But it's just gotten bigger, Mr. Blackmann, and there's nothing I can do about it, and I was afraid to tell you. I was afraid you'd be mad. I was afraid you'd—" But he calmed her with his palm atop her head and held her, and their breathing fell in unison, and her sobs steadied and she looked up, blinking away the tears: "You aren't mad, are you?" He said he wasn't. He wasn't angry. No, in fact he was more frightened than she, for with her news he felt the sucking flush of fortune's drain, drowning his piercing but unspecific hopes for another life. A vision came to him, as clear as a photograph: there he was, old and stooped and poor and dying in the groundsman's cottage. Then Edith was fishing in her coat pocket and pulled out a sack bound with leather twine and opened it and dumped its contents onto the bed, onto the mattress where they had made love during the hours after her choir rehearsal, and said, "I've stolen it from my Papa. He's out to sea. He won't be back until tomorrow night. He keeps his money in an empty lobster pot with a trick bottom. Look, Mr. Blackmann! Three thousand dollars! Everything he's ever made." She ran her hands through the wadded bills and the stray coins and tossed some up into the air as if they were confetti. "What have you done?" he said. "We'll run away," she said, hugging him, pecking him with her pretty lips— puffy shell-pink lips that had first attracted Blackmann and that, one might say, would inevitably cause her downfall. She kissed him more and more, lips like two satin cushions upon his throat and face. "We have to hurry," she was saying. "We should leave tonight!"

"What are you talking about?"

"We'll go west. We'll go to California. We'll marry on the way. Out there, no one will ever know. We'll arrive on the train as Mr. and Mrs. Andrew Blackmann. Way out there, no one will ever guess the truth!" She was playfully pounding her fists upon his breast and he took her wrists and cuffed them roughly and her face fell still as she became afraid. Would he not go to California with her after all?

"We'll leave at dawn," he said, and the smile returned to her face and she buried herself within his thin, strong arms. And Mr. Andy Blackmann, groundsman, and Miss Edith Knight, daughter of a lobsterman, slipped beneath the covers of a bed wide enough for one, the money repoured into the sack and stored within his boot. They fell asleep while the winter wind blew old snow across the path and Edith dreamed of a land of sunshine and orange trees and her baby in a shaded carriage, and Blackmann closed his eyes and pretended to sleep. His mind turned not with notions of elopement but with plans of escape, and it was while he lay there, as the charred logs shifted in the fire, that the name "Blackwood" first came to him, and an hour before dawn, while Edith lay curled like a kitten, he slipped out the door with nothing but his coat and the sack of money and boarded the first train headed west, transferring in Albany and again in Chicago and then scarcely budging from his seat until he spotted the billboards twenty miles outside Pasadena advertising the hotels JUST LIKE PARADISE and the endless orange groves and the available LAND! LAND! LAND! By the time he stepped down to the platform at the Raymond Street Station, the young groundsman from the women's college in Brooklin, Maine, Andy Blackmann, had reimagined himself as Andrew Jackson Blackwood, a real-estate man eager to invest in the right piece of land.

"Daydreaming, Mr. Blackwood?" Mrs. Nay reappeared on the landing with its view of the mountains.

"I'm afraid you caught me, Mrs. Nay."

"You look as if something had just carried you back to the past."

"Yes, something."

"So there you have it, Mr. Blackwood. Chambermaid gossip and a little reporting helped fill in the stories over the years."

"And that's how you know all this?"

"Of course, some things Linda and Bruder told me themselves."

"Mr. Bruder doesn't seem like the type of man who would say anything about himself."

"Oh, but he is. All you have to do is figure out what it is he's bursting to say. All silent men are like that: Find the key, Mr. Blackwood. Find the key!" And then, with a face clearing itself as if it had been wiped clean with a rag, she added, "But I don't want you to think that all I do is trade in dirty laundry. It's only that this house has a history so very different from any other."

Together they crossed the threshold and stood beneath the portico and looked at the Imperial Victoria, which somehow looked somewhat *less* between the pillars. "You'll call me if your interest continues," Mrs. Nay said. Blackwood sensed something skeptical in her voice.

"I *will* call, Mrs. Nay. Once I find another free day." He would be careful to wait a week or so before ringing back. "The house is ready for delivery, I presume. There's no one residing here at all? Not even a maid in an attic somewhere?"

"Not a soul but the jays in the coral tree."

"Good luck with your match, Mrs. Nay."

"Thank you. In eighteen matches against Becky Touchett, I have yet to lose a set. And I don't intend for that to change today."

"No reason it should, Mrs. Nay. No reason there's anything different about today."

"Good to know you, Mr. Blackwood." A supple hand extended itself, bangle bracelet tinkling, diamonds dull in the shade. His hand met hers, and Blackwood's callused roughness surprised her, and Cherry Nay took note. She would have to think carefully about what she would report back to Bruder: "Yes, I showed it to him. His interest is difficult to gauge. What's that? Does he have the necessary funds? You might not think so, but he does. The funds and the will. What I mean is, Mr. Blackwood has much to gain from buying a property like the Pasadena. Yes, that's right. He's keen on moving up. Of course he's wrong, but he thinks that moving into a mansion will help him along in this town." She and Bruder would share an informed, but not cruel, laugh. But already she anticipated that Bruder would say he was inclined to do business with Blackwood. After all, did Bruder have a choice?

"Until next time, Mrs. Nay," said Blackwood.

"That's up to you. As they say, the ball is in your court, Mr. Blackwood." On the hood of his car they found a white-faced kestrel crying *killy, killy*. Its black, hawkish eyes turned to them and its blue-gray wings opened. "Oh, look!" said Mrs. Nay, and the bird flapped and flew off in the direction of the orange grove.

In the front seat of the Imperial Victoria, Blackwood put his hands to his head and found his temples damp, as if from nerves, which wasn't like him at all: as if the house had extinguished his usual sunniness. In his rearview mirror he saw Mrs. Nay fiddling with the flap of her purse. He backed the car between the portico's pillars and slowly made his way down the hill, and when he reached the bottom and passed through the gate, the radio found its reception and the announcer on the afternoon news reported further advancement in Germany and the young man reminded one and all to do their part. "The more we do, the sooner the boys'll be home." And, ever efficient, Blackwood noted that he would have to get to work if he was going to be ready to take advantage of their return.

But he had a hard time drafting a legitimate plan for the Rancho Pasadena's future. Instead, he returned over and over to the story of Linda Stamp: the girl had made her way to Pasadena, but how? Blackwood realized that Mr. Bruder had something to do with it. From the way Mrs. Nay had told it, theirs was a doomed love; why they hadn't seen this from the get-go, Blackwood couldn't understand. Two ambitious hearts can never unite; if Blackwood knew anything, he knew this. He repeated in his head Mrs. Nay's description: "She loved him but at first refused to hand over her heart," Mrs. Nay had said. "Some are like that. Nothing frightens them more than surrendering. As if love were about being taken prisoner, or being smothered by a pillow."

Mrs. Nay had said, *How about you, Mr. Blackwood? Always a bachelor?*

That was when Blackwood had said it was time to go, leaving Mrs. Nay to her stories and her impending tennis match, returning to his sycamore-shaded house, where he lived alone with his advancing plans for the future and with the wall mirrors that reflected a man who was not who he claimed to be.

2

STINKY WAS UNIMPRESSED with Blackwood, and his dissatisfaction came through the telephone line. It transferred to Blackwood himself, who sat in his echoey house—he had lived there for years, but there were so few personal items it looked as if he had moved in the month before—not entirely certain how he had left the Rancho Pasadena without visiting the orchards—*the most valuable part,* Stinky declared, to Blackwood's annoyance (for he was well aware of that). "It's just that Mrs. Nay kept me busy with some old story," Blackwood tried to explain. "How much are they asking?" Stinky asked, and even more surprising, especially to Blackwood himself, was that he had left Mrs. Nay without obtaining the price. "All in all, it sounds like a wasted morning," said Stinky, hanging up.

But Blackwood disagreed.

For the next few days, the stories about the fishergirl and the onion farm stayed with him. In his second-floor office on Colorado Street, running his pencil tip down the green-lined ledger, he couldn't think of much besides what Mrs. Nay had told him. He couldn't say why, but he felt certain that Mrs. Nay had chosen him, had found him more trustworthy than most, and he took pride in the knowledge, unconfirmed but true nonetheless, that she didn't unfurl upon just any old one. Mrs. Nay had seen something in Blackwood, he was sure.

In fact, she had seen the hesitancy behind his still youthful, typically confident eyes, and the flushed cheeks wounded by rejection, and, not least important, the swollen wallet of a man ready to invest. Mrs. Nay knew that life would not move on, either hers or Bruder's, until the Pasadena was sold and reincarnated. "The dead must be buried," she sometimes said. Anyone who works in real estate knows that properties house ghosts, and Cherry felt obliged to free Bruder of his past, to release him on his way. She was thinking of this as she drafted a letter to Blackwood on Nay & Nay stationery; and the next day, Blackwood was thinking of Linda and Bruder buried in the landslide when, shuffling through his mail in his office chair, he came across the soap-blue envelope from Nay & Nay.

In a fine penmanship, Mrs. Nay thanked Blackwood for visiting the Pasadena, saying that she was always *on the stand-by* should he have further questions. If his day had begun with doubt, all that fell away by the time he reached Mrs. Nay's closing sentence: *Mr. Bruder remains anxious to sell.* Blackwood folded the letter into his breast pocket, thinking again and again of Mrs. Nay's postscript: *You seem like the type of man who understands the responsibility of carrying this property out of the past.*

On Christmas morning, Blackwood realized that Stinky's vaguely promised invitation for the Sweeney family crispy-skinned holiday goose would not come. Nor had any of the men Blackwood knew professionally asked him into their homes for hot grog and rounds of hearthside carols. Blackwood woke up without an engagement, and he tried not to let it overwhelm him with sadness or a windy sense of isolation; but he asked himself, as he did on occasion, what it would take for Pasadena's triple-bolted doors to open to him; never could he have guessed that a community could seal itself so tightly. He wondered whether a grander life—residence in a mansion rather than in his modest (albeit satisfactory and well-built) bungalow—would make others realize that there was more to him than met the eye. Hadn't one of the clerks at the bank let it slip to *anyone* just how many zeros yawned bold and black on his well-thumbed passbook? For the first time he thought about upgrading the Imperial Victoria—she was hardly new, after all— but that would be too much for Blackwood.

He lay about in bed, something he frowned on in others, and the birds shrieked in the cypress that pressed against his window. It was a sunny morning, not especially warm, and he supposed that the best part of having nowhere to go on Christmas was the freedom from the endless civic discussion that was circulating on how New Year's wasn't really New Year's without the Tournament of Roses: "This damn old war!" On the rear wall of Vroman's Bookstore, someone had painted this: "No Milk or Meat, OK. But Bring Back the Parade on New Year's Day!" No, he wouldn't have to participate in the citywide *tsk!* of regret over how the Germans and the Japs had reached their sneaky hands all the way into Pasadena civic life! No one was expecting Andrew Jackson Blackwood, not anywhere. He didn't think of it this way, but the truth was: Blackwood was on the mind of no one this morning, no one in the world.

But Linda Stamp was on his, and so was Mr. Bruder: how had he come into so much property—Condor's Nest *and* the Rancho Pasadena? Bruder, who had started off with even less than Blackwood? Nothing impressed Blackwood more than a man who had made himself, and he was keen to learn how Bruder had gone about it. He was sorry they hadn't gotten on better. Standing at his living-room window, Blackwood surveyed the arroyo, the sycamores green and glassy with dew. He thought of his parents, dead and buried beneath the Maine snowdrifts. Lungs sopping with influenza all those years ago, but Blackwood had managed on. When he thought of the past, his memory became imprecise. He had forgotten that he had been a thievish child, that in fact he had stolen first from his father: eggs pocketed from the hen's nest, cream skimmed from the cold-handled pail, potatoes smuggled to market in his long yellow stocking cap. On an especially busy day, with deals ringing through the telephone and deeds transferring from one vault to another, if you were to ask Blackwood what had happened with the red-haired girl at the women's college, he would say he didn't remember. Everything about those days Blackwood did his best to forget, and he proved adept at his art.

And so on Christmas morning Blackwood went for a drive, the Imperial Victoria offering its own company. The radio played nothing but Christmas symphonies and holiday carolers and church services broadcast from cathedrals in New York City and Washington, D.C. On KNX, a clergyman by the name of Father Crean asked everyone to remember the boys, their feet ice blocks in their dicebox boots, and indeed Blackwood remembered the boys, he thought of them every day. One thing he had said to Mrs. Nay: "I'm cautious, but once I make up my mind, I move fast as a hawk." He had swooped his arms in emphasis.

Under the weak Christmas sun, the car crossed Suicide Bridge. The

Rose Bowl sat idly, waiting for the football enthusiasts—of which Blackwood did not count himself a part—to return. His was the only car on the bridge, and the sky was a flat winter blue, and he saw no one in the arroyo beneath him. The city felt empty to Blackwood, and he enjoyed the sensation as if it were a sign of things to come: the world his for the taking. The morning was crisp, the air brittle with pine and cedar, and Blackwood drove on, listening to the Christmas sermon and then the on-the-hour news from the front, where the bombs continued to fall and the boys ate rations of foil-wrapped chocolate and navel oranges "shipped from the great state of *Cal-ee-for-nye-aye!*"

Blackwood found himself at the gate of the Rancho Pasadena. He nudged it, and it opened as easily as before. As he drove up the switchback road, once again the radio's reception fell away. He hadn't planned on returning to the property but here he was, driving by the great lawn—a total of eleven acres, Mrs. Nay had finally revealed—and carefully steering between the portico's columns.

But Blackwood didn't stop at the house as he had before. Today he continued along the drive, which returned to dirt as it descended the hill into the narrow valley of the abandoned orange grove, where stillborn fruit clung to the branch. At the foot of the hill, Blackwood parked at the camp of outbuildings and barns and sheds and the long ranch house shaded by a pepper tree. The buildings were not in an advanced state of disrepair but they looked sadly empty; dust frosted the windows and sweet clover sprouted at the foundations. Beneath the pepper was a worn wood table and a bench and a rusted steel drum overturned and spilling old coal and ash. The outbuildings and the ranch house sat in a corner of the orange grove, and the trees, with their knuckled orange-and-black fruit, appeared, through squinted eye, like those along Christmas Tree Lane, decorated and gaudy and a child's delight— except not this year; no excessive lights anymore, by rule of law.

Blackwood justified his trespassing with the knowledge that he could not make any investment decisions without a full set of facts. On foot he followed a road into the grove and soon saw that nearly a third of the trees were dead and leafless, their trunks gnawed by fruit rats and their bony roots pushing through the soil like a corpse's arm rising from the grave. The other trees grew bushy and unkempt, their skirts of leaves dragging in the soil. The irrigation ditches had eroded into shallow ruts and a few wood-slat crates lay on their sides, their stenciling faded: RANCHO PASADENA, THE SOUTHLAND'S BEST. They looked a bit like lobster pots, and again Blackwood thought of the girl.

Except for the wind chiming in the waxy leaves and a woodpecker's busy drilling, the morning was silent and Blackwood was alone. He walked between the trees down a narrow lane, and soon he saw only grove. It did not occur to Blackwood that he might become lost in the orchard; his sense of direction was too great for something like that. Besides, the grove, for all its display of former wealth, wasn't all that vast. It was only a little more than a gentleman's ranch, Blackwood sniffed, and when he stopped and held his ear aloft he heard more than the wind and the woodpecker: from beyond, in what direction he couldn't be sure, Blackwood heard the cars careening down the Arroyo Parkway. Blackwood took comfort in the noise of progress, in the din of development. More than once he had regretted that he hadn't known enough to get in on the parkway at the beginning. Someone had once said to him, "Nothing like the business of rolling out roads." But, unusually for Blackwood, his ear had turned away from the tip.

He had been walking for several minutes when the grove ended at the foot of a hill. There before him was a white temple of some sort. Blackwood was as surprised to come upon it as he would have been to find at his feet a trunk of gold. It was of Greek design in its circular peristyle, a dome of milky marble supported by a double ring of columns. It made Blackwood think of the Jefferson Memorial, opened in Washington last year to celebration. In fact, this little orange-grove temple was nearly similar in design (he remembered the pictures in the *Star-News*), although smaller and, most certainly, in memoriam to an event or a person of much less significance than Mr. Jefferson—about this, Blackwood was sure. Maybe it was a temple to the mighty orange, or to the god of oranges—who was that? Blackwood made a note of looking it up in his Bulfinch; not that the Bulfinch was actually his, it had belonged to Edith; there'd been a couple of months when she'd loll in his arms and read him myths, like the story of Cupid and Psyche. Blackwood mounted the steps and inspected the cold white box beneath the dome. Only then did he realize that he had come across the family mausoleum Mrs. Nay had pointed out. At once he understood that he was inspecting an aboveground tomb housing the unburied dead.

The fact of it shocked Blackwood, and he withdrew his hand from the frigid marble, aghast, as if he'd been touching the corpses them-

selves. The tomb was taller than he, perhaps as long as the Imperial
Victoria, and inscribed with five sets of initials: WFP, ACP, LP, LB,
WFP II, Cpt.

Blackwood scratched his head. It became clear that Mrs. Nay had
not finished her story. He checked the other side for dates or other information but found only these words:

> Shall I strew on thee rose or rue or laurel,
>   Brother, on this that was the veil of thee?
>   Or quiet sea-flower moulded by the sea

"What brings you to the Rancho Pasadena, Mr. Blackwood?"

The voice came from behind a column, and Blackwood turned to
find Mr. Bruder. Blackwood felt the deep red of embarrassment sweeping his face. He removed his hat, and it fell from his fingers; he retrieved it from the mausoleum's icing-white floor. "I hope you don't
think I'm trespassing, Mr. Bruder."

"But you are."

"No, not at all." Blackwood's hands were up in the air in protest.
"I've been shown the property by Mrs. Nay. I've come back for a second look. We didn't get to see the orange grove at the time."

"Mrs. Nay told me. I'm glad you've returned."

Bruder's hair blew against the pillar, and he stood in angled sunlight. There was a phantasmagoric quality to him, and Blackwood
rubbed his eyes. Maybe he hadn't woken yet and was having a Christmas dream? But Bruder interrupted this reverie: "May I show you the
groves myself?"

He took Blackwood by the elbow and escorted him down a lane of
orange trees. Bruder's boot came down on the withered fruit littering
the soil, stomping hard, crushing the inedible oranges, and leaving a
trail of squashed rinds.

"Did you have any questions in particular?"

"Quite a few."

They returned to the yard outside the ranch house, and Bruder
seemed to collapse onto the bench, dropping his face into his hands.
For the first time, Blackwood noticed the meatless shoulders pressing
sharply against Bruder's shirt and the neck thin in the collar. Blackwood's antennae sensed decay. Not only had the good times passed for

the Rancho Pasadena, they had passed for Bruder as well. Deals were made under such duress, Blackwood knew, and hadn't Mrs. Nay hinted at Bruder's exigency?

"So much for a warm Christmas," said Blackwood, approaching the bench. "All this land is a lot to have on one's mind, I'm sure." Up close, Bruder's weariness was obvious: the scrubby chin, the saucered cheek, the tendons in the throat, the blood-threaded eyes rimmed by yellow and the moon-blue on the lids; he clearly needed a shower and some rest. Blackwood moved closer and suggested that they sit on the Imperial Victoria's quilted front seat, with the heater running. "Let me turn on the radio. How about a little *fa-la-la-la-la*?"

In the car, the heater blew gassy air. Bruder's knees pressed the dash and he said, "What would you do with it?"

"The land? Why, I'd develop it, of course." Blackwood was careful not to reveal too much about the potential profit. An investor keeps his ideas to himself, Stinky had taught Blackwood. Yet Blackwood couldn't help but share the idea that popped into his head just then: "My hunch is that an offshoot of the parkway could run right up this valley to connect Glendale with South Pasadena."

"A highway through the orange grove?"

"It's one of the many possibilities. But you'll see, Mr. Bruder. The trolleys are already on the decline."

"And the house?"

"Condominiums are the way, Mr. Bruder." Blackwood felt the need to add, "The mansion itself doesn't need to come down. It could be divided up into a rooming house. I have experience with walling up a mansion. Or it could be turned into something more useful for the community, like a home for the elderly or the indigent. Something that contributes and gives back. Naturally, the modern man is too busy for such a large house. No one could live there on his own."

"It isn't for yourself?"

"It'd be too much for me." Blackwood added, "Not too much money, but too much waste." His face flushed with pride. "Then again, maybe I would enjoy such a big house."

Bruder didn't respond; his head hung heavy in his palms. The orange in his breast pocket sagged strangely against his chest, and he took it out and coil-peeled its rind and held aloft the dry white fruit. "You can't eat it," he said. "Not even good for juice." He threw it out the car's window. It hit the ranch house and split apart, and the small hard sound of it, the *thonk*, hung with them. Finally Blackwood put forth the question that had long been on his mind, "How did you come to own the Rancho Pasadena, Mr. Bruder?"

Bruder shifted in the seat, his boots leaving dirt clods on the foot mat. He turned to Blackwood, and this made him think of a raccoon lifting its eyes. "We'll get to that."

"Get to it?"

"In a minute. But let's start at the beginning. Do you have another question, Mr. Blackwood? Don't you want to know how I came to Pasadena?"

"How, then?"

"I was born here."

"On the ranch?" Blackwood eyed the ranch house, and it didn't take much for him to imagine a young servant with black hair birthing a baby boy beneath the tin roof. As Blackwood thought this, a sympathy rose in him, for Bruder had started off with things piled up against him; and Blackwood knew about that.

"Not on the rancho," said Bruder. "No one knows where."

"Mrs. Nay mentioned an orphanage."

Bruder's chin jerked. "The Children's Training Society. The woman who ran it, Mrs. Banning, at first she refused to tell me anything about my mother, even when I begged and begged. When I got older, I begged a little more forcefully."

"No one wants to help you out, isn't that right? You have to forge ahead on your own." Blackwood added: "We're of the same lot, I'll have you know."

Blackwood felt his first connection with Bruder, as if they shared something, a disdain for antecedents and inheritance, perhaps, or the knowledge that each man was meant to find success in a solitary life. Nothing more specific than that, but a glance at Bruder's softening brow suggested that he too was feeling the same just then.

"What did she tell you about your mother?"

Bruder said, "Why do you want to know?"

"I lost mine when I was young too."

"It's a common story," said Bruder.

"Aren't they all?" said Blackwood. "They're common unless they're our own."

Again Blackwood sensed that Bruder's estimation of him was rising. "She was a chambermaid," said Bruder. "At the Hotel Maryland, working seven days a week in apron and cap. She worked in what they called Bungalowland, cleaning all the little houses where the heiresses from Chicago spent their winters flirting with the valets."

"That's a bit coarse of you, Mr. Bruder."

"But it's true."

"Mr. Bruder, what are you trying to tell me?"

"The truth."

"Ah, yes," said Blackwood. "Then go on. You didn't ever know your mother, did you?"

Bruder shook his head. He told Blackwood about the orange crate left at the Training Society. Then Bruder did something that Blackwood could interpret only as a gesture of intimacy: he produced from his pocket two small photographs. He passed the first to Blackwood. It was of a thin, sable-haired girl in a bonnet standing beneath the Maryland's pergola, her feather duster held as demurely as a bride clings to her bouquet. "What was her name?"

Bruder didn't answer, saying, "I have this picture that Mrs. Banning gave me. It was taken for the hotel's brochure."

Blackwood didn't know why Bruder was confessing all this, but he took it as a sign of some sort of effort to reach a deal. Trust is another factor in the real-estate equation, as important as the numbers, and trust has to come from both sides: this was Bruder's way of saying he trusted Blackwood. And only then did Blackwood notice that Bruder was wearing the coral pendant; it dangled as smooth as a sucked mint against his flesh.

"Is the other picture your father?"

Bruder shook his head, offering the second photo.

"Is this you?" Blackwood inspected the picture more closely: it showed Bruder as a young infantryman, his hair cropped close, sturdy under a sixty-pound pack, one stiff nailed boot resting jauntily on a boulder, rifle in hand. Hanging from him, as if he were a rack at the Raymond Street hardware store, were a bayonet and a collapsible shovel and ammunition pouches stuffed with a hundred rounds. Bruder must have been only eighteen or nineteen then, and this struck Blackwood, because there was something about Bruder that could make you believe he had never been young. Next to him, blurry in the

face, was another doughboy, although Blackwood could make out
nothing about him.

"Is this France?" Blackwood asked.

"Saint-Mihiel, not far from Verdun."

"I had to sit it out," said Blackwood. "Bad knees."

Bruder was motionless and pensive and said, "It changed everything, that war."

Blackwood nodded, although the idea seemed a bit quaint now: that
war, the one they had naïvely called "the Great War," the doughboys
sent over in spring and snugly home by Christmas. Sure, kids had done
their part, but it wasn't like today. Bruder could have stood in a trench
and never fired a round; that was the difference between 1918 and now,
thought Blackwood. "I'm sure you were a fine soldier," he said.

"Drive up to the house," Bruder ordered.

Once they'd parked beneath the portico, Bruder asked Blackwood
in. To Blackwood's eye, Bruder looked more like a burglar than a land-
lord, fumbling with the front door and his boots dragging in field dirt.
The library blinds were drawn, and Blackwood's eyes adjusted to the
dim light. His hand was up as he oriented himself, and it fell to Bruder's shoulder; and then he saw the tapestries and the stepladder with
the ostrich-skin railing. It struck him again that Bruder must be among
the richest men in Pasadena. Or maybe not; maybe that's why he was
selling: nothing erects a FOR SALE sign faster than an empty pocket.
Bruder sat on a chair that resembled a throne, roses carved in the gilt
frame, but Blackwood doubted that Bruder would ever think of himself as a king on a throne; and no doubt his dirty pants would ruin the
raw silk.

"What else did Mrs. Nay tell you?" asked Bruder.

"Very little."

"She said you spent the entire morning here."

"There's a lot to see. She told me some stories and such, but, Mr.
Bruder, you underestimate the way I inspect a property."

"Did she tell you about the war?"

Blackwood shook his head.

"And that's why I've returned today. Just as I told you before."

"Did Mrs. Nay tell you how I came to own the Rancho Pasadena?"

Blackwood shook his head again.

"Did she tell you how I first met the Poores?"

"She did not."

"It was at the Valley Hunt Club."

A thorn of envy pressed into Blackwood. "Are you a member, Mr. Bruder?"

"Me? You haven't been paying attention, Mr. Blackwood. I used to work in the kitchen." And Bruder said that when he was fifteen, Mrs. Banning had sent him to work there as a pot-scrubber, and as long as he lived he'd never forget how they had treated him: the snapped fingers; the "Boy, over here!"; the members' children telling him to stop looking at the girls, *Keep your eyes off her legs!,* telling him to go back into the kitchen, *Go back home,* wherever that was, *Go to wherever it is you belong!* "El Brunito," they'd call him.

"Yes," said Blackwood. "Mrs. Nay mentioned your, ah, nickname. But did they know your real name?"

"No, never, not in those days." No one had called him Bruder: he was merely the wandering orphan, or the boy who wanted to learn to read, or the kid with the criminal stare, and no one today would remember that all those years ago it had been Bruder whose foot received the poke of a sterling-silver walking stick; that it was he who was pushed into the swimming pool, his burgundy velvet uniform shrinking tightly across his swelling adolescent body. They weren't all like that, but Bruder remembered the names and the eyes of those who were: the blue eyes flecked with gold of a blond-mopped boy named Willis Poore; the deeper blue of the eyes of his sister, a girl named Lolly, frail in her tennis dress. One day the Santa Anas were blowing violently, and the wind pulled free Lolly's hair ribbon. It blew through the kitchen window, landing on Bruder's shoulder. There it lay, green satin and three feet long. Willis Poore had yelled: "Keep your stinking hands off her things!" Lolly Poore, fourteen and birdlike, had smiled through the window, her chin dipping to her chest. Bruder passed the ribbon over the sill and set it in the small hummingbird of her hand, and Willis Poore, hands on hips, marched to the club manager and had Bruder fired and escorted out the gate.

Blackwood said, "Yes, but if the Rancho Pasadena belonged to Willis and Lolly Poore, how did you manage to become its owner?" He wondered if something criminal had occurred.

"Let me start at the beginning."

"Yes, at the beginning."

"The first Willis Poore built the ranch, and when he died it passed to his son, the second Willis Poore."

"When did the first Poore die?" said Blackwood.

"You mean to say Mrs. Nay didn't tell you *that*?" Blackwood said that she had not. "What on earth *did* she tell you?" And then, "The Rancho Pasadena transferred from father to son on a cloudless day in 1913, when the dirigible crashed into the Arroyo Seco."

"The what?"

It was a pod-shaped balloon, said Bruder, with a sight-seeing car hanging from its belly. The bag was made of gray silk, and it was filled with city gas, and the balloon would take ten passengers up twelve hundred feet so they could survey their properties from the air, snapping pictures to show off at their dinner dances. It was the first commercial dirigible in the country, reported Bruder, and Mr. Poore, the senior Mr. Poore, took his wife up to take aerial photos of his ranch. Mrs. Poore had told her two children to watch from the rim of the arroyo. The dirigible motored around the city sky, and the children waved into the glare. Lolly would always say that she could see her mother's face in the little suspended car, that she saw her mother blow a kiss just as the silk tore—like a run in a stocking on a giant thigh—and the balloon collapsed souffléishly and plummeted to the ground.

"It's a terrible story, Mr. Bruder. Is it really true?"

"Of course it's true. It's the story of how the Pasadena was passed from father to son. That's why I'm telling it."

"And the story of how the Pasadena passed from son to you?"

Bruder rubbed his chin, and the two men sat silently on Christmas morning, the house groaning and stretching, as an empty house will, and each turned over the facts in his mind, conjuring a world sealed off from the present. A window or a door must have been open somewhere, because a whispery breeze ran into the library, from nowhere in particular, and Blackwood thought of Mrs. Nay demonstrating how gossip traveled down the dumbwaiter and up the heating ducts. The rustling noise lifted like a child's cry, and Blackwood turned to Bruder and asked, "What *is* that?" And Bruder said, "That? That's the house. It, too, is thinking of the past."

Blackwood thought to say, "She sounds like she was quite some girl."

"Who are you talking about now, Mr. Blackwood?" His voice was weary, like that of an invalid whose energy has left him before his visitors depart.

"Linda Stamp."

"Why do you say that? What do you know about her?" And then: "Has Cherry been telling you stories? I hope you've learned by now that embellishment is Cherry's finest talent."

"She said that you two were close."

"Is that what she said?"

Blackwood hesitated. "Not in so many words."

"She was a whore."

"Sorry?"

"The girl you keep asking about, she was a whore. She sold herself."

"Isn't that a bit harsh, Mr. Bruder? She was quite young when you knew her."

"I can see that Mrs. Nay didn't finish the story, Mr. Blackwood. There was more about Linda than you know. She could be like two different people. But I don't have to tell you about the doubleness of life, do I, Mr. Blackwood?"

"You don't, Mr. Bruder."

"You of all people should know what that means."

"Indeed, indeed." But then Blackwood wondered what Bruder was referring to. As far as Blackwood knew, no one in California knew of him as anything but a singular man; the name Andy Blackmann hadn't been uttered since that night in the cottage at the edge of the tiny Maine college, when Edith had delivered her news and gripped his collar and cried, *You still love me, don't you, Mr. Blackmann!*

"How is it, Mr. Bruder, that you came to own the ranch?" said Blackwood.

"Why are you so eager to know?"

"This is a significant purchase, and I feel I have the right to know of any"—and here Blackwood's voice found its lowest register—"ghosts."

"You are right, Mr. Blackwood," Bruder said softly. "I am sorry. There are ghosts. And no matter what I do, they won't go away."

The man had grown so morose so quickly that Blackwood felt everything turning his way. Another question pressed upon him. "How did the girl first come to Pasadena?"

"I asked her."

"You asked her?"

Bruder paused. He touched the coral around his throat and bit his lip, drawing blood, a teardrop of garnet bubbling up and then catching in the corner of his mouth. Once again Blackwood had the impression that Bruder, lost in his dreams, was traveling to another world, or being visited by one. At last Blackwood had discovered Bruder's weakness. Blackwood would involve the girl when he opened his negotiations for the Pasadena. And just as the idea took shape and form—the notion that Linda Stamp could help things along even after she was dead—Bruder said, "I asked her to come to Pasadena to be with me."

"Did you own the ranch then?"

"It wasn't mine, but it was slated to become mine."

"How is that, Mr. Bruder?"

"I shall tell you. Are you in a hurry?" His face had gone pale in a peaceful way.

Blackwood said he wasn't.

"We were talking about the war. I was telling you about 1918. I was on the front with Willis Poore."

"The second Willis Poore?"

"Yes, of course," Bruder snapped. "If you listen, the pieces will fall into place." Then: "We were together at Saint-Mihiel, along the Meuse. We were both in Motor Mechanics Company 17, First Regiment."

"Mechanics?"

"It wasn't what it might sound like today, Mr. Blackwood. This was the first time the automobile was taken into battle. We were much more strategic than you'd think. There is a purpose to everything I'm telling you," said Bruder. "I'm telling you for a reason. I'm answering your question."

Blackwood knew he would have to indulge Bruder. Selling property can stir up sentiment in even the most hard-hearted, and Blackwood understood that there was something about his round, chipper face that had caused many men and women to tell a final tale before signing a contract. Mrs. Nay had hinted that Bruder had something to say, but no one to say it to, and Blackwood was not surprised that Bruder had chosen him.

"Of course, by the time we arrived," Bruder began, "the front had been in stalemate for years. Up the Meuse, at Verdun, there'd been the terrible battle in 1916, four hundred thousand dead and no ground gained. By 1918, the French were weary, the Germans were drowning in influenza. I sometimes think America won the war simply by show-ing up."

Bruder explained that the front was a network of trenches, from Nieuport winding down across Europe to the foothills of the Vosges, near the village of Bonfol. The wire ran from the North Sea to the Alps in the shape of a backward S. Blackwood wondered what this had to do with the Rancho Pasadena, but he told himself to be patient.

Bruder turned in his chair, as if the pain were wearing him down by the minute. "Saint-Mihiel is at the edge of a forest of beech trees, and several streams and small hills rise to form the heights of the Meuse. There the medieval forts, although battered, still stood in the summer of 1918. This part of the front had been deemed passive, Mr. Black-wood, although nothing upon our arrival suggested that. The no-man's-land between the trenches was a landscape of craters, craters within craters, and craters that had blown apart previous craters. There were two lines of trenches, two miles apart, but the front here, like everywhere, had the feeling of the infinite and the interminable."

Blackwood leaned forward; he was falling under the spell of Bru-der's voice, and he nearly felt himself disappear.

"One fine summer afternoon, one of those days when the sky is lavender at dusk, Company 17 drove the forty-odd miles from Bar-le-Duc to Verdun along the supply road known as 'La Voie sacrée.' Willis Poore and I were not in the same platoon, so I was surprised to find my-self sitting next to him in the back of a truck on a bench scarcely six inches deep. The truck bed was so overcrowded that his left thigh and my right one pressed together for the entire afternoon, and by nightfall our legs were still next to each other, as if they had become a pair, and it was then that Willis Poore and I became a pair in actuality. The truck followed the road along the front to the mountains, and every ten miles or so it would slow and the captain would point to two men and throw them into the forest. As the summer moon rose, the truck slowed and Willis and I found ourselves next in line to jump out. We landed in a ditch of tallgrass, and I was lying on top of Willis and he was cough-ing from the dust and the truck's exhaust and he had a dazed look to him, as if he were still in disbelief that he was in France and being asked to fight a war. He asked me what we were supposed to do now, and the question came in the same voice that I imagined he used when asking his butler what was for dinner.

"You see, even at this point, Willis Poore did not recognize me. Nor did he think to ask me where I was from. If he had, he would have learned that I was a fellow Pasadenan. From one of the other soldiers I already knew that Willis thought I was from Mexico and wondered what I was doing in the American army. They say the army can change a man, but what they don't tell you is that the army can also make a man reveal his truest nature, especially if that nature is an ugly one. But I'm getting ahead of myself.

"We found ourselves in a dry ditch along a road cutting through the forest. Before we'd left Bar-le-Duc, every other man had been told the nature of our mission—a safety precaution—and I knew why we were there but Willis did not. He shouted, as if to test his voice against the trees, and the forest replied in kind, as did an owl, whose long *hoooo* caused Willis's eyes to widen with fear. Only then did Willis think to ask my name. I told him. When he introduced himself as Willis Poore, I said, 'I know.' Willis was the uncurious type, and it did not occur to him to ask how I knew his name. If he had, I would have told him. If he had asked, I would have told him everything.

"I had been informed in advance that where we were dumped would at first appear desolate, but that we would find a tiny road hidden behind a mound of branch and shrub. The moon and a crudely drawn map led me to the road, but when I stepped into the forest, Willis called from the ditch, 'Where are you going, soldier?' I told him that our mission was down the road, but it was clear that Willis didn't want to enter the forest at night. As I cleared the branches and located the two tire tracks in the dirt, it became even more clear that Willis didn't want to be left alone. He shouted at me to wait for him, and soon enough he was at my side again. We marched down a road that was barely a road, more like a path curving between tree trunks and boulders. 'Are you sure this is the right way?' Willis kept asking. 'Maybe we should camp right here and wait for daybreak.'

"What I knew that Willis did not was that nearby, in the forest, sat one of the Allies' secret motor depots, where trucks and light whippet tanks with engine trouble were hauled. We marched no more than half a mile on that warm August night, Willis thinking this was a fine time to inform me that he came from the Rancho Pasadena. 'I inherited it outright,' he said proudly, but Willis did not tell me a single thing about himself that I didn't already know. What I have never understood about

Pasadena—and I suppose it's no different than any other community in this regard—is why certain people remain unaware of the gossip they fuel. Nearly everyone takes pleasure in speculating about the sins of the powerful, but the powerful seem to believe that people only enjoy discussing their virtues. Willis Poore was living proof of this.

"After our short march, we arrived at a clearing. There were four or five trucks parked with their hoods flung up, and a little two-bay garage attached to a small barrack, no more than a cabin. The depot looked both busy and abandoned, and once I had lit a kerosene lamp I explained to Willis why we were there. 'We're fixing engines,' I said, peering into the barrack, where there were two bunks side by side separated by a tin crucifix nailed to the wall. 'This is home, soldier.'

"At this point, Company 17 had been in France for most of the summer. Before arriving in the forest, we'd been at the front, in the chalklands of Artois, where we had to make camp in a trench floored with duckboard plank and with bunks shelved into the chalky walls. That was where Willis made a name for himself, swapping oranges for his place in the trench raids. So, despite the depot's eerie isolation, you can imagine the pleasure this camp brought to Willis's face. He found the water barrel, wiped down his brow and throat, unrolled one of the cot mattresses, and hopped into bed. It was the first time in months that his pillow wasn't caked in dirt. 'Night, soldier,' he said, sighing like a settling dog. I remained outside, staying awake with a cigarette.

"Willis wasn't asleep for more than ten minutes when a slow rumble rose in the forest. It was a terrible sound of clacking iron and steel. As it approached, the ground shook and the trees trembled and Willis leapt out of bed and came to my side and whispered like a child, 'What *is* that?' I didn't know either, so we took up our rifles and hid behind a truck with a missing front grille and waited. Willis had stripped to his shorts and there had been no time for him to pull on his pants and now, although the night was warm, he was shaking. I'm sure people have told you how slight he was. Well, Willis was even slighter then—a boy, really, not a single hair on his chest. I would be lying if I said I wasn't frightened too, for I knew that my companion would be of no use in fighting back a German raid. The rumbling continued until it was so loud that it consumed the forest. I held my eye on the road, expecting a German A7V to lumber into camp at any minute. I was prepared to face the tank with the Iron Crosses painted on its side and the cannons aimed at us. I shouted to Willis that we could take anything, but he couldn't hear me and he kept saying 'What? What'd you say?' and then all of a sudden out of the forest rattled a rickety Tin Lizzie painted camouflage-green. Two American boys no older than twenty were driving the Model T, and when they saw us they stood up on the seats and said, 'Do you think you can fix 'er?'

"And that was how we spent the month of August. At nightfall the trucks and the cars drove in or were towed by horse into our camp, and we worked under the hoods until dawn. To my surprise, Willis turned out to be good with the wrench and knowledgeable of the carburetor. Within a week, we had earned a reputation as one of the best depots along that part of the front, and the cars lined up through the forest each night. By six in the morning, the depot's visitors were gone and we had the day to sleep or read or splash thigh-deep in the stream that ran through the forest. It was a hot summer with almost no rain, and some days Willis would lie on the table outside the garage stripped down to nothing and bathe his body in the sun, his rump turned up like a little ham browning in an oven.

"Although we worked and slept alongside each other, we didn't talk much, so a couple of days passed before Willis said, 'Say, Bruder, did you know that orphan in Pasadena? El Brunito? Something about you reminds me of him. He was a bad kid, they say. Once he dropped an ice block on the delivery boy. He isn't by chance any relation to you?' Sometimes people are called stupid unfairly, but not in this case. It wasn't until I told Willis Poore that little El Brunito and I were one and the same that the pieces fell into place in his small mind. You should have seen him. A face frightened and frozen, as if prepared by the taxidermist. He said, 'I thought El Brunito didn't speak English. I heard that you had half a brain. They must've gotten it wrong about you. You're not as bad as all that.' That is exactly what he said, unembarrassed by his misunderstanding and for some reason holding me to blame for it. As you can guess, we spoke even less after that, and the only time thereafter that any sort of camaraderie existed between us was when Willis and I pushed our faces beneath the same hood to inspect a burst valve.

"The ancient poet said long before I, 'That war is an evil is something that we all know.' It does not matter the century, nor the skirmish. Yet war can produce good too, bravery and honor, although less of it than you might guess. Nonetheless, I found much less than bravery and honor in the form of Willis Poore.

"September came but the summer heat remained, as did the steady nighttime traffic of trucks and ambulances and light tanks, although occasionally a thirteen-ton Schneider-Creusot rumbled into the depot complaining of an oil leak. The soldiers brought good news and bad, and occasionally a soldier would return two or three times and a friendship would strike up between him and Willis and me—for everyone else thought us an inseparable pair. It troubled Willis much more than I when one of these soldiers with whom we had bartered cigarettes and whiskey for a new rubber belt failed to return to the depot and word of his death reached us instead, usually accompanied by the vivid details of a shrapnel decapitation or the gagging asphyxiation brought on by the green-cross gas. Willis would quake when he heard the stories, and his eyes would fill with tears, but I was always convinced that he was not disturbed on behalf of the dead soldier but merely frightened for himself.

"As I was saying, in September the summer continued and so did the war and then the Americans began the battle to retake the village of Saint-Mihiel. We knew this because one night not a single truck turned up and Willis and I waited silently on our cots until dawn. No one came and no word, and at first Willis took this as a good sign. But the next night was the same as the previous, not a single broken-down truck, although the sky was illuminated by shelling, and the thunder of the German long-range gun that the doughboys called 'Big Bertha' clanged above our heads. The war was nearby, and each hour it seemed to be getting closer, and just before dawn we heard something approaching. We drew our rifles, and just at the moment when the night sky cracked with morning yellow, a spindly International MW truck pulled into the clearing. The truck's tires were missing several of their sixteen spokes, and there wasn't a seat—the driver was standing behind the wheel. And when he pulled the truck's brake, Willis stood up and waved, calling, 'Engine trouble, soldier?'

"But this particular private was having more than engine trouble, I'm afraid. Upon cutting the ignition the young man, who appeared rather orderly from our defensive position behind the water barrel, fell limply from the truck to the ground. We ran to help him and found him on his back, a bleeding hole in his side, and his eyes already glassy and dead. This set off poor Willis, who broke into a fit of tears. He spent the day crying and cursing both me and the war, declaring nearly everything in his life unfair. It was a pitiable sight, but after a few hours of it, with the shelling continuing overhead, he became more annoying than pathetic, and I told him to shut up or leave the depot. I saw it then: the child's panic flickering in his eye, that desperate look of hunting for a mother's breast. I poured him some whiskey and brought the cup to his lips and made sure he got enough down to twist his tongue. I was tired of listening to Willis Poore.

"You must remember that we were alone in the forest, and that almost three days had passed since word had come about the war's progress. We did not know if France was falling or if Germany was relinquishing territory. We did not know if the gray-clad soldiers would arrive to execute us or if a new truckload of doughboys would turn up to tell us it was time to return to California. We knew nothing other than the fact of the mounting shelling and the very real sense that the heavy guns had been turned our way. Great explosions erupted in the forest, and it was easy for me, and even easier for Willis, to imagine a shell cratering a tract of woodland the size of the depot's clearing. Willis made the suggestion—rather bold it seemed at the time—that we abandon the depot and escape. We weren't far from the Swiss border—two or three days by foot, as best we could tell—and he offered a plan of running from tree to tree all the way to the mountains. He went on to say that he knew a water spa in Montreux where we could rent rooms and sit out the rest of the war along the shores of Lac Léman. He was nearly delirious as he described the fresh perch served in lemon butter on the spa's terrace. Needless to say, I told him that he would have to flee to Switzerland alone, a prospect I was certain he would find more frightening than dying in my arms.

"By nightfall it was clear there was nothing to do but wait. We hadn't slept in more than two days, and we thought it best to lie down on the cots. I said to him that it might not be so bad to be executed in our sleep—which might sound cowardly to you now, as you sit here in the great comfort of peace, but in the reality of war a fast and painless death does offer its own enticements, even to a man like me. Under the bright stars of gunfire we went to sleep and I passed into a heavy dream, although even to this day I cannot recall what it was about. This has vexed me since that September night in 1918, for I am sure that I was dreaming about something portentous and prescient. At some point in the middle of the night I found Willis's cot empty. I still do not know whether it was in my dream that I pondered the empty cot—where had he gone?—or if in fact I was awake. But I lay there, both awake and not. From my pillow I could see through the barrack's door into the yard, and a figure came slowly into focus. He was a silhouette and he was busy with a large tin can, haphazardly dumping water or some other liquid. Again, I did not rise, for I cannot tell you if I was awake or asleep, although I firmly believe I was both at the same time, which might sound unlikely but isn't. I watched the figure, who I gradually realized was Willis, continue with his dumping, and I could hear a distinct sound of water spilling onto hard dirt or being thrown against the door of a truck. Willis moved about on his toes in a clumsy effort to maintain silence. He would pour the contents of the tin can upon the side of the garage and then refill the can inside and then continue with his dousing and refilling. It came to me like that, little by little, until at last my mind lit up and I was more awake than I had ever been in my life. I realized that Willis was splashing the depot with petroleum, and I leapt from the cot and ran into the yard. For a second or two I couldn't find him. The shelling had stopped, leaving the night black. There was no moon, as if it too had been shot down, and I peered around. And just as I thought that perhaps I *had* been dreaming, I saw Willis crouching deep within the trees, lighting the kerosene lamp. He stood and swung his arm and was about to toss the lamp into the gasoline-drenched truck yard when he saw me. This caused him to hesitate, and as we both well know, you and I, a moment's hesitation can change the course of events forever; for then something miraculous occurred before my eyes. Willis had performed his work sloppily, and petroleum must have soaked its way up his sleeve, and suddenly, with both his eyes and mine aghast, we watched a flame shoot up his hand and sleeve, across his shoulder and up the nape of his neck. Neither of us could believe it. His oily uniform and his greasy flesh were burning like pigskin over a flame. He stood motionless with shock, his arm extended and on fire.

"I ran to him, and there were several seconds—no more than three or four but they felt like an hour or an entire night—when Willis burned, his eyes watching me come to him. Only as I reached him did Willis realize that the lamp in his fist was the source of the fire, and he made a great gesture, one that I am sure he believed would be the last of his life, and hurled the kerosene lamp in a long arc over my head to the depot. The lamp glass shattered, and then everything was silent until a great *whoosh!* swept the truck yard. I smothered Willis in my arms as the depot exploded with mushrooms of orange and black flame. I turned to see a fireball rising so high that I am sure they could spot it in Berlin.

"Willis's fire transferred to my head—that is where this small scar at the temple came from, Mr. Blackwood. But I managed to extinguish him and then to drag him out of the scalding heat of the burning depot and into the beechwood forest. I pulled him several hundred yards, far enough from the breath of the fire but still within range of its fumes and smoke. I dragged him as far as I could, but he was wounded and I was too, although less so, and we lay on the hard forest floor as the sun rose and day broke. As we sit here right now, with the sun pressing through the blind and the hearth empty, I'm sure you can imagine for yourself the lulling qualities of a fire. Well, a large fire, even one shoot-ing truck shrapnel into the trees, can be that much more soothing, es-pecially if you are hurt and tired and desperately scared. I don't hesitate to tell you that that is what I was: scared for my life, although without any sense of regret. But scared, as any man would be.

"Eventually the explosions stopped, but the fire continued. Willis and I were huddled against each other and soon we fell asleep. Later, the sunlight through the trees woke me up. I didn't know what day it was, although it would turn out to be only an hour or so after the first ex-plosion. The fire was still burning, consuming everything within it but for some reason not spreading into the forest beyond. I sat up and Willis stirred, moaning with pain. His arm was less burned than you might think, for the flame had consumed more of his sleeve than it had his flesh. But his neck was badly burned, the flesh open and weepy. He could not sit up. He was ashen in the face, and he kept clearing his throat with a terrible thirst. With his eyes he begged me to do some-thing for him, but I didn't know what I could do. He pressed together his lips and whispered, 'Water.'

"I stood to survey what had happened, but as I did so, my own shirt fell away as if it had been woven of ash. For in smothering Willis's fire, my clothes had burned too, and I was down to a pair of trousers dotted with holes and my diceboxes loosely laced and the little piece of coral around my throat.

"Again, Willis begged for water. Needless to say, the water barrel had overturned, and the stream was on the far side of the depot, a quarter of a mile from where we were. I tried to lift Willis, but the pain overtook him, and as urgently as he had begged for water he now begged me to release him and leave him lying. I scoured the strewn debris for a tossed canteen, but there was nothing but bits of fender shredded to the size of tin-can openers. I told Willis, 'I'll go to the stream.'

"Due to the hot summer the stream ran low, but there was enough current and flow for me to sink my face into it. The water was a great relief to the patch of broiled flesh at my temple and to my own dry throat. I hadn't realized how much oily smoke I had breathed until I washed out my mouth. But there was no way for me to bring water back to Willis. When I returned to him I said, 'I'm sorry, I couldn't find a cup.'

"His eyes met mine and it was clear that he was disappointed, although not with me. No, it was as if, for the first time, he was disappointed with life. With fate. I told him that the explosion had been so great that it was unlikely we would have to wait much longer for a couple of soldiers to come along to investigate. Willis tried to take comfort in this, nodding as much as he could, but the fire had chewed the flesh so viciously from his nape that even a tilt of the neck hurt him more than a man, even a man like Willis Poore, should be asked to bear. I knelt by him and asked what I could do to make him more comfortable. He told me to help him adjust his head, and doing my best to ignore his horrible wincing and shrieking I rearranged him so that his cheek was resting against my thigh. And in that position we waited.

"The morning sun reached noon's peak, and still no one arrived in the forest. In war, a lack of response can be a good sign or something more ominous, there's no way to be sure, so I knelt patiently, and my leg fell painfully asleep.

"Willis was too uncomfortable to sleep, and eventually he gave up trying. His open eyes met mine, and there was a long intimate moment, his head in my lap, of us looking at each other, like two animals thrown together in a cave, one might say, or perhaps the way man and wife cautiously study each other across the conjugal bed on their wedding night. Willis and I shared a deep sense of not knowing what to expect from the other, and I believe that he both trusted and feared me at the same time.

"Willis lay wounded in my lap, which is where men dream of finding their enemies one day. Isn't that the case? Wouldn't you agree?"

Bruder stopped talking and stared at nothing for a long while. His face looked like that of a man in prayer.

"Now I've come to the final part of my story. As I was saying, Willis Poore was dying in my lap. Given my past encounters with him, to say nothing of his murderous arson attack, I'm sure you would think that I would relish this moment, that I would nudge him toward death, that I would search for a pinch of salt to throw onto his open pink wound. I might even have thought this myself. But in fact that wasn't the case. I surprised myself by becoming concerned for Willis, and after we'd stared into each other's eyes for some time, I said, 'Willis? What can I do?'

"His lips parted and his tongue emerged and then he spoke slowly, like someone who must ponder the creation of each word. 'I was going to pull you out of the fire,' said Willis. 'I planned on rescuing you.' I told him to stop, he didn't have to tell me anything, not now, but he persisted. 'I had a plan,' he said. 'A plan to make it look like we'd been shelled. Then we could have fled.' Here I insisted that he stop his explanation. It could change nothing now.

"I don't know if I believed him. I don't know even today. But I know my fortune forever changed at that moment.

"I told Willis to stop speaking, it would only exhaust him more and leave him in greater need of water. Several more hours had passed, and the burn on his neck seemed to be worsening, as if it were continuing to eat at his flesh and dig down to the knuckles of his spine. It was a terrible sight, as close as anything to seeing into a man's soul, a hole so open and deep that I could have launched anything—a louse, a villainous thought—directly into his brain. The thirst was overcoming him, and he returned to begging me—in that California way—for water. I told him I didn't know how to get him to the stream, and he said, 'Please bring me some water, please, do anything.'

"The other thing that interests me about death is how clever it can make a man. As Willis struggled to maintain consciousness he pointed at my boots, the old diceboxes that had reshaped my feet into hard red blocks. 'Bring me water in your boot.'

"In my boot? I had to admit it was a good idea on his part, and I told him so. I ran to the stream, removed my right boot, and filled it with water. Of course the boot leaked, but I believed it would suffice as a vessel and I ran carefully back through the forest. Needless to say, a boot is not meant to transport water, and it spilled its contents as I returned to Willis. By the time I reached him the boot was wet but empty, its laces grimy and limp. Willis's disappointment was apparent in his eyes. I said, 'I'll try again.' But he was becoming desperate now and he said, 'There's no time.' His chest rose and fell, and he said, 'Bring me water in your mouth.'

" 'In my mouth?' He began to nod, but the pain of it caused him to scream. He was right to ask for this, and I returned to the stream and knelt at its bank and pushed my face through its surface. I drank for a long time and then filled my cheeks and began to make my way back to Willis.

"Have you ever run with a mouthful of water? It isn't as easy as it might seem. The water slips down the throat, especially if your throat remains greasy with smoke; it pushes its way out the nose. No, as we all know, God created no vessel more leaky than the mouth. My telling you this is a prime example. In any case, by the time I reached Willis, there was little water left behind the dam of my lips. But I knelt beside him, and he chose to bear the terrible pain of lifting his head to me, and with surprisingly little embarrassment we brought our lips together. And when I opened my mouth to his waiting tongue, only drops of spittle transferred. But Willis was so thirsty that he began to suck the moisture from my lips, and I had to push him off me or he might have slurped the flesh from my face.

"By now it was clear to me that Willis had stepped upon death's threshold, and that if something did not happen he would leave me alone. And it was clear to him as well. He gripped my leg and said, 'Go back to the stream. Bring me more.' At first I resisted, thinking I had run a quarter of a mile there and a quarter of a mile back to carry a single drop of water. After all, what was the point? I am fatalistic that way. But Willis clawed at me, and his pleas filled the forest. 'Go! Hurry!' 'But, Willis,' I said. 'I didn't bring you any water. You were drinking the spit from my tongue.'

"The mood of a man in Willis's position can change instantly, and he released his hand from my thigh and fell back and said, 'You are right.' He was silent with resignation for a while, and then he said, 'Bruder? Will you tell them I died honorably?'

" 'But you did not,' I said.

" 'But will you tell them that I did?'

" 'How can I?'

"Willis asked me to come closer, to bring my face within inches of his. I did so, and I could feel his breath upon me when he said, 'Don't tell them that I was trying to flee. Don't tell them that I burned the depot. Tell them that we were shelled. That the enemy brought me down.'

" 'But it isn't true.'

" 'We can make it true.'

"Was I shocked at his request? No, I wasn't shocked. Desperation produces desperate acts. But I was surprised by my willingness to listen. What was it the poet once said? 'I can endure my own desperation, but not another's hope.'

"Willis looked into my eyes and said, 'I have a proposal for you, Bruder. A proposal for a transaction.'

"I asked what he had in mind.

" 'A transfer of property.'

"Willis motioned for me to lean in even closer, so that now our noses almost touched. He said, 'I'll give you anything you want if you tell them I died an honorable man.' I asked him what he meant, and he repeated, 'Anything.'

"Although I was young, and in many ways still an unformed man, even then I knew precisely what I wanted. Yet until that moment I didn't know how greedily I had desired it. I did not know what I was willing to do to acquire it.

"I held Willis's face in my hands and said, 'I want the Rancho Pasadena.'

"I expected Willis to protest, to say that that was the one thing he could not give me. Yet of course in many ways it was the only thing he had. He did not flinch. He only closed his eyes and opened them and said, 'All right.' From my pocket I produced a scrap of paper and a pencil. With significant effort Willis sat up, groaned, and began to write something down. While he worked on his note, I said, 'How do you know I will keep my word?'

" 'I don't,' said Willis. 'But with this paper you know I will keep mine.' He handed me the note and I read it: 'Upon my death, I, Willis Fishe Poore II, leave the Rancho Pasadena to Private Bruder of Company 17.' The note was short and spontaneous but legally irreproachable. What shocked me most about that day in France was the note itself. It looked as if a seven-year-old had written it. The letters were elementary and oversized and very much in the hand of a child. And I suppose that that was the case. But the note left me profoundly sad, and I genuinely felt compassion for the young man—a boy, really—dying before me. I did not take pleasure in the great treasure that would soon transfer to me. My life had changed with that note, and it actually felt—at first, at least—that Willis's murderous disgrace was falling away. 'The ranch is yours,' he said. 'Treat my sister kindly. You must make sure that Lolly does not suffer.' I said that I would indeed look after Lolly. 'And no matter what, you must not tell anyone how I died. Please always call me a hero, from this day on.' I said that I would. And it was that simple. The deal was done! Willis's disgrace had been erased, the truth of his impending death had been twisted into an unrecognizable form, and I had become one of Pasadena's greatest landowners.

"Do you see what war can do? Everything can change with a single shot. In an afternoon, history, both personal and national, can turn itself around.

"But I did not have time to think of such things there in the forest. Willis was suffering greatly, and I knew that he wanted nothing more than another drop of water. 'I'll try again,' I said. I ran through the trees, stopping only to tuck the note into my one dry boot. It was late afternoon by now and a shadow had fallen across the stream, as if someone enormous were standing over it. I knelt at the stream's edge, but this time I closed my eyes for a minute. I cannot say whether or not I knew enough to pray then, but I stopped to think about the fateful day I had just survived; I relived it in my head and told myself to always remember it as it was, not as it might have been, or should have been. No, I would hold history correctly, artlessly. Then I pushed my head beneath the surface and filled my cheeks with water. Under the water, I thought I heard a clanging like cowbells, yet I was sure it was nothing but the stream running over the rocks. Willis was waiting, and I knew that I must return to him with the final drops of water he would ever drink. I pulled my head out of the stream and shook the water from my face. It was a great relief to the burn at my temple, but there wasn't time to think about that; no, I had to get back to Willis Poore. But when I stood and turned around, there, not ten yards from me, was a little man with white hair and a white beard and a wide rack of tin cups and pans and canteens strapped to his back. He was wearing a little cap with earflaps, and it was clear that he wasn't a soldier but a salesman. What was he doing and who was he?, you ask. Oh, that's simple to say. It was Dieter Stumpf, hawking his tin cups up and down the front, from trench to trench, and on that day in September 1918, Dieter reached up over his shoulder and plucked from his rack a tin cup with a curled lip and said, 'Need a cup, soldier? Only five cents.' He moved toward me, the cup extended, and when he was at my side he said, in a voice that could have sold me anything, 'I've also got a first-aid kit for that burn of yours, soldier. It can be yours for a dime.' "

3

BRUDER'S STORY STAYED with Andrew Jackson Blackwood as he drove home from the Rancho Pasadena on Christmas Day, and he returned to it many times during the following week. It began to explain things, at least sort of, and he felt as if he had succeeded at a difficult task in getting Bruder to unravel his past.

Blackwood alluded to this when he called Mrs. Nay the day after New Year's, but she was furious with him for going to the property without her: "Your relationship with the client should be via me." She scolded him for behaving unethically, prowling around the ranch like a thief, and Blackwood tried to explain that his interest had grown so intense that he couldn't keep himself away. "Then meet me at the house this afternoon," she ordered, "and I'll show you the rest."

In truth, Cherry Nay didn't want Bruder to tell the story; even though it wasn't about her, she felt it was hers to recount. Hadn't she been the one who tried to sort out things in the end, for Bruder's benefit? She saw it as her role—and her right.

"I told you already, Mrs. Nay," said Blackwood. "I managed to see the orange grove. Mr. Bruder graciously showed me around."

"Meet me anyway," she insisted. "Come at three, and I'll show you the rose garden and the empty swimming pool and . . ."

"And?"

"And I'll tell you the rest of the story." She paused; and then: "Don't be late, Mr. Blackwood." She returned the receiver to its cradle and hurried to the tennis courts, where, once her mind was clear of all this talk of the past, she would continue her winning streak, completing her climb up the ladder. She acknowledged that Blackwood was a curious and inquisitive man, and she anticipated their conversation. He would ask her: "If Mr. Bruder had become the heir to the Rancho Pasadena, why did he go to Condor's Nest in the first place? Why didn't he just return to Pasadena and the land that would one day be his?"

And Cherry Nay would reply: "From the day he met Dieter Stumpf by the stream, everything Bruder has ever done has been for her."

"For who?" Blackwood would say.

"For the girl we used to call Linda Stamp."

REAP

{ *part four* }

Thou didst purchase by thy fall
Home for us and peace for all;
Yet, how darkly dawned that day—
Dreadful was the price to pay!

EMILY BRONTË

1

ON AN OCTOBER AFTERNOON in 1924, Linda Stamp—now twenty-one and almost six feet tall—stepped off the Pacific Electric at the Raymond Street Station. Since the death of her mother, her coltishness had given way to a handsome solidity: her ankle descended sturdily to the platform, her sea-worn fingers held tight the handle of her kettle-pot bag, and her hair was cut pragmatically away from her face. On the platform Linda stood erect, her head large atop her throat, and anyone kneeling to tie his shoe or to jiggle the latch of his traveling trunk would look up and see her almost as a giantess before the brittle Sierra Madres, her profile in line with the pale dry mountain range. For more than four years she had lived alone with her father, assuming her mother's farm and kitchen chores, and what Linda didn't know about herself was the lust-inspiring nature her beauty had acquired. The mirror told her nothing of what she could stir in the hearts of others, and her life since the landslide had been so solitary that there was no one to tell her of it either. It was a beauty of contrasts: the pelt-dark hair against the pale cheek, the high, wide brow above the narrow but deep eyes, the unsettled soul of a girl now inhabiting a woman's body. Her hair, which had once grown in ropes down her back, thick enough to lose pencils and fishing hooks in, had gone unshorn since Christmas 1919, and now that she'd cut it she couldn't get used to the lightness of her head or the fact that she could no longer hide behind the curtain of her bangs.

On the train, Linda had worn an overcoat with a green felt collar and her hat with the white eagle feather, which she had purchased, at last, for the journey, and the coral pendant around her throat. In the car's window she found her reflection agreeable, dressed smartly as she was for what Margarita had called a fancy-pants town. But Margarita's tales of Pasadena and its luxury hotels—the Vista above the arroyo, the Maryland with its long pergola, the Huntington with its distant ocean views—and its civic societies—the Twilight Club, the City Beautiful Committee, the 100 Percenters—sounded as if everything she knew had come from the society page. "You can learn a lot from the *American Weekly*," declared Margarita. "You wait and see. Won't be a soul up there who doesn't read every last word. There's a columnist named Chatty Cherry who keeps everyone abreast of the goings-on. Linda, you should look her up," Margarita suggested, although Linda couldn't imagine why.

But on the train, the scab-kneed boy next to Linda had left a thumbprint of guava jelly on the wrist of her coat; and when she opened the window, the eagle feather loosened and blew away. By the time she'd arrived in Los Angeles, dust and soot powdered her nose, and the coat hung limply on her arm. While waiting in Union Station for the four o'clock to Pasadena, Linda was asked for money by a burn-scarred man in an army uniform. When she said that she had very little, he yelled at her, his voice echoing. A heavily made up woman farther down the bench looked up from her compact and said, "Don't make him mad, doll." It was warm for October, summer's final sticky grab, and during the long day on a woven-wool train seat and, now, this depot bench, she had heated up, a dewiness collecting on her throat, and she hoped he wouldn't notice the weariness the trip had brought her.

The miles of track from Los Angeles to Pasadena cut through scrub-land and arroyo, crossing a bridge spanning a dry riverbed and running alongside acres of orange grove. Through the open window came the scent of citrus bud and green waxen leaf and the singed odor of soil that had gone without rain for more than six months. A team of men—hoes and hooks in hand, burro idle in yoke and cart—was clearing the brown, brittle fennel weed from the lanes between the orange trees, readying the orchards. The harvest would begin soon, and the lanes would fill with men buttoned into shoulder picking sacks. Then the train tracks curved away from the orange grove, the trees retreating. Linda's window sped past an abandoned grape orchard and a dairy and a sign promoting THE WORLD FAMOUS SOUTH PASADENA OSTRICH FARM & HOTEL. Another billboard advertised the VALLEY CASH FEED

& FUEL CO.: HAY!——WOOD!——COAL!——80 LB. SACKS OF SCI-
ENTIFICALLY MIXED MASH! Two or three houses with red-tile roofs
appeared next to the fields, then more houses, Victorian in eave and
turret, painted fescue-green and sunshine-yellow and scarlet. Soon
paved streets ran neatly out of the fields, and the fields gave way to
empty lots bordered by quartered sidewalks, and the empty lots gave
way to more houses, now side by side, white stucco and iron grate and
Tudor beam, wooden porch and cedar eave, and then the conductor
called, "Pasadena! Next stop, Pasadena!"

She hadn't seen Bruder in more than four years. The landslide had
buried him in a foot of mud, the bulbs of his onion-white eyes peering
through. Once free, he had dropped to his hands and knees and dug
like a dog, mud shooting behind him. He said he knew exactly where
she was, as if he'd caught her scent: "I knew I'd dig the hole and pull
you out and you'd be there. I knew it more certainly than I've ever
known anything." When he did, Linda was crying and he wiped the silt
from her lips and held her, her suit of mud cracking away. But only then
did she ask: "Where's Mama?" This time, however, Bruder's hound
skills failed. They didn't find Valencia, curled into a delicate, hard ball,
until the next day. He departed before they could bury her, the Vulture
House door snapping behind him. Linda followed him across the field
to the road, but when he reached the pavement he told her to turn
around. She asked where he was going, and he said, "Home." "I
thought you didn't have a home," she said, and then he was gone, and
atop her pillow Linda found the piece of coral.

Had she known where Edmund was, Linda would have sent a
telegram—MAMA'S DEAD—but he might as well have been dead too,
gone and with no word, off with Carlotta. Accompanied by Father
Pico's trembling recitation of the rosary, Linda and Dieter buried Valencia beneath the tulip tree, in a field just beyond the shadow of the
Vulture House. She held Dieter, frail in his epaulets, the winter sun
blazing in a cloudless sky. "You'll take care of me?" he asked; she said
she would, and that first night she worked Valencia's apron strings
around her waist and shucked a pot of beans. She rolled the *tortillas* and
fried the eggs while Dieter sat at the table, napkin tucked into his collar,
his eyes fluttering with sleep. "Papa? Are you all right?" He snorted pig-
gishly and woke up and sucked on the long white whiskers around his
mouth. A sense of dread overcame Linda: not only was Valencia dead,

but now Linda would have to assume her mother's life. She thought of how Valencia had changed after landing at Condor's Nest; the girl brave enough to dance at Café Fatal and swim the Pacific had learned— and this Linda was beginning to understand—to yield. How disappointing it was to Linda; and rinsing the beans at the sink, the apron strings tight on her waist, Linda shuddered at the suddenly limited possibilities of her future.

After Valencia's death, little changed at Condor's Nest, little except that Valencia's many duties—how had Linda not known there were so many?—were now Linda's own. She cooked for Dieter—baking the *conchas,* boiling the onion kraut—and strung his yellow-stained wash and mended his trouser knees and sacked the onions until she thought she would never be able to scour the odor from her thumbs. She rinsed the dishes and repaired the curtains and stacked the furniture on the table when it was time to lye-mop the floor. She maintained the farm log: eleven hens, three roosters, two burros—Tristan and Isolde, Dieter called them. She hauled the onions to the market on the pier and sold her catch at the gutting house to a wholesaler named Spencer, whose thick, square face, the shape of a book, always made Linda think he was cheating her. At night she eased Dieter into bed, tucking the sheets around him, pulling his stocking cap over his ears, tamping the ash in his pipe, propping the pillows to help him sleep upright. Quickly she came to know better than she might ever have hoped Valencia's life, the life gifted to her mother as recompense for a brief moment in Dieter's barn; had it been a moment of pleasure? Linda would never know. It occurred to her, after living in Valencia's apron for many months, that her mother would never have stayed at Condor's Nest had she not become pregnant with Edmund. She'd been on her way to someplace else, to another life. Over the years, Linda had wondered how her mother had transformed from a girl smuggling herself in the ocean to a hausfrau, and now Linda understood: There'd been no choice. It was a hard, jagged thought to tuck into the soft folds of her mind, but there it sat, pointed and true. The only comfort came in Linda's certainty that it wouldn't happen to her—even after it already had.

During these long months, and then years, Linda tried to imagine how Bruder was spending his days. She guessed he worked in a field, on a farm or a ranch somewhere, and with an inexplicable certainty she knew he wasn't far. Beyond Baden-Baden-by-the-Sea, surely, but not far away, Linda would tell herself; sometimes she'd write it in the margin of a book: her daydream guess of where he might be. The books had belonged to Bruder, and the elegantly scrawled annotations she found here and there were as foreign to her as another language. In *La Vita Nuova,* she wrote:

> Gone! Lost! Down the hill or out to sea!
> Gone now—but he'll come home to me!

On *Don Quixote*'s endpaper, she scribbled:

> In California, up the coast or down,
> In a cove, in a cave,
> But please, God,
> Not in a marble grave!

Did she feel abandoned? No, Linda wouldn't allow herself to believe that someone had betrayed her. She was waiting. For what, she couldn't say precisely. But she would wait, and as time passed she turned the notion around in her head so that it came to feel as if someone were waiting for *her.* She remained at Condor's Nest so that she could be found; she grew another two inches and filled the bust of her mother's apron and spoon-fed her father the delicate pink flesh of apricots and trembling cinnamon rice and his beloved sweet apple butter. Her someone would wait, and so would she. The sun crossed the farm and the full moon halved itself, then quartered, then started again, and Linda remained patient at her old father's side.

And so it wasn't a surprise when the postcard had arrived in the summer of 1924: a picture of a navel grove in blossom with snowy Mt. Baldy in the background, and the words in wedding-cake letters: *Pasadena, Crown of the Valley.* Bruder's note seemed incomplete, referring to information she didn't know: *Captain Poore can never get to me. He leaves me alone, which he knows he has to. We always need help around here. Don't tell Dieter.* For a month she carried the postcard in her apron pocket to the gutting house, where she flayed her daily catch, earning twenty cents a pound. It was the first time in her life that the money she earned was hers, but with it had come little of the satisfaction she had anticipated. The coins sat shiny in a jelly jar above the sink, no one but

she and Dieter witnessing the sunset glinting off them. Only vaguely
did she understand that Bruder had left because of Dieter, and she hid
the postcard from her father, and soon the card chipped and creased in
her pocket as she pressed herself against the rubber conveyor belt that
transported the pale fillets from her place on the line. Then a letter arrived, Bruder's longhand straight across the page. It divulged more than
she would have expected from Bruder: he did not say it in so many
words, but he missed her; he thought of her often; did she think of
him? No, Bruder wrote none of these sentiments, but Linda interpreted his commentary—*The girls of Pasadena are either silly snobs or gossipy
maids, but I have a friend*—as Bruder's longing. A second letter arrived,
and it included a request for Linda to join him at an orange grove called
the Rancho Pasadena.

She knew she couldn't go. She had Dieter to look after, and the
farm, but it was not a week after she posted her reply—*I would come if I
could, you know that, don't you?*—that Edmund returned to Condor's
Nest. One evening he appeared in the kitchen yard, Carlotta's fevered
cheek on his shoulder and their son heavy on his hip. He had lost his
eyeglasses, and he was squinting in a way that made him look old. Edmund said that his lungs were hungry for ocean air, and he and his son,
a boy named Palomar, had the dull eggshell complexion of people who
lived far from the sea. Carlotta, whom Linda remembered as all bust
and mane and red-glass bead, had cut her hair down to a fine cap, and
she clutched a handkerchief hard with dried sweat. Edmund ordered
Linda to straighten up the Vulture House for his family, "Make us a
home, won't you?"

She obeyed, scrubbing the floorboards and polishing the windows,
mending the rocking chair's spindles and planting rust-colored chrysanthemums at the front door and hanging red chilies from the eave.
Soon enough, Carlotta climbed definitively into Bruder's old iron-
spring bed, whence she gave feverish and increasingly demented
commands—most of which involved Linda minding Palomar—and
never again did she climb out, not even to wash or eat or to see her son
on the beach writhing like an overturned tortoise.

Palomar was lumpy like a forty-pound sack of onions, with a barn-
yard smell. His head sat heavy on his sweaty neck, and his wiry black
hair stood up, and his gray eyes moved slowly in slanted sockets. Linda

wondered whether the boy was right in the head, and if his eyes were as bad as his father's. He'd sit for hours propped against the feed sacks staring at the flyingfish dying on the bed of ice, his glazy glare imprecise and unchanging. He rarely cried except when Linda transported him about the farm in the wheelbarrow. She loved the boy, but more from pity for her brother than anything else. And just as she was growing accustomed to Edmund's return—the Stamps glued together almost as they once were—another envelope arrived from Pasadena. Again, Bruder told her not to mention the letter to anyone (Linda had snuck a letter into the post informing Bruder of Edmund's return), but, Bruder insisted, with Edmund back home, wasn't she now free to join him on the ranch? "The woman that deliberates is lost," wrote Bruder, and he said there was a job for her at the ranch, and a narrow bedroom behind the kitchen, and he wrote, "Neither Dieter nor Edmund once hesitated when they left you."

As Linda was preparing to leave for Pasadena, Carlotta, frail and gone mad with syphilis, suggested to Linda that she lop off her hair. "You'll look more like a woman," she said. "And less like a girl." A deathbed beauty tip it would turn out to be, Carlotta boiling in the forehead and wheezing her final *Lieder* and clutching Palomar to her lesion-speckled breast. In the kitchen yard, Edmund cut Linda's hair and it blew in clumps from the bluff, small black ghosts lifting above the ocean and flying off, lock after lock curled at the tip like a talon. Later, Linda would wonder whether Edmund—who had hobbled back to Condor's Nest with a pocket crammed with debt—was in fact shedding his tears over Carlotta's final song or over Linda's hair, tufts of youth carried away, his face broken up with regret. The very fact of moonfaced Palomar explained everything to Linda, everything about Edmund and what he had done and where he had been. She understood that a mistake had transpired at the Cocoonery, maybe even in the greasewood shrub, and in the span of a minute or two, maybe less, his life had been determined for him. Edmund had never really loved Carlotta—he had been trapped by her, a young man handcuffed by obligation and offspring and a justice-of-the-peace marriage certificate. And on the train to Pasadena, Linda had sat rigid on the Pacific Electric seat, certain that the error of passion—a dark hole so many fell down—would never trap her. She had told her father and her brother that she had taken a job on an orange ranch. When they asked why, her throat straightened upon her shoulders and she said, "To see what it's like to be free."

And now, on the platform at the Raymond Street Station, Linda was thinking that so far Pasadena looked just as it had in the postcard, the orange trees round and dense and green, the early fruit glowing like lanterns on the branch. Mt. Baldy rose to the east, its dome pale and brown and awaiting the first cap of snow. She smelled the lavender and the minty eucalyptus, and the sun in the afternoon's corner cast a yellow-pink glow against the tracks. The station wasn't crowded, but the street was busy with cars and clerks in shirtsleeves and black elastic armbands hurrying back from coffee breaks. A long-hooded Sunbeam, driven by a young woman with a shiny yellow bob and a sterling cigarette holder clamped in her hand, maneuvered recklessly between the Model T's and the balloon-tired bicycles. The girl was busy lighting her Violet Milo cigarette and failed to notice until the very last instant the Pasadena Ice Company wagon directly in her path. The Sunbeam skidded and the wire wheels shrieked, causing the wagon's brindled horse to buck and bray and stamp its feet. The girl screamed, and when she finally managed to stop the car she was so close to the horse that its cavernous nostrils were fogging up the car's twin headlamps. "Get that beast off the street!" shouted the girl, and she honked and drove off.

The commotion transfixed Linda, and at first she didn't hear the man's voice saying, "You must be Linda Stamp."

She turned, startled to see a stranger rather than Bruder, and asked, "Who are you?"

"Captain Willis Poore." A buttery rose poked from the lapel of his suit, and dangling from his breast pocket was a military medal on a maroon satin ribbon. He was a young, beautifully handsome man, with a perfectly round head and full, round lips and eyes so blue and flat on his face it was as if they were painted on. He was the type of man newspaper photographers would snap pictures of simply because his face would please all subscribers, old and young, men and women alike.

"Where's Bruder?"

"He got held up at the ranch. He asked me to come along and fetch you instead. He assured me you wouldn't mind. I hope you're not disappointed."

Linda shook her head in disbelief and clutched her bag and wondered if there was a mistake. She asked the man what could have kept Bruder from meeting her, and he said that one of the girls at the house was sick and that Bruder was looking after her. "She hasn't been well lately, and Bruder's taken to seeing to her." Captain Poore's medal reflected the station like a little mirror, and the draft of the departing train lifted the yellow-banded hat from his head and threw it into a ditch, and then Linda's little featherless cap followed, landing next to his. She leapt into the ditch and he followed her, his hand beating hers to the hats. With his sleeve he wiped the dirt from her hat and replaced it atop her head, and it promptly blew off again.

"Welcome to Pasadena." He leaned into her, and the medal swayed on his breast, and to her alarm, Linda felt an awkward inequality next to Captain Poore, like the day last year when Mary Pickford had driven down El Camino Real in a Roi-des-Belges, on her way to a film location at Cathedral Cove: her pretty, delicate head crossing the fields, a chalk-white hand waving, the farmers and the fishermen gulping noisily and checking to make sure their wives hadn't seen the salty leer in their eyes, the envy and desire upon their lips. This event had shocked Linda, for she knew she'd never be able to stir such a response in others. No, Linda could raise a subtler but more profound longing, yet she was unaware of it, as unaware as a baby is of the shimmering pride she engenders. "It was nice of you to meet me, Captain Poore. But I'll wait for Bruder."

"You're free to wait," he said kindly, "but he isn't coming any time soon. He sent me in his stead. The girl's sick, a little stomach trouble, and if I know Bruder he's folding a damp rag across her brow right about now. He's a good man, your friend Bruder." She must have looked shaken, because he added, "It'll be all right. He did say he was looking forward to seeing you. He's always said you're quite a girl."

"I don't know what to do."

"Come with me. I'll drive you home." Captain Poore took Linda by the elbow and led her to a yellow speedster with a rounded back, like a beetle's. He secured her into the passenger seat and hoisted her bag into the trunk. When he turned the engine, the Kissel Gold Bug coughed and Willis Poore whipped the car into the street, where the driver of the ice wagon was stroking his horse's forelock, trying to calm the mare. "Bruder tells me you've never been to Pasadena."

Linda shook her head. Everything around her was so foreign, she felt as if she'd landed in France.

"I'm sure he'll give you a tour before the harvest. After that there won't be much time. But if he gets too busy, I'll show you around. You know how Bruder can be." But Linda did not. "He gets so tied up in the grove. If you'd like, I'd be happy to show you Busch Gardens and drive you up to Mount Lowe and stop in at the ostrich farm." And then, "Only if you want to, Miss Stamp."

"That would be nice of you."

"I want you to feel at home. We're all a big family at the ranch."

As he drove up the street, Captain Poore pointed out Central Park, where the Gentlemen's Tourist Club, a group of retired Iowa feed-corn farmers, met to pitch horseshoes and lawn-bowl and suck on cob pipes, debating the local feuds reported in the newspaper. The car passed the Hotel Green, a Moroccan butter-stucco palace where dignitaries went for iced tea. "Did you ever see that picture of Teddy Roosevelt when he visited Pasadena?" Captain Poore asked. But other than Bruder's post-cards, Linda had seen nothing at all. The Hotel Green sat stoutly upon an entire city block, its two north turrets capped by parasol roofs. Sandstone and teak carved in lacy filigree decorated the balconies and the clover-shaped windows. The accordion awnings extended their shadows to protect the guests, all of whom must be rich, Linda presumed, endlessly wealthy in a way she had never thought of before. Lying atop Linda's stomach, beneath her blouse, was a canvas purse of coins, heavy and bulky and fetus-size, and until this very moment at Captain Poore's side she had deemed herself adequately enriched. But now the coin purse protruded in a ghastly tumorous way, and the pennies—for there were many more pennies in the purse than silver dollars—felt useless and encumbering.

The hotel sat at the head of the park, next to a circular fountain with benches around it where bank clerks and office assistants from the Pasadena Electric & Power Company rested after calling it quits for the day; here gossip about their bosses and the lady clerks and the gloved women who triggered the tinkling brass bell attached to the door traded as rapidly as the jay calls in the pines. Linda noted that the clerks and the assistants, their vented jackets slightly wrinkled and ill-fitting across the back, rested in the shadow of the Hotel Green but not in the butlered shade of its veranda. Quickly, her mind was becoming adept at noting the rungs upon a ladder.

From nowhere Captain Poore said, "And, Miss Stamp. I want you to call me Willis. None of this 'Captain' business from you." She said that she didn't know if she could comfortably accept the informality, but he insisted: "That's just the type of man I am." He laughed boyishly, and his mouth seemed to hold more teeth than other men's mouths, good, square teeth lined up in a gleaming smile. Every so often he would rub his medal, as if to remind himself of a former glory, and when she caught him doing this he blushed, as if he were a child caught admiring his own beauty in the mirror.

As Linda would soon learn, when prodded, which he often was, the captain would recount his wartime heroics neither humbly nor boastfully, simply with the weight of the facts themselves. He told often—because he was asked often—the tale of surviving the shelling of a motor depot along the Meuse. "They gave me this medal for saving a man's life," he would say, and to those whose eyes opened especially wide at the details of the great orange fireball that overtook the depot where he was stationed, Captain Willis Poore would unhook his acetate collar and reveal a pink burn-scar running narrowly but smoothly down his nape, much like a scrap of good leather sewn onto his flesh. The scar was not disfiguring; it merely provided tactile evidence—for it was smooth, and the natural inclination was to touch it, like a shrine—of bravery. To those who clutched their breast upon the conclusion of the tale of Captain Poore's heroic military past he would simply say, "You would have done the same."

"You must have been frightened," said Linda when he told her the story.

"I was," said Captain Poore. "But aren't we all?"

Linda was sorry that Bruder hadn't come for her as he'd promised, but Captain Poore was proving an impressive chauffeur. He must be a busy man, she thought, and she sat rigid with pride that her first impression of this strange city was coming from someone like him. He continued describing the heavy guns on the front and the mists of mustard gas, and if indeed he had a spell to cast, its dust was surely falling upon Linda's brow. Yet she couldn't know this about him, or even about herself, not on that October afternoon in 1924. Not in the angled orange light, with the vines of dusk climbing the date palms and the knife-leaved bamboo; not in the promise of dusk on the manure-spread rose beds, petals weary in autumn, soil hard and crumbly and clumps of it deposited on the street by horses' hoof; not as the firm, dry soil, collecting on the pavement like fossils from another epoch, shot from under the wheels of Captain Poore's lemon-yellow car as he sped through the small gleaming city in the valley. Above them, along the ridge of the Sierra Madres, the lights of Mt. Lowe and the observatory twinkled.

Captain Poore turned at a busy intersection, and soon traffic was all around them—roadsters stuffed with young men in sporty sweaters; a long-bonnet Bugatti driven by a woman in a white fur coat; an open-air Vauxhall with two men and two women in riding helmets holding leather crops between their knees. The women were smoking gold-tipped cigarettes, and as the Vauxhall pulled next to the Kissel, one of the women, with a swirl of hair pasted to her forehead, tapped her cigarette, and the tiny ashes drifted toward Linda. She winked, and Captain Poore honked and leaned toward Linda and said, "Henrietta Cobb. Fifth-richest girl in town, but not for much longer. Her father's still betting on the railroads. You know what they say? Once a robber baron . . ." The girl eyed Linda as she might a maid who had brought her the wrong doeskin gloves.

They passed a horse-pulled wagon, its planks barely held together by rusted bands, carting six Mexicans with their sleeves rolled past their elbows and grime in the folds in their throats; a turnip-shaped man in a striped suit drove the wagon, and the Mexicans didn't look forward but behind. Linda met the eyes of one of them, who tipped his leather-trimmed hat. A red trolley rattled down the middle of the street, a girl in a blue uniform with a patent-leather sash selling tickets at the entry-way, her hair in thick woodcut curls; Linda wondered how she managed to set her hair each morning for a long day on the trolley. A policeman stood on a round platform in an intersection, a whistle lodged in his mouth and his white gloves held up firmly: he waved traffic in this direction and that, and the sun caught his uniform's brass buttons and the gleam in his dust-caked eyes.

"Is this Main Street?" she asked.

"Colorado Street. Isn't it grand? A few years ago, they widened it for all the traffic, pushing the buildings back by almost fifteen feet."

She'd never seen anything like it, although last year she had read in the *Bee* a two-part report on the bustle of San Diego: roads paved all the way to the Mexican border, ribbons of streets unwinding north and south, elevators tossing people twelve floors up. During the years Edmund was gone Dieter had read to her from Gibbon, slowly making his way through the dense history; now she imagined that this was what Rome must have looked like, the yellow afternoon light, the street dust in the throats, all the citizens plying the same thoroughfares, the jostle of exchange and trade. A sign at the train station had declared Pasadena the third-largest city in California, but the sign was already more than a few years out of date; no one seemed to know it, but as grand as Pasadena seemed to Linda, its most glorious days had already passed.

There was too much for Linda to look at: people pushing through the glass shop doors; a newspaper boy in front of the Electric & Power's brownstone building selling the *Star-News;* stockingless women emerging from Model's Grocery with packages wrapped in salmon-colored paper. Through the window of a printing press, Linda could see men in heavy aprons with ink-stained hands. A plume of yeasty smoke rose from a bakery's chimney. A butchery speed wagon was parked in front of the Lincoln Cash Market, a boy in a cap loading deliveries of cross ribs and porterhouses. A man on a ladder painted a sign—10¢ OFF EVERYTHING ON OUR SHELVES—on the plate glass of Pasadena Hardware. Linda took in the careful stack of remedy bottles and tins in the window of the Owl Drug Company: Lydia E. Pinkham's Liver Pills, Dr. Schenck's Mandrake Pills, Foley's Kidney & Bladder Remedy, Jad Salts, Sharpe & Dohme Lapactic Pills, Dr. Pierce's Pleasant Pellets, and a pyramid display of Scott's Syrup of Hypophosphites teetering upon a marble-top table. A sign painted on the side of a brick building said: TURN AROUND! YOU HAVE MISSED THE UNEXCELLED ADVANTAGES OF BROADWAY BROTHERS, 268–278 EAST COLORADO ST.

"I've never seen so many stores."

"A new one opens every day. It's the richest town in California." His hand fell to her wrist just as it had when he'd described the terrible silence before the German shells hit his depot. Captain Willis Poore's nose was long but elegant, and at the crown of his head a cowlick of thick flaxen hair stood erect like a stalk of late-season timothy. On his pinkie finger he wore a star sapphire ring that caught the light in the same way as his blue eyes, and Linda didn't know if she'd ever known such a regally handsome man. The Kissel's dashboard was nickel-plated and reflected the two of them, the fray in her overcoat exposing itself. Also in the dash's shimmering reflection were the brick and cast-iron buildings of more merchants than she'd ever seen in one place and, above everything, the Sierra Madres, where astronomers from the old Throop University were setting up telescopes and, rumor had it, listening stations, antennae and earphones tuned in to the signal of celestial life.

They drove up a hill and into the sun, and then, as the city thinned, a wide arroyo opened before them. Live-oak and sycamore and black walnut sentried the hillsides and a road zigzagged to the basin, but instead Willis Poore turned onto a concrete bridge that stretched casually across the canyon. Bulb-lamp streetlights decorated the bridge, and over the low rail Linda could see up and down the arroyo: the wash sandy and dead, the dry clusters of alder and cottonwood and elderberry, their crisp, dying leaves chiming on the branch. As the car sped across the bridge, the air rushed around her, cool in the late-afternoon shadows of the western hills and fresh with the perfumes of laurel and lemonade sumac, of herb and sage and vanilla-scented scrub. To the north, a great horseshoe-shape stadium—"That's the Rose Bowl; up it went just a couple of years ago"—sat in a flat of willow and toyon and coffeeberry. Linda closed her eyes to imagine the arroyo before the bowl, before the thousand men had come to dig and clear and pound and pour; before the six hundred mules hauled the dirt, sweating and stamping themselves to slow, parched death.

"What do they use it for?"

"The Tournament." He paused, and then: "You *are* new to Pasadena, aren't you? It's a little festival we call the Tournament of Roses."

The Kissel skidded on the bridge's curve and Captain Poore jerked the wheel and Linda's hand fell to his thigh, but just as quickly he regained control and she pulled back her hand and then they sped into the Linda Vista hills. "They call it Suicide Bridge," he explained, chuckling mildly, baring his teeth, and his hair swayed and maybe for the first time in her life Linda didn't know what to say. "You'll like it here, Miss Stamp," he said. "I'm sure you'll get used to us."

He turned down a white dirt road that ran through a eucalyptus alley. On the other side of the trees were outbuildings: a barn and a two-story shed and a stable with an open door. A couple of men were burning a pile of cuttings, but Linda couldn't see their faces, only the orange flame and the pale smoke. An irrigation ditch ran parallel to the trees, its water slow and brown and inviting a gray squirrel to its edge. The road started to climb a chaparral hill, steep and choked with ceanothus and bitter cherry and old lilac and twisted-trunk madrone. Shadows pressed across the side of the hill, and a chill touched Linda's neck. Already the cool, damp scent of night was approaching.

The road ended at a wrought-iron gate suspended between two stone pillars. One of the pillars bore a plaque reading RANCHO PASADENA; the other's plaque read NOT A SERVICE ENTRANCE. The car pulled to the gate and Captain Poore idled the car, his hands on the wheel; after a few seconds he hopped out, saying, "I'll just get the gate."

One of Bruder's letters had described the hundred acres of groves and the dense scrubland, the winter river and the summer wash, the white mansion on the hill, the family named Poore. He had described the gate: "Overgrown with wild cucumber when I arrived. A scraggly eucalyptus alley that hadn't been properly cut back in a decade." Another letter explained: "No one left in the family but a son named Willis and his little sister, Lolly. Spoiled rotten."

The road cut up the hill, and at the crest the holly berry and the laurel sumac gave way to a ryegrass lawn and a long Blood of China camellia hedge. The driveway continued on, leading to a house so big and white that at first Linda thought it was one of the hotels Margarita had spoken of, the Huntington or perhaps the recently opened Vista. Willis drove the car toward it, waving to a Japanese gardener in green rubber boots, and it became clear that this was the Poore House, and that they had entered—as one crosses into a foreign land—the Rancho Pasadena. The mansion was three or four stories, Linda couldn't be sure, the windows shaded with lace that Linda guessed required an army of maids to wash and iron. Several chimneys rose from the pantile roof, and Linda worried over who hauled the wood and stoked the fireplaces and scooped the ash. Were these duties to become hers? A wide balcony set off the second story, and Linda imagined that was where Willis and Lolly Poore resided, in rooms side by side, sleeping in the breeze of a cracked door. She imagined the cans of starch the household would run through in a week, crisping the bedsheets and Willis's detachable butterfly collars. The terrace on the house's south side—its balustrade decorated with urns planted with kumquat—was as large as a lettuce field, an acre of tile; again, Linda imagined the mops and the sudsy bucket water and the ache in a bent spine. "Who cleans it?"

"What? The house? We have some girls around. Rosa and the others. You'll meet everyone."

The driveway narrowed, and the concrete gave way to orange tiles hand-cast in the Teddy Cross Ceramics Studio on Colorado Street, where the kilns burned walnut logs night and day. The car pulled beneath the portico next to a loggia where wicker sofas and a swinging bench waited for lounging souls. Linda next expected Captain Poore— "No, I insist, you must call me Willis!"—to cut the engine and invite her into the house; and a fear overcame her—a fear she didn't recognize and didn't like—that she wouldn't know what to do once inside the house's great hall or in its library or on the vast terrace where, Linda imagined, a maid with a harelip would serve a lobster-claw supper in the glow of sunset. This was a palace, and Linda worried about the jelly smudge on her coat and the small tear in her stockings, the only pair she had ever owned, bought on impulse in a dress shop across the street from Union Station in Los Angeles and pulled up her legs in the station's ladies' room. "Only one pair?" the shop's clerk had asked. "What about a pair of mocha gloves? Only two forty-five?"

But Willis didn't stop the car. "We live here, Lolly and I," he said, accelerating out the other side of the portico, the Kissel rattling as the drive returned to dirt. "I'll show you around one day." The car pulled away from the house, and Linda looked over her shoulder and saw, in a small upstairs window, a girl staring at her with moist black eyes; she had a fragile-looking face: bony, breakable nose and cheeks, forehead like a brown-glass bowl. The girl's white nightdress blew against the windowsill, and she looked as if she might collapse, but her eyes were following Captain Poore's car, following Captain Poore himself, and Linda too, and Linda wondered if the girl was Lolly; Linda wondered why the girl's gaze was blank with longing, but then the car passed a stand of yews and the house fell from Linda's view.

The road descended a hill, and the small valley of orange grove opened before them. Rows and rows of trees, as green as pines, as dense as shrubs, the lowest ground fruit only inches from the hard soil, the highest and sweetest more than twenty feet above the stubby roots. The grove looked ready for harvest, each tree drooping with a thousand cadmium-orange lamps of fruit. A road and an irrigation ditch surrounded the grove, and every hundred feet or so, ten-foot stacks of cordwood stood as neat as bunkers.

"He's probably still up with Rosa at the house," Captain Poore said.

"Will you tell him I've come?"

"He'll be eager to see you."

"Did he say that?"

"Not exactly." And then: "But you know how he is." Captain Poore went on, "I've never hired a girl to work in the ranch house. The packers, of course, are girls, mostly hired over from the orphanages, but they're day workers, gone by sunset, and some might say a ranch at night isn't a place for a young woman. But Bruder told me you could take care of yourself. I said that you could stay up in the house; there's an extra bed in Rosa's room. But for some reason Bruder doesn't think the two of you will get along. It's not fair of him, really—to think like that." Captain Poore paused and then asked Linda how old she was. She told him, and he said, "That's what I would've guessed, but it's funny: Bruder said you were Rosa's age, and she's barely eighteen."

Linda laughed in a confused sort of way, and for the first time she permitted herself to touch the small pink wound Bruder had left upon her heart by not meeting her at the train station. And as if Captain Poore had been reading her mind, he then said, "He's a funny one, your Bruder. He wasn't going to have me come pick you up. He said you could take the trolley and then walk to the gate. I had to insist, because Bruder went on and on saying you could take care of yourself. It's just the way he is, I guess. Of course you'd know better than I."

Linda told Captain Poore that indeed she *could* look after herself, but the truth was she was a little worried. There she was, sitting in the car, quiet, and it wasn't supposed to happen to her: the showy world causing her soul to fold up like a fingered anemone.

Evening was approaching; the sun was bleeding behind the western hills. A purple shadow covered the valley, the orange trees dark and the fruit glowing. The road descended a hillside of chaparral and sumac; the car's path was narrow and rutted and crumbling at the edge, pebbles shooting from the car's rear wheels a hundred feet out over the valley and into the orchard. A railroad whistle echoed against the hills. Those men she had seen on the drive in: for them she'd boil a nightly pot of pink beans and North Burbank spuds, and maybe one of them had been Bruder, and something filled Linda's chest, pressing urgently. She had grown up since he'd abandoned Condor's Nest, and she wondered if he would expect this; or if a chilly shock would climb his spine when he saw her. What if he were to say, "You've become someone else."

At the bottom of the hill, Willis and Linda got out of the car. It seemed as if the grove extended forever: the trees lined up in the soil that crumbled beneath her heel; branches curled against the ground like a dragging skirt; a few lime-green oranges on each branch among the flaring ocher globes. On some of the trees were final sprays of nectary white blossom, and bees swarmed the tiny bleeding flowers. A bee sawed next to Linda's ear and then sat upon her shoulder, and Willis watched her carefully, as if to test her. How would the new girl-hand react to a bee on the shoulder? She'd keep walking, as it turned out, grabbing an orange from the ground and then a second and a third, juggling them as she and Willis listened to an early night breeze rattle the hems of the trees.

"I've got a hundred acres," said Willis. "Eighty-six hundred trees. Last year we yielded nearly eighteen thousand boxes of oranges."

"One hundred acres?" She thought of Condor's Nest, a sliver of land, a third of it swallowed by arroyo, the ocean perpetually eroding everything away.

"We've got a lot more than a hundred acres. Only a hundred are planted. One day I'll ride you around and you'll see."

His stride was short but he walked quickly and he made Linda think of a schoolboy running to class. He looked too young to be a captain, and she could sense his mild petulance, but at the same time he seemed to know everything, she thought. Here was a man twenty-four or twenty-five years old heading up a ranch, a decorated captain, someone who in the course of his day could go from picking and grading oranges to checking the cylinders in his Kissel to fox-trotting and dancing the Portland waltz around the terrace. She knew so little about this type of man—about this type of world, really—that it was like meeting a foreigner: exotic and charming and unknown.

As the sky saddened with the blue of evening, they continued down an orchard alley. Here the lower branches had been cut back, revealing white numbers painted on each trunk. They made no sense to Linda, the three numbers stacked:

5

26

7

A code she had no doubt she'd crack in a few days. She wondered what else waited for her in the morning, the tasks at dawn. Would Captain Poore expect her to run the water in the ditch? Would he tell her what she was supposed to do?

Willis held his hand to his eyes, scanning the ranch. "I don't see the boys." It felt as if no one had been there in a long time, nothing but the trees and the swelling oranges, nothing but three empty field crates turned on their sides—no one but Linda and Willis. Evening darkened their faces, his dimming like a candle dying in a glass shade. She felt the chill of autumn's sly approach; and Willis shivered and stood close to her. "It's not the biggest ranch in California," he said. "But they love our navels." His voice snagged and broke, a pip-squeak's crack, and Linda was touched by this vulnerability, and the way he carelessly rubbed his scar. He wasn't at all what she had expected: no, she had anticipated a cowboy, a sun-worn face beneath a broad-brimmed hat dull with dust, and maybe a leather vest and a belt buckle forged from horseshoe.

"How many years have you been a rancher?" she asked.

"All my life. I was riding bareback when I was four, and when I was eight I drove the final ten heads of steer out of Pasadena. And I've probably picked more than a million oranges since I was a boy." His suit didn't fit him especially well, Linda noted; it was a bit baggy in the chest and the thighs, as if he were still growing into it, but it was easy for Linda to imagine his handsome face in the overcoat advertisement she had seen painted on the brick wall of Perkins & Leddy on Colorado Street. She closed her eyes, and already everything about him had burned into her memory.

They returned to the ranch house, where Willis told her that the harvest would begin in two weeks and that once the pickers arrived she'd be cooking for forty. "They get hungry," he warned. "The Mexicans want beans, and the Chinese want rice, and everyone wants coffee, and no one's allowed to drink. If you see a hand drinking, you must report him to me." They walked in step, the quiet of evening guiding them, the air thick with citrus. A rusty Cooper's hawk circled above, wings calm in glide. She imagined the field mice scampering down holes as the hawk turned and swooped, and a gray squirrel plucked from a live-oak's branch. She looked again and saw the prey already in the hawk's talons, writhing in fear.

By the time they reached the packinghouse, the sky was black. The packinghouse's side door was open, revealing an idle processing hall of conveyor belts and grading equipment and a pile of crate lumber. "In about two weeks," Willis said, "all hell will break loose in there." He said that he liked the ranch this time of year, just before the migrants arrived with their shoulder sacks and their sleeping rolls, and he pointed to a small house nearby with a willow in its yard. "That's the Chinese house. They like to sleep by themselves." The house was empty, but it wouldn't be for long: from all over they'd come, he said, a family named Yuen, brothers and sons and fathers and their great-grandmother, her hair bone-white: "She cooks for them, but sometimes she sleeps through dawn and the Yuen men will come to you for their breakfast."

Willis touched Linda's wrist reassuringly, but his fingers were cold. "You'll get the hang of it," he said. A breeze ran across the triangle of flesh revealed by Linda's blouse, and she sensed that the nights were colder here and that frost could arrive in the dark. "Most of the boys sleep in the bunkhouse down there," Willis went on, "but Bruder and Hearts and Slaymaker sleep in the ranch house, where your kitchen is." He pointed; the ranch house's windows were lit, askew squares yellow and bright in the house's face. Two men were sitting at a table in the yard, their open boots up on a bench and their suspenders hanging from their waists. They were smoking Billy Gang cigarettes, and the glow revealed their eyes as they carefully watched Willis and Linda approach. They acknowledged their employer without rearranging themselves, and Willis said, "Boys, say hello to your new cook."

The two nodded and continued discussing their plans to win a pool-hall tournament. One of the men was tossing and catching a cube of chalk.

"That's Timmy Slaymaker," Willis explained, "and the skinny one, he's Davey Hearts."

Slaymaker flicked his cigarette and tapped a new one out of its pack and held its tip to the flame of the orchard-heater burning warmly at his side. He glanced up at Linda. "What's your name?" When she told him, he said, "I hope you know how to cook."

Davey Hearts rose to his feet and welcomed Linda with a stutter: a narrow nose in a narrow face greeted her, trousers held up by grime, the black of fatigue beneath his eyes. He was young, Linda could see. And then Slaymaker stood too, a hand on the table pushing him up. He grunted, and beneath the layer of muscular fat and the dirt worn into the creases of his hands, Linda could see that he was no more than thirty years old. "You know how to make jellied chicken?"

"Have you seen Bruder?" asked Linda.

"He just came down the hill," said Hearts.

"How's Rosa?" asked Willis.

A voice came from the ranch house: "She'll be fine. A little stomach flu." Then a silhouette appeared in the doorframe, and Bruder stepped into the orchard-heater's light. Except for an oily black beard he appeared almost the same as the last time she'd seen him, as if time had held back, and Linda had to stop herself from running to him.

"I see you made it in time for dinner," he said.

"I'm starving," said Hearts.

"What's on the stove?" asked Slaymaker. "You know how to make livers and bacon?" Linda would learn that Hearts and Slaymaker were a pair, and had traveled up and down the San Joaquin from ranch to ranch, strawberries to almonds to green lettuce to avocados, before settling at the Pasadena. They shared a bunk room in the ranch house and a single towel and a cheap long-toothed hair comb, and when one finished the newspaper he passed it to the other, the stories about water supply, raided pool halls, and the program at the Playhouse circled. Neither man was more boisterous than the other; when one was drunk, so was his mate, and the same was true when sadness descended, or when the brittle winter cough lodged in the lung. If one was more pensive it was Hearts, and Linda would soon learn how his thin face displayed somberness more acutely than Slaymaker's full cheek and jowl. Although both men could be rough—stubbled cheek, orange-bourbon breath, grime capping their fingernails—they were never rough with each other, and what would surprise Linda most about Davey Hearts and Timmy Slaymaker was that with the din of gossip that spun around the ranch, none of it ever involved them. Later, she'd ask Willis about this, and he'd explain that it was because each man tucked a derringer pistol with an ivory grip into his boot, the two guns identical, a pair. Hearts and Slaymaker had each been known to point his pistol in defense of the other. "Once one of them shot a hand charging them with a pitchfork on a vineyard up north," Willis would tell her, "and the man fell dead in the dirt, and till this day neither Hearts nor Slaymaker will say which one of them pulled the trigger."

"Did Willis show you around?" Bruder asked her.

Linda nodded, and then Willis said he'd take her to the kitchen. As they passed Bruder, he stepped out of their way, and the odor of a hard-working man reached Linda and she hesitated but then went on; they would speak later, she thought, when everyone else had gone to bed. And as she entered the ranch house she heard Slaymaker ask Bruder, "She's doing all right? Do you know what it is?" And Linda realized that they were talking about Rosa, not about her.

The kitchen was dark, and Linda could see only Willis's outline, but his breath was rapid in her ear. He fumbled for the light and then a bulb dangling on a wire switched on and revealed a gentle, tentative smile upon his face. "It's wood-burning," he said. He touched the blue-steel Acme range. He seemed to be apologizing, as if she might have expected something more. But Linda hadn't expected anything beyond a stove and a sink and a narrow bed and the minutes in the day she would see Bruder. "Be sure to get the boys to deliver wood," Willis said. "They know it's their job, but they won't do it unless you ask." He turned the faucet. "The water's fine. The ice wagon comes around in the morning. Bruder won't help out with that." And then: "But Hearts and Slaymaker will. They're good men. I told them to look after you."

The shelves were stacked with plates and jelly jars and soup pots and ladles on a hook. There was a sack of flour and a tin of sugar and a half-empty pot of honey. "Where do I get the food?"

"Up at the house. Go to the kitchen, and one of the girls will give you your groceries. If Rosa's feeling better, you'll see her in the morning."

Only now did Linda fully understand that she wasn't cooking for Captain Poore and his sister; no, Linda was nothing more than a ranch-hand cook, and all she would ever see of the mansion was the bolted kitchen door. But she wasn't disappointed, because it meant that her days would be spent near Bruder. It occurred to her she might not see Willis Poore again for a long time.

"How do I get back to the house?" she asked.

He looked at Linda with an odd smirk, as if he was reassessing her. "There's a path up the hill." And then: "You'll let me know if you need a hand? If you can't manage on your own?"

But the hill was steep and she wondered how she'd transport milk and meat for all the hungry men. Was there an extra cart lying around? She wasn't apprehensive; no, instead she simply wondered how best to do her job. The bulb cast a bell of dim light upon them, and his face appeared even younger than before, but out of the evening chill a warmth kindled beneath his flesh and he smiled, and though she couldn't interpret it she felt relieved that Captain Willis Poore had come to fetch her: she suddenly imagined the long trip from the station, the trolley ride and then the long walk, and the loneliness that would have mounted within her if she'd had to enter the ranch on her own.

"Your bed's back here," he said. He opened a door, and together they peered into a narrow room just big enough for a steel cot and a wood chair with a missing arm. The bed was shoved against a window that looked out to the groves, and she could see the outline of the trees and the early moonlight on the leathery fruit; then she made out the dark shape of a coyote crouching in the orchard, its eyes glowing. The animal howled, and Willis looked at her and said, "I hope this'll be all right, Miss Stamp. That you'll be all right."

Linda felt grateful. "I should thank you," she said, and he remained in her small, dusty room for another dark moment, and they said nothing, and the scratch and rustle of the ranchland at night came to them and she finally said, "The boys are hungry, Captain Poore. I should get to supper. Is there anything else I should know?"

He hesitated, and she didn't want him to go just yet, and she wondered if Bruder was noticing the time they were alone together in the house. "I suppose that's it for tonight," he said. "But if you need anything, Miss Stamp . . ."

"I'm sure I'll be okay."

"But if you do, I'm just up the hill." He said something else, and it wouldn't be until later that night that the words would clarify in her ear.

"Thank you, Captain Poore."

A veil of disappointment descended over his face, and this somehow made him appear even more handsome, and she thought of him as the wounded soldier. "This is the last time I'm going to tell you," he said, moving to leave. "You must agree to call me Willis."

She felt the pressure within her chest relent. "All right."

He thanked her. "And from now on I'll call you Linda."

2

THE GIRL HAD BEEN SICK and they were friends and she had asked for Bruder's help and he knew that Rosa didn't have anyone else and he was disappointed in Linda for not understanding. "You promised you would meet me at the station." To her own dismay, Linda had stamped her foot. "If it hadn't been for Willis, I would've been all alone."

Bruder had worked at the Rancho Pasadena for more than four years, and he and Willis Poore had come to an agreement. As foreman, Bruder would oversee the growing, picking, and packing operations uninterrupted, and as long as Willis held up his end of the bargain, Bruder would hold up his. The four years had passed slowly, and when the nights blanketed the little valley and Bruder retired to his room in the ranch house with the swallow's nest in the eave, he would pull his knees up on the bed and read the ancients past midnight, and at the sound of an animal digging or dying outside his window he would look up, and his hardened, lonely face, reflected back in the glass, would startle even him. He had left Linda in order to reunite with her. And after four long years she was at last on the ranch, his ranch.

The orange season ran from November to late March or early April, and during the harvest he was too busy to think of much other than picking a tree clean of fruit, and this had helped his loneliness. But in the long, dry summer months, life at the Pasadena was quiet: Willis and Lolly would spend July and August in Santa Barbara or Balboa, and Bruder would be in charge of the property, and he would have the long blazing days to think about Linda. He liked nothing more than walking the groves and the rose garden in the middle of the night, guided by the moon, imagining all of it as his—and sharing it with her. He wasn't a dreamer, simply a man aware of his future. And he hadn't craved the ranch as a hilltop palace to rule from in isolation; no, he'd imagined it as a place where one day he would bring Linda. But as the years passed, the silence from Condor's Nest had grown louder and louder until one day Bruder had decided he could no longer wait. He wrote to her, and though he knew at first that she would say no, and that he would have to ask her many times, he had been thunderstruck by his great fortune when Edmund had returned to Condor's Nest. Many years later, Linda would wonder if Bruder had had something to do with Edmund's return to the farm, but he did not: it was nothing more mysterious than fate's turning, clicking dial. And if there was a difference between Linda and Bruder, it was this: he believed in the cruel inevitability of fate; and she believed, even now, that the future was hers to invent.

Bruder recognized his place at the Rancho Pasadena, and knew that his voice held as much authority there as Willis's. Rarely did he have to demonstrate this—the others sensed it and respected it. A few, mostly the gossips, didn't like Bruder because he said little beyond his daily recitation of orders; but most were happy to work for him, because if a job was done properly, he left them alone. He made sure that salaries were paid on time and that meals were hot and plentiful. He made sure that thieves went punished and liars were sent away.

The maids in the mansion liked to whisper about Bruder, and he was aware of this. The head maid, a girl by the name of Rosa whose mother had worked at the Pasadena, and died there too, was smart and efficient and could fold two days of work into one, and she and Bruder had become friends. At night they'd sit on a hillside lookout and smoke and talk about their days. Bruder told Rosa about Linda, but Rosa was less open, and perhaps it was her reserve that caused Bruder's own instinctive reticence to fall away. She had encouraged him to invite Linda to the ranch, and promised to look after her, and together in the streaking dusk of late summer, their faces still warm from the day's sun, they had made a plan to bring Linda to the ranch. "She'll come and you'll be together," Rosa had assured him, and her clear-sighted optimism ate at Bruder's hardness, and he posted the first card, affixing the stamps with a summer-dry tongue.

He was thinking of this on Linda's first night at the ranch, as he watched her through the window. She moved expertly around the kitchen, and the restlessness that he had recalled in her, and that she had briefly demonstrated with her stamping foot, was no longer there. Bruder saw a serene young woman whose heart had finally quieted from its adolescent pant. He had been right to ask her to the ranch, and he didn't worry for her, nor for the two of them, and he relaxed with what he thought of as a western sense of relief: that all would work out over time, that things were meant to be.

He had given her a couple of cabbages and several carrots and half a peach pie, and in the cupboard Linda had found a case of canned beef, and with these she prepared her first supper at the Rancho Pasadena. The boys liked to eat outside, holding their hands to the orchard-heater and wrapping themselves in horsehair blankets. They ate their beef and cabbage, and Hearts declared Linda superior to last season's cook, a gentle-faced man who left town after trouble with one of the packing girls. Slaymaker pulled a flask from his pocket and pushed it to his lips and then handed it to Hearts. He offered it to Linda, too, but she declined, and though she knew that she was supposed to report the men, she also already knew that she would never do it. Hearts and Slaymaker laughed at nothing in particular, and Slaymaker said that he hoped Linda wasn't like Licorice Lolly. "I'll bet my last dollar she's a spy for the city council, ready to report the first drop of bourbon on her ranch." Bruder insisted that Lolly Poore was no spy, but Slaymaker said he wasn't so sure, and he pretended his tin plate was a fan and pursed his lips and giggled girlishly, saying in falsetto, "Volstead or death, that's our motto around here, Mr. Slaymaker! You should try licorice, not liquor, Mr. Slaymaker!"

"If she weren't so silly," said Hearts, "some man would come along and marry her and take her away from us."

"She's pretty enough to get married," said Slaymaker. "And God knows she's rich enough. But the trouble with Lolly is she's in love with her brother. It's as plain as a story in the paper."

"What do you think of her?" Linda asked Bruder.

"I don't think of her very much."

"Maybe you should ask what she thinks of Bruder," said Slaymaker.

Bruder threw a log into the fire pit and said that he didn't have much to do with Lolly. "I usually talk to Willis." Slaymaker and Hearts laughed, but Linda would learn that each of them laughed about almost anything, except when a cruel word was said about the other.

"You two know each other from before?" Slaymaker asked, a finger pointing to Bruder and Linda, back and forth. This surprised Linda, for she had assumed that every day since Bruder had left he'd been talking about Condor's Nest; she had imagined her own myth passing from his lips, embellished but true. Why had she thought this? She didn't know, except for the simple fact that every day since his departure she had retold herself the story of the boy who had arrived with Dieter from the war.

"I knew her father first."

"War buddies?"

Bruder's chin cocked as he thought about this and other things, too many for Linda to guess. He was carving a little whale from a bar of soap, and the thin, long shavings flew into a pile at his feet. "We met in the war."

"Ah, yes. Captain Poore's famous Saint-Mihiel."

"I took it in the thigh in a communication trench at Beaumont-Hamel," said Slaymaker. "Missed my soldier by a quarter of an inch."

"Half an inch," said Hearts.

Linda rolled her hands in her lap. She could feel the blood in her cheeks, and she was looking away from the orchard-heater hoping the others couldn't detect that she felt out of place. She was determined to fit in; she had always hated it when down at the gutting house the fishermen had teased her with talk of poles and catch and she had wanted to be able to laugh it off but somehow she couldn't; once, their talk had filled her with such a rage that she had hurled a ten-pound chicken halibut at a boatman, thumping it against his breast. Sometimes the fury would take hold of her and there'd be nothing she could do. "You're ugly when you're like that," Edmund had said years ago. But Pasadena was a new town where no one but Bruder knew her and she could shed the parts of her past that didn't sit well with her idea of herself. Once she'd overheard a lobsterman say of another man's wife, "She's a tough one, that señora," and Linda had deciphered the compliment in the statement and hoped that one day someone would say the same about her. Already she knew that no one would ever admire her for her delicately crossed ankles or her straight silky hair. No, she wanted to be a woman whom men stood back from and watched with awe. Like Valencia had been. Oh! the night when the guard drops and everything changes! Oh, the night.

Linda asked how long Willis had been running the rancho. About five years, Slaymaker said; maybe less, added Hearts. Hearts was the quiet one, and his shyness suggested that he was the one in the pair who remembered facts more firmly. His ears stuck out from the side of his head like handles on an urn. He squinted when he looked at her, and when she asked if there was something wrong he said that he'd lost his glasses last season and was sure to have enough money for a new pair by the end of harvest. He and Slaymaker had been at the Pasadena since 1919, watching it through the idle months when the blossoms bulged and the whorl of leaves folded inward, forming the early tight knot of fruit. The two of them were Bruder's deputies in leading the picking teams who arrived each fall, and were responsible for keeping track of each tree's productivity. During the summer months, Hearts and Slaymaker grew cover crops of vetch or clover down the grove's alleys—the middles, they called them—plowing them under in September to add humus and nitrogen to the soil.

"But that's not all we do around here," said Slaymaker.

"Oh no," said Hearts. "There's a whole lot more."

"We work every day but Christmas and New Year's."

"We never work New Year's," said Hearts. "Every year, Slay and I enter the chariot races. I think this year's going to be our lucky year and we'll take home the hundred bucks and the wreath of yellow roses."

Linda asked Bruder if he had ever entered the chariot races, and he said that Willis wouldn't lend him a horse.

"That's not the reason," said Slaymaker.

"It's not the reason at all," added Hearts. "It's because Miss Lolly says it's too dangerous and she won't let her foreman risk his life."

Bruder turned his shark knife in his palm, the heater's flames catching the blade, and he hurled the knife across the table and over Hearts's head into the trunk of the pepper tree. "Stop telling lies, boys," he said softly, and he walked off into the dark grove. He didn't want anyone revealing him to Linda; he would do it in his own careful way. The story of the ranch and his life there was his, and he would tell Linda over time. As intelligent as he was, Bruder didn't realize that the stories inevitably would come from all mouths, not only his, and that any myth he hoped to create would be embellished and retold by more eager tongues.

By the time Slaymaker and Hearts went to bed, Linda had cleared the table and washed the dishes and found the oats and the eggs and the coffee for breakfast. She returned to the yard, where Bruder sat with his feet on an orange crate. A low blue flame burned in the heater, and he was motionless, looking heavenward. She didn't know if he saw her standing there in the doorframe, but without turning he said, "Ever see the Little Dog?" His finger led her eye to three stars. "It's Orion's other hound."

"Where'd you learn that?"

He pulled a chair close and offered it to her. "The constellations? I guess I learned about them at our depot in the beech-wood forest."

"Were you with Papa?"

"Not until the very end. But I was with Willis, and he and I would lie on the ground on the late-summer nights and stare up at the black sky and we wouldn't talk about much except the stars."

"You were with Captain Poore?" Bruder said nothing, and Linda said, "It must have been lonely."

"No more lonely than everything else."

She didn't believe him; or, rather, she wouldn't allow herself to believe him. His letters had been a call to soothe an isolated heart. She had to believe this. What else did she have? "Captain Poore must've been a brave soldier."

Bruder shrugged. "You should ask him yourself for the real story."

"Why don't *you* tell me?"

"When we got to France, he didn't know much about fixing an ignition's trembler coils, and he barely knew how to dig a hole. He could shoot all right, but his head was small and his helmet kept slipping off and he was too vain to report that the smallest regulation helmet was too big for him. The only good thing about him were the crates of oranges that would arrive from the patriotic committee of Pasadena's Board of Trade. He loved to hand them out to the other boys, and they were so desperate for fruit that they'd shower Willis with cigarettes and spare socks and iron rations in exchange, anything for an extra orange. One boy swapped six oranges for Willis's spot on a raid into a no-man's-land to fetch a broken-down Mark IV tank. And poor Willis watched the boy blow up before his very eyes. In fact, the boy's helmet blew all the way back to our trench, and it ended up fitting Willis better than anything else. He was upset about that, and though some people say his skin is thick, it's really very thin. But he wore the helmet, and over time he was given his chance to show his bravery. I'm sure he'll tell you about it one day."

"He already has," said Linda.

Stars crowded the sky, the Milky Way a stain of light, and the full, cinereous moon exposed itself like the mouth of a lit passageway. A breeze rustled the pepper tree and prodded the orange leaves, and every now and then a scamper arose in the grove, dirt and leaves and dead stalks of clover kicked in chase. The mellow *coo-coo* of the burrowing owl crossed the small valley. Above them on the hill the white mansion gleamed, gold light pouring from its windows, and if Linda wasn't mistaken, jazz was thin on the breeze: probably the aluminum whine of a disc graphophone.

"Most nights they have a quartet playing on the terrace," Bruder said when he noticed her foot tapping. "Sometimes eight players, and dancing beneath paper lanterns. For no occasion at all. Simply to put an end to the day." The mansion's world was too unfamiliar for any sort of envy to rise in her throat just then. She knew nothing of the marble busts of Roman gods and British naval officers, of the blue-and-yellow Savonnerie carpets and the faded Beauvais wall tapestries, of the aviaries stocked with blue-crested Victorian pigeons and Brazilian parrots taught to say *Captain Willis Poore, Captain Willis Poore,* of the lawn-croquet set with the balls crafted of ivory, the wickets of bent sterling, the ebony mallets. In the mansion lived Willis and Lolly, but Linda knew nothing yet of the pencil-mustached French cook or the puttering Scot valet; of the morning-coated secretary, Mr. Coren, whom Willis would eventually fire because of Mr. Coren's annoying insistence on punctuality and penmanship; of the chambermaids pinned in wool and lace, a tiny-ankled crew led by Rosa; of the Japanese gardeners pruning the acres of lawn with hand shears and tending the thousand rosebushes and the camellia trees: the two-hundred-stamened Snow, the anemone-shaped Splendor, the *C. japonica* 'Willis Fishe Poore.'

The music they heard drifting down the hill was in fact a burl-walnut piano rolled onto the terrace accompanied by a trumpet, a pair of bongos, a wet-reed clarinet, and a singer in sherry-colored velvet— a common entertainment for the Rancho Pasadena, where guests gathered two or three nights a week, the bare shoulders and throats of the women protected by fox wraps and pearls. Societies and clubs made up of friends of Captain Willis and Miss Lolly Poore, clusters of citizens with birthright and acreage in common, often gathered on the terrace, with its view toward Los Angeles. They'd lean against the balustrade and tap their cigarette ashes down the kindling hill and pretend that the fizz in their grapefruit juice came from soda water and not from the crates of Oregon champagne hidden in the cellar behind a trick door. More than a couple of these clubs Willis's father had chaired: the Valley Hunt Club, the Shakespeare Club, the Twilight Club, the 100 Per-centers, this one made up exclusively of men descended directly from Pasadena's one hundred original settlers. Willis knew that one day he too would keep a sharp eye over the membership lists. What was the motto the 100 Percenters toasted to? "City Beautiful, for one and for all."

But on her first night at the Rancho Pasadena, Linda knew nothing yet of this world. Up on the hill the music stopped, and the night crackle and call of the ranchland grew louder, and Bruder said, "Sounds like they're sending everyone home."

"Do you ever join them?"

"He asks me up."

"Do you go?"

"When I feel like it."

"Why did you want me to come here?"

"We need a cook. The boys get hungry." He paused. Should he say more? "Same for me."

"You could've hired anyone."

"You're good enough in the kitchen."

Again, Linda tried to stem her disappointment; but hadn't his letters promised more? Why did he insist upon withholding? And why did she? On the train she had told herself to expect nothing: even before seeing it she had envisioned the narrow room on the other side of the stove wall; and a long line of famished pickers, empty plates and tin cups in their grubby hands; and the pots nearly big enough to curl up in where the Burbank potatoes, a hundred at a time, would boil. That's all she had expected of the job on the ranch, and yet somehow a small pol-ished stone of hope had sat atop her heart. What did she hope for? She couldn't say, that first night; but the cool breeze and the creamy stars and the fruitwood perfume and Bruder's face haloed by the rim of his hat left Linda anxious for a future other than the unremarkable one un-furling before her. What had Willis said before he left her in her room?

Hadn't he said, *I want you to be happy here. You'll tell me if there's anything I can do to make you happy?* She had nodded and touched the coral pendant. The long day had made her think of her mother climbing the bluff from the ocean, surrendering her former self. Linda thought of the nights, after Edmund and then Bruder had left her alone with Dieter, when she had swum in the ocean: breaststroking out to sea as Condor's Nest fell away, a mile out to ocean, maybe farther, Linda indistinguishable from any other fur-coated creature of the sea: an elephant-seal hunter would have spear-shot her from his prow. But the years had passed and Linda had taught herself to inter the longing, and on that first night in Pasadena she cleaned up the kitchen and dried the final plate—and Bruder closed the door to his room, eyeing her through the narrowing crack—and after the mansion fell dark and the ranch house quiet, Linda went to bed alone.

3

SHE WOKE BEFORE DAWN. The ranch was still and dark and the iron springs groaned as she pulled herself from bed. In the chest of drawers she found a yard of cheap Zion lace. Later, she would sew a curtain for her window and, if there was enough left over, a second, for the window at the kitchen sink. But at this hour the black of early morning poured through the paned glass, comforting her. The wind had died and the orange trees were large huddled masses, shouldering one another—kneeling beasts, they looked like before dawn—and there was a glimpse of the house on the hill. She had been tired and dreamed of nothing, and she woke with a clarity of mind that reminded her of the days—they now seemed so long ago—when she rose with the coydogs at Condor's Nest and sank hook and worm into the gray-dawn waves. Edmund had asked her to write every night before going to sleep, and now she was already behind on her promise. The loneliness he had confessed had upset Linda, leaving her uncertain as to what he wanted from her. She didn't know how to respond to his desperation; or to the awkward way he held Palomar on his knee; or to how, at the very end, he had ignored ailing Carlotta, who died in the Vulture House bed, her hair fanned around her as if she were floating in a brook. He had sobbed when Linda departed, the choke simmering in his throat. "Go, go," he had said. "If you must." He walked her to the road, struggling with her bag, leaving Palomar crying in the sun-killed yard.

From her window, Linda saw something stir among the trees, a moving silhouette, and as dawn began to streak the sky the sight of Bruder took shape: his arms spread and gripping the handles of a pushcart, trundling it down a middle and stooping to clear the oranges dropped from the branch. She cracked the window and held her breath and heard his boots on the hard soil. There'd been talk at the table last night of when the first rain would come, before or after Thanksgiving; Slaymaker and Hearts had gone back and forth and then Bruder had said, "It'll be early this year. No later than the first of November." He had looked at Linda and thought, If you trust me, you'll see that I am right.

Later in the morning, after the coffee and the oatmeal and a general inspection of the pantry and the oilcloth nailed to the kitchen counter, Linda set out up the hill. The sun was quickly wiping up the glossy dew, and the sycamore and oak offered speckled shade, but much of the road stretched blankly beneath the hard daylight. She came across a rattler exposing its white belly to the morning. Linda threw a rock and it landed squarely on the snake's head, and with one quick flick of its baby-rattle tail the snake died. She couldn't be certain how many rattlers she'd killed over the years, dozens and dozens, and with her pocketknife she neatly removed the rattle and wrapped it in a handkerchief. There'd been a time when she and Edmund would ceremoniously present each other with their bagged rattles, the tips withered and crisp, and each would sleep with them beneath the bed.

At the top of the hill, Linda came upon a wire fence with redwood posts covered in pink-and-white Cherokee roses. It separated the ranch's scrubby hillside from a formal shade garden of Satsuki azalea and pineapple-fruit cycad and spotted-leaf calla. The road continued, the ruts smoothed and the rocks cleared, until it passed a tiered circular fountain with four spewing dolphins. Linda leaned over its rim to rinse the snake blood from her hands. The fountain sat at the head of a long lawn, walled on both sides by camellias and barrel-shaped holly bushes and a colonnade of towering fan palms. Italian stone figures—warriors in skirt and shield, cherubs at the foot of bare-breasted virgins—stood on pedestals along both sides of the greensward. The lawn led to the rose garden, a graded field of bushes flower-heavy in autumn, swollen blossoms of butter yellow and fish-gill pink and summer-sky white and night purple: forty beds separated by path, bordered by pergola, alive with the entire history of the rose. At the time she knew nothing about the flower, and how could Linda have guessed on that first morning at the Rancho Pasadena that she would come to learn the name of each species and cultivar, their bud size and bloom life: the yellow Sun Flair, the pinkish-red Altissimo climbing the pergola's latticework, the pink-and-white summer Damask, the hybrid teas grafted together in the humidity of the glasshouse under the gloved care of Nitobe-san. Linda wandered along the edge of the garden in the direction of where she guessed the kitchen door might be, but only in the shadow of the house itself did she realize that there wasn't a kitchen door as she might think of one, that the stove's smoke and flame most likely billowed and burned deep within, at the house's pit.

Through a window, Linda saw a room that must have been Willis's library. Perhaps he was in there at the partner's desk or up on the stepladder with its ostrich-leather rail, but instead Linda saw the girl she'd seen in the upstairs window on a stool lifting the lid of a ceramic urn, feather duster poised. She was a few feet from Linda on the other side of the glass, and her hair was springing from her cap, and she was whistling *O Sweet-a-Lee, O Sweet-a-Lee,* and she was, Linda noted, quick with her work. A mirror above the mantel offered the girl a picture of herself, and she took the time to inspect the reflection, turning to see front and back and the way the apron fell across her lap. Linda thought about rapping the window and asking the way to the kitchen, but she feared she might startle the girl, who soon enough climbed off the stool and departed the library. Someone was calling, *Rosa! Rosa!*

Around the corner Linda found the terrace, and she was on the steps before she realized that there were people there. She stopped, her hand on the rail, and wondered if she should turn around, but she didn't. Willis was sitting at a table littered with the remains of breakfast, and standing next to him was a young woman, her spine alert and erect, holding several pages before her. His tie matched the soft peach color of the woman's petal-sleeved dress, and the two looked alike. The loose sleeves and the petunia-cut hem of the woman's dress emphasized her boniness and her zinc-pale flesh—her face was so white that Linda wondered if she ever got out onto the land. A rope of pearls hung heavily to her waist, and it looked as if her head might spring back were she to remove the necklace.

It was clear to Linda that this was Lolly Poore, and she was reciting something. Neither she nor Willis saw Linda: he nursed his coffee and scanned the *Star-News,* and Lolly shuffled the papers and said, "Willis, tell me what you think of this one. Maybe it's good enough."

"What's it called?"

" 'Pasadena, the Bride.' "

"Who wrote it?"

"Mrs. Elizabeth Grinnel. She also wrote that not-so-bad sonnet 'Our Feathered Friends,' the one you said you liked somewhat." Lolly arranged herself against the balustrade and the backdrop of the valley. "Willis, are you listening?"

He murmured that he was.

Again: " 'Pasadena, the Bride.' "

> She is the bride, Sierra's fairest daughter,
> The hoary-headed East has won her hand;
> His cherished household jewels he has brought her,
> And turned his back upon his native land.

"Please stop. It's awful."

"I suppose it is, isn't it? But what am I going to do?"

"Stop reading me bad poetry."

Lolly sank into her chair and riffled the pages, her face distressed by everything she read. "What about this one: it's called 'Pasadena, Atlantis Ye Shan't Be.' "

"You read that one yesterday."

"It was terrible, wasn't it?"

"Excruciating."

"Why do only bad poets enter poetry contests?" She folded her arms and sighed.

"Why did my sister agree to be the judge?" The newspaper hid his face and Lolly turned in her chair, leaning over the back, and it was then that she saw Linda. "Who's that?"

Willis folded back the newspaper and smiled and called Linda over. "Lolly, dear. That's Linda Stamp. She's the new cook down at the ranch house."

Lolly didn't stir.

"Lolly, remember I told you about her? She's a friend of Bruder's."

Linda apologized for disturbing them. She explained that she was looking for the kitchen, and an unfamiliar deference took over, one that felt as uncomfortable as an outgrown dress. It quieted Linda, and again the vastness of the Rancho Pasadena came into focus: the balustrade running the length of the terrace, and the valley beyond, and the far hills, gold in October. Did the Poores own all of it? The terrace had the feeling of a broad stage with a secret world hidden behind it in the house. Clipped, round pillars of brush cherry grew tall in planters, and a giant coral tree cast a webbed shadow over the breakfast table. The terrace faced south down the hill, and she saw that the orange grove covered only a portion of the valley; beyond it ran the wash of an arroyo, a trickle of white rock and sand frozen in arid gleam. The Pacific Electric's tracks glinted in a long arc parallel to the dry river. The rest of the land was open scrub, live-oaks canopied on a field of yellow grass and the beige blur of sycamores knotted in the foothills. One or two houses dotted the far hills, plank-cottage stations for the former cattlers and the secret vintners who tended five acres of grape hidden by a ring of walnut trees. To the west were more hills, their morning faces bright with needly chamise and the blue-blossomed deerweed. The tracks ran through a pass in the western hills, and beyond them Linda saw the flicker of city, the cast iron and brick and stucco of Los Angeles that she had seen from the train's window. From this distance it was no more distinct than a phantasm, shimmering and shapeless and alive, teeming with unknowable life; that was how she had felt upon pulling into Union Station, frightened not by the dangers shadowing a concrete alley or by the red mustache of a confidence man but by the palpable prospect of losing herself to the sprawl. A great relief had come to Linda as the Pacific Electric left Los Angeles and the canyons of the San Gabriel Valley opened before her. Pasadena was a city, but it remained planted amid the wilderness, and the view from the hilltop now reassured her—the river dead in autumn, the neat lanes of the grove, the great, green mass of the coral tree growing at the terrace's corner. And then in the west, beyond the wink of Los Angeles, something flashed and burned, a flat sheet of blue-gray, and she said, "Is that the ocean? Can you really see it from here?"

"On the clearest day you can see Catalina," said Willis, whose tonicked hair reflected the dull red of the tiles. He said that he hoped she'd slept all right. Lolly coughed delicately and said, "The ranch house isn't so bad." She was a year or so older than Linda, and maintained a clear ceramic face of youth; her cheek was decorated sparingly with brush and rouge, with an imperceptible amount of powder on the hood of her eye; Linda noted it, the powder glittery in the sun, but she didn't feel plain in comparison. No, Linda merely wondered what it was like to sit

at a dressing table with a view of the valley and apply the makeup with
the careful help of a chambermaid and then descend the stairs to meet
Willis on the terrace. Linda wasn't envious but she wondered, as any
girl might wonder, and she asked Lolly about the poetry contest and
this perked up Lolly as she exclaimed fiercely, "The first-prize winner
will be printed on the front page of the *Star-News* on New Year's Day.
And in the Tournament's brochure. We've had hundreds of entries. All
I can hope is that our Browning will turn up."

Then Rosa arrived, and Linda got the sense that Rosa already knew
who she was. Rosa collected the plates and never took her eyes off
Linda, who worried that she had said something wrong, or was in fact
in the wrong place. It occurred to her that the terrace might be off-
limits to her, and never before had Linda felt so out of place. She was
angry that Bruder hadn't escorted her up the hill that first morning, and
she planned to tell him that he should have shown her the way to the
kitchen, and the longer Linda stood there the more lost she felt, and
then Willis said, "You're looking for the kitchen? Let me show you the
way."

In the pantry, Rosa asked Linda what she needed from the larder. Then
she said, her voice low, "Be careful around them."

"Around Willis and Lolly?"

"Keep your eyes open."

The pantry was narrow, with glass-door cabinets holding groceries
and copper-bottomed pots. Every morning, Rosa inventoried the stores
with a checklist and a red pencil and then called Chaffee's with an
order: for, say, a case of PictSweet peas, or a half dozen cans of M.J.B.
coffee, or the bricks of Sea Rose codfish that Willis liked to eat at midnight, after the musicians went home. Rosa was a beautiful girl with
beautiful eyes and a body hard from mansion chores and breaststroking
naked in the swimming pool when the others slept. Her lips were full
and poutish and gave her a pretty, dimwitted look—which was altogether inaccurate. She was eighteen and in charge of a troop of five
maids, and she knew, without rage or brooding, that had she received a
proper education she would have gone on to become a famous lady
mathematician. She held numbers in her head easily and perpetually
and multiplied instantly, as if there were a button and she knew where

to push it, and she could order the groceries and tally the prices without the assistance of an abacus or scratch pad. She helped Bruder predict the orange yields, and she helped determine the number of pickers the ranch would need for the season, and the number of field crates. Lolly relied on Rosa's numerical skills for calculating the tonnage of manure required for her rose garden, and Willis relied on it when re-estimating the value of his land.

Rosa's mother had been one of the late Mrs. Poore's maids, and one day as a four-year-old, Rosa fell down the dumbwaiter and lay unconscious in the shaft for a long summer's day. Everyone at the Rancho Pasadena, including young Willis, believed that the girl would be damaged in the head, but when the concussion and the goose-egg bump subsided, Rosa continued on her way to superior intelligence. But her mother needed her help around the mansion, and after several, but not enough, years at the Titleyville School, Rosa began working for her mother six days a week. She polished and hemmed and swabbed and dusted and swept until a fever overtook her mother and a colony of weepy lesions ringed her torso, and then Rosa's mother up and died, mop in hand.

"I've been here my whole life," Rosa told Linda in the pantry. "I know them better than they know themselves."

"Then what's she like?"

"Who, Lolly? She isn't very kind."

The two young women fell quiet, and they looked at each other, and what either knew of the other she had learned from Bruder. Then Linda asked: "What about Captain Poore?"

"I can't stand him. It's a long story. One day, you'll see." And then, "No, I take that back. I hope you never see." Rosa was loading a box with food for the ranch house: a sack of H.O. oats, a pound of Purity Oleoa, a box of Not-a-Seed raisins, three pounds of boiling beef. "I was going to give you a couple of cans of tomato juice, but they drank them all last night."

"Did they have a party?"

"Another silly Poverty Party."

Linda asked what that was, and Rosa pursed her mouth, as if she was wondering whether it was worth explaining. "For a good laugh, they ask their friends to show up dressed like paupers," said Rosa. "The men arrive in filthy suits like bums, and the women turn up as if they're working the street. It's their idea of fun." Rosa folded back the news-paper and showed Linda the morning's society page:

POVERTY PARTY AT THE RANCHO PASADENA
By Chatty Cherry

Captain Willis Poore and his sister Miss Lolly Poore hosted one of their much-loved Poverty Parties at their orange-ranch home in West Pasadena last night. A band of 4 Negroes played on the terrace and a Mexican girl by the name of Anna Ramirez serenaded in bare-foot and authentic twirling peasant dress. The party was in honor of Miss Connie Muffitt's 22nd birthday. Prizes for the most creative "poverty" costumes were awarded to Mr. and Mrs. W. O. Walker, who dressed as a pair of shoeless orphans, gruel-bowls looped to their belts. Among those in attendance were Mr. and Mrs. Richard Murphy, in railroad hobo get-ups, Mr. and Mrs. Charles New-hall, costumed like sub-continent beggars, Mr. and Mrs. Walter White, chic in his-and-hers maid and butler uniforms, the Misses Felt, dressed as urchins, Miss Jett, carrying a migrant farm-worker's picking sack, and Harry Brooks, who arrived with coal smudged on his face. Captain Poore wore torn trousers with scallions in his pocket and introduced himself as a bankrupt onion farmer. The party raised more than $1000 for Mrs. Webb's Home for Indigent and Orphaned Girls.

"Captain Poore can't sit still," said Rosa. "Like a little boy who can't stay put in his chair. He has people over almost every night, and they play pool and shoot their pistols at the stars. Sometimes Willis stays up all night."

As she said this, a deep smear of red appeared in Rosa's cheek, and Linda instantly realized—the way you realize the sky is clear or the flower is pink—that she shouldn't trust Rosa. She was the reason Bru-der hadn't met Linda at the station. Rosa lay her hand upon Linda's arm, and her fingers were rough-tipped and a little sticky, and Linda could see in Rosa's blown-glass face that she resented her arrival at the ranch—nothing Rosa said could be believed, Linda warned herself. And just as Rosa handed Linda the box of groceries, Lolly appeared in the pantry.

She ran her finger up and down the doorframe, as if to say, Don't mind me. "I've called the butcher and ordered a box of porterhouses," she said. "His wagon will deliver them in the afternoon to the ranch house. Mr. Hearts likes his with onions, and Mr. Slaymaker likes his gray as a goose, and Mr. Bruder likes his rare with blood. Willis scolded me for not ordering one for you, Linda, so I called back and ordered you the biggest one of all."

Then Lolly left, and Linda felt even more certain that everything Rosa had said was a little less than true.

Lolly was a poetess. Twice the Tournament of Roses had printed her sonnets in its annual. Two poems, each of two stanzas, "Mt. Lowe the Lovely" and "Roses in Arcady," and Lolly took as much pride in her work appearing within the Tournament's brochure as she did when the early rosebuds, as tight as the skin on a grape, took shape in the trembling March wind. Once *The Century* awarded her second prize in an ode contest, an event that occasioned the *Star-News* to headline an article LOCAL POETESS PUTS PASADENA ON THE LITERARY MAP. When meeting someone for the first time, Lolly had a habit of declaring herself frail, patting her temples and alluding to a childhood infirmity. But other than a fashionable boniness and a pile of curls susceptible to the Santa Anas, there was nothing feeble in Lolly—except her odd insistence that she was still a child. "Part of her doesn't want to grow up," said Rosa. Lolly had yet to retire her collection of hair bows, more than a hundred stored and displayed in a special closet with a wooden rack Bruder had crafted. A few years back, she had contemplated college and even bought herself a floor-length beaver; but then she learned that the pretty Northampton snowdrifts could top ten feet and remain in place until early May and that at least once each winter a girl would disappear in them, frozen and lost until the thaw. "I wouldn't survive," Lolly had said, throwing out the college pamphlets but keeping the beaver, wrapping it in layers of scarlet tissue paper during the summer and wearing it on the winter nights that promised frost.

Lolly was ten months younger than Willis, and when they were little some people confused them for twins, especially when he wore his hair long. "Even now he anxiously corrects anyone who thinks they're a pair," said Rosa. He shared his sister's smallness, but in his case it was beautiful, and nearly a year in a captain's uniform had roughed up his complexion to a respectable maturity. "One of his greatest daily concerns is keeping his hair in place," said Rosa, explaining that the Eau De Quinine hair tonic wasn't always successful against his resilient crop of bangs. He knew that his floppy hair, like puppy ears, added to his image of youth, and so he never left the ranch without his comb and a tin of pomade. He owned a pocket mirror framed handsomely in teakwood, and although he didn't carry it with him all the time, he carried it more often than not. This was another habit he shared with his sister, and a second reason others considered them of the same litter.

Lolly knew what power she possessed over her brother, and that a tilted chin and a chest lifted in mid-sigh could get him to agree to any-thing. Because she was undernourished, her breasts were small, and she hid them under a corset that flattened them against her ribs, as if it were her intent to conceal her body's every curve. If one of the maids were to accidentally see the dark rosy circles of her nipples, Lolly would fling herself atop her canopied bed as if she had been violated. She was a woman obsessed by preservation, not of her home or her land or her city or even her happiness, but of her childhood's odorless, bloodless flesh. She saw this pursuit as her greatest virtue, and because she had achieved it with near success, she perceived herself as too innocent to be flawed.

Willis, on the other hand, was just mature enough to recognize a few of his shortcomings, and one of those was his weak skill, and limited in-terest, in ranching. And this was why he needed Bruder. At least that was how Rosa explained it to Linda. "Not that he doesn't enjoy the life of an orange heir." Landholdings vast and wired off, fence posts bent from golden bobcats rubbing their backs against them. Willis kept horses down at the ranch house, and even now, with pavement creep-ing closer to the Pasadena's perimeter, each week he rode once or twice into his land, along the bottom spine of the dry arroyo, in the purple cleave of a foothill canyon, shading his horse beneath a live-oak older than California itself and vital with the delicate *seee, seee* of a waxwing. Yet despite the occasional pleasure of the rusty buckwheat catching in his cuff, if it were up to Willis he'd never clip another orange. His father had had hair as bright as a tangerine, and in his lifetime he'd picked and packed a hundred million oranges, he estimated with admirable exag-geration. When Willis was five, his father had given him his first bam-boo ladder and a pair of picking gloves and a shiner pole, and from that day on, Willis perpetually hunted an excuse to avoid the harvest. Noth-

ing had really worked until the war rumbled along. After the eleven
months in France he spent a semester at Princeton, admitted as a war
hero. More than once he'd passed out in a pile of elm leaves on Nassau
Street, his tongue pickled by the best bathtub gin in New Jersey. He
hadn't minded the cold descending autumn; he battled it in a coyote
coat that dragged along the campus paths, and he told his prissy east-
erner friends about shooting lynx from his bedroom window and wrestling grizzlies. He promised a couple of sophomores to bag them
green-eyed cougars over the Christmas break. These were boys raised
in woolen-felt topcoats trimmed with burgundy velvet, sons of stock-
brokers and the presidents of rubber-belt manufacturers, young men
who felt connected to the wild by donning a penguin-skin top hat.
Drunk in a secret paneled room deep within a Gothic, gargoyled hall,
Willis would often ask the eastern boys how they could even be sure
they were *alive*? They promised to take Willis to New York, to a hotel
near the Bowery called the Baby Bijoux, where the bonnetless girls
would prove they were all *much more* than alive. "But then there was a
shipwreck that lost a quarter of the harvest," Rosa explained. "No one
knew why Willis had put his oranges on a boat. Lolly made him come
home to oversee the property. I helped her write the telegram. 'Ranch
in trouble. Your return expected immediately.' She paid Western Union
with trembling hand."

And then Rosa revealed something, coyly tossing it out as if she
knew how it would ring against Linda's heart: "That's when he asked
Bruder to come up to the ranch."

"But why Bruder?"

"Because of what happened in France."

"What happened in France?"

"You don't know?" And then, with a careful face: "You *don't* know,
do you? So many secrets slip out of this house, I forget which ones
the roof has held tight. It's nothing." And Rosa sent Linda down the
hill with the box of groceries, the carton heavy and awkward and the
sunlight in her eyes. Linda thought of the oranges on the beach and
the pregnant girl in the mouth of the cave and she knew that Willis
couldn't be the man Rosa was describing, and just then Linda decided
not to believe anything Rosa had said, nothing at all.

And when Willis caught up with Linda on the road he took the box
from her and said, "I hope you know enough never to listen to her." He

said that Rosa was a hardworking girl: "Too good to fire—no, I'd never do that. Her mother was like a mother to me. I'd never think of throwing her out. But trust me when I tell you that Rosa . . ." And Willis hesitated until his eyes had caught and secured Linda's stare. ". . . is a girl made up of lies."

4

BRUDER WAS RIGHT, and by the first of November rain arrived, the sky low and turning like the underside of the ocean, and a two-day downpour softened and loosened the hill road into a muddy chute. The irrigation ditches ran with dirty water, yellow foam quivering, and the kitchen roof leaked and the window by Linda's bed swelled in its case. One morning while returning from the house with the groceries Linda slipped, the box of food sliding out of her hands and over the edge of the road, a pot roast ("For *you*!" Lolly had said) lost to the coyotes. Then Bruder met her on the road and opened an umbrella over her. The mud had splattered her skirt like bloodstains and her hair lay wet and flat round her face. He found her beautiful like this—strong, but quiet; and during the moments when Linda needed him most, Bruder could imagine a future that held them together in its palm. "You'll need better boots," he said. In the ranch house he gave her a box from the Pasadena Grocery & Department Store, and inside, beneath leaves of lettuce-colored tissue, were two red rubber boots lined with checked cloth. He knelt and dried her feet and then helped her put them on. He had seen them in the window and thought of Linda, and now, as he told her this, she felt a stir within. She tested the boots down the long narrow hall in the ranch house, her hands on her hips. He leaned in the doorframe and watched, happy that she liked the gift, and Linda said that she would wear them through the season, and because Bruder was guileless and had nothing to hide—or so he told himself—he cheerfully said, "I bought Rosa a pair, too."

"Rosa?"

Bruder failed to see the hardening pique in Linda's eye; he missed the jealousy curling her fists. She said that she was busy and had to return to the kitchen. She said good-bye efficiently, and again Bruder didn't correctly read her emotions, and he left Linda for the packing-house content—as much as a young man like Bruder is ever content— that he had brought simple joy to two girls, and he pondered the similarities between Linda and Rosa and he came up with more than a few.

Why did Bruder misunderstand Linda so completely? It was a question she asked herself, flipping about in her bed, but one he never put upon his own conscience. If he had, he might have realized that over the years he had come to expect people to speak their minds. He had grown up with Mrs. Banning sucking her cheek and saying to him, "Sometimes you make me wonder if you're all there." And the children at the Valley Hunt Club, screaming through the window of the kitchen where Bruder sweated as he mashed the bananas for the angel-cream pies: "Freak! Freak! Bruder can't speak!" And Rosa, a young woman with a wise soul, leaning into him softly: "I don't know what I'd do if I didn't have a friend like you." She was the closest he had to a friend, and Rosa knew of his desire to marry Linda and build a small cabin on the far side of the orange grove, and when Rosa asked if Captain Poore would permit him to do that, Bruder said, "He doesn't have a choice." He couldn't step back and see himself this way, but the truth was that in Linda's presence his own heart became as inscrutable as hers. The truth was that Bruder could plainly see the bald motives, the good and the evil, of everyone in the world but Linda and himself. And Rosa had said, "That's true love," and Bruder had replied, "I wouldn't know."

But when the rain stopped two days later, Bruder was too busy to further ponder the delicate mysteries of the heart. He was a workingman and he had work to do, although what drove him was greater than the simple need of wage and food. The hands were arriving for the season—boys short and tall, all of them underfed and silky-whiskered and in patched cotton trousers. They were no more than a year or two out of the orphanages in Tecate and Mexicali or along the Rio Grande, floaters who traveled up and down California's long fertile belly from orange ranches and lettuce farms to strawberry fields and white-grape vineyards, and they were still young enough to be grateful for work and willing to sleep on any bunk or floor. They arrived at the Rancho Pasadena in the buckboard, fetched from the Raymond Street Station by Hearts and Slay. Each carried a tiny sack with his blanket and his poncho, his picking gloves and a second pair of socks and any mementos the nuns at the orphanage had given him in memory of his parents. They were sixteen or fifteen or fourteen years old, downy cheeks, trembling Adam's apples, early hair on concave chests. A handful had worked at the Pasadena last season, but most were new, and Hearts and Slay spent two days explaining how to efficiently pick a tree clean while Bruder checked their sacks and bedrolls for guns and knives. One boy was carrying a bowie knife in his underpants, and when Bruder found it in a frisk he kept the knife for himself and drove the boy to the Pasadena's gate and sent him off with a silver dollar.

This year's hands were especially young, and Bruder worried about their inexperience. On the loggia, he complained to Willis and Lolly, interrupting their game of backgammon, that the ranch needed a better set of pickers. "Relax, Bruder old man," said Willis. But Lolly echoed Bruder in a tiny chirp: "Willis? Maybe he's right?"

During their first days at the ranch, Bruder lectured the hands by holding up a long bamboo pole and asking, "Any of you know what this is?" The boys shook their pimply chins. "It's a shiner pole. After you've picked a tree clean, I check to make sure there aren't any oranges left. If there are, they'll shine like a light in the dark. If any tree has three or more shiners, I'll send you back to finish it off yourself." The boys were sitting on crates with their hair-sprouting knees out, and they looked at one another and each was thinking that the season would be all right if they stayed clear of Mr. Bruder. Each boy saw Bruder's enormous hands—hands that were both thick and quick—and each boy could imagine the fingers tightened into blocklike fists or stroking a rifle barrel. And when they saw Captain Poore—starched collar, and hair bright as gold, and the medal thumping against his breast—each boy easily believed that Captain Poore would feed him more and pay him more if old Bruder wasn't around to tell him not to. The boys were young and new to Pasadena, and because of this they could clearly see how things were at the Rancho Pasadena—or so they thought.

The days after the rain had stopped were cold and windy, and the small valley dried out the way parched land quickly gives back its first drink of water. In the morning the orange grove appeared freshly painted, the fruit dewy and illumed like glass balls. A carpet of lime-green clover had pushed its way through the topsoil, and the rubber-aproned gardeners, commandeered by Nitobe-san, began rolling and reseeding the mansion's lawn. Shortly after dawn one morning the ice wagon delivered the Yuen family. Rosa had said that the Yuens shuffled around the ranch in silk pajamas and conical hats, but this wasn't true at all and Linda didn't know why she'd said it. No, the Yuens arrived in work trousers and shirts patched with burlap from pistachio sacks, and they said they were ready to work: "Let's begin today!" a young man cried, but Bruder slowed him down, saying that there was work to do before the picking could begin. Linda watched the Yuens unload their furniture from the ice wagon, bedrolls and a red-lacquer table and heavy bags of rice and a rocking chair, and they settled so quickly into the adobe house that Linda didn't know how many had arrived until she knocked on the door and it turned out there were only four. A young man named Muir Yuen, peering through the crack of the barely open door, told Linda that they preferred to cook for themselves, and then an old, blue hand opened the door farther and a woman asked Linda in for tea. Mrs. Yuen laid out a tray, and cups painted with cranes, and a dented tin pot. She and Linda spoke about the upcoming harvest, and Mrs. Yuen, who was ninety-two, tapped the ring of jade around her wrist and declared it to be a good year for the orange. Her mouth was a soft line clamped upon the rim of her teacup, and she said, pronouncing Linda's name as Valencia once had—*Leen-da*—"You must watch out for yourself, Linda." And then, "Some things never change."

In the mornings, Linda would return to the pantry and Rosa would greet her, and although Linda disliked Rosa she did her best not to show it. She said little as Rosa packed the crate, and though Linda assumed that Rosa didn't like her either, nearly every day she sent Linda off with an extra treat in her box: a sack of walnuts, a bag of Cupid chips, a tin of butter crackers cut into the shapes of kings and queens. And often Lolly would send Linda back down the hill with a special package of meat wrapped in bloody paper: "For the men," Lolly would say.

During the final days before the harvest, everyone was busy nailing the packing crates and the field boxes, sewing the flaps onto picking bags, mending bamboo ladders, and test-running the equipment in the packinghouse. The conveyor belts were tried out and repaired, the rind-brushers replaced, the hoses tightened and taped. A representative of the California Fruit Growers Exchange, one Mr. Griffith, a lumpy man in serge suit and vest who looked as if he'd never picked an orange in his life, came to measure the scales. Willis was at the ranch house to meet Griffith, and relief entered his face as Griffith told him that all was fine with the packing scales. The man drove off in his pressed-steel Tipo 8, his great round head lolling behind the wheel, and later Rosa told Linda that every November, Bruder had to pay Griffith off: "And Captain Poore is too oblivious to know that's how things are done." And again, Linda didn't believe her. This time she told Rosa so, and the girl's face froze with surprise. She said, "Linda. I'm only watching out for you."

At night, the hands saved a chair for Linda at the table beneath the pepper tree, and she smoked the Vasquez cigarettes that Hearts passed around in a cigar box and listened to the ranch-hand stories, and sometimes she told the boys about Condor's Nest.

When Linda asked, Davey Hearts said he didn't have much of a history to speak of: born in Wisconsin's North Woods and chased out of town by a man with a Stevens tip-up pistol who falsely accused him of pestering his wife. "It couldn't have been true," said Slay. "She was a hausfrau," said Hearts. "Older than my mother. The man was trying to extort me, it's as simple as that." Bruder had warned her never to listen to Hearts or Slay once the cap was off the flask, but it seemed to Linda that they were honest men. Once a week, Davey Hearts shaved his head in a mirror nailed to the pepper tree. He'd lather up his scalp and then go around waking up the other hands, and as the dawn cracked he'd whistle "Break Out the Oars!" while he dragged the blade across his scalp. He was strong in a lean sort of way and had a surprisingly small appetite, often turning down Linda's syrupy curds and returning his plate to the kitchen with his beans untouched. He'd met Timmy Slaymaker on the train to San Francisco and they'd been a pair since the end of the war, when one of them shot a bear-faced man in defense of the other. That was up in the mountains on the road to Tahoe, and the deputy sheriff took a look at the dead man curled at the foot of a red-wood and thanked Hearts and Slaymaker for ridding the road of a pirate toll-collector and said, "Self-defense, you say?" Then the deputy sheriff advised Hearts and Slaymaker to get off the Sierras by the end of the day. That's when Slaymaker led Hearts home to Pasadena. "He told me we could get a pair of jobs in one of the hotels and wear tuxedo uniforms," Hearts recalled, but their grimy, worn clothes had prevented them from entering even the back door of the Huntington or the Green, and Slaymaker had taken Hearts instead to the Rancho Pasadena.

Timmy Slaymaker had first turned up at the Pasadena when he was twelve. He said he had no family, but the ranch hands who shared the bunkhouse with little Slay spoke of the boy talking in his sleep in a strange tongue. In the middle of the night, the hands would stand around his bunk and listen to the spitty babbling, trying to figure out what language he was speaking. "I think it's French," said one. "That ain't French. It's Portugee." A third said, "It ain't Portugee either. It's Irish." Everyone then agreed that the burbling possessed a Gaelic quality, and the hands returned to bed, relieved to have solved the puzzle. But Slaymaker had never known his parents, and he didn't know that the language of his peat-farmer ancestors wafted through his memory. The hands told the boy that he was a black Irishman, and for a season everyone at the Pasadena called him "Black Lad," which evolved into "Black Boy," and then Timmy Slaymaker—by now a large young man with a boy's heart buried beneath a stocky hide—quit the Pasadena, crying into his fists on the train to San Francisco. "That's when I met him," said Hearts. "We hooked up like a couple of links."

"You never see them apart," Bruder would say of the two. "They know something the rest of us don't." Sometimes he would join them at the table, listening to the hands swap stories, a knife cold in his palm. Linda would wait for him to tell a story of his own but he never did, and Hearts and Slay knew not to bother asking, and the Mexican boys were too frightened of Bruder to inquire much. One night, Linda said that it was his turn—"Don't you want to tell us anything? About the war, maybe?"—and the pit fire leapt in his eyes and he turned the deer-foot knife in his hand and told everyone beneath the pepper tree that he'd let others tell those tales. One of the boys asked if Bruder had ever killed anyone, and Bruder said, "You should be asking Captain Poore."

One boy who liked to slay lizards with a slingshot said, "Captain Poore must've killed a million Germans to get a medal like his." The other boys peeped like kittens, as they were always more interested in Captain Poore than in Bruder—for who would envy the latter's life over the former's? The boys had traveled in railcar and buckwagon and pickup truck, and they'd slept in open asparagus fields, their heads resting on their rolled long johns; in their short lives they'd seen the West, they liked to say, up and down, north and south. Yet they were still young enough to become frightened when Bruder said, as he did around the table, that there wasn't much difference between killing a man and killing a mountain lion. "If it's going to happen, it's going to happen," he would say.

"Is that really true?" the boys would ask. "Doesn't anything scare you at all?"

And Linda said, her voice light in the dark, "I bet you never killed anyone at all."

Bruder wasn't trying to be coy, but he wished Linda would realize that he wanted to say very little in front of the men who worked for him, for Bruder believed that respect came from inscrutability. Once, after the hands had gone to bed, he said to her: "One day I'll tell you what you want to know," but it was after midnight and the arm of her alarm clock was turned to five and she said, "What makes you think I'm going to sit around and wait for you?"

She left him, but the next day he came to her kitchen and pulled the butcher knife from her hand and tugged her wrist. "Come with me." He said he wanted to show her some things on the ranch, and there was a new and awkward tenderness in his voice and in the delicate, tentative way he touched her, his fingers falling to her hand. Rosa had said that Bruder was at heart a shy man, but Linda disbelieved this more than anything else Rosa had said: "Bruder? Shy? That's the silliest thing I've ever heard," Linda had said, laughing in a way she hadn't for several years.

They walked through the grove, and pride was bright upon Bruder's face, as if the orchard were his, and his vanity surprised her; but if he was proud, it was because whatever order and efficiency existed at the Rancho Pasadena was due to him. She didn't know this, and Bruder would never say it in so many words, but after the war Willis was slow to return to the ranch; and when he did he thought about shutting it down. But Lolly had cried, "No, no, you can't!" Months of indecision led to general neglect—mice in the packinghouse, red spider in some of the trees. "In a grove, every day there's more work," Bruder would say, and it was his attention—an eye that could be cruel in its relentless exactitude—that had returned the Pasadena to full capacity. He told Linda some of this, as much as a proud but modest man could say, and she skipped a few paces ahead of him and she was both impressed by the land—at the bottom of the little valley, the ranch felt almost as endless as the ocean!—and unable to fully recognize the intimacy Bruder was offering. She instructed herself to ask Willis for his version of the ranch's death and rise, and she was pleased with herself to have acquired a skeptical ear. No, she knew enough not to accept one version of events. Only a few weeks in Pasadena had taught her that.

They continued walking, and once or twice his hand dropped to her shoulder or to the small of her back, causing her at once to pull away and then, as she realized that the gesture was gentle and kind, to lean back into him, welcoming him. She didn't know she was doing this; and she didn't know that her body was tossing a circle of heat that Bruder sensed, one that betrayed her most private longings. It was a hot afternoon, the sun bare and high, and Bruder stopped to show her the irrigation system, the open flumes that ran along the border and the plowed furrows between the rows of trees and the cement heads and the standpipes. Bruder explained that the ditches ran at a slight downward pitch, thus the water seeped into the earth to the root systems. During the summer and fall they ran the water every three weeks, but now they probably wouldn't have to run it until spring. He predicted more rains and she asked how he knew and he said he didn't know, "I just get a sense." And then: "Don't you ever feel that way, Linda? Feel certain about what's to come?"

"It's like waiting for a flood," she said, and the past that lay between them opened, deep and exposed, and she peered into it and Bruder stood at the rim and peered over as well. Linda thought to ask why he had left Condor's Nest so quickly.

"It's complicated," he began.

"Tell me."

"I wanted to earn your affection," he said. "I wanted it to come from *you.*"

She didn't understand this. In her pocket she found another one of Edmund's letters, one of the small spit-sealed envelopes that now arrived almost daily, with a few pleading queries inside. She was quick to tuck them into her pocket and she didn't read them until late at night, after the boys had gone to sleep and she was lying on her bed, the window cracked to perfume her room with the oranges. Then she would decipher Edmund's wobbly hand, his notes about loneliness and Palo-

mar, who, he wrote once, had gotten sick from eating sand. He wrote of
the fresh soil atop Carlotta's grave, next to Valencia's near the tulip tree,
sited by a wooden cross that the first rains had toppled. In each letter
Edmund asked Linda to return to the farm: "As soon as you can, or
sooner." He wrote that she didn't belong in Pasadena, how could she
survive so far from the ocean? Each night she meant to write Edmund,
she meant to tell him that she would return at the end of the harvest,
that living far from the ocean wasn't so bad. Over and over she would
start a letter, "From the terrace of the house you can see the Pacific, far
far away . . ." But almost immediately she'd fall asleep with the pen in
her hand, the blue-black ink bruising the breast of her nightdress. And
the night would take Linda, its hand upon her.

She said, "Why would you have to leave to become mine?"

And Bruder admitted more: "Some promises made long ago,
Linda."

The sun pressed on their necks, and Linda wiped her lip and felt the
heat trapped in her dress. Bruder was walking close to her, his arm
swinging near hers, and when she'd take a long step his hand would
graze her elbow or her hip and his heat would transfer to her, a spark up
the wick of her spine. Again, something was pulling her to lean into
him, and as she did he leapt over a puddle, his shoulder out of her
cheek's range. She believed that everything he did was deliberate,
which was true, and in his eyes she read a desire to torment her, which
was wrong. But she thought she smelled it in the musk seeping from
him, and in the way the sweat hung from his short beard, drops suspended whisker by whisker and then lurching down his throat. She
didn't like to admit it, but loneliness would reach her late at night, on
the iron-spring bed, where the air from the cracked window ran cool
across her flesh; once or twice she had removed her nightdress and let
the breeze touch her, the orange oil in the air caressing her; and then
her own hand. She would fall asleep like this, naked in the anteroom
between waking hours and sleep's chamber, an eruption of desire over-
taking her. But it was no longer clear what Linda longed for;
it felt as if her world had doubled, or quadrupled, since moving to
Pasadena, and each night as she drifted toward sleep she thought of
them: pale Edmund and silent Bruder and the golden hair of Willis
Poore and the gems of his eyes.

"And now I'm earning it," he said. "I don't need to buy it."

"What are you talking about now?"

It wasn't precisely what Bruder had meant to say; no, what he'd meant to say was that he knew Linda would love him. But his words had warped the sentiment, and, embarrassed, Bruder hurried back to the subject of the ranch tour. Oh, Bruder: how often he thought he wasn't meant to reveal his heart.

"It's a mature grove," he explained, pointing this way and that to the ranch's property lines up in the foothills, a mountain to the east and to the south, a hill like a camel's hump. "First planted in the 1880s," he said, and now the best trees rose more than twenty feet. He told her that he and Hearts and Slay had spent most of September erecting canvas tents around each tree, fumigating for scale. "You always have to be on guard for an infestation." They'd spent most of October hosing down the trees for red spider, dragging the four-hundred-gallon tank through the grove, Slay and Hearts two-fisting the nozzle, its pressure so fierce that their teeth rattled as they held the hose. Each afternoon they'd return to the ranch house drenched, as if they'd spent the day floating at sea. "We'd strip down to nothing but our boots and sit on the bench and wait for our pants to dry on the line," one would say, and the other would grin.

Bruder stood next to one of the oldest trees, a canopy of branch and leaf and early fruit. "We call this one 'Decameron.' There's always at least two oranges on it, no matter what time of year." The name meant nothing to Linda, but Bruder continued, "There's the poem about the pair of lovers who bathed in orange water and a courtesan who drizzled orange perfume into her bedsheets." He paused as he realized that she had no idea what he was talking about, and it hurt him that she showed no curiosity. At Condor's Nest, wouldn't she have inquired?

"It's just an old poem," he said. And she said she would have to look it up one day. But she wasn't the type to look up a poem, and Bruder wondered if she'd ever become such a person; and at the same time Linda wondered where Bruder had read the poem about the bathing lovers. Did Captain Poore invite him into his library? And then a jealous image entered Linda's head: Bruder following Rosa into the library, silently shutting the door behind him, whispering, "They're outside. We'll have to hurry." And the soft, brown mound of Rosa's feather duster dropping to the floor.

The orange tree shadowed Bruder, and the sweet perfume was almost sickening, and the endless rows of trees and the long brown-water ditches and the hard blue sky and the Sierra Madres rising purple in autumn all loomed over Linda, greeting her with pitiless beauty. She closed her eyes, and a view of the San Gabriel Valley came to her, its stretch and reach, the dry rivers and the parched yellow foothills and the dusty arroyos and the red-roofed city with its creeping neighborhoods and spewing cars and the coyote's cave and the wild grape choking an electricity pole and the two-hundred-year-old live-oak depositing an acorn into broken-up soil, and among it all, here stood Bruder, next to her. He was yet another, but somehow greater, breath among the inhalation and exhaust of nature's panoply, and so was she. There they were, Bruder and Linda, their eyes locked. The breeze down an orange alley tugged at his shirt and popped a button and exposed the flank of his chest; and nothing had changed since his arrival at Condor's Nest. Nothing and everything had changed, and Bruder leapt across the running ditch and extended his hand for her, but Linda didn't take it. She jumped with her hem in her fist and landed, her breast against his, and at last she remembered why she had come to Pasadena, and in the sunlight they kissed.

5

IN THE MORNING, Willis turned up at the ranch house, honking the Gold Bug's horn. It was Sunday, and everyone was asleep but Linda. "We're on our way to church," Willis called from the car. He pointed up the hill, saying that Lolly was waiting. Linda looked up to the house, where the terrace was partly hidden by drippy Montezuma cypress and cork oak and conifer. She couldn't see Lolly, but Linda knew that she was there, leaning against the parapet, waiting, watching. "Lace up your hiking boots and let's go to the mountains," Willis proposed. "I'll fetch you after church." And before she could ask if Bruder was coming too, Willis was gone.

While she waited for them to return from the First Presbyterian, Linda wondered who else would join them on the hike. Maybe Willis would invite Muir Yuen, whom Willis liked to ask up to the house to impress him with his collection of porcelain snuffboxes and blue-and-white ceramic elephants. She assumed that Lolly would come too, her face shaded by a broad-rimmed hat with an ostrich plume, pigskin gloves tight on her wrists. Lolly loved archery, and Linda expected her to arrive with a quiver slung across her back; her small face and her gold curls would make her look like a hungry cherub floating on the path. When at last Bruder woke up, Linda told him about the outing.

But Bruder had no intention of hiking with Willis, and he told Linda—the words coming more harshly than he intended—that he didn't care what she did, he had things to do on the ranch. "The harvest begins in the morning, the first packers will arrive at dawn, and I can't go." He expected that she would stay with him; the sunlight would needle through the pepper tree and the day would be warm and they would work together—this was his hope.

"But I want to go," she said. Surely he would yield and join them, and she imagined his hand reaching for hers as she mounted a granite boulder cold from oak-branch shade.

Neither imagined that each would refuse the other, and then at exactly this moment Willis drove into the yard and Rosa appeared on a path leading down from the house. Willis honked and called, "Hop in!" And Rosa shielded her eyes from the sun and said, "Bruder, will you be around later?"

Linda and Bruder said nothing, and they wouldn't look at each other, and as she slid into the car, he went to Rosa and asked her how she was feeling. The car knocked a cloud of dust and exhaust into the yard, and through it Bruder was a retreating silhouette to Linda's eye. It had happened in a flash, a mistake too late to correct, and before Linda and Bruder knew it, they were separated. She would blame him and he would blame her, and each had expected the other to yield.

Captain Poore drove her out past the Rose Bowl and beyond Devil's Gate and into the foothills, where the dirt road narrowed to a lane barely wide enough for the car to pass. The thorny hands of the chaparral pressed against the hood, snapping and scratching dryly. Mexican elderberry and toyon and holly-leaf cherry and sugar sumac grew all in a parched tangle until a thicket eventually chocked the road, and the Kissel's engine sputtered and stopped.

For a long time they followed a path through the oak scrub, Linda behind Willis. His neck above his collar was pink, and soon his scar was slick with sweat, and he plucked a handkerchief to swab it dry. He asked if she was warm and she said she was fine and Willis said, "Yes, Bruder tells me a little heat never stopped you."

"Is that what he said?"

In fact, over the years Bruder had told Willis almost everything he knew about Linda; and the more Bruder revealed, the greater Willis's interest had surged. In his estimation, Bruder was a heartless man. They had known each other under the direst of circumstances, and Willis, he liked to say, had seen Bruder when it counted most—when a man's true soul is put to the test. "I thought Bruder was incapable of feeling for another human being," he now said to Linda, "and then I realized he had a peculiar, fraternal fondness for you."

Willis was carrying a six-shooter, its pearl handle carved with an ox-head design, and every now and then he'd pull it from his pocket and twirl it on his finger. She had heard that he was a good shot, and when he saw her looking at the revolver he held it up and said, "Just in case." Then he stopped and straightened his arm and fired down the path. Surely he was showing off, she thought, and if he imagined a bullet would scare her he was wrong; but then they reached the headless squirrel twenty yards down the path, dead with an acorn in its tiny black claws. Willis held it up by the tail and said, "I used to chase grizzlies out of the grove."

Despite the early rain, everything in the foothills remained in need of water: the brush rabbits scampering and sucking on sumac leaves; the gray-bellied towhee fluttering out of the live-oaks in a desperate search for seed; the tree tobacco, thick with the limp ghosts of its yellow trumpet flowers; swaying, crackling garlands of climbing penstemon; tiny creamy aster fragile as lace coral; fairy tarweed, yellow-white and beaten down by the sun; the small terminal leaves of the drought-defying mimulus; a thistle, its red-purple color drained away; wild oats pinning Linda's skirt with barbs; the cockle's egg-shape seedpod falling before bloom; a twelve-foot yucca blossom toppled across the trail. The littered autumn hillside waited for visitor, rain or fire, and no one dared to bet which would come first to sweep it clean.

Willis lifted a string of barbed wire for Linda to climb beneath. "Left over from the Rancho San Pasqual. The sheep used to graze up this high." They were at a lookout, and below was the sloped table of the San Gabriel Valley, the busy cluster of Pasadena laid out on grids of white concrete, and the outlying farms and ranches and groves, and the long gleam of the railroad tracks. "Imagine this. Not even fifty years ago, all of this was a single rancho. A big old Victorian house, a couple of lean-tos for the hands, some barns, hundreds of miles of barbed wire, and thirty thousand head of cattle. That's what was here. Nothing but scrub and cow dung and fifty thousand sheep. Fifty years ago, two people owned a hundred thousand acres, maybe more. They owned so much that no one was really sure *what* they owned; the parchment surveys only described the property line as running from the sycamore with the heart-shape hole to the dead spring and everything in between.

And no one bothered to even wonder what they owned until they started selling it off."

She could imagine it, not needing to close her eyes to see the past with its endless vista of scrubland and dry riverwash and the mesas and the dust clouds driven heavenward by stampeding hooves. She had seen the growth in Baden-Baden-by-the-Sea, but it was nothing like this: there the village measured progress by the pier's extending length and El Camino Real's widening macadam and the electricity poles rising on the horizon—but not much else. The number of farms and families had changed little, a few more one year and a few less the next; and except for the increasingly heavy wave of spring-seeking tourists, their cars leaving pools of motor oil in the dirt, the village had remained an outpost between Los Angeles and San Diego. But Pasadena, even Linda could see, teemed with growth, its soil practically sprouting houses and roads: a population doubling in ten years, doubling again in twenty; how long could the valley hold it back?

"Fifty years ago there were maybe fifty people out there," said Willis. "Now there are fifty thousand spread around."

"Where did they come from?"

"The same place they all come from. Someplace else."

She wished that Bruder were there to share the view, and she said so.

"Bruder? I asked him along. He didn't want to come."

"You asked him?"

"You know how he gets. He waved me off. Told me to make sure you had a good time."

The familiar disappointment returned to Linda, and Willis must have noted it because he said, "I'm sorry you're not enjoying yourself."

But she assured him that she was.

His medal sent a blinding reflection of sunlight into her eyes, and for a short moment she couldn't see him: she only knew instinctively that a man unlike any man she'd ever known was at her side.

During her weeks at the ranch, Linda had learned from Hearts and Slay and from Rosa something of the Poore family. They said that Willis Senior had arrived on the Rancho San Pasqual in 1873 and convinced the owners to sell him four thousand acres. Where he got the money for it Slay and Hearts couldn't figure out, but he turned around and sold fifteen acres to a hundred soybean farmers from the Illinois-Indiana border, and in a single afternoon he had founded the Indiana Colony of

California. "They say it was quite a sight on that January morning in 1874," Slay had said. "Wagons and buggies of every kind coming up the arroyo, and each laying claim to fifteen acres. Each colonist waving a piece of paper scrawled in Willis's illegible hand. He was famous for terrible writing. It was so bad, some said he didn't know how to write."

"You never know about a man's past," added Hearts. "Those settlers rode into town, and from what I've heard it was unlike anything seen in the San Gabriel Valley since God created it and the mission first rose. Nothing but dust and men and women and babies in baskets and skinny horses and stupid mules eating flies. Wagons loaded with rockers and trunks and cooking pots stacked eight feet high, and weary, patient faces beneath sunbonnets looking for a man named Willis Fishe Poore."

"And there he was," said Slay. "Handing out a hundred deeds and declaring the establishment of a new colony and then walking away with his twenty-five hundred acres and plans for an orange grove and a mansion on the hill."

"Hey, Slay, do you think he was a crooked man?" Hearts had asked.

"No more crooked than the next."

Now, on the path, Willis told Linda they had another mile before reaching Paradise Canyon. Then, in a gesture that resembled a hummingbird landing at a fat-faced rose and flying off, Willis took Linda's hand for a tiny, fluttering moment and then released it, leaving it suspended between them, fingered with his oils. She looked at her hand as if it belonged to someone else, and Willis cracked the small spell by saying, "I hope you'll like Pasadena. A lot of good people here. Not everyone's like the folks you read about on the society page."

"I mostly read about you."

"Then I hope you know enough never to believe what you read." Each morning when Linda arrived at the pantry for the groceries, Rosa would fill her in on what had taken place at the house the day before. "Yesterday was Lolly's Orchid Club. Rummy all afternoon." Or, "The University Club ladies were here to discuss their upcoming pageant, something called 'The Mexicana.' " And once: "Willis and his friends were over last night shooting in the trout pond. Didn't you hear their guns?" Linda wouldn't ever have believed Rosa if she didn't also open the *Star-News* to the page that reported on these events and the city's other social activities: the Friday Morning Club putting on Shaw's

"How He Lied to Her Husband"; the Sunshine Society's bridge tour-
neys; the Masque Ball at the Hotel Maryland; the Bierlich Trio's concert at the Hotel Raymond; horseback trips up Mt. Wilson; lessons in
portraiture by Miss Mabel Watson, 249 E. Colorado; dancing instruction in the Huntington's ballroom; fashion shows sponsored by
Fuhrman's French Millinery. And all over the page, Linda would find
Willis and Lolly Poore's names: as a mixed doubles team on the Valley
Hunt's ladder; as members of the College Club's book discussion
group, led by Leslie Hood of Vroman's Bookstore; as runners-up in an
archery tournament sponsored by the City Beautiful Committee. At
least once a week there'd be a picture, and Rosa would say, "Doesn't
he look awful, with that little sneer of his?" But Linda would hold
the newspaper and study the smile of Willis Poore, posing in his bathing tank suit, winner of the swimming and diving championship at
the Water Carnival. The suit would reveal his small but muscular arms
and the water sparkled in his hair and the trunks were cut high on his
stocky, powerful thighs. She had leaned on the pantry counter, bringing
the newspaper close to her face, and Rosa would say, "Doesn't it make
it worse that he's so beautiful?" Once Linda ripped a photo from the
paper and took it back to her room, folding it into her pocket next to
Edmund's unanswered letters.

The day was hot on the trail, and Willis's shirt was now soaked with
sweat. As if something obscene were exposed in front of her, she tried
not to look at his narrow pink flanks, yet there was nowhere else to look
except at the quilted muscles of his back.

"I suppose you know all about Bruder," said Willis. "I suppose he's
told you everything himself."

Linda asked what Willis meant.

"He's not from Pasadena, not like Lolly and me."

"Nobody's like Lolly and you."

"That's not what I mean." And then: "He was a strange child."

"Weren't we all?"

"Did he ever tell you about the boy he killed?"

Something gripped at Linda and she said, "Not in so many words.
But what can you expect? He was at war."

"I was at war, too, but that's not what I'm talking about." Willis said
that as a child he was told about the little dark-haired boy at the Children's Training Society. "The widow who ran the place didn't know

how to keep him under control," he said. And she'd run to the Presbyterian minister to confess her exasperation at the six-year-old who refused to speak and who spit at strangers like a camel. "The newspaper used to write little stories about the boy they called 'El Brunito,' and the minister said that the only way to calm him down was to get him into the fields from dawn to dusk. He said that this 'El Brunito' was like an animal, that if you didn't work him he'd go crazy on you—a little black stallion, snorting, growing an inch a day. They decided that working him was better than sending him to school. Everyone in town knew about him—had read about him, at least—but because he was so young they didn't put his picture in the paper or print his real name, and Mrs. Banning was too good to him to allow that. And so when I was growing up there was a fear around town that any half-Mexican boy encountered on the street was El Brunito, and if some sort of mischief had occurred, like a rose bed sprinkled with lime, everyone would blame him."

"You never met him?"

"Not then, not when we were so young. Sometimes Lolly would wake in the middle of the night and say she heard something, some sort of noise on the trellis, and she'd run down the hall and jump into my bed crying, certain it was El Brunito.

"Then one day, when Bruder was just leaving his boyhood behind, he was helping with the ice delivery at the City Farm. He was working the iron tongs, and the next thing that happened—but how, no one really knows even today—the delivery boy was dead beneath a block of ice. They say you could see his red curls and his broken nose through the three-foot slab.

"It was in the newspaper. Every day for a month another article, more speculation, interviews with Mrs. Banning, quotes from the manager of the Pasadena Ice Company, a picture of the poor kid's grave. The police determined it was an accident, but it was a fishy accident, and there was no one's word to go by but Bruder's. The police believed him but no one else did, and once the whole thing died down, for a few years after, he stopped talking altogether. He'd plow the fields and pick the lettuce and the grapes and the lemons, and he said nothing all day and stayed up all night with a book borrowed from the library. They never ran his picture or used his name, but most people thought they knew who he was. Women would cross the street to avoid passing any dark boy who they thought might be El Brunito. Men, too. The only one who knew anything about him was the librarian, Miss West-lake, who checked out book after book for him—one a day, as I've heard her tell it."

"Doesn't it make you feel sorry for him?" said Linda.

"Lolly and I used to send books to the Training Society. He never knew who they were from. Probably doesn't, to this day."

Willis explained that he first met Bruder in a beechwood forest, not far from the banks of the Meuse. "That was the summer of 1918. When the mechanic in line next to me said that he was from Pasadena, imme-diately I figured out who he was, and I'd be lying if I didn't tell you it made me a little scared. I thought he might kill me."

"But he didn't kill you."

Willis hesitated. "No, he didn't."

"Did you save his life? Is that how you got your medal?"

"We were all saving lives." And Willis fell silent.

There was a step up in the path, and he offered his hand, and his palm was slick and left a ripe scent on Linda. At last they had reached Paradise Canyon. It was a narrow blue cleft between two peaks in the Sierra Madres, bottomed by a dry wash glittered with mica. A wall of granite headed the gulch where, Willis said, in spring a waterfall rushed white and cold and deadly. "You should see it in April, everything alive and in flower. Every fall, before the harvest, I hike in here to see the dead gully. Then in the spring, after we've picked the last orange, I re-turn. We'll come back, Linda, you and I, and I'll show you. Look at it now, remember what it looks like now, dead like this, dried up like this. In April, you won't believe it. There'll be thickets of sweetbriar and masses of feathery greasewood and wild buckwheat and prickly pink phlox." He moved and she felt something near her, his shifting heat. "We'll come back and you'll see the larkspur and the Indian pink. And hundreds of mariposa lilies and thousand of golden poppies. Poppies everywhere, in the ravine and in the crook of a tree and peeking from the crag. Everything bursting and alive, and in April you forget that rain is half a year away, you forget that everything shrivels and dies, every last thing."

The shade of the canyon wall reached them, sending a chill across her neck. His shoulder touched hers, and she smelled a blend of musk and tonic. The part in his hair had disappeared, replaced by a tousle of blond falling into his eyes. He smiled, and she wouldn't know it then—how could she know it then?—but his eyes were alive with plans for her, and even Linda couldn't explain or reclaim the forlorn, desperate sigh that just then pressed from her chest. If she'd ever doubted what she wanted for herself, it was now, and Willis found a dry wild rose, its heart brittle and white, and pinned it at the throat of Linda's blouse.

6

THE FOLLOWING MORNING, at shortly after seven, the ranch hands divided into teams of four and walked down the grove lanes. Each team propped its bamboo ladders against a quadrant of trees and stacked its field boxes, their identification numbers painted bright on the sides. The buckskin picking gloves cost each man seventy-five cents, and at night they slept with them beneath their pillows, because the first thing to tempt a ranch-house thief was a pair of picking gloves. A pair of citrus clippers cost $1.75, and the hands would sharpen them before bed and then chain them to their cots. From time to time a representative from the Growers Exchange would arrive unannounced, and Bruder would scramble to find Willis, and together they would walk the man—typically, Mr. Griffith—through the groves to inspect gloves and clippers. There was a mandated method to picking a navel orange, whose easily damaged rind, if bruised, could succumb to decay spores, spoiling an entire box and then a ranch's reputation. It was the job of Slay and Hearts to make sure the boys knew how to handle the oranges, and on that first day they walked up and down the rows and shouted into the trees. "Clip it off, don't pull it. Be sure not to cut the stem's button. And don't dare pack an orange with a stem longer than half an inch."

The ranch hands wore burlap trousers held up by suspenders and solid-colored shirts to mask the dust. Everyone but the youngest boys wore a workman's coat or vest, and some wore aprons; some carried more than one gunnysack over the shoulder; they hauled crates that could hold twenty pounds of fruit when the oranges were neatly packed like eggs. Each man had his own ladder, and a bamboo prodder, and they worked in rows, their faces only partly protected by thin-brimmed bowler hats. The occasional hand wore a loose bow tie, as if expecting something great to occur in his day.

One team of hands, boyhood friends from the orphanage of the Catedral de la Ascensión in Hermosillo, called themselves the Naranjo boys. They were seventeen or eighteen—even *they* didn't know—and they traveled from ranch to ranch, picking the navels in the winter and the Valencias in the summer, and they made only one demand of the foremen: four beds in a row. They would climb the trees and clip the oranges and pull their floppy, feathered hats down against the sun. Throughout each day they would chatter as if they hadn't seen one another in weeks, amusing themselves with stories about their unknown mothers. Pablo was the smallest, with a moony forehead and a corn-silk mustache of six or seven limp whiskers. His hair was mysteriously blond, and he told his friends that his mother was a Pima princess and his father an admiral in the Spanish navy, cousin to the king. Juanito was the oldest—or at least his beard suggested that—and he had luxuriant, wavy hair and a bump on the ridge of his nose, and he'd tell the others, from his bamboo-ladder perch, that the actual explanation for the blond hair was that Pablo had been born into a family of yellow-headed blackbirds, one of the thousands roosting in the trees of Plaza Zaragoza back home. The Naranjo boys would laugh, even Pablo, and Linda would find them giggling in the branches, their picking sacks full, when she arrived at noon with the crew lunch. She brought a chicken *tamale* to each boy and an orange soda and a single *polvorone* wrapped in white kitchen paper. They'd descend their ladders for the noon rest, their picking hands swiftly replaced by gray-rumped mockingbirds. With the Naranjo boys she'd sit in the shade and share a *tamale* and assure them she'd say nothing as they quartered a pint of white tequila—for by now Linda knew that if she were to report the alcohol on the ranch, every last man and boy would be thrown out. "No one's dry," Slaymaker would say. "How else could we accept our fate?" The first time the Naranjo boys offered Linda a sip of tequila, she declined; and the next day they offered again, and she declined again; and every day it was like that. Bruder had told her to watch out for them (they told her the same about him), and she sat with the tequila fumes itching the tip of her nose, confident that there was no one she had to watch out for—nothing could infect her; she thought of what Willis had said on the hike out of Paradise Canyon: "I'll keep an eye out for you." She thought of Edmund's letters, growing in desperation: *Who will look after you, Linda?*

Bruder's job was to oversee the hands in the groves and the gossiping girls in the packinghouse and just about everything else during the harvest and to report to Willis the daily yield. "What do I care if the girls don't like me much?" he said more than once when Linda pointed out that he should be careful not to shout so much: "Nobody likes to be barked at." The identification numbers painted on the field crates helped Bruder figure out who was clipping carelessly and packing sloppily, and nearly every day as she delivered lunch to the teams Linda heard his voice rising above the trees: "That's coming out of your wages!" He told her to cut down on the lard in the *polvorones* and the chicken in the *tamales* and the ice cooling the sodas, and when she asked what he cared about it, he said he cared about everything at the Pasadena: "Everything here is my concern." He said this with that familiar look in his face, his eyes narrowed and nostrils flaring, and Linda couldn't interpret it any more now than she could years ago at Condor's Nest—that hard gaze that seemed a terrible mixture of love and hate, all of it shadowed by his patchy beard. She wondered where his loyalty to the ranch came from; his love for this particular stretch of land in this particular valley was too specific for it to be merely professional fidelity. Certainly Willis didn't return the sentiment: after all, hadn't he said, "Sometimes I think Bruder isn't quite from this world." Hadn't Willis leaned in and whispered to Linda, "Isn't quite human, do you know what I mean?" But Bruder wasn't thinking of Willis; no, Bruder was concerned with himself and his future, and if ever he was going to have a tract of land to call his own—for was there a greater security in California than a V-shape fold of fertile soil?—it would be the Pasadena. It was owed to him, he reminded himself often, and sometimes he'd take the piece of paper from beneath his mattress and reread Willis's childlike scrawl. But when Bruder said things about the land becoming his, Linda would ask, "What on earth are you talking about now?"

Mrs. Yuen, old but strong, helped Bruder oversee the packinghouse. Every morning she welcomed the girls to the ranch with a dish of burning incense and a gleam in the braid coiled atop her head and a little yellow steaming bean bun. She assigned packing stations to the girls, most of whom traveled by truck and wagon each morning from Titleyville or the Webb House, an orphanage and boardinghouse that each Christmas raised money by sending to the finer Pasadenans, including the Poores, pamphlets describing the home as a place where "everything is done to develop the Little Mexican Women into useful American citizens." At the height of the season the packinghouse would employ more than fifty girls, and Linda would stay up late each night stuffing the *tamales* for the next day's lunch. It shocked her the first day she went to the packinghouse and found Bruder yelling at one of the packers, a girl with frizzy hair around her brow. Her name was Constanza, and she held down her pear-bottom chin as Bruder complained about undersize oranges slipping into a packing crate. When at last he stopped she lifted her head, and her watery eyes, lit by the slender shaft of sunlight coming through the window beneath the eave, made Linda think of diamonds, like the teardrop stones she'd seen pinned to Lolly's ears.

"Do you have to yell at everyone?" Linda asked one afternoon in the ranch-house kitchen.

"If they don't do their job."

"I'm sure at least once someone's yelled at you, and I'll bet it didn't make you feel all that good. I should think you'd try to remember that the next time."

"No one's ever yelled at me. No one but you."

But Linda knew this wasn't true, and she said, "What about when you were a boy? I've heard the stories." She added, "Sometimes I think I can't believe you."

She wasn't sure who was more startled by her having said this, Bruder or herself. He was holding a glass and his knuckles whitened as anger ran through him; she flinched, knowing that the glass would momentarily shatter, but then Bruder set it down and left her. Since her arrival in Pasadena, so many people had told her so many things about Bruder—shards of history that contradicted his own version—that she wondered if she could ever believe him again. "You've succumbed to gossip," he said when she asked him about his life at the Training Society. "Did they really used to call you 'El Brunito'?" "No one's ever called me anything but my name." But this, too, wasn't true—he just *wished* it were true, and he wished that Linda knew him only as the man he was today. The shame that came from memory struck Bruder, and he was sorry that Linda couldn't perceive it blowing him about; if she were to stroke his cheek she would have felt the heat in his flesh, the blood rising in concussion. He was a wounded man, and sometimes it was all he could do to protect himself.

"I'm just trying to run the ranch," he'd say.

Every morning before dawn Bruder picked up most of the packing girls at the Webb House and drove them to the Pasadena. The girls were fifteen or sixteen years old, many of them born in East Pasadena and abandoned at the Pasadena Settlement House because their mothers, whoever they were, knew that the Pasadena Hospital not only refused adult patients whose flesh wasn't dairy-white but also turned away babies with any flecks of cocoa in their skin. The Settlement House was at California and Raymond, and its black-clothed administratrices prayed at Our Lady of Guadalupe and arranged for milk for any and all babies of Pasadena no matter the origins of the suckling mouth, and eventually these ladies—who prayed for a sighting of the Virgin Mary in their wall mirrors—placed the infants in the orphanages around town. This was how most of the packing girls first came to the Webb House, and even though they were natives to Pasadena, no one who ran the city considered them as such—for the girls were familiar with little beyond the orphanage and the neighborhoods of Lamanda Park and Eaton Wash, where Spanish floated from *casita* to *casita* through the jacarandas. The girls who packed the oranges weren't refined enough to work in the mansions along Orange Grove and Hillcrest—or so they'd been told most of their lives and now they believed it. "I've raised my girls to be workers," the *Star-News* quoted Mrs. Emily Webb, the Webb House's headmistress, in an article about the Community Chest. Along with the girls from the Webb House, there were packers from all over the valley, from the Junior Republic and the Rosemary Cottage, where girls of a certain slowness studied kitchen crafts; from the Altadena foothills, where adobe houses burrowed into the chaparral, abutting mountain-lion dens; from East Pasadena bungalows where every child, no matter the age, contributed to the shallow, well-scraped pot. They came from the cottages tucked behind mansions, where extended families slept in bunks and hammocks and bedding rolls, and where a grandmother with arms as soft as avocados woke everyone before dawn to send them off to their jobs: the men to the citrus ranchos and the alfalfa and corn fields that still grew along the underbelly of Pasadena, the women to hotel laundries and galleys, through the back doors of mansions, down to basements where washtubs waited, spitting suds. But the girls with the strongest arms and the ugliest hands and the faces that didn't look pretty beneath a maid's pastry-puff cap met up with Bruder's truck at the Raymond Street Station and rode out to the Rancho Pasadena, where a long day in the packinghouse paid slightly less than a chambermaid's wages at the Hotel Vista.

Every day at one o'clock in the packinghouse, the rubber belts stopped and the water-spray washer hissed to a trickle and an exhausted silence fell over the sizing bins as Linda arrived with lunch. A packer named Esperanza would help her distribute the *tamales* and the orange soda, passing the stations with a bottle opener. For thirty minutes the packers sat slumped on their stools, their canvas caps askew and their cheeks damp. A few would step outside into the pepper tree's shade for a cigarette, but most ate inside and gossiped and wiped their throats. Esperanza, whose sister was a wet nurse in the home of a chocolate-bar heiress, aspired to become a seamstress, and practiced her needlework on her apron and the other girls' aprons too, embroidering them with a bunch of red grapes or a climbing rose or a yellow-sailed schooner cutting a wave. As she helped Linda pack the *tamales,* she told her that one day she hoped to work in the mansion, hemming Miss Poore's clothes and embroidering Captain Poore's handkerchiefs with gold stitch.

It seemed like a strange ambition to Linda, who spent more and more time imagining the house's silent and dark hallways, brocade drapery beating back the sun. Life in a cage, she thought, but Esperanza had heard from her sister that being on a mansion's staff meant warm meals in winter and cold drinks in summer and a tiled bath shared with only three others and a bed shared with no one at all. Every time Willis passed through the packinghouse, Linda would notice Esperanza tucking her hair up into her cap and shaking out her apron so that he could properly see the navel orange stitched to her breast. Whenever Willis spoke to Linda, she felt Esperanza's eyes on her, and she slowly realized that more eyes than Esperanza's studied each interaction between the captain and his ranch-house cook. What they were looking at, she didn't know.

Just as she didn't know that no one's eyes followed her as closely as Bruder's.

That year's harvest began as one of the best in memory, and the Naranjo boys and the other teams of hands sent to the packinghouse

hundreds, eventually thousands, of boxes of oranges. In a typical year
the Pasadena's most mature trees each produced enough oranges to fill
two field boxes, but this year the boys were clipping from the best trees
enough oranges to fill almost three. Slay and Hearts's wagon was on a
constant run between grove and packinghouse, a blue tarp across the
boxes to protect them from the sun. At the packinghouse door a mound
of oranges almost nine feet tall waited to be processed, and this backlog
etched a new crease across Bruder's brow. He would shout to the girls
to work faster, but it was clear to Linda that they were already at capacity, and when she suggested that he hire a few more packers, Bruder
told her to stay out of it or he'd put her on the packing line as well. And
she would have joined them if she wasn't so busy in the kitchen, finishing breakfast and turning immediately to lunch, then to supper. Her
first quiet hour came just before midnight, her last ended in the pitch-
black at a quarter to five.

Once hauled in from the groves, the field boxes stood for two days
at the packinghouse, to allow some of the rind moisture to evaporate,
enhancing the oranges' sturdiness. The sight of hundreds of boxes laid
out tested Bruder's patience even more—*Idle!,* as he put it—especially
when Willis inspected the boxes, turning the dimpled oranges in the
sun: "When will you get to these?" Once, Willis brought Lolly with
him. They were on their way to a tennis match, he in a white vest and
calico pants and she in a pleated skirt with a white band across her forehead, and she refused to get out of the car, instead peering into the
packinghouse with hand-visored eyes.

"He's a fool," Bruder would say of Willis.

"He's got a lot on his mind," Linda would reply.

"So do I."

When she wasn't helping Linda, Esperanza worked as a washer, submerging the oranges in a warm bath and scrubbing the dust from the
rinds with a soft brush. She'd rinse the oranges in a cold shower, and
then rollers would carry them beneath a blast of hot air, so that they
were dry by the time they reached the grading table. At first the packinghouse reminded Linda of the Fleisher gutting house, but the packinghouse was more sophisticated than that, the graders as precise as
jewelers sizing orange diamonds. During the harvest, Willis spent
much of his time surveying the grading table, for he knew that this was
where his money came from. He'd watch the canvas belt carry the or-

anges past the graders, who examined them for size and quality, separating them into classes. The graders were experts, trained under the oily eye of Mr. Griffith, and Willis liked to stand behind them and watch how they scooted the different grades of oranges onto the four separate belts that carried them to the proper sizing machines. "These people pay for the ranch," Willis was known to say. Or, on a bad day, "Those graders are going to make me a poor man one day." The graders wore white lab coats and gloves, and they inspected the fruit with a seriousness that impressed Linda, in part because they seemed to ignore Willis when he disagreed with them: "That orange was perfectly fine!" One grader, a red-nosed man named Mr. Foote, pretended not to hear Willis at all, and when Willis demanded that he be fired, Bruder refused. "Then I'll do it myself," Willis declared, but Mr. Foote remained firmly at his station atop his stool, running his gloved hands over the rolling oranges and pulling out the dross.

After they rolled by the graders, the oranges passed between two wood rollers that ran alongside each other like the arms of a V. Each orange shuffled up between the V's yawning limbs until it reached the place where it no longer touched either roller, and then it plopped into a canvas bin collecting exactly that size of orange. It was an efficient procedure, refined over the years by Willis's father, who had always searched for methods to remove manpower from the harvesting process. "He hoped to one day run a handless rancho," Willis would say. "Get rid of everyone but his family."

The packers at the collecting bins quickly wrapped each orange in tissue and then carefully placed it in the shipping box. If they were slow, or if the orange haul was too heavy, the bins were emptied in piles on the floor while the girls, their skin reeking of orange oil, packed crate after crate. They would complain about the scent, and Bruder would tell them that there'd been a time in France when no bride would think of marrying without an orange blossom upon her breast. "Think of the French girls," he'd say, dismissing his packers' dissatisfaction.

A packer might be expected to fill almost seventy-five boxes in a day, but by the beginning of December, Bruder was telling each girl she'd have to nail lids into ninety crates before the wagon would return her home at dusk. It was Bruder's idea to require the packers to deposit a ticket in each crate so that he could trace lazy work. More than once on the packinghouse floor he ceremoniously opened a crate returned from the Growers Exchange, publicly firing the girl whose careless packing had spawned a pretty green wrapping of mold. It was an awful sight, his big hand enclosing the girl's wrist, holding it up as if she were the winner of some sort of contest, while the other girls stood around in their aprons silently loathing him and the packinghouse and everything about the Rancho Pasadena. Sometimes they wished the pay were worse so they could quit without hearing the screams back home at the kitchen table, the *¡Maldito sea!* from the soft-armed grandmother, from the pencil-mustached brother, from the father in the yellow-collared shirt, from the slutty sister, from the toothless, milky mouth of a newborn. The girls who lived at the Webb House had it even worse: were they to return to the orphanage having lost their job, Mrs. Emily Webb was likely to fold her mole-dotted arms and say, "Well, then. I've been thinking a few things over. Perhaps it's time you thought about leaving the Webb House." Her narrow shoe-shape face, its leathery texture attacked nightly by a generous application of Ingram's Milkweed Cream, would remind the unemployed girl what she already knew: that the Webb House shut its doors upon the indolent, the dishonest, the syphilitic, the pregnant, and the whore—not necessarily in that order. It did not occur to Mrs. Emily Webb—and why should it?; she was born in a taffeta-draped nursery on Orange Grove Avenue and married a banker whose only fault was long ago to have stepped in front of a Pacific Electric trolley on New Year's Day—that a girl could lose her position at the Rancho Pasadena for any reason other than insouciance or laziness; no, Mrs. Emily Webb was unfamiliar with the subtleties of injustice. "Lost jobs are our own faults," she was known to say, each morning at a quarter to six, ringing her cowbell to wake the girls in the dormered attic. "In our world, a girl is given but one chance in life. After that, her fate is sealed."

Linda learned this when she took the girls back to the Webb House one night. It was the first time she had driven the buckboard on Pasadena's streets, and only from the vantage of the plank bench did she see how the city no longer accommodated horse and wagon. The roadsters and the Tin Lizzies buzzed around her; the cow-spotted mare shied from the honking and the tailpipe shots. Linda drove down into the arroyo and up the opposite hill, over toward the intersection of California and Raymond. Esperanza sat on the bench with Linda, and a dozen girls rode in the wagon bed. The early-winter evening blanketed the valley with timid dusk as the horse clopped along and the yellow lights in the store windows flickered on. The bird rouge on Esperanza's full cheeks had turned waxy during her packing shift, and her teased bangs sprang from her cap. She was no taller than five feet, but she was one of the older girls at the Webb House, almost twenty, and she was careful to stay in good standing with Mrs. Webb, who thought enough of her to have given her a tiny muffin-size sewing box on her last birthday. "Sometimes Mrs. Webb says I'm the only one of her girls who'll manage to stay out of trouble," Esperanza confided to Linda.

The wagon continued down California Street, past the diaper laundry and the enormous window of the P. F. Erwin Electrical Distributorship, where footlights shone on a display of its endless electrical wares: Telechron clocks, plug-in waffle irons, coffee urns, casserole dishes, hot plates, Hoover uprights, lamps with skin shades painted with scenes of hummingbirds, massaging pads, torchères, and silver-plate milk warmers. The store was so modern and brightly lit that it, and all of California Street, felt to Linda like another world. The wagon passed through the pool of yellow light cast from Erwin's window, and Esperanza leaned in toward Linda and whispered, "You know what's above Erwin's, don't you?"

But Linda did not.

"It's where Dr. Freeman is," Esperanza said, pointing at the brick building. "He's the only one in town, and the trouble is, he charges a month's wages for a visit." The three windows on the second floor were blacked out by roller shades, but Linda saw a crack of light at the sill. As the wagon passed the building, a girl in a slip-on sweater emerged from a door in the side alley that Linda guessed led to the upstairs office. The girl was arranging a china-blue beret on her head, and her face was pretty and round and her eyes were turned up. The light from Erwin's window bathed the girl in a gold glare as she stood in the alley, her arms extended and her palms out—as if she was startled to find herself there. In the golden light the girl seemed to be presenting herself to the alley: a creamy school-age cheek half hidden by mink-brown hair, fluttering eyelids, ankles wobbly in gunmetal-leather shoes. She dug through her purse for a handkerchief, and Esperanza said, "They say that Dr. Freeman was in love with his own sister, and after she died he went into this sort of business. They say he only does it for the money. They say—"

But Linda had stopped listening to Esperanza. Instead, she watched the girl walk tenderly down the street, her hand against Erwin's window for balance, her feet spread awkwardly.

"Each night I pray to God I don't end up at Dr. Freeman's," Esperanza chattered on. "Mrs. Webb says it ends up happening to almost every girl at the House. But not me, she says. Mrs. Webb says I'm smarter than the others."

Again, Linda looked at the girl on the sidewalk, who was tentatively peering up and down California Street, checking her watch, as if expecting someone. Out of the pool of light from Erwin's, the girl's face turned dark, and Linda wondered, from the way the girl's shoulders rolled, if she was crying now.

"Do you suppose she was there getting it done?" said Esperanza. "Why do you think it costs so much?" And then: "What would you do, Linda, if it were you? Would you—"

Again, Linda stopped listening. She snapped the reins and clucked her tongue, and the mare trotted on. Linda looked once back toward the girl: still her eyes were searching up and down the street; but no one came to meet her, and then, as if in resignation, she moved gingerly down the sidewalk, in the opposite direction of the Webb House, and disappeared.

Linda pulled up in front of the Webb House, and Mrs. Emily Webb waited on the porch. Clutched in her hand was a box of the chalky, pellet-shape Dr. Warden's Female Pills, "for female troubles and diseases peculiar to our sex." Mrs. Webb patted one pill into each girl's palm, reminding them to swallow, never chew. Her fingers were sharp and schist-cold, and she waved abruptly to Linda, and Mrs. Webb's choir-trained voice hooted, "Come in, girls, come in! Hurry up and come in from the night!"

From then on it became part of Linda's routine to drive the Webb House girls home, while Bruder, meanwhile, crossed town with a truckload of the Titleyville packers, who would wave good-bye and giggle in a manner suggesting that they whispered about him behind cupped palms; and the girls would jump down from his truck and clasp hands and walk down the darkening palm-alleyed street, spinning stories of running away and never returning to the Rancho Pasadena. From behind the wheel he would watch them, silhouettes on the narrow street where teeth-white porches faced one another, and he enjoyed knowing that the girls who worked for him simultaneously feared him and longed for him. It wasn't a sadistic impulse, only an efficient one—for Bruder didn't know a better way to inspire productivity. If he was selfish, his motivation was not greed but self-protection: early this season he had increased by a nickel each girl's pay for every box packed, and he'd done so without consulting Willis; everyone on the ranch knew it, and they all talked about it: that, once again, Bruder had done as he pleased. One might presume that he never thought of others, but this too wasn't true: Rosa hadn't been feeling herself for several weeks now, and in the mornings Bruder would show up at the pantry in the big house and ask what he could do for her: haul the laundry, pack the groceries, carry the ice, he would do anything—for there was nothing around the ranch he hadn't done. There was a fraternal feeling between them, and once she asked if, on his way home from Titleyville, he could stop at the Owl Drug Company and buy her a box of soda crackers and a bottle of Dr. Petal's All-Pure Antidote for Female Pain. "I'm not feeling well in the stomach, and down there," she said, and this caused no awkwardness between them, only sympathy. Bruder sometimes wondered whether if his heart were clear of Linda, would he love Rosa? He never settled the issue—it was too hypothetical—but unlike so many men, his firm, muscle-bound heart had a capacity limited to one, and it never really became a quandary for him; he was as loyal and patient as the ravine that waits patiently for the annual melting snow.

Often, as he returned from Titleyville, Bruder would catch up with Linda on her way back from the Webb House, and he would slow the truck and follow her, and by now it would be dark and the stars would sparkle like the ice-dust on the ice-house floor. She would be sitting erect on the wagon seat, pulling and snapping and tucking the reins with small, confident movements of her hands, like a seamstress who could perform expert work blindfolded. The *clop-clop* of the hooves would compete with the cough and gasp of the old truck, and she would turn her neck and the sliver of her smile would gleam. She hadn't been in Pasadena long, but even so she was settling into a patterned day, and Bruder's heart lurched, as he watched her steer the wagon out of the Arroyo Seco and up onto Park Avenue and into the Linda Vista hills, because her routine had yet to fully incorporate him.

From time to time he wished he had known her before he had gone to war, before he had become the man he was; then she would understand him better. It was an illogical desire—for didn't he know Linda precisely *because* of the war?—but wasn't that the case with most things a man wants? Why bother to yearn at all, if not for the unobtainable?

And yearn he did—steadily, like a low, blue flame—and Bruder knew that one day he would be a wealthy man and would share his fortune with Linda, and he decided then, on a crisp night as Linda's wagon and his truck reached the rancho's gate, that he would no longer allow her to push him away; he couldn't wait anymore.

And during these evening trips home, Linda, guiding the wagon into the foothills, would be aware of Bruder's eyes on her, and she knew he was thinking of her and she thought of many things but mostly of him: and it was as if the wagon crossed the city on its own, as if she were blind and merely being led along. The truck was loud but soothing, gently overwhelming the horse's stomping and snorts and rubber-lipped bray, and it wouldn't be long, she knew, before the horse would remain forever on the ranch, corralled by a sagging string of barbed wire, and the wagon would be broken up, its planks cut down for orange crates.

On each trip to the Webb House a different girl would sit up on the seat next to Linda, and each girl would eagerly tell her something about the ranch. "Bruder scares me," said one. "I don't think Captain Poore likes Bruder very much," said another. The girls were still young enough to speak dreamily, holding their chins in their unjustly rough fists while the slow mare pulled them along. After a week of runs to the Webb House and back—Mrs. Webb waving from the pink-trimmed porch with her suspicion retreating a bit further each night—Linda realized that the girls perceived her as somehow different from themselves, as if her slot in the ranch's order was far above their own. It was true, of course, and she pondered over how she had managed this fate, and it confirmed her suspicion that her life was hers to plan and achieve. Those who say they are pawns of a cruel, invisible will don't know what they are talking about, Linda would think. Once, Esperanza asked, "Would you mind speaking to Captain Poore for me? About my taking on some of the sewing in the house? I'll do it at night." At first, Linda had stared at the girl, startled by the notion that she, Linda, had any more access to Willis than anyone else. How had Esperanza known this before Linda realized it herself? At first, it was difficult for her to see that the more time she spent at the Pasadena, the more possibilities were opening before her. But that was the case, and Linda gradually came to believe that her improving future was a matter of her own doing.

Despite herself, she wondered what the mansion was like inside, and how it felt to stare out of the many-paned windows rather than in. Through a window she had once seen the double staircase that rose from the gallery, and Linda imagined herself upon the carpeted landing, her fingers on the hand-cast rail. She had seen dozens of Lolly's lace-trimmed and silk-lined dresses lying flat and lifeless on the ironing board, Rosa's strong arm pushing out the creases. But Linda was slow to recognize the tendrils of envy creeping about her heart; she failed to recognize the wingflap within her chest. Her longing was soaring but aimless, and would remain so until the day it found its nest.

One Sunday evening a few weeks before Christmas, Linda served the hands their supper and washed the teetering stack of dishes and cleaned the kitchen for the upcoming week. The weather was cold and the men were tired, and before she finished her work most everyone had gone to bed. The previous night, an isolated frost had settled on a few low-lying acres of the grove, and half a dozen hands had to divide the night into three shifts, stoking a few orchard-heaters in the spots where the cold air tended to get trapped. The paper reported that this night would be warmer, but Bruder wouldn't let them take the risk: six men were to spend the night among an acre of trees, their breath fogging their faces. Nothing made the hands grouchier than a frost, and they'd stumble through the dark cursing the winter and Bruder and Captain Poore, who tonight had sent word down the hill that the mansion needed an extra cord of firewood right away. A couple of men delivered the wood and returned and said, "Those two were meant for each other." Then the hands drew lots, and the losers wrapped themselves in blankets and headed into the grove, lighting the small platoon of heaters. They'd let them burn for an hour, then put them out and drag them twenty feet down the grove to the next quadrant of trees. It was a cold, tedious, sooty task, and no one wanted to do it, despite the extra two dollars Bruder paid each man, money that came from his own pocket, something no one knew.

The kitchen was at the far end of the ranch house, down the dark hall, and the faint sound of doors latching traveled to Linda—first Hearts and Slay's, then Bruder's, the click and fall of the guillotine-shape bolts. The window over the sink displayed the ranch in the winter-dark, and the grove was like a night ocean, calm waves of trees, the flickering heaters the deck lights of a distant ship. She thought she saw Bruder hauling a heater, but that didn't make sense, for hadn't she heard his door close just a minute before? And she thought she heard a shout in the grove, but the coyotes were crying and the wind whistled down the hill and maybe she hadn't heard his door latching after all. She heard yelling again, this time someone calling, *"¡Cuidado!"* The men would ruin their picking gloves carrying and lighting the heaters all night, and she felt bad that they'd have to pay for new pairs out of their wages, and she thought that perhaps in the morning she'd recommend to Bruder that he forgive the cost of the gloves. And if Bruder said no, she would appeal to Willis. She didn't know that Bruder had already bought the men new gloves; there was so little she knew.

Linda finished her kitchen work after eleven and set four pots of water on the stove for her bath. In the corner of the kitchen was a coffin-shape zinc tub, its lip brittle and cold. Linda filled it with hot water and drizzled in some orange oil, the drops gold and glistening. The steam touched her throat, and she drew the curtain, sewn by her own needle, across the kitchen window. A small oval mirror revealed her face, and it struck her that there were times when she didn't recognize herself anymore: she had become a woman different from the one she'd imagined. Years ago she had thought that one day she'd become the captain of a fishing boat; or maybe a clerk at Margarita's counter; or perhaps she would grow old overseeing Condor's Nest. Even six months ago, how could she have guessed that the ocean farm would fade so quickly away? She thought of Edmund, and she imagined him down the coast: stoking the fire and struggling with the fishing rods and bundling Palomar into his blankets and easing Dieter into bed. There'd been more letters, and she had failed to answer them yet again. They were in a pile beneath her pillow, and when she saw them she turned sharply, wishing they'd go away, and the longer they went unanswered the more she resented her brother for having written in the first place. She turned off the kitchen light and sat on the tub's lip and unbuttoned her blouse and stepped out of her skirt and saw in the mirror the way the straps of her camisole fell across her shoulders and cupped her

breasts, and despite the crisp night she found herself warm within her
body's coves. The steam softened her skin and dampened her underclothes, and she looked forward to slipping into the water and sitting
knee-to-chin until the water chilled. She hung her clothes on a hanger
and began to peel a strap from her shoulder, and just as she was about
to shimmy into nakedness, the doorknob shook and the door opened
and in its frame was Bruder.

His mouth opened and he struggled to speak and a hot wave of embarrassment soaked him: "There was no light in the window," he said.
"I thought you'd gone to bed. I didn't mean to . . ." He was so surprised
that he didn't move, and the kitchen was dark but for the moonlight
that exposed her bare arms and legs, the long, pale stem of her throat,
and the square of flesh beneath her shoulders and above her breasts,
crisp and fresh and white. "I wouldn't have come had I . . ." Bruder
tried again, and again he couldn't finish. His hand remained on the
knob, and Linda remained in her camisole on the lip of the tub, and despite the cold night she became even warmer, the steam reaching up for
her, turning her flesh sticky, and it felt as if Bruder was shooting his heat
at her too, and he could see this—he sensed her face opening and ripen-
ing before him. She couldn't move, and Bruder had succumbed to the
same desire, and they stared at each other, their faces as clear as they'd
ever been, and maybe for the first time each understood what the other
wanted, and the night was black and the stars distant but bright, and
Linda stared at him and said, "You were looking for me."

Bruder inched toward her, and before either of them knew it he had
crossed the kitchen and was taking her in his arms and they were kissing. A coyote howled, and she jumped, but his hand held her firmly to
his chest. Beneath the camisole she was wearing nothing, and he could
feel every shiver of her skin through the fake silk, and the tiny straps
slipped from her shoulders, and the last thing she was wearing fell away
and she was naked against his clothed body, and he held her and it felt
as if his hands could touch her all at once and his fingers began to knead
and stroke and search and find; and he sighed, "My Linda."

She murmured "Yes? Yes?" and the time fell away as if a black cloth
had been laid over the clock's face. His buttons slipped through their
holes, and his leafy scent met her nostrils, and in the dark he led her to
her room and together they lay in the narrow bed. They were alone.
Each was happy in the same simple way. Good fortune had found them,

but they'd both forgotten that this was rare and that they were the few among the many. It was too much to ponder on a night of pleasure, and there they were, Bruder and Linda—as they were meant to be—and for a few hours each pondered nothing but the other's body.

The night moved to dawn, and Bruder never let go of Linda and she never released him, and then they slept for an hour. With their eyes sealed and their cheeks fused into one, they could not have seen the heaters flickering and extinguishing, the hands returning from the night shift; nor the stars fading; nor the moon turning out its lantern. Bruder and Linda did not see the first stain of dawn, or the early lights up at the mansion. And they failed to see the pair of eyes peering through the window beside the bed, eyes noting the scene, studying the rise and fall of the breathing, dreaming mound of flesh, eyes blinking indignantly and then dashing away.

It was daylight when they woke, and Linda said softly, "They'll be wanting breakfast soon," and Bruder kissed her again and again and he left. He returned to his room, and she brushed her hair in the kitchen mirror and drained the cold water from the tub. The spore of happiness that had lodged in their hearts remained. They were certain of the secret joy that had at last found them, and as the sun rose above the valley, burning back the dew, up the hill Captain Poore was hearing of indiscretions upon his land.

His reaction was swift and unbending. He ordered Rosa to help Linda pack her things. "She'll be living in *my* house from now on. I should've known better than to have a woman in a ranch house." And he sent Rosa with the news that from that day forward, Linda would sleep in a new bed.

7

BUT ROSA SAID that because of the harvest there wasn't a free bed in the servants' quarters, and Captain Poore himself ordered Linda to stay in one of the guest rooms, upstairs, at the end of a hall. The room overlooked the terrace and the orange grove, a slender double door opening onto a balcony wide enough for two with a black rail that would retain the sun's heat even after twilight. Linda's first night there, she lay in bed staring up at the flesh-colored canopy, the pillows nearly swallowing her. She was thinking of the long day that had followed her night with Bruder—how those hours alone already felt like years ago. On the nightstand, a porcelain man in a cherry coat held a small gold clock in his tiny fingers; the clock's hands seemed frozen, the night inert, and Linda waited impatiently for the slow lurch to dawn, when she'd return to the ranch house and to Bruder. Earlier in the day he had tried to stop her from moving into the house, but Willis wouldn't relent and Lolly had turned up saying, "I'll make her feel at home."

"She's not a child."

"Please don't worry about me," Linda told Bruder. They weren't alone, and she didn't take his hand. And so in the end he sent Linda up the hill with a hard pleading look in his eye.

When she arrived at the mansion, she passed Willis in the pantry but refused to look at him.

"Don't be angry," he said. "I'm only thinking of you. You should watch out for yourself. You don't want to end up like the other girls, do you? He's not what he seems."

"No one is." She left Willis, following Rosa up the tunnel of the back stairs. The steps whined as they climbed, each step moaning louder than the previous one, and Linda realized there'd be no sneaking out in the middle of the night. Upstairs, Rosa led Linda down to the dark end of a hall. "He wants you here." Her lips were as red as jam with a new lipstick called La Petite Fille.

"Can this be right?" Linda asked as the door opened. "Isn't his room down there?" Linda asked whether there mightn't be a room she could share with one of the other maids. But Rosa rolled her eyes in the direction of Captain Poore's door at the opposite end of the hall and repeated, "He wants you here." The eight-paneled door gleamed from its daily polishing, and Linda instructed herself not to imagine the goings-on behind it, the sighs in the night. No, she would endlessly try to keep herself from pondering Willis in such a way. But when she did—when she pictured him asleep, his hair folded across his eye, a curled fist rubbing his nose—she hurried her imagination onward to something else, back to Bruder and the elusive, dark beauty he had presented her as he slept in her arms.

"Lolly's room is that one over there." The two young women looked toward a door with a gilt knob cast in the shape of a tightly puckered rose.

"This can't be right," Linda said again, but Rosa assured her it was.

The other maids slept either in the attic on the third floor, where in summer the rafters trapped the heat, or in the narrow rooms behind the kitchen, where the buttery air left their faces slick with grease. According to rumor passed around the ranch house, Rosa slept upon a locket of her mother's blue-black hair, and her tiny room, which she permitted few people to enter, was kept just as it was the day her mother died—thin, white sheet stretched across the mattress, pillow flattened down to a small square pad, colored-pencil drawings of Rosa and her mother holding hands in the garden. The room was on the third floor, with a single dormer window that let in the dawn light, and from it she could see everyone arriving at the ranch. "Keep an eye on the comings and goings around here," her mother used to tell her, and all her life Rosa had clung to this advice as if it were the only thing her mother had left behind. Her mother's death had brought a heavy sadness to Rosa at a young age—sad eyes in a fragile face. She was delicately boned, but not in a girlish way; no, her comportment was more like that of a widow—she was a tiny-wristed woman who appeared frail but was in fact strong, hardened by the life she was required to live. Rosa never encouraged the flirtations the ranch hands tossed her way—like an enemy's grenade, she thought of their playful words—and she ignored the sucking noise they made through their teeth; *¡Rosa! ¡Mi Rosa!* She tried not to spend much time at the ranch house, where crusty-lipped whistles were offered as sincerely as valentines. If one of the boys hooted at her, she'd ignore him, but her detachment would spur the young men even more. Some of the hands would ask Linda or even Bruder for news of Rosa—what could they do to make her smile? One hand was caught sneaking up the hill to serenade her, his spit on his harmonica lit by the moonlight. Others spent a week's wages on silly gifts like an abalone-shell music box, or a pink rose suspended in a wax globe. But Rosa was occupied by something else—and most assumed that it was grief. She ignored the boys. She dismissed the attentions of every man except one—or so Linda learned when she was unpacking her things in her new room, folding her few blouses and skirts into the cherry-wood dresser, its drawer deep and finely crafted. There was a rap on her door, and she was afraid she knew who it might be, but then Linda heard Esperanza asking if she could come in. The girl was carrying samples of her needlework and she pushed them into Linda's hand. "Will you show him for me? This one I did especially for him." It was a little felt sack with a flap, stitched with Captain Poore's monogram. "It's for his medal. A place to store it at night when he's asleep."

"I'll see what I can do."

"You'll try, won't you? For me?"

And then Esperanza proved herself craftier than Linda had realized by saying, "Did I mention I saw Bruder and Rosa out together yesterday afternoon? I guess they were on a Sunday outing of some sort." She released a single spurt of laughter.

"Bruder and Rosa? Yesterday?" Linda didn't say it but she thought: Only hours before he came to me?

"They were at the orange combine. At the end of the day. It was almost evening. I saw them sharing a soda. They were listening to the graphophone."

Had Bruder bought Rosa an orange soda, Linda wondered, and maybe a wedge of orange cake drizzled in icing thin as frost? Esperanza, whose thumb was spotted with needle-pricks, said they seemed to be having a good time. "I wondered where you were, Linda, I really did."

"I was at the stove. I was at the sink." And Linda too wondered what she had missed and how it was that this assignation between Bruder and Rosa had preceded her first night of love. A chill found her and she shivered and it felt as if she were alone in the world, and later, when Willis timidly poked his head in her door, she welcomed him. "Everything's all right?"

She thanked him for his kindness.

"Can I get you anything?"

She said he'd already done enough.

After unpacking and setting the coral pendant on the dressing table, Linda escaped down the back stairs and returned to the ranch house. She spent the day as she had spent her previous days, grinding *masa* and rolling *tortillas* and boiling beans with cubes of ham and lard and whole onions and carrot coins. She delivered lunch to the Naranjo boys and the other teams, and Esperanza helped her pass out to the packers *taquitos* rolled in wax paper. She found Slaymaker on his wagon in the grove and gave him an extra *tamale,* and she noted a sternness in his face that she guessed was exhaustion; Hearts was next to him and he didn't say anything either, just tucked away a tentative grin. Slay silently accepted the *tamale,* dividing it for him and Hearts, and they understood—even before Linda did—that something had changed. She asked them if they'd seen Bruder. Slay shook his head, the fold in his neck as soft as a bolster. "He was late picking up the girls this morning," said Hearts. Then they turned to their *tamale* and their soda and Linda left them on the wagon, their long shadows merged into one on the ground.

After lunch, she was busy with a roast studded with bacon; the moist scent of chilies and brisket and pork fat overcame the kitchen. The fatty sludge at the bottom of the pan she'd collect and mix into bread dough. While the meat cooked, she made an orange flan for the boys. As she melted the sugar into caramel, she told herself that her days at the Pasadena would be no different than before, except that now she'd have to rise earlier to walk down the hill before everyone woke. The long day would pass in the kitchen, and she'd deliver the food to the hands and the packers, and she'd return to the mansion late at night, after the musicians had left the terrace and the candles in the paper lanterns had been extinguished. She was living in Captain Poore's house but nothing had changed, she carefully reassured herself, and she would have believed this had the boys not been so silent and deferential when she served them the roast later that night. They ate quickly and sucked their fingers and the steam shivered off the meat and no one said anything except, *Is there more?*

She brought them the orange flan, and Hearts asked, "What is it?" When she told them, their faces fell, and then Bruder arrived and said, "Don't you know that the boys hate to eat what they've picked?"

But no one had ever told Linda. The boys left the table disappointed. When they were gone, Bruder asked about her new room.

She shrugged and told him it was nothing special.

"Nothing special? Have you gone spoiled already?"

"How's Rosa?"

"Why do you ask?" She didn't answer, and he said, "How many times do I have to tell you? Rosa's my friend. One day *you'll* wish you had a friend like me."

"One day," she said, and leaving Bruder in the yard she returned to the kitchen with trays of greasy dishes.

The dirt was dry and cold beneath his boots, and his breath puffed so densely that he could nearly hold it in his hands. The kitchen curtain was shoved aside on the rod, and he could see Linda moving about inside. Last night the window had been dark and its darkness had invited him in; the drawn curtain was the sign he had waited a long time for. He had hoped to find Linda just as he had. It had been a plan, but then the plan had unfurled wildly from his hands. Bruder didn't know what had prompted Willis's suspicion this morning, and he was angry that gossip was spuming from the ranch house, but he couldn't guess from whom. It wouldn't have been Hearts and Slay, and it wouldn't have been Rosa—no, she wouldn't do that, not after what she'd told Bruder late Sunday afternoon at the orange combine. They had sat atop a picnic table and for almost an hour she had talked, confessing that she had done something silly, something even Rosa was surprised she had done: she'd gone and fallen in love with Captain Poore, and what was she supposed to do? Bruder had listened but said nothing until she sobbed over her empty soda bottle. "Do you think he might love you?" he said. No, she didn't think so, nor did Bruder, for that matter, and they'd sat for a long time as the afternoon slipped away and the reality of Rosa's life sat up in all its apparent truth, and the picnic bench was rough with splinters, and carved with graffiti professing eternal teenage love. Bruder didn't have to deliver any advice, for Rosa knew what she must do.

She was young but sheltered a knowing soul, and this had been her only lapse from sense; she could add things up better than most. "I know I should give up on him," she said, resigned to the truth but slightly afraid that Bruder would find her childish for even confessing it. Bruder said, "He'll use you." Rosa nodded, knowing that he was right. The late-afternoon sky hung above them, the beautiful rosy light too delicate to last. Bruder promised he'd never tell anyone, not even Linda, and Rosa knew she could trust him, and it didn't occur to him to break that promise, and many years later—after it was too late—he would regret that he had ever believed that a kept secret was an honorable thing.

By the time Linda returned to the mansion, it was past eleven. A firm weariness had entered her, and she made her way up the back stairs with her eyes nearly closed and gritty with sleep. The lights were off and the house was still and the handrail guided her, and she looked forward to the wide canopied bed and the perpetual tick of the little porcelain clock, and just then at the top of the stairs, out of the darkness, Willis said hello. "Do you have everything you need?"

She thanked him, and he said he'd told Rosa to get her whatever she wanted. "I'm sorry you were put in that position," he said. "You'll need to be more careful."

"I've always taken care of myself."

He turned to leave, hesitated, and said: "I'm at the other end of the hall. Just in case."

Linda nodded, and they were two shadows saying good night, and neither could see the other's face, and this was for the best.

On the canopied bed, the silence kept Linda awake. The window was locked, the heavy drape pulled. She was used to the ruckus of the natural world at night—the thrashing ocean, the osprey's emphatic *kee-uk,* the kangaroo rat busy in the underbrush, her father's rattling snore reaching every corner of Condor's Nest. In her narrow bed in the ranch house she used to listen to the soft, toadlike trill of the nighthawk before its plunge into the groves to snare a pocket mouse, and the screams of coyotes in love. Once a cougar had descended from the foothills to pick through the trash, and as she lay in bed listening to his icy hiss she came to realize that something was wrong; if the cougar ate from the trash more than a couple of times, he'd forget how to hunt raccoon. It had happened before, Bruder had told her. The only solution was buckshot between the shoulder blades; and there was another glassy-eyed trophy for Willis's library, where grizzly and bobcat lay filleted on the herringbone floor.

But the mansion—"It's really just a big house," insisted Willis—was sealed off from the world. Linda resigned herself to the lifeless peace, to the motion strangled from the night except for the small gold clock held up by the porcelain man and the senatorial gong of the longcase in the gallery below. Nothing stirred in the house but the click of a door's latch down the hall and a bare foot tentatively landing, and loitering, on the plush runner outside Linda's door.

8

SOME THINGS ARE KNOWN and others reveal themselves over time, and much later Linda would learn that Willis had wanted her to stay in the house from the beginning. It was Lolly who had asked, peeling a persimmon, "But heavens, why?"

Willis profoundly believed that his soul was more generous than his sister's, but he didn't fault her for this; he merely accepted it as fact. Whether or not it *was* fact was almost beside the point. Over the years, Captain Willis Poore had known a number of girls and he'd come to think of them in two ways—or so he explained it to Linda one day. "Girls from Pasadena, and girls from somewhere else. My world's divided up like that."

"Which do you prefer?"

"What do you think?"

She remarked that it was an imbalanced division, wasn't it? How many young women were from Pasadena, anyway? "Even less than you'd guess." He rattled off a list that could be counted on the fingers of two hands: Henrietta, whose family owned the oil fields out by the ocean, not that Henrietta ever visited the greasy wells herself; Margaret, whose family owned a handful of newspapers—not the *American Weekly* or the *Star-News,* she would quickly point out; Dottie Anne, whose family maintained the largest ranch in California, where she spent her holidays inspecting the lambs. Others too: a girl named Eleanor, daughter of a banking family with branches in Nob Hill and San Marino, freckled and tall, sporty on horseback, who years ago had asked Willis to escort her to the debutante ball but then changed her mind. And Maxine, who had a strange ambition to become a scientist, and who hung around the Cal Tech campus and followed the chemists into their labs; she dropped by the Pasadena every now and then, once with a cow's eye floating in a jar. And there was Lolly's best friend, Connie Muffitt, who lived in a redwood Greene & Greene bungalow that featured, in its parlor window, a stained-glass poppy. Connie painted her own teacups with a calligraphy brush and was known around town as an *artiste*. She and Lolly organized an annual production at the Shakespeare Club, and over the years Willis had seen Connie play Ophelia, Goneril, Juliet, and Lady Macbeth, a range that he found impressive if not convincing. To each role she brought the same gold bob, tiny feet, and gentle lisp. At a Shakespeare Club party last spring there'd been an awkward moment of Connie's hand moving to Willis's lap, her hot sugar-rum voice in his ear: "I shall obey, my lord." He told Linda this—not to disparage Connie, he said, but to inform Linda of what kind of man he was. Willis had become known for resisting all the girls who years before had written notes of sympathy on ecru cards when his parents had plunged to their deaths; there had been a line of them at the funeral, beneath black veils, prodded by pearl-braceleted mothers, each waiting her turn to offer condolence and a fine, teenage gloved hand.

Some of this Linda learned from Willis himself, each morning as he walked her down the hill. But the rest came from Rosa. Linda had come to understand that the information Rosa passed along on the stairwell sometimes contradicted Willis's version of events, and Linda had carefully decided that Willis had more reason to tell the truth than did his first-rank maid. There was the time Willis told Linda that he had rushed off to France to fight, "so eager I packed my own rucksack." Rosa etched a more vivid but less credible scene of frightened tears running down Willis's cheek and his boyish face pressed to Lolly's breast. But if Willis had been so scared, how could he have won a medal for courage? Willis told Linda that the one thing he hated about his sister was how she often pretended to be ill: "She does it to get my attention, but I can tell the difference between the flu and folly." Rosa, however, reported otherwise: "She'll stay up all night, coughing into her pillow so he doesn't hear." But if this was true, how was Lolly capable of overseeing the mansion, managing every last floorboard waxing and window polishing and often taking the rag from a maid's hand and saying, "I'll just do it myself." Willis told Linda that he had saved a man's life on the banks of the Meuse; and Rosa said that someone had saved his.

There was no reason not to believe Willis, and one morning on the walk down the hill he said, "I hope Rosa hasn't been telling you any tales. She's an okay girl but tends to make things up. It's her way of not talking about herself." He added: "Or about her mother."

Linda asked what Willis meant.

"She didn't tell you? Her mother died a whore." It was a cruel thing to say, said Linda, and he said, "Cruel but true." He said that he was unlike a lot of other people in Pasadena, and he was only interested in telling the truth, even when it wasn't so pretty. Then Willis startled Linda by saying, "In some ways my mother was pretty much the same as Rosa's."

"How can you say that!"

"I'm only telling the truth."

What type of man would call his mother a whore? Despite the years, Linda's memory of Valencia had never sweetened the truth, and she'd never forget the story of her mother's arrival at Condor's Nest, and of the morning deed in the barn—sunlight gilding the hay, Dieter grunting as he finished up. Once Valencia had admitted to Linda, "All women arrive at the same fate." And Linda had cried, "But not me!"

"I loved my mother," said Willis. "Don't misunderstand me. I think of her every day." A dreaminess descended upon his face, and now he looked more vulnerable than Linda had ever seen him. His eyes were damp and pretty and blue, and his cheek was like a ball of dough, and she thought that if she were to touch it, her finger would sink softly in. If he wasn't a captain, if the medal wasn't hanging from his lapel, if he didn't own the sprawling ranch, he could have been any young man on the street, his eyes lifting to meet hers. It happened often, and she had grown to love it—to *want* it, even: a stranger's eyes widening before her, taking her in, telling her at that tiny instant in his life that he would do anything for her.

"My mother wouldn't want me to tell lies about her," said Willis. "She was an honest woman. She was never one to care about what people said. I guess I'm more like her that way than Lolly is. She was from Maine, my mother, and she came west when she was fifteen."

"Why?"

"Did you say why?" He began again: "She was fifteen. She lived in snowy Maine. Of course she was looking for something else. To become someone else."

He said that his mother was a soprano and had come to Pasadena to sing at the old Moorish Grand Opera House that once stood on the corner of Raymond and Bellview. She was giving a series of bel canto recitals with Donizetti and Bellini on the program—the sleepwalker's aria and Anna Bolena's prison-cell lament—and one night in the audience she saw a handsome man with hair as orange as a tangerine. She later would say that even with the stage lights in her eyes she couldn't miss his hair, like a fire in the second row, burning around a strong, square, durable face. And there was no doubt that Annabelle was beautiful herself that night. She was a honeycomb blonde, with a mouth like the bottom of an apple and two blue eyes big enough to take in the fifteen hundred faces staring up at her as she trilled up to the mountain range of high C's, leapt from peak to peak, and then carefully scaled back down. Her nickname was "the Bluehill Baby"—a label she invented for herself after departing for good the whitewashed village where her mother and father rested in flinty graves.

"My father didn't care much for music," said Willis. "He always said it required too much sitting around." Willis's father, he said, was a strong, compact man who sneered at fanciness even as he surrounded himself with marble and gilt. From years of his riding about the rancho, his skin was as tough and rich as hide. Picking oranges had bulked up his forearms to the firm shape of two meaty drumsticks. He talked with one corner of his mouth cocked and made sucking noises as emphasis, and he almost hadn't gone to the concert at the opera house that night. "Who is this Bluehill Baby anyway?" But word reached Willis Fishe Poore that a young woman of exceptional beauty was singing and that every night she caused the audience to stomp its feet and shout for more. As an encore to the Donizetti and the Bellini on her program Annabelle would sing two songs of a more folksy quality: "The Girl with the Crab-Red Hair" and "Sweet Casco Bay." Between the bel canto and the Maine folksongs, Annabelle would change out of a leaf-colored dress sewn with Bohemian crystal and into a velveteen gown the color of blueberries that revealed a ballerina's neck and small, beautiful shoulders. Across these shoulders lay a patchy brown stole of indeterminate fur, like a dead deer slumped across the rump of a mule. Annabelle Cone's voice wasn't especially big, and it wobbled like a truck as she drove up the peaks of the high C's. Nor was her diction impressive; in fact, most of the time she couldn't be understood, and not just because the songs were in Italian. This was Donizetti and Bellini, and the audience was filled with Pasadenans, and women, and men too, in this town were known to study up on a libretto before going to the opera house. No, her vocal talent was limited, destined to earn her a living as long as she was healthy and young but—and Annabelle Cone knew this better than anyone else—the day her beauty began its inevitable retreat, her career would end.

What was all the fuss?, Willis Fishe wondered impatiently in the audience. But then in the interludes Annabelle would lift her hem and display ankles in pinky-brown stockings, and she would dance across the stage in a quick, proud trot, her calves as pretty as sweetmeats beneath the lights. As she finished each song she'd throw a prop—a country-white rose, a paper fan, a handful of peas—into the audience, which swayed en masse trying to catch them. And on that fateful night her leopard-lily corsage landed in Willis's lap, the rusty stamens staining his fly. The man next to him received a dark, wet handkerchief that smelled like old roses fallen to the ground. Three rows back, a man caught an empty Eau-de-Moi perfume bottle shaped like a mermaid, with a pretty fake-gold cap.

But it was during the encore—as the Bluehill Baby belted out "She had crab-red hair, that made me long and stare!"—that Willis Fishe Poore knew he must meet the soprano. After the recital he went to leave his calling card with the opera house's manager, a bald, happy gentleman who walked home every night with his cash in his boot. But to Willis Fishe's surprise, the manager told him that Miss Cone was waiting for him backstage. Willis Fishe found her at her mirror, pinning her hair into a plump chignon. Years later, he would often describe the scene as virtually the reunion of a brother and sister: "It was as if we had known each other all our lives, separated at birth or something of the such." Their eyes met thrice in the three-panel mirror, and never again did they look away. But in fact they didn't speak that night. They kissed on the dusty backstage and Willis Fishe repinned the leopard lily to Annabelle's bosom and stroked her cheek, which he always said was as cold as north-face snow.

After that, Annabelle and Willis Fishe began a short-lived correspondence, his letters delivered by wagon from the ranch, the driver instructed to wait for Miss Cone's reply. "One long furious week of love written on the page," said Willis Fishe's son. After one week the mar-

riage proposal arrived, in Willis Fishe's nearly illegible hand. Annabelle
Cone accepted it at once and arrived at the Pasadena on a September
morning in 1898 in her bridal gown, ivory lace hiding her face. The
mayor of Pasadena was fetched, and in a little ceremony on the lawn,
Willis Fishe Poore and Annabelle Cone were married, the maids, including Rosa's mother, throwing rose petals and whispering behind
their cupped hands. As the mayor read through his rigmarole, Willis
Fishe realized that he had never heard his bride-to-be speak, and he anticipated the voice of the smallest, prettiest bird. But when she declared
"I do," he learned how wrong a man can be. Only then did he discover
that her beautiful if somewhat strained soprano coexisted with a speaking voice not of liquid gold or fruitwood oil or the small trill of a song-
bird but as fierce, and as difficult on the ear, as a peacock's scream.

But this last part Linda didn't learn from Captain Poore. No, this
aspect of the story came from Rosa, who had learned it from her mother.
"It's how mistakes are made," said Rosa. "And lives ruined." She described the lawn wedding as rushed and private—"Annabelle was so
thin, she would show within the month"—and how several weeks later
the police shut down the Grand Opera House after discovering that it
was the front for a brothel. Linda said that she didn't believe her, and
Rosa said, "Fine, don't." But during the raid, it seemed, the police had
discovered a secret chamber, occupied à deux, that the arrested house
manager, in confession, called "Annabelle's Attic." And a second room,
with walls padded in blue velveteen, identified as "Miss Cone's Candy
Cove."

9

DURING HER FIRST DAYS in her new room, Linda learned more
and more about life in the big house and in the little city endlessly
expanding nearby. The more she discovered, the deeper her interest
ran, and the further Bruder felt from her. Despite herself, everything
about the Rancho Pasadena fascinated her, nothing more so than Captain Poore himself. Each morning he walked her down the hill—and
often he'd walk her back up again at night—and once or twice he visited her in the ranch-house kitchen and leaned against the table while
she dressed the chickens or chopped the onions; and the sweet, eye-
burning odor would rise to her nostrils, carrying her back to Condor's
Nest. Willis would comment, "Even after growing up on an onion
farm, they still make you cry," and she'd dab her eyes with her sleeve.
He asked about her mother, and she told him the stories; twice he asked
how she had died, and the third time she described the landslide. This
was on a cold December night when the kitchen's warmth draped the
windows with opaque moisture and the ranch on the other side of
the glass was blurry. Linda realized that no one could see clearly into
the kitchen, that anyone passing by would see only fuzzy shapes of
movement. She talked of the steady ache and said she doubted it would
go away. Willis said that his heart too had collapsed when he saw the dirigible deflate, the silver balloon sinking in the sky.

But on many nights Willis was busy with meetings and committees
and hearings about various issues, including a proposed motor parkway
connecting Pasadena to Los Angeles (he was in favor) and the Bakewell
& Brown design for the new City Hall (he was in favor of a belfry, but
others wanted a dome).

Lolly was equally busy in her own pursuits. The Monday Afternoon Club would meet in the Ladies' Lounge of the Huntington Hotel to discuss literature and geography, and the Women's Committee of the Valley Hunt Club gathered to put the finishing touches on the New Year's ball and the flower-draped carriage for the Tournament of Roses. Lolly was as aware of her responsibilities to Pasadena's civic advancements as her brother was, and the seriousness with which she pursued them gave her a tight-faced appearance, like the skin atop a cup of warmed-over milk. Despite her slightness, and her frequent but unspecified infirmities, Lolly was an energetically organized, determined, and carefully bunned woman who kept a tidy appointment book and, folded and tucked into her sleeve, a list of things to accomplish during each day: write the mayor about the dangers of the chariot races; discuss Christmas goose with Cook; beat the carpets; "swim 1 mile"—the 1 then crossed out and changed to a 2. Her efficiency—she could be a tall, slender blur in the hall—further contradicted Rosa's description of a soft-fleshed invalid, gasping for breath and strength. It was true that there was a silliness to her repeated recitation of her iron deficiency and her struggle to stay afloat in the pool because she lacked "a normal person's buoyancy of fat." But she was not the *little girl frozen in time* Rosa had depicted; nor was Captain Poore a *selfish little boy.*

They were rich and they were spoiled and they were eccentric, but they were always kind to Linda.

On her own, Linda came to this conclusion—that Rosa depicted the Poores unfairly—just as she realized that the ranch and the city constituted a whole, full world, one that she believed more and more could make a small place for her. Each evening as she rested her cheek upon the spiny down pillow, the silk canopy stretching above her and the little clock ticking, she grew ever more accustomed to the room that had seemed so foreign that first night. And just as she had grown used to living in the house—referring to the pretty little room as "mine" without knowing she was doing so—Bruder asked when was she moving back to the ranch house.

"I can't return *there.*"

"I understand. But you don't want to get too used to it. It'll be hard to leave when the season ends."

"I'll be ready to go when the time comes. It's just a big old house." And she put her arms around him and tilted her head in that way she

had discovered could affect him more than anything she could say. She
didn't know that she wasn't speaking the truth—she didn't know her
heart well enough to be so calculating. No, she simply said things she
knew she should, even if they were false. She implied that she would
return to the ranch house if Willis would permit her, and against his
best judgment Bruder believed her. He said, "I'll talk to Willis." "I've
already tried," Linda said quickly. "He won't budge. Besides, what difference does it make after all? Nearly all my time is spent right here in
the kitchen, where I've always been." And then: "With you." The raw,
unpainted shelves, the floorboards so widely spaced that they perpetually trapped the dirt, and the stained oilcloth suddenly depressed her;
was this really how she'd been meant to spend her days? But she continued, "Nothing's really changed. I might as well be sleeping in the little room back there," and she pointed to where they had shared their
night; but now that Linda knew better, she realized the room was nothing more than a closet; in fact, Lolly's closet, shown to Linda by Rosa,
was more than twice as large.

But just as something almost imperceptible was shifting within
Linda, a new sense of trust was taking shape within Bruder. He hun-
grily believed her, just as he recalled every detail of her body: the strong
lines on the inside of her arms, her narrow, moon-white hips, the pink
nipples upturned and greeting him, the flash of dark, dark hair between
her thighs. He had been only with whores, and he never really looked
at them, never wanted to look into their eyes, and with them his hands
would find cool, hard flesh in the dark and he'd go about his business
and finish up and always he'd say thank you. He was the type of man to
pay in advance, so that the girl would know his word was good and his
money real and so she could relax a little—if that was possible; Bruder
didn't fool himself about what the girl was thinking. But it was as if he
had found an entirely different type of pleasure in Linda, and the short
hours holding her had left him desperate for more. Nightly he reminded himself of the virtue of patience, and once or twice he thought
that if he was to marry her, they could at last be together and Willis
would have to let Bruder build a cabin at the far end of the grove, and
there, together, they'd wait for fate to run its course. No matter what,
Bruder remained committed to his belief in fate: they were meant to be
together, and the time would come, and if he didn't have this, what else
would he have? He would say to her, "We'll be together."

And she would say, "I know."

When there were moments to steal, they kissed, and rubbed the dusk-cold from their hands, and Bruder failed to taste the hesitation on her lip or feel it in her fingertips. When she asked about Rosa, why he was spending so much time with her, he failed to hear the skepticism in Linda's voice. "How many times do I have to tell you? She's my friend, and I've made a promise." When he said that she should be careful around Willis, Bruder was oblivious to her averted eye. He never saw the joy lifting Linda's chin when Willis stopped by the ranch house. Bruder might have been suspicious of others, but not of her. "There's nothing duplicitous about Linda," he confessed to Rosa, who replied, in a distracted way, "I'm sure you're right."

One night, Bruder asked Linda to stay with him. "Let's sit by the fire and watch the stars," he said. "There are so many tonight." And she agreed. "But let me go up and wash my face and change my dress." He told her that she looked beautiful right then, and she said, "I've been working since five o'clock. Let me go and change." And he tugged her hands and she slipped out of his grasp and ran up the hill.

In her room there was an oval mirror in a wooden stand, and in front of it she changed, and brushed down her hair, and tried a little of Rosa's lipstick and clasped the coral pendant around her throat. The dress was old, but Esperanza had embroidered pink and yellow roses on the cuffs and the collar, and Linda unwrapped the stockings she had bought all those weeks ago, the silk now flimsy and dead-feeling in her hand. She wished she had a new dress and a new pair of stockings, but she didn't; and she reminded herself of what Bruder was always saying about patience. He would say that it would bring both of them their true fate. She liked to challenge him: "But what if I'm meant for something else? Shouldn't I hurry up and chase it? Grab it?" And she'd clutch his shirt and pull Bruder toward her, and if no one was around they would kiss. Once Hearts and Slay saw them in an embrace, and one of them said, "Uh-oh. Looks like trouble," and the other laughed, and Linda and Bruder, holding on tight, each laughed into the sweet musk of the other's hair.

Then there was a knock on her door. "Linda? Are you there? Lolly wants to know if you'll come down and join us."

Through the door she said, "I can't tonight."

"What can't wait until morning?"

She thanked Willis and asked if she could join them another time, and he said, a bit impatiently, "Why not tonight?"

She said she needed to return to the kitchen. Willis promised there'd be music and he lowered his voice and said he had a good bottle of champagne on ice and Lolly wasn't going to have any and wouldn't it be a shame for him to have to drink it alone. "Linda? For a little bit?"

She hesitated, and the reflection in the mirror showed a beautiful girl dressed for an evening grander than a night by the ranch-house fire. "I can't," she tried again.

But then Willis was saying, "Do this for me?" He knocked impatiently on the door, and then the knob turned (when she'd first moved in, she'd noticed that there had once been a lock on the door but that it had been removed), and Willis was standing at the threshold. He was dressed in his dinner jacket, and his hair was tonicked down, and he was handsome and held a white-hearted rose in his palm. "For a few minutes?"

And Linda, who sometimes lost track of herself, agreed. "Just twenty minutes. Then I'll have to go back to the ranch house."

She stepped into the hall, and the music greeted her. They followed it, descending the stairs, passing the window with its view of the mountains; the lights from the observatory burned like low-hanging stars. On the loggia was a graphophone in a richly oiled wood box, its great petunia horn pumping jazz. Lolly was on a wicker swing reading the newspapers. Willis said, "May I get you some cider?" He winked and disappeared and, in a minute, returned with two brown mugs filled with champagne. Linda brought her mug to her lips and sipped; she coughed then, the bubbles tickling her throat, and it felt as if at once a bubble rose and popped in her head. Giddiness took her by the hand.

"Have you been ill, too?" asked Lolly. "That cough of yours?"

"Let's get some real music going," said Willis. He switched records, resetting the hummingbird needle. A rhythmic version of "Rumble, Tumble" began to play, and Willis kicked his feet a little and the champagne sloshed in his mug. His shoes were shiny, and his medal looked as if it too had been polished. He had gone to the barber recently, and the shell-pink scar was exposed and he mindlessly rubbed it with his handkerchief before wiping the spilled champagne from his thigh.

"Do you like to dance?" he asked Linda.

"Of course she likes to dance," said Lolly. "What girl doesn't?"

"You don't, sister."

"That's different." Lolly rolled her eyes and they turned in their sockets like two large, handblown marbles. It was as if she had said, *Men!* Or, *What will I ever do with him?* She pulled the *American Weekly* insert out of the *Star-News* and shook back the pages and burrowed into the stories with an *Oh goodness me,* like a sighing dog curling up for sleep. But soon she was emitting noises as she read the gossip: *Aha* and *Mmm-hmm* and *Uh-huh* and *Tsk-tsk* and a short, whiplike "I knew it." Her commentary continued as she read along:

"That figures."

"I saw it coming."

And once, "I always knew she should've been more careful."

"Anything good in the paper, sister?"

"Just the usual odds and ends," she said, although her perusal of the society page was performed with an earnestness and exactitude that swelled beyond casual interest. On the days when she opened the newspaper and found neither herself nor Willis mentioned, she was both relieved and disappointed. "But the last place you want to end up is in Chatty Cherry's column," Lolly would say, pushing her face into the newsprint and clearing her throat and saying, more to herself than to anyone else, "Now let's see what old Cherry's dug up this time."

She read the column while Willis fiddled with another disk, and Linda felt the champagne rise in her head. "Listen to this one," said Lolly, who, Linda could see, managed to tap endless reserves of energy to make her way through the gossips. Lolly denied that she was *hooked.* "I only read Cherry's column with any regularity. The others I just skim. Besides, the *American Weekly* recently gave her twice the space, so now she coughs up all sorts of useful news." As if to prove that Chatty Cherry's column was of greater merit than those pecked out by other society reporters, Lolly opened to it, cleared her throat, looked up to make sure Willis and Linda were listening, and began:

ANOTHER WEEK IN THE VALLEY
By Chatty Cherry

I wonder whose daughter didn't fit into her debutante dress the other morning when she went to try it on? They say screams could be heard across several San Marino estates, all the way down to the

old mill, I was told, disturbing even the swallows. Was it one too
many "ile flotantes," this season's dessert of choice at the Valley
Hunt Club, or was it something of an entirely different nature?
Meanwhile, did anyone notice which railroad man's wife was strap-
hanging on a competitor's line last Monday? Where was she going
anyway, and what was in her Broadway Brothers bag? I didn't know
she shopped there, did you? Could the not unattractive woman
have been on her way to that young bride's first attempt at throwing
a ladies' luncheon? Probably not, but in any case sources say the
naive hostess spent too much time preparing her hair and face and
not enough worrying over her canapes and her tennis-special
punch. All in all, a failed afternoon, many women agreed as they
walked in wet ivy to fetch their cars since the valet boys either forgot to show up or were never hired. But it provided plenty to talk
about the next day on the Garden Club's tour, didn't it? That is,
until the tour reached the Linda Vista yard where a workman was
found sleeping shirtless and sweaty in a cart. The Garden Club,
made up almost exclusively of ladies, collectively averted its eyes,
except for one pretty blue pair belonging to a not old woman who
has shown previous interest in household staff. The man was fired
and the Garden Club left before viewing the narcissus patch behind
the tennis court. And while we're on the topic, guess which ladies
tennis champion seems to think there's room for her at the Midwick's bachelor bar? They say even the club manager can't throw
her out, but who am I to say what's right and wrong?

"Where is that reporter from?"

"Who, Cherry?" Lolly brought a ringed finger to her chin. "I don't
really know. She turned up only a few years back. But I don't know anyone in town who doesn't read her."

"Have you met her?" asked Linda.

"Met Cherry? Of course not. You never want to meet Cherry. She's
a lurker. Hanging around a hibiscus shrub to get a story—that sort of
business. No one wants to talk to her. No one answers her phone calls."

"*Somebody* must talk to her," said Willis. "*Somebody's* feeding her the
news."

"The maids are, that's who," said Lolly. "It's a problem for everyone.
You've got to watch your gals."

"Not ours," said Willis.

"I wouldn't trust that Rosa with my middle name."

"Be kind, sister. Rosa's a good girl, and you know it."

"I'm sure she's the one who spilled the news about my anemia."

"Ah, sister, put the paper down and let's dance."

Willis pulled Lolly from the swing and she complained about her legs and protested that she really shouldn't, *the doctor said* . . . Yet as soon as they began to two-step, her eyes narrowed and her lips pressed together and she concentrated on the task of dancing around the loggia. The song had a long refrain—*Rollick frolic! Frisker whisker!*—and each time it came around Willis would plunge his sister so low in his arms that she'd become a board nearly horizontal above the floor and her hair would loosen from its knot and fill out like fruit swelling on the branch. Linda watched them, and she wondered what was the likelihood that her old pal Charlotte Moss had moved up the coast and reinvented herself as Chatty Cherry. It seemed unlikely that she could have attained such influence in four short years, but after all, weren't transformations often seemingly completed overnight? You go to bed one person, and wake up as someone else. Wasn't that the point? To shed the past like a layer of grime running down the drain?

When the record ended, Willis redeposited his sister in the swing. Lolly was flushed, and her chest rose and fell as she caught her breath, and she swabbed her throat with a piece of lace. Her eyes were pale and sensitive and trained on Willis.

"Now it's your turn," he said to Linda.

She moved to him, but Lolly said, "Oh, she doesn't want to dance with you. She must think we're so silly. She's too grown-up for such horsing around."

But Linda said that indeed she *did* want to dance, and soon Willis's arms were around her and holding her close. His hand upon the small of her back made a subtle circling motion as he guided her around the loggia, and it was as if he had found a spot on her flesh she herself didn't know: his strong fingers working the flesh beneath her cheap, thin dress. Willis hadn't even noticed the embroidery, Linda realized; it was as if he had seen right through everything she wore, as if she might as well have worn nothing at all.

And Linda closed her eyes and imagined that it was Bruder holding her, leading her round the loggia. No, what she imagined in fact was more complicated than that: she dreamed that Bruder was Captain Poore, that Captain Poore's world was Bruder's, and that she and Bruder could live like this, together and alone and comforted by the vastness of the ranch cradled in the valley. It was simple for her to envision, an entire world formed bright and green behind her eyelids, and it couldn't have been further from reality, but there it was in Linda's mind, every last detail of her desired world conceived.

The evening continued, but every time Linda said she had to be going, Willis would bring her a refilled mug and say, "One more dance." Linda would refuse, but he'd pull her hand and she'd relent, and she wanted both to leave and to stay and her impulses were crossed and confused. Willis put on a new record and took turns dancing with Linda and Lolly. While he danced with Linda, Lolly would return to the gossip columns and she'd read the *especially good* items aloud, and her gleeful chuckle was as close to a cackle without being a cackle as was possible. And while Willis danced with his sister, Linda would lean against a pillar and listen to the breeze in the philodendron leaves and the trickle in the fountain. After almost an hour he said, "I'm worn out," and he plopped onto the wicker sofa and lay on his back with his feet on the floor and he looked like a teenager slouched and drunk. Then he popped up and refilled his mug, and Linda's as well, and Lolly said, "Maybe I'll have a little cider after all." But Willis was quick to say, "Sister, do you think you should? Didn't the doctor say to count your sugar? Cider's nothing but."

"Maybe you're right." And Lolly tugged a long woven-silk sash that hung from the ceiling, and a tinny little bell, like the kind on a shop's door, jingled. She yanked it until Rosa scurried onto the loggia, asking what she could get Miss Poore.

Lolly ordered some tea. Before she left, Rosa looked at Linda in a way that embarrassed her, and Linda felt that she was being accused of pretending to be someone she was not. She wanted to defend herself: *He invited me! I didn't ask to be here!* She wanted to go to the kitchen with Rosa and help with the tea; she wanted to touch Rosa somewhere where her flesh was bare and vulnerable and say, "Promise me one thing? You won't mention any of this to Bruder? I'm not trying to hide anything, but you know how he is. . . ." But Rosa had turned on her heel too quickly for Linda to say anything at all. She and Bruder had never discovered how Willis had learned about their night together in the narrow bed, and Linda had concluded that it was Rosa. "She's spying on us," Linda had said to Bruder. "She told him." But Bruder held her fists and kissed her forehead and said, "Don't be silly. You don't know Rosa the way I do." He said, "It was just a coincidence. He doesn't know what happened. He's a suspicious man. He could see something between us, that's all. That's why he made you move up the hill. Don't think about it. And don't blame Rosa. Linda, she wants to be your friend." But Linda said, "I know how a girl like Rosa can be."

It was an unkind thing to say, and Bruder told her so, adding, "I don't like it when you're cruel." And this pricked Linda sharply and she pulled back and said, "I didn't mean to be. You're right. I won't think about Rosa like that anymore." But Linda couldn't stop herself; the accusation swelled in her mind every day.

While they waited for Rosa to bring the tea, Lolly and Willis began arguing over what Linda quickly surmised they'd been arguing about for several days: whether or not to pave the road that ran from the front gate up one side of the hill and down the other to the ranch house. "I refuse to live through another year of mud," said Lolly, folding her arms.

"You make it sound like the mud lasts forever. We have our rainy days, and by February the skies are mostly clear and the mud dries and it isn't all that bad. We're not living back east, after all."

"Even so, when it's muddy, the road can become *impassable*. Dangerous, even!" Her fingers fell on Linda's hand in emphasis, or warning.

Willis changed the record again, and soon the Bubb Brothers were singing, according to Willis, "authentic Harlem jazz-a-roo!" The song was about a girl named Maggie who'd been lost on a street corner, and the Bubbs crooned and their voices were more intoxicating than the champagne. When Rosa returned with the teapot, Linda asked if she could help, but it was an ill-timed question, for what was there for her to do now that the tea had been delivered? "I'll see you in the morning," said Rosa, and the look on Willis's face suggested that he thought that was a rude thing to say to Linda, no matter that it was true—unless, of course, something were to happen to Linda between now and the morning. But what could happen? she thought, reminding herself that she'd have to emphasize to Rosa and to Bruder and to Hearts and Slay that it was only by chance that *she* had ended up in the room at the end of the mansion's hall, and not one of *them*. It hadn't been her doing at all.

Once Rosa was gone, Willis pulled Linda up again and held her firmly to his chest. The space between them narrowed to a nearly imperceptible gap, and soon his heartbeat echoed in her breast. Willis said that he wanted to teach her a step called the Grizzly Bear. It involved two or three low sways and then a heavy pounce. "And be sure to curl your fingers like claws." Together, Linda and Willis swayed and pounced, and he growled like a cub.

She had never known anyone like Willis, and she couldn't yet anticipate him. Once, Willis left a note on her pillow for no reason at all: "Sleep well. Dawn will be here soon." The next night he left a second note, and Linda tore it open, her heart racing over their flowering friendship, but then stopping with disappointment: "We're having sixty for dinner tomorrow night. I'm sure Rosa could use an extra hand."

They continued to dance, and the wind rose in the yews, and then rain began to patter in the fountain and on the carpet of ryegrass. Rosa emerged from the house and began to roll down the canvas shades that enclosed the loggia like a tent. Linda moved to help, but Willis pulled her and said, "Let Rosa do it." Linda said that it would take only a minute—the shades needed to be fastened down, like sails, to the floor and to the side pillars—but when she tried to take one of the shade's corners, Rosa shook her head. "No, keep dancing."

Soon the rain had turned heavy, pelting the canvas and shaking the fabric in gusts. The loggia had the feeling of a sultan's grand tent, candlelight flickering against canvas wall and orchids folding demurely in the chill, and as the rain grew in intensity it seemed as if the tent were under siege. It had turned even colder, and Rosa rolled out a heater— the same kind used to warm the orchards—and lit a blue flame in its chimney. But Willis wanted to continue dancing; he riffled through his stack of record disks and held up one and said, "You'll love it." And he was right, Linda loved the music, the soft cry of a song called "Valley of the Night" and the harp in the ballad "Mountaintop for Two."

The storm was pelting the canvas walls so hard that Linda was sure it must be hailing too. She shivered, and Willis rubbed her spine in a friendly way, pressing out the cold. Their bodies touched in many places, their chests and thighs and knees and the simmering skin of their cheeks. The orchard-heater's gem-blue flame burned clear and hard, and something warm spread across Linda, a seeping feeling, and Willis was saying something—*Isn't it nice to have you here,* she thought it was—and for some reason Linda was confused by this: she wasn't sure if he meant her or Lolly, who remained on the swing enjoying the news, her fingertips now smudged with ink. The record ended, and the music gave way to the blowing night. The rain was falling in waves, and it made her think of the nights she used to lie awake, Siegmund at her side, listening to the surf. A clap of thunder startled her, and Willis too, and they pressed together, and it felt as if something passed from Willis to Linda, nothing more visible or tangible than a current of electricity or the pulsing wind, and whatever it was, it was small and hidden from the eye, but nonetheless it was there and had transferred, between them. The needle continued to scratch, and Lolly got up and changed the disk. "This one's my favorite." Soon a creamy-voiced man was singing about the night he found his love, *Up in the air! Up up in the black, black air!* Linda had never heard the song before, but it was beautiful, and Lolly must have sensed the pleasure on her face because she said, "Why don't you and I dance? It's time we kick old Willis aside."

The two girls danced in circles and took turns leading each other, and the song started off slowly but broke into a stomping, giddy cakewalk, and the next song was a Virginia reel. Lolly's skin was cold, and up close she appeared both old and young at once, and it was easy to imagine sixty years into the future when she would appear, except for her surely sugar-white hair, nearly the same as she did tonight. "You're a good dancer," she complimented Linda, the flattery sounding sticky on her lips. "You should teach me some time." Linda said that she had learned from watching her brother. "He used to go to the dances at the Cocoonery," she said. The girls said nothing more as the song and the rain continued. The canvas flaps shook somberly, and the wind tried to snap them from their hooks, and Linda worried that the rain was coming down too hard for December. Was the ranch ready? The grove protected? "I should get down to the ranch house and check on things."

Willis was lying on the swing with a cigar lodged in his mouth. "We pray for nights like this. It'll be snowing in the mountains."

Lolly said, "But, Willis, maybe she's right. Maybe you should look to see if Bruder has everything under control." And not a single second passed after she said this—not even a heartbeat in the fastest, most excited heart—when one of the canvas shades flapped open and Bruder

appeared, his shirt pasted wet to his skin. His arrival was so abrupt that
Lolly gasped, and simultaneously she and Linda let go of each other, as
if guilty of something.

"Get your coats," ordered Bruder; his face was calm but serious, and
if the music hadn't already ended, his grave stare would have brought it
to a halt. The rain dripping from his brow smudged his eyes. The scene
before him was what he had expected—the stuttering graphophone's
arm and Lolly's newspapers thrown about and Willis's champagne-
pickled breath and the dancing-scuffed tiles—all of it was familiar and
expected, except for Linda. He noted the embroidery on her dress and
the arrangement of her hair, something she must have learned about in
one of Lolly's beauty magazines. The pink lingering in Linda's cheek,
and the oil on her eyelid, suggested champagne too. If the freezing rain
weren't driving down so hard, he would have accused her then. But
with every passing minute the ranch could be losing another tree, and
he cared about the land as much as he cared about anything; it was
where he believed his future lay—*their* future—and he would confront
her later. His hurt would have to wait, as it always would.

"Everything's freezing over fast," he said. "We need everyone."

The road down the hill had already turned to mud, and Bruder's
half-ton truck began to skid, and he and Willis got out to inspect the
slick dirt while Linda sat at the idling wheel. They told her to try the
truck again, and when she released the brake and pulled the choke,
she feared the truck would glide off the road and over the hillside. Even
in the dark the icy crystals in the hard mud were bright, and the road
looked like a slow, dark river. Eventually she got out of the truck and
told them they were wasting time, and the three ran down the hill,
hunched in their coats, the balloons of their breath pelted and popped
by the rain.

Behind them they heard, "Wait for me!" Lolly was running toward
them, her beaver coat swinging heavily. Willis told her to go home, and
she said that it was her ranch too and she was going to help, and a tiny
goddammit! peeped from her mouth, and even Lolly seemed surprised
by her assertion. "There's no time for this," said Bruder. "There's no
time."

Down in the yard the hands were busy pulling from the shed the
smudgers and the portable tanks of distillate oil, the tanks' caps lost

long ago and replaced by potatoes. The men tried to fight the cold in their hats, and their tight Stockinette jackets buttoned to the throat, and their ponchos worn over aprons worn over knit sweaters worn over nightshirts on top of their Sunday solesette shirts. They stamped the cold from their feet and stood with their shoulders close to their ears and dragged the smudgers into the yard and up into the wagon's bed. The base of each smudger was disk-shaped, like a curling stone, and painted red, but the years had dented the steel and scarred the paint. From the base rose a four-foot chimney with a sheet of mesh over the flue. The chimneys were black and, soon, so were the men, the soot imprinting their gloves and their thighs, their guts, the skin around their eyes.

Slaymaker was organizing the men into a line to pass the smudgers along from shed to wagon, but the men wouldn't stay in place, instead yelling at one another to wrap the horses and the burros, and Hearts was yelling at Slay to tell the boys to keep still. Muir Yuen and his cousins were in the yard as well, but they wore nothing warmer than blue fireman's shirts as they fastened burlap and rope to each mule's back. The real work hadn't even begun, but Linda could see that the men were already angry about the cold and the rain, and she asked Willis if he didn't have anything warm to lend them—scarves or blankets or anything?

"We'll need some coffee," he said, the youth draining rapidly from his face.

The smudgers held two and a half gallons of fuel each, and Slay was complaining that for a few years now he'd been telling Willis to buy five-gallon tanks. "They'll burn up their gas before sunrise," Slay warned, and the other men realized it too. Linda could see it in the downward etch in their faces, these men who knew that the long night's work of distributing the smudgers throughout the groves was only the beginning; by the time they'd laid the last smudger and lit its greasy flame, they'd have to return to the first to refill its tank. Everyone seemed to know that they'd lose trees in the night—many more than they had lost in several years—and quite possibly a hand or two, quitters who'd ice up in the fingertip and walk off in the direction of Los Angeles, where a train would take them to better-managed strawberry fields in the San Joaquin. And each man knew that if he wasn't careful, a flame could leap from one of the chimneys to his coat. There wasn't a hand at the Rancho Pasadena who hadn't seen a buddy burn from wrist to wrist on a black freezing night.

Bruder was complaining that there weren't enough smudgers for the grove, and yelling that they'd have to light brushwood fires in the ditches. He ordered Hearts to take five men into the groves and start piling up the cordwood. "Dump a little gasoline on the logs, and let the fires go." The rain was beginning to stop, which meant that the night would turn only colder, and Bruder predicted that by two or three it'd be so cold that they'd need a smudger for every tree—and at last count they had only a thousand. "It's going down below freezing. Twenty-seven or twenty-eight," he said. He knew the San Gabriel Valley as well as anyone, and he knew the way the cold caught in the foothills and the arroyos and how the eucalyptus emitted its green scent as the temperature dipped. "Everything's going to be ice. The oranges and everything else." He yelled at Lolly, "You should go back up and wrap your roses."

But Lolly said that she'd come to help, and at once the men looked at her and took note of her hooded beaver and her velvet slippers peeking from her hem and her fists curled as tight and white as stones. "Then get in the wagon," said Bruder. She extended her hand, seeking his assistance, but Bruder loaded another smudger and Lolly climbed onto the wagon bench next to Slaymaker. "That muskrat?" he asked.

"Where's the coffee?" Bruder shouted. "Get the coffee on." He no longer frightened Linda when he was like this. She believed that she could now anticipate him, and it was as if suddenly the most mysterious man in the world had become predictable. She watched him as he grabbed hold of a smudger and hoisted it into the wagon. The two-and-a-half-gallon tanks were empty, and they echoed with cold. Bruder let Lolly try to lift one, but it fell to the wagon bed with a hollow clang that rose above the yard and called out to the fluffy ears of a screech owl, who responded kindly with a series of low, short whistles.

Bruder had to calculate the best way to hold off the frost. He decided that they'd set out one heater for every four trees, leaving some trees unheated except for the ditch fires. He knew certainly that some of the oranges would freeze before dawn, but he told his men that he'd rather lose a harvest than a tree. But Willis disagreed with Bruder's calculations, and argued that they should spread the smudgers evenly

across the grove, one for every eight trees. "Maybe we won't lose anything. Maybe it won't get any colder than this."

"I'm not willing to risk anything with your hopeful wishing," said
Bruder, counting the hands off into teams. "One heater for every four,"
he called through the megaphone of his hands. "Now get out there!"

"You seem to be forgetting whose ranch this is," said Willis.

"I'm not forgetting anything." And then: "Maybe it's you who's
forgotten."

There was a current in the air that everyone could feel as it ran between Willis and Bruder. Many of the hands were surprised that Bruder would speak to the captain like that, and even more surprised that
the captain would let him.

And soon Willis was conceding, "There's no time for arguing. Get
the boys to work."

By midnight everyone was in the grove, a chain of men down each
row of trees. One hand would dig a shallow hole, and another would
drop the smudger into it. Then they'd pull out the hose from the fuel-
tank wagon and fill the smudger's base. They'd light the smudger and
an oily flame would catch at the chimney's mouth, grimy black smoke
lifting and settling on the men's faces. Lolly helped with the fuel tank,
and Linda and Mrs. Yuen ran the coffee from the stove to the men
while Willis took orders from Bruder like any other ranch hand.

After the coffee was made and a sloshing pot was hung from the
back of each wagon, Linda said she was going to work in the grove as
well. She looked around for something to do, and—inevitably, it
seemed to her—she found herself working alongside Willis, she digging a shallow grave for the smudger and he guiding it in, laying it
down.

Willis didn't say much as they worked. She asked him if he'd ever
lived through a freeze and he said, "Not in a couple of years." She could
sense that he was aware of what everyone was wondering: why was the
grove so poorly prepared for the winter? Eventually he said, "The last
big icing was in 1912. They said it was a once-in-a-century freeze. I remember Father telling me I'd never live to see it so bad."

Lolly was enjoying herself as she turned the nozzle on the oil tank,
filling a smudger and then cutting the flow. "And now!" Bruder would
yell, and Lolly's raspberry gloves would turn the crank and she'd throw

her body against the tank. "Off, Lolly! Cut the oil!" Again Lolly would follow orders. By now her hair had loosened entirely, and it was thick and shiny across her shoulders, and her beaver coat was slick and skidded with grease. Distillate oil matted patches of the coat, but as far as Linda could tell, Lolly was having a good time. Willis was muddy, and soot smudged his face and his calfskin gloves were torn, and from the way his eyes hung sadly he looked as if he'd burn everything he was wearing once he returned to the house. His nose was red, and eventually he took Linda by the shoulders and said, "You're cold, your nose and ears look frozen." He asked her if she wanted to return to the kitchen and bring out more coffee. A couple of the hands hooted in agreement, and Linda set out across the grove, the fish scales of hoarfrost breaking beneath her foot.

She stopped for a minute at a smudger burning alone; hundreds of yards separated her from the others and from the ranch house. In the distance, on the other side of a row of trees, was a string of burning flames, the oil hissing. The sky was black, and she pulled an orange from a tree. It was hard and dull in color, and Linda knew it would be scrapped, that eventually the Rancho Pasadena would fill train cars with dented brown fruit that had no use except to feed freckle-backed swine. At the stove, coffee brewing, she wondered how long she'd remain at the Pasadena, and if Edmund and Palomar and Dieter would welcome her back to Condor's Nest. Maybe her brother would turn her away, and the dread of the unanswered letters visited her again. Where would she go after the orange season? Would Bruder ask her to stay? She had nothing more than the clothes she was wearing and the piece of coral that hung coldly against her chest. Even now, all the men in her life could still tell her what she could and could not do, where she could and could not go, where she could and could not sleep. If Edmund didn't want her, and if Bruder didn't want her—what then? She imagined herself following the Naranjo boys around California, up to the vineyard where they worked in the summer, up north, where, as the boys said, things were different and the world left you alone. She imagined herself turning to Willis, head bowed, and asking for help. She hated her dependence, and she began to question whether in fact she could determine her own destiny.

Through the kitchen window, she could see the heaters and the fires flickering and convulsing. She smelled the smoke and the oil, and knew that in the morning the entire valley would be veiled with an acrid odor; even the hearts of Lolly's roses would be slimy with grease.

When Linda returned to the crew with the pots of coffee, she discovered that Willis had left. "He gave up," said Bruder.

"He didn't give up," said Lolly. "He's been sick."

"Sick?" asked Linda.

But there was no time to talk, and Bruder asked Linda to help him refill the oil tank, and she drove with him and Lolly back to the shed where the distillate was stored.

"Your brother's going to ruin this ranch," Bruder said, offering his hand to Lolly to help her descend from the wagon.

Together they ran the hose from the portable tank to the great iron pot in the shed, inserting the hose's head into the pot's rusty pink canal. Soon the oil was running and the bitter fumes swirled. Lolly said she couldn't bear it, and she went to sit on a crate a hundred yards away.

"Cut the oil in another minute," Bruder told Linda. She watched him follow Lolly and sit beside her, and Linda couldn't be sure but their shoulders looked as if they were pressed together, blocking out the cold. When a minute had passed, she pulled back the lever and the tank shook on its iron feet and the hose sputtered. She disconnected it, and the nozzle sprayed her with oil. She called to Bruder and Lolly, saying that the tank was full and they should get back to the trees. They were far enough away that she couldn't see their faces, and then Bruder's voice reached Linda: "In a minute." But Linda wouldn't wait. She ran to them; she would get them on their feet at once. And as Linda, whose brow was holding back a feverish fury, approached Bruder and Lolly, she looked up the hill and saw that the house was dark except for a light in Willis's room. She stopped, and for a long time she watched the house, hoping he would appear in the window, but nothing stirred in the mansion as it loomed above the cold valley and the groves, framed by the yew trees. Then, at the opposite end of the mansion, a light came on, two windows brightening to gold, and Willis's silhouette entered the room where Linda now slept. She watched Willis—what was he doing? what did he want? He was a black outline in the light, still and careful and faceless, and then he came to the window and gazed down into the valley where she stood, down into the wide span of the freezing night.

10

IT TURNED OUT that Bruder had been wrong, and by one A.M. the temperature leveled, and by two it rose above freezing. They had burned through twenty-five hundred gallons of oil and half a ton of cordwood for almost no reason at all. No trees were lost, and Hearts and Slaymaker estimated that the frost had browned no more than a thousand oranges. As the night waned, the ranch turned quiet with relief. The hands were exhausted and angry about the chaos. The blame that had been falling upon Willis's shoulders shifted to Bruder's. "Who's in charge here, anyway?"

By the time Linda returned to her room, she had only a few minutes to change her clothes before she'd have to go back to the kitchen. Willis hadn't touched anything—or, if he had, he had replaced it carefully—but she sensed his presence, looming over the bed, the air disturbed, inhaled by him and released. She expected to find his fingerprints on the silver stem of the hairbrush or on the hand mirror; but no. What had he wanted? Had she not been wearing the coral pendant, he would surely have cupped it in his hand—she could imagine this. And then she saw the little hat she had bought for the trip to Pasadena. It sat upon a needlepoint chair, and it appeared reshaped, its felt pressed and molded, and the band that had held the bald-eagle feather now captured a sturdy, flaxen feather from a golden eagle. How had Willis known? Who had told him?

But Willis hadn't known. It was Rosa.

Soon dawn would spill over the valley, and the air was already as clear as glass. Linda wiped the oil from her hands and face and returned to the ranch house, and for the first time, Linda—sleepless and weary—descended the hill resentfully.

She brewed more coffee and boiled the oats and baked four dozen *conchas,* and then she waited as the thin near-solstice dawn pushed itself farther up. The morning sky was without color, and the sun was dull, but the chaparral on the hillside had turned green with fresh shoot and leaf and bud. The early rains had polished the scrub and the live-oaks, and except for the orange trees, everything pushing from the earth looked as if today were the first day of spring. But nothing stirred except for the coffeepot's trembling lid; all else was still.

Linda moved down the hall of the ranch house. She heard the bleating snores from the room Hearts shared with Slay. She leaned her ear toward Bruder's door, but there was no sound, and she turned to go back to the kitchen.

"You were looking for me?" said Bruder, pulling his door open.

She said she wanted to know if he was awake. "There's coffee . . ."

He took his coffee to the damp table outside. "The ranch is officially shut today," he said. "The boys have the day off. No one will be up for hours."

She needed to speak to him, but she didn't know how to form the words. She knew that he felt that she had betrayed him, but she had not. How to explain it, even if only to herself? Can a heart lurch two ways at once? Can a man appear handsome in the dark, and loathsome in the dawn? "He insisted that I join them in their little party," she tried. "I work for him, after all. How could I say no? I was on my way to you."

"Nothing is as it seems. You don't have to listen to him. You can move back to the ranch house tonight."

"It's easy for you to say. You can come and go as you like, and you can find work and Willis listens to you because . . . because . . ."

"Because?"

She couldn't go on: she didn't know why Willis listened to Bruder. She was going to say that it was because he was a man, but she knew that it was more than that. It was almost as if some sort of debt were being paid off.

Bruder said, "I asked you to come to Pasadena to be with me."

"It's no longer so simple." She moved to his side, and her hand shook almost imperceptibly.

"Why do you spend your time with him?" he asked.

"I work for him."

"You work for me."

As morning pressed onward, she could see the red in his eyes and the bruise-color in his tired lids. She thought of what she might say, but there was so much, and a small planet of fury began to orbit in her chest—would the day ever come when she worked for no one? If Bruder blamed her, then he knew nothing of the fate she was perpetually fighting against. She said, "Rosa's in love with you; you realize that, don't you?"

"You're being silly. This has nothing to do with Rosa."

She said that she didn't believe him and that time would tell—*won't it, Bruder?*—and Linda was crying and she was upset with herself for breaking into tears, for she liked to think of herself as the type of girl who didn't cry; but her eyes were wet and the tears spilled over and ran down her cheeks, and she had no choice but to mop her face. In her pocket was one of the handkerchiefs embroidered by Esperanza— "You'll show it to Willis for me? You'll do that for me, Linda?" But Linda had forgotten about Esperanza's handiwork and had never shown it to Willis, and now she wiped her face with the little white square of cotton stitched with a happy, breaching humpback whale.

On their day off, the hands usually left the ranch and went into Pasadena for a matinee at Clune's or an afternoon at the pool hall, where orange bourbon swirled in soda bottles, or they dropped by the whorehouse behind the bakery, where the bedsheets smelled of yeasty rolls and the narrow by-the-hour rooms overlooked the racks where the baker cooled his cherry pies. The hands would buy themselves pies and *taquitos* from the open-fire stand, or drink so much that they'd forget to eat, and one or two would pass out at the whorehouse and have to empty his pockets to pay for the time he slept in a girl's bed. None would return before dark, and some wouldn't make it back to the ranch before dawn, and Linda wouldn't have to cook until the next morning, and the day was hers, too, and she realized she was momentarily free.

After her argument with Bruder, suddenly exhausted, she returned to her room and climbed into bed. She hadn't been napping long when there was a knock on the door. Her heart leapt, as she expected Willis's voice to pass through the keyhole, and Linda pulled herself out of bed and ran to the mirror and pinched her cheeks and witnessed her own disappointment as the voice said, "It's me. Rosa."

It was the first time Linda had ever seen Rosa out of uniform. Her dress was a dull brown-gray color, and it hung loosely upon her frame, and Linda felt sorry for her that she was doomed to wear such plainness. Its only brightness was the silvery-white orange blossom Esperanza had stitched upon the breast. Rosa wore a small, round straw hat, and the embroidery and the hat, with its pink ribbon, pointed to her refined, fragile beauty, like that of a ceramic figurine.

Rosa appeared upset; her eyes were cast down. "I have a favor to ask," she said. "I need your help."

"Why don't you ask Bruder?"

"I need *your* help," she said. "Will you meet me in Central Park? At one o'clock?" She said that she had to make a visit and didn't think she could do it alone, and when Linda asked where she had to go, Rosa's eyes flooded with tears.

"But why me?"

"Just meet me, won't you?"

Linda hesitated, but Rosa's desperation was raw, irresistible. "Does it have to do with Bruder?"

Rosa's body convulsed and her face twitched and her chin shook, and Linda had no idea whether Rosa was saying yes or no.

"Should I bring anything?" Linda said.

"I have the money," said Rosa. "I don't need anything else." And then: "Don't say anything, Linda. Promise me you won't. Not even to him."

"To who?"

But Rosa was gone.

An hour later, Linda emerged from her room, and she was just descending the stairs when Willis intercepted her. "Lolly's sick again. She shouldn't have been out last night. I'm on my own today." He asked where she was going, and when Linda said that she was running an errand in town he said, "I'll give you a ride." Linda declined, saying she would ride one of the rancho bicycles. Willis said again that he'd drive her, and she declined once more, but then he insisted and Linda followed him down the stairs and out the front door and slipped into the low leather seat that had first greeted her when she arrived in Pasadena.

It was the Saturday before Christmas, and the lamps on Suicide Bridge were decorated with garland and wreath, and an electric banner welcomed visitors to Pasadena. Willis sped past the orange combine, where teenagers sat upon picnic tables drinking orange juice and a couple of girls were dancing in the sun, a circle of boys hooting around them, and the man who sold the orange juice looked bored, as if there was nothing he hadn't seen.

"I need to stop by the Vista," said Willis. "Do you mind?"

The Hotel Vista sat on the bank of the arroyo, just south of the bridge. Recent improvements—a new colony of stucco bungalows; miles of cleared bridle paths; a reservation agent who'd say *Not this season, I'm afraid* if he didn't like the sound of your name—had made the Vista, even Linda knew, the most luxurious hotel in town. Each week the *Star-News* and the *American Weekly* wrote of the hotel's new arrivals, sending reporters to lurk in the oleander and spy on the steel tycoons, the cattle scions, the railroad barons, the citrus heiresses, and the cautious or gleeful widows tumbling out of their Bugatti limousines, gloved hands shielding their faces from the sun and the cameras' flash. But equally interesting to the newspapermen were the bee-yellow or lipstick-red speedsters supplying the Vista with head-scarfed movie actresses, gangsters in gray suits, traveling sopranos, Savoy Theatre chorines, petal-mouthed mistresses, and the Negro boys dressed up as musicians who delivered tequila and rum in saxophone cases. Since November, the hotel's arrivals had increased weekly, and by now more than five hundred guests—"We are *complet, complet, complet!*" the reservationist was quoted in the paper—had unpacked in suites and bungalows, each with a private butler's button, and scouted the lobby and the pool, discreetly asking, "Who else is here?"

Of course Linda had seen the Vista only from the bridge, where it loomed at the western entrance to Pasadena like a great fortress, one that would admit only, as the reservationist was also quoted, "a certain *kind.*" A couple of the stem-throated packing girls had confided to Linda their ambition to get jobs on the hotel's staff, where if given the right assignment they could close a week with twenty dollars in tips. "Tips to your ass," one of the other packers had said, a girl whose taste for dresses that revealed her bread-brown shoulders would soon get her kicked out of the Webb House. "I'd do just about anything for twenty dollars," one of the girls had said.

The hotel lobby was decorated with potted palms and folding screens behind which men and women sat in oak rockers, their knees touching and their highballs clinking, cigarette ash drifting to the carpets. Large pillows sewn from scraps of old Persian rugs were thrown about the floor, for children or dogs or anyone with lubricated knees who felt like lying down. Arched doorways divided the lobby into a maze of alcoves and semi-private chambers; alabaster planters on the walls spilled fuchsia vines and perfumed the hotel with an odor Chatty Cherry had described in her *American Weekly* column as "suggestive of something ripe." A great eyebrow of a window overlooked the terrace and the pool and the Arroyo Seco stubbled with early green, and three small girls pressed their faces against the glass, begging to be released into the children's playground, where a high swing looped to an ancient live-oak would fling anyone under seventy pounds out over the arroyo and back. The Negro bellboys, in boxy hats and epaulets, and the Mexican chambermaids, in silky chignons and flesh-tight blouses, were more numerous than the guests themselves, and moved about the lobby with alert eyes; the stories they took in were sold, at least by the more entrepreneurial staff members, to the *American Weekly* at the going rate of fifty cents if the anecdote involved money, and a dollar if sex lay at its pulsing heart. The bellboys hurried across the lobby shepherding leather-trimmed trunks, and the chambermaids transported vases of white roses and freshly shampooed poodles and tea for twenty and decks of suede-backed playing cards and cubes of fudge sprinkled with gold leaf. The bellboys said, "Good afternoon, Captain Poore," and the chambermaids nodded and curtsied.

Down a side arcade was a row of small boutiques, each no bigger than a stable stall and specializing in a careful selection of winter jewels or touring-car hats or pleated tennis dresses. Willis stepped into a furrier's shop while Linda waited in the hall. Through the plate glass she watched him speak with the shop's owner, a middle-aged woman whose flouncy crêpe de chine dress revealed a V of sunburned flesh beneath her throat. The woman disappeared behind a curtain, then reappeared with a glossy white box. When Willis exited the store, its bell tinkling, he held up the box and said, "For New Year's Eve. There's a party at—" But he stopped himself. "Never mind. It's all too dull to talk about. How about some lunch?"

"I have to meet Rosa."

"Just a quick bite. Old Rosa won't mind."

Linda protested, but Willis said they'd be fast, and she agreed because the truth was, she *wanted* to dine at the Vista, and she thought
about the letter she'd write that night to Edmund describing the French
food, the open western view, the expensive people running about.
When they stepped onto the terrace, the sunlight reflecting off the pool
blinded Linda, her pupils contracting like water down a drain, and
Willis's fingers were on her elbow, guiding her into a chair, and all she
could do was look around and stare.

He ordered for her a lobster *farci* and two cold quail legs and told the
waitress, a worried-mouthed girl with a pretty, plump nose, that they
were in a hurry. "Of course, Captain Poore."

Linda wondered whether Rosa would wait for her, but as Linda sat
on the terrace, Rosa's trouble, whatever it was, began to feel remote, as
if such mysterious dangers would not—could not!—intrude upon
Linda. She wouldn't be all that late, forty minutes, no more than an
hour, and what was the hurry?, and after all, why wouldn't Rosa wait?
And at this very moment, Linda couldn't imagine *anything* that would
require urgency. Most girls in her situation wouldn't have agreed to
meet Rosa, Linda thought. Most girls would've told her, "You're no
friend of mine." But Linda wasn't like most girls; in so many ways, she
believed, she was different from the rest. Once Willis had said, "You're
a proud girl, aren't you?" And she said that she was, unaware of the insult that perhaps lurked beneath the compliment.

The table overlooked the pool, and some sort of swimming game
called Treasure Hunt was about to begin. Twenty boys, and a few girls
in bathing dresses down to their knees, were lined up impatiently along
the pool's rim. One boy jumped in the pool before the whistle and was
disqualified, which brought an explosive screech from his deep little
lungs. Everyone around the pool, and the diners at the tables too,
stopped talking and leaned forward. Linda pressed against the rail beside the table and saw the light flashing on the water, and then she saw
something winking at the bottom of the pool like a fleck of gold in Sut-
ter's river, and she saw another and another. "What are those?"

"In the pool? Coins, I would imagine."

The lifeguard blew his whistle and the children threw themselves
into the water and swam to the bottom, where, Linda could now see,
lay hundreds of coins: gold and silver dollars and quarters and nickels

and a few pennies. Air bubbles rose as the children fished around the pool bottom, fighting in nine feet of water for a silver dollar. Soon the first clamped fists punched through the surface, and all around the pool, mothers and fathers and governesses were shouting at their children, screaming at them to look in the deep end or on the step, cheering when the children delivered the clean, wet, sparkling coins to their feet, yelling at them to return for more. The children, when their small faces broke through the water, screamed—*I got one! I got two!*—and there was as much cheering and roaring as would spill over the lip of the Rose Bowl on New Year's Day. And Linda watched, her chin on the hot iron rail, and out of the corner of her eye she could see that Willis was watching her. Why had he brought her here? The waitress delivered their lunch and Linda picked at the lobster tail, disappointed that it was not a California rock lobster but a clawed Mainer, doubtless railroaded across the country in a sloshing water tank. She heard someone say, with an incensed *tsk,* "Did they really only plant a hundred dollars today?" The yelling and the cheers continued, and women who otherwise would sit straight-backed were jumping up and down and clinging to men's arms and to one another. The men were clapping and whistling and coaching the children—"There's a goldie just over *there!*"—as if they were training championship puppies. And the children themselves retrieved the coins with smiles and wagging tongues, depositing them in the slots between their fathers' feet: towheads and pigtails and cowlicks and a shaved, deloused head diving and breaching and diving again. After a few minutes the cheering died down as the children swept the pool bottom clean and hauled themselves out of the water, heaving and wet on the concrete, their black suits glistening, like panting seal pups. After a careful tally, a little girl with fat-padded arms was declared the winner, having snatched up a total of $17.34, and Linda heard her say, "I'm going to buy myself a bunny-fur muff!" The parents laughed and the governesses toweled down the children and the diners returned to their lunches and the sunbathers leaned into their pink terry chaises and tilted the parasols and closed their eyes.

A wall of cabanas stood on the far side of the pool, and every other cabana door had a large brass M on it, and large brass L's were screwed to the doors in between. Men and women in swimming suits and bathing robes went in and out of the cabanas, and Linda noticed a man in a white linen suit entering a stall at one end of the row, followed by a tiny-waisted woman stepping into the cabana next to his. Five minutes later he emerged, still in his white suit, and a minute later she strolled into the sunlight, touching her crocodile belt and arranging her hat's netting around her face. A suspendered man took the first man's place, and then nothing happened for several minutes, until a pretty girl with an urn-shaped head entered the cabana next door. Linda studied the two closed doors, and she thought she saw one of the knobs tremble, but the door remained shut, and outside the lappers were backstroking up and down the pool and wives were coconut-oiling their husband's lumpy chests. The children, sitting in little circles on the patio, were all eating *tacos,* and the lifeguard in his red trunks was talking to a widow in a white fur stole, and no one noticed the urn-headed girl rush from the cabana, one sparkling button unhooked. The suspendered man appeared a few minutes later and looked blearily into the sun and then sat down at a table and ordered minced veal on toast. By the time his lunch arrived, two others had occupied the far cabanas, a young man in baggy tennis whites and an older woman who lodged a mint beneath her tongue as she passed through the door.

"I see you've noticed the sheds," said Willis. His smirk told her that he liked her witnessing these things. He was playing with her, she realized, but she wasn't going to let him think that he could upset her. She sat back and said, "You're more of a devil than you let on."

"Linda, that's not fair." He offered his sincere, boyish face, apologized, and said they should leave. He wadded his napkin and half rose from his chair, and she felt something press down upon her shoulders, and she looked up but there was nothing there: just Willis across the table, in that bent angle between standing and sitting. There was nothing by Linda's shoulders other than the breeze and a blue jay's wingbeat. "Or we'll stay if you want." And Willis sat back down. A shadow descended upon their table and a breathy voice said, "Willis, I didn't see you."

Linda recognized the girl she'd seen the day she arrived in Pasadena, the careless driver who'd nearly smashed into the ice wagon. A silver part cut so precisely through her yellow hair that it was almost like a gash. Her toe cap of a chin was tilted up, and she fluttered her eyelids as she spoke. "Who's this?" Two fingers landed on Linda.

Willis introduced Connie Muffitt. By now he was standing, leaving Linda in the shadows, and she felt like a child looking up at them. She stood and shook the woman's hand and saw that they were nearly the same height, she and Linda, and that Connie was more beautiful than anyone else around the pool. "Stamp, is it? Haven't I seen you somewhere before?"

"She's not from Pasadena," said Willis.

"In Pasadena for the season? Staying at the Vista?"

Connie didn't even pretend to wait for Linda's response, and said to Willis that she hoped to see him New Year's Eve. "Where will you be?"

"I haven't decided yet. It depends—"

"Don't forget to bring Lolly." Then Connie was gone. It struck Linda, the pool throwing the sunlight into her eyes, that she hadn't come to Pasadena for this. She thought of Bruder, alone in the groves shoveling the charred wood out of the ditches; he'd be so damp with sweat that his pant legs would stick to his thighs, to the mass of hair spreading there. His palms white with blisters and his throat hoarse after the yelling last night, and then speaking to no one today, not a soul. It was his fault, she told herself; she was here with Willis because of him. But it wasn't too late, and the season would stretch on until spring, and she would cook for Bruder until the last orange was picked, and she imagined climbing aboard the Pacific Electric with him, waving good-bye to Captain Poore and his sister through the window. To tell the truth, Linda couldn't imagine a future other than that one; Willis was like a game, like the Treasure Hunt itself. And she told herself that she would go to Bruder and say that she had forgiven him, and she didn't consider that he might be incapable of forgiving her. And Linda surprised even herself when she leapt up from the table and said she had to go, she'd walk downtown, it wasn't far, but she had to go *now.* Willis caught up with her in the lobby, the furrier's box stuffed under his arm, and took her by the wrist, his fingers uncomfortably tight, and he steered her behind a folding screen painted with a pagoda scene, shushing her and whispering, "No, no, I'll drive you. But don't be upset, I didn't bring you here to upset you." She shook her head, saying that she wasn't upset by any of this. She said she'd promised to meet Rosa, and now look at the time! Willis handed her a handkerchief, but Linda wasn't crying or sniffling; her breath was as slow as a somnambulist's; she felt her face harden and she stood erect and she felt cold. She returned the handkerchief, and Willis struggled to return it to his pocket while holding the furrier's box. He snapped at a bellboy to help him, and the boy in the little square hat lay his manicured hands around the shiny white box and fell in step behind Willis and Linda, who said, "Thank you for bringing me here. Now I see." With its own will her hand made its way to his elbow as she descended the hotel's front steps, just as the coco-buttered hands of all the other women on the steps slid around the elbows of men; Linda Stamp was one of a dozen young women entering or leaving the Hotel Vista, hems high upon shins, silk headbands tight across brows, hands squeezed roughly in the paws of a man. As she stepped into the *porte cochère,* the petroleum fumes greeted her, and Linda thanked Captain Poore for lunch.

She was almost two hours late, but Rosa was still waiting on a bench in the park, staring at the fountain and the old men throwing horseshoes. Her glassy face looked as if it would shatter to the touch and her eyes were threaded with blood. "I don't know if he'll still see me," she said.

"Who?" Linda apologized as she recognized the gravity of the afternoon that lay before them.

They walked down Raymond Street, squinting against the glare. With each step, Linda came to sense Rosa's fear. The skin around her eyes flinched. Linda didn't know where they were going, and Rosa, whom before today Linda had chosen never to believe, now seemed like a different person: young as a schoolgirl, vulnerable with honesty, marooned atop the great cresting wave of fate. But Rosa wasn't a different person. No, in fact, Linda was merely seeing more of Rosa than she had before. She took Rosa's hand. "Everything will be all right."

"I'm not so sure, Linda."

Not far from the Webb House they crossed California Street, and before Linda knew it they were in front of the P. F. Erwin Electrical Distributorship. Mr. Erwin himself was in the window, rotating his display, plugging in an electric juicer and arranging a pyramid of oranges, and he was too preoccupied to see the two girls hesitate in front of his building. Linda finally realized where they were and whom they were visiting, and she rubbed the cold from Rosa's fingers and they stood silently in the December sun, the City Beautiful Committee's Christmas wreaths swaying in a breeze on the lampposts. Traffic passed, but the world felt no larger than the square of sidewalk where they rested, the cars and the exhaust pipes receding into another, distant world. Rosa's fingers were sticky and soft like ice-plant leaves, and Linda led her into the side alley and to the door with the bubble-glass window etched with a simple sign:

RING BELL FOR SERVICE

They waited at the door for so long that Linda rang again, and she began to fear that Rosa had missed her appointment because of her. They'd have to return another day, and Linda imagined Rosa's horror at having to wait. Again Linda whimpered an apology: "He said we weren't going to be—"

But just then a shadow appeared on the other side of the glass, and a walrus-size nurse opened the door and quickly waved the girls inside. "The doctor was about to leave." The nurse heaved her tremulous legs up the stairs, her uniformed backside as large and white as an icebox. She pulled herself along by the rail and called over her shoulder, "Come on, girls." The stairwell was dark, walled with unfinished redwood panels, and the steps creaked and Linda couldn't see beyond the woman, her body filled the stairwell so completely. The nurse panted and said, "You coming?" At the top of the stairs she fiddled with a ring of keys at another bubble-glass door, working three locks and then scooting Linda and Rosa into Dr. Freeman's office.

"Which one of you is it?"

Rosa took a small step forward, as if offering herself. The office was crowded with a desk and a Bar-Lock typewriter on a stand and a daybed upholstered in russet figured velour. A glass-doored cabinet held trays of pliers and scalpels and rubber-tipped pincers and wads of cotton and glass jars of clear liquids that made Linda think they might explode if dropped. On the top shelf was a sharp foot-long instrument like an ice pick, its steel handle cross-hatched for grip, and lying across it a loop-shaped steel knife.

"You're lucky the doctor didn't go home. I told him to wait another fifteen minutes. But usually the ones who keep him waiting never show up at all."

Linda and Rosa sat on the daybed while the nurse squeezed around the furniture, moving so indelicately that Linda was sure she would knock something from the desk or slam into the cabinet or topple the fern stand. The nurse was humming and then looked up and said,

"Don't be frightened. That'll only make it worse. He's a good doctor. You've come to the best."

Linda continued to hold Rosa's hand, and they both jumped when the door opened and the doctor appeared. He was a young, darkly whiskered man, bespectacled and narrow-chested, and he shook the girls' hands and then sat behind his desk. "You met Miss Bishop?" He nodded in the direction of the nurse, who had propped herself on a spinning stool, her body spilling over the seat, its mass rolling the casters.

The doctor looked at Linda and said, "I presume you're Rosa."

"No, I am."

The doctor's eyes remained on Linda and he said, "I'm sorry. For some reason I thought it was you." Then he shifted his attention to Rosa. "I have some questions. Then we'll begin."

The nurse nodded her plush, plucked chin, and one of the coils in the daybed groaned, and Linda whispered, "If you want to go, I'll take you home."

"How old are you?" Dr. Freeman began.

"Twenty."

"Where were you born?"

"In Pasadena."

"Any family?"

"My mother's dead."

"Are you married?"

"No."

"Why are you here today?"

"I have a . . . I'm in . . . Doctor, I thought you knew." Her hand curled into a ball and rubbed her temples. The tendrils of her hair were moist around her ears, and her eyelids were dewy and her cheek was damp.

"How long has it been, Rosa?"

Rosa hesitated, and Linda wished she could answer the questions for her, help her some way at all. But Linda knew nothing more than the doctor and Miss Bishop did. She found herself leaning toward Rosa and wondering how long it *had* been, and then she asked herself the inevitable question: And with whom? How long ago, and with whom? But Linda knew the answer to at least one of those questions, and she was too worried about Rosa right now to unlock her own anger and hurt. That would come later, but Linda had promised to see Rosa through this appointment, and she had almost broken that promise, and now she would keep it, just as Bruder had kept his.

The doctor removed his eyeglasses and looked to Miss Bishop and then stood and leaned over the desk. "Rosa, dear. It's important that you answer all my questions." He grinned in a way that he must have thought friendly but that Linda found coldhearted, as if what Rosa might say next were the most *fascinating* news he would hear all afternoon.

"A couple of months." And then: "I can't really say."

Miss Bishop began removing instruments from the cabinet: the cotton balls, a scalpel, the looped knife. She passed through the doorway behind Dr. Freeman's desk, and Linda could see the rubber-padded examination table that waited in the back room. Miss Bishop wheeled an enormous lamp on casters to the table's side, positioning it to spray Rosa with bitter pearly light.

"Have you had any related illnesses?" Rosa stared blankly, clutching Linda, and Dr. Freeman continued, "No? Nothing? Gonorrhea? Chancroid? Syphilis?"

Rosa let out a little gasp.

"Rosa?"

"No. Just this."

"I'll give you some arsenic, just to be sure."

Next to the cabinet was a window, its shade drawn, but the sunlight pressed around it, framing the dingy sheet of canvas. It reminded Linda of the bright day outside and the Vista's terrace where she had visored the sun out of her eyes with her hand. Had that been only an hour ago? Everything felt so far away, and she turned to Rosa, whose cheek raged pale.

"Why don't you go see Miss Bishop now," said Dr. Freeman. Rosa stood, and Linda got up too, and Rosa hugged Linda awkwardly, her breasts soft and her quick breath warm on Linda's throat and her body a slender column of bones.

Rosa entered the next room and Miss Bishop closed the door, and through the bubble glass Linda could see Rosa's silhouette as she removed her coat and then unhooked the buttons of her dress. Dr. Freeman remained at his desk, gazing into space, his glasses secure in his hands. Linda could see that he was a handsome man who suffered from a daily beard so bristly and black that by afternoon he looked forlorn. On his desk was his wedding picture, angled so that Linda could just make it out, Dr. Freeman in his Navy uniform and his bride pinned with a corsage. "She'll be fine," he said.

"How long will it take?"

"Not long at all. But she'll need to rest a couple of hours. If you like, you can leave and come back for her around five." Linda said that she would wait. "She'll be uncomfortable, but that's normal. I don't want you to worry. Is she your sister?"

"A friend."

The doctor put on the white coat hanging from the wall and entered the next room and the door closed. Linda sat on the daybed and felt a weariness overtake her, the sleepless night catching up. The dim office settled her pulse and her eyelids grew heavy and she wasn't sure how much time passed before she heard the terrible shriek and the sob. "Nurse!" Dr. Freeman called, his voice urgent but without panic, and again a scream rose from the other side of the door and Linda moved toward the panel of bubble glass and heard his calm, firm voice, "Miss Bishop, hold her down. Keep her down." Rosa was crying, and Linda tried to see through the glass but she made out nothing more distinct than two dark shapes moving around, and it was like seeing two patrolling sharks through fifteen feet of water. She turned the doorknob but it was locked, and the sounds on the other side quieted, the silence broken by sniffling and a heave. She remained at the door, but for several minutes there were no sounds from the other side except for what reminded Linda of the familiar clink and splash of dishes being washed in a sink. Linda went to the window and pulled back the shade and saw that the office looked across the alley and a tar-paper roof over to the Webb House. The white Victorian house gleamed in the late afternoon sun, the slanted light a pinky orange on its clapboard. The house's scallop-trimmed turret shimmered, and two of the packing girls, enjoying their day off, sat in the turret's window seat, the western sun lighting their faces. Their idle poses suggested to Linda that they were chatting about anything but the orange grove. On the porch, Mrs. Webb stood in an iron-gray skirt with her hands on her hips, and she looked around as if she knew, *she just knew,* that some girl somewhere was getting into some sort of dilemma that only Mrs. Emily Webb could resolve. *What would they do without me?,* Linda imagined Mrs.

Webb thinking. In her chest, Linda felt a breaching sensation, her allegiance turning on its side.

From the examination room a lone sob traveled to Linda's ear, and she returned to the daybed and several minutes passed before Dr. Freeman appeared. "She's resting, but she'll be fine," he said. Dr. Freeman sat at his desk and folded his hands and Linda tried to stay alert, but once again sleep overtook her and gradually she slumped against the bed's round, padded head and she slept while Rosa slept behind the bubble glass. At a quarter to six, Dr. Freeman called the Black & White cab service, and a kid in a billed cap too large for his head drove them in a taxi with a black roof and a black body and whitewall tires to the rancho's service gate.

Later, when at last she was alone in her room, Linda found on her bed a letter from Edmund. He had written again with news from Condor's Nest—*I've sold a few more acres to the highway men*—and reiterated his careful, fraternal inquiry: "Are you all right? Please write to tell me that everything is all right. That no one has hurt you." She would have to send word but not tonight, she was too tired tonight, and as she leaned against the pillows, her feet still on the floor, she closed her eyes. And then there was a knock on her door, followed by a second rap, and Willis was saying, "Linda? Linda? Will you be coming down to dance tonight?"

11

HE DIDN'T LIKE to talk about the war. One might think that Bruder
had never seen battle, he said so little about being a soldier. Others
might accuse him of forgetting his martial past: That scar in the forehead? Shrapnel that had affected his memory. But Bruder hadn't forgotten anything. He thought of the beechwood forest every morning as
he knocked about between sleep and the waking hour; and again when
he retired to his room with Thucydides; and again, an hour later, when he
gave up on the day and returned to sleep. And throughout the work-
day, too—especially when he saw him and the sunlight burned upon
his medal, giving him an aureate, convincing—but false—appearance.
They'd been soldiers together, and in a desperate hour they had cut a
deal to keep a secret. *I'll give you this, and you give me that.* Wasn't that how
progress came about? Progress of land and property, of possession and
fortune, even progress of the heart? Someone has something that is
more valuable to someone else. Bruder was a man of few words, but
those words he uttered he meant and kept, and here he was on the eve
of 1925, foreman at the Rancho Pasadena, a man of an indeterminate
but youthful age, although already sore in white bone and blue bloody
joint, living by the deals he had struck; and even now Bruder would
never reveal the secrets he had promised to keep. To whom had he
vowed a particular silence? First to Willis, then to Dieter, now to Rosa.
Each for a different reason, each to a varying degree of selfishness, but
hands had been shaken, and although Bruder had thought he was gain-
ing by his agreements, he now saw as plainly as the snow-topped Sierra
Madres before him that he was at risk of losing some things. Not prop-

erty. No, that would come. He was losing Linda. He blamed himself, and he blamed her.

And one day he would speak of it all.

At twelve noon on New Year's Eve day, Captain Willis Poore rode into the orchards on his quarter horse, White Indian, and charged up and down the middles calling to the hands that they were off duty until the second of January. The hands left the empty field boxes in the groves and threw their ladders over their shoulders and returned to the packinghouse, where the girls were nailing shut the final crates. The boys talked about where they'd go that night to find a drink, and the girls made plans to sneak away from the watchful eyes of their grandmothers, or Mrs. Webb. Some of the hands and some of the packing girls would meet up in one of the brick alleys off Colorado Street, at a plain black door through which *marimba* music would thump. They'd pay their entry in coins, and inside they could dance and spend more money on foamy, milky *pulque,* and as the night wore on most of the boys would give up hope of saving any money for the morning and they'd buy tequila for themselves and the three or four girls they were eyeing, and by midnight their pockets would be empty—unless they were lucky and someone's pretty hand wormed its way in for a New Year's visit, but that would cost money that most of the boys didn't have.

After Willis dismissed the crew, only Bruder continued working, picking clean the trees one after another, moving and resetting his ladder and keeping to his work as if he had no idea that the rest of the ranch had come to a halt. But he knew, and he wasn't going to stop midday. He wouldn't stop until the last orange was picked at the end of the season. From the branches he had an open view of the house, and he looked to it and wondered how Rosa was today. She had been ill but she hadn't told him why, and he wondered if it was what he feared: but what he feared wasn't as grave as the truth. Nonetheless, Rosa had seemed to Bruder to be on a collision course with Willis, and Bruder had done his best to steer her out of her employer's path. But Bruder had known all along that she would ignore his counsel—just as Rosa had known that though Bruder was right, she still couldn't heed his warning. Bruder asked Linda what she knew, but Linda would only say "I've made a promise to Rosa not to tell." Linda was known for many things, but keeping a secret wasn't one of them. She said, "I'm sure you don't need me to tell you what's wrong." She said, "I'm sure you don't need me to tell you the importance of my keeping my word."

Bruder sensed that Linda blamed him for something, and he moved to hold her. He knew that there was a misunderstanding, but he didn't suspect its depth. If there was one thing he was certain of, it was that no one would ever mistake Bruder and his deeds for Willis and *his*.

But in fact Linda had done just that, and she told Bruder to leave the kitchen, that she wanted to be alone. All this time she had believed that he wanted to be only with her, with Linda, and she had known not to trust Rosa from the first day at the Pasadena. And though Linda had tried to stay vigilant, questioning Rosa's every word, everything she did, after a while Rosa's apparent sincerity had remained constant, and Linda's skepticism had nearly fallen away. Until now. The hours waiting on Dr. Freeman's daybed had taught Linda that if she wasn't careful, her destiny would slip from her hands and she would be carried along by a cruel and manipulative fate, and she still believed that this was not how she had been meant to live; maybe others, but not she, and if she didn't believe this, what else would she have?

And this was why, when Willis told Linda that Lolly was sick and he didn't have a date for New Year's Eve, Linda said, "Is that so?" Willis removed his hat and his bangs sprang up and there was a bright beauty to him, especially next to the row of dusty, half-picked trees. The day was fine, the sky bluer now that the cold had passed, and Willis was wearing the star sapphire ring that seemed to capture on his knuckle all the sun and the sky. It was a funny thing about Willis Poore and the way he carried himself. His slightness would come and go, and by now Linda could perceive the change: when news was bad around the Pasadena, his shoulders would sink and his neck would hang and he would take on the stature of an adolescent; but when Willis was in a good mood— after shooting a rabbit, say, or moving up the tennis ladder—his full size returned, and this was when Linda saw him differently, as she did now. "There's a ball over at the Valley Hunt," he said. "We'll leave at eight."

Later, up in the house, she told Rosa about Willis's invitation.

"You're not going, are you?"

"I don't have a choice."

"Oh, Linda. Don't you understand?" Rosa began to cry into Linda's sleeve. Her recovery had been a series of good days and bad; a drained lifelessness would send her to bed, followed by a day of vigor and fully circulating blood. Dr. Freeman had predicted this, and Linda interpreted Rosa's tears as a symptom of what Dr. Freeman had described as "a heightened state of female emotionality."

"Don't you remember," said Rosa, "what I just went through?"

Of course Linda remembered, and wasn't that the point? There was comfort in a man like Willis Poore; she couldn't be more secure than at his side. "But if you want me to stay with you," Linda volunteered, hoping Rosa would say *No, no, go ahead.* For Linda didn't want to miss this opportunity, this chance to peer further into life in Pasadena, and she'd be on Willis's arm and she'd meet—she'd be introduced to, presented to!—the people she had read about on the society pages, in Chatty Cherry's column, and wasn't there a chance of Linda's name appearing in the paper too? And in her imagination, Linda herself wrote the headline: MYSTERIOUS BEAUTIFUL WOMAN VISITS PASADENA.

But Rosa said nothing at all, exhaustion and pity causing her face to fall. She turned in her bed and began to pick at the wallpaper. Beneath the thin blanket she was a tiny mound; the blanket was old and dingy and frayed, and it wrapped Rosa like a shroud, and her breathing was slow, and Linda waited for Rosa to say something, and Linda waited for a long time, for what felt like a minute and then like forever. "Rosa? Rosa?" But Rosa had fallen asleep and Linda left her, a girl drowned by fatigue and scar.

Later that afternoon Linda was downtown, making her way up Raymond Street, alone. She had never been into the city by herself, and with each step she inhaled the conifer-minty air of Central Park and felt free in a way she had never before. She was thinking of no one—not Willis or Bruder or Edmund—no one but herself, and her mind was clear and her breath was loud in her ears. As she passed the Hotel Green, its veranda filled with people in wicker chairs, Linda became more and more aware of the isolation she had endured during her months at the Pasadena—the world reduced to the isolated fortress of the rancho. Rosa had said, "The city's no different than the rancho. It's a small, walled-off place too." But again, Linda didn't believe her—how could this be true? Why, look at the city before Linda: men and women filling the sidewalks, children walking small white dogs, and other girls like Linda out alone, out for an errand or a stroll and dependent on no one at that particular moment. Free to go wherever they wanted! No one looking at them, no one expecting anything from them, no one but themselves aware of where they were, what they would do next, which shop they would enter, what would *happen to them* next! It would have overwhelmed her if Linda didn't feel as if she'd been waiting for this her whole life, and roaming the heart of Pasadena nearly made her forget why she was there and what she was looking for.

At the intersection of Raymond and Colorado, a white-gloved policeman on a box was directing traffic. His lips were clamped around a silver whistle, and he blew and blew, and his hands pointed to cars and pedestrians. A small stone of worry caught in Linda's throat as she thought that he was pointing at her and telling her to stop, as if she didn't have a right to be there, to go wherever it was she was going. But the policeman wasn't pointing at Linda; he saw her only for what she was, or what he and so many others thought she was: a pretty girl in a plain dress, a worker of some sort, her toil apparent in her red knuckles, in her long, firm arms.

Linda passed volunteers on ladders decorating streetlamps with garlands of evergreen and yellow and white rose. Ribbons of rosebuds trimmed store doorframes, and in the display window of Model's Grocery was a fleshy standing rib roast, pale red roses wired to each bone. The people on the street had come alive with flowers as well, moss roses and blood hibiscus in coat lapels, poppies pinned to tightly knotted coifs, lilies yawning from a purse; one woman, lumpy in a brown knit dress, wore a pineapple in her hat. A girl with a narcissus corsage hurried past Linda, but the sweet, erotic scent of the tiny, papery flowers lingered, engulfing her in their perfume. The city was preparing for the Tournament of Roses, and the street felt like a garden in early spring.

She had come to town to buy a dress, and her pocket was full with her cook's wages, and she imagined herself in something white and long and of a nearly blinding sheen. After her nap, Rosa had said that Willis would wear a white tie, "But what will you wear, Linda? You don't have anything to wear." Rosa suggested she pilfer a dress from Lolly's closet: "She'll never know." But Linda didn't want one of Lolly's

dresses. Rosa offered Linda her confirmation gown, a dress with a ruffled, biblike front. But the small tear in the skirt and the almost imperceptible yellow stain at the throat made Linda a little sad. After all, Linda
hoped for more. "I'd never fit in it," she said, returning the dress to
Rosa.

Linda had read the women's page in the newspaper, and next to the
recipes for creamed orange tart and "Alma Pudding" and the advice column written by a secret citizen known as "the Kewpie," she found the
advertisement for F. C. Nash offering gowns and dresses under the
promise of "High Drama for New Year's!" Silk shifts with crêpe de chine
wrappers, tunic dresses with black feather collars, and, "for the daring
woman of Pasadena," a cream blouse and skirt beaded in the manner of—
or so the advertisement claimed—the ceremonial wardrobe of a Tongva
Indian princess. "Come in and ask about our reduced prices!" But a
smaller, more refined advertisement had caught Linda's eye:

DODSWORTH'S DRESSES

EUROPEAN STYLES ONLY

EXCLUSIVE DESIGNS

FOR THE VALLEY'S MOST DISCERNING LADIES

In Rosa's washtub Linda had seen Lolly's dresses with the Dodsworth's
label, and now Linda found herself in front of Dodsworth's window. A
mannequin was posed in a silvery silk dress fringed with sea-foam lace,
and next to it on a little stand a sign read: OUR LATEST FROM PARIS.
The glass reflected Linda, and in the angled afternoon light the effect
was that of her face superimposed upon the mannequin's head. A small
black terrier with two rosebuds clipped to his collar lounged in the window on a needlepoint cushion, beside another sign that read: BY AP-
POINTMENT ONLY.

But Linda was determined. She tried the door and was surprised to
find it bolted. She rang the bell and heard an ugly buzz from inside and
waited at the glass door while people passed her on the street. She told
herself not to feel self-conscious: no one knew whether or not she
had an appointment, no one knew whether or not she belonged, *no one
knew who she was!* And she wondered if there was a more liberating
thought—more liberating than the freedom of thinking itself—than to
know that she was a stranger to this entire city and could blend in and

become anyone she wanted. She felt as if people were looking at her, but they weren't, no one paid any attention to Linda at all until a woman—surely this was Mrs. Dodsworth herself, Linda thought—appeared on the other side of the door and turned the bolt. "Yes?"

"I'd like to buy a dress."

"Do you have an appointment?"

"I was hoping you'd make an exception."

"Your name, Miss?"

"Linda Stamp."

Mrs. Dodsworth touched the blue-and-white cameo at her throat. She was of a grandmotherly age, and her white hair was shellacked around her face, and she seemed to Linda rather simple in appearance to own such a fancy store. "I was interested in the dress in the window," said Linda, emboldened, and she touched her coat pocket, where her money was rolled in a wad.

Mrs. Dodsworth looked skeptical, but she cracked the door farther and decided to admit Linda. "It's New Year's, after all."

The dog greeted Linda coolly, sniffing her shoes, and Linda knelt to pet him but Mrs. Dodsworth stopped her. "Mr. Huggins doesn't like to be touched. Now, it's the silver dress you're interested in?"

Linda mentioned the ball at the Valley Hunt Club, and the patchy eyebrows of Mrs. Dodsworth, who was a 100 Percenter herself, lifted and she said, "I see. You said your name was Linda Stamp?" Mrs. Dodsworth moved to fetch the dress from the mannequin, and from behind the partition her voice rose, like a neighbor's over a wall: "You're visiting Pasadena, Miss Stamp, is that it?"

"For the season."

Mrs. Dodsworth cooed approvingly, for nothing was better for business than an heiress camped at one of the hotels for three months. But Linda Stamp's coat suggested she wasn't an heiress at all. "Perhaps you saw our holiday fashion show at the Huntington?" Mrs. Dodsworth probed. Linda said she was sorry to have missed it. Mrs. Dodsworth returned with the dress lying delicately in her arms.

In a little closet with a curtain and a mirror, Linda tried on the dress. It was soft and as silver as a coin: "Platinum silk," said Mrs. Dodsworth from the other side of the curtain. The sleeves cut off at the elbow, and the collar opened to reveal the cove of her throat. The silk lay smoothly against her flesh, and it felt almost obscene, touching her everywhere like that. "Is it too short?" called Mrs. Dodsworth. "We can let down the hem."

Linda emerged from the dressing room, and Mrs. Dodsworth, doing up the buttons at Linda's back, clucked with approval. "Doesn't she look handsome, Mr. Huggins?"

The store's three-paneled mirror showed Linda off, and but for the coral pendant she wouldn't have recognized the girl staring back: a girl Linda had wanted to become, and now there she was, tall and shimmering, and she knew that no one could possibly fail to notice her. She pushed her hair behind her ears, and Mrs. Dodsworth said, "Much better," and Linda knew that Willis would stagger for words when he saw her, and that the men at the Valley Hunt Club would whisper *Who's that?,* and that the women would know she had shopped at Dodsworth's. And suddenly, all of this mattered to Linda: again, she was aware that she was wrestling, and beating, her fate. She held out her arms, and only then did she notice the little tag hanging from the sleeve.

Linda knew that the dress would be expensive—maybe two or three times more than the nicest dress at Margarita's—but she had brought all her money and was certain that she could afford it. So when she turned over the little tag, she gasped, and immediately she became warm and could feel the blood rushing to her cheek and her body break out into a beady sweat and she worried about staining the silk.

"I know it is a bit *chère,*" said Mrs. Dodsworth. "But of course it's just come in from Paris. I'm sure I don't have to tell you that everyone at the club will be looking at you. Examining you."

Linda looked at the tag again—maybe she had misread it—but the little red zeros remained: as agape as a row of children's mouths.

"May I wrap it for you, Miss Stamp?"

"I'm afraid I'm not going to take this one."

"But heavens, why?"

Linda said that she wasn't sure the dress fit correctly, but Mrs. Dodsworth, her eyes screwing up, said, "Nonsense. I told you we can let down that hem." She stared at Linda as if she were reappraising her. "Then may I ask what it is you're looking for?"

Linda hesitated. "Something a little less . . ."

"Yes?"

"A little less . . ."

"Extravagant?"

"Yes, extravagant. It's not really my style, as you can see." And together Linda and Mrs. Dodsworth looked at Linda's plain dress hanging limply on a peg.

"Is there a budget you had in mind, Miss Stamp?"

Before moving to Pasadena, Linda had never thought of herself as either rich or poor, but now she was aware that she had nothing and that she would always have nothing, and that a cook's wages would bring her nothing too. "Maybe I could buy the dress on credit," she said. "I didn't bring my purse."

"Where are you staying, Miss Stamp?"

"At the Rancho Pasadena."

"At the Pasadena? Are you a guest of the Poores?"

Linda shook her head, and Mrs. Dodsworth said, "Sorry, what did you say?" and Linda said, "I work there."

"You work there?" And again: "You *work* there?"

Linda knew it wouldn't help things, but she said: "As a cook."

Mrs. Dodsworth snorted and began pulling her curtains and closing up her shop, and Mr. Huggins followed her around, snout turned up at his mistress's heel, and Mrs. Dodsworth was saying she *didn't have time for games,* she *didn't have time for things like this,* and *Have a nice afternoon, Miss Stamp.*

"I'm sorry if I've caused you any trouble." Linda was boiling up under the silk, and she could smell her heat rising from the bodice, and she longed for a glass of water. She felt behind her for the buttons but couldn't reach. Mrs. Dodsworth was chattering at Mr. Huggins, and she pulled down the door's roller shade and turned over a sign in the window: CLOSED.

Linda's heart quieted, as if it had left her just then. She felt like an impostor, the silk soft against her skin, the dollars in her pocket as thin as lint. The dress touched her everywhere, caressing her, and as she looked at herself in the mirror one last time, she wanted the dress even more, and a spike of desire drove into her, again and again. "Would you be willing to take less, Mrs. Dodsworth? Seeing that it's New Year's Eve and you're closing up?"

"What do you think I run? A bargain emporium?" Her arm lay like a gate across her breast. Mrs. Dodsworth wagged her finger, and her scent of hair shellac and rose water reached Linda, and Mr. Huggins sucked marrow from a bone. Linda needed help with the buttons, but now she was too ashamed to ask, and she wished that she could disappear from the store. How could she have been so naïve? "You're not from here," Bruder had said weeks ago. "Never forget that, Linda. If you do, they'll remember it for you."

The telephone rang. Mrs. Dodsworth hurried to it while snapping at Linda to take off the dress. "I can't," said Linda, and Mrs. Dodsworth hurried back to Linda and unbuttoned the dress with quick, cruel hands and then lunged for the phone. Back in the changing room, Linda let the dress fall away, and in the mirror she saw her flesh that the silver silk had brought to life and the body that Bruder had seen and held, and the heat of her present shame. From the other side of the curtain she heard Mrs. Dodsworth say, "Yes, she is. Yes, she mentioned that. No, I had no idea. Right. Yes, I understand. No, no, I will. Yes, indeed." There was a pause. "Yes, of course. No, thank *you.*"

When she was dressed in her own clothes, Linda pulled back the curtain and returned the dress to Mrs. Dodsworth. It looked like a deflated balloon, limp and lifeless. Mrs. Dodsworth shook the dress out and said, "It is a pretty one, isn't it?" and she laid it over a length of red tissue paper while humming to herself, and as Linda moved to the door Mr. Huggins growled and Mrs. Dodsworth said, "Don't you want the dress?"

"I thought I—"

"May I show you anything else, Miss Stamp?"

"But, Mrs. Dodsworth—"

"Do you have the right shoes for tonight?"

Linda protested again: Why was Mrs. Dodsworth putting her through this? Her money was worthless here. She might as well have come in with nothing in her pocket.

"Stop your worrying, Miss Stamp. It's all been arranged. Now, do you have a wrap? The evenings can turn cold."

"Mrs. Dodsworth?"

"That was Captain Poore. He said he saw you come into the store. He wants to make sure I send him the bill. I'm sorry about the misunderstanding. I should have been listening more carefully, Miss Stamp. I didn't understand at first." Mrs. Dodsworth moved to Linda, and Mr. Huggins rubbed against her leg, his snout twitching damply. Outside on the sidewalk, two of the girls from the packinghouse appeared and pressed their faces against the store's window. Their moony eyes admired the clothes in the shop and the boutique's plush air. The girls didn't recognize Linda—they looked through her, and she might as well have been someone else. They were holding hands and they looked at the dresses they would never own, and then they were gone, and later that night at the party behind the door in the alley, each girl, as she was being groped by a boy as poor as she, would wish that the dress that was being pushed up her thigh had come from Dodsworth's.

Mrs. Dodsworth said, "Is there anything else you wanted to see, Miss Stamp?"

Linda was too startled to speak.

"A shawl, perhaps?"

Linda didn't know what else she would need. Would the dress be enough to get her through the night?

"Or a hat?"

"A hat, Mrs. Dodsworth?"

"I have a lovely one, white, with a crystal-studded veil."

"A veil?"

"Or this one just came in. Look at it, Miss Stamp. Isn't it pretty? All white and fluffy like a snowball! It's one hundred percent bald eagle." She flapped her arms, like a large hawk.

"Eagle feathers?"

"I know what they say about conservation and all, but I saw it in a catalog from New York and I ordered two. The first one's already been snapped up. Now's *your* chance!" She placed the cap atop Linda's head, and together the two women—one old and one leaving youth behind—stared in the mirror, and Mr. Huggins gnawed his bone, and Linda felt something leaving her, a ripple in the mirror's reflection, nothing more than the cold sensation of early regret passing through her.

12

THAT EVENING, when he came for her, Willis was wearing a raccoon coat and a beaver hat and boots covered in shaggy polar bear. As it turned out, the ball had an Antarctic theme and everyone would be wearing furs. He held up a grizzly coat for Linda, and inside on the lining was a loopy monogram stitched in gold:

LP

"Is it Lolly's?"

But Willis didn't answer. The coat was heavy and the fur was thick and woolly. Linda slid her arms up the sleeves, and the coat's dense weight immediately restrained her.

"Do I have to wear it? Won't I be uncomfortable?"

"You don't have to do anything," said Willis. "Everyone else will be in a fur, but if you don't want—" He stopped. "I want you to fit in."

Willis drove, and he didn't say much as the car wound down the hill and passed through Linda Vista and crossed Suicide Bridge. Linda didn't know what to expect at the Valley Hunt Club, and as she looked at herself in the mirror, the worry was apparent in her face. Beneath the grizzly coat she was heating up, and she felt the sweat bubbling on her lip. She had borrowed some of Rosa's lipstick, and her red mouth beamed in the car's dark cab and her lips tasted waxy and somehow not real, what a doll's lips might taste like, she thought, a beautiful little doll; and this made her think of the day that Rosa, tiptoeing down the hall, led Linda to a locked door and opened it with one of the keys from her ring and together they peered into a room crammed with hundreds of Lolly's dolls, their bodies naked and pink and chipped like an old empty plate.

"Did you say something?" said Willis.

"Nothing."

Linda cracked the window and let the cool air rush around her, and on the breeze was the scent of lavender and ryegrass and the bitter car exhaust. And, faintly, the orange groves.

"We'll have some fun, won't we?" said Willis.

And Linda, who once had been a fearless girl, heard the hesitancy in her voice, the wobble of an adult's fright: "Do you think they'll like me?"

"Oh, Linda," said Willis, and his hand left the steering wheel and found its way to her shoulder and rocked her through the bearskin. "Will they like you?" His laugh wasn't cruel but he laughed hard, and when he saw that she wasn't laughing he said, "Don't be silly."

She welcomed the intimacy, the way she had once welcomed Edmund's hand patting his bed, asking her to sit beside him while they talked—or was there more to it than that, and would Linda admit it if there was? What kind of girl was Linda Stamp? What kind of girl had she become? She looked out the window, at the mansions on Orange Grove, one after the other, where maids in the windows were drawing velvet blinds. Where am I going?, Linda asked herself, staring out into the night, and as they sped past the damp lawns and the lights reflecting in backyard swimming pools, Linda fell down into a well of echoing, mossy thought, a deep narrow well where the thoughts dripped like water *plip-plip-plip* and it was only Willis's hand that pulled her out again. His hand was still upon her shoulder. It was a small but strong hand, and as he touched her—one hand on Linda, the other flat palm steering the wheel—his raccoon coat opened and his white tie peeped out like a bright, toothy smile in a dark empty room.

The clubhouse was decorated with thousands of flowers, lilies round the banister, sweet peas framing the *plein-air* paintings of Eaton Canyon and Devil's Gate, snapdragons biting the air. In the ballroom, a "1925" sign made of button chrysanthemums hung above the orchestra stage, and the waiters wore Pink Perfection camellias in their lapels. There were hundreds of people, members and their guests, and all were buried beneath coats and ponchos and sweaters and shawls of animal skin: tawny cougar, grizzled coarse coyote, black seal and buff sea lion, mule deer, pale gray elk, glossy otter, hognose skunk, long-tailed weasel and marten, white-tipped fisher, winter-coated ermine, mink and silver-flecked sable, red fox kit, yellow-gray ringtail, black bear, old zebra and jaguar, and stiff-feathered penguin.

A man with a hothouse orchid pinned to his goatskin vest welcomed Linda and Willis. He introduced himself as Carlisle Waud, Willis's cousin. He was slight in frame and heavy in limp—he'd been shoved into the path of a buggy by his sister, Greta, when he was six—and he walked with a sterling-silver cane. Carlisle took one of Linda's arms and Willis hooked himself to the other, and they steered her through the pelts into the ballroom, where eyes lifted with curiosity.

Flimsy hands like calla lilies extended. "How d'you do?"

It didn't take long for Linda to realize that her existence if not her reputation had preceded her: that the story had passed—as a flea hops from one hide to the next—that Willis Poore was escorting a stranger to the New Year's ball. Linda heard a voice floating somewhere above the music: "Who is *she*?" Other voices wafted around the ballroom, coming from here and there and everywhere: from the women propped up in sturdy, fuzzy columns of silver fox, from the manicured men in their frontier coats, from the orchestra in white dinner jacket playing a Viennese waltz.

"They'll jazz it up later on," Willis said. "Then we'll really cut into it." Someone asked where Linda was from, and a little circle of silence fell upon them when she told them. Then Carlisle asked, "From Baden-Baden-by-the-Sea? Do you fish?"

"I trapped lobsters." This caused eyelids to lift and necks to extend. "Lobster pots?" said a woman. "At the bottom of the ocean?" A man sputtered, "You mean to tell me you'd catch the lobsters yourself?" Another woman said, "I just love lobster. I bet you didn't know that about me, did you, Gregory?" (But Gregory said that he did.) Someone asked, "Where does one go about buying a lobster pot?" And Linda said that she built them herself with a mallet and scrap wood and a knitting needle. Someone squealed, "All by yourself?" And one of the women exclaimed, "You actually swim down to the bottom of the ocean with all those *fish* around you, *nibbling* at you?" The woman pushed out her mouth curiously, and the others at the table—each rich and handsome or rich and fat or rich and homely or rich and shy—propped their chins in their fists and leaned in as Linda told them about the blue shark.

"You didn't!" screamed one woman. "You *did not*! Didn't you look at him and just want to *die*!"

A petite, damp-eyed girl wearing a condor-feather cap twirled over to their table and landed herself in Willis's lap. "Captain Poore, where's Lolly tonight? You haven't locked her up again, have you?" The young woman rose, her pleated skirt swirling so high that everyone could see her garters and her silver silk underwear. She said she was off to the pool house: "Ship ahoy!" Several others followed her, and soon Linda was alone at the table with Willis and Carlisle.

"Where'd you find old Willis, anyway?" said Carlisle.

"I didn't," she said. "He found me."

Twenty minutes later, one of the men returned from the pool house, his cheeks and eyes glowing. He said, "Won't you join us, Miss Stamp?" His girl, whose red hair was curled like sausages, slapped his hand and said, "Hugh, now cut it out." Others returned to the table, a greasiness slicking their eyes. They spoke more slowly, as if their tongues had thickened in their mouths.

"Come on," said Willis. "Let's go outside." He led Linda to the terrace. In the swimming pool, the moon of the underwater lamp glowed, and hundreds of magnolia blossoms floated on the surface like stars. One woman was standing on the ladder, her gold sandals dangling from her fingers and her river-otter coat wet at the hem, and she was leaning back over the water and her husband was begging her, "Millie, get off that thing," and she was saying, "Oh, Jimmie, relax, would you? This old otter came from the water." A fat young man had shed his jacket and was bouncing on the diving board, and back in the clubhouse Linda could see the members—for that was how she heard everyone refer to themselves throughout the night—dancing and smoking and slurping oysters and sucking the covert alcohol from gin-soaked celery sticks. About twenty of the club's junior members were crowded in the pool house, where flasks passed from fist to fist and wrists emptied their contents into highballs of orange juice and tomato juice and even cups of coffee, and a few young men brought the silver-rimmed flasks to their chapped mouths, their furs wet with sloshed and drooled drink, and their young wives or girlfriends or sisters swatted them with their fans and then grabbed the flasks for themselves.

"Should we have something to drink?" asked Willis.

Linda agreed, and someone passed her a cup of orange bourbon distilled in a pair of six-foot Chinese vases at the hearth of a mansion just up the street; it smelled like petroleum so she swallowed it quickly, and it tasted even worse than that.

"Are you all right?" someone asked from behind her, but Linda wasn't sure who it was. She turned around, and there was Connie Muffitt in a short leopard coat and an anaconda shawl, her blond hair pasted to her skull like a gold-glass Christmas ball. She waved with her pinkie and was coming toward Linda when a man in an elephant-skin top hat snatched her, pulling her to the dance floor.

The bear coat and the cramped pool house had left Linda hot and weary and thirsty, and she felt the perspiration dotting her face and collecting inside the silver dress, leaving stains on the silk. Linda looked around for Willis but saw only shiny faces and fur. He had left her, and the drink had scampered straight to her head and she felt dizzy and sticky and warm, and someone, a stranger, stopped her and said, "Oh, what a pretty dress!"

Another said, "What a pretty coat!"

Someone else said, "I was just hearing about your fascinating life!"

By now Linda was drunk, and she thought that perhaps these people weren't so bad, and she relaxed and for a moment forgot that she was new to all this; for a blinking moment, it felt as familiar as her own life.

Linda returned to the pool deck, and the fat young man was still bouncing on the diving board, his suspenders hanging from his waistband, and there was a commotion among a cluster of old women, their faces powdered poodle-white, about this being *the last straw*. Members of the club's steering committee arrived to try to talk the man off the board, but he continued to bounce and then flung himself, his lumpy back first, into the pool, resounding with a horrible slap to his fleshy flesh. At once, the night became too much for Linda: she longed to leave, but she couldn't see Willis anywhere, and something in her decided not to return to the ballroom alone but to sit in the night on a cold bench and count the white stars. She walked out to the pavilion overlooking the tennis courts. It was quieter there, the music distant and the wind rustling the high palms, the ivy turning crisply. Linda leaned against the rail as the far-off orchestra played a song that caused nearly everyone at the club, even those around the pool, to raise their arms and refrain in sloppy voices, *Yes-sir-ee! Yes, indeed! Yes-I-can, Ma-dame!*

A hand fell on hers, and something caught in Linda's throat.

"We're not always like this," said Willis.

She pulled her hand away.

"They're just having a little New Year's fun. Letting off some steam." And then: "Linda—"

She turned, her shoulder shifting away. She felt the sudden need to bathe, to sit in a hot bath and let the steam rise around her. It was what she would do when she returned to the Pasadena, and just then Willis said, "I want you to like it here. I was hoping you'd want to stay."

"What are you talking about?"

"Linda? Don't you feel the same?"

The same?, she said, but did the words emerge from her mouth? Had she managed to speak at all?

"You don't really want to go back there, do you? To the little farm? To your old lobster pots?"

She said that she did, she said that she *had* to go back, she had her brother and her nephew and her father to look after, and they would expect her in the spring, and she couldn't spend the rest of her life in a ranch-house kitchen, could she? It wasn't what she wanted for herself. She wanted more, and she realized that Willis understood this—perhaps even more profoundly than she did.

"That's not what I'm talking about," said Willis. "I get the sense you like it in Pasadena."

She didn't know what to say, but the truth was that with every passing hour, with every ticking minute of New Year's Eve, Condor's Nest fell farther and farther away, and now it felt that her life had become a double life: Linda Stamp from Baden-Baden-by-the-Sea distantly bound to this young woman, who at midnight would turn twenty-two, her durable shoulders hoisting a grizzly skin and her throat singed from orange-based bootleg. They were two, like an oyster halved and flapping open on its fragile hinge, and if she were asked to, Linda wouldn't be able to identify herself just then.

A man and a woman searching around for a private love nest climbed up onto the pavilion and peered into the dark. "Who's there?" the man called. "Who are you?" whispered the girl. They saw the out-

backing her up, until she was leaning over the pavilion's rail, and his arms held her aloft and at once she wanted him both to let go and to never stop. He led her to a wicker bench behind the pavilion and laid the grizzly coat over it. He kissed her as the moon continued to throb, and his heat on her flesh surprised her, causing her to gasp, and Willis continued and Linda kissed him in return, as she imagined she should, and the dancing one-two'd on and on across the ballroom's parquet, and Willis's hand, smooth from years of avoiding work on the ranch, made its way down her neck and over the bodice of the dress he had bought for her, paid for, worth more money than she had ever earned, than she would ever earn, unless . . . unless . . . and he made his way with such assurance that it was as if he had the right, as if he owned the dress, and didn't he? And Linda wanted him both to stop and to continue, and she didn't know how to say either, how to say both at once. That's what Willis did to her: stole the words from her throat. His hand went farther, and she pushed it away; and it was back, and she pushed it away; and Willis's hand returned again to her breast, to her stomach, between her legs. "Willis, no," she cried softly, but one arm clasped her and the free hand roamed and she wiggled playfully and then she writhed and his arm pinned her to him. She had let him fool her: the boy was a man; that's all he was. The grizzly skin pricked her flesh, and Willis was wet with sweat, and his quick, greasy hands roamed over her, and she tried one last time, "Willis, what if someone comes?" but he wasn't going to stop, couldn't stop now; and the orchestra conductor introduced a trio called The Night-Men, and the crowd inside the ballroom roared and a sax and a trumpet bled into the cold New Year's night. And Linda Stamp would remember the night like this: she didn't have a choice. The fate she had held at bay for so long broke and crashed around her, and the New Year washed in and Linda hadn't decided any of this for herself. Linda, so strong in spine, a spine that now trembled under Willis's kneading hands, let the night pass over her and let Willis press himself into her and the hands worked the dress effortlessly, as if he had previously studied every hook and button, and he panted into her breast, "Oh, Lindy! Lindy!" And she wondered who he was calling after; that wasn't her name. "You can have all this," he said. "All *what*?" But Willis didn't answer, and again: *Lindy!* And as he thrust on and the sweat poured from his brow into her eyes and her mouth, causing her to cough and gag, the distinction between his heartbeat and hers blurred, she heard the name again and again—*Lindy Lindy Lindy*—and she felt something shift beneath her— the wicker sofa cracking, the silk ripping, the grizzly coat almost growl- ing as if it were being buried alive—and a pair of fast, pink-palmed hands beat the bongos on the orchestra stage and Willis's mouth was hot and wet on her throat, biting, nipping, and there was the salty ocean scent of blood, and his medal for heroism, still pinned to his breast, pressed into her flesh, imprinting her with its reverse image, stamping her like a sizzling brand, and Linda at last gave up and fell limp beneath him and let the New Year ring in and flood down upon her, and the band's music ran like a river into the night, they would play until dawn, and Captain Willis Poore said again and again, whispering, now, almost tender, the two of them drenched as if emerging from the water, his voice soft, singing, nearly a song:

> *O, she was born in the ocean*
> *And came from the sea*
> *A woman of devotion*
> *My li'l Lindy*

13

BY THE TIME THEY LEFT the Valley Hunt Club, dawn was arriving behind the mountains. Willis and Linda emerged beneath the *porte cochère* and found a crisp frost on the clubhouse lawn. It was so late that the valets had gone home, and Willis left Linda to fetch the car. While he was gone, a man in a bowler hat appeared from behind a hedge. "Enjoy yourself tonight?" he asked.

Linda said that she had, pulling the coat tight around her, buttoning herself in.

"What made it so special?" asked someone behind the man. Linda couldn't see who it was, but she was so tired that she spoke without hearing herself: "The music and the dancing. And those hundreds and hundreds of furs."

"Is that your bear coat?" It was a woman's voice, and the man bent to pull a camera from a bag at his feet and Linda saw that the woman behind him was small with silvery curls, and young but somehow already hard in the face. The face was familiar, and the woman smiled knowingly, as if she were aware of something that had yet to click in Linda's mind.

Then Linda knew. "Charlotte? Is it you?"

"Sure it's me." And Cherry Moss handed Linda her card: REPORTER—SOCIETY AND NEWS. "But, golly! Take a look at my old friend Sieglinde Stumpf. Wally"—and she elbowed the man—"be sure to get a shot of her. I knew her way back when."

Wally clicked his camera and an enormous tin-colored flash erupted on the lawn and Linda's hand flew to her eyes. She was blinded for a second or two, disoriented, and she found herself reaching at the empty air before her. "Charlotte?"

"Cherry's right here. Did Wally get you in the peeps?"

Linda's eyes cleared, and she found Cherry standing at her side with her notebook, biting her lip in that way of hers. She stood with her feet planted firmly, as if she were boring in for a long day, and a great dreamy confusion overcame Linda and she wondered if it was the drink, or something else. She was both cold and hot, and the grizzly was nearly suffocating her.

"Do you mind telling me who you came with tonight?" asked Cherry.

"Captain Poore." As she said this, the car pulled beneath the portico and Willis ran to Linda, yelling at her to get in at once. When she didn't move, his arm moved around her and she leaned into him, and the magnesium flash startled her again. Then Willis yanked Linda into the car. They drove off in the direction of the bridge. Linda looked over her shoulder and saw Cherry, her head down, busily writing in her notebook, and when Willis said under his sour breath, "Goddammit, Lindy, never talk to the gossips," Linda understood.

Cherry's curls bobbed against her throat, and her pencil scratched her notebook as the car sped up the boulevard, and when Cherry lifted her head, the distance was too great, and her face, to Linda, was a blank oval. And so much had happened in the night that Linda thought maybe, just maybe, it was a ghost or a memory or a premonition, anything but the cold truth of the grinding daily news.

But the daily news arrived the next afternoon, printed in gray ink that smudged Linda's thumbs as she held up the *American Weekly*.

ORANGE HEIR ESCORTS COOK IN BORROWED BEARSKIN!
By Chatty Cherry

Guess which one of Pasadena's founding sons escorted his ranch-house cook to the Valley Hunt Club's Antarctic Ball? The girl was snuggled into the brown fur of a bearskin coat borrowed—unknowingly, perhaps?—from the bare shoulders of the orange heir's little sister, who remained at home, bedridden. I wonder what was ailing her?

The accompanying photograph, blurry and dark, caught Linda and Willis in a moment of exhausted happiness, his arm around her shoulder and her head tilted toward him. It revealed, even in the dull newsprint, her glowing eyes, and anyone shaking the *American Weekly* out of his newspaper—for the *American Weekly* was distributed in the grimy folds of a thousand of America's finest and filthiest papers, including the *Star-News*—would recognize the dewiness of Eros on the lips and throat of Linda Stamp.

Certainly Bruder recognized it when he folded back the newspaper, and the ranch hands craned their necks to see the picture at the table beneath the pepper tree; they hooted and whistled at Linda's silhouette moving in the ranch-house window, preparing their breakfast, and Muir Yuen and the other men joked about Linda not working in the kitchen for much longer. Bruder sat at the head of the table with the newspaper spread in front of him, his forehead propped in his hands. He didn't want to believe it, but the evidence was before him. He had always hated Charlotte, or Cherry, or whatever she was calling herself, but now, even as he despised her, he was grateful for her having captured the truth. It was the same truth Linda herself had been presenting Bruder, but somehow he hadn't been able to see it in her averted eyes. Only the newsprint clarified what he should have known for a long time, and Bruder was silent and enraged. The hands must have known that he had been betrayed, everyone must have known, and Bruder sat with his humiliation, too stunned to nurse it.

"Don't believe everything you read," said Linda.

"And the picture?" said Bruder.

"It's nothing. It might give someone the wrong idea." She laughed falsely, and her voice, high and sweet, didn't sound like her, and she didn't know how to explain what had happened even to herself. Her future had arrived, but she didn't know where it was.

By nightfall, Willis had relieved her of her kitchen duties, driving her up the hill once and for all, and by the next night—although she wouldn't know it for four or five years—a speck of flesh in her loin had reddened with chancre, and Bruder had quit the ranch, running off beneath the shattered moon.

14

SEVERAL WEEKS LATER, Willis bought Linda a return ticket at the Raymond Street Station and left her on the platform with his command to *think about it, Lindy. What else can you do? I don't understand why you can't say yes right now.*

Burdened by headache and fatigue, she rode the train down the coast, her coat with the jelly-stained cuff wadded in her lap. Her fingertips pressed against the swollen nodes in her throat and wiped at her simmering brow, and she felt as if she were someone else returning to Condor's Nest, an offshoot of her former self. She had lost weight, and her face was thin in the window's reflection; beneath her skirt, upon her upper thigh, a mild rash blossomed red, like a colony of ant bites, but Linda thought little of it. There was the morning nausea too and her sluggish blood flow and Linda was not herself—that much she knew. She had even said to Willis, "I'm not feeling myself," and said it to Rosa; and when she wrote Edmund, announcing her return to Condor's Nest, she had also said: "Haven't felt myself lately." And then: "But nothing's wrong."

Linda pressed her face to the glass as the train raced along the coast. The dimpled ocean was calm and the tide was out, and she saw fishermen wading and buoys bobbing and, on the horizon, two people in an outrigger canoe. The window was cracked and the damp, salty air fell like a veil across her face, and she smelled the beach and the heaps of drying, flyblown kelp, and the train passed a cove where a group of boys and girls were prodding with sticks a beached pilot whale, and throwing rocks at its huge, rubbery head.

She was going home because she didn't know what she should do.

She would talk to Bruder. She would ask Edmund for his help. No one knew her better than he, she told herself, and his letters—all but one unanswered—were piled in her bag, bound by twine, smudged and ripped, the ink of one smeared by an overturned flute of champagne. After New Year's he had written that Bruder had returned to Condor's Nest. "He's kicked me out of my cottage. I'm living with the boy in the Vulture House. He acts like he owns the farm, and then he told me that he does."

When Linda reached Baden-Baden-by-the-Sea she walked down the paved lane toward Condor's Nest, bag in hand, the silver dress, re-sewn by Esperanza, folded in tissue within. She expected that Edmund and Dieter would run out to greet her, and Bruder behind them. They would hug her beside the field, and their oniony scent would flood her nostrils, and their dirty, working hands would hold her, smudging her blouse, and they would say, "You're home at last! Welcome home!"

But no one came to meet her, and she found herself standing next to a sign that someone had erected:

CONDOR'S NEST
STAY OUT

Linda called out for her father and her brother and then Bruder, but her voice was swallowed by the grumbling ocean. She yelled again, but there was a wind running up the bluff and she could barely hear herself and Linda felt alone. Something small and sharp and laden with regret sat beneath her breast.

She found Edmund in the Vulture House, struggling to get Palomar out of a pair of muddy overalls. Edmund looked too burdened with work to be happy to see her. The boy was babbling and fighting with his father, and his bare hips were white and aglow against the blue blanket on the bed. He was kicking, and Edmund was yelling at him to stop, and the boy kicked his father in the chest, and Edmund slapped his son.

"Can I help?" she said.

"I didn't believe you when you said you were coming home." His face was soft and tremulous. "I don't believe you're here right now."

Little Palomar ran to Linda, the overalls plunging around his knees and his flesh mottled from the cold. He wrapped his arms around her shins, nearly toppling her, and she knelt and guided him out of his overalls and into a clean pair of pants.

Then Dieter appeared, and he struggled to recognize Linda. "Back from the war?" he said. "Back from France?" His face was snow-blue and his eyes were vacant and his right hand was a lame, flaky claw. He was old, and his brain had emptied before his body. "One day he woke up and he was gone," said Edmund, snapping his fingers to demonstrate the swiftness of a fleeting second, of a life. "Didn't you read my letters?"

But Edmund appeared hollow too; the household chores that once had been Linda's had drained him. With both Dieter and Palomar to look after, Edmund's days were long: he rose before dawn and went to bed late, feeding his father and his son and washing their clothes and their bodies and changing their bedding and stewing the white cabbage Dieter liked to slurp on and baking the corn *tortillas* Palomar sucked on for hours and lye-mopping the floors after one of them, or both, had made a mess. The endless quotidian work had left Edmund with the feeling that he had buried himself and was being forced to lead another's life.

"I've come to see you," said Linda.

"Why now? After all these months?"

"I've come to talk to you. To tell you what's happened—" But Linda was interrupted by something moving outside the window, in the field. She looked, and it was Bruder trundling a pushcart. Because of her fever, she almost wondered if he was a ghost: he looked just as he had when he first arrived at Condor's Nest. She sat upon her brother's bed and their thighs touched and he plucked her hand from her lap and stroked it with cold fingers. There was a cruel honesty: at once she realized that their lives had diverged, but at the same time their childhood felt only an hour away. She said his name. And he said hers.

Siegmund.

Sieglinde.

What Linda didn't know was that as Bruder worked the onion field in the twilight he could see them on the sagging mattress, like two old people clutching each other against the sucking brutality of life. In one of Bruder's pockets was the picture from the *American Weekly* and Cherry's article; in his other pocket was the deer-foot knife. He had left

Pasadena with nothing but it and the newspaper and a hard vow of revenge.

There's a question that some people ask: When does a man become the man that he is? For Bruder, he would always think of New Year's, 1925. He had believed in her, and then that day he stopped believing, and although he would always love her, he would never forgive her. Despite himself he wished her dead, but that glance into the future stung his eyes with tears, and the onions in his cart reeked and rolled around like lopped heads, and Bruder went down to the beach to roam the black night.

He no longer wanted anything from her—except the coral pendant, which one day he would take back. He imagined his fist snapping the necklace from her throat, yanking the pendant free, and at precisely the same moment, Linda imagined this too, sitting up in her bed and touching her throat as if a hand had been squeezing her windpipe. At first she didn't know where she was, and then she recognized the crashing surf and realized it was the middle of the night. At first she thought that she was a little girl, and that Dieter and Valencia were asleep in the cottage next door, but then Linda remembered everything. Spread around her were the gifts from Willis: a detachable polar-bear collar, mother-of-pearl opera glasses, the silver dress hanging from the window sash and fluttering in the breeze. She got out of bed and examined the rash on her thigh. It was hard and red and the pits of her arms were tender with swollen glands, and she didn't understand what was happening, not at first. Rosa had said, "It happened to me too. It comes in the first month or two." Then: "How's your stomach? And your sleep? And the queasy feeling buried deep within? Are you tired before dinner, and in the morning?" Linda answered yes to all of Rosa's queries. "Then you'll be visiting Dr. Freeman soon," Rosa had said.

Something outside Linda's window moved. When she pulled back the curtain, she saw Edmund at work in the barn with mallet and hewing ax. Leaning against the door were tiny wooden rods of white pine, and Linda couldn't guess what he was doing. Edmund screwed the rods into a rail-board, and slowly she figured out that he was building a small bed for Palomar. The barn light cast a gold electric halo onto him, and Linda saw the smooth peace in his face as he two-fisted the mallet, his lips clamped around a pair of screws. Edmund knelt at his task, securing a rod with his screwdriver and then rubbing at it with his sander. It was as if Edmund were in a trance, protected from the reality that had descended upon all of them. Linda could see this in his concentration, his eyes open but blank behind his spectacles, in the way his hair fell round his brow. He screwed another rod into the molded rail, and Linda could sense that he was prepared to help her—there had been a detour in their lives, but all would be right soon.

She had come to Condor's Nest to correct things, and she would no longer wait. In her nightdress and bare feet she went to him, the dress billowing as she crossed the field. The moon spun its silver upon her face, and she moved to Edmund as if she were being carried across the yard—a young woman just twenty-two, Linda Stamp, floating moth-like to the gold light in the barn door. As she approached him she knew what she would tell him, she knew. She would ask Edmund for his advice, she would tell him the truth about New Year's Eve, and about how her heart had sent Bruder away, and now she wanted her brother's help in bringing him back. The night was moist with sea mist. The quake in her stomach returned with an oceanic lurch, a cold, fish-thick wave swimming through her. Edmund, busy at his task, didn't see her approach. A pink ribbon ran through the nightdress's collar and sleeves. It was a gift sent over from Dodsworth's; the necklace of pea-size pearls too. "You'll need something other than that piece of coral," Willis had said. A woman in an oyster-white gown approached Edmund, and when Linda stood over her brother he looked up, and the peace that she had witnessed in his face broke away in chips and shards, like a mallet smashing a vase's round cheek.

She knelt beside him in the doorway of the barn. Their knees touched, and the moist air greased Edmund's face. "It's for Palomar," he said, screwing the base of the spindle, turning the screwdriver with a thrust and then finishing with a swift smack of the mallet, a *crack!* in the night.

She said it softly: "I need your help." He didn't stop, wrists twisting, the single grooved screw tight between his lips, its tip beneath his tongue; was the iron taste seeping down his throat? Had Edmund heard her plea?

What she needed to say was simple, but now she feared she couldn't bring it to words. Could the narrowness of a sentence hold the brimming truth? But her life had come to this: one man wanted her, and she didn't fully understand why; and another man didn't want her, and she couldn't understand why not.

"I've come into some trouble," she began.

Edmund's hands stopped. His chin turned cautiously toward her. His eyes screwed up as if someone were hurting him. His mouth was an open blank hole.

"Edmund," she said. "I'm going to have . . ."

She tried again. "I'm, I'm . . ." She shook with humiliation and uncertainty, and then there was a lone, horrible sob. "I don't know what to do."

"What did he do to you?"

Edmund gripped the mallet, his knuckles glowing dark and amber, and like a bird taking off he propelled himself up and soared across the field, his arms outstretched, the barrel head of the mallet catching the moonlight. His feet and the wind carried him at full wingspan: gliding, running toward the bluff, like a turkey vulture scampering into flight, his head bobbing angrily.

Linda stood: *Edmund! Edmund!* She didn't know where he was going, why he was running from her. He reached the cliff, and as quickly as a sparrow darting away, over it he ran.

Linda began to run too, calling his name. It came to her then, as Edmund's scream rose from the beach: "You'll never touch her again!"

As Edmund called out for Bruder, his voice echoing up from the sand, Linda understood. An image had entered Edmund's head, one of her lying down in the orange grove, Bruder descending upon her. Was the image in her brother's head similar to those that had visited her late at night, in a hot sleep, the sheets twisted between her legs?

Linda ran to the edge of the cliff: "No! Edmund!" And then: "Leave him alone!"

For Linda Stamp—*Lindy! Lindy!*—would not yet admit to herself that the decision had already been made for her; that she had made her own decision. How could it have happened without her knowing?

"It's fate," Willis had said. "You and me."

A voice in the breeze, crawling up the cliff, struggled to reach her.

She stood at the edge, rocks skittering down the bluff: a calm tide, black ocean, whitecaps frothing, shooting and spraying and spilling in dollops, a glimmer on the wreckage of the staircase. She reached the

beach but didn't see anyone. The sand was soft, footprints molded deep. Linda followed them down the shore, south around the bend and past Jelly Beach. Her feet ripped up the sand and she ran until it was hard to breathe and she kept running.

She heard them before she saw them: "I won't let you take her from me!" Edmund cried, and there was a crack like wood splitting, a *snap!* like something out of memory, and then the sand gave way to a field of rocks and she arrived at Cathedral Cove and at once she saw them: Bruder's raised arm was coming down swiftly, as if he were hurling something. Edmund was falling at Bruder's feet. There was a strange sound, like a hoe slamming into mud. A small coin of metal winked atop Edmund's head, and the ocean moaned. And then all was still. She saw them but she didn't know what she had seen.

And time would pass, weeks and months, years, before Linda could know for sure what had happened.

She stopped at the edge of the cove. She heard Bruder crying in the darkness. He yelled at her not to come any closer. Linda was frightened and she obeyed and she stood on the beach and peered at the two figures, one standing and one lying down. Then something inside her told her to look away. She turned and looked north up the coast and thought of the beach's long endless span, across inlets and coves and around harbors it ran, and her mind traveled up the coast with it. She thought of the orange groves and the white house on the hill and she thought of her future and she thought of her past. She made one last attempt to come to Bruder's side, but she fell on the rocks, slippery with laver, and cut her palm, and her blood was bright on her blouse, and Bruder, a faceless silhouette in the night, hollered, "Linda, go back home! Stay away!" And then he said in a voice so soft that perhaps he hadn't meant for it to reach her ear: "There's nothing you can do now. You've come too late."

DEED

part five

All Heaven's undreamt felicity
Could never blot the past from me.
No; years may cloud and death may sever
But what is done is done for ever.

EMILY BRONTË

1

BY THE LATE WINTER of 1945, Andrew Jackson Blackwood had yet to make a move on what Mrs. Nay described as *the opportunity of a lifetime.*

"Something like this comes along but once," she said one day when they ran into each other on Colorado Street. The sun was high and the rains were over. She added that as the months had passed, Mr. Bruder had grown more and more anxious to *unload.* "Imagine it, Mr. Blackwood. You: the master of the Pasadena. You'll have come quite a ways, wouldn't you say?"

It was one of the few instances in which her sales pitch became, to Blackwood's ear, excessive. She discreetly inquired whether or not Blackwood had the funds, leaning in and whispering in a mildly insulting fashion. Blackwood politely assured her that he was more than capable of buying not only the Rancho Pasadena but also Condor's Nest, should Mr. Bruder be interested in selling both.

"Both? In the same deal? It's not a bad idea," said Mrs. Nay.

"It was, after all, the onion farm that first caught my eye." They were standing on the sidewalk in front of the former Dodsworth's, shuttered so long ago.

Mrs. Nay said that she couldn't promise anything but would float the idea. And then she was off to a meeting of some sort about the many abandoned buildings on Colorado Street—the Committee to Eradicate Our Eyesores, the group called itself. But she turned on her heel to tell Blackwood one more thing: "I just received a letter from George. He says the Reich is falling faster than even in the newspaper accounts. The first boys could be home by summer!" She waved a tissuey envelope from a hotel in Washington. Her smile was full of the joy of prospective peace. Cherry longed to see her husband after these many months. Their relationship was unusually amiable: George and Cherry Nay— comrades, they thought of themselves. When she was young, she had built herself a somewhat shameful life—rushing from one sordid story to the next!—but back then her options had been limited. At the time, there wasn't much else for Cherry but living off her words: she had been young and smart but not especially pretty, and in possession of no connections, and the world had offered little to a girl like Charlotte Moss. She'd done her best, although she admitted to herself, when the regret rose in her throat, that sometimes she had done less than that. But then she had helped out Bruder when he needed help the most, and at nearly the same time she had found George; in a matter of months, everything had changed for her. She understood her good fortune, her lot improving *just like that!,* and now, every time she wrote a letter to her husband—*My Dearest Friend . . .*—she reminded herself that in the end, fate had dealt her a fine hand.

"Good-bye, Mr. Blackwood."

"Good-bye, Mrs. Nay."

"We'll be speaking soon, I am sure."

The following morning began with an unpromising sunrise, diffuse and white, and a forecast of an early heat wave. But then a bald eagle alit on the telephone pole at Blackwood's curb. Its hooked yellow bill was clasping something papery and green, and it looked to Blackwood like a dollar bill. He took this event as a sign of good fortune and he rushed for his folding telescope. But upon inspection the greenback turned out to be nothing but a leaf of mountain mahogany. Although hardly symbolic, this incident prompted Blackwood; and he coated himself in his customary cheerful self-confidence, and then and there, in his mint-green pajamas, he decided to pursue what he now thought would be his greatest accomplishment, that for which he would be remembered: to take control of the Rancho Pasadena. He would transform it into something useful and profitable, hauling it into the modern age. This would be the transaction that would forever rechart his destiny—once and for all moving him up the greasewood ladder that over the years had lodged so many splinters in his thumb. All would change for Blackwood; he would become a different man, and the world would have to accept him differently. The world that hadn't acknowledged him would begin to mail invitations to his red-flagged mailbox. He looked in the mirror and saw the flickering of someone else.

In early March, he arranged for Mrs. Nay to lead the men from the bank on a tour of the Pasadena. It was the time of year when the middles should have been stacked with field boxes and tracked from the picking trucks, but everything at the ranch was idle and, one could say, dying, if not already dead. While the bank men in their gray suits inspected the land and peered into the abandoned packinghouse and marveled at the California history that lay untouched at the western boundary of their progressive city, Blackwood sat in the Imperial Victoria, listening to the news that became more promising by the day.

Nineteen forty-five was turning out to be the year—for the good of the world and Andrew Jackson Blackwood. Matters would settle in his favor, he realized.

After the tour, he and the bankers returned to the conference room next to the bank's vault. Blackwood made a formal presentation, unrolling a map of the ranch's small valley, each square in the grid representing an acre. "What will you *do* with so much land?" one of them inquired phlegmatically. "Do?" "What are your plans, Blackwood?" Blackwood admitted that his plans were not yet firm. "The Pasadena is one of those properties that you buy when you can and figure out what to do with later. I'm sure you don't need me to tell you that the opportunities are endless." He added, "Wouldn't you agree that it's best for the city if this land falls into the hands of someone like me? Someone whose goals are in alignment with our mutual notion of progress?" The men around the white-oak table murmured inscrutably. Blackwood knew that plucking the civic strings often did the trick in Pasadena, and that the bank men (100 Percenters, they used to call themselves) were also directors of the Tournament of Roses and the First Presbyterian and, over on Euclid, All Saints. But they were cautious men in a cautious age. Way back in 1930, a couple of them had bet money that the Arroyo Parkway would run one direction, but the river of concrete had ended up flowing another route. The bank had also sunk money into the Hotel Vista, expecting its reign to last a hundred years. Blackwood hadn't been around during those days, but they said it was once the spot—movie stars and gangsters and orange heiresses all around the swimming pool! And now look at the Vista: the most luxurious hotel in California converted to an army hospital, the bridle trails and the bungalows and the carpets sold off for pennies on the dollar, the swimming pool as deep and empty as a socket without its eye. No, the Vista hadn't turned out well for the bank, but this would be different, Blackwood assured the men, their cheeks gray and bloodless, and these were different times. Why, just today, March 1, 1945, the siege lines were forming around Cologne. "The war is almost over," Blackwood stated in his meeting at the bank. "The boys will be coming home to California. Shouldn't we ready the city for them, gentlemen? After all they've done for us? Don't they at least deserve an apartment with a covered garage?"

Blackwood didn't need the bank's assistance to buy the ranch, but if he wanted to put up a condominium city he'd need their involvement, not really for the cash but to spread the risk. If Blackwood knew anything, it was that you don't open a condominium complex on your own. The chances of going belly-up were too great. He would say, "Be a bull, be a bear, but don't be a pig." Besides, the men of the bank belonged to the circles Blackwood aspired to, and he imagined each of the men at dinner later that night saying to his wife, "Honey, that Blackwood's a fine-enough man. We should ask him over some time." Blackwood imagined their post-debutante daughters, idle and in patriotic khaki, greeting him at the front door: "You must be Mr. Blackwood!"

Blackwood's final argument in front of the bank's Investment Committee ended with the chairman, a thoughtful, hard-whiskered man by the name of Dr. Freeman, saying, "We will have to think about this a little further, Blackwood. This may not be the time."

"Not the *time*?" Blackwood said with dismay, sensing that they were more opposed to him than to the idea itself. Who was this Freeman, anyway? A graduate of Old Throop and then medical school back east; he'd gone on to make a small fortune in women's health. Blackwood had nosed around and learned that Dr. Freeman had a secret past, just like the rest of them. Imagine it: Blackwood thwarted by a man who had performed quite a few illegal procedures in his day. Not that anyone said these things about Dr. Freeman; no, only the most clever knew it. Blackwood wouldn't stop; he would go to others. Or maybe he would abandon the Investment Committee altogether and pursue the Pasadena on his own. Blackwood had always done well on his own. And then a fear overtook him: What if Freeman and the others were to buy the property from beneath him? Would Mrs. Nay protect Blackwood? Was Bruder an ethical man? These questions left Blackwood with a new sense of urgency: he would have to pounce.

In the evening, after the meeting at the bank had ended inconclusively, Blackwood was sitting on his sofa with his chart before him. The telephone rang. It was Mrs. Nay, inviting him to the Pasadena for one last visit. "To be certain, Mr. Blackwood."

"Certain?"

"Certain that you're the one meant to carry this property into the future."

"I'm not sure I know what you mean. But I would like to see you again, Mrs. Nay." And they agreed to meet the following afternoon.

Cherry arrived at the rancho early, and she sat on a chair opposite the Cupid statue and pondered the urgency of Bruder's most recent call. He'd been coughing, rasping with fluid, and he spoke slowly, hesitating often. The pauses had made her guess that he was rubbing his temple between his sentences. She had asked if he had seen a doctor but the question was dismissed; she should have known that Bruder was the type of man who would refuse medical help until it was too late. He was fatalistic about these things, Cherry knew, often saying *What good will it do?* But for a man resigned to what he called *a greater evil force,* he had become awfully busy making arrangements for his estate. "Sell the ranch," he insisted. "I want the memories to go away." Bruder wasn't a naïve man, but Cherry thought this was rather simplistic of him. If only recollected horrors could be sold off! Cherry imagined the auctioneer calling out to an empty hall. Who would buy someone else's history?

But she had agreed: "I'll do my best." He thanked her and said, "Cherry, you've saved me once again."

She opened the iron-and-glass door and greeted Blackwood. Ushering him down the gallery she said, "I realized you never toured the complete grounds."

Blackwood didn't argue, although in fact he had seen nearly every corner of the Rancho Pasadena—the sickly groves and the sugar-white mausoleum and the abandoned packinghouse, where years of heat and disuse had disintegrated the rubber conveyor belts into crumbling black webs. She had shown him the parched crater that had once been the trout pond, "where Mrs. Poore used to go when she was lonely, casting a bamboo rod from the pavilion." With Bruder, Blackwood had inspected the rusting bunks in the ranch house and the overgrown paths through the camellia garden and the sun-blazed corner of the property where Lolly Poore had tried and failed to grow a cactus garden. What was left for him to see?

"Why don't we go out to the rose garden? It's a mess, but it is salvageable, I'm told. That is, if you intend to keep some of the property as it is."

"We took a quick look at it, Mrs. Nay. Don't you recall?" Her imprecise memory startled him.

"Of course I remember, but let's see it again, Mr. Blackwood." He followed her across the terrace and down the far steps. She was telling him about the word that had come from her husband. "All looks well, doesn't it? Good news on the horizon, as visible as the far hills. We're coming to the end, aren't we, Mr. Blackwood? The boys home and everything. A new era about to begin."

"Everything's pointing that way."

"It's why I wanted to see you. Mr. Bruder hopes we can come to terms as soon as possible."

"And so do I."

"He's worried that you've bogged things down with the bank. The paperwork can take months. The due diligence would ask questions that might be painful for him to answer, might force him to remember things he's spent several years trying to forget."

Blackwood asked Mrs. Nay what she meant.

"Mr. Blackwood, I shouldn't be telling you this, but Mr. Bruder doesn't have months to close a deal."

"Mrs. Nay, whatever do you mean?"

"What I should say is that he's eager to be rid of this land at once. He's sent me to find out whether you have the money right now."

"I could have the money right now, if I chose." He said this proudly, and registered the twitch upon Mrs. Nay's lip: he could see that she was impressed by both his resources and his negotiating skills. But actually, that wasn't the case: Cherry Nay was simply relieved, for she wanted to close the deal for Bruder's sake. He had nearly begged, "Do this for me, Cherry?" She knew that Bruder could no longer bear the ache that the Pasadena lodged within him.

She stopped at a tulip tree, its fallen pink-and-white blossoms littering the ground. "She planted this tree."

"Who did?"

"Mrs. Poore."

"You mean Linda Stamp?"

"That's correct, Mr. Blackwood."

"Can I ask you a question, Mrs. Nay?"

"I'll do my best to answer."

"How did you know that she'd be at the Valley Hunt Club that night? It turned out to be such a fateful night for poor Linda. How'd you know where to find your story?"

"Don't you remember what I told you about the leaky house, Mr. Blackwood?" He said that indeed he remembered, and he mentioned the heating ducts.

"Yes, but this was even more direct than heating ducts or whispering dumbwaiters. In this case, Rosa called me up. She was the one who gave me the tip."

"Rosa? The maid who had the—" But some things Blackwood couldn't say aloud.

"Yes, Rosa."

"But why?"

"To protect Linda."

"To protect her? From what?"

"From Captain Poore, I'm afraid."

"Because he wasn't who he said he was?"

Mrs. Nay nodded.

Each of them hesitated, pondering the world and its falsities.

"By the time she married Willis in the spring of 1925," said Mrs. Nay, "he was calling her Lindy. And soon enough, everyone else was calling her Lindy too. It didn't take much time for most people to forget that Lindy Poore had ever gone by another name."

Blackwood eyed Mrs. Nay, thinking that she was no different. She too had transformed herself in just a few years. Reinvention doesn't require much time, thought Blackwood—not around here. In the past several weeks he had become something of a self-reflective man, and now he thought to himself: *And look at me.* Lately, a terrible pang had interrupted his sleep and he would find himself sitting up in the dark, clutching his chest. He'd be breathing hard and he would realize that he'd been dreaming; typically, Blackwood was the kind of man who never remembered his dreams, but now they stayed with him as clearly as if he had just read them in the newspaper. In his sleep, the girl was visiting him, Edith Knight with her red hair blowing and a white panic in her face.

"Mr. Blackwood? Mr. Blackwood? Is something wrong?"

"Mrs. Nay?"

"You look as if you've seen a ghost," she said. "You're as white as a sheet."

He brought his fingers to his cold cheek. He blinked, and a shudder released him from the spell, and Blackwood moved to fold up and put away his past. He unpacked it so rarely that when he did, he ended up startling himself. Was that really once Blackwood, the campus dirt per-petually ground into his knees? A few days ago he had called to find the girl, to send her the money with interest, but the operator for Isle au Haut turned up no one who once might have been Edith Knight: "You said red hair? Don't know anyone with red hair but Shelley Stone, and she's but sixteen." He had written out a note of apology, asking: *Is there a child?* But there was no address to mail the letter to, and Blackwood tasted the regret upon his tongue as he assured Mrs. Nay that he was fine.

"You were daydreaming."

"I was, I'm afraid."

"This place takes you back down the tunnel of time, doesn't it?"

Their shoes ground the sticky cup-shaped blossoms into the earth and they continued along the property.

"We all hold a past, don't we, Mr. Blackwood?" He said that she was more than right, but he worried that an awkward color had risen in his cheek, revealing something. But Mrs. Nay continued, changing the subject, "The men at the bank. They're all fine men."

"They are, Mrs. Nay."

"Sometimes they have trouble imagining the future. They aren't vi-sionaries. Not like you."

Blackwood succumbed to the flattery. "That they aren't."

"Mr. Bruder doesn't want to get bogged down in their red tape."

"You said that, Mrs. Nay."

"That Dr. Freeman, the Investment Committee chair—"

"Yes?" If anyone's opposition to Blackwood's plan had been most difficult to bear, it had been Dr. Freeman's. His probe had proven uncomfortable, like a prong reaching inside.

"He treated her, of course."

Blackwood was silent.

"He was Lindy Poore's doctor at the very end. It was 1930, and New Year's Day of 1931."

"What was?" said Blackwood.

They had reached the rose garden. Years of neglect had left it a wide thicket of tapering branch and stillborn bud. Blackwood knew that Lolly Poore had once tended the most coveted rose garden in the San Gabriel Valley: more than nineteen hundred cultivars and species, plants from every period of the flower's history, going as far back as those described by Herodotus. Lolly had hunted for cuttings and rootstock, importing them from as far away as China, where a velvet-red climber perfumed the pagodas. But now thorn and bitter rose fruit snarled the garden, and the climbers were working to pull down the pergola. Willis Fishe Poore had staked out the rose garden on this spot for its view of the valley, but on this day in 1945 that view was smudged by a yellowish haze. Just this morning, the *Star-News* had written about something called "smog." But Blackwood didn't believe it: that the Imperial Victoria's rear-pipe cough could get trapped up against the mountains, although that was what the newspaper had implied. The notion was laughable—that the sky wasn't endless!, that the heavens weren't infinite! It was like saying that a tear shed into the Pacific was enough to pollute the ocean.

"I'm not sure I know what you mean, Mrs. Nay. Dr. Freeman looked after Linda Stamp?"

"She was Lindy Poore by then, but yes."

"Dr. Freeman, of the Investment Committee?"

"Mr. Blackwood. Do you mean to tell me you haven't pieced together the ranch's history by now?"

"I think so . . ." But he didn't know exactly what Mrs. Nay was referring to.

She must have read the puzzlement in his face, because she said, "You don't know what happened, do you?" He shook his head. "Then it's my mistake for saying this much already. I was under the impression that you had put the pieces together by now. They are open secrets, after all."

Blackwood took a stab at it. "The Lindy Poore buried in the mausoleum is Linda Stamp."

"Of course that's who I'm talking about. And her husband is at her side. Which is a tragedy in its own right." Captain Willis Poore had died in early 1943, Cherry went on, while making preparations to ship out to North Africa. He had spoken of returning to glory. He'd been adhering to a self-imposed regimen of calisthenics when he collapsed and died. Sieglinde discovered him on the terrace, as frail-looking as a downed bird. She cried for help, but her calls echoed off the coral tree; by then, no one lived at the ranch but the two of them; the maids' rooms were empty and shrouded in dust, the kitchen silent but for the greedy mice.

"What about Mr. Bruder?" asked Blackwood.

"What about him? You know him yourself. You know what sort of man he's become." Even so, Blackwood said, it seemed that he had been in love with the girl. How had they ended up apart?

"The same way so many people end up with the wrong person," said Mrs. Nay. "Or alone."

Blackwood said that he didn't understand.

"Come now, Mr. Blackwood. You've never made a mistake of the heart?"

But Blackwood ignored that subject and asked, "And what about Edmund? Her brother?"

"Dead, as you know. Another terrible mistake." She waited a moment before continuing. "We all make them, don't we, Mr. Blackwood? Edmund thought that Linda had given herself to Bruder, but he was wrong. Poor man. If you ask me, the cards were stacked against Edmund from the day he was born."

Mrs. Nay had arrived at their meeting in a white tennis dress with oranges and lemons embroidered on the skirt: "Esperanza has a little shop over on Fair Oaks, and the ladies of Pasadena are mad for her needle and thread." Now Mrs. Nay was leading Blackwood to the tennis court, which hadn't been resurfaced in almost twenty years. The Long Beach earthquake had split the baseline in two; the cracks in the concrete sprouted weedy gold poppies and sweet fennel with feathery leaves. Blackwood and Cherry needed each other, they realized separately, and this brought them a mutual comfort.

Mrs. Nay told Blackwood to sit on the broken bench at the court's side. It was clear that she wanted to continue reviving history: her face was set firmly, as if she was preparing herself for a solemn task. And indeed, Cherry felt a compulsion: she hadn't done her part at the time—she'd been too selfish in pursuit of a story—and now, for the sake of her conscience, she wished to sort things out. George had written: *My Dearest Cherry, no one is entirely proud of his past. But it's never too late to make amends. It's never too late to try to change things. Even for those who are gone.*

"After Edmund's death," said Cherry, "he was arrested. There was a trial."

"Arrested? Who was?"

"Mr. Bruder. I'm afraid he wasn't very cooperative. He had hardened by then. He was on his way to becoming the man you now know."

"Was Mr. Bruder charged with murder?"

"It was a sad day. But maybe I shouldn't say any more, Mr. Blackwood. What's done is done, and that's the way it is."

"You can't stop now, Mrs. Nay."

She plucked a fraying thread from one of the embroidered oranges. Then she began again. "I'm telling you, Mr. Blackwood, because you seem to want to know. You seem to recognize that the history of this ranch goes back to her."

"And back to him."

"Yes, and back to Mr. Bruder." She paused. "I covered the trial as a reporter. It didn't last more than a couple of days. There was very little evidence. Besides him, she was the only witness. There was no one else to call. She testified first, and after that the jury never heard any of what Bruder had to say."

"You're talking about Linda Stamp?"

"Yes, but she was Mrs. Willis Poore by then, ready to give birth, stomach swollen out to here. It was hard for her indeed, speaking against Mr. Bruder. But she did it for her brother. You can imagine what a struggle it was for her, deciding what to say. What to do."

It was the end of the summer, said Mrs. Nay, and the trial was held in Oceanside. There weren't many people in the courtroom—a judge with a German-sounding name ("Dinklemann," Cherry said, pulling it up from her memory) and a porcine quality to his face, and the prosecutor, Mr. Ivory, a trim, groomed man who raised his voice as if the courtroom was large and there were people in the last row straining to hear. But that was not the case: it was a small courtroom with a glazed tile floor and a few rows of oak benches worn smooth and brown. It was a jury of ten men and two women, both of whom had bought a special lipstick. No one but Cherry Nay and a cub reporter from the *Bee* sat through the trial, and there were times when the ceiling fan made the only noise in the room.

Lindy Poore was called to testify, and she settled into the witness stand uncomfortably. She told the court that she was expecting her first child in the early fall, but in truth the baby would arrive before the week's end, nearly nine pounds and screaming and fully formed. Lindy had spent her final trimester in bed, receiving her daughter's kicks, and through the hot August afternoons it had felt as if the unborn baby were boxing her mother, fists to the lining of her womb, a steady beating, Lindy's stretched flesh rising from beneath.

"Will you be all right, Mrs. Poore?" asked Judge Dinklemann.

She had come alone, her husband grateful that the trial was held far from Pasadena, and although word had seeped through the city, staining conversations about the new Mrs. Poore, the story remained remote. The question lurked: What precisely happened that night, and how had Edmund died? There was speculation of self-defense on the part of Mr. Bruder, but it was somewhat laughable when chatter compared the physiques of the two men. Had it been an accident? "Mrs. Poore, we hope you'll explain what you witnessed that night," prodded Judge Dinklemann.

Of course, Bruder was in the courtroom as well, seated and under the supervision of a bailiff in a sand-colored uniform. On the trial's first day the jury listened to Mr. Ivory's re-creation of the events and his preview of what he promised would be Mrs. Poore's forthcoming and convincing testimony. At the time, Lindy did not know that her words would settle Bruder's fate, but nonetheless she sat before the small courtroom with a firm understanding of what she was being asked to do. She hadn't seen Bruder since they'd buried Edmund, and now here he was, erect in his chair and waiting for her to speak. His gaze was upon her, and it took all her will not to begin to weep. She wasn't well, and she blamed the fatigue and the fever and nearly everything she felt on the writhing baby, whose unborn anger Lindy feared. It was hard for her to concentrate but she would, she told herself, and she looked to the small panel window above the door, where a blood-bright bougainvillea tapped the glass. She looked to the coral-pink lipstick worn by one of the women in the jury, and to the bow tie at Mr. Ivory's throat. His sterling-handled cane was hooked over the arm of his chair, and he seemed too elegant of a man for this kind of work. "Your name," he said.

"Lindy Poore."

"What is your maiden name?"

"Linda Stamp."

"Who is Sieglinde Stumpf?"

"That was my name as a girl."

"And now you are the wife of Captain Willis Poore?"

She had married Willis in a small ceremony on the ryegrass lawn. She wore a snow camellia on her breast and a veil so gauzy that she couldn't see more than two feet before her; her new husband's face was as obscured as if it were behind white smoke. Lolly was there, of course, in somber navy serge and a hat with black netting that hid her teary eyes. She clutched Palomar at her hip as if he were a toy of some sort, and little did anyone know that from that day on she would never, as long as she lived, release him from her grasp. Also present were a handful of 100 Percenters and members of the Valley Hunt Club, shading themselves from the sun with their Books of Common Prayer. Rosa had helped Linda dress, and she asked the trembling bride about the rash on her thigh and was told it was nothing; and Rosa, who had seen the chancre rise and kill her own mother, said, "Nothing is nothing." But Linda insisted that Rosa not worry about her, and by the time Linda returned to the bedroom to remove the veil, she was now Mrs. Willis Poore, Rosa's mistress, and she made it clear that her maid would not inquire into that which was not her concern.

"You haven't been married very long?" said Mr. Ivory. He posed other questions to establish the facts of Lindy's life, and throughout them she sat with her hands resting on her belly and tried to catch Bruder's eye, but now he refused to look at her. She was afraid, although she didn't know of what. She planned to tell the truth: that she didn't know what had happened; that she'd arrived just as Edmund was falling but that it was too dark to see precisely how he had been killed. During the drive down the coast she had anticipated the prosecutor's final question: "Did Mr. Bruder kill your brother?" Over and over she had repeated her answer: "I cannot say."

It was warm in the courtroom, and one of the bailiffs moved to open the window above the door with a long, clawed stick. The window tilted open and the jury shifted and mopped their throats and during this interruption Lindy found Bruder looking at her again. He was studying her carefully, almost the way she expected she would one day study her baby. Nothing about Bruder appeared distressed—or, at least, he didn't seem concerned for himself—but while the bailiff returned the clawed stick to the corner, Lindy thought she saw anxiety for her rise in Bruder's eye.

Mr. Ivory asked Lindy to explain what had happened the night Edmund was killed. The long summer in bed, the heat trapped in the second-floor room, had prepared her for this. Over the months she had retold herself the story many times, and nothing about it remained mysterious, except the very end—what exactly had happened, she could not say. Did she think it was an accident? This was the one question she hoped the prosecutor would not ask, for it was the one that invariably prompted her to weep. She didn't know whether or not it had been an accident, and she feared the truth. During those first months married to Willis, Lindy hadn't feared anything else. The brief illness that had come during her first weeks of pregnancy, and the weepy chancres lining her thighs, had faded, and she wasn't afraid when they returned in the final months of her pregnancy: the small red pustules near her groin, the hot ache in her joints, the fever, coming and going like the Santa Anas off the desert. None of this had she feared. Her life had inverted itself and she didn't fear any of it: not the new husband or the new sister or the new house or the city that was now hers; not even the violent baby taking over her womb; no, she had feared only the truth of what she didn't know about that night on the beach.

"Now, Mrs. Poore. Tell us what you saw. What you saw happen to your dear brother, Edmund Stamp."

"I didn't see much," she began.

"But you saw *something*."

She explained how she had woken up and found Edmund in the barn. She was careful not to say that they had argued. "We discussed some things."

"What things, Mrs. Poore?"

"My marriage to Captain Poore. We discussed this, but Edmund was upset, and he ran off."

"Why do you think he was upset?"

Lindy realized that she couldn't tell the entire truth, but she didn't hesitate as she said, "He had recently lost the farm to Bruder. He was still angry about it."

"How did Mr. Bruder take the farm from you and your brother?"

"My father gave it to him."

"Your father?"

"Yes."

"Is your father not senile?"

She said that he was.

"And he signed over his only property to Mr. Bruder?"

"Yes," Linda said again. The men in the jury had opened their coats, and a few fanned themselves with their hats and the women's face powder was melting. Mr. Ivory stood in front of the judge, crisp in summer linen, and he was plainly proud of what he had stirred up. "I'm sure that the ladies and gentlemen of the jury," he said, "could use some help understanding the reasons a man would leave his land to someone other than his children. Would you explain that, Mrs. Poore?"

Lindy realized something. "I'm not exactly sure myself. My father never told me. But he had his reasons, I know he did."

"Is it possible that Mr. Bruder took advantage of your father's declining state?"

But before Lindy could answer, the question was withdrawn and Mr. Ivory asked her to proceed with her story of the fateful night: "Edmund ran off, you were saying."

Again, Lindy looked to Bruder, and now she found his stare tender, as if the only person he was worried about was her. She tried to return the sentiment in her glance. Her eyes were moist, and she wondered if he could see the tears. "He ran down the bluff to the beach," she said.

"And you followed him?"

"Yes."

"Was he carrying anything?"

"A mallet."

"Where did you think he was going?"

"I didn't know."

"But you know now." She assented. "Where was that?"

"Down the beach to Cathedral Cove." She described the inlet and the cave, and the jury sat dully, as if they couldn't imagine such a place. But it wasn't so far up the coast from the courthouse; hadn't any of them been? The baby kicked and punched Lindy, and there was a sharp pain deep within that felt as if the baby were shredding her. Lindy was certain that if someone were to inspect her womb, he would find it black-and-blue.

"Who did you see when you arrived there?" asked Mr. Ivory.

"Edmund and Bruder."

"What were they doing?"

She explained that it was a very dark night, and the clouds were passing before the moon, and as she ran along the beach, following Edmund's footsteps, she didn't know what she would find. When she rounded the bend at Cathedral Cove she couldn't make out what was happening.

"Was there a fight, Mrs. Poore?"

"I don't know."

"What did you see?"

"I saw my brother falling."

"Falling?"

"As if he had jumped, or been pushed."

"Pushed?"

"I didn't see anyone push him," she said.

"But he was falling down?"

Lindy nodded; it had been as if Edmund had lunged and he had struggled with himself while Bruder stood by.

"What did Mr. Bruder do?"

"I couldn't see what he was doing."

"Did you find him next to your brother?"

She said that from far off, it had appeared that way.

"Did you see him raise his arm and bring it down swiftly while your brother was falling to the sand?"

She said that she had.

"Was there something in Mr. Bruder's hand?"

"I don't know."

"Is it possible that he was smashing the mallet into your brother's head?"

"I don't know. It was dark. I couldn't see much more than their silhouettes. I was at the edge of the cove."

"Now I'd like to show the jury some pictures," said Mr. Ivory. "And perhaps you, Mrs. Poore, can tell us what they're of." In the corner was an easel draped in a black cloth, and Mr. Ivory unveiled it as if it were a work of fine art. Propped on the easel's ledge was a board with a photograph pasted to it. It was of pieces of wood on a beach. "What is that, Mrs. Poore?"

"It looks like driftwood."

"These pictures were taken at Cathedral Cove the night your brother was killed. Could the tide have brought in this driftwood?"

Lindy didn't understand what Mr. Ivory was pursuing. "Anything can wash up on a beach," she said.

"How many lobster pots did you keep in the ocean?"

"Eight."

"Where did you keep them?"

"Straight offshore from Condor's Nest."

"Could these pieces of wood have come from your lobster pots?"

"I don't know."

He brought the picture to Lindy for closer inspection. The strips of wood were dark but dry, and it was hard to know what they had come from. "Does it still look like driftwood to you?"

"It could be."

"Carried in on the tide?"

"That would make sense."

"If someone were to claim," said Mr. Ivory, "that this pile of wood was one of your lobster pots smashed to pieces, what would you say?"

"I'd say I can't tell from this picture."

"Do you remember seeing this wood when you reached Edmund?"

"I never saw this wood. I never went to his side."

"Is it possible that this wood was carried in by the rising tide? *After* Edmund died?"

"I don't know, but it sounds possible."

"And so you were saying, the next thing you knew, you found your brother dying, with the mallet in his temple. Is that right?" The memory was a terrible pain, as bright and awful as any she had known: but more would come. "Would you tell the jury for yourself, Mrs. Poore?"

She said that Edmund had died at Bruder's feet.

"Did he have the look of a murderer?" This question, too, was withdrawn and Mr. Ivory shifted his interrogation. "Tests have found Mr. Bruder's fingerprint on the mallet's handle. Did you know this, Mrs. Poore?"

Lindy hadn't known this, and she wondered if it was possible. Could Mr. Ivory be twisting the evidence the way she had twisted the truth about her final conversation with Edmund?

"Mrs. Poore?"

"Yes?"

"Did Mr. Bruder kill your brother?"

"I can't say. I didn't see it."

"But if you had to explain it, Mrs. Poore, wouldn't you say that Mr. Bruder is guilty of killing your brother?" She said neither yes nor no, and she met the gleaming eyes of the jury, which told her that they had quickly snapped the story into place, the lock clicking. "Mrs. Poore?" said Mr. Ivory.

She looked to Bruder, but he would no longer look at her. He had given up on Linda Stamp.

"I didn't see him do it," she said, but it was too late. Her hesitation had spoken. The jury was shifting in their seats, conclusions reached circumstantially, and Cherry flipped the page in her notepad, and eventually Lindy Poore stepped off the stand and left the courtroom. Later that night, Willis—who sometimes she could hardly believe was her husband—would come to her and stroke her throbbing belly and say, "All you did was tell the truth."

2

NO MATTER HOW HARD he tried, Blackwood could not shake from his mind the story of Linda's testimony against Bruder. It must have been a gruesome sight for her, her brother felled at her lover's feet. And then to meet him in the courtroom. Blackwood wasn't surprised to learn that things had come to this—Linda's heart had been wayward, after all, staggering this way and that. We pay for such behavior, thought Blackwood: the debts mount indeed. He recalled his first meeting with Bruder and the blood smeared across him; hadn't he taken delight in the death of the barracuda, in inflicting unnecessary torture? Hadn't there been a murderous gleam in his eye? Blackwood was convinced that Bruder was capable of sinking a mallet into a man's head, certainly in the name of love. "I assume that Mr. Bruder was convicted of this horrible crime, Mrs. Nay?"

"Yes. He was sent to San Quentin. A cell with a little window overlooking the bay. Everything smelled like salt and the marsh."

"You visited him, Mrs. Nay?"

"Remember, I was still a reporter at the time. I went to talk to him. I knew there was another story to tell."

"Another story?"

"His version."

"Was it different from hers?"

"They always are."

"What was his version, Mrs. Nay?"

"Oh, Mr. Blackwood. Should we really go into it now? Aren't we here to discuss your purchase?" An unfamiliar modesty touched Cherry, as if this one story, the one that was truly about her, shouldn't be relayed. In the end she'd done her part, and she took comfort in that. Bruder had acknowledged her deed, and wasn't that enough for Cherry? No, she wouldn't tell Blackwood what she had done for Mr. Bruder fifteen years ago.

"Of course we're here to talk about the property," said Blackwood, "but I'd like to know if I'm entering into a transaction with a . . ." He stumbled across the word. "A murderer."

"Don't think of him like that."

"How can I not?"

"You're jumping to conclusions."

"Now I'm confused. From what you just said—"

But Cherry stopped him and plucked his sleeve and pointed out the graceful sight of a bald eagle landing on the telephone wire that ran from the mansion to the ranch house. "All is not lost," she said mysteriously.

"Sorry, Mrs. Nay?"

"Nothing is as it seems."

Later, Blackwood was thinking of this conversation as he drove down the coast. He was considering what this type of betrayal might do to a man—to be sent to San Quentin by the testimony of the woman he loved. Bruder must be storing a violent well of hatred within him, to have killed Edmund and then to have to sit in a narrow cell with a sliver of view of the Golden Gate. Typically, Blackwood would be wary of dealing with a man with a felonious past (he'd made that mistake once before), but it was too late, and now Blackwood wanted to speak directly with Bruder. Blackwood felt that he could no longer rely on Mrs. Nay as an intermediary. He was certain that the final terms of the deal could be settled if only he and Bruder met again.

There was only one last thing standing in Blackwood's way: the agreement upon a fair price. Given all he had learned, Blackwood felt confident that Bruder would have to offer a steep discount and terms tilting in Blackwood's favor. If Blackwood didn't make a bid, who else would? And he drove down the coastal highway, certain that a deal could be reached before the end of the day.

In a letter, Bruder had urged Blackwood to visit him at once, and by the time he reached Baden-Baden-by-the-Sea, Blackwood was bursting with confidence. He raced along the road that somewhere, a few miles back, had split from El Camino Real. It was a cool, cloudless day, the type of day that would begin and end in cold, drippy fog, and the kid announcer on the radio news could hardly contain himself with the flurry of optimistic headlines pulsing on the wires: Cologne had fallen; the Allies had engulfed the Ruhr area; the Russians had reached the Baltic; and a smaller item, of less import but equal interest: The German government had confiscated the last available coffins in Berlin, banning citizens from burying them. Coffins, the kid announcer read from his transcript, have now been declared vital for the war effort. "The Reich government declares that any citizen attempting to bury a coffin will be shot."

Blackwood parked next to the farm stand and went to inspect the girl's display. Today's catch was a bucket of rock lobsters, and the girl pulled an undersize one, live, from the water. It lifted its small tail, and its slender, branched antennae tapped the air as Blackwood inspected it. "Where are its claws?"

"They don't have pincers round here."

"Did you catch them yourself?"

"I've got eight pots at the bottom of the ocean."

"Do you have anything bigger?"

"This is as large as they come, Mr. Blackwood. The ocean's being picked clean."

"Did Mr. Bruder tell you I'm buying the Rancho Pasadena?"

"He said you wanted to buy it but you don't have the money."

This shocked Blackwood, that Bruder would tell lies about him, especially to a girl who certainly couldn't understand such things. And although Mrs. Nay had provided him with more pieces of the Pasadena's story, only just now did he realize that this girl, Sieglinde, had been born at the ranch. But how had she ended up here, with Bruder? "You used to live there?" he said. Sieglinde nodded. "For how long?"

"A long time."

"When did you leave?"

Her attempt to answer was interrupted by Palomar's arrival. Again he wore the striped overalls with the red satin heart, but there was a griminess to them—the heart was stained black with something that had dribbled down it. "Bruder sent me to fetch you, Mr. Blackwood. He wants to see you in the cottage."

"I'll be down in a minute."

"He wants you to come now."

Blackwood didn't like being told what to do. But he acquiesced, anxious to get on with his task. As he parked his car in the dooryard, Bruder emerged from the cottage. He waved Blackwood inside, and only when the two were standing close, at the hearth, could Blackwood fully see the frailty that had overtaken the man. He was thinner than before, and it was obvious that he couldn't stand for long and that many pains in bone and blood pressed upon him. He had shaved his beard, exposing hollow, sallow cheeks. He sat in the small rocker by the hearth, his knees and elbows sticking out awkwardly, and he rocked himself next to the smoldering heap of ash as a trail of smoke rose from the blackened logs. The scar at his temple was dark and throbbing.

"Can I throw some more wood on it for you?" Blackwood offered.

"That would be kind."

After doing so, Blackwood sat in the opposite rocker, and their feet nearly touched on the braided rug. The clear March sun pressed through the windows and the low tide was distant and clement, like someone sleeping in the next room.

"I was having a chat with Sieglinde. She said some things." Blackwood said this to see what nerves might flinch in Bruder's face, but his flesh did not move. "Mr. Bruder, are you all right? May I get you something?" Bruder's hand rose to his throat, touching the piece of coral. Moments in the quiet spring day passed while Bruder idly stroked the pendant, and Blackwood told himself to be patient and to wait for his opportunity.

"I understand," Bruder began at last, "that you have mucked things up with the bank men. That you bothered to involve Dr. Freeman and his gang."

"Is that what Mrs. Nay said?"

"You realize, I trust, that they aren't good men. They look out only for themselves and their kind. If you're not one of them, you'll never be."

"Isn't that a bit critical of you, Mr. Bruder?"

"Did you know that just yesterday Dr. Freeman sent a telegram inquiring about the Pasadena? He said that the committee would like to meet with me right away."

Blackwood stammered: "But it's mine!"

"It isn't yours, Mr. Blackwood." Bruder's eyes rose to the bookshelf, where the telegram sat crumpled in a ball.

"I was here first."

"Calm down, Mr. Blackwood. I haven't answered Freeman." Bruder paused, and his sudden stillness frightened Blackwood. Was the man ill? He couldn't tell whether Bruder was succumbing to disease, or if this was nothing graver than weariness.

"Mrs. Nay reports—" Blackwood tried.

"I know everything Mrs. Nay has told you. We are friends, you forget." And then: "Why have you come to see me, Mr. Blackwood?"

"It was you who asked me down."

"Of course it was. But have you come with serious interest, or have you come to waste my time?"

Blackwood assured Bruder that he was a sincere man, and Bruder said, "And that's why I'm speaking to you. I have no intention of doing business with men like that."

"Like what?"

"Come now, Mr. Blackwood. You understand Pasadena as well as I."

The conversation was proceeding so strangely that Blackwood was unsure whether or not he was making progress. Even so, he sensed he must attempt to wrest control of the negotiations. "As you know, Mr. Bruder"—and Blackwood inhaled deeply—"your ranch has sat on the market for many, many months. The longer it goes unsold, the less desirable it becomes. Now that I know the ranch's history, the story of all that went on there, I am here to discuss a fair reduction in your asking price."

"Do you know the ranch's history? Do you know *all* that went on there?"

"Mrs. Nay has gone on quite a while with her stories. And you yourself have told me others."

"Are you sure you know everything?"

Blackwood hesitated, and he felt silly with presumption.

"You were saying, Mr. Blackwood, that you're looking for a reduction?"

"One that we both agree is fair."

"How could something be equally fair to you and to me? Doesn't one of us have more power than the other? Isn't that always the case?"

But Blackwood plunged ahead. "Some would say it's a tainted property, Mr. Bruder. It carries with it a number of, as they say, undesirables. A dead orange grove. A mausoleum filled with a dead family. And you being a . . ."

"A what, Mr. Blackwood?"

"A . . . a, well, a man with a past of his own. This might frighten off the more timid."

Blackwood expected Bruder's face to fill with rage, but it did not. He continued: "A ghostly abandonment pervades the house and land. Many potential buyers will turn away from it, Mr. Bruder."

"Ghostly, you find it?"

"To tell the truth, yes. Its rapid decline—in less than a generation—is rather shocking to a potential investor."

"How do you mean, Mr. Blackwood?"

"Less than twenty years ago, this was one of the great houses of Pasadena. And now look at it. Everyone who lived there is dead and buried in a crypt."

"Not everyone. You were speaking to Sieglinde just now. She seems very much alive to me."

Blackwood thought of the girl: she resembled Mrs. Nay's description of Linda, but it was as if the girl's father was missing from her blood. "Aside from Sieglinde," said Blackwood, "the family's now gone. People don't like such misfortune attached to their real estate."

"You and I both know that you are right, Mr. Blackwood."

Bruder's agreement startled Blackwood, leaving him so emboldened that he proceeded with his next statement before he knew what he was saying. "And another thing, Mr. Bruder. It is very strange that you are the Pasadena's owner and not Miss Sieglinde. Your ownership is another—and not insignificant—pall cast over the property."

Bruder was silent and everything but the ocean was quiet too. Then he spoke: "Mr. Blackwood. Don't you recall my story of the beechwood forest? Don't any facts stick to that mind of yours?"

"Of course I remember. Every last detail. But something was missing."

"Missing?"

"Missing, indeed, Mr. Bruder."

"Your challenge surprises me. I told you the truth."

"You didn't tell me everything."

A tiny smirk appeared on Bruder's lips. "I see. You're a better listener than I thought."

Blackwood noted the appreciation in Bruder's grimace. "You never told me why you followed Dieter home from the forest. You never told me why you came to Condor's Nest in the first place. There was no reason you should have ever met Linda Stamp."

Bruder's chest rose and fell with slow breath and he stroked his chin, as if his fingers were feeling for the shaved beard. He grunted, a pain passing through him.

"And Mrs. Nay never spoke of it," said Blackwood.

"Cherry doesn't know."

"I thought she knew everything."

"Almost. It was another promise I made long ago. Another promise to hold tightly to the truth. Another promise no longer worth keeping." Slowly, Bruder pushed himself up from the chair, and he motioned for Blackwood to follow him. They moved to the doorway with the sheet strung along the rod. Bruder pulled it back, and together they peered into the narrow room on the backside of the chimney. There was a small window covered with gunnysack cloth and a kerosene lamp flickering a low flame, and on the bed a tiny, flour-white man was curled like a cat. His beard fluttered as he slept, and his eyelids were as thick as window shades, and his hands cradled an onion.

"Is it Dieter?" said Blackwood.

Bruder nodded.

"He must be a hundred years old."

"Nearly."

"I didn't know he was still alive."

"Did someone tell you he was dead?"

"How long has he been like this?"

"Twenty or twenty-five years."

"Who takes care of him?"

"Sieglinde mostly. Pal, too."

Bruder let the sheet fall and returned to his rocker. Blackwood followed, but stopped at the window and watched a pelican soar over the ocean and then plunge for chub. There were five rows of waves crashing, a surfboard riding one of them, and beyond the waves were the buoys and a shark's wake and then the Pacific was endless and blue.

"He has seen a lot of history, hasn't he?" said Blackwood.

"And much of the history you've heard from Cherry and me begins with him." Bruder paused. "If I didn't tell you, Mr. Blackwood, no one would ever know the truth."

"I can keep a secret, Mr. Bruder."

"I could take it to my grave."

"Is that fair?"

"Fair to whom?"

"I don't know. But if you have something to say, I should think you'd want to share it with at least one man before—" But Blackwood stopped himself; he knew enough not to try too hard.

"Why should that be you?"

"Because one day I might be in possession of your land."

"It always comes back to that, doesn't it, Mr. Blackwood?"

"Back to what?" Now Blackwood didn't know what Bruder was talking about. There was no way he could. Even so, he sensed everything going his way and he nearly expected to depart Condor's Nest with the deed to the Pasadena rolled up in his glove compartment. Blackwood was so certain of his prowess as a negotiator that he was startled when Bruder interrupted his thoughts by saying, "Dieter gave me his daughter."

Blackwood's eyes screwed up. "Sorry?"

"Yes, he gave Linda to me. In a trade."

"Mr. Bruder? I'm not sure I'm following you."

"It has to do with the war."

"Like so many things these days."

"I'm talking about the previous war, of course. That one really kicked off the century, didn't it."

Blackwood said yes, but he didn't know what precisely he was agreeing to. As he waited for Bruder to continue, Blackwood suddenly thought of Edith Knight: he should try to look for her again. He decided just then that he would hire a private investigator out of Boston, sending the man up to Maine. Blackwood would instruct him to search from Portland down east, in every steepled village on every rocky cove. Across from Blackwood, Bruder was turning in his rocker, seeking a comfortable position before he began another story. As Bruder prepared to—to use Mrs. Nay's word—*unload,* Blackwood realized that one day he too would become overwhelmed by the need to stare his own history in the bruised eye. He shuddered, afraid of himself for the first time. What had Blackwood done? Who had Blackwood become?

"May I take you back to the beechwood forest, Mr. Blackwood?"

"I'm listening, Mr. Bruder."

"You recall how I first met Dieter?"

"Along the stream. He sold you the tin cup that saved Willis Poore's life."

"Yes, exactly. Dieter was a one-man supply store walking up and down the lines. He was selling tin cups and tin bowls and tin canteens, and entrenching spades and haversacks packed with field dressings and iron rations, and vials of morphine and tobacco kept dry in bullet shells. Anything a soldier might need when cut off from a supply line."

"Is it why he went to Europe?"

"Dieter never forgot that fortunes were made in supplying desperate men."

"I can understand that," said Blackwood.

"Because I met Dieter that day by the stream, Willis Poore recovered long enough to be picked up by an ambulance. He was transported to a hospital outside Paris, where he convalesced under the care of hobble-skirted nurses. He told me afterward that his bed lay in a shaft of sunlight and that he would close his eyes and feel the warmth on his face and dream he had returned to California. Every day his mind would carry him back to the rancho, and his strength returned and the wound on his nape closed and healed and buckled and scarred. While in the hospital he was promoted to captain and given his medal, and when the nurses came to sponge him down he'd show it to them, and soon he learned how its gleam brought a profoundly respectful smile to anyone who looked at it, and especially to those who fingered it against his breast. Captain Poore was released days before the Armistice, and he spent the winter roaming the cold alleys of Paris, and like many dough-boys he succumbed to the whistles and calls shot from darkened door-ways. It was there, I presume, that he first acquired his taste for the whore."

"Mr. Bruder!"

"You've never sampled the wares yourself, Mr. Blackwood?"

"Indeed I have not." And this was true, technically speaking.

"Don't think you're a better man for it."

"I do not." And then: "But what does this have to do with our deal, Mr. Bruder?"

Bruder ignored the question. "And while Willis was lying atop the ticking-striped mattress in the convalescent hospital, I was left to defend the burned-out depot. A platoon of soldiers arrived as reinforcement, and they were shocked when they saw the destruction, barracks burned to ashes. Every time a new soldier arrived he'd say, 'That was a hell of a gun the Germans shot. You must've done something to make them really mad at you.' I'd made my deal and so I said nothing, and the men would kick the char and soon we got to work on rebuilding the depot. Within a couple of days you would never have known what had happened there unless you stumbled across the pile of blackened rubble dumped in the forest.

"It was only a few days later that the line gave up some territory and the front moved closer to our station. Now we could hear the battle day and night, and the howitzers traced the sky and the wounded stumbled into our depot, and soon we were no longer fixing trucks, we were fixing men.

"Every night around eleven o'clock, Dieter would arrive in the forest, his tinware clanging like cowbells, and the men one by one would slip away into the beechwood stand and buy themselves some tobacco or morphine or whatever it was they could afford and needed. Supplies were low and the road that had first brought me to the depot was under siege, and we never knew what was coming or when. Every soldier who'd been in France more than a week knew that in the woods behind the lines were traveling salesmen. And not just Dieter. Most of them were Frenchmen, and some were boys too young to shave, and they were quick to adapt to the soldiers' needs, always supplying a demand. When canned beef was low at a camp it could be found in the forest, and when supplies of scurvy pills were gone they could be bought for a dime. The doughboys called the salesmen Vultures, and when things were calm, sometimes word would arrive at a camp or a station that five hundred yards into the forest, a Vulture had arrived with girls for sale. That business went on, French maidens lying atop mounds of moss, and soldiers would pay for what they needed most. They'd hand over every last *centime* for a turn. Why the face, Mr. Blackwood? It was war, and the men needed comfort and the girls needed food, and other than

the syphilis there was nothing more tragic about this than about everything else."

"The Vultures!" said Blackwood. "What terrible men!"

"Mr. Blackwood, you of all people should think before you con-
demn."

At some point during Bruder's tale, Pal and Sieglinde had slipped
into the cottage and curled their legs up onto the window seat. They
were leaning their heads upon the panes, their faces turned toward the
ocean, but both boy and girl were silent, as if Bruder's story had sent
their minds traveling too. Sieglinde's knives and whetting stone sat on
the floor beside her, but she ignored the work; her face, in the light
through the window, was—Blackwood imagined—identical to her
mother's.

"As I was saying, I was at the depot and one night the guns fell silent.
At this point, as you might imagine, I was having trouble sleeping. To
tell the truth, never again in my life would I sleep through a full night.
It was a moonlit evening at summer's end and I got up, took my rifle,
and went for a walk. If I told you I wasn't looking for a certain thing, I'd
be lying. It was very late, and typically the Vultures had come and gone
by midnight, but I went to see anyway. I followed a path and I leapt
across the stream and still I found no one. I walked for almost an hour.
Then I gave up on finding one of the men and his girls, and I stroked
the coins in my pocket and told myself to hold them in reserve for another night. The sky was as blue and dark as the ocean, and the moonlight seeped through the forest's canopy, and there was something
about this night that carried me on, and the fear that I typically bore had
fallen away. It occurred to me that perhaps the battle that had been wag-
ing had ended and that word had yet to reach us of the outcome. I continued walking, thinking I should scout for information. The line
wasn't far, and I knew that if I walked another half mile or so I would
come across something to tell me what was going on, some sort of battle debris: the abandoned clips of ammunition, the pockmarked shells,
the scraps of military leather, shredded and mildewed, the bits of flesh
as pale and bright as bread crumbs on a path.

"The forest became even more dense, and I pushed my way through
the low branches and stomped upon the soft ferns and sometimes the
sticks cracking beneath my boot echoed in a way that startled me, and I
would stop and stare into the silvery darkness and wonder if anyone

was there. But no one *was* there, and I continued, and there's a funny thing about fear: once you recognize that you're afraid, you become less so, as if you've somehow thrown a saddle across its bucking back.

"I kept walking, and after a quarter of an hour, through the stand of trees, I saw something move. It was dark and small and at first I thought that perhaps it was a bear, but then I figured that every bear along the front must have been killed long before. Then there was a second figure and a third, one large and one small, but they were only black outlines in the forest and a careless eye wouldn't even have seen them. I'm sure *you* would have, and I saw them too and I dropped to my knees. I wasn't close enough to sense what was going on, but then one of the figures moved away from the other two and walked twenty or thirty yards into the forest, until it seemed to sit upon a felled tree. Then there was a glow like a firefly and soon I could smell the burning tobacco.

"I didn't know what I had come across, but I held my rifle tightly and thought that maybe I was somewhere I shouldn't be. In the distance I could see the cigarette burning, the orange glowing brighter as a pair of lips sucked upon it. Back over where the two others were, they were standing close and making some strange motions and it was impossible to tell what was going on. Suddenly, one dropped to the forest floor and the other followed, and soon horrible cries were traveling through the forest, grunts and pleas and it was then that I heard a voice.

"It was a girl's voice, and she was crying in both German and French, *'Nein, nein, nein . . . non!'* I moved closer, and the forest rustled beneath me, and then the heaving and the panting stopped and I held still and it seemed as if the glowing orange tobacco was the only thing alive in the night. For a few minutes I didn't move, and the figures in the dark held still, and after a long while someone said, in German, *'It's nothing, there's nothing there.'* And soon the girl repeated her cry, and I heard her French accent, and then I realized what I had stumbled across.

"Just as there were Vultures on the Allied side of the front, there were Vultures on the German side as well, and at some point I had crossed the line, for in the final months of the war the front slithered back and forth, and there were points in the forest where no one knew *who* was in control. And it was at such a point that I had found a Vulture selling a French girl to a German soldier.

"My heart was racing, but I wasn't shocked. I realized that I had simply come face-to-face with my enemy. In some ways, certainly every soldier awaits this moment, and I inched forward, carefully sweeping the way with my hands, and every time a twig snapped I prayed to God the soldier wouldn't hear me. But by now he was so engaged in the act of raping the girl that he wouldn't have heard anything—he was moaning and grunting and drowning out the owls. I knew I wouldn't have much time, and soon I found myself no more than ten yards from the mossy clearing in the forest.

"I arranged myself as silently as possible and aimed my rifle, and as I peered through the sight the moon appeared from behind the clouds and the soldier's face came into my view. He was a common infantryman with a spiked helmet camouflaged by a field-gray cover. Beside him was his backpack of stiff, undressed hide, and his ten-pound rifle and bayonet were propped against it, and he was so young in the face that under any other circumstances one would have assumed that the gun and the bayonet were toys. His cheek was flushed, and his nose was small and round, like a lamb's. But he was thrusting himself violently against the girl, and his black bluchers dug into the soil. Then his neck stretched like a turtle's and his lips parted and he gasped embarrassingly and I witnessed him reach his moment of pleasure. All of him shook and trembled, and I thought that perhaps this was his first time.

"Beneath him, the girl was in a sundress printed with sweet peas. She was as young as he, but it wasn't her first time—her stoic face told me that. Her skirt was pushed beyond her hips and her bodice had been clumsily opened and her breasts were small and white. Even in this terrible position she maintained a dignified beauty, holding her mouth grimly, refusing to contort her face. Her eyes were open and she was looking into the soldier's face, and I saw that she was braver than he because he wouldn't look at her, he was overwhelmed with pleasure, and then the moment was over, as it always is.

"The soldier stood and pulled up his trousers. His leather greatcoat hung from him heavily. He was shockingly thin, with a waist that was fleshless and bony, and it touched me that he had spent his money on the girl rather than on food, and isn't that the way men are? Choosing one hunger over another?

"In any case, I wasn't there to philosophize. I was there to kill. As he adjusted his buckle, I squeezed the trigger and felt the hot bullet pulse through the barrel. The shot went swiftly through the soldier's temple, and for the shortest instant in my life his face cleared, as if he'd been ac-quitted of all the crimes that he'd ever committed, and he looked like a happy teenage boy, a smile upon his lips, guilty of nothing.

"This moment, too, did not last. At once he fell over dead, and the girl screamed and leapt to her feet and bent to arrange her tattered stockings, and the dark figure off in the forest stubbed out his cigarette, and there were footsteps and branches snapping and the girl was crying and a man's voice came to her in French, telling her to *be quiet, it was all right, they'd be fine.* And I remained in place, prepared to kill the German Vulture, and when the man reached the girl I saw through my sight that he was Dieter.

"I was as surprised as you, and with a steady voice I told the man not to move, and I rose from the ferns and then he spotted me, my rifle aimed at his heart. His hands went up slowly and I told him to step away from the girl, and he obeyed. I don't think he recognized me at first, and I could see his eyes turning as he tried to hatch a plan. He began speaking in English, his German accent nearly concealed, and he was thanking me for killing the soldier and I yelled at him to shut up. The girl was weeping and I told her to leave, but she didn't move, and Dieter told her in French to run home. The girl looked at me with frightened eyes to see if I was really freeing her or if I was going to kill her, and Dieter told her, again, to run.

"She left us, and to this day I can recall her skirt fluttering and her legs as long and fast as a deer's. Then she was gone. Dieter remained, his hands up and waving like two white flags. Behind him was his trav-eling rack of tinware, the dented cups and the lidded bowls and the forks that bent in the fist. He said, 'The German took the girl from me.' I told him to shut up again and I told him I had eyes and I told him not only had I caught him hawking girls, I'd caught him selling them to the enemy. Dieter tried to convince me that I was wrong, that it'd been too dark for me to see things correctly. But my patience was thinning and I yelled, 'Do you know what they do to traitors?'

"He was protesting with his hands that I was wrong, and he was such a small man that it was hard for me to believe that he was peddling such evil but I'd seen what I'd seen and I said to him, 'Maybe I should shoot you now.'

" 'Shoot me?' he squealed. 'For selling a girl? I'm out here trying to stay alive like everyone else. Her family will eat tonight.'

"I told him to drop to his knees, and when he didn't I shoved my rifle barrel in his direction and he was soon down on the ground and his hands were clasped and he was begging: 'Oh, please, please, I'll do anything. Anything you want! Just let me go free. What harm have I done? You've killed a German because of me. I'm not the enemy, he is.' And he turned to the poor boy, dead with the happy smile eternally upon his face. 'What can I give you? I'll give you anything you want. I'll give you any girl you want. Tell me what you like, soldier. Do you like brunettes? Do you like them blond? Or dark in the eye? I can get you any girl. I can get you enough cigarettes for your whole company. Tell me what you want. Please—'

" 'I don't want one of your whores,' I said.

" 'Every soldier wants a whore. What about Sylvie? The girl who was just here? She's fifteen. You can have her. You can marry her. I can arrange it.'

" 'I don't want her,' I said.

" 'There's more!' He fished a photograph from his pocket and said, 'What about her? Do you like her?' He pushed the picture toward me but I didn't want to take it, something told me not to take the picture, and I resisted but he continued to dangle it between us. 'Go on,' he said. 'Have a look. She's the most beautiful girl I know. Go on, have a peek.' I told myself not to look, I sensed even then the mistake of looking at this girl, and I told Dieter to put the picture away but he didn't. 'This one's special,' he said. 'Tall and strong, hair as black as the sky tonight, and flesh as white as milk, and you've never seen a girl like her, soldier. Go on, take a look.' The voice remained in my head, warning me not to look, but urges mount us, don't they? I wondered what made this girl so special. The picture was a small square in Dieter's fingers and I found myself pulled toward it as if it were magnetic, and I found my hand reaching out for it and I felt Dieter's horny fingers graze mine as I took it from him and brought it to my eye.

"Dieter hadn't lied. She was the most beautiful girl I'd ever seen, eyes dark and deep and a throat rising from her blouse in a way that would make any man want to kiss it. She was a young girl, but her eyes were a woman's. I tried to resist her and I said, 'I told you I don't want one of your whores.'

" 'She isn't a whore,' said Dieter. 'This one's special.'

" 'Who is she?' I asked, even though I knew I shouldn't.

" 'She's my daughter. She can be yours.'

"I cupped the picture in my palm, and her eyes held me, and I fell in love with Linda then and there, as the dawn cracked above the forest, and before I knew it I was under her spell and Dieter could see this; he was always a clever man. He said, 'I can see that you like her. She can become yours.'

" 'Where is she?' I said.

" 'In California.'

" 'In California?'

" 'Do you want her, soldier?'

"In the pale glow of early morning I nodded obediently.

" 'Then all we have to do is make a deal,' said Dieter, 'and you can come home with me to Condor's Nest.' "

3

MUCH LATER, Blackwood found himself slumped in the rocker, Bruder across from him. After finishing his story, Bruder had fallen into a pitiable sleep, but then Blackwood too had allowed his neck to slacken, and the two men had wheezed through sleep that brought them to the dawn. When Blackwood woke, he could see that Bruder was motionless but alert. Pal was gone, and Sieglinde had thrown more wood into the hearth, and the fire burned upon the black oil of Bruder's eyes. He was wheezing through heavy lungs, and coughing into a rag, and as Blackwood rubbed the sleep from his eyes, Bruder's decline became even more apparent. And now Blackwood understood: from the beginning, Bruder had tried to manipulate Linda's fate, and now he was suffering for it.

"You haven't been well, Mr. Bruder?"

"Nothing more than the years catching up with me."

"You seem to have something in your chest. Have you tried that new miracle drug, penicillin?"

"I have not."

"I saw a special announcement that beginning on April first, Kalash's Pharmacy will be able to supply it. Civilians will get to try it for the first time. The next time you're in Pasadena, you should give them a call. Their number is Sycamore 2-1704. They're saying it's the greatest miracle the century has brought us. They say right now there's no limit to what it can cure. One little pill can take out any old illness, the Spanish flu, pneumonia, even syphilis. Anything, I should imagine. It makes you feel for the poor souls who had to go without, doesn't it, Mr. Bruder?"

Bruder's story had clarified nearly everything for Blackwood. But what of Edmund's death? Bruder said nothing of it, alluded not at all to the years on the peninsula in San Francisco Bay, sunlight slanting through the iron bars. Now that Blackwood knew the whole story, it made even less sense—if Bruder would save Captain Poore, if he'd save Dieter Stamp, then why would he go on to kill Edmund? It didn't add up, and Blackwood wondered if Linda had sent Bruder to prison on false testimony. Blackwood looked up. Had Bruder been framed?

But then Bruder startled Blackwood by saying, "Let's get down to business, Mr. Blackwood. I'd like to know about your plans for the Pasadena."

"My plans?"

"If it were to become yours, what would you do with it? How would you make your money back?"

"Well, I . . . I suppose I . . ." But Blackwood still didn't know what the correct answer was; he didn't know what Bruder wanted done with his property.

"Would you live in the mansion?"

"In the mansion? I don't think so. It's a bit large for a bachelor."

"A man needs his castle, Mr. Blackwood."

This cheered Blackwood, and he sat up in the rocker and leaned forward so that again his knees almost touched Bruder's. "Indeed, a man must reign over something. Look at you, Mr. Bruder. You have Condor's Nest to set your throne upon."

"I'm only waiting to pass it on to Sieglinde and Palomar. When I'm gone, they'll do what they want with it. It's really theirs, anyway."

"You'll be the King of the Coast for quite some time, I'm sure. If you were to call Kalash's—"

"Penicillin can't save everyone, Mr. Blackwood. But enough of this. Tell me, what would you do with the land?" Blackwood thought over his answer carefully; he still did not know what Bruder wanted to hear. Now he was angry with Mrs. Nay for not providing him with more insight—but hadn't she? "What would you do with the orange grove, Mr. Blackwood?"

"Yes, what would I do with the grove? I suppose they'd have to be felled, those trees, wouldn't they, Mr. Bruder? From what I understand, their roots have been infected by the nematode. Besides, there's no room for citrus in a modern city."

"That's correct, Mr. Blackwood. An infestation has overtaken the orchards. Cut the trees to the ground and burn the soil. That's what you'll have to do." Bruder fell silent, as if he were imagining the fire just then. "And what would you do with the land?"

"It would be a lot of open space indeed. Tracts of land that large don't come up anymore, do they? The frontier's been filled in. Yes, what would I do with it? Of course, I'm a real-estate developer, Mr. Bruder. I feel I've been open about that from the get-go. I would develop the land, of course."

"Yes, but how?"

"There remains talk of a second branch of the parkway. The cars are proliferating like rabbits. They say that our lovely Arroyo Parkway will reach its capacity within a few years, cars backed up from Los Angeles to the Hotel Raymond's hill. It's hard to imagine the traffic as bad as all that, but that's what they say. I should think that after cutting down the trees I'd talk to the highway men about bringing a six-laner up the valley."

"And if they wanted to build an eight-laner?"

"I would be open to that."

"Very good, Mr. Blackwood. A river of concrete pouring into Pasadena, that would be best for the old orange grove."

"It seems it's what the citizens want these days. Modernity. Convenience. Speed. People want to live in the future now, don't they?"

"The past is of little use to them."

"Can you blame them?"

"Tell me, Mr. Blackwood. What would you do with the gardens and the scrubland around the house?"

"The gardens?" By now Blackwood's confidence had returned, and at once he could imagine a plan for the entire 160 acres. When Blackwood was done, no one would know that the street they stood on had once been an orange ranch; no one would see the arroyo beneath the asphalt. "In the gardens I'd put up a community of those condominiums that are becoming all the rage. Call it something like Blackmann Court."

"Blackmann Court? Who is Blackmann, Mr. Blackwood?"

"Did I say 'Blackmann'? Yes, well, he's a long-lost friend. A friend of my youth, you might say. I thought I might make the gesture."

"You're too modest, Mr. Blackwood."

"All right then, perhaps I'd call it Blackwood Court."

"That does sound pleasant, Mr. Blackwood. It would evoke the natural past without giving too much away. It'd be a shame to call the place Orange Grove Terrace, or something of the sort. Why turn the mind to the torn-up past?"

A terrible pain entered Blackwood's chest, and all at once he recalled his moral crimes, even those that he'd never thought of as criminal until this very minute: the Spanish courtyards he'd ripped up for warehouses; the gulleys he'd paved; the meadows replaced by motor courts. He thought of Edith Knight and the three thousand dollars that had once felt like the greatest sum of money known to man. Hadn't he promised himself as he fled west on the train, spring rising outside the window: "With this money I'll make good."

"It sounds like you have an excellent plan, Mr. Blackwood. Your goals and mine are in conjunction. Run the highway up the valley, cover the hilltop in condominiums. All of this would help haul Pasadena out of its past. Rid it of its past. And do you know what I like most about your idea?" said Bruder.

"What's that?"

"You'll be able to survey all that you have done from your terrace. It will be a good life for you, Mr. Blackwood." And then: "I want you to have the Pasadena."

The pronouncement had come so quickly that Blackwood wasn't sure he heard it correctly. He ventured, "I want it too."

"You must put your money together by the end of the week."

"That won't be a problem."

Sieglinde brought them tea, and Blackwood and Bruder sat silently. The tide had come in, and it was thrashing the bluff. Finally Bruder said, "I will cut you a deal."

"A deal?"

"On one condition."

"What is that?"

"You may do what you like with the property. I don't care what happens to the house or the land, as long as you destroy everything as it was."

The regret tasted like rust on Blackwood's tongue.

"Everything but the mausoleum."

"The mausoleum?" said Blackwood.

"Where she rests. It's where I'll lie down at last, too." Bruder brought the pendant to his mouth, sucking on it as gently as a nursing infant.

Once again, Bruder seemed swamped by his dreams. "How do I know you'll preserve the mausoleum?" he said.

"You have my word."

"Yes, a man's word. It's all I can have. It's all I've ever had."

Eventually Blackwood thought it was time to leave; he was unsure whether or not the Pasadena had passed to him in the course of the conversation. In fact, it had, but Blackwood did not know this yet, and he remained uneasy. What would happen to Blackwood if after these long months he came up empty-handed? If the men from the bank came in and scooped up the ranch from his grasping fingers? It'd be quite a blow, he thought; but when in a few days he found the Pasadena's deed folded in the Imperial Victoria's glove compartment, he wouldn't be quite certain how he had accomplished the task. What was it Mrs. Nay had said to him last week? *You seem like a man unfamiliar with himself, Mr. Blackwood.*

Blackwood cleared his throat. "I have a final question for you, Mr. Bruder."

Bruder didn't stir.

"I've been wondering this for a long time now."

"Sieglinde," said Bruder, "please leave us alone." The girl leaned against the waxed slickers on the hook and folded her arms across her breasts and said she wouldn't leave. "So much like her mother," said Bruder. "Go ahead, Mr. Blackwood. I'll do my best to answer."

"It's a bit personal, if you don't mind."

"Mind? Why should I mind now?"

"What happened to Linda?"

"It's rather straightforward, Mr. Blackwood. She became Mrs. Willis Poore. They called her Lindy."

"Why did you let her marry him?"

"It wasn't my intention."

"Then why did you ask her up to the ranch in the first place?"

"To be with me."

"You misjudged her, Mr. Bruder."

This touched Bruder in a way Blackwood hadn't intended. "I'm not sure why I thought she'd be more patient. Had she waited, one day we would have lived on the ranch together."

"Yes, but what happened to her?"

"Sieglinde, please go."

"No," said the girl, and she brought a chair to the oval rug and sat by the fire. Palomar returned to the cottage smelling of fish, and his pant legs were wet, and he lay on the rug like a dog drying himself, his head upon his cousin's feet. Of course, Blackwood had never met Linda and Edmund, but even so he could see the resemblance in the girl and boy.

"Do you really want to know?" Bruder asked. Blackwood said that he did. "Then I'll tell you. What happened to her is what happens to anyone who betrays her own heart." And then: "But it was worse than that."

"Worse?" said Blackwood.

"First she betrayed mine."

"How do you mean, Mr. Bruder?"

"Can't you tell by now?"

"It makes me wonder. How did Captain Poore learn about the two of you? About the night she was taking her bath? It seems to me that your fortune, and hers too, turned that night."

"That's very perceptive of you."

Blackwood thanked Bruder for the compliment. He went ahead and made a guess: "Did Linda tell Captain Poore herself?"

"Linda tell Captain Poore about our one night of love? Even she wasn't capable of gross betrayal like that. She scratched in a subtler, deadlier way."

"Was it Rosa?"

"Rosa? Oh no. Rosa was all good. She never did anything to hurt anyone. Of course, that didn't stop Captain Poore from hurting her."

"Then how, Mr. Bruder? How did Captain Poore know to move Linda up to his house? How did he know to take her away from you?"

Bruder leaned forward in his chair. His breath was strained and his eyes were vacant and his hand trembled, and he was the closest Blackwood had come to seeing death. "Yes, how?" He paused. "I can tell that Mrs. Nay hasn't told you everything. Go back to Pasadena, Mr. Blackwood, and ask Mrs. Nay to finish. Ask her to tell you about Lolly Poore."

Soon Blackwood was shaking Bruder's hand, unaware that he'd never shake it again, and the sunlight outside the cottage blinded Blackwood, and when his pupils adjusted he looked over his shoulder and waved good-bye.

INFEST

{ *part six* }

It is not pride, it is not shame,
That makes her leave the gorgeous hall;
And though neglect her heart might tame
She mourns not for her sudden fall.

EMILY BRONTË

1

ON AN AFTERNOON in July 1930, during the third year of the long
drought, Lindy Poore was driving Willis's Gold Bug west on Suicide
Bridge. The sun was in her eyes and one of her headaches was attacking
her as densely as a blow to the temple, and that, combined with the sun,
made it nearly impossible for her to see. But there was no room on the
bridge to pull over and so she slowed, her foot heavy on the brake. The
car behind honked viciously and Lindy signaled for the man to pass, but
the oncoming traffic prohibited him. Again he pressed on his horn and
she could see that he was yelling, a bush of wiry gold hair about his
mouth. He continued to honk, and when the traffic cleared he overtook
her on the narrow bridge, craning to leer and shout at the *lady driver!*
Then the man was gone and Lindy inched along the bridge, and up rose
the brittle scent of the arroyo, desiccated since the drought began in
1928. A pale dust drifted from the dead riverbed, and the Rose Bowl sat
dull and cracked and alone, radiating its own heat like an enormous
cauldron. The newspaper had said the temperature would top off at
109, and it felt as if the sun were igniting Lindy as she lurched the car
toward the bridge's western end, where she would pull into the orange
combine and rest in its shade.

She was on her way home from a meeting of the Monday Afternoon
Club, held in the Ladies' Lounge of the Huntington Hotel. The club,
made up of twelve women, met on the last Monday of the month to
discuss literature and geography and anything else proposed for its
agenda, such as the new but distressing problem of unemployed chambermaids loitering at night outside the Raymond Street Station. On

this particular Monday afternoon, the ladies—including Mrs. Ellie Sickman, Mrs. Sarah Woolly, Mrs. E. B. Rocke, and Mrs. Connie Ringe—
had discussed—and *tackled,* as Connie Ringe declared—Gibbon's Rome.
In the days before the meeting there had been a flurry of midnight
reading in a dozen upstairs suites across Pasadena, on shady Oak Knoll,
on wide-avenued Hillcrest, on olive-lined Lombardy, in the skunk-
and-coyote Linda Vista hills: a lone window bright with gold light, a
fine-boned, determined hand turning page after page while the neighborhood slept and the wind bent the stalks of cypress, while the husband snored and emitted his sour nighttime effluvia and the children
sighed and picked the paint from the bedposts and the governess
moaned in her dreams. But the members of the Monday Afternoon
Club were achievers, women capable of nearly anything they set their
minds to; such was their motto, and inscribed on the inside of their
white-gold membership bracelets were the words of Abigail Adams:
"We have too many high sounding words, and too few actions that cor-
respond with them." In due time each member had finished studying
Gibbon and was prepared to discuss the subtleties of a civilization's decline.

But two weeks before the meeting, Lindy hadn't been able to locate
Gibbon in Willis's library. Most of the books were his father's, and over
the years she had learned that few left the shelves for any reason other
than to be caressed by Rosa's feather duster. At Vroman's Bookstore,
Lindy asked one of the clerks, Mr. Raines, for an edition. He brought
her the books, the three volumes held to his chest by shirtsleeved arms.
Mr. Raines, a young man from Stanford, was responsible for the history
section, and while Lindy inspected the three volumes he leaned against
the oak shelves, one meaty, half-exposed arm crooked above his head.
Behind him was a glass case displaying Adam Vroman's collection of
sun-pale Hopi kachinas and folded Navajo blankets and dozens of
carved Japanese netsuke purse-beads. Hanging above the bookshelves
were photos of Hopi Indians: a chief silhouetted on a ridge and a
braided woman peering into a basket of squash and a penny-colored
child in a mesa village. Mr. Raines said that though he himself was a
specialist in the history of the West, he had learned at Stanford to look
to the ancients for certain truths. He adjusted the items in the cabinet
while Lindy inspected the books.

"Behold," says the laureate, "the relics of Rome, the image of her pristine greatness! Neither time nor the Barbarian can boast the merit of this stupendous destruction: it was perpetrated by her own citizens."

"Is there anyone more useful than Gibbon in these trying days?" said Mr. Raines, seeing Lindy to the car. He suggested that she visit him when she had finished her reading, to share her thoughts. They could have a book chat in the Spanish Library Room, he proposed, glancing in the direction of the courtyard. His eyes returned to her, and there was something behind them, a warmth Lindy no longer could take comfort in. The young man was offering friendship, but Lindy couldn't accept it. She hesitated before she made any promises, and Mr. Raines, who was twenty-two or twenty-three, stepped backward on the sun-swamped street: "I hope I haven't said anything disagreeable, Mrs. Poore. I wasn't suggesting—"

She assured the man that he had not.

Two weeks later, the Monday Afternoon Club met in the Ladies' Lounge, with its upholstered window seats and the passion-fruit relief scrolling around the room. They picked at radishes and spiced peaches and cooled themselves in front of electric fans, discussing both Gibbon and the recent downturn in civic fortunes. Ellie Sickman chaired the Committee for Reforming the Poor, and she told the other Afternooners that her task had become so much more difficult this year. "Ladies, 1930 is not 1929. We are living in a different age," she said knowingly, her husband's ice fortune collapsing even as she spoke. The Sickmans would go on to lose their "gals," as Ellie called her three crow-haired maids. Then the Sickman house on Orange Grove would close, its fescue lawn that cost a thousand dollars a year to irrigate burning to straw; and the Sickmans would sneak off in the night, bags and baby tucked underarm. But of the future, what did Ellie Sickman know during the July heat wave of 1930? What did any of them know, in the Ladies' Lounge? They had gathered to discuss the past. One of them, Sarah Woolly—whose long, boxy mouth and heavy-lidded eyes possessed a bovine quality that grew even more prominent when she discussed her mother's dairy fortune—said that the Afternooners held a unique responsibility to summon history when others were too busy worrying

about the day-to-day. "Ladies, we are privileged in that regard," said
Sarah, who was the club's chair for 1930 and therefore stowed in her
purse the cherry-wood gavel that kept meetings in order and on agenda.
The Woolly dairy empire would survive heartily into the future, for
with the decline in beef sales came the rise in the consumption of cottage cheese, a trend that would continue for fifteen years, conferring
upon Sarah's daughter the unspoken but oft-thought moniker "Pasadena's Cottage Cheese Princess."

Yet Lindy's vision into the future—whether her own or that of the
city that had become her home—was imprecise. When she tried to look
forward, one of her headaches would descend and its blow would prod
her to look back: the years with Willis had passed somehow both urgently and in one long rolling gait, and the baby would turn five in September. "I'm not a baby anymore!" Sieglinde would scream, her fists
pounding Lindy's thigh or the wall next to her bed as she flipped and
flopped and refused to go to sleep. Sieglinde was a dark-featured girl,
eyes like two chips of coal and a black tendril of hair growing down her
neck. People would say, "She doesn't look a thing like Captain Poore.
She's all you, Lindy!" Lindy would correct them, "You're wrong. She
looks like her Uncle Edmund too." The girl loved to roam the open
chaparral, slingshot in hand, and hike into the foothills above Devil's
Gate, hurling arrow-edged rocks at the squirrels. She learned to swim
at twelve months, tadpoling across the pool into Lindy's arms, and how
to ride at the age of two, in Willis's lap on White Indian. But as much as
little Sieglinde loved to run barefoot through the groves and ride in the
truck with Hearts and Slaymaker, the girl loved even more the boxes
sent from Dodsworth's and the bunny-fur hoods ordered at the furrier
in the Vista's lobby. She was only half her child, Lindy knew, and with
this came both love and disappointment; and when her headache
throbbed, and her joints ached feverishly, Lindy's regret would pool in
her chest even more.

Sarah Woolly continued to steer the conversation away from Gibbon
and toward what might be done for the less fortunate of Pasadena. The
girls released from service in the half-empty hotels and the shuttered
mansions were "becoming a blight," said Ellie Sickman. They gathered
at night in search of what the Monday Afternoon Club called "romantic
work." "I would just *die* if I ever saw one of my gals out there, waiting in
the night," said Ellie, although, when this event transpired a year later,

Ellie Sickman did not in fact die; she merely wondered how much a girl could earn between dusk and dawn. Ellie Sickman would go on to say, "I suppose for many gals there's no other way."

"We must do *something*," Sarah Woolly implored. "These girls have no training other than housekeeping and cooking, so what are we to do with them? They're steps away from desperate lives."

"We should educate them," said Connie Ringe. In the time that Lindy had lived in Pasadena, brass-haired Connie Muffitt had married and divorced a man named G. W. Ringe, a Hollywood producer who shortly after their marriage found himself ensnared in a tax-and-bribery scandal. The incident of her brief marriage—the twelve-hundred-guest wedding, the oak-shaded *finca* in San Marino where no one could hear her midnight screams, the teary drive home to her parents on Bellefontaine—had chiseled away Connie's hardness, leaving her with supple cheeks and hands gloved in empathy. They had become friends, Lindy and Connie, each with one foot in and one foot out of the lives others expected for them; together they had hunted lynx in the foothills until hunting became illegal and they played doubles at the Valley Hunt, climbing the ladder as fast as ivy. They made sure that the boys at the Children's Training Society and the girls at the Webb House each received a winter sweater and a pamphlet on birth control, respectively. Connie showed Lindy a side of Pasadena that Willis knew nothing of: the poetry circles and the scientific lectures at Cal Tech and the Pasadena Arts & Crafts Society, where men and women in smocks and berets painted dreamy oils of the sycamores. "We should organize a school," proposed Connie to the Afternooners. "Some place where these girls can learn less domestic and more modern work."

"Yes, a school for girls," said Lindy. "A place that can prepare them for the future."

"Afternooners," said Sarah, "let's each of us talk to our husbands about starting a fund."

"A fund for a school for girls," someone said.

"If we don't do it, who will?" asked Lindy.

No one thinks about the girls' futures, the women agreed.

But the Afternooners were unsure what precisely they could teach the unemployed maids and cooks and seamstresses and nannies and house girls and washerwomen. "What will the future demand that these girls can supply?" The question hung in the Ladies' Lounge and buzzed around the Monday Afternoon Club's ears: What indeed? And Lindy thought too, but not about the abstract future. For what *could* be done? Wouldn't fate go on and have its way? She recalled, rubbing her temple, how certain she had been that a girl's life was her own to steer, that no single misfortune could thwart a young girl's plans. And yet at some point the truth had flashed her, both obscenely and indisputably. At night, tucking Sieglinde into bed, Lindy tried to tell her daughter that things would be different for her. "No one will tell you what to do," Lindy assured her. "But, Mommy. You're always telling me what to do." The girl was too young to comprehend, but her eyes sparked as if the notion was registering. It was all Lindy could hope for.

Over the years, Sieglinde and Palomar had become best friends, and Lindy would come across them—Palomar's melon-round face molding slowly into an image of Edmund—tying flies on the edge of the trout pond, which Willis had stopped restocking in 1929. Lindy had cared for Palomar after Edmund's death, and when she married Willis, the boy came as her only dowry. Willis had mistakenly thought that with Edmund's passing, Condor's Nest would become Lindy's; but, no, she had had to explain: the farm is Bruder's. "But he's been thrown away." "And from prison he's ordered that no one step foot on his land," she said. Even Dieter had been moved into a room behind Margarita's; Lindy mailed a check each month to pay for his board and care. When all this was revealed to Willis, Lindy could see her husband registering the news: *I've married a strange girl,* his eyes told her. No, Lindy brought nothing to the marriage but herself and Palomar, and the forming lump in her stomach, which kicked and beat through the nights and days.

Lindy's love for her nephew was rivaled only by Lolly's possessive affection. Lolly, who was held permanently under youth's glass bell, had fallen for the boy the way a little girl falls for a yellow-maned pony, or a china-head doll. Side by side, Lindy and Lolly raised the children while Willis, unwilling to hire a new foreman, oversaw the groves and shaved his landholdings as bid after bid came along: small tracts—four, seven, thirteen acres—to housebuilders and macadam mavens and the automobile companies buying up right-of-ways. Over the years he would entertain any offer: "What do I need with all this land?" Soon enough he stopped mentioning his business transactions altogether: if he sold a parcel, she would learn of it only on the *Star-News*'s "Notices and Holdings" page.

But in the idle summer of 1930—with the number of unemployed citizens doubling each month, with the chambermaids and the private secretaries released from the mansions by the truckload, with the undershirted construction crews standing around in the heat, their cement mixers still—there was little on Captain Poore's mind but the deal that would, as he put it, seal the Pasadena's—and Pasadena's—fate. Captain Poore and a developer named George Nay led the men proposing a motorcar turnpike running from Pasadena to Los Angeles, a bending river of concrete its proponents hoped would pave the floor of the arroyo and the sandy riverbed. It had become a great distraction to Willis, a pursuit that kept him irritable and away from the ranch, in planning meetings in the Valley Hunt Club's paneled library, in the tiled, resounding corridors of City Hall, its courtyard fountain tinkling; and it kept him away from Lindy and her fevers, her red eyes, her tender nodes. Captain Poore and the other 100 Percenters were busy hatching plans for the parkway, as they referred to it, emphasizing the *park*. Their enthusiasm was based on their intention to keep Pasadena at the helm of civic advancement; that, and to sell their spare scrubland at the highest possible price. The men were much like Willis himself: former mayor Hiram Wadsworth, whose white billy-goat beard children liked to stroke; Wallace Burdette, an Ohio industrialist who erected a castlelike mansion in Linda Vista modeled after Byron's Château de Chillon; Charles Sutton, a fair, wispy man with an El Segundo oil reserve that gushed a thousand barrels a day; Milford A. Puddington, grandson of a robber baron, whose open disdain for railroads ("A car'll beat 'em every time!") had brought a seizure upon his ninety-nine-year-old grandmother's tiny, rich heart.

In August 1930, the parkway was nothing more than a dream, although in the developers' minds a vivid one. Not everyone supported the idea of a six-lane concrete river flooding down the Arroyo Seco. More than a few "naturists"—as Willis called them—predicted traffic of more than five hundred cars per hour, a vision into the future Willis scoffed at as both "hysterical and factually unfounded." "These are people who have yet to rip down their stables," Willis would say. "People who dream backward to the days of wagons and mules." Willis Poore was not such a man, he was fond of saying; like his father he looked only forward, and sometimes at the breakfast table he would emphasize this by thumping his breast, or by talking with a mouthful of raspberry

jam, which would prompt little Sieglinde to giggle. On a regular basis
he would make a speech of some sort to Lindy, as if he were testing his
resolve in front of an audience, and she would say, if she was listening,
"Once you've destroyed something it can never return."

Their first argument was over the baby's name: When the nurse
handed Lindy the greasy, shrieking infant, she realized at once that she
wanted to name her Sieglinde. "What kind of a name is that?" said
Willis. "Sounds like an immigrant." That was exactly what kind of
name it was, Lindy protested, and a dread settled upon the new
mother's breast. In her bedroom she cried that no one would tell her
what to name her daughter, and her screams rose above the baby's, and
the sweat running down her sides mixed with the blood on the sheets.
This behavior erased the happy, new-father grin upon Willis's face, and
she knew that she had frightened him, as if he had for the first time
peered down the tunnel of her soul, carbide lamp in hand.

Over the years, Willis had come to realize that it was less effort to
keep things from his wife than it was to argue with her. He hadn't told
her that earlier in the summer of 1930 he had sold to the Pasadena
Parkway Corporation two hundred acres, a corner of the rancho that
was wild and untouched and where Lindy had taught Sieglinde to ride
a colt and shoot an old Winchester Model 1873, a gun with a barroom
nude etched into the silver plate. No, Willis failed to mention the transaction, and only by reading the *Star-News* had Lindy discovered it.
When she asked about it, he said that he had sold the land not to destroy
the Pasadena but to preserve it. "We want the parkway running by our
front gate, don't we? It's going to be like the railroads," he predicted.
"You don't want to be left out of its path." But Lindy doubted he was
right; from the flock of roadsters and Hispano-Suizas rushing down
Colorado Street, *beep-beep*ing by the trolley cars, she had a clear sense of
what was to come. When she ventured to tell her husband, he would
hush her: "Why should *you* be worrying about such things?"

During the past year—especially during the summer, when a feverish
malaise overtook the city, and Lindy and Willis suffered through the hot
nights on the sleeping porch—she had thought about leaving Pasadena,
even if only for a short time. The longing for someplace else was both
imprecise and permanently lodged. She didn't know what she hoped to

find beyond the gate, beyond the Sierra Madres' long morning shadow; there were days when more than anything she wanted to see the ocean and feel the salt dry stiffly on her skin. Occasionally she would bundle Sieglinde into the car and they'd drive to Santa Monica. On the beach in front of the Jonathan Club, Lindy would sit in a canvas chair and watch her daughter erecting a dam of sand. There were rules, unstated but firm nonetheless, against mothers joining their children in the tide. The younger women—the seventeen- and nineteen-year-olds with the narrow white hips—bathed in their rubber and worsted-wool suits, rubbing coconut oil into one another's long limbs, but never the mothers and the wives. Up the beach and far off from the Jonathan Club's roped-off sand, Lindy could see the Mexican families bodysurfing, mothers younger than she walking naked infants into the waves. The fathers would dig pits in the sand and burn driftwood, and they'd be opening baskets of *conchas* and *tamales* for sunset picnics while Lindy and Sieglinde made their way across the beach to the parking lot. Those young mothers and their shiny-bottomed children, and their husbands and brothers with mustaches drooping around their mouths—Lindy knew that they would stay to witness the sun slip beyond the horizon, when the clouds in the sky singed orange. But Willis didn't like Lindy driving at night; he'd say he didn't like the idea of Sieglinde eating anywhere "public"; he didn't approve of his wife returning to him with a fine layer of salt across her warm and red face. She used to argue with him, but not anymore. She used to scream from the bottom of the stairs, her hand upon Cupid's foot. Willis would hurry down the steps and kiss her forehead and say, "No, no. I would never dream of telling you what to do."

But in fact he did.

Yet other than the day trips to Santa Monica and the afternoons beneath the Valley Hunt's latticed tennis pavilion or along the hiking trails in the foothills, Lindy had nowhere to go. Willis, whose self-worth extended as far as his gate, didn't like to leave his ranch: "Who's going to look after things? Rosa? Hearts and Slay?"

Sieglinde had been born only a few days after Lindy gave her testimony in Bruder's trial. The baby arrived in the world with the bloody cord tight around her throat and her face blue and bruised. When Dr. Birchback cut the baby free, a frightening shriek emerged, one so high-pitched and glassy that nurses from two wards down peered into the

Labor Room to inspect what variety of devil had arrived. They held their fingers to their lips as they looked at the large blue baby girl, and thought, *The poor mother . . . what she must've gone through.* Within two weeks, though, Lindy returned to working on the ranch, helping Hearts and Slay prepare the bunkhouse for the soon-to-arrive hands and scrubbing the plank floors in the Yuens' adobe. But soon word came that Bruder would be sentenced, and Lindy drove down the coast to hear Judge Dinklemann read aloud Bruder's future. She insisted on taking the baby with her, and Sieglinde, who typically screamed herself hoarse every day, slept in a mysterious silence throughout the sentencing. Not once did Bruder turn around in his chair, and Lindy didn't know if he had seen her. She hoped that her daughter would wake up and scream and cause everyone in the courtroom to turn. He would see her; he would see that she had come. But Sieglinde slept as if she'd been drugged; nothing would nudge her from her dreams, not even when Lindy pinched the baby's leg, twisting her skin.

The bailiff led Bruder out of the courtroom, and just as he was leaving he said to Judge Dinklemann and Mr. Ivory, "I'll be back for it." Then he was gone, and the judge and the prosecutor looked equally perplexed by Bruder's final statement, and soon they were folding papers into files and their day was done.

The next day, a package arrived for Lindy. It was from Bruder, and he'd sent it just before being taken to San Quentin. She carried it to her room and told Rosa to leave her alone, and on her bed—where she had gone to sleep during her pregnancy and where she would sleep most but not quite all of her nights alone—she tore through the brown paper to find Valencia's old apron, its strings dingy and frayed. She shook it out, expecting a note to tumble from the heap, but there was nothing, and when she held the apron to her nose, again nothing—nothing lingered, nothing remained.

It had been Bruder's last message to her, and now, almost five years later, no word had carried up from Condor's Nest or down from San Quentin. Dieter had been moved to an oceanside house for the aged and the infirm, and when Lindy would drive down the coast to visit him she would enter her father's room and he would have no idea who she was. He would be wearing his military jacket with the epaulets and babbling in German, and Sieglinde would be frightened of her grand-

father, and soon they'd leave, a crate of oranges the only thing to tell
Dieter that he'd had a visitor.

And now, parked at the orange combine, on her way home from the
Monday Afternoon Club, blinded by a fever that Dr. Birchback once
dismissed as "a feminine response to the heat," Lindy Poore felt as if she
too hardly knew who she was. Five years ago, when Willis had found
her mother's apron hanging limply from Lindy's bed, he had inspected
it, laughing, "Was this once yours?" And Lindy had struggled to answer,
for she didn't know: she no longer knew what was hers, which life was
hers. The old smudged apron was both familiar and foreign, and it was
stiff with dirt and smoke, and when Lindy told her new husband that it
wasn't hers, Willis ordered Rosa to throw it away—"Unless you want it
for yourself."

During her first orange season as Mrs. Willis Poore she had continued to rise at dawn and walk down the hill and drink coffee with
the hands. Willis had hired a new cook, a girl from Salinas who spoke
haltingly but with great deference to Captain Poore. Her name was
Carnación, and the bud of her mouth would pinch whenever Lindy—
whom Carnación would call only *Señora*—entered the ranch-house
kitchen and peered into a pot. Lindy continued driving the truck to the
Webb House to pick up the packing girls, and now that they understood
the vast difference between themselves and the rancho's mistress, none
of them would sit up front with Lindy. Through the little window in
the truck's cab the girls' gossip would reach Lindy's ear, and she took
comfort in knowing that they still talked about the same things, in
knowing that each girl would close her weary eyes at the end of a long
day in the packinghouse and dream what every orphaned girl had ever
dreamed of. In the rearview mirror, Lindy would watch the girls study
the mansions along Orange Grove Avenue. Lindy knew that their eyes
were looking to the bedroom windows, and she also knew that if she
were to warn the girls of what waited behind one of those Roman
shades, they wouldn't believe her. For all they had to do was look at
Lindy as evidence of what was possible, even for them. "If you're pretty
enough . . ." Lindy heard one of them say.

The season of 1925–26 was the last rainy winter for several years,
and it would also turn out to be the last Willis would permit Lindy to
work. "Lindy, sweetheart, you can do anything. Why do you want to

spend the day in the orange grove? It doesn't suit you." For a while she defied him, returning to the grove each morning and sharing coffee with Hearts and Slay as the sun rose. She continued to oversee the packing, carefully monitoring the girls: when one became too hot upon her stool, Lindy would lead her to the fan standing in the corner and to the water spout. She'd bring Sieglinde with her, and the baby would sleep in an orange crate Hearts had lined with flannel. Sometimes, Willis would send Lolly to request that Lindy return to the house. Sometimes, Lolly would say, "He's worried about you, Lindy."

During the first year or two of his marriage, Willis had urged his sister to bring Lindy into Lolly's social world. "Now that we're sisters," Lolly would say, telling Lindy what to wear and where to shop and that her women's clubs, while limited in membership, would only expand Lindy's mind. Lindy went along to the tea dances and the cotillions, her husband and her sister-in-law hooked to her elbows. They took her to all-night jazz parties on the Vista's terrace or around the Midwick's swimming pool. Willis took her to balls where she had to strangle her arms in elbow-length kid gloves and stand within her husband's clasp, unless he excused himself "for some fresh air on my own." There had been a period of time when Lindy wanted to fit in, and she learned from Lolly how to curl her hair with an iron and from Willis how to get tipsy from lemon-wedge fruit punch. Lolly took her to Dodsworth's for evening dresses and to Nash's for linen suits, but almost immediately upon opening the boxes on her bed Lindy would discover a familiar loneliness, one she had tried and failed to tuck away. Once, when Lindy and Lolly were strolling through Carmelita Gardens, Lindy spotted a man on a bench beneath a conifer. His back was to them, and his black hair spilled over the collar of his suit. A robin bobbed around on the bench beside him, inching its way closer. It's Bruder, Lindy thought, and she stopped as the sun throbbed and the heat rose from the garden path and the small great instant Lindy had known would come finally arrived: Bruder had returned. "Do you know him?" said Lolly, and she looked to the man as well and then said, "Is it Bruder?" Both women, now sisters, approached the bench, the anticipation between them palpable, like heat radiating from sunburned flesh, and just as they reached the bench the man turned around and revealed himself to be no one they had ever seen before.

No, it couldn't have been him, for Bruder was sitting on a wooden bench beneath a barred window, the breeze rank with salt and the stench of the mudflats. Her husband's words remained with Lindy: "You put him away."

It had been in the autumn of 1929, not long after the Crash that had kept Willis up late at night in his library, that the fever returned to Lindy. It arrived swiftly and vigorously, with sweat and chills and the sensation of a vise clamped to her head. As Lindy lay in bed, Sieglinde would tug on her sweaty hand—"What's wrong, Mommy?" But Lindy didn't know what was wrong, and neither did Dr. Birchback, who held his talc-soft finger atop her pulse and said, "Female trouble?" Then he saw himself out, careful not to investigate further—"I'm not that kind of doctor, Mrs. Poore." There was no reason to think that the fever wouldn't simply come and then go, as they do; there was no reason to believe that the open sore where her leg met her hip wouldn't fold itself up and heal. Lindy didn't really know what was happening, and so she wasn't worried. She kept herself from Willis, who in any case heard Dr. Birchback's report of a female malady and stayed away. No, it wasn't until Rosa said "We should see Dr. Freeman" that reality, with all its infectious truth, presented itself to Lindy.

Just as it was doing right now.

And in the July heat wave of 1930, three years into a drought and several years before its end, at the western end of Suicide Bridge, a couple of miles from the Pasadena's gate, Lindy Poore leaned her head against the Gold Bug's steering wheel. Her headache thumped and the sunlight flashed through the combine's canopy and the volumes of Gibbon sat upon the passenger seat and all of her past sat up in her mind, jumbled but there. History presented itself to her as a great dark light behind her eyelids and she looked into it, seeing nothing but sensing everything that had once touched her. The past was there, more firmly rooted than her present life, than this very day, more real than the breath leaving her lungs just now, and then someone was rapping a knuckle on the Gold Bug's window and at first she thought it was the headache but then came the *Hello, hello?,* and for a moment—a tiny moment when her overturned heart uprighted itself—she thought that Bruder was at last free; after all these years, he had come for her, on the other side of the glass.

But the knuckle continued to rap and the blur cleared from her eyes and Lindy looked up and there was Cherry, saying, "Lindy? Are you all right?"

They hadn't seen each other in years, not since Cherry reported on Bruder's trial, and Lindy felt a sudden tenderness for her old friend, someone who had known her before her present life. Lindy told Cherry that she was merely tired, that she had had trouble sleeping in the heat, but Cherry interrupted her, saying, "Lindy, I've seen you driving around town. You haven't looked yourself."

"Myself? What do you mean, Cherry?" She paused. "Have you been following me, Cherry?"

But Cherry denied this, saying she was giving up reporting. "I was worried about you."

Lindy asked why she would give up being a reporter when she had always loved it as much as anything.

"I'm getting married, Lindy."

"Married?"

"To George Nay. Do you know him? He moved to Pasadena a few years back. The real-estate developer? He and Willis are working together on the parkway."

Lindy had only heard Willis sniff at the man's name.

"He told me he wouldn't marry me unless I gave up reporting," said Cherry. "He says it's not a lady's pursuit, writing stories about other people's lives."

"And you're listening to him?"

"George is right. It's a crummy business, living off others. I'm ready to give it up."

Lindy said she didn't understand—and maybe it was because she was feeling dizzy; everything around her was dimming.

"Just one more story, Lindy," said Cherry. She lowered her voice. "One more that I hope will do some good. After that, I'm putting down my pen." Lindy said that she had to get back to her daughter, and Cherry said, "I can tell something's wrong with you, Lindy. You'll let me know if I can help? You'll call me, Lindy?"

Through the glass, Lindy promised that she would.

2

BY AUGUST, many people had left Pasadena for the cooler airs of Santa Barbara or Balboa or La Jolla cove, and those who remained in the city made up their cots and hammocks on their sleeping porches. Cherry's inquiries had startled Lindy—it dismayed her that her old friend could sense her decline—and a week later, Lindy passed through the rancho's gate and drove into town. The sun was hot and she was thirsty, and near the entrance to Suicide Bridge she pulled over at the orange combine. The juice stand was in the shape of a giant navel orange, with a dirty awning, and a radio was playing a song Lindy had heard a trio play at Connie Ringe's the night before. Lindy had danced with Willis by the pool, beneath the pink paper lanterns strung between the oaks. The trio played *My girl with the blue, blue eyes,* and Willis was cold to her touch, but he held her tight and it felt as if he wouldn't let go and then he said, "You haven't seemed yourself lately." She asked what he meant, but then Connie cut in, shooing Willis away, and Lindy swayed in Connie's arms while across the yard Willis pushed himself in a swing in the sycamore. "Everything okay?" Connie said, lifting Lindy's chin with a gloved finger. "I can see you've got the five-year blues." No, Lindy said. It was more than that. "It'll pass," Connie assured her, fox-trotting Lindy around the pool while the man in the coat with the plum-silk lapels sang "Jazz Me, Baby."

The girl behind the counter dropped an orange into a machine and it tumbled down a metal chute and was pushed against a triangular blade, the two halves carried along a conveyor belt to the juicer. The girl asked Lindy if she wanted to try the new orange sherbert: "Tastes like heaven in your mouth." At a picnic table next to the stand, a boy was spooning sherbert into his girl's mouth and she was giggling and swinging her feet and saying, "That's enough, Billy. Okay, stop." But the young man, his broken nose reset crookedly, continued feeding the girl and she kept laughing, her mouth open and her tongue orange and creamy and the sherbert dripping down her throat. "You're too much, Billy!" she was saying, and then: "No, Billy. I mean it this time, please stop. Billy! Stop, it's too much, you're making me sick—" And then a voice: "Ma'am, nothing but the orange soda?" A pause. "Ma'am?"

Lindy parked not far from the Webb House. As they always would, a new crop of girls had moved in, and the two frizzy-haired girls on the porch didn't recognize Lindy Poore when she passed. A year or so ago Mrs. Webb had run into some sort of trouble, something about taking a cut from the girls' wages. There'd been headlines and a picture in the papers of Mrs. Webb in a high-collared cape, and one girl charged her with the often-repeated accusation: "Twentieth-century slavery!" Mrs. Webb no longer ran the home; she was retired, they said, to a cabin outside Avalon, where she tended a herd of wool sheep.

Erwin's had closed at the beginning of the summer. There'd been an EVERYTHING MUST GO sale one afternoon, but no one had turned up, and Mr. Erwin had stood at his door and asked people in from the sidewalk. Two days later, he turned over the sign in the door—CLOSED— and moved to Flagstaff, leaving a display of electric vibratory devices in the window, there to catch the dust and stares. Now the dark window offered Lindy a reflection of herself, thin in a belted dress, her hair recently cut short in a style the hairdresser had called "the Downturn-Do." "It's very *you*, Mrs. Poore. Very, very *you*."

She rang the bell and waited in the hot alley, and then a figure appeared on the other side of the bubble glass, dark and slow. The locks turned and Miss Bishop waved Lindy up the stairs. "He's running late," the nurse said, fiddling with her key ring at the top of the steps. Lindy recalled how heavy Miss Bishop was the first time she had come to Dr. Freeman, but now Miss Bishop was a skeleton swimming in a suit of loose skin. The folds of flesh hung from her like laundry on the line and she looked exhausted, as if scooping up the hems of her skin had worn her out.

Lindy sat on the daybed and Miss Bishop watered the fern, saying, "You're feeling all right?" The same, said Lindy, describing the feverish aches, the fatigue. "Poor you," said Miss Bishop. "Let me check on the doctor." She disappeared behind the bubble-glass door and there was a muffled conversation and then the door opened and Dr. Freeman appeared, asking Lindy to come in. He left the examination room while Lindy undressed. She hung her dress on the coat-tree and sat on the padded table in her slip, the rubber warm against her thighs. Miss Bishop, standing in front of a black-bladed fan, bought on sale at Erwin's closeout, commented on the heat. "I told the doctor to get two," she said, her bangs fluttering. Miss Bishop said that the doctor had been inexplicably busy lately, *tsk*ing about his workload and the stress it put upon him. "He had to cancel his holiday next week," Miss Bishop said, recounting her own vacation plans, a drive down the coast to San Diego, two nights in Tijuana, a third in Ensenada Beach. Miss Bishop had a friend named Molly Pier, and the two rented a bungalow together in Altadena, and they would drive to Mexico and back in Molly's Dodge Delivery. Miss Bishop was going on about needing some sort of special insurance to cross the Mexican border when Dr. Freeman reentered the examining room.

"How've you been, Mrs. Poore?" She said again that she was the same: no better and no worse. "No new symptoms?" She described the headaches and the aches in her joints and the occasional pain in her eye. "Like a needle going through it. It's hard to see at times. The left one." Dr. Freeman looked into her eye with a penlight and made a note.

"You've been taking your bismuth and the salvarsan iodide?"

She said that she had, and she wondered if they had made her feel even worse. Flipping through her file, Dr. Freeman said, "I've given you both arsenics, haven't I?" Lindy nodded yes: arsphenamine and neoarsphenamine administered intravenously, long afternoons on the rubber table with a needle in the crook of her arm and a distant cold sensation running through her. He had administered mercurial rubs, the cold paste massaged into her pores by Miss Bishop, who had worn a blacksmith's apron. Dr. Freeman had put her through fever therapy, two hours baking in a lightbulb-lined coffin called the Electronic Cabinet of Kettering. Dr. Freeman had had an arrangement with Mr. Erwin to rent the cabinet, and when Erwin's closed, Freeman had said he might give up on that particular hyperthermia treatment anyway: "In the end, I'm not sure how much good it does." For almost a year Dr. Freeman had instructed Lindy to soak in near-scalding baths, a habit that Willis had found peculiar and wasteful. From time to time she would fall asleep in the green-glazed tub, waking only when her nose slipped beneath the water.

"Any new lesions?" asked Dr. Freeman.

"Just the one on my thigh." She opened her legs for the doctor and he bent to inspect the rubbery tumor. He pulled a ruler from his pocket and pushed it against Lindy's flesh and said, "Miss Bishop, the gumma is one third of an inch in diameter." Miss Bishop wrote this down, and Lindy leaned back on the examination table and looked to the ceiling as Dr. Freeman poked at the tender lump. She had learned that Dr. Freeman did this sort of work for no other reason than the money, wads and wads of it collecting in his pocket. Once, in an unusual moment of intimacy, Miss Bishop had said, "He's glad he can help out all these girls, but he wouldn't be here if it didn't pay so well. He's earning so much money now, he *can't* walk away." Lindy understood this; she wouldn't be here either. Their lives wouldn't have crossed; how far Dr. Freeman's office, down the little alley, felt from the rancho's gate. It was like traveling forward in time, Lindy sometimes felt when she sat on the velour daybed. She was warm, the moisture sticky beneath her breasts and in the pit of her arms, and then Dr. Freeman asked her to remove all her underclothes and he turned to his chart while she stepped out of the ivory silk; her clothes were in a pile on the floor and it made her think of Sieglinde, who liked to strip down to nothing at the pool. Dr. Freeman's left hand lifted her right arm, and his free hand traced the flesh around her breast. He lifted her left arm and did the same, gently pushing her breasts one way and the other, inspecting the flesh in between. She found the examination neither humiliating nor exciting, only numbing, as if she had stepped out of herself as the doctor pushed her back onto the table, eyeing her, prodding, taking notes, checking her reflexes with a rubber-headed mallet.

After she dressed she returned to the velour daybed, and Dr. Freeman sat behind his desk and Miss Bishop perched on the windowsill, the Webb House's shingled turret behind her. The fan's blades whirred in the black cage and the limp fern fluttered in its gust.

"You've been coming to see me for almost a year," Dr. Freeman began. "I'm afraid we've seen very little progress." He explained his regret, as he had before, that she had not sought treatment when she was first exposed, when the first chancre had erupted on her loin. But Lindy hadn't known, she said, as she said every time she visited Dr. Freeman.

"It looked like nothing more than a few spider bites." He scolded her gently for not looking after herself, lumping her with "all the women who inexplicably fail to do so." Miss Bishop's gaunt face shook, as if she knew that in these matters the doctor lacked insight. The second lesion, eight or nine weeks after the first, had gone unnoticed in the spring of 1925. There had been a fever and a flu-like exhaustion as she watched Edmund's coffin sink into the soil out by the tulip tree, no one there with Lindy except Dieter and Father Pico and Margarita and Cherry Moss, taking notes and eyeing Bruder, who stood fifty feet from the grave, awaiting the deputy sheriff's arrival. Palomar had cried, grabbing at Lindy's hair. And Willis had sent word that he was sending a car to retrieve her. No, she hadn't tended to herself, Lindy admitted to Dr. Freeman. "There wasn't any time." And then, "I didn't know."

"You're entering what we call the early tertiary stage," said Dr. Freeman. "There's now more of a chance the disease will advance from chronic to . . . well, to a more debilitating phase." He said that at this point the spirochetes would concentrate in either her cardiovascular system or her nervous system. "Or both. Cardiovascular syphilis degenerates the aorta and other tissue around the heart; the heart itself too. Neurosyphilis can damage the brain, resulting in—" He stopped, as if wondering if he had already said too much. "I suppose the best way to describe it is personality change. A change of the self. You may be Lindy Poore, but you might act like someone else. Sometimes the patient doesn't recognize herself." He must have seen the bloodless fear in Lindy, because immediately he was stumbling: "But I've seen no signs of this in you, Mrs. Poore. Nothing suggests that your case has turned that particular corner. Everything about you suggests you know quite well who you are."

The daybed was soft, and it nearly swallowed her. She inched herself to its edge and with great effort stood. Once again, the inconsolable doubleness of life hit her: Dr. Freeman's news was at once shocking and expected. All those years ago the red chancre, no more dense or fierce than a boil, had both looked like nothing and alerted her to her future. There were times when Lindy could see the clarity of today and the vision of the rest of her life, like seeing at the same time ten feet in front of the car and the long white strip of the road ahead.

"Why hasn't Willis become ill?"

"I'm sorry, what was that, Mrs. Poore?"

"My husband? Why isn't he sick as well?"

"Your husband? Well, not having examined him, I can't really say. You know for a fact it was he who gave this to you?"

The question shocked her: Who else, if not Willis? There was no one else. Lindy told Dr. Freeman she was sure.

"In that case, sometimes it'll lie latent for years and years," said Dr. Freeman. "There are many who never become sick. It's another one of the disease's great mysteries. Who it chooses, I suppose you could say. Who it singles out." Dr. Freeman led Lindy back to the daybed, settling her against its humped headrest. "I trust you've discussed this with Captain Poore."

She didn't answer, thinking of the night she had gone to Willis, saying, "There's something I need to tell you." He had looked through her, somber with shock and certain of his innocence. He denied that he had known anything about this: "How do you know you didn't get it before? From *him*?" She told him she knew exactly how the spore had first settled in her blood, but Willis demanded that she tell no one: *You haven't told anyone, have you, Lindy? It could ruin us, Lindy. Ruin you!* But who was there to tell? "I don't want to hear you mention it again," Willis had said. "I want to pretend you never told me any of this. I'm going to pretend I've dreamed this and it's a bad dream and now I'm waking up." And he hurried to the sink, where he scrubbed his hands with a wire brush. Long ago, Lindy had learned that she'd married a coward. To expect more of him was to deny this simple, awful truth.

Dr. Freeman returned to the chair behind his desk and said, "Now, Mrs. Poore. If you're willing, I want to try something new." Miss Bishop looked up from Lindy's chart as he said this, as if this was news to her as well. "Mayo is reporting success with malarial treatment. The reports are promising." He continued, "It's a form of fever therapy. You come in, and I'll give you an intravenous inoculation of five to ten milliliters of malarial blood." Dr. Freeman explained that she would become ill with chills and fevers and eventually go into a febrile convulsion. "It runs in cycles, a convulsion every two or three days. Optimally I'd want you to undergo ten or twelve convulsions, and then I'd abort the attacks by administering quinine." He added, "You'd be sick on and off for a little more than a month."

Lindy leaned into the daybed. She would continue to bear this alone. Not out of shame but because she had no choice—the same way when, years ago, she hadn't wanted anyone to know that she could bleed. She wasn't yet thirty and refused to become an invalid. Yet more acutely, she refused to admit that there'd been a mistake; that perhaps *she* had made a mistake. After Sieglinde was born she had returned to the room with the canopy bed, and for a year or two Willis would knock on her door late at night when he wanted her. He was always polite, asking if she minded. And at first she didn't mind, his fingers kneading away the loneliness, releasing the longing. But it had been a long time now since he'd kissed her, and Lindy hoped, the velour soft on her cheek, that he would never try again. From time to time she liked to close her eyes and imagine herself as a young girl in the grove, a fisher-girl graduated to the orchard, with her life ahead of her, a future unfurled; but it was no longer true. What was it Lolly had said when they were in Dodsworth's last week? "You've become just like the rest of us, Lindy. Most people can hardly believe you weren't born in Pasadena."

"Mrs. Poore?" Dr. Freeman was saying. "Mrs. Poore?"

Lindy shook herself back to this August day, to the office above the alley.

"I'd like to begin right away," said Dr. Freeman. "Next week." Miss Bishop flipped the appointment book and proposed a time. "Will that be all right, Mrs. Poore?"

"What?"

"Can you come back next week? You'll have to make some arrangements in advance. You'll be out of sorts for the month. Can you do that, Mrs. Poore?" The voices trailed away, and Lindy saw in the window's reflection that she had misbuttoned her blouse. She fixed it, but the reflection was of someone else; was it really she? Another woman stared back, pocketbook hooked over wrist, hair cut and pinned in place, mouth grave and expressionless, and something came for Lindy, a large gentle hand, and led her through the office door and down the stairs and into the alley, where the sun reflected off the garbage canisters, and past Erwin's empty window, and the exhaust from the traffic rose around her and Lindy found herself behind the wheel of the Gold Bug, the seat scalding, the dash burning her fingertips. In the heat wave that had spilled from July into August and would burn toward September a fever came on its own to Lindy; she was damp with sweat and her eyes

3

HE FOLLOWED HER, through the hills and to the overgrown gate, and in the rearview mirror Lindy watched Bruder, and she thought of those evenings years before when they would return together to the ranch, she in the wagon and he in the truck behind her. But Bruder, his hair wired with gray and a deep frown carved around his mouth, now appeared as if more than five years had passed. His skin had darkened and coarsened, and his beard was dense and woolly, and he looked uncomfortable in his suit. He was visoring out the sun with his hand, but he couldn't take his eyes off the Gold Bug's rounded back and the sight of Lindy's dark hair above the driver's seat. She glided the car up through the curvy hills, and the sun seeped through the live-oaks, their trunks nearly encased in pavement. He knew that she was thinking that he looked older, but the same was true of her, although her beauty remained. A part of him had expected it to have faded by now—she'd pressed her face too close to the sun—and it would have been easier for him to return to Pasadena if she'd thickened in the middle and her posture had sagged under the life she'd chosen. She was thin, he noted—Cherry had alerted him to that—but the contrasting beauty was there: black, beautiful eyes darting fast in a somber face.

But Bruder had come to Pasadena not to pursue what he'd already lost, and he shook the longing from his mind, a shiver traveling down his spine.

Lindy's hands were trembling on the wheel; it was like seeing a ghost. She had assumed that she wouldn't meet him for another fifteen years—if ever. She had assumed that by the time he emerged from the gates of San Quentin and ferried across the bay to the railroad station and then traveled south, she would be old and Bruder would be old too. She had assumed that all those cruel cold years would snuff the final flicker of desire, and that it would be safe to greet her former lover in her husband's house, and the two would share a memory of twenty years before—there's nothing as harmless as a tempered memory, thought Lindy. But she'd been wrong, for here Bruder was right now, holding his hand up to blot out the sun, and she wondered if he'd bought the seersucker suit to impress her. Had he escaped, had there been a riot, prisoners digging to freedom with coffee spoons? A secret swim across San Francisco Bay, his head in the water as black and slick as a harbor seal's?

And in the Pierce-Arrow, Bruder knew that she was turning over the possibilities of how he'd come to arrive in Pasadena. He couldn't see her face, but he knew; just as he knew that the reason for his freedom was the one reason she'd never suspect.

Lindy got out of the car and opened the iron gate, a cloud of yellow dust rising, veiling her, but through it she could see him, and he never lost sight of her, of the whites of her eyes peering out. The sun was hot and Lindy's headache remained, but the fatigue that had mounted in her the past several weeks was receding. She thought that if she had to, she could run up the hill—all the way to the great lawn and the loggia—and her blood was racing. And she thought it would be fun if the two of them left the cars at the gate and ran up the hill together, and she imagined their chests rising and falling with panting breath, and she imagined their hands clasping as she slowed before the lawn, and she imagined the great heat each of them would cast upon the other and she imagined the smell of sweat, the musk of a working heart.

She was standing next to her car dreaming of all this when the Pierce-Arrow's door opened and Bruder got out: "Linda? Are you all right?"

"Lindy."

Bruder cocked his chin.

"They call me Lindy now."

"Lindy?"

"Lindy Poore." Bruder got back into the Pierce-Arrow and yanked the door shut. Her daydream collapsed upon itself, and she got back in her own car and they drove up the switchbacks, like any two cars in traffic. Her radio lost reception at the turn just before the hillcrest. She drove around the brittle summer lawn with no sound but the wind flushing through the car and the grind of the Pierce-Arrow behind her. As she approached the house, she felt the tent of her soul collapse with disappointment: Willis and Lolly would be on the loggia, listening to music and reading the newspapers, the children playing at their feet. Already Lindy felt duplicitous, and she grew quietly angry at Willis for making her feel this way. Her husband would be alarmed that she had brought a fugitive to the house; Lolly would blanch with fear, a balled hand fluttering upon her breast. They had always found Lindy reckless; "My girl of the Wild West," Willis would say. "I pulled her off the frontier," he would proclaim, shuddering at the thought of what California had once been, and comforting himself by what it had become, what it was on its way to becoming. They say that the only constant in California is its rapid rate of change, and Willis had tried to track down who had said it first, but he hadn't found the answer; the researcher over at the Romanesque library on Walnut called back with an unspecific response: "My guess is they've been saying it since long before the Spanish arrived, Captain Poore." Nonetheless, Willis would use the quote in his next presentation about the proposed parkway.

Now, as Lindy approached the house in her car, she feared her husband's reaction to Bruder. Willis would study Lindy as she talked to Bruder; he would note that she hadn't smiled in months and that now, on this afternoon in early August, her cheer had returned, her shoulders pulled back and her head leaning in to listen to her visitor. Lolly would coo and fan herself and look at the man through her fingers; she would rise from her chair and turn and offer a silhouette so thin in crêpe de chine that one might wager she wasn't even there, or was merely a delicate pillar of bones held together by translucent flesh. She weighed only eighty-five pounds, and Lindy had heard the screams behind the bathroom door when the round-faced scale told Lolly that a new pound of flesh had latched on to her fragile pile. Lindy had seen Lolly's lips seal upon themselves as the platter of *filet de boeuf au jus* moved around the table. Now Lindy imagined Lolly offering Bruder a lemonade and a licorice stick, and she and Willis would inspect him as if he were a delivery man from Model's.

But Lindy couldn't anticipate what Bruder would do. She still didn't know what he was entitled to. She didn't know that the scrap of paper with Willis's written last will and testament was in an envelope in Bruder's breast pocket; she didn't know that it was all he had arrived at prison with, and that it was the only thing they'd returned to him when he departed last week.

She drove the Gold Bug through the *porte cochère,* and there they were, her family: Willis in a fan-backed chair and Lolly on the swinging bench, one foot hooked beneath her. She was reading and he was examining papers and they had a soft, clayish appearance in the heat. The children were building a house of wood blocks, and Sieglinde was insisting that Pal didn't know the correct way to erect a barn. Lindy had never felt it so distinctly, but the sensation pulsed through her that she did not belong to her family. They were strangers, except her daughter, and her heart felt what a heart feels for a stranger—very little beyond common compassion. Did Lindy feel even this? No, she felt even less for those who had become her own. She tried to stamp out the embers of this smoldering pitilessness, but she failed. Every now and then we stop loving those whom we love, she told herself, Bruder's face still filling her rearview mirror. Love isn't constant, it skips across a gap—does it not? She thought so, knowing also that more than once she had failed to navigate those bottomless ravines. In the mirror was Bruder, but it might as well have been her entire past, a memory sailing from one edge of the mind's sea to the other. He'd come in a new seersucker suit, but he'd brought everything with him, every last memory.

When Willis saw Lindy, his face folded grimly upon itself. Lolly lifted her head and waved childishly and the Arcadia orange trees planted in the porcelain saki barrels were so sweet in the heat that their perfume caused Lindy to gag, and she didn't stop the car but continued to steer through the pillars and past the house, down the other side of the hill to the ranch. She didn't wait to see her family's reaction to who was following her, and she sped along and Bruder remained behind her, the Pierce-Arrow clearing the pillars by a few inches and then emerging free from the *porte cochère,* and both cars gathered speed down the hard dirt road into the valley where summer sat in a haze.

They parked beneath the pepper tree and Linda got out of her car and Bruder slammed his door and the afternoon was silent, the grove dry and aching, the leaves parched and crisp, the irrigation ditches dead, the sun flashing off the packinghouse's corrugated roof. Through the haze the mansion appeared white and faraway in a smudged white sky. "Nothing's changed," said Bruder.

And she said he was wrong.

He inspected himself and shrugged, as if excusing the suit and the tonicked hair. He had his reasons, and they didn't have anything to do with Lindy, not anymore. He reminded himself of this each time the wind lifted her hair and pressed it against her throat, each time her face opened up and she said, "I don't believe you're here."

She asked where he'd come from and he said Condor's Nest and she said she didn't understand. "I sold a couple of acres and bought myself a suit and a car," he said, and again Lindy didn't know what he was telling her. There'd been no word since the wadded apron arrived in the mail more than five years before. She'd written him two, maybe three times, but each letter was returned unopened, stamped REJECTED BY PRISONER. Over the years, whenever she read in the newspaper an item about San Quentin—another convict sent away for life—a precise vision would press upon her of Bruder in a colorless jumpsuit standing alone in a bleak yard, fingers curled through a fence, the clear, blank sunlight bringing a permanent squint to his eyes. He would be looking to the bay and the yawning mouth of Golden Gate, where the sea lions paddled with silver fish in their mouths. On some days she did her best not to think of him, but she almost always failed, and there was a terribleness to what she had done, or hadn't done. Yet hadn't she seen what she had seen, and what she hadn't seen? Hadn't she testified as precisely as she could? And she reassured herself that she hadn't chosen Edmund over Bruder; no, she had chosen the truth, or what she knew of the truth. But even as the years in Pasadena had passed, and especially in the 109-degree summers when it was hard to think plainly at all, Lindy never forgot that Bruder had testified after her. She hadn't been there, but Cherry had told her afterward: he took the stand and he was wearing a tie for the first time in his life and he told a story of Edmund's eyeglasses flying from his face and his tripping over a lobster pot and the mallet twirling in the night sky. He carefully recounted his version, but it was too late: the jury had reached its conclusion even before he laid his hand atop the court's warped Bible. "If this is the case, then why didn't Mrs. Poore tell us about it yesterday?" Mr. Ivory had asked. He was a man with fleshy ears that had made Lindy think of a hound's, and his quivering nostrils too, and what else could have happened that night other than what she thought she saw, and what the jury had agreed she must have seen? She had come to realize that Edmund and Bruder had always been destined to destroy each other, each in his own way, each to remove the other from her life. All in one night her path to the rancho's gate had been cleared. And now it all felt like fate—as the inevitable always does. It now felt as if she'd never lived anywhere else; as if Edmund and Bruder were men she had read about in a book pulled from Willis's library or selected for her by Mr. Raines at Vroman's— characters who remained in her head through her dreams and who felt more real than anyone she knew in Pasadena. Real because they weren't real, not anymore. And yet, look there now, here was Bruder circling the ranch house, Panama hat in hand . . . And oh, Lindy, Lindy! Why were you saddled with the burden to never really know the men around you? To never really know yourself?

"You're free," she said. She said she didn't understand what had happened—hadn't the sentence been for twenty years?—and the fever in her hips caused Lindy to wince. Did Bruder see it, her creased eyes? Yes, for he came to her and said, "I've been back at Condor's Nest almost a week."

She wondered if he knew that earlier in the summer she had thievishly visited the farm, lurking in the yard and stealing memories? Had her fingers left prints in the dust on the knobs? Prints waiting for him as he returned? He didn't say. Instead, he spoke of catching a barracuda almost five feet long, and of the lobster pots he had mended and returned to the ocean floor. He asked where she had sent Dieter. "I want to bring him home," Bruder said, and she wondered if his voice held an accusation within it.

They were standing next to each other and a watery sensation passed through Lindy, as if Bruder were transferring something to her; as if he were a spirit passing through her. She felt something brush against her arm, but when she looked it wasn't Bruder, who was two feet away, next to her but a small, treacherous gap away from her. She felt the pull and the resistance at once. She felt her heart rise high in her chest like a turnip-shape buoy lifted by a wave; she felt her pulse working. For the first time she feared he might find her silly. "Silly woman," Willis would say about Ellie Sickman or Connie Ringe or even Lolly; "Don't be silly, Lindy," Willis would say. It was an insult Lindy would fight off with fists upon her husband's lapel, but from Bruder it might simply crush her, its crinkle of truth.

"How did you come here?"

The ranch-house door opened and soon Hearts and Slaymaker were shaking hands with Bruder and slapping his back and they were standing close to each other, their arms folded against their chests as they were congratulating him for busting out.

"You're living proof that truth is freedom," said Slaymaker.

"I told you you should've never left us," said Hearts. Time had touched him kindly in his lanky frame. But age had fallen swiftly upon Slaymaker, whose hair had whitened like sagebrush gone dry. The flesh around his throat had continued to pile up, his jowls sloppy, but his eyes remained blue and clear. Over the years Hearts would say, "It's all in his eyes. I see straight through them, all the way down." Now both men said that it was nothing but hard luck for a man to be thrown in like that, only to have the truth pull him back out five years later—and that's five years too late, said Hearts. The two hands were jumping up and down, so excited were they to see their old foreman; and Hearts and Slaymaker confessed that they had missed Bruder, though they knew Bruder well enough not to hope for a similar confession in return.

Hearts pulled the newspaper from his pocket and said, "We were reading it just now in the afternoon edition. I read it and ran across the groves to tell Slay."

"I thought someone was dead the way he was running after me, waving the paper. He had it folded up like he was about to hit an old dog, and he was saying, 'You'll never believe it! You'll never believe it!' "

"I don't think I'd have believed it if you weren't right here," said Hearts, and he tossed the paper onto the table, and it opened as if on its own, and on the back page was a story by Cherry Moss—she had abandoned the "Chatty Cherry" moniker sometime last year—with the headline:

CONVICTION OVERTURNED; JAILED MAN FREED

There wasn't a picture, only two columns of newsprint, and Lindy brought the newspaper to her face and began to understand. She was shaking and the paper was blurry before her and there was a moment when her eyes wouldn't focus—as if she didn't know how to read and the letters didn't fit together into words—but then she blinked and understood.

"Can you believe it? The tide was going out, not coming in," said Hearts. "Leave it to Cherry."

That wasn't the whole story, but they didn't say anything else. Lindy read the newspaper in silence, and when she was done she said, "You've been free for a week?"

"What was the first thing you did?" asked Hearts.

"Did you take the ferry into the city and drink yourself down?" asked Slay.

"I would've rented me a fancy hotel room," said Hearts, "with sheets starched harder than ice, and gone to sleep for three days."

"I would've taken the bus out to Sunset Beach," said Slay. "Stripped down to nothing and gone for a swim, just to feel myself as free as a fish."

"What'd you do, Bruder?"

"I went home."

Hearts and Slaymaker nodded, this made sense to them—except that by now the old ranch house at the Pasadena was their only home.

"Everything okay around here while I was gone?" Bruder asked. His eye cast about the property.

But Hearts and Slaymaker told Bruder that everything hadn't been okay since he'd left. There was plenty of talk of running the motor parkway up the valley, and Willis seemed more interested in concrete than citrus. The recent winters had been dry, and everything was brown and dead in that California way—when everyone gives up hope of life ever pushing through the cracked earth again. After a few years of drought it was hard to imagine a river in the riverbed, or a carpet of grass upon the foothills, or the delicate gold cup of a poppy. For the first time in as long as anyone could remember, the mountains had gone without snow, their spines patchy and pale like a half-starved dog. The spring's runoff had trickled down the arroyo, murky and slow. "I could piss more than that," Slaymaker said. "Go up to Devil's Gate," said Hearts. "Take a look at the reservoir. This city's living on its last gulp. Everything's gone to hell since you were sent away."

They were dutiful men, Hearts and Slaymaker, but they were like many others in the San Gabriel Valley, living high when the winters were wet, and then living drowned when the waters flooded the canyons, and then, once again, scraping hard when the winters dried up. Their memory was deep but imprecise, and in the years of rain they forgot the cycle of drought, and in the long, skinny years of drought they scratched their heads and forgot that the mountain springs had ever spurted their ice water. Of course, many men had grown accustomed to the burbling waters ferried along miles of concrete from the Owens Valley, but Hearts and Slaymaker remained suspicious, certain that one day a great hand from above would reach down and turn off the faucet. That water, white as foam, had never seemed to belong to them, running to Los Angeles and charged for like motor fuel at the pump, and Willis Poore never liked buying his water from a stranger in another county. No, he had his land, and his men, Hearts and Slay, would draw from the wells. "When the last one dries up, boys, it's time to go home," Willis would say. It was a joke because Willis never believed that his wells would dry up, not all of them; he didn't believe because he was certain that his father, dead so many years now, would never have picked out a bum tract of land. But by the summer of 1930 the wells echoed and the water trickled up, a pathetic dribble barely strong enough to wash the worry from the eyes of Hearts and Slay.

Bruder left them, walking off into the grove, and soon Lindy followed. She didn't know what she should say, what she should offer just then. If Cherry's story was true, did it mean that the version Lindy had delivered was false? It didn't make any sense, and yet here Bruder was, corroborating the report: a prisoner freed, a conviction overturned, a ruling thrown out. Lindy's word had been held up to the light and discarded as useless. Something in Cherry's article had stuck out: "Mrs. Willis Poore had testified against Mr. Bruder, but even she, according to transcripts, once admitted that the night had been too dark to see, as she had put it, 'what was what, who was who.' "

"The ranch is too quiet," said Bruder. "What's been going on here?"

She didn't understand why he was so interested in the ranch's well-being, but she told him about how three years ago Willis had shut the packinghouse, handing the whole operation over to the Growers Exchange. The hands no longer lived on the ranch for the season; instead, there were day pickers whose heavy field boxes were trucked immediately to the co-operative's packinghouse in Burbank. "I begged him not to close it," Lindy said. "I told him to think of the girls. What would happen to them? He said it wasn't up to him to feed every girl in the San Gabriel Valley."

"He's right. You can't run a ranch on sentiment."

"The girls came to me, every last one of them, and asked for jobs cleaning floors or sewing hems or preparing the baby's dinner. But I could hire only Esperanza. Now she sleeps in the room next to Rosa and helps Lolly with Palomar."

But Bruder showed no interest in the fate of the girls. He inspected the groves in a way that made him look both official and coldhearted. He turned an early orange in his hand and with his deer-foot knife peeled its rind into one long coil. The orange was skimpy and hard and dry, and Bruder frowned. He lifted a tree's skirt of branches and kicked the soil around the roots. The deeper they walked into the grove, the more he shook his head. Lindy wondered what he was doing and why he had returned to Pasadena to examine the orchards; he seemed more interested in their health than in hers. She wondered what he had learned about her life over the years. What news had traveled through the prison gate? Did he know, for instance, about Sieglinde's difficult birth? The evil scream that all of Pasadena had heard—or so it seemed, from the way people continued to whisper of it? No, Lindy thought, he couldn't know about that, for if he had, he would have written her. She took comfort in this, even if it wasn't true. Nothing had come as promised, but Lindy had to acknowledge that there had never actually been any ribbons of promise, only those tied up in her mind. It was hard to accept that she was no different from any other woman, that her fate was common and forever repeated. But Bruder's return—his hand grazing the sleeve of her blouse just now!—suggested that maybe this wasn't the case. Just maybe, it wasn't too late to defy her future. Just maybe, Bruder was concocting a plan to help her run from the inexorable path! Something was turning behind his eyes.

But oh! how wrong she was when she thought she was capable of reading Bruder's mind. He was planning nothing for Lindy at all. When he was thinking clearly and coldly and with both eyes cast solely upon his future, he thought of her only as one more obstacle between him and that which he was owed. There were times when the cold calculation melted away, and Bruder's heart warmed with fond memories like that of any other man. But now he struggled against those lapses, wrestled them to the ground.

They walked toward the mausoleum. The trees growing up into the foothills had weakened in the last two years, the top branches skeletal, the lower ones producing less and less fruit. Willis had sprayed for whitefly and aphid and citrus mite and melanose, and the sulfur had left the fruit with a rusty burn. The six or so acres around the mausoleum were in decline, half-dead trees rimming the marble temple. Bruder pulled a leaf from one of these trees and rubbed it between his fingers, and the orange oil smelled sharp.

"You know what he's got, don't you?" said Bruder.

She shook her head, thinking that perhaps Bruder was speaking about her: what Willis had in a wife like Lindy. She had always been loyal to him, as loyal to Willis as she'd been to Edmund—and loyal to Bruder, in her own way. But how do you consider the mind's wandering, and the fluttering heart? Loyal in the most technical sense, to be precise. Again she thought of the lesson she had come to understand: Love can come and it can go and it can return. No one can love someone the same amount every single day. Was this true? Lindy could only hope; she had to believe in it, for hadn't she lived by it, even without knowing it at the time? Yes, she could rely only on the truth of the rising and falling commitment of the heart, for if this wasn't true, and she was the exception, then she would have to acknowledge that which everyone struggles to deny: that her own heart lay in her chest slightly blacker than the rest.

"Spreading decline," said Bruder. He sat on the mausoleum steps and sealed his eyes. She asked him what he meant. He explained that the nematode had burrowed into this part of the grove. "It eats away the small roots, cutting off the food supply. The trees die slowly over the years." The spreading decline, he said again. "You've got it." He said this with a greater concern than she would expect from him; and Lindy took this as a promising sign. She asked what could be done. "Nothing. Cut the trees down. Burn the soil." The burrowing nematode didn't attack an entire grove, he said. Just swaths, leaving gashes of dead trees across an orchard.

"Why wouldn't Willis have known about it?"

"Maybe he did." And then he startled her by saying, "You're happy, I suppose."

She didn't answer.

"You don't look happy," he added.

"After all this time, do you really think you're capable of recognizing my happiness?"

"You might not recognize it yourself, Lindy."

His abruptness hurt her and she recoiled and again she wondered why he had come to see her. She was expecting tenderness from him, and an illicit arm about her waist. Instead he said, "Pasadena suits you, I see." His voice was soft but accused her of falsehood and she said, "It's my home now."

He asked after Lolly, and Lindy said she hadn't changed. "She's a little too watchful over Palomar."

"She probably loves the boy," said Bruder. "Loves him as if he were her own—in a way that you can't." This insight surprised Lindy, as if he knew everything about their lives. "Maybe more than you love him." Lindy said that she loved Palomar, that she had done much more for the boy than most people realized. "That's not who I mean," said Bruder.

If not Palomar, then who? "Willis?" she said, but Bruder stopped her and said, "You didn't tell the truth."

"I told them what I knew. What I saw."

"You saw only half of it."

"I saw what I saw." And then, "What happened that night?"

"You read it yourself in Cherry's article."

"Tell me," she said.

He paused because he wasn't sure he wanted to tell her; he thought that maybe she deserved to know about it only from the paper, like everyone else. But for five years, hadn't he thought about this? Every night, as he lay atop his bunk in his cell, he imagined the day he'd see Linda again and tell her he hadn't killed her brother. He imagined their reunion; he imagined her tears; he saw himself cuffing her flinging wrists. He practiced the words: "And didn't each of them want to kill me? Each for his own reasons?" Linda would ask who he was talking about, and Bruder, as he imagined it, would say, "First Willis, then Dieter, and finally poor, bumbling Edmund."

And so Bruder launched into his version of the story that Lindy had gotten so terribly wrong.

"I was down on the beach," he said.

"I saw you. Why were you there?"

"Why are you only asking that now? Things might have been different if you'd asked a long time ago."

His voice was grave and his eyes intense upon her, but she wasn't frightened.

"Why were you there that night?"

"Your brother was a vengeful man."

"What makes you say that?"

"He hated me."

"Can you blame him?"

"He was intent on destroying the farm. But he wasn't any good at plotting destruction. Except his own."

"Did you come here to tell me this?"

"I came here to see the ranch, to see what trouble has surely sprouted here."

"None, I should say."

"Are you sure, Lindy?" He reached for her hand, but she recoiled and held it to her chest; it felt like all those years ago, when she was a girl and had struggled to understand what sort of man Bruder was. "As I was saying, what you don't know about your brother was that he spent the last days of his life trying to destroy Condor's Nest. He sprinkled the onion field with lye and tried to set a fire in the arroyo but couldn't get the sagebrush to catch—everything was too green in March. It was a series of desperate acts: snapping the fishing poles over his knee and releasing the hens onto the road and shoveling manure down the well. He thought I didn't know what he was doing but I watched, slowly deciding when I would catch him and maybe hang him or just throw him off the farm once and for all. I know you thought he was an intelligent man, Lindy, but he wasn't. No matter how much he read, he learned very little. There are men like that, I'm sure you know. Lessons of history do not hold."

Lindy said that she wasn't going to listen to this, but Bruder said that she would—*You won't get up and leave, you never could, Linda*—and he was right, she stayed at his side. "You want to know," he said. "You should know the truth."

Bruder continued: "He thought of himself as a secret agent, sabotaging the harvest and destroying the tools. Earlier that day, while you were in the cottage with the boy, he paddled the outrigger to the buoy and cut the pot warp."

"Why?"

"No good reason. Just to make sure your old pots never trapped another lobster."

"It doesn't make any sense," said Lindy.

"None." And then: "Except it does."

"How do I know you aren't lying?"

"Because I'd never treat you as you've treated me." She began to protest, but Bruder stopped her, continuing with his story. "Earlier in the evening the lobster pots washed up in Cathedral Cove, and I was down on the beach collecting them. They were your pots, Lindy. Your craftsmanship deserves my praise. Over the years, with a few repairs, they remained finely constructed. At the time, I remember thinking that at last you had ceased to surprise me, but that night you managed to do it again, your handiness with mallet and nail and wood slat apparent and estimable. And that was my mistake—you see, I freely admit to my own mistakes. It was my mistake to think you could no longer surprise me. But you had a few left in you, didn't you, Lindy?"

"A few what?"

"Let me finish, Mrs. Poore." Their few happy months working together—she in the kitchen, he in the groves—had come to feel like a large wedge of history, longer than the skimpy weeks they actually were. "They were perfectly good pots and they had washed up on beds of kelp. Six of them had surfaced at Cathedral Cove, and I stacked them atop one another near the mouth of the cave. All of this I told the jury, but they weren't inclined to believe me, were they, Lindy? I was down there doing the work of a fisherman, no more or less, and it was then that I heard your brother, yelling and running toward me.

"As you've been so careful to point out, Lindy, it was a dark night, darker than most on the beach, as if the great iridescent light in the ocean had been switched off. I heard Edmund, heard the strange calls and the nervous yell of a man who does not yell naturally. I even saw the wink of something metal in his hand, but what it was I had no idea. I stood near the stack of lobster pots, and I want you to imagine what six lobster pots stacked more than six feet high might look like on a dark beach. Do you have any idea, Lindy? They look like nothing. Nothing?, you ask. That's right, nothing. The slats black, and the gaps between the slats black too, and you can see through a lobster pot, just as you can see through a barred window. But that's something I would know about, not you, Mrs. Poore.

"I stood and waited for your brother and I didn't know why he was so angry, why his mission had gone from secret to overt, but he ran toward me and it was no more frightening than watching an old dog lumber to your heel. I waited for him. It was too dark to see his face but he was yelling things about me and you—and only you, Lindy, know if he was right or wrong.

"Edmund was running with the mallet and there was only a second to realize what he was about to do before he was doing it. I saw his eyeglasses fly off his face but this didn't slow him, he continued his charge, just as a bull will run into a blade. The next thing I knew your brother had leapt atop a boulder and was jumping toward me, the mallet raised. Only then did it occur to me that he was trying to kill me, but this seemed laughable enough and then, together, both Edmund and I realized that he had made two grave errors. The first was small, and not necessarily fatal. The boulder he was propelling himself from was covered with rubbery Pacific laver, and he lost his footing, causing him to leap with much less arc than I imagine he had planned. The other error was more ghastly, however. You see, only when his foot was leaving the slippery rock did he see the nearly invisible stack of lobster pots between him and me, and by then his body was hurtling and he did not land on me but on them. The crack was like an iceberg breaking free from its translucent blue shelf.

"The lobster pots, which I'd just been admiring for their construction, broke beneath him, and Edmund was thrown several feet toward the mouth of the cave. And even more surprising, both to Edmund and to me, was that the mallet had sprung from his grip and was flying up and up, twenty, then thirty, feet into the air, stopping and suspending itself in the night for a brief long moment. Up there it winked, its violence as distant as a star's. Then it began to fall, head over grip, boomeranging down, faster and faster, and as it passed me I tried to snag it but I couldn't although I want to emphasize that I tried, hence the fingerprint. But before anything else could happen, its head sank into the temple of your brother."

"Why didn't you tell the court this?"

"I did. But they'd already listened to you. Don't you remember the picture Mr. Ivory showed you? The driftwood?"

Linda said she remembered everything about it.

"It was your pots broken to a thousand pieces by your brother."

"I told Mr. Ivory I didn't know what it was. How could I know that, Bruder?"

"Don't you remember Mr. Ivory insisting it was driftwood brought in by the tide *after* Edmund was killed? Do you remember that, Lindy? Do you?"

She said she did.

"Cherry proved he was wrong."

"How did she know?"

"She came to visit me and she asked. She's a good reporter. Half-truths never stopped her. She went to the police archives and found the film shot by the officer sent out from Oceanside. Remember him? His freckled nose twitching at the sight of the night flies landing on the fatal wound? Shielding himself with his camera. Taking pictures up and down the beach and asking only you, never me, 'Now, what happened here?' You do remember him, don't you, Lindy? Cherry sent the film out to be blown up. When the pictures came back they showed the body, which proved nothing new, and the mallet, also useless, and the ocean—beautiful, but not helpful. But one picture was of a pile of split-up wood. 'Why are you showing me that old picture of driftwood?' said the prosecutor when Cherry took it to his office. She didn't have to say anything. In her head already she was writing her article: *Dear Reader: Do you remember the story of death on the beach from five years ago? . . .*

"Then Cherry produced a tidal report from the spring of 1925. It turns out that when Edmund was killed, the tide was going out, not coming in. That wood didn't wash up after he died. It was already there. Right in Edmund's path. And when they studied the enlarged picture again, both Cherry and Mr. Ivory saw the eyeglasses in the pile, and the driftwood now looked like nothing but broken-up lobster pots."

Lindy and Bruder remained on the mausoleum steps for a long time, and the wind descended the foothills and shook the dying trees. Their scent of citrus was sharp but faint, overwhelmed by the husklike odor of parched ranchland. Leaves whirled about the pillars, blown at the base of the tomb.

"I understand you haven't been well," said Bruder.

Was this why he'd come? To inquire about her health? Had he driven from far away, his foot on the pedal heavy with concern for her?

"Who told you?"

"Cherry. All she said was, something's wrong."

Lindy rested her grateful cheek upon his shoulder. "Is it why you're here?" She was prepared to describe the fevers and the lesions and the shameful pain in her loins.

"I came to look in after the ranch," he said. "I heard it was dwindling by the day."

His cruelty mixed with kindness startled her, and she failed to see the pattern of his heart. She was as blind to it as Edmund, forever losing his spectacles, had been to the world. She pulled away from Bruder and moved to stand, but her body didn't follow, her joints sore and the headache's tide coming in. She meant to rise and walk away but she remained on the steps at his side. A space no more than a foot separated them but the air felt as flinty as a stone wall. "I thought you came to see me," she said.

Why, oh why can't we understand that the heart both loves and repels at once? Lindy and Bruder were sitting close, but they might as well have been separated by the ocean. Bruder steeled himself against feeling anything, a skill he was on his way to perfecting. And Lindy felt the blade of old love. The August sun burned against the Yule marble and silhouetted the leafless branches in the dying trees. Then a rustle rose in the grove, footsteps in the soil, and someone approached the mausoleum.

"Lindy?" Willis called.

His face flushed and his chest was heaving. "Lindy," he said. "Please come to the house at once. Sieglinde was looking for you. So was I."

Lindy rose and moved to her husband, and when she looked over her shoulder Bruder was gone.

Later, next to Willis on the stairs, Lindy said: "Why do you always have to behave like that?" Her husband said nothing as he inspected her, as if he hoped to find a slip of paper pinned to her dress that would explain her. She watched him, eyes dull and flecked with gold, and she saw a man at a loss; but she was at a loss too.

"I thought you were happy," he said.

"I'd be happier if you treated Mr. Bruder as you'd treat any other guest of mine."

His face fell, a tremor in the chin. "You don't see yourself the way I do, Lindy. Even a mirror can't show you your burning cheek. You don't know it's there, but I see it. And he saw it too."

"What did he see?" Willis attempted to rest his hand on her, but she shrugged him off. "You don't know him," she said.

"But I do, Lindy. It's you who doesn't know him." And then: "Please don't see him again."

"I can't say whether or not he'll come to visit." She said this not knowing that Bruder wouldn't return to the Pasadena for years and years—and then, in fact, only to close it down and sell it off. Despite their conversation, Lindy thought he still might return for her.

"If you love me, you won't see him again."

"If he shows up at the door, I can hardly turn him away."

"You can."

"But I won't."

"No, I know you won't."

From the nursery, Sieglinde called for Lindy. She was crying, thirsty from the heat, and Lindy thought of her daughter's fists rubbing her eyes, her hair in moist curls around her ears. "Mommy!"

"The baby," said Lindy. Dusk was approaching, the yellow light framing the stalks of cypress outside the window. Willis opened it, and they heard the trickle of the dolphin fountain and the clang of copper pans in the kitchen. Sieglinde cried again, and Lindy looked up the stairs, telling her husband that she must go. There were others who needed her: that's what her face relayed to her husband. She didn't mean it, but long ago her heart had been quartered and divided among a few. Once, she had assumed that her love could continue to blossom from her heart's bloody bulb, one red-faced flower after another, pressing upon the world a weeping bouquet of love; love as endless as spring feels on an April night, when white flowers shawled the orange trees; enough for everyone. But that was long ago.

"Mommy!"

"I wish she wouldn't scream like that."

"Mommy, I'm thirsty."

And then from the room across the hall came Pal's bristly voice: "Lolly! Lolly, come tell her to shut up!" The children began to scream at each other from their bedrooms.

Lindy moved up the stairs. She felt her husband falling away as she climbed the steps, the chandelier's treelike shadow cast across his face. She mounted the steps slowly, her knees wobbly, the flare in her hip, the red weltish chancre dense with pain, a pain that prescribed her future, and as she reached the top Lolly pushed by Lindy, a blur of skirt and tightly wound hair, and she was calling, "I'm coming! Pal, I'll be right there!"

4

BUT BRUDER DIDN'T RETURN to see Lindy: no letter in the mail, the telephone in the cabin beneath the stairs silent, the bell at the gate dead and rusted over. She asked Rosa if she'd heard anything. "Only that he's taken a bungalow at the Vista." Cherry said she'd spotted Bruder around Pasadena, at the Midwick tennis courts, in the window of the bakery, seeing a matinee at Clune's. "And he's not always alone."

"Who's he with?"

"Now, Lindy, I thought I told you I've given up reporting gossip. That was another me. Another Cherry."

One afternoon, Lindy and Lolly drove the children out past Devil's Gate, where the water sat low and black in the reservoir. At the trailhead the children ran ahead, their little feet scaring lizards into holes. Lolly, equipped with silk parasol and goatskin canteen, marched up the path. The children were out of sight, but Lindy could hear Sieglinde's peevish squeals and Pal's gentle laugh. Lolly seemed to be energetically sulking over something, and at first Lindy was curious about her sister-in-law's vigor: the parasol beating the evergreen out of the path.

They paused and passed the goatskin. Lindy asked if something was wrong.

"That day, when Bruder came by," said Lolly. "You didn't ask him up to the house. You kept him to yourself."

"Willis didn't want him in the house."

Lolly was contemplating this answer and her face told Lindy that she didn't find it adequate. They continued walking, and the heat was all around them. The scrub was dry and brittle and scratched at their

clothes and their bare forearms. Were a spark to fall, the entire mountainside would sway with waves of orange flame.

The women stopped again, and Lolly called after Pal to come for
water. He called that he didn't want any, and then his crackling footsteps told them that he was continuing up the path. "Will you invite
Mr. Bruder to the house?" Lindy saw it then: a glimpse of betrayal in
Lolly's eye. "You're trying to keep him from me."

"Away from *you?*" Despite the years, Lolly was still a child-woman
stunted in a household that gave her no reason to grow up. Up the path,
the children's voices had fallen away and Lindy called after them,
and there was a moment of silence when the only response was the jays
in the pines and the squirrels scampering in the underbrush, and then
Sieglinde answered, "Mommy, we're right here!"

"Did you love him, Lindy?"

Within Lindy something broke; she had dammed herself for too
long and now there was a surge. She scolded Lolly for being childish.
"What do you know about love?"

"I know what love is."

"Mommy?" cried Sieglinde. "Mommy, where are you?"

"Right here."

"Mommy, come now. Mommy, I'm scared. There's someone here."
Then the girl screamed, a shriek crossing the canyon, followed by a cry
from Pal.

Lindy and Lolly ran up the path. The voices were coming from behind a thicket of sumac and the children were screaming and Lindy
thought, *What's happening?* A cold panic entered her, and when Lindy
and Lolly reached the children, she found them shaking in the long
shadow of Bruder.

He was standing over them, his hand spread atop each of their
heads. His suit was dull with dust; a grass stain shone bright on his
knee. He said, "Out for a hike, I see."

"What are you doing here?" said Lindy.

The children ran from him, Sieglinde hugging Lindy's leg and Pal
taking Lolly's hand. The girl's nose was quivering, as if she were both
scared and excited at once. Pal was motionless next to Lolly. He reminded Lindy of Edmund: his sorrowful, nearly adult face attached to
a little boy's body, the drooping eyes and the early wrinkled brow and
the downturned mouth.

Lindy expected Lolly to berate Bruder for scaring the children but she said nothing, only lifted her chin and smiled.

"We were just talking about you," said Lolly.

"I doubt I could be of much interest in any conversation of yours."

A door flew open in Lindy. It felt as if her emotions were stampeding out to this spot in the chaparral, trampling the path and the felled sycamore where Bruder's foot rested, his ankle exposed to the sun. She feared that he and Lolly and even the children could read everything in her eyes: the jaundicing jealousy, the tearful regret. She wanted to cry out and tell Bruder—but what would she say? How could she begin now? For many years, words had sat tasteless on her tongue. Again she wondered why he did not know how she felt; wasn't it as obvious as smoke rising from a far fire? But perhaps he did know; perhaps he knew and he no longer cared. She realized that what she had feared most was true: He has seen my heart and rejected it. . . . The door to her soul banged shut on its hinges.

"Mommy, I wasn't scared," said Sieglinde. She twirled in her sunflower dress and performed a curtsy.

Pal's eyes were wide and he twisted Lolly's skirt in his fingers, and in his hesitation Lindy could sense that the boy was recognizing something about Bruder.

"Pal wants to leave," said Lolly. "Good-bye, Mr. Bruder." She took the boy's hand and together they ran down the path and the afternoon was silent again.

When they were gone Lindy said, "Lolly was just now confessing her affection for you."

"For me?" His grin was curious, and Lindy wondered if it was at her own expense.

"There's something you should know about her," said Lindy. "It was Lolly."

"What was?"

"She was the one who told Willis about that night."

"You remember it, do you?"

"Don't play with me."

"How do you know?"

"Willis told me."

"Why would she do that?"

"Because she loved you even then."

"Lolly? In love with me?" He thought about this. "What use would I have for her?" He grinned mysteriously, and she saw that he was going to tell her nothing.

The years had been like a sentence for her too. Bruder wasn't the only one who had stared out a window longing for freedom. The rancho had become her prison, its staircase creaking beneath her descending foot, always causing Willis's voice to rise from the library, "Lindy? You aren't going out, are you?" The rose bed had snared her, the front gate had trapped her, and now the illness strapped her to the bed. There was so much to tell Bruder, but his grim face told her that he would no longer listen; his eyes told her that he had learned all he needed to know about Lindy Poore.

After reading the article, she had called Cherry. "What did he tell you?" she asked.

"Everything he told me is in the story," Cherry answered.

"What did he tell you about *me*?"

"Nothing, Lindy."

"When you went to see him. Did he ask about me?"

"No, Lindy. Your fate was already clear to him."

"How did he know?"

And Cherry, who was planning her City Hall marriage to George Nay, said, "Lindy. How is it that you don't know?"

"You'll let me know if I can help you?" Cherry had said. "Lindy, call when you need me." The phone line clicking dead had stayed in Lindy's ear for a long time; she could almost hear it now amid the calling jays.

Lindy and Bruder found themselves seated on the sycamore log. A spear of exhaustion entered Lindy and her fever rose. "Sieglinde, come sit beside me." Lindy extended her hand, but her daughter instead threw her arms around Bruder and sat in his lap and pecked his cheek.

"She could only be your daughter."

The afternoon had spoiled and Lindy shut her eyes, stopping the painful sun. The breeze ran through the oak scrub and she thought of that day years ago at the mineral spring, as she had awkwardly attempted to explain herself, and he had tried to confess what was in his heart. But her memory of that day was imprecise: she recollected it as if he had revealed secrets about himself, when in fact he had said almost nothing. She had come to convince herself that she was the only one he had opened his heart to. For a moment she thought of them as lovers again, an afternoon in the sun, dust caking their eyelids, their throats dry, pulses panting. Time had passed and nothing had changed and she transported herself to one of Bruder's first days at Condor's Nest; with her eyes shut, she carried herself away from the trail above Devil's Gate. She traveled home.

But then Bruder broke the spell. "Imagine it," he said. "Lolly Poore and me." If Lindy had opened her eyes she would have seen the predatory smile and the frozen, preylike fear in Sieglinde's face. But she sealed her eyes against the hot reality of the day, and then Bruder laughed, and his laugh echoed in the canyon, a dark chuckle climbing up from somewhere deep and filling the brown, burned hills above Devil's Gate.

5

A WEEK LATER, Lindy drove to Dr. Freeman's, this time with Rosa. The sun-whitened dirt in the arroyo was blinding, and the KHJ radio news said that the afternoon's temperature would reach 110. The hot wind rushed around them as they crossed the bridge and drove into town. There was more talk of the future speedway up the arroyo and an even wider bridge spanning its yawn. Lindy could imagine the pavement running endlessly, strips crisscrossing and eventually filling everything in, every last gopher hole stopped up with concrete; she shut her eyes and then opened them, and in the dark instant she had seen a narrow white road running from the Pasadena's gate to Condor's Nest. It was free of oil and rubber stain and it seemed as if someone had rolled it for her.

In Dr. Freeman's office, Lindy and Rosa waited on the daybed. Over the years its velour had gone bald in spots, and the fern had grown into a large tattered shrub that filled the window and spilled across the file cabinet. The fern filtered the sun, casting a green light on the office and on Lindy's hands and legs. It gave them a sickly color, Rosa's face too, and while they waited for Dr. Freeman behind the bubble-glass door, Rosa took Lindy's fingers in her own. Miss Bishop was with the doctor in the examining room and the two young women were alone, the heat touching them everywhere, the thin velour bristly, the fan blowing, its neck clicking. They didn't need to say it but both were thinking about Rosa's mother, and all the other women felled by the reeking, weeping tumors. "Somebody gave it to her," Rosa said, "and she gave it to nobody, and she didn't know what she had until she was sick and then she knew exactly what she had." But then Rosa realized what she was doing to Lindy and she said, "But she never took mercury. She had nothing but her rosary."

And what did Lindy have?

"Due to your somewhat advanced stage," said Dr. Freeman, "I'm going to give you the full ten milliliters." She was lying on the rubber table, her blouse hanging limply on the coat-tree, and the rubber was almost gooey against her back. Lindy stared up. Since her last visit, someone—Miss Bishop, no doubt—had taped to the ceiling tiles a picture of a beach, gentle waves rolling in, children playing. It looked like Dana Point, but it could have been anywhere up or down the coast, fat-kneed children crouched in the wet sand and two mothers standing watchfully behind them, hands on hips.

"One good thing about the times we're living in," said Dr. Freeman.

"What's that, Doctor?" said Miss Bishop.

"Plenty of donors willing to sell their blood. I had no trouble getting a pint that's smear-positive for Plasmodium vivax."

Miss Bishop nodded, agreeing that that *was* fortunate, and through the bubble glass, Lindy saw Rosa's blurry black figure. "Can she come in?"

"Who, your maid?"

Miss Bishop opened the door, and Rosa came in and seated herself on a steel stool; the stool's plate-shape seat looked like the only cool thing in the examination room and Lindy longed to press her cheek against it. Even without her blouse she was warm and sticky, the rubber mattress sucking at her. She thought of Willis, who'd be sweating it out down in the groves. He had spent the past week figuring out what to do about the spreading decline. The worms had taken no more than thirty trees, but there was no way to know where they would stop, burrowing deep until they found cold, moist soil and the teat of a root tip. They had tried spraying, Hearts and Slay and Willis misting the trees with zinc, borax, and manganese, which left the dying trees covered in a brittle gray film. The nematode lived in the soil, and flooding the rootstock with six parts water to one part chlorobenzene had done nothing either, the flammable runoff collecting in the ditches and sitting in the sun as combustible as gasoline.

Dr. Freeman nodded indifferently in Rosa's direction, and Lindy could tell that he didn't recognize her. But Miss Bishop did: she had said, "And how are *you*?" Miss Bishop once said that she never forgot

any of the girls who visited Dr. Freeman. While they lay on the examination table, humiliated by Dr. Freeman's probe and prod, Miss Bishop
would study each girl's face, and she'd store the memory in a carefully
indexed mental file. Sometimes Miss Bishop would scold Dr. Freeman
by saying, "The girls might be coming to you with the same problem,
but don't forget, Doctor, if you asked each girl what happened, each
time you'd hear a different story." "You're right, Miss Bishop," Dr.
Freeman would say. "But there isn't time to ask, is there?"

On the wall was a diploma, Old Throop, class of 1914. Lindy imagined Dr. Freeman buttoning himself into his white coat for the first
time, taking up his scalpel with intentions of bringing good to the world.
Lindy was struck by the sadness of a man's inexorable transformation—
from the bright hope of youth to the dull, limited options that come
from years of compromise. No one could imagine for himself a future
that entailed the daily walk up the dark staircase, the turning of the lock
in the bubble-glass door. Yet here was Dr. Freeman, Miss Bishop too;
and here was Lindy as well, and her future and her present life had long
ago parted ways. Sieglinde would be five in a few weeks; when Lindy
was five she was trapping puma and casting her lancewood rod into the
surf and chasing Siegmund up the arroyo. At once it felt as if it were
both yesterday and a lifetime ago, and again the relentless doubleness of
life stroked Lindy, soothing and frightening her in the same grasp.

Miss Bishop swabbed the crook of Lindy's arm, and the alcohol was
cool and the fan blew on it and Lindy began to relax. She looked again
to the picture of the beach, and in it the ocean waves stretched to the
horizon and far out she saw a little boat and she couldn't be sure but it
looked like an outrigger canoe, two people paddling to shore and cresting a wave. Miss Bishop saw Lindy looking at the picture and she said,
"I bought it on my vacation."

"Where is it?"

"A little run-down beach village. Baden-Baden-by-the-Sea. Do you
know where it is? Down south of Capistrano and north of La Jolla cove.
You ever go down to that part of the coast, Mrs. Poore?"

Dr. Freeman told Lindy to release her fist and to breathe deeply. He
said that the inoculation wouldn't take long. He flicked a syringe and
prepared a vial of blood, and before she knew it he had inserted the needle into her arm and something warm seeped toward her shoulder just

beneath the skin. While he held the vial in place and the blood transferred to Lindy's vein, he said that the first ague would set in at any
point in the next three or four days. "It's a quartan malaria. The chills
will return every fourth day." He said he hoped that Lindy would be
able to hold out until the tenth or even twelfth bout. "You'll feel hot
and cold all at once, and an icy sweat will cover you, and it'll be hard to
think straight. But I don't want you to worry because that's normal,
that's what's to be expected, Mrs. Poore. It'll pass within a few hours
and you'll be tired, and the next day you'll feel a little better."

"Should I give her anything?" said Rosa.

"A cold rag and some water and, if she wants it, some ice chips, in
case she's gnashing." Lindy thought of what she might say to Willis if he
was to find her shaking and drenched in her bed; she'd only have to say
that it was *a woman's problem* to send him scurrying down the hall, his
curiosity squelched. She would tell Rosa to keep Sieglinde away during
the ague hours. "Tell her that Mommy's gone to bed." Lindy couldn't
quite envision it now, on the rubber pad, but she had a vague, misty
sense that those words would echo in the house over and over during
the next few months, up the dumbwaiter and down, transported by
aluminum heating duct: *Mommy's gone to bed.*

Dr. Freeman removed the needle, but this felt no more uncomfortable than a hand releasing her arm. "Rest for a bit, Mrs. Poore," said
Miss Bishop.

"Whenever you want," said Dr. Freeman, "I'll interrupt the treatment and administer the quinine. But I want you to try to hold out.
The fever is burning the spirochetes out of your blood. The longer you
let the agues run, the better chance we have."

She was both hot and tired, the warm, fan-prodded air holding her
against the rubber pad. Rosa took her hand and they waited together
while Dr. Freeman moved to his office and continued his paperwork
and Miss Bishop reset the instrument table. "Everything's going to be
okay," said Rosa, and Lindy knew that Rosa was right. The Mayo Clinic
was reporting a success rate greater than fifty percent, Dr. Freeman had
said. "Almost seventy percent, depending on how you look at the numbers."

"By success, do you mean cure?"

"It isn't so simple, Mrs. Poore."

But Lindy had no doubt that she would outmaneuver fate one more time. She was emboldened by the sense that good fortune waited ahead, and she felt her strength returning, running up her legs.

A few minutes later, Lindy stood at the window, buttoning her blouse. Outside, the tar-paper roof looked as if it were melting into a black skin of oil. The Webb House's turret flashed the sunlight back into Lindy's eyes, and she tucked the blouse into her skirt, and soon she and Rosa moved to leave. Miss Bishop was saying, "Don't forget to call if it becomes too much."

When she got home, Lindy felt in fact better than she had in several weeks, and the headache had subsided and the fever had disappeared. She thought that perhaps the treatment was working already. Sieglinde was out with Lolly and Pal at the swim tournament at the club. Lindy changed into her old work clothes and hiked down the hill, looking for Willis.

At the ranch house she found Hearts and Slaymaker strapping themselves into knapsack sprayers, the brass pumps burning in the sun. Hearts was in his work pants and his boots and nothing else, and the skin of his chest was glistening and the heat rose off it in iridescent waves. The yard smelled like petroleum, and the boys were greasy about the face, and they looked as if they might burst into flame right then, and when they saw her Hearts said, "About a thousand degrees today." Then they helped each other into nickel-plated masks bound in chamois skin, Hearts adjusting the elastic band around Slay's head and Slay doing the same for Hearts. There was only one pair of goggles, though, and each told the other to put it on and their voices were muffled like a holler into a tin can and finally Slaymaker insisted and helped Hearts adjust the goggles. His eyes were huge and worried-looking behind the smoky glass. He said something that Lindy couldn't make out. Hearts put his hands atop his head, and the pits of his arms were white. He and Slaymaker walked slowly into the grove, the four-gallon tanks lurching on their backs, their boots coughing up dust.

They were off to spray the trees around the mausoleum with a fine mist of petroleum, and to douse the roots. In the past they'd sprayed the grove with fuel to fight off fungus and mites, and as no one had any better ideas of how to stop the spreading decline, Willis decided they had nothing to lose. Hearts and Slay hated the spraying more than any other job on the ranch. For a week they'd smell of bitumen, the vapors off their flesh so strong that Clune's wouldn't sell them tickets to the matinee. Following them down a middle, Lindy thought it was like being stuck behind two old belching Tin Lizzies, the petroleum fumes trailing them. She ran ahead and asked where Willis was, and Slaymaker mumbled through his metal mask, "He's out here spraying too."

When they reached the mausoleum, she found Willis slick with fuel sitting on the steps, his sprayer at his feet. He looked worn and small, his eyes dull in his greasy face and his clothes damp-dark with sweat and fuel. The far end of the grove smelled like the Richfield filling station, where the serviceman in the jumpsuit with the eagle stitched to his breast stacked the quart cans of Richlube in pyramids eight feet high.

"I've come to help," said Lindy.

She expected Willis to turn her away, and she was prepared to fight to stay and work with them, but he simply ran his hand through his hair and said, "All right. Take my sprayer." And he heaved it up and worked the leather straps over her shoulders, tightening the buckles and adjusting the mask over Lindy's mouth. And then he saw the cotton taped to the crook of her arm. "What happened to you?" She said that a bee had stung her, but the mask garbled her words and no one heard her lie. No matter, for Willis was already busy explaining how to use the nozzle, showing her the stopcock, maneuvering the rubber hose. His demonstration released a cloud of petroleum mist that immediately cooled the air around them, but then it changed, the vapor heating in the sun, thickening to something both invisible and deadly. Even behind the mask her nose and throat burned, and it made Lindy think of the lion's-mane jellies on Jelly Beach, invisible, almost a product of the imagination, until a long yellow tentacle snared a girl's thigh, burning the flesh off in strips.

The sprayer tank was half full but it pulled on Lindy, and she shifted her hips, trying to find a spot of balance on her back; she leaned forward heavily, fearing that if she were to stand up straight, she might teeter over. "I'll help you up the ladder," said Willis, and they walked to a tree at the mausoleum's rim and he set the ladder inside the branches. She climbed until her nozzle reached high and then she waved at Willis to stand back. He walked down a middle into a place where the trees were full-canopied and green, and she watched him scurry away to the ranch house for shade and water. From the ladder the grove stretched before her, nestling the bottom of the valley and rolling up into the foothills. She saw from here how the mausoleum echoed in its design the house on the hill, both white and rising from the surrounding chaparral. Willis had installed a special telephone line between the house and the ranch house, its thick gray wire strung down the hill along stripped ponderosas, and the wire looked as if it were crackling in the heat. Several yards away, Hearts and Slaymaker were up in the trees too, gingerly working their nozzles through the branches, spraying and turning their heads, spraying and turning away.

Lindy adjusted the sprayer on her back, aimed the nozzle, and flipped the stopcock. She released a mist of petroleum and the sunlight caught it, illumining each particle as if it were a shattered diamond blown aloft. The small cloud descended and veiled a section of the tree, its leaves turning greasy. The petroleum fumes reached her through the mask and she coughed and held on to a slick branch while a dizziness arose in her, fluttering her eyes, seeping the blood from her head. But the spinning stopped, and she sprayed again and again, dousing the tree down to the trunk and then misting the roots through the hard dirt, each spray causing a lightness in her head. By the time her first tree was complete, her tank was empty and her clothes were wet.

She returned to the fuel shed, the mask hanging around her neck. She called after Willis but couldn't find him. She began refueling her tank, the petroleum running hot through the rubber tube, and she smelled nothing but the burning fumes, as if they had sprayed the entire ranch. There was nothing in the air but fuel, petroleum lining the breeze, a river of fuel mist for the grove jays, a spring of fuel air for her thirsty throat. Her eyes were watering and she touched her cheek and found it hot with grease, and when she closed her eyes she felt her mind boiling. The tank overflowed with fuel, a rivulet running across her feet, saucing her boots and ankles, and Lindy shut the valve.

Her first attempt to reload the sprayer onto her back ended in her falling over. The second time, she crouched into the straps and slowly pulled herself up. The galvanized tank loaded with fuel was heavier than a rucksack of bricks, and she was so bent over she could nearly touch her toes. She fleetingly thought about leaving the spraying to Hearts and Slay, but she didn't want to walk away from the work. She made her way back to the mausoleum, each step heavy and clumsy and painful. By now her forehead burned, the coat of grease intensifying the heat of the sun, her skin turning pink and then red. It felt as if there wasn't a clean breath to be had in the valley, as if all the air would be hazy and toxic until the winter rains swept in to scrub the atmosphere.

And she realized, as she set the ladder in the next tree, that Bruder wouldn't return to the Pasadena for her. He would leave Pasadena and live at Condor's Nest and she might never see him again. Lindy flipped the stopcock and the petroleum sprayed out and she hung to the top of the ladder, panting. What was it he had said? "You've chosen, Linda." He didn't understand, she reassured herself; something might look like a choice but was in fact inevitable. She knew, even then, that the first fever would come before morning. Soon she would be trembling in a cold bed of sweat. It didn't frighten her; she knew what to expect. Her mind would grow dark, her vision would close down, her teeth would chatter, a clamminess would dress her, her hair would lay damp against her throat. She would wait out the ague, teetering at the brink of delirium, and Rosa would ice her forehead. She would call to Willis through the door that *everything was all right, go back to bed.* Rosa would tell Lolly that Lindy wanted to be alone. Sieglinde's will was harder than the others', Lindy knew; she might cry at the door, kicking it, flinging herself against it until her Mommy let her in. Sieglinde would blame Lindy for turning a bolt upon her, but Lindy would burn through the icy fever saying nothing, biting back the groans, and then as dawn rose over the oily valley, the fever would recede, the yellow-pink restored to Lindy's cheek. She had steeled herself to last the dozen bouts, and only then to request the quinine. She wanted to return to Dr. Freeman and say, *I have done as you said. Am I healed?* She believed that she would recover. She believed that her future would be long. Now, she believed it more than anything.

Up in the orange tree, Lindy asked herself if she might die, and she said *No.* She considered it and dismissed it and she was certain; and Lindy Poore would never ask herself again. It was what kept her from being afraid: her ability to ignore the embers of evidence. She aimed the nozzle and sprayed her way down the second tree, resetting the ladder four or five times. By the time she was in the third tree, Willis had returned with a cart loaded with barrels. He called Hearts out of his tree to help him. When Hearts removed his sprayer there were red ribbons of welts across his shoulders. He didn't bother to examine them, just gave Willis a hand unloading a barrel and dumping it at the base of a tree. The barrels were filled with water and a curdy layer of petroleum, and Willis used a broom handle to stir it up before dumping it into the soil. "If this doesn't get that goddamn worm, nothing will." He and Hearts continued turning the barrels over, and Willis was cursing the *fucking nematodes,* the *goddamn evil worms* from *fucking hell!* He was coiled and stooped and red, and Lindy watched him from the treetop. In their five years of marriage he had taken on a leathery quality about the neck, and his hair had gone wiry. He was thicker in the middle, not yet soft but on his way, and when the City Beautiful Committee meetings didn't keep him busy outside the ranch, draw poker and Santa Anita did. Sometimes, when he was exasperated with Lindy, he would say, "For Christ's sake, don't you love me anymore?" In spots he had roughened, just as she had hardened in patches, and both were aware of the sparking friction between them, both smelled the early smoke. He was good with Sieglinde, when he was interested. Sometimes, not always, Lindy looked at Willis and thought that soon he'd be gone—not dead but far off—and no longer would she be Mrs. Poore; she didn't cling to this, nor articulate it specifically, but it remained a possibility, like the inevitable chance of good fortune walking up your path.

"Need a hand with the ladder?" Willis called. He helped her set it into the next tree but then he said, "You look worn out. Maybe you should take a rest." He tried to help her out of the sprayer's straps but she resisted. She wanted to keep spraying and she climbed up into the branches. Down the lane, Slaymaker was up in a tree and he waved, and behind him it seemed as if the afternoon sun was continuing to rise, throbbing more and more with each hour, and it felt as if everything in the valley would catch fire and explode—the sky white, the sun white, the dirt drained of any color but the rainbow beads of petroleum water. And just then, in the span between a rising and falling breath, something did catch—sun through the prism of blowing petroleum mist, a spark shot from the sizzling telephone wire, two flinty rocks falling in the foothills—but no one would ever know exactly what, or where. White smoke rose in the mountains far above the ranch, at first as lazily as a lonely drift of ocean fog. Slaymaker wasn't waving hello: he was pointing out the smoke far off in the distance. He pulled his mask from his face and called, not urgently but with respect, "Fire."

It happened as Lindy knew it would: she leapt from the ladder and she was dizzy and Willis ripped the sprayer from her shoulders and took her hand and they ran to the ranch house. Hearts and Slaymaker were behind them, and they panted in the pepper tree's shade while Willis telephoned the house, but no one answered and he was yelling, "Come on, where is she? Where's that sister of mine?" He held the receiver to his ear and the sweat ran down his face and he hit the wall with the palm of his hand and at last he said, "Rosa, call the fire department! What? No, no, no. She's here. Just call!" The fire was miles away but they didn't know which way it was traveling, and they didn't know if it had just taken hold or had been burning for hours and only now turned down a canyon to come into sight of the ranch. At first, only slow, lazy smoke rose from the mountainside and it was far enough away that it was more beautiful than menacing. But soon they could smell it, the bitter burning coming down through the foothills, and each of them inhaled the smoke and Slaymaker said, "Pine smoke." A light flurry of ash drifted down.

When the first gold flames came into sight, no one was surprised. Hearts propped his ladder against the ranch house and they climbed up on the roof and passed a pair of binoculars around. They saw a platoon of flames standing erect in the mountains, idling as if deciding which direction to run. A hole in the pineland opened for the fire, and Willis and Lindy leaned against each other, and Hearts and Slaymaker leaned against each other, and the afternoon burned toward gloaming and the fire swayed, orange as the Pasadena navels. The smoke blew up the foothill chimneys, and the fire lay against the Sierra Madres like a huge fluttering blanket. Lindy thought she heard a distant roar, like the steady sound of traffic on Colorado Street: the flames sweeping away the sumac and the toyon and the lemonade berry. Hearts had turned on the radio in the ranch house and the announcer's voice filled the yard and greeted them on the roof: "This just in: Fire in the foothills." Almost at once the smoke changed from white to black, fueled by single-leaf pinyon and the blue-black berry cones of the western juniper. The afternoon was closing, but it was hotter than ever in the valley, and Lindy felt the ripple of fever behind her eyes. She touched her ears and found them hot as flame and she reached for Willis. Was the smoke drifting through the Linda Vista hills and across the Arroyo Seco, passing the Hotel Vista's terrace? Was it sending word?

The wind shifted and the fire flapped like a sheet being shook out, and then it leapt both up the mountainside and down, and soon they heard the fire engines pass the service gate. Willis and Hearts and Slaymaker climbed down from the roof, and they were yelling and pointing while the fire picked its way in no discernible direction—now it was retreating west, now it was lurching east!—and Lindy, in the tin roof's glare, felt herself erupt with fever as she waited for the valley to explode. She waited and she began to tremble and she was becoming cold and she clung to the brick chimney. Its mortar loosened beneath her grip, and the dusk swallowed the afternoon, just as the fire swallowed a swath of scrubland, climbing up into the mountains, and by night it was certain that the ranch would be spared even as the fire burned out of control. She thought she could hear the gray squirrels screaming and the black bears weeping and the bobcats hissing for help and the liveoaks falling as the fire burned into the forest, devouring the mountain, hungry for the entire range. By nightfall, firefighters from all over Los Angeles and in from Riverside were in the hills cutting firebreaks and hosing down cabins and trying to hold a line. As a precaution, Hearts and Slay had flooded the far end of the grove, and the trees sat in a foot of water and the mausoleum was covered with snowflakes of wandering ash, and late at night the fire was an orange strip on a far-off ridge, rancid and distant; but the smoke was reaching them, coming for them. Onlookers from all over drove into the rancho's valley and up into the mountains to see the fire, to smell it, to stick out their tongues and taste the ash. They would park their cars at lookouts and drink from glovecompartment flasks and bet which way the flames would next dash; and some of them would make love for the first or the last time; and some of them would make love as if there were nothing special about tonight. And all the while the fever would continue to burn in Lindy, and eventually Rosa would drive her up the hill and escort her to bed, where she would shake through the night atop cold, damp sheets. She would lie awake alone, her arms crossed over her breasts, and patiently wait, her breath nearly stopped. She could withstand anything, she told herself as she lay her hand on the cold brass rail and lifted her foot to climb the stairs to bed, and just then, with Rosa's hand at the small of her back, Lindy saw the note propped against the Cupid statue. At the landing, the far-off hills burning outside the window, she would read the note and learn—while Rosa gasped and Sieglinde cried upstairs in her room—that Lolly had taken Palomar and eloped with Bruder to Condor's Nest.

6

ONE MORNING IN SEPTEMBER 1930, between the sixth and seventh fevers, Lindy drove down the coast, Sieglinde at her side. Over the
years the road had expanded, the strip of bitumen widened just as they
had widened Colorado Street last year, lopping off fifteen feet from the
façades of buildings in order to make way for more automobiles. The
road followed the ocean, slicing through the beach villages where pink-
stucco motor hotels clustered like giant autumn weeds. The late sea-
soners hung their striped towels from balcony rails, and little bluff-top
shops sold picture postcards and soda and ice cream and strips of fish
fried in dough. At one of the stops Sieglinde ate a dish of sherbert, and
Lindy thumbed through the rack of penny postcards and she stopped at
one that showed the same image as in the picture taped to Dr. Freeman's ceiling.

Back in the car, Sieglinde sat with her legs crossed and asked where
they were going. "The beach," Lindy said, and Sieglinde asked if they
were going to the Jonathan Club, where they planted torches in the
sand and organized sand-castle contests for the children. "Another
beach," said Lindy, and Sieglinde, whose face was as bright as a pane of
glass, said, "Are we going to Condor's Nest?" Yes, said Lindy, telling her
daughter about the lobster pots and the blue shark; but Sieglinde was an
impatient child and she turned in her seat to face the ocean, her finger
idly tracing the horizon.

"We're going to pick up your grandfather," said Lindy.

"Who's he?"

The day was hot, the sky empty of clouds, and Lindy told her
daughter to pull down her hat and Lindy tightened her own head scarf,

the knot hard at her throat. Each fever had been more and more difficult—the blue-lipped chills, the icy sweat flooding her bed, her wet
hands flailing up and tearing the peach canopy. Rosa had fed her ice and
wagged Lolly's peacock fan. She would open the window and let the
breeze run across Lindy's body, thin in moist eyelet, until she would cry
out for Rosa to shut it again, *she was freezing;* it went like that for several
hours, Rosa tucking Lindy into blankets until she had sweated her way
out of them, and then the cooling down until her hands turned blue.
Lindy's memory of the malarial hours was imprecise: a remote buried
heat, like a fire in a coal mine, that was how she thought of it; she could
recall the misery—her trembling, exhausted body told her of it—but
she retained no knowledge of how she had borne it. She would remember talking with Rosa, but later, when the fever's tide had ebbed,
she wouldn't know what she had said. Once, between the second and
third fevers, Rosa said, "I still don't know why you never told him."
Lindy looked at her puzzled: "Told him what?" And then: *"Who?"* Another time, when Rosa was easing Lindy into the bath, she said, "He
loved you, Lindy." Lindy was under the fever's spell and required an
hour's soak in the scalding, steaming water. As she stepped out of the
water and into the towel spread in Rosa's arms, Lindy managed, "Who
loved me?"

At night, when her head was clear and the moon was bright enough
to read by, Lindy would worry that she had revealed too much to Rosa;
as if the fever had scratched at the lock on her heart. Over the years,
Lindy had learned that the house talked, almost on its own—the windows like eyes, the doorways like ears, the heating ducts like mouths. It
traded secrets with its inhabitants as freely as a breeze crossing a threshold. Lindy no longer believed that Rosa would betray her; she regretted
that she hadn't trusted her long before. But the house itself was capable
of betrayal—as if its walls could read her mind and relay everything to
Willis. And Lindy had to concede that her own face, lit with memory
and emotion, could betray her more than anyone else.

When Rosa spoke of Lindy to one of the new girls, she would warn
the young maid to watch out for Mrs. Poore's shifting moods, especially the onslaught of anger. "You can see it rising red in her throat. Be
sure to leave the room right away. Tell her a faucet is running somewhere, a hot iron is waiting, anything. Just get out of there." Rosa
warned all the girls to avoid passing Lindy's door on the afternoons

when she stayed in bed. "Don't even tiptoe by. Find another route." When the girls, who sucked on gossip as if it were cherry-flavored candy, asked what was wrong with Mrs. Poore, Rosa would say, "Trouble of the heart." The girls, feather dusters in their fists, would cluck and sigh, for they too had witnessed this common tragedy, over and over: their mothers, their sisters, each wrongly betrothed, each mending fissures in their souls. Yet no matter the evidence, each girl believed that such a cruel fate would spare her; for why should she—she with the blood-red lips or the black-velvet hair or the twenty-inch waist—err where so many women had erred before? The odds were against her but she would triumph—*love would triumph, at least for me*—and Lindy would know that each girl was thinking this as she brought Lindy her warm milk, the words unspoken but glued with teenage spittle to her lips. "I'll either marry for love or not at all," one of the younger girls told Rosa. Her name was Antonía, and she wore her hair in a long plait, and she had lost her job waxing the Huntington Hotel's ballroom floor; the nightly affairs—debutante balls and midnight suppers and Donner Party–themed dinner dances for a thousand in gown and tuxedo—were now less frequent than a full platinum moon. "It won't happen to me," said Antonía, tilting her head. But Rosa pushed the girl into the laundry room and said, "That's what she thought too."

The dumbwaiter's station was outside Lindy's door and she could hear everything said in the house, soft-voiced news rising from the cool wine cellar up through the pot-clanging kitchen, into the echo-filled gallery, and traveling upstairs to Lindy's ear. During her first year married to Willis, she would stamp her foot angrily whenever she heard Esperanza or anyone else talking about her: *I never thought she would marry him. She can't really love him, can she?* If Rosa caught the girls gossiping she'd warn them, "Don't discuss what you don't know." Lindy would thank Rosa for her loyalty; Lindy said that next time, she wanted Rosa to fire the girls. "I'm not going to allow a girl to tell lies about me in my own house." But Rosa's glassy face met Lindy's with unflinching honesty: "They might be talking, but they aren't telling lies."

Lindy had learned not to mind, just as she was learning to withstand the pain of the fevers. She would anticipate her returning health as she wrapped herself in the towel after bathing out the last of the day's fever: Rosa's hands would be cold to her shoulders and Lindy would grip her fingers, as if to say, *We've made it through another. Recovery can't be far off!*

The light reflecting off the lime-green tiles would cast a leafy pallor across Lindy's calm, naked body and she would say, "I'm free for another four days." And last night, after the bath had concluded the sixth fever—a bout that had boiled her temperature to 104—Lindy had said, "Tomorrow. I'm going to drive down there." And Rosa, tamping the water from Lindy's breasts, had said, "Yes, I know."

The salty wind ran through the open car and Sieglinde's face remained turned away from her mother and Lindy drove on, squinting against the glare. She was halfway through the treatment: six more fevers to bear, and not once did Lindy doubt that she would make it. Eventually one of the fevers would surpass 106 and there would be hours when she'd slip into a short coma and would feel as if she were lying in a coffin of ice—all of this Lindy expected, and at the same time she knew she could withstand it, *would* withstand it. Lindy was prepared.

"Are we really going to that smelly old onion farm?" Sieglinde took an Automobile Club map out of the glove compartment and opened its paper wings and pretended to read it, studying the matrix of roads. Lindy warned her to put the map away, that the breeze would pluck it from her, but Sieglinde ignored her mother, and when Lindy warned her again, the wind lifted the map and off it flew, folds extended like a white gull in glide.

When they reached the dirt lane, Sieglinde asked, "Mommy, where are we?" and Lindy saw the sign:

CONDOR'S NEST
STAY OUT

The Vulture House appeared abandoned on the far side of the field, and there was a worn look to the dooryard and the cottages. The arroyo was dry, the dam's stacked remains nearly imperceptible to the unknowing eye. Lindy got out of the car, and Sieglinde ran to the bluff's edge, and Lindy became frightened as she watched her daughter dash to the lip and then stop as the sandy soil crumbled over the edge, sending a pair of snowy plovers into flight. "Whose farm is this?" Sieglinde asked, but Lindy didn't answer. She went to her old cottage's door, but it was locked. She peered inside and saw the iron bedstead and the matted puma-pelt rug, and memory's flood washed away the years—but only for a moment. The other cottages were locked as well and there was no sign of life and Sieglinde asked, "Mommy, who are we looking for?"

Together they peered over the bluff to the skeleton of the half-built staircase. The sailor-carved table remained in the yard, and Lindy and Sieglinde sat on the bench. The sky stretched endlessly to the sea, no clouds between Condor's Nest and San Clemente Island, a canopy of faded blue. The surf filled their ears and Sieglinde said, "Are we looking for that man?"

"And your Aunt Lolly."

"What about Pal?"

"And Palomar."

"And what about Grandpa?"

"And Dieter too."

In the clarity that came with the most recent fever's subsiding, Lindy had made a decision. When the treatment was over, she'd leave her husband. She wasn't sad about it. No, in fact she was happy with the promise of her future. She had no plans. This trip to Condor's Nest was to help her prepare. She didn't know what she'd do or where she'd go, but one night she and Sieglinde would pass through the gate and she'd watch the rancho fall away in the rearview mirror. They'd pick up Dieter, propping him in the Gold Bug's tiny seat, and they'd be off— and she would figure out the details between now and when the malarial treatment ended. She knew she was healing, and she knew that later in the fall she would act. She would leave. She'd take her jewelry and the cash she had collected in an envelope: three thousand dollars: "Just in case," she'd say. She would leave everything behind. She'd even drop his name. She'd sign her letters *Linda Stamp*.

Together Lindy and Sieglinde checked the barn and peered through the windows of the Vulture House and hopped into the arroyo to look around. "Maybe they're on the beach," said Sieglinde, and Lindy took her daughter's hand and walked her back to the car. "Why don't we go down to the beach, Mommy?"

But Lindy wanted to look around in town. Maybe she could find a place for them to live?

They drove back down the dirt lane, past the sign and then the tulip tree, and Lindy drove into the village, not knowing what she'd find on Los Kiotes Street. What would she do if she found Bruder and Lolly sharing a pan-fried turkey supper on the Twin Inn's veranda? Would she stop to say hello?

After it had become clear that the fire would spare the ranch, Willis had returned to the house and read Lolly's note. He had cursed his sister, and his contorted face, frozen in the instant when one realizes that all hope is lost, reminded Lindy of Edmund. Willis went to Lolly's room and tore the mattress from the bed and shredded the lavender-silk bolsters and ordered Rosa to remove Lolly's clothes from the closet and her hair ribbons from the rosewood stand carved especially to hold them. He dumped open her mother-of-pearl jewelry box and found its velvet-lined compartments empty. "Get rid of all her things," he ordered Rosa, who packed the taffeta dresses and the porcelain-faced dolls and the poetry diaries into tissue-lined crates. In the morning the crates were hauled to the attic, and Lindy did her best to hide the *American Weekly*'s headline from Willis:

ORANGE HEIRESS ABANDONS FAMILY FOR LOVE

The story was written by the man who had taken over Cherry's column, and he'd gotten it wrong. The story was about love, but he had arranged the facts incorrectly. Did it matter? Was there a reason to do anything other than shred the article from the newspaper and tuck it in with the tissue in one of the packing crates? There for another generation to find. Rosa and Lindy used Dieter's mallet to close the lids, its worn head sinking each nail through the yellow pinewood with a single blow.

The drought had devastated Baden-Baden-by-the-Sea. The mineral spring had gone dry, and the tourists had stopped coming, and the real-estate speculators had fled. Half of the Twin Inn had been boarded up, and a peeling VACANCY sign swung on the door, and when Lindy and Sieglinde stepped into the hotel's entryway, a man in a visor greeted them. "Need a room?"

"I was looking to see if someone was in the dining room."

"The dining room's closed. Had to shut it up last winter." Lindy touched the flocked wallpaper, and Sieglinde pulled on her hem, saying, "Let's go, Mommy."

They drove up Los Kiotes Street, but no one was on the sidewalk and Margarita's old porch had been walled up since the beginning of the summer.

An old sign shredded by the wind announced a sale on everything in the store, bolts of dimity, Princess beauty products, eagle-feather hats— EVERYTHING MUST GO!

Lindy and Sieglinde drove past the mineral spring, but the platform around the weeping rock was abandoned and the stands that sold the bottled water were shut and the baths had closed. A faded sign flapped in the breeze: DRINK A CUP OF PURE APFELSINE WATER AND CHANGE YOUR LIFE!

Lindy drove on, with no idea where else to look, following the road along the rim of Agua Apestosa. The lagoon was low with turgid water and the receding waterline had left bright salt powdering the mudflats. It reflected the sun, and Sieglinde hung her head over the car door and pointed. They reached the far edge of the lagoon, and Lindy thought that perhaps she would show her daughter the schoolhouse and the bushes around the outhouse that Miss Winterbourne used to make her cut back with a scythe; Sieglinde wouldn't believe that her own mother had lived like this, Lindy knew. But when she rounded the eucalyptus grove, she found that the schoolhouse was gone. In its place was a mission-style filling station, half built and then abandoned before the first delivery of gasoline. The eucalyptus grove cast a net of shadow over the station, and the pair of bulb-headed pumps looked like two small, ghostly children whose faces had been wiped blank. This was a strange thought, one that released a chill upon Lindy, and she feared that perhaps the seventh fever was coming early; her fingertips found her forehead damp and her ears burning. But she wasn't shaking, and she assured herself that she was fine. She had three more days until the seventh fever; Dr. Freeman had promised that four days would separate them, there would always be a gap of four days. "It's as predictable as the calendar itself," he had said, and she had believed him.

The filling-station window reflected the Gold Bug, and there was a sign on an iron post, but no one had even got around to painting it and the blank white rectangle swung in the wind.

"Mommy? You went to school *here*?"

They drove out through the lettuce fields, and on the outskirts of the village everything was as it had been for fifty years, and Lindy felt the relief settle in her throat that something had stayed the same. The electricity poles ran along a distant ridge in a column, tilting toward one another, and the wires drooped in long cautious smiles. The red-leaf lettuce fields waited dormant for the first winter fog, the crumbling soil blowing about. They came upon Miss Winterbourne's house, and the shades were drawn in the front windows, and Lindy thought she saw a finger peel back the corner of a shade. Maybe Miss Winterbourne would become Pal's teacher and he would grow up reading Edmund's books.

Lindy parked the car in the dooryard and told Sieglinde to wait. Lindy had never been inside Miss Winterbourne's cottage—as far as she knew, no one ever had. The paint on the paneled door was peeling, and the knocker was dull with grime. When Lindy knocked, the entire door fell in, as lightly and quietly as if it were a model made of balsa. She stepped through the doorframe and the cottage was tidy but empty, nothing left inside but the roller shades and, on the mantel, a pair of cheap black-glass earrings, dusty and warm in Lindy's palm.

"Mommy, when are we going home?"

Lindy and Sieglinde drove farther east, where the grasses grew in brown-and-gold carpets up the hills. The macadam ended and the car picked its way along the stony lane and Lindy felt the vibration in her cheeks. Yesterday, during the fever, Willis had come to her door, but Rosa had turned him away, telling him that his wife was resting with *the female business*. But Willis had persisted, knocking again and rattling the doorknob and pressing the door so hard that it trembled in its frame. Lindy was lying naked on her bed, ice in her fists and more ice melting atop her forehead and on her breasts and stomach, the cold water lurching between her thighs. The room was hot and the air was thick, and the open window brought no relief. Lindy felt trapped, as if she were being buried alive in a sludge of fever. Willis continued, now flinging himself at the door, and then the wood cracked, like the ice cracking behind her ears, but the door held, and from the other side Willis called, "Lindy, when will you come out?" She tried to mouth the words but nothing formed on her tongue, and so Rosa said again, "She'll be better in a few hours. Let her rest." In the evening, after her bath, Lindy had sat with Willis on the loggia. The moon was bright enough to reveal the burn-scar running up one of the far hills, and the swath of black burnout in the distant mountains. The fire had been contained within three days; only a dozen houses had been lost, and a corral of roan-rumped mares. People liked to name the fires after women, and since this one came so close to devouring the orange ranch, the local fire-fighters and the onlookers with their collapsing nickel telescopes and the lovers backseat-kissing in the glow of forty-foot flames officially dubbed this fire "Valencia." "But we grow navels here, not Valencias," Willis had tried, unsuccessfully, to explain. Nonetheless, the fire entered the logs as "Valencia": houses burned, 12; acres scorched, 4,400; stock killed, 9 mares; lives lost, just 1—a girl of nineteen or twenty burned so badly no one could identify her. There was speculation over who she was and how she had ended up in the fire's path, but in the end no one knew and no one came forward to offer the girl's story and she was remembered briefly as Valencia's only victim—a *Star-News* picture of the perfect outline her body had preserved in the dry gold grass. A reporter wrote in his column that the girl was a runaway who had lived in an abandoned bobcat cave, but there was more speculation to that story than truth, and three or four people wrote the newspaper saying *Let the girl rest in peace,* and so Pasadena did just that, never thinking of her again.

The same dry gold grass covered the hills east of Baden-Baden-by-the-Sea, and Lindy turned down a narrow lane and crested a hill and saw the glint in the field of an old rail line. She drove to the top of the hill, and where she had expected to find the glass-walled Cocoonery there was nothing but a giant water tank, shaped like an onion and painted with a sign: WATER DEPT.

"Mommy, what are we doing all the way out *here?*"

She didn't know what she expected to find, but something told her she had to go out and look. Before the sixth fever, she had visited Dr. Freeman and he had asked how Willis was holding up and Lindy, knotting a pear-patterned scarf about her head, said, "Nothing gets to Willis." The doctor had looked into her eyes with a penlight and kneaded the flesh in the pit of her arms and around her breasts and held his ruler against the gummy tumor. Expressionless, he told Lindy that he found her the same as before, neither healed nor in further decline; but she knew better. She lingered on the daybed, the fan blowing in her face, the fern limp in its pot, and after several minutes Dr. Freeman looked up from his desk and said, "Did you want something else, Mrs. Poore?" And then again: "Mrs. Poore?"

"Don't you see any improvement, Dr. Freeman? Can't you tell?"

In the afternoon, Lindy and Sieglinde returned to Condor's Nest. As the Kissel made its way down the dirt lane there was no evidence of Bruder's return, but Lindy sensed something and she knew he was there. In the dooryard she called, but only the wind mounting the bluff greeted her. In the barn a horse sneezed and a cow groaned, udder-sore and craving salt. The bantams had pecked the yard clean of grass, and the breeze threw dirt and sand around her ankles. Lindy and Sieglinde went to the door of Dieter's old cottage but, as before, it was locked. Through the windowpane she found everything as it once was: the mantel carved with pilot whales, the shelves tidy with Dieter's books, the gold stamping on the three spines of Gibbon catching the light. Next, Lindy checked the cottage where Valencia had made her kitchen. It too was locked, and Lindy pressed her face against the window above the sink and saw that nothing had changed in there either: the oilcloth on the table, the shelves of dishes neatly stacked, a hunk of cheese on a plate, humid and ripe. It was as if the farm had held back the fists of time. Sieglinde's hand was sticky in hers, and the girl rubbed her eyes with her thumb and her dull dark hair blew wildly about her face.

Lindy led her daughter to the third cottage, and at the plank door Lindy said that *this was where Mommy grew up.* Again, Sieglinde's face screwed up: *here?* The door was locked, and the two stood on the stoop, and the chilies hanging from the post were red and fresh, and when Lindy leaned in against the window a cold fear raced through her and she dropped her daughter's hand to cover her own mouth. Inside the cottage the two beds remained, the balding horsehair blankets tucked tightly beneath the mattress. The hand-colored etchings of Germany's cathedrals were tacked to the walls, and Siegmund's old stocking cap was planted on the post of his bed. In his old pillow was the ghost impression of someone's head. And on Lindy's old bed—not Lindy's but Linda's, but not really Linda's either; no, Sieglinde's—on the bed that once belonged to Sieglinde Stumpf lay Dieter, his arms folded funereally across his chest and his ankles tied to the bedstead with what appeared to be clear silk trolling line.

Lindy banged on the window crying, *Papa! Papa!,* but her father didn't move. His eyelids were closed and everything in the cottage was still and time ran forward and out of Lindy's grasp; she was panting, the palm of her hand rapping the window, banging the door. The window was too high for Sieglinde to see in and she said, "Mommy? What is it, Mommy?" And Lindy's face twisted in what must have been a horrible fashion, for Sieglinde's lip began to quiver and her eyes spilled over with tears and she too screamed, an icy child's scream rising above the ocean roar and piercing the ears of the hovering gulls and filling the remaining ten and a half acres of Condor's Nest. But nothing stirred, and Dieter lay motionless on the bed, his ankles turned awkwardly, his legs spread unnaturally, the silk line like a gossamer chain, and Lindy and Sieglinde stumbled into the kitchen yard and looked up into the glare. They held each other at the edge of the bluff and looked out to the beach at low tide, the beds of green surfgrass limp against the rocks.

"Why are we crying, Mommy?" Sieglinde thought to ask, but Lindy didn't answer. Sieglinde's face cleared, as if she thought that perhaps this was a game, and she began to skip in circles round her mother, singing the song Lindy had taught her: O, she was born in the Ocean, and died in the Sea! Sieglinde didn't remember the rest and she repeated the first line over and over and Lindy stood in the flash of sunlight for what could have been a minute or an hour, she didn't know, but it was long enough for her to sense the sun shift, the tide inch forward, and the afternoon make its first gestures of closing down.

She was still standing at the bluff when the cottage door opened and there was Lolly, pushing Dieter in a wheelchair onto the porch. "Lindy? What are you doing here?"

Lindy was so startled that she couldn't answer, and hadn't she seen, as plain as the rays of sun, the trolling line looped cruelly about Dieter's ankles? And the lifeless waxiness of his forehead? Lindy couldn't explain any of it, and she felt the grip of fear tighten about her heart. She didn't believe that her eyes had deceived her; no, Lindy wasn't capable of believing that. Deception would come from anywhere, but not from within—this Lindy knew: she would fatally cling to it. "Lolly, what did you do to him?"

Lolly began sweeping the porch around Dieter, and she had an empty look to her, her blue eyes milky and unfocused. She giggled and said, "What are you talking about, Lindy?"

Lindy said she'd seen it with her own eyes, Dieter's legs turned in a funny way and the trolling line wrapped about his feet and anchoring him to the bed.

"Lindy, you must be seeing things. Why would I tie Dieter to the

bed?" She spoke without looking at Lindy; Lolly's head tilted toward
the sand on the porch's planks and she continued sweeping the same
spot over and over, dreamily embracing the broom handle. Lindy asked
if Lolly was all right, if something was wrong. "I'm fine, Lindy. It's you
I'm worried about. You don't look well, Lindy."

"Where is he, Lolly?"

"Who?" Lolly moved to the porch corner, bending to reach the dirt
beneath the bench. Lindy asked again and Lolly said nothing, humming
to herself, and in profile Lindy could see how thin she was—she could
disappear behind the porch post. Lindy peered through the open cottage door and saw the bed, delicately dented with the outline of Dieter's
body, but she didn't find any fishing line. Under the mattress? Beneath
the pillow? Nothing; had she imagined it? But the snarls of line had
been there: colorless but identifiable, like a jelly floating in a wave. Lolly
took up a rake and was sweeping the yard and she ignored Lindy altogether.

"I saw him there," said Lindy.

"Lindy, you might want to visit the doctor. You're clearly seeing
things. You sound like you're going mad."

But Lindy was healthier than she'd been in months, maybe even
years, and she knew what she knew; she knew what she'd seen . . . but
did she?

Lindy and Sieglinde climbed into the arroyo and down to the beach.
They removed their shoes and stockings and rested them atop a rock.
The ocean was bath-warm and gentle across their feet and they walked
along the lip of the tide, into the glare, Sieglinde running up ahead and
back, like a dog. As Lindy hurried down the beach the years fell away,
and the only thing to remind her of who she was now was her daughter; if Sieglinde hadn't been there, Lindy would have slipped trancelike
into the past, tracing the tide's sash, reverting to the days when the
world began and ended in Baden-Baden-by-the-Sea. Yet Sieglinde kept
snagging Lindy out of her nostalgic reverie. *Mommy! Mommy!* "Where
are we going, Mommy?" To find him, said Lindy. "Who, Mommy,
who? Daddy? Is Daddy here?"

They rounded the blueschist bend and then crossed Jelly Beach and
reached Cathedral Cove. He was where she expected to find him,
standing in the tide in trousers, and shirtless, a fishing line cast into the
surf. The water beaded on his chest and the hairs across his stomach

were damp and limp like the surfgrass and he was shaking water out of his eyes. Lindy believed that he was waiting for her, and at once she became vain in that old way of hers and she wondered how she looked and the fear returned cold-fingered about her heart: Would he recognize her, had she strayed that far?

"What is Lolly doing to him?" Lindy called. She stood at the edge of the tide, her skirt in her fists, and she kept jumping back as the waves ran toward her. She yelled again and again: "I saw him with my own eyes!"

Bruder was ten feet into the surf, the waves passing through him at waist level, his line tight as it angled into the ocean. As a wave swept out she moved closer to him, but then she back-stepped with the next. This continued for a minute or more, Bruder's back, quilted with muscle, facing her. She said it again: "What are you doing with my father?"

"I brought him home. That's all." He didn't turn. He continued jerking his cork-gripped rod and adjusting the quadruple reel. She watched the nearly invisible line for a tug, and she thought how long it had been since she had set bait into the ocean.

"Will you come out of the water?" Lindy called. Bruder said he couldn't, he had a line out, and she should be the first person to understand that.

"I've come to see you."

"I thought you came to see your father."

Then Lindy realized that Sieglinde was no longer at her side and a quick panic entered her, but it fell away when she saw the girl crawling around at the mouth of the cave. "Be careful," Lindy called. The voice emerging from her throat didn't sound like her.

But if Bruder wouldn't come to Lindy, she would go to him. She stepped farther into the tide and watched the stain of water creep up her skirt and Lindy pressed on, the water taking her in like the baths Rosa prepared. The beach was rocky and the stones were sharp to the arch of her foot and the water reached up her thigh and touched the tumor— a mound no bigger than an infant's fist, no uglier than an old red rose, no deadlier than the deadliest blue shark in the ocean's grave—and she was next to Bruder, everything about her wet and warm. The waves sloshed her and she reached to him for balance and even with her fingers around his arm he didn't stop adjusting the reel, turning the bone handle, pulling up on the rod's tip. Her skirt was spread about her, floating on the water's surface, and Bruder said, *"Her clothes spread wide; and mermaid-like, awhile they bore her up,"* and Lindy said, "What are you talking about now?" Bruder jerked his chin and told her to forget it. A wave cut through them, and their bodies rose together as if two great hands from above had plucked them and pulled them up and then, after the wave passed, their feet were returned to the ocean floor and something sharp cut into Lindy's toe.

She cried out and held Bruder tightly while she hopped on one foot, pulling up her other. Through the green water she and Bruder watched the inky blood seep. She had stepped on an old double hook, one tip sunk into her toe, the other tip as bright as a fish gill under the water. The blood flowed in dark clouds. The initial sharp pain was gone, and looking at the snared foot through the water it was as if it belonged to someone else. Bruder passed his rod to Lindy—"Hold this"—and he knelt in the water, his head swallowed by the surface, and with a doctor's concentration he carefully pulled the hook from her flesh. He stood back up and gulped for air and his hair was flat and glassy on his skull and the water had washed the sullenness from his face: it was as if the saltwater had etched away the years. "It'll scar," he said.

He took back the fishing rod and began reeling the line in and he said, his eyes cast upon the horizon, "I wanted you to love me, Lindy." San Clemente Island was visible in the distance and it looked like the hump of a sea monster, and how could Lindy know then that the sky over Condor's Nest would thicken with filth, and that in a few years the island would slip behind a scrim of haze, to be spotted from shore only on the clearest, bluest days. She couldn't know this, nor could Bruder, but as the heart perceives the future before the eye, Lindy realized her world was gone. "I wanted to earn your love," he said. "I already had you but I wanted to earn you. And you wouldn't let me."

And then, flicking the rod, he said, "That's all there is."

She said he was wrong. He didn't know her heart, no one knew her heart! He slowly raised his hand and moved it to her and she expected his fingers to stroke her chin, to touch her thin, fever-hollowed cheek. But instead he yanked the gold chain from her throat and pulled the coral pendant off her, his tug so hard she thought her neck might snap, but it didn't, only the gold chain, like a fishing line breaking under the weight of a bluefin.

You're wrong! she was about to cry again, but before the words left

her she asked herself—and would ask herself through the next six
fevers, and the months of remission, and the illness's final visit next
spring—Who? Who was wrong?

"I'll be back for my father," she said.

"And I'll be here."

Lindy returned slowly through the water to shore, her clothes hanging heavily from her. She pulled Sieglinde from the mouth of the cave.
"Time to go," she said. "Don't argue." What a girl cannot know about
her mother, thought Lindy. What no one can know.

They returned up the beach and up the arroyo, up the highway and
up the coast, up the white dirt road and the chaparral hill. Lindy returned home, to her room and the canopied bed, where she would
sleep through the nights and days alone, planning her exit from the
world that was never hers, and outside her window the nematode
would creep through the orange grove and spread the spreading decline, and the six-cylinder plans for the parkway would hurtle forward—six lanes! eight lanes! ten lanes! And many weeks later a night
would come when the moon would fail to rise and Rosa would be snor-
ing and Willis would be wheezing with orange-bourbon breath and
Sieglinde would be sucking the flesh from her thumb, and everything
in the house would be as quiet as the dead, except for the canopy flapping in the breeze, its silk torn by Lindy one night in a feverish bout,
but all else would be still, all else would be gone, and Lindy would
stand at her open window and look out across the small valley and
strain to see the black ocean—almost always hidden now behind the
sulfuric haze—and she would blink and blink again and all but the
shimmering phantasm of memory would fall away. She'd go to bed and
pull the white sheet taut to her chin, and as she drifted into a cave of
dreamless, bottomless sleep, Lindy Poore would be certain of her recovery.

UPON THE BREEZE

epilogue

Bless thee, Bright Sea—and glorious dome,
And my own world, my spirit's home;
Bless thee, Bless all—I cannot speak:
My voice is choked, but not with grief.

EMILY BRONTË

ONE DAY IN AUGUST 1945, Mr. Andrew Jackson Blackwood was walking through his orange groves when he arrived at the mausoleum. He had owned the Rancho Pasadena for a month, and although he had visited the lonely property several times he had yet to explore the orchard's outer reaches. It was a dry, desertlike day, the sun burning through a wad of permanent haze. The grove sagged with abandonment and the dirt was as hard as concrete. The mausoleum appeared before him, white and agleam, just as it had the time he discovered Mr. Bruder there on Christmas Day. How long ago that felt now—war yet raging in frozen-mud Europe and the Japs still defending the bayonet-sharp tallgrass of the Pacific atolls. And now it was all over and Blackwood, like every American, had learned how to say "peace" in half a dozen languages. *It's a new world!,* the news reports had been claiming for a week.

The sun had left the marble hot to the hand. It was midday, and the mausoleum provided little shade except directly under its dome, and there Blackwood found himself, master of a great tract of western land, leaning against a family crypt. A sense of loss touched Blackwood, and at once, in one swamping wave, he recalled everything Mrs. Nay and Bruder had told him.

He traced his finger across the Swinburne quote and walked around the high, sealed box to study the newest name, added only days after Blackwood took possession. Mrs. Nay's telephone call had come as a great shock. "He's dead, Mr. Blackwood," she had said. "Taken in his sleep." Of course it was how Lolly had died years before, her little heart giving up. As distressing as the news of Mr. Bruder's death was Mrs.

Nay's own grief, the sob traveling across the line. Blackwood had heard the regret in her voice, and he understood.

He returned up the hill to the terrace, to the shade of the coral tree. He leaned against the balustrade and surveyed all that was now his. On his first visit to the Rancho Pasadena as its new owner, the sense of pride he had expected did not come. And on each visit thereafter, the view of the valley had stirred him even less. In the past week, Blackwood had asked several visitors to the rancho: a man who built peach-stucco houses by the dozen, a highway man whose complexion was as rough as asphalt, and a man in an unventilated wool suit who was scouting property for a new power plant. Yet after each meeting Blackwood had felt nothing certain about the future, except the need to wash his hands.

In August the hills were husk-brown and dead, the grasses and the scrub too brittle to sway. The newspaper predicted a deadly fire season, and yet he noted that the newspaper predicted that every August. Might as well report that the sun is hot, thought Blackwood.

He did not live at the ranch, nor would he. There's no point in trying to live a life that isn't yours, he had come to understand. Blackwood was a dealer, not a baron, and although once he'd had the desire to live like a rich man, not anymore. That inclination had departed Blackwood, crawling away from its cave. His small but comfortable house would be more than Blackwood would need for the rest of his days.

And it was at this moment of summer contemplation that Cherry Nay came across Blackwood slumped over the parapet.

"Am I interrupting, Mr. Blackwood?"

"Not in the least." He wasn't expecting her but her visit didn't surprise him either, and he greeted her warmly.

"You haven't checked your mailbox, Mr. Blackwood." She handed him the envelopes and the flyers.

"My mailbox? I suppose I'm still not used to this place being mine. I don't even know where the mailbox is."

"Down by the gate, draped in wild cucumber," said Mrs. Nay. And then: "Guess what the mail brought me today, Mr. Blackwood. My George is on his way home. Released from service."

"You must be very happy, Mrs. Nay."

She said that she was. She was looking forward to resuming their dawn-lit tennis matches, and their evening gin on the patio shaded by the avocado tree, and the quotidian regularity of peace and prosperity. George had written that he was eager to return to business. "The boys are coming home," the letter said. "We'll be busy for many years, my dear Cherry."

Blackwood shuffled through the mail and found that it was mostly notices from the utility companies and something from the Growers Exchange addressed to Mr. Bruder. Seeing Bruder's name typed out like that reminded Blackwood of the cruelty of death: the mail continuing even when you cannot.

Blackwood came across a small envelope with a return address in San Marino, from someone named Mrs. Connie Ringe. The envelope was made out by hand, and at first Blackwood thought it must have been misdelivered, but he looked again and saw that it was indeed addressed to him. In the letter, Mrs. Ringe apologized for writing even though they had never met. She was writing on behalf of a group called the Committee for Reforming the Poor. At once he realized that it was a solicitation letter, and he nearly stopped reading. He figured now that word was out that he owned the Rancho Pasadena, many people would conclude that he was a rich man, there to donate to their cause. But then the name grew familiar to Blackwood.

"Connie Ringe? Wasn't she a friend of Mrs. Poore's?"

"Who, Connie? Yes, in the end they were friends. Why do you ask?"

Blackwood continued reading. Connie Ringe and some other women had raised money to open a school for underprivileged girls. "It's something we've been working on for nearly fifteen years," wrote Mrs. Ringe. She said that over the years the group had held drives and sought out bequests. They were now in a position to buy a modest property. There were plans to hire a small faculty and open a high school.

"I'm sure your plans for the Rancho Pasadena involve much profit-producing development, but if you would be kind enough to agree to meet with me, Mr. Blackwood," concluded Connie Ringe.

"They're hoping to open a girls' school," said Blackwood.

"Yes, they've been at it for years and years. I understand that someone recently died and left them a sum of money."

"An admirable mission," said Blackwood.

Cherry agreed, and together they looked out to the valley. The afternoon was still and the birds were quiet and Blackwood looked behind him to the mansion and imagined the cry of girls running in the gallery between classes. He imagined the sight of a row of shiny heads bent over an exam in the library. A school for girls? At the orange ranch?

"I hope you don't mind," said Cherry. "But I brought Sieglinde and Pal with me."

"What? The children? Where are they?"

"I left them at the service road. They wanted to visit his grave."

"Is that why you came?"

"They didn't feel comfortable coming on their own. They didn't want to trespass, Mr. Blackwood. I hope you don't mind."

He said he didn't, and sometime later, when he looked again, he saw the two figures walking about the mausoleum. They were far away and the distance smudged their faces, but he could make out which one was Pal and which one was the girl. She was standing beneath the dome, examining the crypt. The young man waited for her on the steps.

"How are they doing?" asked Blackwood.

"It's hard to lose the only world you know." Bruder had left them Condor's Nest, and Cherry said that they had torn down the Vulture House and tidied things up in a way that hadn't been done in a generation. "They've set out to rebuild the stairs to the beach. The boy is giving up on onions. He's starting a flower farm."

"A flower farm?" said Blackwood.

"Gladiolus, poppies, narcissus."

"Is the soil right?"

"Anything will grow there. Any old thing."

Blackwood thought about this for a long time, motionless with contemplation. If Cherry had learned anything about Blackwood during the past many months, it was that he was a nostalgic man. The past stroked at him, like a cat's tail winding around his ankle. She made use of this vulnerability now by asking him, "Have you made any plans, Mr. Blackwood?"

"None yet, Mrs. Nay." Later in the afternoon, Stinky Sweeney was dropping by. Stinky had an idea for an instant village for all the commuters who worked in the office buildings in Los Angeles. "Roll out a branch of the parkway down the bottom of the valley, and I guarantee it, Blackwood, you'll be richer than even *you* thought possible."

What Cherry had never revealed to Blackwood, or to anyone else, was that in all of George's letters during the war he had pressed her to negotiate with Bruder to take control of the ranch for themselves. George wanted to develop the land, and often he inquired on the Pasadena's status and she had been vague, careful never to lie outright to her husband. But sometime ago, Cherry had realized that George's work—her work, too—wasn't always for the best. She had developed a hope—in this instance, at least—to guide the ranch into the hands of a man who might preserve it. Early on, she had sensed that Blackwood would be her best chance. In his face she had seen a conscience bubbling with remorse; and it reminded Cherry of herself. All those years ago, Lindy Poore had said, just before she died, "Cherry, you'll look after things for me?"

"Mr. Blackwood?"

"Yes, Mrs. Nay?"

"Would you ever consider handing the property off to a charitable organization? Something like a school for girls?"

"I never thought of it," he said. "It wouldn't be a good return on my investment, would it?"

"I understand, Mr. Blackwood. It's a lot to ask."

Down in the grove, Sieglinde and Pal had disappeared, and for a while Blackwood and Cherry stood on the terrace, waiting for nothing in particular. They didn't speak, and the wind brought nothing to them—no scent of citrus or trilling birdcall—nothing but the streaming rush of the traffic on the parkway behind the hill. More cars now than even a year ago, thought Blackwood and Cherry simultaneously.

When Sieglinde and Palomar reached the terrace they were flushed with heat, and Blackwood asked if he could get them some water. They refused, shading themselves beneath the tree, and they stood close to each other, and the resemblance was faint, except in their bottomless eyes. Blackwood wondered if in fact he now knew more of their history than they did; he wondered what it was they regretted. He wondered how they got through their days—what with the past of others yoked to their shoulders for them to bear.

Cherry hadn't said why the girl had gone to live with Bruder after Captain Poore had died a few years back. Of course, the ranch had passed to Bruder at that point, but why hadn't the girl gone someplace else? She was in an ivory dress that revealed a strong neck, and everything about her spoke of Linda Stamp. In the mansion, Blackwood had found an old picture album, and he had studied the photos of Captain Poore. None of him had shown up in his daughter.

"He'll be happy there," said Sieglinde. "Buried with my mother." Her face was dreamy with grief.

Palomar took her hand, and their expressions turned somber as they looked down to the mausoleum. The girl was beautiful, in a handsome way. Her hair was blowing about her face and she said nothing else, content in her silence. In the searing afternoon, Blackwood watched her for a long time, and when she moved to leave he came to realize why she looked nothing like Captain Poore. Just then Blackwood had taught himself one more fact about Linda's story, and he thought of Bruder in his grave.

Huddled side by side, like a couple growing old together, Sieglinde and Palomar left the terrace, heading to Mrs. Nay's car.

She moved to follow. "Good-bye, Mr. Blackwood."

"Good-bye, Mrs. Nay."

"You'll enjoy your ranch, I'm sure."

He said that he would.

"I'll be curious to hear about your plans."

"You'll be the first to know."

Something pushed up from within Cherry and she felt obligated to say: "There's a need, Mr. Blackwood. It would be a grand gesture. Grander than most men are capable of making."

"I'll have to consider all my options."

"The house could be used for classrooms. The ranch house could be a dormitory. Think of all the poor girls, Mr. Blackwood."

"I'll try," he said. Several weeks ago, the private investigator had called with bad news: "There's no Edith Knight in the whole state of Maine. And another thing, Mr. Blackwood. I found nothing to suggest there ever was."

"They would name it after you," said Mrs. Nay. "The Blackwood School for Girls."

"I'm not looking to have a school named after me."

"Then they'd let you come up with the name, Mr. Blackwood. The Orangeridge School for Girls? The Pasadena School for Girls?"

"Aren't you getting ahead of yourself, Mrs. Nay?"

She apologized, and her sun-worn hand extended itself, its grip tennis-strong, and Blackwood took it. In the August glare, Andrew Jackson Blackwood thanked Cherry Nay for all that she had done. She returned the gratitude and hurried to her car, certain that something had been saved.

For a moment, Blackwood lingered on the terrace. He listened for the birds, for the chiming leaves. But still there was nothing at all, the entire valley empty and alone and burned dry. The traffic hidden behind the hill was the only sense that life would continue, barreling on.

Blackwood entered the mansion, taking refuge in its shade. All was silent in the gallery, but then up through the vents came a ghostly call of some sort, a strange whimpering, almost like a girl crying. "Just the house settling," Mrs. Nay had said. But this noise was spirited and small and alive. Blackwood asked if anyone was there, but no reply came. It continued, sounding like a child who is either happy or sad, only she can say. "Tell me if you can hear me," Blackwood whispered into the empty house. His heart was pounding in his ears and the sound continued for another moment and then it died and there was nothing but his echoing breath.

Later, Blackwood would discover the source of the noise—an open window in an almost forgotten room at the end of the hall upstairs, a bed's torn canopy flapping in the breeze—but in the meantime he dashed out the front door and climbed into the Imperial Victoria. He drove down the hill and through the gate, in the direction of Suicide Bridge, and in his rearview mirror a black cloud of exhaust rose from his tailpipe, and in its haze the Rancho Pasadena passed away.

AUTHOR'S NOTE

Although this is a work of fiction, it takes place in a world that once existed (or could have existed) but no longer does (or no longer could). Several resources invaluably assisted my imagination in creating it. I started and concluded the novel in the Pasadena Public Library's Centennial Room, where a collection of Pasadena history and arcana is housed behind wire-gate doors. The research staff at the Huntington Library welcomed me with their vast knowledge of Southern California history. The upstairs stacks of the Carlsbad Public Library introduced me to the history of San Diego's North County. Many books informed this novel, and among those I consulted most often are *Seekers of the Spring: A History of Carlsbad*, by Marje Howard-Jones; *Historic Pasadena: An Illustrated History*, by Ann Scheid Lund; *The Valley Hunt Club: One Hundred Years, 1888–1988*, by Ann Scheid; *A Natural History of California*, by Allan A. Schoenherr; *Underwater California*, by Wheeler J. North; *The National Audubon Society Field Guide to California*, by Peter Alden and Fred Heath; *The Huntington Botanical Gardens, 1905–1949*, by William Hertrich; *The Botanical Gardens at the Huntington*, by Walter Houk; *Fifty Years a Rancher*, by Charles G. Teague; Kevin Starr's incomparable series, *Americans and the California Dream*; *Oranges*, by John McPhee; and *The First World War*, by John Keegan. I am indebted to the careful scholarship of each of these authors.

ACKNOWLEDGMENTS

This book owes much to the generosity of many. My agent, Elaine Koster, encouraged me when it was an early idea, and again when it was a long manuscript. At Random House, Sunshine Lucas, Liz Fogarty, Tom Perry, Carol Schneider, Gaby Bordwin, Amy Edelman, Stacy Rockwood, Casey Hampton, Libby McGuire, and Ivan Held are among my many colleagues who applied their great publishing skills to my work. My copy editor, Benjamin Dreyer, brought his beautiful expertise to these pages. Evan Stone, Maria Massey, and Daniel Burke read the final drafts with thoughtful precision. Ann Godoff edited this book with patient, knowing care. For that, and much else, I am grateful to her.

ABOUT THE AUTHOR

DAVID EBERSHOFF is the author of *The Danish Girl,* a *New York Times* Notable Book and the winner of the Rosenthal Foundation Award from the American Academy of Arts and Letters and the Lambda Literary Award. His collection of stories, *The Rose City,* was named one of the best books of 2001 by the *Los Angeles Times.* His books have been published in more than a dozen countries to critical acclaim. Since 1998 he has been the publishing director of the Modern Library. He has taught at New York University and at Princeton, where he is presently a visiting lecturer. Originally from Pasadena, he is a graduate of Brown University and the University of Chicago. He currently lives in New York City and is working on a new novel. He can be reached at www.ebershoff.com.

ABOUT THE TYPE

This book was set in Bembo, a typeface based on an old-style Roman face that was used for Cardinal Bembo's tract *De Aetna* in 1495. Bembo was cut by Francisco Griffo in the early sixteenth century. The Lanston Monotype Machine Company of Philadelphia brought the well-proportioned letterforms of Bembo to the United States in the 1930s.